C000196969

THE ULTIMATE
DISCWORLD
COMPANION

Also by Terry Pratchett

THE CARPET PEOPLE
THE DARK SIDE OF THE SUN
STRATA
THE UNADULTERATED CAT (with Gray Jolliffe)
GOOD OMENS (with Neil Gaiman)
NATION
THE LONG EARTH (with Stephen Baxter)
THE LONG WAR (with Stephen Baxter)
THE LONG MARS (with Stephen Baxter)
THE LONG COSMOS (with Stephen Baxter)
THE LONG UTOPIA (with Stephen Baxter)
DODGER
A BLINK OF THE SCREEN: COLLECTED
  SHORT FICTION
A SLIP OF THE KEYBOARD: COLLECTED
  NON-FICTION

The Bromeliad
TRUCKERS
DIGGERS
WINGS

Johnny Maxwell
ONLY YOU CAN SAVE MANKIND
JOHNNY AND THE DEAD
JOHNNY AND THE BOMB

The Discworld® series
THE COLOUR OF MAGIC
THE LIGHT FANTASTIC
EQUAL RITES
MORT
SOURCERY
WYRD SISTERS
PYRAMIDS
GUARDS! GUARDS!
ERIC
MOVING PICTURES
REAPER MAN
WITCHES ABROAD
SMALL GODS
LORDS AND LADIES
MEN AT ARMS
SOUL MUSIC
INTERESTING TIMES
MASKERADE
FEET OF CLAY
HOGFATHER
JINGO
THE LAST CONTINENT
CARPE JUGULUM
THE FIFTH ELEPHANT

THE TRUTH
THIEF OF TIME
NIGHT WATCH
MONSTROUS REGIMENT
GOING POSTAL
THUD!
MAKING MONEY
UNSEEN ACADEMICALS
SNUFF
RAISING STEAM

Discworld (children's)
THE AMAZING MAURICE AND HIS
  EDUCATED RODENTS
THE WEE FREE MEN
A HAT FULL OF SKY
WINTERSMITH
I SHALL WEAR MIDNIGHT
THE SHEPHERD'S CROWN

Discworld non-fiction
MORT: A DISCWORLD BIG COMIC
  (with Graham Higgins)
GUARDS! GUARDS! (with Graham Higgins)
THE PRATCHETT PORTFOLIO (with Paul Kidby)
THE STREETS OF ANKH-MORPORK
  (with Stephen Briggs)
THE DISCWORLD MAPP (with Stephen Briggs)
A TOURIST GUIDE TO LANCRE: A
  DISCWORLD MAPP (with Stephen Briggs and
  Paul Kidby)
DEATH'S DOMAIN (with Paul Kidby)
THE COMPLEAT ANKH-MORPORK
  (with The Discworld Emporium)
NANNY OGG'S COOKBOOK (with Stephen Briggs
  Tina Hannan and Paul Kidby)
THE WIT AND WISDOM OF DISCWORLD
  (compiled by Stephen Briggs)
THE ILLUSTRATED WEE FREE MEN
  (with Stephen Player)
THE ILLUSTRATED LAST HERO
  (with Paul Kidby)
THE ILLUSTRATED ERIC (with Josh Kirby)
THE ART OF DISCWORLD (with Paul Kidby)
WHERE'S MY COW? (with Melvyn Grant)
MISS FELICITY BEEDLE'S THE WORLD OF
  POO (with Bernard and Isobel Pearson)
THE DISCWORLD IMAGINARIUM
  (with Paul Kidby)
THE ANKH-MORPORK ARCHIVES: VOL. I
  (with Stephen Briggs and Paul Kidby)
THE ANKH-MORPORK ARCHIVES: VOL. II
  (with Stephen Briggs and Paul Kidby)

THE ULTIMATE
DISCWORLD
COMPANION

Terry Pratchett
and
Stephen Briggs

illustrated by
Paul Kidby

This edition first published in Great Britain in 2021 by Gollancz,
an imprint of The Orion Publishing Group Ltd
Carmelite House, 50 Victoria Embankment, London, EC4Y 0DZ

An Hachette UK Company

1 3 5 7 9 10 8 6 4 2

Text copyright Dunmanifestin Ltd. and Stephen Briggs 1994–2021
Illustrations copyright Paul Kidby 1993–2021

Discworld® and Terry Pratchett® are registered trademarks of Dunmanifestin
Limited. All trade marks are used under licence.

The moral right of Terry Pratchett and Stephen Briggs to be identified as the
authors of this work and the moral right of Paul Kidby to be identified as
the illustrator of this work has been asserted by them in accordance with the
Copyright, Designs and Patents Act 1998.

All rights reserved. No part of this publication may be reproduced, stored in
a retrieval system, or transmitted without the prior permission of both the
copyright owners and the above publisher of this book.

All the characters in this book are fictitious, and any resemblance to actual
persons, living, dead or undead, is purely coincidental.

A CIP catalogue record for this book is available from the British Library.

ISBN (Hardback) 978 1 473 22350 9
ISBN (Export Trade Paperback) 978 1 473 22351 6
ISBN (eBook) 978 1 473 22353 0

Designer Alex Stott
Art archivist Vanessa Kidby
Copy editor Linda Antoniw

Printed in Great Britain by Clays Ltd, Elcograf S.p.A

MIX
Paper from
responsible sources
FSC® C104740
FSC
www.fsc.org

TerryPratchett.com
OrionBooks.co.uk
StephenBriggs.com
PaulKidby.com

CONTENTS

TERRY PRATCHETT

Professor Sir Terry Pratchett OBE was the creator of the hugely successful Discworld series of novels and during his lifetime became Britain's bestselling author of adult fiction.

His first published story, *Business Rivals*, was printed in his school magazine and then published in *Science Fantasy* magazine when he was just fourteen. Using the proceeds, Terry purchased his first typewriter.

He left school aged seventeen and worked as a journalist for his local newspaper, the Bucks Free Press. His first novel, *The Carpet People* – developed from stories he had written for the weekly children's section of the newspaper – was published in 1971.

In 1979 Terry was appointed publicity officer for the Central Electricity Generating Board, where he remained until 1987. During this time, he wrote the first four Discworld novels – *The Colour of Magic, The Light Fantastic, Equal Rites* and *Mort*. In September 1987, after completing *Mort*, he gave up his job at the CEGB and devoted himself fulltime to writing.

His interests were wide-ranging and eclectic, and are reflected in his books, which are littered with esoteric ideas and wisdom – from beekeeping, folklore and cheese-making, to quantum mechanics, astronomy and the finer aspects of Morris dancing.

Terry was appointed Officer of the Order of the British Empire (OBE) in 1998 and knighted for services to literature in the 2009 New Year Honours. He used the latter accolade as justification for forging his own knightly sword – Thunderbolt Iron – using iron he smelted himself.

In 2001, he won the Carnegie Medal for *The Amazing Maurice and His Educated Rodents* and went on to receive many literary awards, ten honorary doctorates and the World Fantasy Award for Life Achievement, eventually earning the full title of Professor Sir Terry Pratchett, OBE, Blackboard Monitor, Adjunct of the Oscar Wilde Centre for Irish Writing and the School of English at Trinity College Dublin.

In 2007, Terry announced that he was suffering from posterior cortical atrophy, a rare form of Alzheimer's disease. Despite this embuggerance, as he came to call it, he subsequently penned a further twelve bestselling novels, made several award-winning documentaries and campaigned tirelessly for Alzheimer's research and the right to die with dignity.

Terry died peacefully in March 2015 at his home in Wiltshire, with his family by his side and his cat asleep on his bed.

His final request was that the hard drive containing his unfinished novels be either crushed by a steamroller or fired into space. His assistant and friend, Rob Wilkins, chose the former, having decided that launching a rocket from their rural office in Wiltshire might be impractical.

STEPHEN BRIGGS

Stephen Briggs was a collaborator with, and friend of, Terry Pratchett for more than 20 years.

They worked together to build the city of Ankh-Morpork, to create the Discworld on which it stands, and to put together a *Companion* to Terry's wonderful world.

Stephen went on to collaborate with Terry on a number of spin-offs which expanded on the institutions and geography of his possibly fictional world. He has also dramatized twenty-two of Terry's novels (so far) and recorded Terry's unabridged audio books for various publishers in the UK and US.

Terry used to say of Stephen: 'He knows more about Discworld than I do'. Less flatteringly, he described Stephen as Bosworth* (sic) to his Dr Johnson... hopefully, he was joking.

---

* *For those unfamiliar with British history, Bosworth was the battlefield which saw the death of King Richard III – the last English monarch to die in combat. Dr Johnson's sidekick, as Terry well knew, was called Boswell.*

PAUL KIDBY

Paul Kidby has been wielding a pencil all his working life. As a young school leaver he was determined to teach himself the skills and discipline required to become a designer and illustrator. Paul read his first Discworld novel in his late twenties.

This was a seminal moment. Inspired to design and illustrate characters from *The Colour of Magic*, he hand-delivered his artwork to Terry Pratchett after queuing to meet him at a book signing. It was the beginning of a dynamic creative collaboration between author and artist, Terry wrote that he liked the reality of Paul's work, and the feeling that he had 'just strolled into the books with a sketchpad'.

Almost thirty years and many publications later, Paul has an astonishing archive of Discworld artwork, some of which can be seen here for the first time.

WHERE AM I?

'Toto, I've a feeling we're not in Oxford any more.'

When I look back over the years since I last revised the introduction to the *Companion*, I am staggered at how much has happened.

My original introduction to the first *Discworld Companion* said: 'Six years ago I was a civil servant who dabbled in amateur dramatics (er... I still am)'.

I've now left the civil service; it was taking over all my time. I don't think that the work/life balance exhibited by Scrooge and Cratchit at the start of *A Christmas Carol* is actually a sound way forward ... in fact, I firmly believe that a work/life balance is intended, implicitly, to include an element of 'life'.

As many of you know, I fell into Discworld backwards, as if I'd been leaning on a rickety old door in a walled garden and I'd suddenly found myself in a magical kingdom full of snow, fauns and benevolent lions. I hadn't meant to be here, but I'm jolly glad that I am.

I came across Discworld while looking for books to dramatize for my amateur drama club. We were the first people – anywhere in the world – to dramatize the works of Terry Pratchett. When I first wrote to Terry back in 1990 to ask permission to dramatize *Wyrd Sisters*, I little realized that in choosing that book to dramatize, I had made a really BIG life choice. I can still remember how worried we were when the author (then Mr Terry Pratchett) actually telephoned me – in person – to say that he wanted to come and see our little production. Would he like it? Would he let us do any more?

Wyrd Sisters went so well that we went on to stage twenty more Discworld books (so far!) plus three written for use by schools. Most of these have now been published, and have been staged by amateur drama clubs all over the world – Australia to Zimbabwe, Indonesia to Bermuda, Finland to France, South Africa to the USA. Even in the Antarctic – how cool is that? Along the way, they've raised tens of thousands of pounds for the Orangutan Foundation from their royalties.

Anyway, back to 1992. One day, when I was working on only my second Discworld play, I mentioned to Terry that I was convinced from my reading that Ankh-Morpork had a distinct shape. He doubted it – he said he'd just put buildings and streets in wherever the plot required them. I said that in this world they got put in wherever History demanded them and I was sure the city was mappable. Fine, he said. Go ahead.

And that led to *The Streets of Ankh-Morpork*, published in 1993, possibly the first map ever to get into the bestseller lists.

The arguments ... er, discussions ... and constant reference-seeking involved in that project led me to wonder out loud if it wasn't time for a guide to Discworld.

And *The Discworld Companion* was born.

Since then, my own little 'backlist' has grown to include three maps, those dramatizations of twenty-two of Terry's books – *Wyrd Sisters, Mort, Guards! Guards!, Men at Arms, Maskerade, Carpe Jugulum, The Fifth Elephant, The Truth, Interesting Times, Night Watch, Feet of Clay, Lords and Ladies, Going Postal, Making Money, Monstrous Regiment, Unseen Academicals, Dodger, The Rince Cycle* (a mash-up of *The Colour of Magic, The Light Fantastic* and snippets of *Sourcery*), *Terry Pratchett: the Shakespeare Codex* (a mash-up of *The Science* of *Discworld 2* and lumps of Shakespeare!), *Hogfather, Johnny & the Dead* and *The Amazing Maurice and his Educated Rodents*, six diaries, a cook book and a graphic novel. Oh, and *The Wit & Wisdom of Discworld* – an excellent reminder of your favourite bits – or a way to ease newbies into the world of Terry.

It is still weird, when friends return from foreign travels to tell me they've seen the maps in a bookstore in Munich, the *Companion* at a French airport or, much more surprisingly, one of my plays in a bookshop in Zimbabwe.

The weirdness factor is compounded when, from time to time, I get a small package from Colin Smythe (Terry's and my agent) containing translations of some of the above – the cook book in German, the *Companion* in French, a diary in Bulgarian or a map of Ankh-Morpork in Polish.

Several years ago now, I recorded a couple of lines to go into Dave Greenslade's *From the Discworld* album ... this was another happy accident, as I'd only gone along to the studio to dress up as Death for some publicity pix. From those two lines ('The turtle moves' and 'Nevertheless, the turtle does move'), I moved on to record many of the unabridged books (initially for Isis Publishing, and latterly for Harper Audio (US) and other audio companies). These were a tremendous responsibility. It was nerve-wracking enough to have to replace the established artist (Nigel Planer), who had a loyal following among those who listen to the books on tape or CD, but I was also all too aware that Terry and his family used to receive – and listen to – early copies of the completed recordings.

Along the way, and again virtually by accident, I had found myself selling a range of Discworld merchandise to Terry's readers across the globe. It all started with an Unseen University scarf, but went on to include enamelled badges, T-shirts, key-rings, tea towels, aprons, etc. Sadly, the pressures of my real-life job (as was) had obliged me to drop that little 'spare bedroom business'.

Before I met Terry, I had no access to email or the internet at all, but now I am of course totally immersed in email, Facebook and Twitter, with email, Messenger and WhatsApp having replaced the paper-based alternative for 99 per cent of my correspondence. Even so, and much to Terry's amusement and disgust, this *Companion* is still based on material captured on an old-fashioned card index. I used to remind him, though, that the cards are still as readily accessible as the day I wrote them. Any 1990s computer indexing program would be much more of a challenge!

Discworld has been very good to me, and I welcomed the limited chances I used to get to meet Terry's readers, either at the conventions, less formal get-togethers or on those occasions when the publishers used to let me tag along to a book launch. It was really strange to see people wearing badges and shirts I'd created, or offering for signature diaries, maps, plays that I'd helped to create.

I wouldn't have missed it for worlds.

TERRY PRATCHETT

Terry and I shared a sense of humour and an interest in the crazy stuff in our Roundworld which we later had to tone down to make it believable on his Discworld. But apart from that, I wasn't an obvious choice – I wasn't a fan, I didn't read fantasy fiction, I wasn't in publishing and I didn't make things. I was also a Luddite about technology and didn't even have an email address.

Terry and I became friends and (as you may know) we worked together on lots of projects. We had fun – touring the Royal Opera House and attending *Phantom of the Opera* to research *Maskerade*, running lines from *Life of Brian* at signing queues … 'Crucifixion? Good … line on the left, one cross each'; or flying to Germany just to watch a production of *MacBest* (*Wyrd Sisters*), drink beer and eat Bratwurst… We also nurtured privately the illusion that we were the only people in the world who'd seen *The Keep* (1983 film) .

Socially, Terry was funny, fun, challenging and good company. To work with, he was challenging, engaging, entertaining and bluntly honest. He was a loyal and hospitable friend – and he's the person who first introduced me to *The Princess Bride*.

It was awful to learn of his 'embuggerance' – posterior cortical atrophy – a form of Alzheimer's, and to know that it would, inevitably, steal him from us. It was a hammer blow when he died. It seems really odd to be producing this edition of the *Companion* without Terry's cheerful and challenging input.

I still think about him every day – and I feel extremely fortunate to have been included in his Venerable Order of the Honeybee – with its responsibility to honour his Discworld.

But Terry's books live on. When I left school, I worked for a couple of years for the Bodleian Library. I used to handle books that Henry VIII would have thought of as old. In 400 years, Terry's books will still be here. His plots, characters, humanity and humour will be there to delight generations to come.

THIS FINAL EDITION

This edition, of course, now takes us all the way to *The Shepherd's Crown*. It has been a sad task to put together what will be the final *Discworld Companion*. Both Terry and I expected him to carry on writing into his nineties, with me producing updated Companions every few years or so. Fate had other ideas.

When I revised the *Companion* in around 2002, I had to act like Legitimate First, gravedigger at the Cemetery of Small Gods (see *Night Watch*). I had to move some people out of the main cemetery of the Companion and into the charnel house of my card index to make room for all the new people, from new books, struggling to get in. So we lost quite a few more of those characters whose only function was to support a gag line, or to bop Rincewind on the head. Some of them still held on – Terry and I retained a soft spot for the bit-part players on the great stage of life. For this, Ultimate, edition, I went back to the original card index which we used for the first edition and I have added back in all the character references we dumped in Terry's old office as we pieced together that first *Companion*. Background artistes from subsequent books have still had to take their chances; for them, just exisiting as a name isn't necessarily enough.

So, sad to say, it means there really wasn't room for Bob-Bob Hardyoyo, Germaine

Trifle, Dozy Longfinger or Ronnie 'Trust Me' Begholder. Muted apologies to them, and many others – including Mrs Gibbons of 12 Dolmen View, Pant-y-Girdl, Llamedos (who, as you know, can be relied on to take in post for Evil Harry Dread).

One of the delights of the *Companion* is that it allowed Terry occasionally to expand on random aspects of Discworld; on topics he wasn't able to cover in detail in the novels – such as Magic on Discworld. In that spirit, I have still incorporated material from those Discworld diaries which Terry and I wrote together. They contained some good background material, which I enjoyed researching and we both enjoyed writing. It gave Terry more chances to play with the backgrounds and histories of some key institutions in a little playpen that needn't intrude into or slow down the actual plots of novels. It would have been a pity to see it all disappear because the diaries, by their nature, are only transient… they wither away like the purple lilac once their year is over.

In total contrast to my card index, trying to access the text of the original *Companion* from what counted as state of the art IT storage back in the 1990s has been a little more of a challenge. Technology, eh?

SPOILERS

Spoilers? Not a word we knew in this current context when we wrote the first *Companion*. It is really, really hard (even with Terry's help) to avoid spoilers when writing about characters – especially those whose plots advance significantly during the books…. We have done our best – aimed to not give away too much about characters' plot lines but, here and there, there may be the occasional spoiler. Please tread carefully. Darth Vader is Luke's father – oops ..!

RANDOMNESS

Terry and I delighted in being a bit arbitrary in who was included and how much they were included. I have retained this 'personal' approach. This is, in effect, the original *Discworld Companion*. It's just that it now includes all the Discworld novels.

At some point in the distant future, a much drier and more complete Index of Absolutely Everything will be produced for those studying Sir Terry Pratchett for their doctorates.

Hopefully, you doctors of Pratchettology will also search whatever replaces bookshelves to locate and read this book, too.

Stephen Briggs
Oxfordshire 2021

ILLUSTRATING DISCWORLD

'I like nonsense; it wakes up the brain cells. Fantasy is a necessary ingredient in living; it's a way of looking at life through the wrong end of the telescope. Which is what I do, and that enables you to laugh at life's realities.'

Dr. Seuss

It has been almost thirty years since I first discovered Discworld, when my sister sent me a copy of *The Colour of Magic*. Until then I had been working freelance in magazines, advertising and product design; the work wasn't exactly creative and I was feeling uninspired. This gift introduced me to a writer who portrayed life with what Lewis Carrol described as a 'visual squint' – the books were funny, cynical, richly layered and teeming with idiosyncratic characters. There was depth and a serious commentary on society, yet written with the lightest touch and wrapped in a warm humour that made me laugh. Discworld was the fresh inspiration I craved and the next step in my professional journey beckoned...

My route to becoming the Discworld illustrator was not straightforward. I grew up in suburban London in the 1960s and '70s. As a boy, there was a house on my street that I found fascinating. In the window was a skeleton. When I heard what the resident lady did for a living, I found her house all the more intriguing. But I was well into my teens before I dared knock on the door of Miss Ockendon, artist and creative taskmaster.

At that time, I had just dropped out of sixth form and was on one of Mrs Thatcher's 'Youth Opportunity' Schemes, making false teeth. I had been interested in art from an early age and this apprenticeship was the closest I could get to being a paid creative. Throughout my childhood I had always drawn for pleasure (and luckily had plenty of pens and paper as my dear dad was a stationery salesman). As a teenager I drew imaginative pieces influenced by my two main interests: fantasy literature and contemporary music – *The Lord of the Rings* and Kate Bush, *The War of the Worlds* and The Clash.

Aged seventeen, I finally plucked up the courage to introduce myself to Miss Ockendon. She had taught at The Ealing School of Art, the alma mater of Freddie Mercury, Ronnie Wood, Pete Townsend and one of my own art heroes, Alan Lee. She had also worked as an anatomical artist in operating theatres and was an adept draughtswoman and calligrapher. In no uncertain terms she told me that if I was serious about becoming an artist, I had to learn the nuts and bolts of my craft, starting with perspective, anatomy and composition. I had to ditch my imaginative illustrations and start drawing from life. I visited her every week, and she would set me challenges; technically I learnt a lot from her – but the most important thing I took away was that to be successful as an artist (or indeed anything else), you need discipline and an investment of serious time. That was the very beginning of my artistic development – and, eventually, a life-changing process.

By the early 1980s I was designing and hand-painting roller blinds in a factory. I was working, but not hard. My friend, Tony, and I would clock in and then go jogging around the Park Royal Guinness Factory (until Tony developed a yeast allergy and started frothing at the mouth). We then turned our attention to making bows and arrows to shoot across the department into giant rolls of cardboard. This stopped after we thought it would be fun if the arrows were flaming and we almost set the whole workshop on fire. Tony taught me to airbrush and I taught him what I had gleaned from Miss Ockendon.

By the mid 1990s I was a young dad, working as a commercial illustrator, first as a freelancer in London, designing greetings cards and packaging for videos and computer games, and later at Future Publishing in Bath, where I painted covers for magazines such as *Commodore Format*, *Sega Power* and also *GamesMaster* editions 1–34 . I had the energy and optimism of youth but it did mean working a lot harder, the days of firing arrows were well and truly over. As the graphics of the games improved, I could see that it was only a matter of time before hand-painted artwork for these magazine covers would be superseded by computer graphics – it was time to find a new line of work.

That fateful twenty-ninth birthday gift from my sister was therefore timely. Terry's characters in *The Colour of Magic* leapt off the page into my imagination and I felt compelled to draw Rincewind, Granny Weatherwax, Nanny Ogg, Magrat and Cohen. I was unaware of Terry's popularity, and it was a surprise to me when, in October 1993, I had to queue for two hours at the Bath branch of WHSmith to meet him. When my turn finally came, I handed him an envelope containing photocopies of my character drawings and my telephone number. I didn't hear anything, and frankly I wasn't surprised. It was a number of weeks later, when his signing tour was over, that Terry called me and enthusiastically suggested that we collaborate on some potential Discworld projects. It was a dream come true.

We began with *The Pratchett Portfolio*, published in 1996, and a series of prints, maps and diaries followed. I then illustrated Terry's short novel *The Last Hero*, my first big Discworld project. When, sadly, Josh Kirby died in 2001 Terry asked me to take over the Discworld cover designs, an undertaking that left me feeling daunted and honoured in equal measure.

The characters depicted are such clear and recognizable 'types' that drawing them is a constant delight. I appreciate the way the writing pins the persona but in abstract terms, such as 'predatory flamingo', this gives me plenty of leeway for artistic interpretation. As Terry was fascinated by science and engineering, his fantasy is buttressed by a logic that makes it believable, with a limited amount of actual magic. My artwork celebrates this approach, and, like Terry, I also enjoy creating a sense of historical realism shot through with humour, so I feel his words and my pictures have a pleasing sense of unity to them. Terry liked to pepper his novels with cultural and literary references, from Shakespeare to Asimov, and sometimes it is fun to do something similar with my artwork, but only when the right and fitting occasion arises. Over the years I have parodied, amongst others, Peter Blake's Beatles album cover, *Sgt. Pepper's Lonely Hearts Club Band*, Munch's *The Scream*, Joseph Wright of Derby's *An Experiment on a Bird in the Air Pump* and Rembrandt's *The Night Watch*.

For the past three decades my work has been devoted almost exclusively to Discworld and my archive is expansive. To be able to assimilate this large collection for *The Ultimate Companion* is a treat for me, and there has been much rummaging in cupboards and extensive searching on hard drives for long-lost images.

I was delighted to have an excuse to draw some of Terry's more obscure creations, such as one of Death's garden gnomes and Horace the Cheese. Other illustrations have very rarely, if ever, had an outing in print, so this is their chance to be seen playing an integral part in the rich and intricate tapestry that is Discworld. Recently, I was asked by one of my Facebook followers if I ever get bored with re-drawing the same characters; my reply was that I view my work as progressive, I am always developing the character designs and pushing the proverbial envelope both with technique and portrayal – so, in short, I am never bored!

It was a joy to work with Terry and I consider myself very fortunate to have had the opportunity to realize his creations. Being an artist in his own right, he had a good sense of design and a keen eye for illustration. Sometimes he would challenge me by requesting I draw particularly complex subjects, such as the Floral Clock, and his brief for the cover of *Snuff* was a veritable shopping list of things to be included – all of which I managed to incorporate, even the chickens. We shared many meetings of collaborative creativity where we discussed the physical attributes and personal foibles of his characters. Special memories remain – such as the night he rang to invite me over to look at Saturn's rings through his telescope and the afternoon he helped clear my pond while we chatted about ideas for new stories. Not all of those stories got written and his loss is felt by many, including me, every day.

Following his untimely death, I was honoured to become one of 'The Venerable Order of the Honeybee', a group of twelve people entrusted by Terry himself to oversee the safe future of his works. As I continue to illustrate Discworld and reinterpret the people and places that he wrote about so vividly, I endeavour to always give my artistic best to Terry's wonderful legacy.

Paul Kidby
Dorset 2021

NOTE

A name or word in SMALL CAPITALS indicates that it is the subject of a fuller, separate entry; regular references such as Ankh-Morpork, Granny Weatherwax and Unseen University are not normally flagged (they're certainly not *consistently* flagged!).

The book where the character or reference first occurs is indicated with the following abbreviations. These are given at the end of each entry.

AGD	*Assassins' Guild Diary (2000)†*	POD	*Post Office Diary (2007)†*
CCDD	*A Collegiate Casting-out of Devilish Devices*****	RM	*Reaper Man*
		RS	*Raising Steam*
CJ	*Carpe Jugulum*	SALF	*The Sea & Little Fishes*
COM	*The Colour of Magic*	SG	*Small Gods*
DD	*Death's Domain*	SM	*Soul Music*
DM	*Discworld Mapp*	S	*Sourcery*
E	*Eric*	SN	*Snuff*
ER	*Equal Rites*	T!	*Thud!*
FOC	*Feet of Clay*	TAMAHER	*The Amazing Maurice and His Educated Rodents*
FGD	*Fools' Guild Diary (2001)††*		
GG	*Guards! Guards!*	TB	*Troll Bridge***
GP	*Going Postal*	TDA	*The Discworld Almanak*
H	*Hogfather*	TFE	*The Fifth Elephant*
HFOS	*A Hat Full of Sky*	TGD	*Thieves' Guild Diary (2002)†*
ISWM	*I Shall Wear Midnight*	TGL	*A Tourist Guide to Lancre*
IT	*Interesting Times*	TLC	*The Last Continent*
J	*Jingo*	TLH	*The Last Hero*
LF	*The Light Fantastic*	TOC	*Theatre of Cruelty****
LL	*Lords and Ladies*	TOT	*Thief of Time*
LTD	*Lu-Tze's Yearbook of Enlightenment (2008)††*	TSC	*The Shepherd's Crown*
		TSOD	*The Science of Discworld**
M	*Mort*	TSOD2	*The Science of Discworld 2**
MA	*Maskerade*	TSOD4	*The Science of Discworld 4**
MAA	*Men at Arms*	TT	*The Truth*
MM	*Making Money*	UA	*Unseen Academicals*
MP	*Moving Pictures*	UUD	*Unseen University Diary (1998)†*
MR	*Monstrous Regiment*	W	*Wintersmith*
NOCB	*Nanny Ogg's Cook Book*	WA	*Witches Abroad*
NW	*Night Watch*	WFM	*The Wee Free Men*
P	*Pyramids*	WS	*Wyrd Sisters*

*   *In fact, there's still very little included from* The Science of Discworld *series – the books are borderline canonical – so characters unique to those books (many of whom are from Roundworld) are not necessarily included. After all, the elves in the* Science of Discworld *series specifically sneer at the idea of being called Peaseblossom – even though that is the name of a major elf character in* The *(canonical)* Shepherd's Crown. *A couple of named people may have managed to sneak out of Roundworld into this book. The Science of Discworld approach has also been taken with the later spin-offs (some diaries and a railway guide), to which Terry was not able to contribute personally in the way he used to.*

**   *Short story published in* After the King *– it is, technically, not Discworld, but it made it into the first* Companion *and has now earned its right to stay.*

***   *Short story published in W. H. Smith's* Bookcase, *now a collectors' item.*

****   *Short story included in* A Blink of the Screen.

†   *Collected in* The Ankh-Morpork Archives *Vol. I*

††   *Collected in* The Ankh-Morpork Archives *Vol. II*

There was not a lot that could be done to make Ankh-Morpork a worse
place. A direct hit by meteorite, for example, would count as gentrification.

– *Pyramids*

Abbot, The. The 493rd Abbot of the History MONKS is an old man with wrinkled hands when we first encounter him during the events of *Small Gods*. And, by the time the events of *Thief of Time* occur, this dear, kind man's teeth are giving him trouble and he is not walking very well. That is because, by then, he has been born again.

Although he is mentally around 900 years old and extremely clever, he has never mastered the art of circular ageing (crudely known as 'immortality'). He has therefore been forced to achieve longevity in a more circular way, via serial reincarnation. The Abbot, in short, goes round and round, while managing to remember all his past lives; by *Thief of Time* he is a mere baby, although he is off the wet nurse (something of a trial for all concerned, in the circumstances) and onto less embarrassing fare, such as rusks. He travels around the Oi Dong Monastery in a sling on the back of an acolyte, often wearing an embroidered pixie hood to keep out the cold. His speech wavers between the sensible outpourings of a wise and very old man, and loud outbursts of babytalk when the infantile body takes over. He uses his wide selection of toys as apparently unintentional weapons against his recalcitrant colleagues, and many a monk has been struck by a random rubber yak, wooden giraffe or large wooden brick hurled from the Abbot's pudgy little hands. It may well

be, perish the thought, that having so recently had to put up with these people patronizing him and shouting things in his ear, he treats these juvenile periods as a welcome opportunity to settle a few scores. [SG]

Abbott, Jack. A lumberjack in Lancre, who lives with his mum in a rickety little hut. He was treated for a foot injury by Granny Weatherwax. [TSC]

Abbys, Bishop. Prophet of the Omnian Church, to whom the Great God OM is said to have dictated the Codicils to the Book of OSSORY. Little is known of this great man except that he had a big beard, because this is essential wear for prophets. On the subject of beards, the famous Ephebian riddle about them – All men in this town do not shave themselves and are shaved by the barber. Who shaves the barber? – caused some head-scratching when it was printed in an almanac that got as far as LANCRE. People there couldn't see what was so philosophical about the statement because Lancre's barber is one Mrs Deacon, who is open for haircuts, warts and teeth two mornings a week. [SG]

Abraxas. Ephebian philosopher, also called Abraxas the Agnostic, and 'Charcoal' Abraxas (because he had been struck by lightning fifteen times – which suggests that being an agnostic requires an enviable strength of mind, not to say thickness of skull. His own comment, just before the fifteenth stroke, was 'They needn't think they can make me believe in them by smiting me the whole time'). He was the author of 'On Religion', and the man who found the Lost City of EE. And presumably lost it again. He was readily identified by the smell of burnt hair. [SG]

Abrim. Grand Vizier of AL KHALI. A tall, saturnine wizard, with a long thin moustache and wearing a turban with a pointy hat sticking out of it. He was once refused entry to Unseen University because they said he was mentally unstable. Given the apparent mental equilibrium of many of UU's faculty, one can only wonder at this exclusion. Driven by the ARCH-

CHANCELLOR'S HAT, Abrim was destroyed in a battle of magic. 'Never trust the Grand Vizier' is a popular Discworld saying, which many oriental adventurers would have survived a whole lot longer by knowing. [S]

Aching, Granny. Her maiden name was Sarah Grizzel. She died two years before the events of *The Wee Free Men*. Her memory is a major part of Tiffany Aching's life and career. She was an expert shepherdess and her memory is reinforced by the remains of her shepherding hut, which still stands on the chalk hills overlooking Tiffany's family home. There isn't much to see now, just the iron wheels sinking into the turf and the pot-bellied stove with its short chimney.

Granny used old words, and came out with odd, old sayings. She didn't call the downland the Chalk, she called it 'the wold'.

Near the big black stove in the Aching home was the shelf, still called Granny Aching's Library by Tiffany's mother, who liked the idea of having a library. Everyone else called it Granny's Shelf.

There were only five books, if you didn't include the big farm diary. One of these was '*Diseases of the Sheep*', which was fat with the bookmarks that Granny Aching had put there. She had been an expert on sheep, even though

she called them 'just bags of bones, eyeballs and teeth, lookin' for new ways to die'.

Other shepherds would walk miles to get her to come and cure their beasts of ailments. They said she had the Touch, although *she* just said that the best medicine for sheep or man was a dose of turpentine, a good cussin' and a kick. Bits of paper with Granny's own recipes for sheep cures stuck out all over the book. Mostly they involved turpentine, but some included cussin'.

You hardly ever saw Granny Aching indoors in the spring and summer. She spent most of the year sleeping in the old wheeled hut, which could be dragged across the downs after the flocks.

So – who was Granny Aching? The answer is: what Granny Aching was, was *there*. She was always there. It seems that the lives of all the Achings revolve around Granny Aching. Decisions are made, things are done. Life goes on in the knowledge that, in her old wheeled shepherding hut on the hills, Granny Aching is still there, watching. [WFM]

Aching, Tiffany. When we first meet her in the series, Tiffany is a nine-year-old girl. What does she look like? Start with the boots. They are big and heavy boots, much repaired by her father and they'd belonged to various sisters before her; she wore several pairs of socks to keep them on. They are *big*. Tiffany sometimes feels she is nothing more than a way of moving boots around.

Then there is the dress. It has been owned by many sisters before her and has been taken up, taken out, taken down and taken in by her mother so many times that it really ought to have been taken away. But Tiffany rather likes it. It comes down to her ankles and, whatever colour it had been to start with, is now a milky blue.

Then there is Tiffany's face. Light pink, with brown eyes, and brown hair. Nothing special. Her head might strike anyone watching as being just slightly too big for the rest of her, but perhaps she'll grow into it. We also meet Tiffany at the age of eleven (*A Hat Full of Sky*), thirteen (*Wintersmith*), not quite sixteen (*I Shall Wear Midnight*) and early adulthood (*The Shepherd's Crown*).

Tiffany Aching

She was born and brought up on Home Farm, the farm her father, Joe, rents from the local Baron. Her name means 'Land Under Wave' – Tir-far-thóinn – although her late and much lamented grandmother, Granny Aching, used to call her 'jiggit'.

She has a brother, Wentworth (*see* ACHING, WENTWORTH) and two sisters, Hannah and Fastidia. The family also owns a dog – Jester.

She gains three pieces of jewellery in the course of the books: two pendants – a silver horse (resembling a chalk horse on a local hill-side) and a golden hare – and a ring, which she had the local blacksmith make from an iron nail. It has a dull shine; it'll never rust while she wears it, because of the oils in her skin. It has little snowflakes cut in it with a tiny chisel. She also gains a shepherd's crown, though, as a fossilized sea urchin, even a small one would make a fairly lumpy brooch.

Tiffany has substantial magical abilities which, combined with a bucketload of common sense, a real skill at cheesemaking and a close friendship with the Nac Mac Feegle, should serve her well in her future. [WFM]

Aching, Wentworth. Tiffany's younger brother is two years old when we first meet him (he was seven by the time of *Wintersmith*). At that age, anything could make Wentworth sticky. Washed and dried and left in the middle of a clean floor for five minutes, Wentworth would be sticky. It didn't seem to come from anywhere. He just got sticky. But he was an easy child to mind, provided you stopped him eating frogs. By the time he was seven, little Wentworth was always running after the men, always wanting to be one of them, always trying to help. By the time he's in *I Shall Wear Midnight*, he's happy to fight much bigger boys in the village to defend his sister's honour. [WFM]

Aching Family, the. The Achings all live at the Home Farm. Tiffany's father rented it from the Baron, who owned the land, but there had been Achings farming it for hundreds of years, and so, her father said (quietly, sometimes, after he'd had a beer in the evenings), as far as the *land*

knew, it was owned by the Achings. Tiffany's mother used to tell him not to speak like that, although since Granny had died, the Baron was always very respectful to Mr Aching, calling him the finest shepherd in these hills, and was generally held by the people in the village to be not too bad these days, it paid to be respectful. Besides, said Tiffany's mother, the poor man had sorrows of his own.

But sometimes Tiffany's father insisted that Achings (or Akins, or Archens, or Akens, or Akenns – spelling had been optional) had been mentioned in old documents about the area for hundreds and hundreds of years. They had these hills in their bones, he said, and they'd always been shepherds.

And for as long as she could remember Tiffany had heard her father, an otherwise quiet, slow man, make 'The Joke', the one that must have been handed down from Aching to Aching for hundreds of years.

He'd say, 'Another day of work and I'm still Aching', or 'I get up Aching and I go to bed Aching', or even 'I'm Aching all over'. They weren't particularly funny after about the third time, but she'd miss it if he didn't say at least one of them every week. They didn't have to be funny, they were *father* jokes. Anyway, however they were spelled, all her ancestors had been Aching to stay, not Aching to leave.

Achmed the Mad. Klatchian necromancer, who taught himself magic partly by trial, but mainly by error. Author of the '*NECROTELICOMNICON*'. It is said that he wrote it one day after he had drunk too much of the strange, thick Klatchian coffee (*see* FOOD AND DRINK), which sobers people up too much. Achmed preferred to be called 'Achmed the I Just Get These Headaches'. He is also the author of '*Achmed the I Just Get These Headaches's Book of Humorous Cat Stories*', the writing of which was said to have driven him mad in the first place. [MP]

Aeron. Secretary to the Low King of the Dwarfs. Moist von Lipwig views him as a dwarf version of DRUMKNOTT, although one might detect a slightly closer relationship with his monarch. The King's secretary is slim for a dwarf, almost nimble and quick, and decidedly ubiquitous, his long beard follows him like a banner as he goes about on the King's business. He carries a sword, not traditionally a dwarf weapon. [RS]

Agantia. Queen of Skund. Just one of those people who turns up. CASANUNDA the dwarf claims to have received his title of 'Count' by performing a small service for the Queen; but since Skund is almost entirely forest and has next to no population, let alone a royal family, this is what is called, in historical terms, a lie. [LL]

Agatean Empire. Capital city: Hung-hung. Principal and only port: BES PELARGIC. Pop.: about 50,000,000. Old, cunning and very, very rich empire on the COUNTERWEIGHT CONTINENT, also called the Aurient, because of its gold deposits. Once ruled by the Sun Emperor, who was considered by his subjects to be a god (i.e. someone who can kill you instantly for no reason and not have to say sorry). Following the events of *Interesting Times*, it was ruled for a while by Ghenghiz COHEN. Agatean architecture is inclined towards squat pyramids; there is a wall built round the entire Empire, around twenty feet high and sheer on its inner side. In the bad old days, it was patrolled by the Heavenly Guard in very heavy boots to jump on the fingers of the terminally inquisitive. Ladders and tall trees anywhere near the wall were emphatically discouraged.

There is only one port because the Empire did not encourage more contact with the outside world than was absolutely necessary. To be a citizen of the Agatean Empire was felt to be the most fortunate of mortals, and the old government wanted its citizens to remain steadfast in that belief; it was important, therefore, to encourage the suggestion that anywhere else was a mere barbaric wasteland, inhabited by legions of vampire ghosts. The benefits of a period under the rule of a genuine barbarian invader have yet to make themselves shown outside the walls.

Aggy, George. Senior Postman Aggy is a wizened old postman, with a tin leg and a badge for having had fifteen dog bites and still being standing. He is the Chairman of the Ankh-Morpork Order of the Postal Workers Benevolent and Friendly Society and a Member of the Brotherhood of the Order of the Post.[GP]

Agony Aunts, the. Dotsie and Sadie. Possibly sisters. Possibly even real aunts.

Most of the Guilds have their own laws and some means of enforcing them. The Ankh-Morpork SEAMSTRESSES' GUILD is no exception, although what they police are not so much laws as acceptable standards of behaviour. There are some things the ladies of the Shades will not put up with, in short. But no one wants the Watch clumping around the place, putting everyone off and ogling at people who have reasons for not wishing to be ogled, and so when the traditional troll with a big club is not sufficient the Agony Aunts are sent for.

Dotsie is short and plump, Sadie is tall and thin with a pale, oval face. They never run and neither smiles much, at least not at the things most people would find amusing. Both always dress in black, with old-fashioned black straw bonnets. Dotsie's handbag and Sadie's parrot-headed umbrella are used by them as weapons. Their actual mode of operation is unclear, but at best an offender will wake up in the street without any clothes and covered in paint in a place where turpentine is really going to hurt. Or he may find himself on board a ship headed for the incredibly distant island of Sumtri by way of Cape Terror. Or if the offence warrants it, he may never be found again at all; it is rumoured that merely killing someone is only about half way up the Aunts' scale of punishments.

They are seldom required these days, and generally spend their afternoons taking tea in some small tearoom somewhere. Rarely are they seen talking to one another, except about matters currently in hand; the impression is that they did all their talking a long time ago.

The position of the official Watch on the subject of the Aunts is typical of that pragmatism which is the soul of Ankh-Morpork. Since they know that the Guild has a very flexible approach to what is acceptable and, indeed, natural, they take the view that anyone even capable of complaining to them after the ministrations of the Aunts got let off lightly. But a bottle of turpentine and a scrubbing brush is kept at Pseudopolis Yard for the more pathetic cases.

Ahmed, 71-Hour. Prince CADRAM's policeman in Klatch. He studied at the ASSASSINS' GUILD in Ankh-Morpork, and takes the view that after surviving a posh public school a man can survive anything.

Ahmed is a skinny man of uncertain age and below average height. He has a cast in one eye and his face is a network of scar tissue, surrounding a nose like an eagle's beak. He has a sort of beard and moustache, but the scars affect the growth so much that the hair sticks out in strange bunches and at odd angles. He looks, in fact, like he's been hit in the mouth by a hedgehog. Said mouth is full of gold teeth and strange exhalations, because he chews cloves. He wears a huge curved sword on his back and acts as policeman, judge, jury, executioner and sexton for criminals in the far-flung regions of Klatch. [J]

Aimsbury. He works as the chef at the Royal Bank of Ankh-Morpork, along with his daughter Peggy. He is allergic to the *word* 'garlic'. Not the vegetable. Just the word. [MM]

Aix en Pains, Marquis de. A well-known Quirmian wine grower. The Marquis is a young, forward-looking nobleman, who courageously decided to marry an Ankh-Morpork girl. Vive la difference. [RS]

Ajandurah's Wand of Utter Negativity. Weapon used by MARCHESA to control Rincewind and Twoflower. Its use does not cause the victim simply to cease to exist, but also to have never existed. An extremely dangerous device discouraged at Unseen University. [COM]

Aktar. Welcome to Aktar, the first character from the original card index to make it back into the *Companion*. He was a sergeant in the Divine Legion. [SG]

Albert. DEATH's manservant. (*See* MALICH, ALBERTO.)

Albrechtson, Albrecht. A candidate for the position of Low King in ÜBERWALD. Albrecht is very much a traditionalist, and dresses in the cone-shaped leather-flapped robes favoured by the deep underground dwarfs. He resents the reforms that are affecting dwarfdom, and would be happy to see Ankh-Morpork burned to the ground. [TFE]

Alchemists' Guild. Motto: *OMNIS QVIS CORVS-CAT EST OR*. Coat of arms: a shield quartered with, on the upper-right and lower-left quarters, gutt es d'or on a field, azure. On the lower-right and upper-left quarters, a creuset, sable et enflamm on a field, gules.

The Guildhall, located on the Street of Alchemists in Ankh-Morpork, is always new. It was explosively demolished and rebuilt four times over one two-year period – on the last occasion without a lecture and demonstration room, in the hope that this might prove helpful to its long-term prospects.

This tiny, despised Guild largely devotes itself to the aid of widows and orphans of those alchemists who had taken an overly relaxed attitude to potassium cyanide, or who had distilled the juice of some interesting fungi and had drunk the result. There are, in fact, not very many widows and orphans, because alchemists find it difficult to relate to people long enough to form such relationships, and women often find it difficult to grow attached to people who have laminated themselves across the ceiling.

Alchemists are uncooperative in every other respect; every alchemist is a solitary individual, working in darkened rooms or hidden cellars and endlessly searching for the one longed-for breakthrough – the Philosopher's Stone, the Elixir of Life – or, failing that, enormous amounts of cash. This success has never been achieved, but they have succeeded in creating celluloid and popcorn (or, as they styled them, octo-cellulose and banged grains – the basis for the brief Discworld moving-picture industry centred around HOLY WOOD) and have managed to fail to discover nuclear power, computers and electricity. The only real skill that alchemists have developed is how to turn gold into less gold.

They tend to be thin, pink-eyed men, with that vague, unworldly expression that you get from spending too much time in the presence of boiling mercury.* They also tend to be nervous individuals – it comes from not knowing what

the crucible they are experimenting with is going to do next.

The current head of the Guild is Thomas SILVERFISH, although in the nature of things there is a regular turnover – and, indeed, rise and fall – of senior Guild members.

Alfonz. Sailor on the *Unnamed*, a trading boat belonging to CHIDDER's family. Its purpose was largely that of moving things from one place to another without disturbing people, particularly those people of a revenue frame of mind; its appearance was that of a slow merchant ship, which often led pirates to engage in actions which they briefly regretted. Alfonz himself is a mere walking canvas for so many instructive tattoos of a carnal nature that, stictly speaking, he should be dressed in a plain brown wrapper. [P]

Alice. Also called 'Princess'. She is a thirteen-year-old girl, who works in Tower 181 of the Clacks system. [GP]

Aliss, Black. *See* DEMURRAGE, ALISS.

Al Khali. City on the Hubward coast of KLATCH. It is rather like Ankh-Morpork, but with sand instead of mud. Popularly called the Gateway to the mysterious continent of Klatch, Al Khali's temple frescos are famous far and wide, at least among discerning connoisseurs (tours leave hourly from the Statue of OFFLER in the Square of 967 Delights** but are restricted to males over eighteen and married women).

The city is also known for its wind, blowing from the vastness of the deserts and continents nearer the Rim. A gentle but persistent breeze, it 'carries aromatic messages from the heart of the continent, compounded of the chill of deserts, the stink of lions, the compost of jungles and the flatulence of wildebeest'.

The Seriph's palace, The RHOXIE, occupies

---

*   Hence the phrase 'daft as an alchemist', for exactly the same reasons as those behind 'mad as a hatter', another profession that spent far too much time physically around mercury and mentally in orbit around Jupiter.

** The Khalians are meticulous about things that interest them.

most of the centre of the city that isn't covered by the artificial paradise constructed by Seriph CREOSOTE in his search for a more cerebral life. The patron deity of the city is Offler, the Crocodile God, a popular deity on the continent. [S]

Alls Fallow. The one night of the year, according to legend, when witches and warlocks stay in bed. This is probably just a legend; the witches so far identified on the Discworld go to bed when they damn well feel like it. It is worth noting that no practising warlock has ever been found on the Disc and, indeed, no one even knows how many legs one should have. [COM]

Al-Ybi. Undistinguished Klatchian desert city, known in folklore as a place where criminals always claimed to be when accused of a crime. The Seriph of Al-Ybi was once cursed by a dyslexic deity, so that everything he touched turned to GLOD, a small dwarf. That was the most interesting thing that ever happened in Al-Ybi. In Al-Ybi, it is said, the Klatchians invented the concept of zero. That tells history everything it needs to know about what there was to do in Al-Ybi of an evening. [WA]

Amanita. *See* DEVICE, AMANITA.

Amonia. Queen of LANCRE for about three hours. The guests played hide-and-seek at the wedding party; Amonia hid in a big, heavy chest in an attic and was not found for seven months. It seems she is remembered in Discworld legend because the story is considered to be romantic. [LL]

André. A member of the reformed CABLE STREET PARTICULARS, although when first encountered he is a piano player at the Ankh-Morpork OPERA HOUSE. André is a fair-haired young man with a pleasant laugh. He is also a member of the MUSICIANS' GUILD (Memb. No. 1244). [MA]

Andrews, Altogether. One of the Canting Crew – a group of beggars living under the Brass Bridge in Ankh-Morpork. Andrews' personality contains eight separate personali-

ties – Jossi, Lady Hermione, Little Sidney, Mr Viddle, Curly, the Judge, Tinker and Burke. The accepted view is that Andrews was some innocent and hospitable person of a psychic disposition who had simply been overwhelmed by the eight colonizing souls. [TT]

Anghammarad. A very old talking golem. Actually almost 19,000 years old. Born in the fire by the priests of Upsa in the third Ning of the Shaving of the Goat (that should help you to place him accurately), he was given a voice so that he could carry messages. His eyes burn a deep ruby red, and a chill of time radiates off him. On one arm, just above the elbow, he had a metal box on a corroded band which has stained the surrounding clay. This was used to deliver items for King Het of Thut 9000 years ago. [GP]

Angua. Captain and chief tracker of the Ankh-Morpork City WATCH. Her full name is Delphine Angua von Überwald, and she is a werewolf. Her father (sire) was Baron Guye von Überwald (also called Silvertail); her mother was Mme Serafine Soxe-Bloonberg of Genua (also called Yellowfang). Angua had two brothers and a sister. Her sister, Elsa was a YENNORK (she was always in human state) and was killed by their brother Wolfgang von ÜBERWALD. Her brother, Andrei, is a yennork who is always in wolf state. He was driven away by Wolfgang and currently lives as a champion sheepdog in Borogravia. Angua is a classic biomorph: for most of the month she is a well-developed

Angua von Überwald

girl with ash-blond hair (which she washes in Willard Brothers' 'Good Girl!' Flea Shampoo), and at full moon she is a werewolf, with blond hair as long as a mane around her ears. She has a human intellect but with certain additional powers, such as the ability to smell colours and tear out a man's jugular vein.

Angua has a long-term liaison with Captain CARROT Ironfoundersson, also of the Watch. Well, a bit more than just a liaison. It appears that Carrot, whose main hobby is ambling the byways of Ankh-Morpork on foot, has been more than happy to forgo the slight monthly dampener on the relationship in exchange for a girlfriend who is always ready for a nice long walk. [MAA]

Animals of the Disc. The Discworld has a wide range of creatures that are peculiar (in both senses of the word) to it. Many remain decently shrouded in mystery, while others have been the subject of more detailed observation. Some of the more prominent of them include:

Albatross, Pointless. It can fly from the Hub of the Discworld to the Rim without landing. When it does land, however, it seems to do nothing except wander around for a while taking a few photographs. [SG]

Aphodius maximus. The Giant Dung Beetle. [TLH]

Basilisk. [S]

Blowfish, Deep Water. An extremely delicious but deadly fish, parts of whose body contain the poison which is distilled by the Assassins' Guild into 'bloat', the effect of which is to make the eater very briefly impersonate a Zeppelin. A very skilled cook indeed is needed to prepare the dish; his job is to make sure it contains no trace of the toxic liver, stomach and digestive tract. [P]

Bog Truffle, Klatchian Migratory. Pale, brown, warty and now extremely rare. Once whole bogs would appear to be on the move. Delicious on toast. [M]

BOOKWORM, .303.

Burglar Crab. [H]

BUTTERFLY, QUANTUM WEATHER. The existence of this breed (identified, apart from its noticeable effects, by the interesting fractal patterns on its wings) probably owes a lot to the Discworld's precarious balance on the cusp of reality, where a good metaphor stands a fair chance of becoming real. In brief, the QWB can change the weather at a distance merely by flapping its wings. This probably originated as a survival mechanism – few predators would tolerate a very small but extremely localized thunderstorm. [MAA]

CHIMERA.

Coit, Three-banded. [WA]

Combovered Eagle. Can vomit over three countries at once [UA]

Common Creed Waggler [SN]

Crowhawk, Lancre. [LL]

CUCKOO, CLOCK-BUILDING.

CURIOUS SQUID. [CJ]

Deep-Throated Frog-Eater [SN]

Elephant, Hermit. A very shy, thin-skinned species, which for preference wears abandoned huts for protection and concealment. It does not find these hard to obtain. Few people remain in a hut once an elephant has joined them. [MAA]

Fighting Tiger Limpet [H]

Fox, Lancre Reciprocating. Little is known of this creature except that, from context, it appears to act like a warrior about to go into battle, i.e., it probably drinks a lot and makes love as often as possible. [LL]

Ice Bear [H]

Lemma, Shadowing. A possibly invisible creature which stalks and eats mathematicians. [MAA]

Lipwigzers. A breed of fierce guard dogs [GP]

Mongoose, Inflatable. In this creature, evolution has found an efficient way of dealing with burrowing snakes. It is impervious to all snake venom, and its liver is highly prized as a result. [P]

Octarsier, Tree-dwelling. [COM]

Parkinson's Warbler [SN]

Pig breeds. Lancre Stripe, Sto Saddleback. [LL]

Puff Eel, Deepwater. Caught only for its bladder and spleen, which contain a deadly yet tasty poison. [M]

PUZUMA, AMBIGUOUS.

Ramtop sheep. Known for its wool, which can be knitted into vests of almost chain-mail quality. Known breeds include Habbakuk Polls and Lowland Cobble-worths. [GG, W]

RIMFISHER.

SALAMANDERS.

SCALBIE.

Spikefish. [RM]

Stripefish, Red. [RM]

Tharga beasts. It is known that some creatures have a secondary brain. Tharga beasts, herded in some parts of the Ramtops for their meat and hair, have four – one for each leg. A tharga progresses by means of consensus, and therefore is frequently found stuck in crevasses, backed into thorn bushes, plunging over cliffs, etc., its only consolation being that it got there democratically. [M]

Thrush, Lancre Suicide. Many thrushes break open snails by banging them on a stone; this species attempts to dive-bomb them. [MAA]

Überwaldian Deep Cave Land Eel. An ugly, newt-like creature. It emits a burst of DARK LIGHT when startled. [TT]

VERMINE.

Vurms. Glow beetles which grow in deep caves in Llamedos. They have no teeth, and eat organic matter when it gets 'runny'. (T!)

WORRIER, LAPPET-FACED.

YETI.

Yok. Horned beast of burden and food, used by nomads in the Hub regions. Like a yak but heavier. [M]

Ankh, River. This mighty river flows from the RAMTOPS down to the CIRCLE SEA, passing through the great city of ANKH-MORPORK, by which time it is tidal, and very sluggish. Even before it enters Ankh-Morpork it is slow and heavy with the silt of the plains; by the time it gets to the seaward side of the city, even an agnostic could walk across it. The citizens of Ankh-Morpork are strangely proud of this fact. They say that it is hard to drown in the Ankh, but easy to suffocate.

Owing to the accretions of centuries, the bed of the river is in fact higher than some of the low-lying areas; when the winter snows swell the flow, some of the low-rent areas of Morpork flood – if you can use that word for a liquid you could pick up in a net. By the time it has passed through the city, it can be called a liquid only because it moves faster than the land surrounding it.

There are said to be some mystic rivers, one drop of which can steal a man's life away. After its turbid passage through the twin cities, the Ankh could be one of them. Citizens of Ankh-Morpork, however, claim that the river's water is incredibly pure in any case: any water that has passed through so many kidneys, they reason, has to be very pure indeed. There are fish, of a sort, that have adapted to life in the Ankh, but their shape is not recorded because they explode when exposed to air or fresh water.

There are big river gates where the river flows out of the city. These, and the gates on some of the city's bridges, are used in time of fire to flood the city. It says a great deal for the stoicism of the citizens that being drenched in the waters of the river is considered preferable to being burned alive.

The Ankh is probably the only river in the universe on which murder investigators could chalk the outline of a corpse.

Ankh-Morpork. Mottoes: *MERVS IN PECTVM ET IN AQVAM* and *QVANTI CANICVLA ILLE IN FENESTRA*. Coat of arms: a shield, supported by two Hippopotâmes Royales Bâillant – one enchainé , one couronné au cou – and surmounted by a Morpork Vautré Hululant, bearing an Ankh d'or, and ornée by a banner with the legend '*Merus In Pectum Et In Aquam*'. The shield bisected by a tower en maçonnerie sans fenêtres and quartered by a fleuve, argent and azure, bend sinister. On the upper-right quarter a field, vert, of *brassicae prasinae*; on the lower-left quarter a field, sable. On the upper-left and lower-right quarters, bourses d'or on a field argent. Below the arms a ribbon with the legend '*Quanti Canicula Ille In Fenestra*'.

Pop.: 1,000,000 (including the suburbs).

Chief exports: manufactured goods, most of the processed animal and vegetable produce of the fertile STO PLAINS, trouble. Main 'invisible' exports: banking, assassination, wizardry, trouble.

Imports: raw materials, people, trouble.

The shield shows the TOWER OF ART, the oldest building in the city, and also celebrates both the River ANKH and the vast surrounding expanse of brassica fields which have combined to produce the city's prosperity and, to a great extent, its smell.

The younger of the two mottoes, *Merus In Pectum Et In Aquam* (lit.: 'Pure in mind and water') was devised by a rather high-minded committee in the early days of the First Republic, and is considered a jolly good laugh.

The older – and, strangely enough, the more popular – is *Quanti Canicula Ille In Fenestra* (lit.: 'How much is that small dog in the window?'). Its origin is the subject of urban legend but can be traced, as can so many of the city's oddities, to the reign of King Ludwig the Tree.

Kings cannot become mad; this is self-evident. Peasants become insane, small traders and craftsmen go mad, nobles become eccentric, and King Ludwig was a little confused and so detached from reality that he couldn't make contact with it even by shouting and prodding at it with a long stick.

King Ludwig's four-year reign was one of the happiest of the entire monarchical period, and people looked forward to his proclamations on subjects such as the need to develop a new kind of frog and the way invisible creatures spied on him when he went to the lavatory. It was less popular among the nobles. Since it would destroy the entire edifice of the monarchical system to admit that the man from whom all power derived actually did go around all day wearing his underpants on his head, an informal system was devised to suggest that, far from being confused, the King was airing an intellect both rarefied and subtle. Monographs were published, agreeing that the modern frog was indeed hopelessly outdated. There was even a brief vogue for wearing head lingerie.

Anything the King said was treated as an oracular utterance. On the day he was asked to choose from three suggested mottoes for the city, his comment, 'How much is that doggie in the window?', was agreed, by a small committee of courtiers, to be the most acceptable of the King's suggestions, the other two being 'Bduh bduh bduh bduh' and 'I think I want my potty now'.

It has subsequently been suggested that the motto is in fact marvellously devised for Ankh-Morpork, since it neatly encapsulates a) the city's intelligent questioning spirit, b) its concern for mercantile matters, and c) its love of animals. Readers who consider this strange should reflect that the motto on the Great Seal of the United States of America comes from a

Latin poem about making salad dressing.*

Ankh-Morpork is the oldest existing city on the Discworld (and known to its citizens/denizens as the Big WAHOONIE). Bisected by the River Ankh, the city is really two cities: proud Ankh, Turnwise of the river, and pestilent Morpork on the Widdershins side, although the pestilence is quite democratic and in fact covers most of the city. Nestling (or, more accurately, squatting) in the Sto Plains, close to the CIRCLE SEA, the city is theoretically built on loam, although in fact it is built on past incarnations of the city, rather like Troy but without the style.**

Ankh-Morpork has been burned down many times in its long history – out of revenge, carelessness, spite or even just for the insurance. Most of the stone buildings that actually make it a city have survived intact. Many people – that is, many people who live in stone houses – think that a good fire every hundred years or so is essential to the health of the city since it helps to keep down rats, roaches, fleas and, of course, people not rich enough to live in stone houses. Each time, it is rebuilt using the traditional local materials of tinder-dry wood and thatch waterproofed with tar.

It is generally accepted that the original building in the city was the Tower of Art, around which Unseen University grew up as a sort of keep, and some small parts of the first city wall are still visible. Over the centuries, however, the city's centre moved downstream as docks were built on the more navigable parts of the river; and fragments of city walls and the general layout of the roads give Ankh-Morpork the appearance, from the air, of a cut onion, although a cut onion smells rather different (i.e., better.).

Over the millennia the city has tried various forms of government; an ancient system of sewers – known only to the ASSASSINS' GUILD (until *Men At Arms*) – and a few other details

testify to a glorious past (glorious being defined as a time when Thousands of People Could Be Persuaded by Men with Swords to Build Big Things out of Stone). There has been monarchy, oligarchy, anarchy and dictatorship. The current system appears to be a sort of highly specialized democracy; as they say in Ankh-Morpork, it's a case of One Man, One Vote – Lord VETINARI is the Man, he has the Vote.

In essence the city is governed as a result of the interplay of various pressure groups. Lord Vetinari positively encouraged the growth of the Guilds, of which there are now some 300 in the city. His reason for doing this may be discerned in his unpublished book 'The Servant', a compendium of advice and precepts to a young man setting out to govern a fictional city (in the book identified only as AM) in a passage which runs: 'Where there are clearly two sides to a question, make haste to see that these rapidly become two hundred.' In practice, the city's political structure consists entirely of a huge number of pressure groups plotting, fighting, conniving, forming alliances, shouting, scheming, intriguing and making plans, in the middle of which one man is quietly doing things his way.

Economically, the city is the profitable bottleneck between the Sto Plains and the rest of the Discworld. It is a service centre for the hinterland in several senses of the phrase, and carries out all the functions that citizens usually perform for their country cousins, such as selling them the Brass Bridge at a knockdown price. It is the big city you go to to seek your fortune. And other people also seek your current fortune, small though it may be, as soon as you arrive.

While it has many of the attributes of the classical fantasy city – Guilds, walls, wizards and so on – Ankh-Morpork is also a working city, with a very large number of small factories and workshops (generally in the Phedre Road and Cable

---

* *Moretum, usually attributed to Virgil.*

** *A lot bigger, though. Troy only covered seven acres, but it did have Homer as its director of tourism and publicity.*

Street areas, and more traditionally along the Street of Cunning Artificers). There is a flourishing cattle market and slaughterhouse district.

Fresh water used to be brought straight into the city centre by a viaduct now barely visible in Water Street, but it fell down centuries ago and, what with one thing and another, no one ever got around to rebuilding it. Water is now drawn from wells, which are very shallow indeed with Ankh-Morpork's high water table. This, along with the slaughterhouses and the cabbage fields and the spice houses and the breweries, is a major component of Ankh-Morpork's most famous civic attribute: its aforementioned Smell. The citizens are proud of the smell; on a really good day, they carry chairs outside to enjoy it. They even put up a statue to it, to commemorate the time when troops of a rival state tried to invade by stealth one dark night; they managed to get only as far as the top of the walls when, to their horror, their nose plugs gave out.[*]

No enemies have ever entered Ankh-Morpork.

This is not entirely true. Technically they have, quite often; the city welcomes free-spending barbarian invaders, but somehow the puzzled raiders always find, after a few days, that they don't own their horses any more, and within a couple of months they're just another minority group with its own graffiti and food shops.

The city's inhabitants have brought the profession of interested bystander to a peak of perfection. These highly skilled gawpers will watch anything, especially if there's any possibility of anyone getting hurt in an amusing way.

The city's 'picturesque' SHADES, with its crowded docks, many bridges, its souks, its casbahs, its streets lined with nothing but temples, all point to its cosmopolitan style. It welcomes anyone – regardless of race, colour, class or creed – who has spending money in incredible amounts.

It has been said that the largest dwarfish colony anywhere on the Disc is in Ankh-Morpork. This may be the case. Certainly the city is home to a large number of dwarfs, a growing number of trolls, and many undead and other special-interest groups. This has caused a number of problems but also some benefits – in jobs, for example. The silicon-based trolls gravitate towards messy jobs because, to them, nasty organic substances are of no more account than sand and gravel would be to a human; vampires tend to end up in the meat business, and often run shops catering for those of a kosher persuasion; undead often undertake dangerous tasks, such as working on high buildings, because nothing can happen to them that hasn't happened already.

The associated problems are more traditional. Trolls hate dwarfs, dwarfs hate trolls. It's a symmetrical arrangement that dates back thousands of years and has accumulated enough ill-feeling that the actual cause is now quite irrelevant. This mutual antagonism has been imported into the city.

Troll skin, which is as flexible as leather but much, much tougher and longer-lasting, is still occasionally used for clothing by the less socially sensitive, and there is a particularly disreputable tavern (and this is Ankh-Morpork we're talking about) which is not only called the Troll's Head but has a very old one on a pole over the door. On the other hand, trolls have been known to eat people (for their mineral content) and the troll game of aargrooha, in which a human head is kicked around by two teams wearing boots of obsidian until it either ends up in goal or bursts, is almost certainly still played in its classical form in remote mountain regions.

So, mingling in the streets of the city are people whose recent ancestors variously ate, skinned, beheaded or in some cases jumped up and down in heavy boots on one another. That there is not a permanent state of all-out war is a tribute to the unifying force of the Ankh-Morpork dollar.

There are two legends about the founding of Ankh-Morpork.

---

[*] *The statue, now sadly decayed, is located close to what is now the Haberdashers' Guild, in a formerly unnamed area known locally as Fetter Lane, presumably a corruption of 'foetid' or 'fetor'.*

One relates that the two orphaned brothers who built the city were in fact found and suckled by a hippopotamus (lit. *orijeple*, although some historians hold that this is a mistranslation of *orejaple*, a type of glass-fronted drinks cabinet). Eight heraldic hippos line the city's Brass Bridge, facing out to sea. It is said that if danger ever threatens the city, they will run away. Nobody knows why the hippopotamus is the royal animal of Ankh-Morpork. The reasons are lost in the smogs of time. Rome had a she-wolf; on this basis, it is possible that the founders of Ankh-Morpork were suckled, or possibly trodden on, by a hippo. But a hippo seems at least as legitimate as a slug, the city animal of Seattle, Washington. It has been speculated that hippos once inhabited the Ankh. If so, they have long since dissolved.

The other legend, recounted less frequently by citizens, is that at an even earlier time a group of wise men survived a flood sent by the gods by building a huge boat, and on this boat they took two of every type of animal then existing on the Disc. After some weeks the combined manure was beginning to weigh the boat low in the water, so – the story runs – they tipped it over the side, and called it Ankh-Morpork. (*See also* CIVIL WAR, LAWS OF ANKH-MORPORK, MONARCHY, PATRICIAN.)

Ankh-Morpork National Anthem. *We Can Rule You Wholesale* was written by Count Henrik Shline von Überwald. The anthem is particularly noteworthy for being the only one that has a second verse *officially* consisting of incoherent muttering. The Count had noted that any group of people singing their country's national anthem never remembers how the second verse goes.

> When dragons belch and hippos flee
> My thoughts, Ankh-Morpork, are of thee
> Let others boast of martial dash
> For we have boldly fought with cash
> We own all your helmets, we own all your shoes.
> We own all your generals - touch us and you'll lose.

> Morporkia! Morporkia!
> Morporkia owns the day!
> We can rule you wholesale
> Touch us and you'll pay.

> We bankrupt all invaders,
> We sell them souvenirs,
> We ner ner ner ner ner ner by the ears,
> Er ner ner ner ner ner ner ner ner,
> Ner ner ner ner ner, ner ner ner ner ner,
> Ner your gleaming swords, we mortgaged to the hilt.

> Morporkia! Morporkia!
> Ner ner ner ner ner ner ner ner ner ner ner ner ner ner ner ner
> We can rule you wholesale
> Credit where it's due.

Ankhstones. Glittery jewels. Like rhinestones, but a different river. [S]

Annagovia, Grand Duchess. Ruler of Borogravia. A childless, plain, middle-aged woman, whose saggy chin and slightly bulging eyes made her look like someone had put a large fish in a dress. She was worshipped by her people, who called her 'The Little Mother'. They pray to a portrait of her, painted when she was aged forty. At the time of the events of *Monstrous Regiment*, she had not been seen for thirty years and was believed to still be in mourning for a young Duke who died a week after they got married. He was gored by a wild pig during a hunt. [MR]

Annaple, Nanny. A witch who lives over the mountain from Bad Ass (no further geographical location has ever been given, which is unfortunate since from Bad Ass everywhere is behind some mountain or other). She owns a billy goat, which is absolutely traditional for a witch. She lost all her teeth by the age of twenty, and has a face so warty it looks like a sockful of marbles; this has led to some coolness between her and Granny Weatherwax, who has never succeeded in looking properly crone-like. [ER]

Anoia. A (minor) Goddess of Things That Get Stuck in Drawers.* Appears as a skinny, tired-looking woman, wearing a sheet draped around her and smoking a dramatically sparking cigarette. She hasn't been doing drawers long. She used to be a volcano goddess. Now, she also finds lost corkscrews and things that roll under furniture. The other gods also want her to do stuck zips (which she is thinking about). Mostly, though, she manifests when people rattle a stuck drawer and call upon the gods. [W]

Anti-crimes. As you might expect on the Disc, even crime has its opposite. Merely giving someone something is not the opposite of robbery. To be an anti-crime, it has to be done in such a way as to cause outrage and/or humiliation to the victim. So there is breaking-and-decorating, proffering-with-embarrassment (as in most retirement presentations) and whitemailing (as in, for example, threatening to reveal to his enemies a mobster's secret donations to charity). Anti-crimes have never really caught on. [RM]

Antiphon. Ephebian writer. The greatest writer of comic plays in the world, at least according to Antiphon (in the plays, the actors hit one another with big sticks every time they make a joke and refuse to proceed until someone laughs). Looks as though he is built of pork. [P]

Anybody, Rob. Big man of the Nac Mac Feegle clan near the village of Tiffany Aching, over on the Chalk. Technically, their Head Man. Smells, as they all do, like slightly drunk potatoes, and has the traditional red hair and tattoo'd blue skin. He also sports a helmet made from a rabbit's skull. Rob is married to Jeannie of the Long Lake, they have seven sons (one of whom is Wee Duggie Bignose) and one daughter. Not a natural learner, but strong-willed and determined, he can soon write his own name, яOB NybO D. [WFM]

Apocralypse, The. The Half-Hearted End of the World. The Triumph of the ICE GIANTS. The Teatime of the Gods. Believed to be the time when the Ice Giants, imprisoned by the gods, will break free and ride out on their dreadful glaciers to regain their ancient dominion, crushing out the flames of civilization until the world lies naked and frozen under the terrible cold stars and Time itself freezes over. Or so it is said. Discworld legend is as unreliable on this as it is on so many other things, hence the name.

Heralding the event – should it ever happen and not just be an interesting tale someone wrote down after too many mushrooms – a dreadful ruler has to arise, there must be a terrible war and the four dread Horsemen (DEATH, WAR, FAMINE and PESTILENCE) have to ride. Then the creatures from the DUNGEON DIMENSIONS will break into the world... Again.

This has all nearly happened once, but it was delayed and then postponed, partly because three of the four Horsemen had their horses stolen while they were enjoying a pub lunch.

Something like a full blown Apocalypse threatened the world during the events chronicled in *Thief of Time*, during which the Four Horsemen actually sided with humanity (why kill off the only creatures who believe in you?) and were aided in this endeavour by the long-lost Fifth Horseman, KAOS, who'd left because of creative differences long before they became famous.

---

* Often, but not uniquely, a ladle, but sometimes a metal spatula or, rarely, a mechanical egg-whisk that nobody in the house admits to ever buying. The desperate mad rattling and cries of 'How can it close on the damn thing but not open with it? Who bought this? Do we ever use it?' is as praise unto Anoia. She also eats corkscrews.

Rob Anybody

Arcanum, Mrs. Owner and proprietor of Mrs Eucrasia Arcanum's Lodging House for Respectable Working Men in Ankh-Morpork. Mrs Arcanum likes Respectable people who are Clean and Decent. She keeps Respectable beds and cooks cheap but Respectable meals for her Respectable lodgers who were mostly middle-aged, unmarried and extremely sober (and respectable). She is not averse to trolls and dwarfs as guests provided they are Respectable. She provides big helpings of food that tastes, well, respectable. One of her lodgers was William DE WORDE. [TT]

Arch-astronomer. Ruler of KRULL. Responsible for the building of the *POTENT VOYAGER* and for the death of Goldeneyes Silverhand DACTYLOS, its designer. [COM]

Archchancellor. Master of Unseen University in Ankh-Morpork and the official leader of all the wizards on the Disc (a polite fiction on a par with the Queen of England also being Queen of Australia). Once upon a time this would have meant that he was the most powerful in the handling of magic, but in more quiet times senior wizards tend to look upon actual magic as a bit beneath them. They prefer administration, which is safer and nearly as much fun, and also big dinners.

The Archchancellor is elected on the Eve of Small Gods. Well, not exactly elected, because wizards don't have any truck with the undignified business of voting, and it is well known that Archchancellors are selected by the gods (which wizards don't believe in). The double doors to the Great Hall are locked and triple-barred. An incoming Archchancellor has to request entry three times before they will be unlocked, signifying that he is appointed with the consent of wizardry in general.

In more recent times, the lifespan of Archchancellors has been seen to be a bit on the short side, as wizardry's natural ambition took its toll. UU has been in existence for thousands of years, and over the last fifty the average Archchancellor remained in office for about eleven months.

UU has had many different kinds of Archchancellor over the years: big ones, small ones, cunning ones, slightly insane ones, extremely insane ones – they've come, they've served (in some cases not long enough for anyone to be able to complete the official painting to be hung in the Great Hall) and they've died. The senior wizard in a world of magic has the same prospects of long-term employment as a pogo-stick tester in a minefield.

It should be noted that Mustrum RIDCULLY, at the time of writing, seems to have had a very successful and, above all, injury-free career as Archchancellor, and appears to be ushering UU into one of its quieter periods.

Other Archchancellors thus far encountered include:

Badger, William
Bewdley
Bigger, Preserved
Bowell
Buckleby
CHURN, Ezrolith
COIN (arguable, of course)
CUTANGLE
Hopkins, 'Trouter'
MALICH, Alberto
RIDCULLY, Mustrum (the current incumbent)
Scrawn
Sloman
SPOLD, Greyhald 'Tudgy'
TRYMON, Ymper (305th)
Wayzygoose, Virrid (didn't actually make it)
WEATHERWAX, Galder (304th)

Archchancellor's Hat. The old hat, now replaced (*see* RIDCULLY, MUSTRUM), was worn by the head of all wizards, on the head of all wizards. (This is to say, *metaphorically* it was worn by all wizards – it is similar to the idea that 'every soldier has a field marshal's baton in his knapsack.')*

---

* *In the case of Corporal Nobbs, his knapsack was found to contain three field marshal's batons, a general's helmet, a colonel's dress dagger, fifteen pairs of boots, some still occupied, and three gold teeth.*

It was what every wizard aspired to, the symbol of organized magic, the pointy tip of the profession. Through the old hat spoke all the Archchancellors who had ever lived. So it was always believed.

In fact, it was rather battered, with its gold thread tattered and unravelling. It was pointy, of course, with a wide, floppy brim. It was covered with gold lace, pearls, bands of purest VERMINE, sparkling ANKHSTONES, some incredibly tasteless sequins and – a real give-away – a circle of OCTARINES round its crown, blazing in all eight colours of the spectrum. It was kept on a velvet cushion in a tall, round and battered leather box. When it spoke, which it did when fighting the Sourcerer, it had a clothy voice, with a choral effect, like a lot of voices talking at the same time, in almost perfect unison. [S]

Archeios. A private in the Ephebian army. [E]

Archmandrite of B'Ituni. A previous owner of the black sword KRING. B'Ituni is little more than a fortified oasis near the Klatch–Hershebian border. [COM]

Ardent. A deep-downer dwarf, who acts as chief liaison with the 'world above' (those who live on the surface of the Disc). He is seen wearing a rigid, pointed black hood and he is otherwise completely shrouded in overlapping black leather scales, with just a narrow slit for his eyes. Has the same, level, way of speaking as Lord Vetinari. [T!]

Argavisti. General of the Ephebian army, involved in the brief war against Omnia [SG]

Arif, Greasy. A fisherman from Klatch. Together with his son, Akhan, he was one of the first people to re-discover the lost Kingdom of Leshp during the events of *Jingo*. [J]

Aristocrates. Secretary to the Tyrant of Ephebe. He is the author of 'Platitudes'. [SG]

Armpit. A really stupid dwarf in the employ of Evil Harry DREAD. [TLH]

Art, Works of. A number of major works of art have recently been named in the series. These include:

Battle of Koom Valley, the (Methodia Rascal) [T!]
Beauty Arising from the Pease Pudding Cart Attended by Cherubs Carrying Hot Dogs and Pies (Unknown art student) [UA]
Countess Quatro Fromaggio at her Toilette (Leonard of Quirm) [RS]
Dogs and Pies [UA]
Don't Talk to Me About Mondays! (Daniella Pouter [T!]
Freedom (Daniella Pouter) [T!]

Goddess Anoia Arising from the Cutlery, the (some bloke with three 'I's in his name, apparently) [T!]

Man with Dog (Lord Vetinari & Wuffles) (William Pouter) [MM]

MONA OGG, THE (Leonard of Quirm) [MAA]

Still Life with Cabbage, Broccoli both Green and Purple, Sprouts, Kale and Elderly Couple being Attacked by Werewolf (Josiah Remnant)

Three Large Pink Women and One Piece of Gauze (Caravati) [T!]

For completeness, I will include a poem:

Oi! To His Deaf Mistress (Robert Scandal) [UA]

Artela. Wife of TEPPICYMON XXVII and mother of TEPPIC. She used to be a concubine. A vague woman who was fond of cats, she died in a swimming accident (insofar as a crocodile was involved). [P]

Arthur. A fellow student of TEPPIC's at the ASSASSINS' GUILD. A little kid with curls. [P]

Arthur, Barking Mad. Member of the DOG GUILD. One-eyed, bad-tempered rottweiler, killed by Big FIDO. [MAA]

Arthur, Wee Mad. He is a gnome, four inches high, and the supplier of rats to dwarf eateries throughout Ankh-Morpork. This enables him to work as a rat-catcher for nothing, selling his rats at half the Guild rate. He is basically humanoid and dresses in ratskin trousers. At least while working, he is bare to the waist save for two bandoliers criss-crossing his chest. He smokes tiny cigars, carries a very small crossbow, and is generally in a foul mood His advertising sign declares:

'WEE MAD ARTHUR
'For those little things that get you down'
Rats *FREE*
Mise: 1p per ten tails
Moles: ½p each
Warsps: 50p per nest,
Hornets 20p extra
Cockroaches and similar by aranjement
Small fees. BIG JOBS

Wee Mad Arthur, who can live more luxuriously on a dollar a day that most humans can live on fifty dollars, is also a very obvious example of the LAW OF UNEQUAL RETURNS. He was raised by a bunch of cobblers but, despite being referred to as a gnome by the careless citizens of Ankh-Morpork, he is an urbanized and solitary member of the NAC MAC FEEGLE.

He now has very gainful employment as one of the smallest officers in the Ankh-Morpork City Watch. [FOC]

Artorollo. Past King of Ankh-Morpork. Little fat man, squeaky voice. This seems to be all that anyone can remember about him. [M]

Ashal, General. Chief Adviser to Prince CADRAM and leader of his army. [J]

AshkEnte, Rite of. Spell performed to summon and bind DEATH. It is generally done with reluctance, because senior wizards are usually very old and would prefer not to do anything to draw Death's attention to themselves. On the other hand, it is also very effective, since Death knows almost everything that is going on because he is usually closely involved.

The Rite has evolved over the years. It used to be thought that eight wizards were required, each at his station on the point of a great ceremonial octogram, swaying and chanting, arms held out sideways so their fingertips just touched; there was also a requirement for dribbly candles, thuribles, green smoke and all the other tedious paraphernalia of traditional High magic. In fact, it can be performed by a couple of people with three small bits of wood and 4cc of mouse blood; it can even be performed with two bits of wood and a fresh egg.

There are in fact ten ways of performing the Rite; nine of them kill you instantly and the other one is very hard to remember.

Ashk-Ur-Men-Tep. A past king of DJELIBEYBI, from the Third Empire. [P]

Asphalt. Very short, broad, troll with show-business experience, mostly to do with mucking out circus elephants and being repeatedly sat on by them. Employed as a roadie by the BAND WITH ROCKS IN. Although shorter than a dwarf, Asphalt makes up for it in breadth. [SM]

Assassins' Guild. Motto: NIL MORTIFI, SINE LVCRE. Coat of arms: a shield, bisected by a bend sinister, purpure. In the upper-right half a poignard d'or, draped with a masque en sable, lined gris on a field, gules. In the bottom-left half two croix d'or on a sable field.

The light and airy Guild building, which looks more like the premises of a gentlemen's club, is located in Filigree Street, Ankh-Morpork. The gates on the sole entrance to the Guild are said never to shut because DEATH is open for business all the time, but it is really because the hinges rusted centuries ago (although by the time of *Men At Arms* clearly someone had done something about this).

The Assassins' Guild offers the best all-round education in the world. A qualified assassin should be at home in any company, and be able to play at least one musical instrument. Anyone inhumed by a graduate of the Guild school can go to his rest satisfied that he has been annulled by someone of taste and discretion, and probably also a social equal. The entrance exam is not strenuous: the school is easy to get into and easy to get out of (the trick is to get out upright).

A BRIEF STROLL AROUND THE MAIN QUAD

Join us on a brief tour of the Guild, starting with the main gates in Filigree Street. Do not neglect the Porter's Lodge, wherein may be found Stippler the porter. His father was porter here, as was *his* father. He has seen it all, and the few bits he hasn't seen he can guess at.

Your path will then lead out into the quadrangle, dominated by its statue of Ellis William Netley, the student who, when playing the Wall Game, first picked up the ball and hurled it with such force that he knocked an opposing player off a second-storey window ledge. He was beaten senseless for this, but his action changed the Game from the rather insipid ball game that it was to the thrilling and bloody spectacle it is today.

To one side of the quad, you can still see the new masonry of the repair to the museum wall after the unfortunate events concerning the removal from office of the previous Master, Dr Cruces.

Looking up, you can see the bell tower, topped by the Guild's famous cloaked man weathervane (known as 'Wiggy Charlie'), which has oft been decked with porcelain chamberpots and female undergarments by waggish students on Wag Days.

Returning to the cloister, we turn and walk along, past the oil paintings and busts of famous inhumees. The first bust, of a former Crown Prince of Brindisi, is now almost unrecognizable as generations of student assassins have patted his regal nose for luck. His plaque records that he 'Departed this vale of tears on Grune 3, Year of the Sideways Leech, with the assistance of the Hon. K. W. Dobson (Viper House)'.

We now turn into the Combination Corridor, leading past the Museum. The Museum is very instructive; time spent in sober reflection there is never wasted. One exhibit which usually exercises the minds of boys for many a long night is the one-armed teddy bear (Mr Wuggle) used by Croydon Minimus to inhume the Baron von Wendeltreppe-Steckenpferd in 1687. Since that fateful day, the Wendeltreppe-Steckenpferds have never allowed any soft toys within 20 miles of their castle in Überwald.

Beyond the museum, we reach Big School, which used to be the Guild's only classroom. It now serves principally as the Banqueting Hall and is also used for indoor sports, assemblies and examinations. Big School is the oldest unaltered room in college and its beams, despite their inaccessibility, have been carved with the names of most of the Guild's most famous old boys.

Just before the multi-denominational Chapel, there is a small door leading up to the bell tower, which houses the Inhumation Bell. This tolls the hours but, as befits the city's most elegant academy, it is always fashionably late.

It also is tolled whenever news comes through of an Assassin successfully completing an assignment and also upon the death of a old pupil of the college. Of course, this may quite often be one and the same event.

Proceeding further around we come to Liming Corridor which leads past Mr Wilkinson's Study to the Library. This is believed to be the largest Ankh-Morpork library outside Unseen University and, in the areas of assassination and other life-threatening professions, we like to think that it exceeds even UU's holdings of relevant tomes.

The Guild extends to five floors, excluding basements, dormer levels and lofts. Much of the building is out of bounds to the Guild's students but, as Lord Downey would say, 'No one became a great Assassin by always obeying the rules. Of course, no one ever became a great Assassin by disobeying the rules *and getting caught*, either.'

At some time in their career, every pupil will see the inside of the Master of Assassins' study. Some will go for a cup of tea, a chat and the automatic avoidance of an almond slice, some will be going for a punishment, some will have been sent up for good and some will be going to receive bad news.

The room is a classic example of a Guild study – impressive, oak-panelled and well-carpeted room – which also serves as the meeting room for the Guild Council. Indeed, to one side you will see the Council's long, mahogany table. The room also contains the Master's own library and workbench – and who knows what mysterious substances may be stored in the dozens of intriguing drawers in his apothecary cabinet?

The room is dominated by the four huge black granite pillars that support the ornate ceiling. Four-square between those pillars, carved as they are with the names of famous Assassins, is the Master's desk, with its wrought-iron rack for birches and canes. These are a relic of the old days. In the modern college, we do not believe in anything so namby-pamby as *corporal* punishment.

SCHOOL PRIZES AND AWARDS

Sending up for Good

Despite its name, this is a good thing: it means a student has produced a piece of schoolwork – practical or written – which is adjudged by their tutor to be so outstanding as to merit their being sent up to the Master of Assassins' study for sherry and an almond slice. Their name is also then featured in the School Magazine.

The Teatime Prize

This will be given after the Hogswatch and de Murforte vacations for the two best papers on the subject 'Who I Killed on My Holidays'. Pupils are not, of course, expected to actually *inhume* anybody, but a team of senior Assassins will assess the pupils' maps, routes, amassed information, professed target and projected methods of 'solution' before awarding the prize for the best *virtual* inhumation. The prize is named after the late Jonathan Teatime, a young Assassin whose plans for the inhumation of Death, the Hogfather, the Soul Cake Duck, Old Man Trouble and several major gods were the talk of the Guild. His body has never been found.

The Blankman Divinity Prize

This is open to all boys in the second and third years for the most realistic representation of the god of their choice achieved using only stale bread and sesame seeds.

Distinction in Trials

Given to the top three boys in every year at end of term Trials (exams).

The Body Trophy

Named after our popular old Under Master, Mr Wilberforce Body, this is awarded to the winning team at the Wall Game.

The Wilkinson Cup

Awarded annually to the boy who scores most consistently high marks at fencing.

The Pendu Illuminated Manuscript

Awarded to the boy who wins the Climbing Competition at the Sports Day. The award is simply placed atop some high building in the city, and the pupil who returns to the Guild with it is adjudged the winner. The opportunities for waylaying, trapping, ambushing and cheating make this a remarkable exercise in Assassin skills.

The Vemificus Chalice

Traditionally awarded at Gaudy Night to the pupil adjudged by the Head of Necrotic Medicine and Applied Pathology to have shown most promise in practical exercises in that specialism.

The Insidiae Plate

Presented on Founder's Day by the Provost of Assassins. The winner is the constructor of the most elaborate trap mechanism in the Show and Tell section at Open Day, although actual killing will result in disqualification.

The Ars Plumaria Cup

This is won by the pupil scoring highest marks for Personal Grooming. A much-contested award.

SCHOOL HOUSES
(AND THEIR HOUSE TUTORS)

Viper House (Mr Nivor)
Scorpion House (Lady T'malia)
Tump House (Miss Band)
Broken Moons House (Mr Moody)
Raguineau's (Baron Strifenkanen)
Pernypopax Dampier (Prof. Stone)
Cobra House (Mr Mericet)
Wigblock Prior (Kompt de Yoyo)
B2 House [day pupils](Dr von Ubersetzer)
C1 House [day pupils](Dr Perdore)
Mykkim House (Mr Linbury-Court)
Mrs Beddowe's House (M le Balourd)
Tree Frog House [day pupils] (Mr Bradlofrudd)
Black Widow House [girls] (Mme les Deux-Épées)
Welcome Soap House (Mr Graumunchen)
Raven House (Miss Smith-Rhodes)

A BRIEF HISTORY OF THE GUILD

Classically, assassination as a profession began in the more mountainous regions of Klatch, where aspirants would partake of a drug known as *hasheesh* which, in sufficient quantities, would cause them to wear flared trousers and listen to really monotonous music with every sign of enjoyment.

Those early 'assassins' then disappeared into history and emerged somewhat later in the form we now recognize them. Possibly their source of supply dried up.

The Guild as it exists today owes a great debt to its founders, Sir Gyles and Lady de Murforte. Sir Gyles was a warrior knight in the days of King Cirone I (Cirone the Unsteady). He quested extensively in Klatch for the greater glory of gold and, during one of his longer crusades against any Klatchians who had money, he learned of the brotherhood of assassins. At this time they were practising their craft for general hire and were already playing an important role in the internal politics of the Komplezianne Empire, rulers of Klatch at that time.* He was so impressed by the skill, poise, intelligence and wit of those Klatchian assassins whom he met (socially) that, far-sighted man that he was, he vowed to form a school for assassins in his native Ankh-Morpork. It was recorded by his clerk that his actual words were 'Onne daye we will neede to beat thys barstads atte theyre owne game.'

On his return to the city, he talked of his plans with his wife Lady de Murforte. She wholeheartedly supported her husband and he altered his will to leave most of his lands on the Sto Plains and many valuable sites in Ankh-Morpork for its construction.

Work on the new school began in 1511. Tutors were brought in from Klatch to train the city's brighter academics and psychopaths in the various skills needed to be a great assassin, so that the faculty should be ready when the building works had been completed. The old building on

the site of the current Guild building had been a warehouse for scrolls and books and it was demolished so that a new, light, airy edifice could be erected to reflect the glory of the new school.

The new school, known then as the de Murfoote School for Gentlemen Assassins, was officially opened by King Cirone II on 27 August 1512. Its first Head Master was Doctor Guillaume de Chacal. Dr de Chacal was not himself known to be an assassin, but had been recruited direct from the prestigious Academie Quirmienne, where his reputation as a strict disciplinarian and moral leader was second to none, if one ignores a few wild accusations by people who were never able to produce any hard evidence.

The school then had eight tutors and seventy-two students, known as King's Scholars. (The King had bestowed the Royal Charter on the school, together with a modest sum to fund the purchase of textbooks, weaponry and anatomical charts. The first influx of students also, as it happened, included Cirone, Prince of Llamedos, his eldest son.) All the students were then housed within the Guild building, in dormitories, or houses in the area which were then named simply after their key code on the architect's plans for the school.

Within a few years, the combination of the royal patronage and the excellent standard of exam results being achieved by the now Royal de Murfoote School for Gentlemen Assassins, had led to pressure from the city's wealthier inhabitants for its doors to be opened to students who, whilst they would benefit from the high standard of education available at the school, might not actually intend to kill people for a living. The King agreed to this extension to the school's charter and places were allocated to twenty-four children of citizens. These students were known as 'Oppidans', from the Latatian for 'town'.

The school went from strength to strength. Over the years, its numbers of students and staff rose, and boys were boarded in houses off-site, run by a number of women known as

---

* *The byzantine and convoluted politics of that lost Empire, which ruled from the now-buried city of Komplez, were in fact responsible for our word 'complex'.*

'dames' because of a then-current tradition of wearing huge white drawers with red spots on and owning a dancing cow.

In 1576, the school was invited by the city's elders to elevate its status to that of a Guild, giving it voting rights in the city's Guild Council. It then changed its name to the Royal Guild of Assassins but, following the events of 1688, it wisely dropped the use of the 'Royal' from its title and restyled itself the Guild of Assassins.

Regrettably, in 1767, following a rash wager by the then head of the Guild, who believed that two pairs could beat any other hand, the freehold of the main Guild premises passed seamlessly to Sir John 'Mad Jack' Ramkin, and has remained in the possession of the Ramkin family until recently, when it became part of the marriage gift of Lady Sybil Ramkin to Sir Samuel Vimes, later His Grace the Duke of Ankh-Morpork, with whom the Guild has a good working relationship.

It now has the original seventy-two King's Scholars (as they are still known) plus 180 Oppidans and a varying number of scholarship boys, the number of the latter usually decreasing as the term progresses. In this form, it has continued to grow in reputation and influence in Ankh-Morpork and throughout the known Disc. Indeed, so great is the reputation of the Guild education that a number of students now come from Klatch.

There are many stories of Assassins meeting, in the course of business, clients who themselves were 'old boys' of the school, and singing a few verses of the old school song together before the inhumation was completed. There have been occasions where the client, shedding tears of joy at the fact that his death would be a part of the ancient and wonderful tradition, signed over a large part of his fortune to the Guild, and many Guild scholarships and bursaries are a result of this. And of course all young Assassins know the story of Sir Bernard Selachii who, upon meeting an Assassin financed by a business rival, spent the entire evening with him, reminiscing about the great days they had shared in Wigblock House, before suggesting that they drink a toast to the old school and

then, while his would-be assassin held his glass aloft, beating him to death with the brandy bottle. Subsequently, Sir Bernard endowed the Sir Bernard Selachii Award for Sheer Coolth, a much coveted prize to this day.

GUILD TRADITIONS

Stealth Chess

New members are always welcome for this exciting and taxing sport, which takes a few hours to grasp but a lifetime to master. It is an excellent test of memory and a remarkable sharpener of that most valuable of skills to an Assassin – rampant paranoia.

It has been argued that a form of Stealth Chess was the *original* chess; this point of view is largely based on the discovery, in an ancient tomb in Muntab, of a preserved corpse with an eight squares by ten squares chessboard embedded in its skull and a pawn hammered firmly up each nostril.

It is entirely unlike its better-known offspring in actual play, although there is only one unfamiliar type of piece. This is, of course, the Assassin.

There are two on each side, outside the Rooks, facing one another down the two outermost files of squares (coloured red and white on the Muntab board, rather than the black and white of the rest of the board). These are known as the Slurks. No other type of piece may enter these. Assassins, as they say, keep to the walls.

Strictly speaking, an Assassin moves one square in any direction, or two to capture. And it may capture *any* piece on the board except another Assassin – that is, a player may sometimes choose to save a usefully positioned

Assassin by letting it 'assassinate' one of its fellow pieces in order to occupy its square, but will never attack an opposing Assassin, because ours is an honourable trade.

So far, that makes it merely a powerful, if slow piece. But it is 'movement in the Slurk' that is the Assassin's forte, and an exciting move it is. It is hard to believe that the ancients had any concept of the Uncertainty Principle, but in short *an Assassin's real movement in the Slurk may not necessarily be in the direction it appears to be moving in.* All the piece is indicating is that it is moving, *not* the direction; it is moving, as the wizards may say, through another dimension. If, for example, an Assassin takes three moves in the Slurk it can on its next move reappear on *any* square three squares from the point where it entered *and then make a one-square move to capture.*

Players of the younger, conventional game find this hard to grasp and, once grasped, hard to live with as silent death appears in the middle of a classic King's Klatchian defence and checkmates the King. Once newcomers pick up the idea, they then find that undue reliance on the powerful Assassins can be unwise if they neglect the opponent's Queen in stately yet conventional progress down the board. Around this point they give up – but for thrills and fascination there is nothing like watching a game between two skilled players with all four Assassins in play and working invisibly with the other pieces, in an atmosphere of concentrated fear.

The acknowledged master of the game is the Patrician, Lord Havelock Vetinari, who won a Black four years running and honed his skill, or so it is said, by playing blindfold.

We can report a very successful season last year, winning all forty-eight games played (five or them by default, the opponent timing out in a terminal kind of way).

The Wall Game

To the unfamiliar, this appears to be a cross between urban rock-climbing, squash and actual bodily harm. It is traditionally played on the walls of the Guild's inner courtyard, but 'friendly' and practice games are played anywhere on Guild property when a wall has

been adapted to mimic some of the original features (such as 'Old Mother Baggy's Washing Line', 'the Window Box', 'the Coke Heaps', 'the Wonky Drainpipe', 'the Place Where the Mortar Is Rotten' and so on). Two teams of three per side are involved, playing with a small ball made of cork wrapped in leather bands. The rules are complex, points being scored by bouncing the ball off walls and opposing players, and only one member of any team may be below 100 inches from the ground at any time. Most games run into injury time, sometimes forever.

Pullis Corvorum

On Soul Cake Tuesday, the Guild chef catches a young magpie and attaches it to a pancake which he then nails to one of the Guild doors, incanting: 'Pullis corvorum invocantibus eum'. The poor bird is then worried to death by first-year students. A small prize, as yet unclaimed for more than two hundred years, will go to the boy who comes up with a halfway logical explanation for this.

Chapel Snoddie

The pews nearest to the high altar are occupied by the Guild's teaching staff. Immediately below them, the pews are reserved for the prefects. Old Prefects by tradition leave small packets of almonds and raisins for their new colleagues. This is known as Chapel Snoddie. It is, of course, a ritualized test; anyone who would eat any old food found lying around wouldn't last a term.

Tumpers

It quickly became a tradition for the whole Guild to process to the Tump, where the new boys would be sprinkled with salt to instil them with wit for their coming years at the Guild, 'sal' meaning both salt and wit, and puns being the lowest form of the latter. Later this became a means of raising funds for Guild charities. Every year on 12 January, boys from the school go out in pairs onto the streets of Ankh-Morpork. One carries a stoneware pot of salt, the other a leather drawstring purse. They accost passers-by and encourage them to make a donation to the Guild. When they receive money, the donor is given a pinch of salt and everyone feels embarrassed.

May Blossom Day

On May Day, if the Master of Assassins gives permission and if the day is moist, the boys are permitted to rise early and collect boughs of May blossom in Hide Park and decorate the windows of their dormitories with them. The boys are, however, not allowed to get their feet wet. For the past ninety years, no boy has bothered to give it a try.

ASSASSIN'S DRESS AND SCHOOL UNIFORM

The correct clothing for any Assassin 'at large' is black, and indeed many Assassins wear no other colour even in their leisure hours, although deep purples and greys will not cause comment.

Boys are not allowed to wear black in their first two years, but may 'take dark' some time in their third if they are making satisfactory progress.

Boys (under 5' 6") in their first year at the Guild must wear the New Bod uniform of a midnight blue coat and knee breeches, worn with cream waistcoat and ruffled shirt, the whole capped off with a black tricorn of beaver pelt.

New Bod Scholars wear white duck trousers instead of the knee breeches and, of course, their heavy woollen Scholars' gown.

Boys over 5' 6" must wear all of the above plus a sheepish expression.

First- and second-year girls of any size must wear a black gymslip or pinafore, black woollen stockings, and round hat known as the 'blonker'.

The purpose of these outfits is to make the pupils feel rather foolish, and hence determined to succeed in their studies and 'take dark' at the earliest opportunity

After 'taking dark', pupils are expected to dress fashionably while eschewing bright colours; young women are enjoined not to dress in a way that might unduly inflame the amorous propensities of their male colleagues. All pupils must wear the Guild's crest on their lapel.

All pupils pursuing post-graduate studies are entitled to dress and conduct themselves as full Assassins.

Only prefects may carry their umbrellas furled.

Apart from their stylish clothing they can also be recognized by their Guild salute – the thumb pressed against the first two fingers of the right hand and rubbed gently, the ancient sign of a man expecting to be paid. Of course, another way of recognizing them is when, at dead of night, someone stabs you. That was them. Presumably someone cared enough about you to pay.

The monetary aspect is vital. The Assassins profess a great regard for the sanctity of human life, and therefore charge enormous amounts for taking it away. As they say: 'We do not kill merely for a handful of silver. It's a lapful of gold or nothing.' Killing for any other reason is an absolute and unforgivable violation of Guild rules, and any Assassin discovered in breach of this rule would find himself at the very pointed end of his Guild's displeasure. By law, they must always leave a receipt.

Incidentally, they do not kill in bulk; they offer a personal service. Even the most famous Assassins never killed more than thirty people in all their lives. They would consider guns and bombs as reducing the whole thing to the level of a farce.

Astfgl. Supreme Life President of HELL. One-time King of the Demons, Lord of Hell and Master of the Pit. *A* Pit, in any case. Despite his undoubted power, he is, like most demons, unimaginative, single-minded and irredeemably stupid in a bureaucratic, industrious sort of way. He favours a moustache, red silk coat, crimson tights and a cowl with two rather sophisticated horns on it, plus a trident (with a loose end). Nevertheless, when he loses control of his appearance, his talons show through his red silk gloves, he sprouts bat-like wings and his skull is framed by great coiled ram horns. Demons have no specific shape and it is assumed that he chose these two forms, which show a certain amount of flair, after seeing an illustration somewhere. [E]

Astrolabe. One of the Disc's finest astrolabes is kept in a large, star-filled room in KRULL. It includes the entire Great A'Tuin–Elephant–Disc system wrought in brass and picked out with tiny jewels. Around it the stars and planets wheel on fine silver wires. On the walls the constellations have been made of tiny phosphorescent seed pearls set out on vast tapestries of jet-black velvet. These were, of course, the constellations current at the time of the room's decoration – several would be unrecognizable now owing to the Turtle's movement through space. The planets are minor bodies of rock picked up and sometimes discarded by the system as it moves through space, and seem to have no other role in Discworld astronomy or astrology than to be considered a bloody nuisance. [COM]

Astrozoologists. Krullian scientists interested in studying the nature of the Great A'TUIN. Specifically, its sex. [COM]

Atavarr's Personal Gravitational Upset. Little-used and hard-to-master spell used by GARHARTRA against Rincewind. It makes the body believe that gravity is acting at right angles to the norm. [COM]

A'Tuin, the Great. The star turtle who carries the Discworld on its back. Ten-thousand-mile-long member of the species *Chelys galactica*, and the only turtle ever to feature on the Hertz-sprung–Russell Diagram. Almost as big as the Disc it carries. Sex unknown.

Shell-frosted with frozen methane, pitted with meteor craters and scoured with asteroidal dust, its eyes are like ancient seas, crusted with rheum. Its brain is the size of a continent, through which thoughts move like glittering glaciers.

It is as large as worlds. As patient as a brick. Great A'Tuin is the only creature in the entire universe that knows exactly where it is going.

Upon its back stand Berilia, Tubul, Great T'Phon and Jerakeen, the four giant elephants upon whose shoulders the disc of the world rests. A tiny sun and moon spin around them on a complicated orbit to induce seasons, although probably nowhere else in the multiverse is it sometimes necessary for an elephant to cock its leg to allow the sun to go past.

After the events of *The Light Fantastic*, the Great A'Tuin was orbited by eight baby turtles, each with four small world elephant calves and tiny discworlds, covered in smoke and volcanoes. They have subsequently begun their own cosmic journeys.

Wizards have tried to tune into Great A'Tuin's mind. They trained up on tortoises and giant sea turtles to get the hang of the Chelonian mind. But although they knew that the Great A'Tuin's mind would be big, they rather foolishly hadn't realized it would be slow. After thirty years all they found out was that the Great A'Tuin was looking forward to something.

People have asked: How does the Disc move on the shoulders of the elephants? What does the Turtle eat? One may as well ask: What kind of smell has yellow got? It is how things *are*.

Auditors of Reality. It has to be understood that the universe of the Discworld is almost entirely animistic. Everything is conscious at some level. The level of reality in the vicinity of the Disc is so low that the distance between the real and the imagined is very small and, frequently, non-existent (hence the *de facto* existence of such beings as the HOGFATHER, OLD MAN TROUBLE, the TOOTH FAIRY and the SOUL CAKE TUESDAY DUCK). On the Discworld, even thunderstorms can think.

It follows – at least, it follows on Discworld – that this inherent consciousness should turn up even at the most basic of levels, such as those involving the very physics of the universe. These are therefore policed by the Auditors of Reality, a race of non-individualized beings whose job it is to make sure the universe functions properly and doesn't just do what it likes. If you travelled faster than light, it is quite possible that it is they who would fine you for speeding.

In appearance they look like small grey empty robes, with a cowl (when they adopt human form, they favour clothing in shades of … grey). They act entirely on consensus; they hate and distrust individuality, which for them is instantly fatal.

It is clear that they regard life itself as being unnecessary, untidy and contrary to good order. The whole purposes of the universe, they know, is to gradually wind down; it is not right, they are sure, that bits of it should wake up and ask questions like 'What's going on?' or grow petals or fly around singing. They are not life-forms. They are non-life-forms. The observers of the Universe. Its clerks. They see to it that things spin and rocks fall. They hate questions. They hate them almost as much as they hate decisions and they hate decisions almost as much as they hate the idea of the individual personality. But what they hate most of all is things moving around randomly. They believe that for a thing to exist it has to have a position in time and space. Humanity has arrived as a nasty shock. Humanity practically is things that don't have a position in time and space, such as imagination, pity, hope, history and belief. Intelligent life is an anomaly. The Auditors really hate things like that.

They can see into human minds. They can see the pop and sizzle of the thoughts. But they cannot read them. They can see the energetic flow from node to node, they can see the brain glittering like a Hogswatch decoration. What they can't see is what is *happening*.

One of their greatest enemies is DEATH, partly because as immortals they fear death far more than humans do (they are like high-stakes gamblers with everything to lose) and partly because of his tendency to tip the scales of history very slightly in favour of humanity. After all, Death more than anyone else depends on the existence of life. It is his living. They avoid death by never going so far as to get a life. They strive to be as indistinguishable as hydrogen atoms, with none of the latter's 'joie de vivre'. [RM]

Aurora corialis. (*Also* Aurora coriolis.) The Hublights. Great curtains of cold fire whose frosty tints illuminate and colour the midnight snows with silent streamers of OCTARINE, blue and green from the roof of the world. Caused by the vast discharge of magic from the Disc's standing field earthing itself in the green ice mountains of the Hub. Spelling is a little flexible, and both versions are correct, depending on what book you're reading

Autocondimentor. Someone who will put certainly salt and probably pepper on any meal you put in front of them whatever it is and regardless of how much it's got on it already and regardless of how it tastes. These people really exist (even on Earth) and fast-food empires have saved millions by recognizing their existence. Mustrum RIDCULLY is such a one; in fact he is one of the extreme variety, who regards any meal as no more than a foundation for salt, pepper, mustard, pickles, ketchup and sauce. [RM]

Autocue. A soldier in the Ephebian army. [P]

Avery, Gwendolyn, Miss. A resident of Schmarm and an early experiencer of the magic of the steam railway. She awoke in the middle of one night to the shaking and rattle of the multiple bottles of age-defying unguents on her dresser. And then she realized that the whole house was shaking to a rhythmic thudding.

When she described this episode in dramatic tones to her friend Daphne the following morning, she said that it was like the sound of a lot of men marching past. She put it down to the cherry

brandy she had had before going to bed whilst Daphne, knowing Gwendolyn's regrettable spinster status, put it down to wishful thinking. [RS]

Awf'ly Wee Billy Bigchin. He is very young, and the current gonnagle (bard and battle poet) in Tiffany's Feegle clan. He is half the size of most grown pictsies (under 3") and always announces himself in full when speaking to new people. He seems to feel that if he doesn't tell people who he is, they'll forget about him and he'll disappear. When you're half the size of most grown pictsies you're *really* short; much shorter and you'd be a hole in the ground.

He is the new gonnagle. A gonnagle is the clan's bard and battle poet, but gonnagles don't spend all their lives in the same clan. In fact, they're a sort of clan all by themselves. They move around among the other clans, making sure the songs and stories get spread around all the Feegles. Awf'ly Wee Billy had come with Jeannie from the Long Lake clan, which often happens. He is very young for a gonnagle, but there's no age limit to gonnagling. If the talent is in you, you gonnagle. And Awf'ly Wee Billy knows all the songs and can play the mousepipes so sadly that outside it will start to rain. [HFOS]

Azrael. The Great Attractor, the Death of Universes, the Beginning and End of Time.

He is DEATH's master, although it is uncertain whether Death is a truly separate entity or

merely one aspect of the whole. He is a creature so large that in real space his length can be
measured only in terms of the speed of light.
On his dark, sad face his eyes are so big a super-
nova would be a mere suggestion of a gleam on
the iris. He is also keeper of the ultimate clock,
from which all TIME originates. Other clocks
tell what time it is – but the ultimate clock tells
Time what it is. [RM]

Granny didn't really keep bees. She took some old wax every year, for candles, and the occasional pound of honey that the hives felt they could spare, but mainly she had them for someone to talk to.

– *Lords & Ladies*

The Band with Rocks In

Bad Ass. Village in the kingdom of LANCRE in the RAMTOPS. Not a large village, and it wouldn't show up on a map of the mountains. It barely shows up on a map of the village. This is a small community, close-knit to the point of a trawlerman's sock, where front doors are used only by brides and corpses and back doors are always left unlocked.

It was named when a donkey stopped in the middle of the river and wouldn't go backwards or forwards. It could have been called Disobedient Donkey.

The valley occupied by Bad Ass overlooks a panorama of lesser mountains and foothills.

From there, you can see to the edge of the Disc. In the long winter snows, the roads out of the village are lined with boards to reduce drifting and to stop travellers from straying. Markers are also carved into the bark of every tenth tree, out to a distance of nearly two miles. Many a life has been saved by the pattern of notches found by probing fingers under the clinging snow.

A narrow bridge over a stream leads to the village smithy, birthplace of Eskarina Smith (ESK).

Baker. A weaver in LANCRE, and a member of the Lancre Morris Men. [LL]

Bands, Musical (names of).

&U ('And You')
BAND WITH ROCKS IN, THE
Bertie the Balladeer & His Troubadour
  Rascals
Big Troll & Some Other Trolls, A
Blots, The
Boyz From the Wood
Dwarfs with Altitude
Grisham Frord Close Harmony Singers
Insanity
Lead Balloon
Snori Snoriscousin & His Brass Idiots
Suck
Surreptitious Fabric, The
We're Certainly Dwarfs
Whom, The

Quite a large number of these are various names briefly assumed and quickly discarded by the band that eventually performed in the famous Free Festival as 'Ande Supporting Bands'.

Band With Rocks In, The. A musical group formed by Imp y 'Buddy' Celyn (*see* IMP Y CELYN), Glod GLODSSON, Lias 'Cliff' BLUE-STONE and, for a brief period when they needed a keyboard player, the LIBRARIAN. [SM]

Bank, Royal, Ankh-Morpork. The facade of the Royal Bank of Ankh-Morpork looks, as major public buildings often do, like a temple. This can seem strange since several major religions are a) canonically against what they do inside and b) bank there.

The architect at least knew how to design a decent column, and also knew when to stop. He had set his face like flint against any prospect of cherubs, although above the columns was a high-minded frieze showing something allegorical involving maidens and urns. Most of the urns, and some of the young women, have birds nesting in them.

In fact, it was originally built as a temple by a previous king of Ankh, around 900 years ago. He had no particular god in mind. It was more a speculative venture – a sort of celestial bird box, awaiting a god to turn up. It then got used for storage in case of a siege, then as an indoor market, until Jocatello La Vice got it when the city defaulted on a loan.

Inside, one notices the hush – mostly because the ceiling is so high that sounds are just lost, but partly because people lower their voices in the presence of large sums of money. Red velvet and brass are much in evidence. There are pictures everywhere, of serious men in frock coats. Sometimes footsteps echo briefly on the white marble floor and are suddenly swallowed when their owner steps onto an island of carpet. And the big desks are covered with sage-green leather. Red leather? Pah! That is for parvenus and wannabees. Sage green means that you've got there, and that your ancestors got there too. On the wall above the counter a big clock, supported by cherubs, ticks away.

In the Undercroft, a grand, vaulted cellar, is the GLOOPER. [MM]

Barbarian Invaders Machine, the. A device apparently invented by Leonard of Quirm. Weight: two tons. Construction: big blocks of wood, and lots of cogwheels. Motive power: weights on a pulley and twisted rubber bands. Purpose: on the insertion of one penny in the slot, the player has the opportunity to fire little spears at the ranks of wooden barbarian invaders as they wobble across the little proscenium. Occasionally a badly carved horseman jerks pasts extra points will be scored if it is hit. A device ahead of its time.

Barnstable. One of the few one-liners who have made it into the *Companion*. A BLEDLOW at UNSEEN UNIVERSITY.

Bashfullsson, Bashfull, Grag One of the most well-known and well-respected dwarfs in the world, according to *Raising Steam*. An enlightened 'deep-down' dwarf – a little young and modern for many dwarfs. He was born in Ankh-Morpork and one of his novel beliefs is that you don't have to be physically deep down to be a dwarf. He lodges in a subdivided cellar in Cheap Street. [T!]

Basilica, Enrico. *See* SLUGG, HENRY.

Battle Bread of B'hrian Bloodaxe, the. This, like the equally famous Scone of Stone, is testimony to the pivotal role of bread products in dwarfish history. The semi-legendary round loaf would, says legend, return to B'hrian's hand after decapitating his enemies like so many hard-boiled eggs, and played a major role (or, possibly, roll) in the battle with the trolls at Koom Valley. Whoever wields it, tradition says, will be invincible in battle and also not short of a meal if really pushed. It is currently in the DWARF BREAD MUSEUM in Ankh-Morpork.

Battye, Sandra, Miss. Miss Sandra Battye first arrived in Ankh-Morpork many years ago to earn her fortune as a seamstress. No, a seamstress. The ones with the needle and thread. Sandra specializes, in fact, in crochet, and made her first fortune out of people's natural confusion. Since the word 'seamstress' had, as everyone knows, been hijacked by the ladies of negotiable affection, very few actual needlewomen cared to work in the city. Sandra made a good living from those poor souls who arrived at the SEAMSTRESSES' GUILD actually looking for someone to darn a sock, or mend a ripped pair of trousers. Having spotted the gap in the market, she stitched it up. [NW]

Beano. A clown, murdered by Edward D'EATH. His only crime – apart, it could be argued, from being a clown – was that he was about the right height (5' 9") and had a room in the right place. [MAA]

Bearhugger, Jimkin. Owner of a distillery in Ankh-Morpork. Manufacturer of Bearhugger's Very Fine Whiskey, Bearhugger's Old Persnickety and Jimkin Bearhugger's Old Selected Dragon's Blood Whiskey – on the bottle of which it says: 'Every bottle matured for up to seven minutes' and 'Ha' a drop afore ye go'. It is cheap and powerful; you could also light fires or clean spoons with it. And probably fuel aircraft.

A recent but short-lived line, which never caught on despite the best scientific recommendation, was Bearhugger's Homeopathic Sipping Whiskey. It is a founding fact of homeopathy that the effectiveness of a remedy increases with dilution. Jimkin decided, therefore, that this idea could profitably be applied to his own product. Strangely enough, the slogan 'Every drop diluted 1 Million Times!' failed to attract custom even though, in theory, merely being in the same room as an uncorked bottle of the stuff should make the purchaser riotously drunk. [GG]

Beavis, Gammer. Witch from LANCRE. Sometimes also spelled Brevis. She is, by Nanny OGG's standards, a bit too educated, so that sometimes it overflows out of her mouth. But she does her own shoe repairs and she takes snuff and that counts her as all right in Nanny Ogg's small world. She wears a hat with a very flat brim and a point you could clean your ear with. [SALF]

Beddsson, Bedwyr. Another one who was lucky enough to earn a card in the Great Card Index. A miner who works in the pits with his pony, Daisy. He has a wife, Bleddyn, and their children attend school in Lancre. [RS]

Beedle, Felicity, Miss. Actually a Mrs; her husband was killed in the Klatchian War. She lives near Ramkin Hall in Apple Tree Cottage, a house that has a direct tunnel into the goblins' hall. She spends some time helping to educate the local goblins and she also finances scholarships for the Quirm College for Young Ladies. She is a small woman with the strange aspect that you see in some people which causes them to appear to be subtly vibrating even when standing perfectly still. You feel that if some interior restraint suddenly broke, the pent-up energy released would catapult her through the nearest window.

She has written many, many books for children, with titles as varied as 'The World of Poo', 'The Little Duckling Who Thought He Was an Elephant', 'Melvin and the Enormous Boil' and 'The War with the Snot Goblins'. [SN]

Beggars' Guild. Motto: *MONETA SVPERVACA-NEA, MAGISTER?* Coat of arms: a shield, quartered. In the top-right quarter, three dragons, courant et or, on a field, gules. In the bottom-left quarter a dragon, gardant et or on a field, gules. In the top-left and bottom-right quarters a pattern of caltraps, argent, on a field, azure.

The question asked most frequently by visitors to Ankh-Morpork is 'Why haven't I got any money left?' The next most frequently asked question, at least by those who already know their way to the areas of the SHADES generally associated with female companionship of the professional kind, is 'What has that coat of arms got to do with begging? Dragons on a field of gools? Doesn't sound like beggary to me.' These people have failed, of course, to understand the very essence of beggary. This is a worn-out, much-patched *second-hand* coat of arms.

This is the oldest Guild in Ankh-Morpork. And also the richest, since the beggars never buy anything they can beg.

The Beggars' Guild predates the formalized Guild system of Ankh-Morpork by hundreds if not thousands of years, and it has a strict class structure and hierarchy all of its own. While all the Guilds are, to some extent, separate societies within society, this is particularly true of the Beggars.

The first mention of the Guild's classes of membership is some six hundred years before the present and says that the Guild includes: 'Rufflers, Uprightmen, Rogues, Wild rogues, Priggers or pransers, People calling you Jimmy, Palliards, Fraters, Mutterers, Mumblers, Freshwater mariners or whipjacks, Drummerers, Drunken tinkers, Swaddlers or peddlers, Jarkemen or patricoes, Demanders for glimmer or fire, Bawdy baskets, Mortes Autem-mortem, Walking mortes, Doxies, Dells, Kinching mortes and Kinchin cooes.' (This list has a certain coincidence with the beggars found in Elizabethan England.)

In fact, however, most of these classes were more correctly various low grades of thief or conman and their descendants have long since decamped to the newer Guilds. Classes of beggars in the city now include: Twitchers,

Droolers, Dribblers, Mumblers, Mutterers, Walking-Along-Shouters, Demanders of a Chip, People who call other people Jimmy, People who need Tuppence for a Cup of Tea, People who need Eightpence for a Meal, People with placards saying 'Why lie? I need a beer' and Foul Ole RON, agreed by his fellow beggars to be in a class by himself if only because no one will share it with him.

While the classes may appear interchangeable to the unpractised eye, their duties are carefully compartmentalized and the demarcation lines enforced. While a Mumbler in good standing might risk an occasional Mutter, he'd be very unwise to try Walking-Along-Shouting until the Guild judged him senior and ready enough to do so. Equally, he would be within his rights to report a mere Dribbler he saw attempting to sneak a Mumble. Especially a mumble in the wrong place; one of the important functions of the Guild is to arrange patrols and shifts so that beggary is properly distributed among the streets.

Pavement artists, people with harmonicas and people who make money by standing still in interesting ways are not beggars. No beggar would dream of providing any kind of service or reward, except to the extent that the donor may feel themselves to be a better person for donating. Doing anything for the money except asking for it is against the tenets of true beggary. Such money as the beggars do make, it must be stressed, is entirely obtained by 1) begging and 2) not begging.

1 is self-explanatory. 2 owes a lot to what might be called the Ankh-Morpork view of social economics. You clearly don't want a lot of beggars hanging around at your wedding or other salubrious occasions, so the accepted thing to do is send the Guild a small sum of money and a kind of anti-invitation, which sees to it that men with interesting running sores and a body odour you could split wood with do not turn up. You'd be amazed at how many will turn up should this small precaution not be taken. This is very similar to the scheme run by the Thieves' Guild, whereby a small payment every year ensures the safety of person and property.

The Guild offers a highly specialized schooling and other social benefits for its members. It is ruled by a council under the chairmanship of the current King or Queen of the Beggars (current incumbent: Queen MOLLY of the Beggars).

Beginning, The. There are various theories about the beginning of the universe. These include the Egg, a theory based upon the Great Egg of the Universe, and the Clearing of the Throat, followed by the Word. Others have also propounded the 'Drawing of the Breath' and the 'Scratching of the Head and Trying to Remember It, It Was On the Tip of My Tongue'. One of the objects of the LISTENERS – or Listening Monks – is to determine, by careful analysis of the very faint echoes, what the Word was. By definition, all theories about the beginning of the universe are true. [LF]

Belafon. A young druid, who delivers rocks for stone circles. When RINCEWIND and TWOFLOWER landed on the 30' × 10' bluish rock on which Belafon was flying, he was carrying a sickle and wearing a long, wet nightshirt and a square of oilskin tied across his head and knotted under his chin. [LF]

Bellyster. Warder at the Tanty. Bellyster is a real old-school screw, a craftsman of small evils, the kind of bully who would take every opportunity to make a prisoner's life a misery. It isn't just that he'd gob in your bowl of greasy skilly, but he wouldn't even have the common decency to do it where you couldn't see him. He picks on the weak and frightened, too. He hates the Watch, and the feeling is mutual. [MM]

Bel-Shamharoth. The Soul-Eater, the Soul-Render, the Sender of Eight. Not Evil, for even Evil has a certain vitality. Bel-Shamharoth is the flip side of the coin of which Good and Evil are one side. One of the old, dark gods of the 'NECROTELICOMNICON'. Although it has never been said explicitly, it is likely that he is one of the creatures of the DUNGEON DIMENSIONS who has managed to survive in this world.

The inner dimensions of his eight-sided temple disobey a fairly basic rule of architecture by being bigger than the outside. It is full of corridors, of tunnels full of unpleasant carvings and occasional disjointed skeletons, hell-lit by a light so violet that it is almost black. The eight-sided crystals set at intervals in the walls and ceiling shed a rather unpleasant glow that doesn't so much illuminate as outline the darkness. The floor is a continuous mosaic of eight-sided tiles, and the corridor walls and ceilings are angled to give the corridors eight sides. In those places where part of the masonry has fallen in, even the stones have eight sides. All routes lead to the centre, where there is an intense violet light, illuminating a wide room with eight walls and eight passages radiating off it. There is a low, eight-sided altar but in the centre of the room is a huge stone slab, eight-sided (of course) and slightly tilted. Under that is a black, tentacled creature with an enormous eye – Bel-Shamharoth – all suckers and tentacles and mandibles. [COM]

Bemery, Queen. A past queen of LANCRE (670–722). [WS]

Bent, Malvolio. Chief cashier ($41/month) at the Royal Bank of Ankh-Morpork. Mr Bent is in every way smooth and uncreased. Instead of a traditional banker's frock coat, he wears a very well cut black jacket above pinstripe trousers. Mr Bent's feet are soundless even on the marble floors of the bank. They are also unusually large for such a dapper man, but the shoes, black and polished, mirror-shiny, were very well made. He is tall and dark and walks like a dressage horse, lifting each foot very deliberately off the ground before setting it on the ground again. Apart from that incongruity, Mr Bent has the air about him of one who stands quietly in a cupboard when not in use.

When he first appeared in *Making Money*, Mavolio Bent had a definition of 'silly' that most people would have considered a touch on the broad side. Laughter was silly. Theatricals, poetry and music were silly. Clothes that weren't grey, black or at least of un-dyed cloth were silly.

Pictures of things that weren't real were silly (pictures of things that were real were unnecessary). The ground state of being was silliness, which had to be overcome with every mortal fibre. Missionaries from the stricter religions would have found in Malvolio Bent an ideal convert, except that religion was extremely silly.

Bent arrived in Ankh-Morpork as a child, on a cart owned by some travelling accountants. He got a job when he was thirteen by sitting on the steps all night until the chairman came to work and then impressing him with his command of numbers. He went from messenger boy to chief cashier in twenty years. Never had a day off for illness, either. He had been with the bank for thirty-nine years.

It seems he may have been born Charlie Benito. [MM]

Bentzen. Captain of Duke FELMET's personal bodyguard. [WS]

Berilia. One of four giant elephants upon whose broad and star-tanned shoulders the Disc of the world rests. [COM]

Bertie. Leader of Bertie the Balladeer and His Troubadour Rascals, a traditional musical group. Wears a gold lamé doublet. [SM]

Beryl. Wife of MICA the bridge troll. [TB] There's also a Beryl married to Kwartz in *The Light Fantastic*. It is a common enough name for female trolls, who are generally named after precious or semi-precious stones.

Bes Pelargic. Major seaport of the AGATEAN EMPIRE. The city includes a Red Triangle District. Little more is known, owing to the Empire's emphatic lack of interest in the outside world, at least until recently.

Bethan. Seventeen-year-old virgin rescued from druidical sacrifice by COHEN the Barbarian. An attractive but pale young lady, she was first encountered wearing a long white robe, with a gold torc around her neck. She subsequently married Cohen. Well, we say married...

It is clear that Cohen 'married' many women during the course of a long and adventurous life, but none of them seems to have been any the worse for the experience and they often ended up richer, since he never mastered the art of spending money. [LF]

Biers. An undead bar in the Shades of Ankh-Morpork, exact location unspecified; it may well be that you can only find your way to it if you are likely clientele. 'Undead' in this case is taken to include werewolves, bogeymen, ghouls, banshees and other foster children of the night. Basically, if you don't need to wear a mask to frighten the kiddies, you can drink at Biers.

Igor the barman serves drinks you tend not to get in other bars. But since he is a barman, and every barman likes to put a bit of panache in his act, he'll put in cocktail sticks with things stuck on the end. *What* things, of course, you may not find out until too late. Therefore it is wise not to order a drink that isn't transparent. And don't order a Bloody Mary unless you are really, really sure of yourself.

Igor's efforts to bring Biers into line with other drinking establishments tend always to have a flaw. We may cite his attempt to brighten up weekday lunchtime by advertising **DEAD GIRLS!!!** It didn't bring in the crowds. Not the right sort, anyway.

Oddly enough, Biers is the one place where the various siblings of the night will leave you alone. There are house rules, after all. You will probably be safer than in most other Ankh-Morpork taverns, in fact, provided you steer clear of the pickles.

The one regular 'normal' customer is Mrs Gammage, who lives nearby. Old, deaf and practically blind, she's been drinking in Biers since it was the Crown and Axe, many years ago. And it's clear that she hasn't realized things have changed. The other clientele, who can be quite kind when the mood takes them, don't discourage her in this belief and she has become a sort of informal mascot. So they keep an eye on her. The occasional attempts by nasty people in the outside world to take advantage of a poor blind widow woman living alone in one of the nastier parts of the town have now ceased, once it became clear that anyone who inconvenienced Mrs Gammage in any way would soon be found dismembered and bloodless in some alley. After all, even the undead have a heart (some have an entire jar full).

It appears that the Igor who runs the place is not an actual IGOR. He's merely called Igor.

Big Cabbage. Theoretically the last town any sensible person would want to visit. It is nevertheless popular throughout the summer because of the attractions of Brassica World and the Cabbage Research Institute, whose students were the first to get a cabbage to a height of five hundred yards propelled entirely by its own juices. Nobody asked why they felt it was necessary to do this, but that was science for you, and, of course, students. Sometimes, a passing location makes it into this book just because Terry had something funny to say about it. [RS]

Big Yan. A huge, muscly feegle. Well, huge for a feegle (7" tall). He has a necklace of four teeth – one for every man he's knocked out. [WFM]

Bilious. The Oh God of Hangovers. He has the appearance of a young male human with a prominent Adam's apple and sporting on his head a little crown of vine leaves. He owed his existence to a collection of magical circumstances that arose from an attempt to kill the HOGFATHER. Whilst the God of Wine spends his entire existence partying and drinking to excess, the Oh God spends his entire existence in the depths of the supernaturally bad hangover which, in justice, ought to be suffered by the God of Wine each morning. What goes down, as it were, must throw up. It is possible that he now does temporary stand-in work for gods who need to take time off. [H]

Bilk, Harrietta. A young witch who'd been doing some aftercare visits to a lumberjack sewn up by Granny WEATHERWAX. Maybe this was Jack ABBOTT? [TSC]

Billet, Drum. A wizard who, in long cloak and with his carven staff, visited BAD ASS to hand his staff over to ESK, the blacksmith's daughter – in the mistaken belief that she was in fact a son. He died after passing over the staff and was initially reincarnated as an apple tree, so covered in mistletoe that it looked green even in midwinter. The tree produced very small fruit which passed from stomach-twisting sourness

Binky

to wasp-filled rottenness overnight. 'Green Billets' are now prized in LANCRE as a very good apple for the making of SCUMBLE. [ER]

Billias, Skarmer. A whiskery, red-faced wizard. Head of the Order of the Silver Star. Resembled a small captive balloon that had been draped in blue velvet and VERMINE. Killed by COIN. [S]

Billom. One of VITOLLER's band of strolling players. [WS]

Binky. The flying horse of DEATH. Binky is a real, flesh-and-blood horse, but while in Death's service he does not age. He is as white as milk, and wears a silver and black harness, with an ornate silver saddle. Behind the saddle is a scabbard for Death's folding scythe, and the saddle bag contains his riding cloak. Binky is extremely intelligent and undoubtedly better treated than most beasts of burden on the Disc.

He leaves no hoof prints in normal circumstances, but when travelling in whatever is Death's equivalent of hyperspace he does sometimes leave glowing prints in the air, because Nature abhors the lack of a special effect. [M]

Bird, Gaffer. When first encountered in the chronicles, Gaffer was head handleman in HOLY WOOD. His hands were stained with chemicals and he had no eyebrows (a sure sign of someone who has been around octo-cellulose for any length of time). He wore a back-to-front cap. Assorted tools hung from his belt. He believed that everything could be repaired with a piece of string, unlike most people in his position in the modern film industry, who believe that everything can be repaired with sticky tape. [MP]

Birdwhistle. Author of the 'Legendes and Antiquities of the Ramtops'. [LL]

Black Celestial Dragon of Fire. Manner in which Agateans expect Death to appear to them. They are wrong. [M]

Black Roger. Huge, jet-black dog, looking like a pit bull terrier crossed with a mincing machine. A member of the Ankh-Morpork DOG GUILD. [MAA]

Blake, Stoker. A 'nom de plaque de pied' adopted by Lord VETINARI during the events of *Raising Steam*.

Bleakley, Rupert. A vampire who works in the slaughterhouse in Ankh-Morpork. [MAA]

Bledlows. (Origin unknown.) The UNSEEN UNIVERSITY porters, who double, with rather more enthusiasm, as its private police, or proctors. They are known more usually by their nickname of Lobsters. They tend to be heavy-set, elderly men with nevertheless a good turn of speed and the sort of head that is made to wear a bowler hat. They are of limited yet highly focused intellect; their whole being is founded on the certain belief that all students are guilty of everything. They are generally ex-soldiers or watchmen and their traditional cry is 'I know who you are!'

They command their nickname for being thick-shelled, liable to turn red when hot and having the smallest brain for their size of any known creature. [T!]

Blenkin. Manservant to Edward D'EATH. [MAA]

Blind Hugh. A beggar at the Pearl Dock, Ankh-Morpork. The nerves in his body tend to vibrate at fifty paces from even a small amount of impure gold. [COM]

Blind Io. Chief of the GODS, by virtue of his constant vigilance. His glowing eye sockets are bound with cloth. The eyes themselves, of which he has an impressively large number, lead a semi-independent life, orbiting around him. It is said that they can see everything that happens everywhere. This taciturn god is all the Disc's

Blind Io

thunder gods, using false noses, different voices and seventy different hammers when he needs to appear to the various different believers. It is also said that he arrived on the Discworld after some terrible and mysterious incident in another Eventuality – a sort of cosmic ticket-of-leave man. Not stupid, but a very traditional thinker. Gods tend to be. [COM]

Bloat. A poison, extracted from the deep sea blowfish, *Singularis minutia gigantica*, which protects itself from its enemies by inflating itself to many times its normal size. If the poison is taken by humans, the effect is to make every cell in the body instantaneously swell some 2000 times. This is invariably fatal, and very loud. You don't need to bury the victims, just redecorate over the top. [P]

Bloodaxe, B'hrian. The famous dwarf king who commanded the dwarfs at the Battle of Koom Valley. He and his … partner are celebrated in the opera '*Bloodaxe and Ironhammer*'. He signed a peace treaty with the Diamond King of the Trolls. [T!]

Bloody Stupid. Camel living in TSORT. [P]

Blouse, Lieutenant. An officer in the Borogravian army. Young, inexperienced, chinless. His face just eases its way into his neck without much to disturb it along the way. His Adams' apple, mind, is a champion – it goes up and down his neck like a ball on a spring. He joins *Monstrous Regiment* straight from headquarters and has no real soldiering experience. His main contribution had been to redesign the HQ filing system. He is married to Emmeline – to whom he writes frequently – and he rides a rather scraggy horse called Thalacephalos.

At school, he was very keen on amateur dramatics, and he played Lady Sprightly in '*A Comedy of Cuckolds*' and Widow Trembler in ''*Tis Pity She's a Tree*'.

His ambition is to have something named after him – like General Puhloaver, Brigadier Galosh or General Anorac. [MR]

Bluejohn. Troll lance-constable in the Ankh-Morpork City Watch. He is very big; so big, he doesn't stand out in a crowd because he is the crowd. People fail to see him because he's in the way. Like many overgrown people, he is instinctively gentle, rather shy and inclined to let others tell him what to do. If fate had led him to join a gang, he'd have been the muscle. In the Watch, he's the riot shield. [TFE]

Bluestone, Lias. A troll. When first seen, he was wearing two large squares of darkish glass in front of his eyes (a troll development to minimize the effects of sunlight). He plays large round rocks, a traditional troll instrument, under his stage name of Cliff – considered by all to be exactly the wrong kind of name for anyone who wants to last any time at all in the field of popular music. Since he is both a troll and a drummer, he could be said to have thrown a 'one' in the great dice game of intellect. [SM]

Bobby, St. The Most Holy St Bobby. Made a bishop of the Omnian church because he was in the desert with the Prophet OSSORY. St Bobby was a donkey and, in the words of Mustrum RIDCULLY, the somewhat irreverent Archchancellor of Unseen University, a righteous ass. [SG]

Boddony. A dwarf. Second in command at Gunilla GOODMOUNTAIN's print room and, later on, husband to… er, wife to… erm, *partner* to Gunilla (*see under* DWARFS for a hesitant explanation). [TT]

Boffo. A clown. Doorkeeper at the FOOLS' GUILD. A very small man, with huge boots. His face is plastered with flesh-coloured make-up, on which is painted a big frown; his hair is a couple of old mops dyed red. He has a hoop in his trousers to make him look amusingly overweight, and a pair of rubber braces to allow his trousers to bounce up and down as he walks. Like most clowns, he was brought up to believe that a custard pie in the face represents the acme of humour. There can be few souls more miserable. [MAA]

Boffo's Novelty & Joke Emporium. Retail outlet at 4, Tenth Egg Street, Ankh-Morpork. Run by Mrs Eunice PROUST and her son, Derek.

Boggi's. Dress shop in Kings Way, Ankh-Morpork. High-class modes for the affluent. [LL]

Boggis, Bengy. Bengy 'Lightfoot' Boggis is the real name of Brother Fingers of the Elucidated Brethren. [GG]

Boggis, Josiah Herbert. J. H. 'Flannelfoot' Boggis. Known for his brown bowler hat. A thief in Ankh-Morpork. President of the THIEVES' GUILD. The large Boggis family includes some of Ankh-Morpork's most respected thieves. [WS]

Boggis, Spooner. A man who was forced, by Mad Lord SNAPCASE, to eat his own nose. [IT]

Bog Truffle, Klatchian Migratory. Despite resembling the Klatchian bog toad in both taste and appearance, this is extremely rare and therefore a delicacy. [RS]

Bonk. Principal city of the Schmalzberg region of ÜBERWALD. Bonk (pronounced Beyonk) occupies a narrow valley with a white-water river winding through it. Its city walls are punctuated with high gates. Bonk's architecture favours steep roofs and wooden buildings heavily decorated with fretwork. One of the city's many embassies is that of Ankh-Morpork, which is housed in a building once owned by the von Überwald family. Visitors to Bonk walk along its cobbled streets to see its famous Rat Clock on the RatHaus, and also to visit the Chocolate Museum in Prince Vodorny Square. The city also incorporates an entrance to the underground dwarf kingdoms of Schmalzberg. [TFE]

Bonsai Mountains. The most testing form of bonsai, practised only by History MONKS and other very long-lived persons who don't mind waiting a thousand years to see what happens next. The mountains are selected while they are small, and their growth is artificially restricted; careful positioning of mirrors and wind screens encourages the formation of the miniature glaciers, forests and lakes that are part of the mountain's original morphic field.

Just any old piece of rock won't do. The trick is to spot the mountains while they are young. In a sense the expert is selecting that piece of rock which, after the normal processes of continental collision and crustal upheaval, will be at the very peak – i.e., from one point of view, the rock with the correct morphic field which will cause the rest of the mountain to form underneath it. A wrong choice here will be bound to lead to disappointment after a hundred years or so.

Books. The Disc is a veritable treasure-house of books. These include:

ABC, The [W]

Achmed the I Just Get These Headaches's Book of Humorous Cat Stories [MP]

Adventures in Acuphilia [GP]

Adventures with Crossbow and Rod [MP]

Almanack de Gothick, The [TFE]

Among the Snow Weasels (K. Pierpoint Poundsworth) [W]

Amorous Adventures of Molly Clapper [NW]

Ancient & Classical Mythology (Chaffinch) [W]

Anima Unnaturale (Broomfog) [S]

Ankh-Morpork Almanack and Booke of Dayes (A. J. Loop) [LL]

Ankh-Morporke, Citie of One Thousand Surprises, Wellcome to [S, MP, RM]

Ankh-Morpork Succesfion, The (Thighbiter) [MAA]

Appocrypha to the Vengeful Testament of Offler [FOC]

Arca Instrumentorum [CJ]

Art of War, The (poss. by One Tzu Sung, or Three Sun Sung) [IT]

Auriga Clavorum Maleficarum [CJ]

Avian Nausea Index (Fletcher) [UA]

Banquet of Worms, A (Col. F. J. Massingham) [SN]

Battle Studies [MR]

Bestiary (Philo) [SG]

Big Directory of Varying Dimensions (Haruspex) [GP]

Biggerwood's Catalogue (mail order guide) [TSC]

Boke of the Film, The (Deccan Ribobe and others) [MP]

Bonfire of Witches, The [ISWM]

Book of Alberto Malich the Mage, The [LF]

Book of Creation [SG]

Book of Etiquette (Lady Deirdre Waggon) [NOCB]

Book of Going Forth Around Elevenish [LF]

Book of Staying in the Pit [P]

Boots and Teeth (Sir Roderick Purdeigh) [DM]

Boy Who Didn't Know How to Pick His Own Scabs, The (Felicity Beedle) [SN]

Bumper Fun Grimoire [LF]

Cabbage, Tau of, The [UA]

Casplock's Compleet Lexicon of Majik with Precepts for the Wise [S]

Cenobile Book of Truth [FOC]

Ceremonies and Protocols of the Kingdom of Lancre [LL, NOCB]

Chivalric Law & Usage (Scavone) [J]

Civics (Ibid) [SG]

Compendium of Odours (Brakefast) [UA]

Compound of Alchemie [FOC]

Cooking in Dire Straights (Superflua Raven) [W]

Cooking With Brains (Aimsbury) [MM]

Cordat, The [P]

Country Dairy of a Gentlewoman [NOCB]

Craft of War, The (Song Sung Lo) [MR]

Dangerous Mammals, Reptiles, Amphibians, Birds, Fish, Jellyfish, Insects, Spiders, Crustaceans, Grasses, Trees, Mosses & Lichen of Terror Incognita (at least 29 volumes and three parts) [TLC]

Daphne and the Nose Pickers (Felicity Beedle) [SN]

De Chelonian Mobile [SG]

Demonologie [E]

Demonologie Malyfycorum of Hanchanse thee Unsatysfactory [ER]

Der Selbst Uberschritten durch das Ganze (Trousenblert) [UA]

Dictionary of Amazingly Uncommon Words [HFOS]

Dictionary of City Biography [GG]

Dictionary of Eye-Watering Words [GG]

Discomfiting Misusage (Birdcatcher) [UA]

Discourse on Historical Inevitability (Ibid) [P]

Discourses (Ibid) [SG]

Diseases of the Dragon (Sybil Deirdre Olgivanna Ramkin) [GG]

Diseases of the Sheep [WFM]

Doors of Deception, The (Fussbinder) [UA]

Doppelte Behrungssempfindung (Von Kladpoll) [UA]

Double Pointers & Flaws [GP]

Ectopia (Gnomon) [SG]

Edible Architecture of Bergholdt Stuttley Johnson, The (Startup Nodder) [NOCB]

Effluence of Reality, The (Von Sliss) [UA]

Ego-Video Liber Deorum (Koomi of Smale) [SG]

Encyclopaedia of Soup, A [W]

Etiquette, Lady Deirdre Waggon's Book of [MAA]

Fairies and How to Avoid Them (Miss Perspicacia Tick) [HFOS]

Farmer's Almanac & Seed Catalogue [RM]

Fencing for Beginners [MR]

First Flights in Witchcraft (Mrs Earwig) [W]

First Steps in Pins [GP]

Five Hours & Sixteen Minutes Among the Goblins of Far Überwald (J. P. Blunderbell) [UA]

Floating Worlds (H. J. Toadbinder) [ISWM]

Flower Magick (Letice Earwig) [TSC]

FULLOMYTH

Gardening in Difficult Conditions [NOCB, SM]

Gaston's Enormous Problem (Felicity Beedle) [SN]

Gd Tak Gar (The Things Tak Wrote) (tr. Prof. W. W. W. Wildblood) [T!]

Geoffrey and the Land of Poo (Felicity Beedle) [SN]

Ge Fordge's Compendyum of Sex Majick [S]

Geoffrey and the Magic Pillow Case (Felicity Beedle) [SN]

Geometries (Legibus) [SG]

Goode Childe's Booke of Faerie Tales, The [TSC]

GRIM Fairy Tales [TOT, TAMAHER]

Guide to Impossible Buildings (W. H. J. Whittleby) [DD]

Guild Houses of Ankh-Morpork, The (Startup Nodder) [TGD]

Guitar Primer, Blert Wheedown's [SM]

Habits of Wolves, The (Capt. W. E. Lightly) [W]

Happy Tales [H]

Harem Frescoes of Old Klatch, The (Lady Alice Venturi) [DM]

Hats, A History of (F. G. Smallfinger) [GP]

Higher Magick, The (Letice Earwig, Witch) [HFOS]

Histories (Marcellus) [FGD]

Hivers: A Dissertation Upon a Device of Amazing Cunning (Sensibility Bustle) [HFOS]

How to Dynamically Manage People for Dynamic Results in a Caring, Empowering Way in Quite a Short Time Dynamically [TLC]

INNE JUSTE 7 DAYES I WILLE MAKE YOU A BARBEARIAN HERO! (Cohen) [S]

Inoffensive Reptiles of the Sto Plains (Walnut) [H]

In Search of the Whole (W. E. G. Goodnight) [UA]

Insects, Howe to Kille (Humptulip) [LL]

Interesting Customs among the N'Kouf (Lady Alice Venturi) [DM]

I-Spy Demons (Prof. Poledread) [HFOS]

Iyt Gryet Teymple hyte Tsort, Y Hiystory Myistical [LF]

Jane's All the World's Siege Weapons [LL]

Joye of Snackes, The (A Lancre Witch) [MA]

Joy of Earwax, The (Felicity Beedle) [SN]

Joy of Tantric Sex, The [NOCB]

Joy of Tantric Sex, with Illustrations for the Advanced Student, The (A Lady) [E]

Koom Valley Codex [T!]

Lacemaking Through the Ages [GG]

Lady Waggon's Book of Household Management [MM]

Laotan Book of the Whole [CJ]

Laws & Ordinances of the Cities of Ankh & Morpork [GG]

Legendes and Antiquities of the Ramtops, The (Birdwhistle) [LL, NCOB]

Liber Immanis Monstrorum (Cuvee) [HFOS]

Little Duckling Who Thought He Was an Elephant, The (Felicity Beedle) [SN]

Little Folks' Book of Flower Fairies, The [LF]

Little Pieces for Tiny Fingers [P]

Lives of the Prophets (Thrum) [CJ]

Lives of Very Dull People (Wasport) [TLC]

Logic & Paradox (Wold) [SM]

Lot of What You Fancy Makes You Fat, A (Nanny Ogg) [TSC]

Magavenatio Obtusis (Witch Hunting for Dumb People) (Miss Perspicacea Tick) [W]

Maleficio's Discouverie of Demonologie [S]

Malleus Malleficarum (Ossory) [CJ]

Mallificarum Sumpta Diabolicite Occularis Singularum [E]

Manual of Swordsmanship, The [W]

Martial Arts [LL]

Mechanics (Grido) [SG]

Meditations (Didactylos) [SG]

Meer von Unvermeidlichkeit (Dr Maspinder) [UA]

Melvin and the Enormous Boil (Felicity Beedle) [SN]

Mis-Draws [GP]

Modal Contextities (Freidigger) [GP]

Monster Fun Book [WS]

Monster Fun Grimoire [M]

Mother Ogg's Tales for Tiny Folk [NOCB]

Mr Bunnsy Has an Adventure [TAMAHER]

Mr Bunnsy's Big Day [TAMAHER]

Mr Cauliflower's Big Adventure [UA]

My Fairy Friends (Letice Earwig) [TSC]

My Family and Other Werewolves [NOCB]

My Life Among the Sponge-Eating Coral-House-Dwelling Pygmies (General Sir Roderick Purdeigh) [COM]

Names of the Ants (Humptemper) [E]

NECROTELICOMNICON

Necrotelicomnicon Discussed for Students, With Practical Experiments [MP]

Nichts des Wissens, das (Frugal) [UA]

Nooks and Corners of Ankh-Morpork (Miss Amelia Cram) [NOCB]

Nosehinger on the Laws of Contract [LF]

Nuggan, Book of [MR]

Obedience of Disobedience, The (Schnouzentintle) [UA]

Observations on the Art of Invisibility, Some (Lord Winstanleigh. Illus., Emilia Jane Greville-Pipe) [NW]

Occult Companion (Boddry) [UA]

Occult Primer (Woddeley) [S]

Octarine Fairy Book [COM]

OCTAVO, The

Old Man of the Woods, The (General Sir Roderick Purdeigh) [DM]

Om, Book of [CJ]

Ominous Encyclopaedia [W]

One Hundred Walks in the Ramtops (E. Wheelbrace) [TGL]

Out with my Flies in All Weathers (Geoffrey Indigo) [RS]

Passion's Plaything (Marjory J. Boddice) [W]

Perfumed Allotment, The, or Garden of Delights, The, [J]

Pictorial Guide to the Lancre Fells, A (E. Wheelbrace) [TGL]

Pin Catalogue (Hubert Spider) [GP]

Pins (J. Lanugo Owlsbury) [GP]

Pins of Überwald & Genua [GP]

Plants, On the Nature of (Orinjcrates) [SG]

Platitudes (Aristocrates) [SG]

Pride and Extreme Prejudice (Jane Gordon) [SN]

Principia Explosia (Affir Al-chema) [J]

Principles of Engagement [MR]

Principles of Ideal Government (Ibid) [P]

Principles of Modern Accountancy [W]

Principles of Navigation (Dykeri) [SG]

Principles of Thaumic Propagation [TLC]

Prudent Advice for Young Women (Lady Deirdre Waggon) [MM]

Pseudopolis, 130 Days of [P]

Psychological Places (E. R. Clamp, D. Thau) [UUD]

Rambling in Llamedos (E. Wheelbrace) [TGL]

Ratty Rupert Sees It Through [TAMAHER]

Reflections (Xeno) [SG]

Religion, On (Abraxas) [SG]

Res Centum Et Una Quas Magus Facere Potest [HFOS]

Ritual Aggression in Pubescent Rats (Dr Vonmausberger) [UA]

Romance of the Broomstick, The (Letice Earwig?) [TSC]

Septateuch [SG]

Servant, The (unpublished work by Havelock, Lord Vetinari)

Seventy Years Behind the Wirecutters (E. Wheelbrace) [TGL]

Show Judges' Guide to Dragons, The (Lady Sybil Ramkin) [TLH]

Shuttered Palace, The (translated from the Klatchian by A Gentleman, with Hand-Coloured Plates for the Connoisseur in A Strictly Limited Edition) [P]

Sieges and Survival (Gen. Callus Tacticus) [W]

Snakes of All Nations (Wrencher) [TLC]

Speech of Trolls (Postalume) [UA]

Spells for Lovers (Anathema Bugloss) [ISWM]

Stripfettle's Believe-It-Or-Not Grimoire [RM]

SUMMONING OF DRAGONS, THE (Tubal de Malachite) [GG]

Survival in the Snow (T. H. Mouseholder) [W]

Synonyms for the Word 'Plimsoll' [GP]

Tactical Defence [MR]

Tacticus: Thye Campaigns [MR]

Temple Frescoes of Old N'Couf [NOCB]

Ten Steps to Witchcraft (Letice Earwig?) [TSC]

Testament from the Mountains (Pastor Oates) [ISWM]

Theologies (Hierarch) [SG]

Theory of Thaumic Imponderability (Marrowleaf) [SM]

Thoughts (Bouffant) [GP]

To Ride a Golden Broomstick (Letice Earwig) [TSC]

Torquus Simiae Maleficarum [CJ]

Toujours, Quirm [NOCB]

Travels in the Dark Hinterland (Lady Alice Venturi) [DM]

True Arte of Levitatione [P]

Trumpet of Equestrianism (Spout) [UA]

Twenty-Four Years Without Eyebrows (Col. Charles Augustus Makepeace) [SN]

Twurp's Peerage [LL, MA]

Unusual Days, Book of (Waspmire) [W]

Use of Pliers in Warfare, The (Sir Roderick Purdeigh) [DM]

Veni, Vidi, Vici: A Soldier's Life (Gen. A. Tactitus) [J]

Vicar Is Coming To Tea, The, and 127 Other Warnings of Social Embarrassment (Dr Bentley Purchase, UU Press) [SN]

Walking in the Koom Valley (Eric Wheelbrace) [T!]

War With the Snot Goblins, The (Felicity Beedle) [SN]

Way of the Scorpion, The [WA]

Wee (Felicity Beedle) [SN]

Wee Wee Men (Felicity Beedle) [SN]

Wen the Eternally Surprised, The Life of [TOT]

Wesentlichen Ungewissheiten Zugehörig der Offenkundigen Männlichkeit, das (Ofleberger) [UA]

What I Did On My Holidays (Twoflower) [IT]

Where's My Cow? [T!]

Whom's Whom [MM]

Why Men Get Under Your Feet (Releventia Flout) [MM]

Why Things Are Not Otherwise (Crumberry) [W]

Woddeley's Basic Gods [H]

World of Poo, The (Felicity Beedle) [SN]

Wormold's Steerage [NOCB]

(*See also* PLAYS, MAGAZINES)

HISTORY BOOKS

The books from which history is derived. Guarded by the History Monks, in their monastery in a hidden valley in the high RAMTOPS. There are over 20,000 of them, each 10 feet high, bound in lead, and the letters are so small that they have to be read with a magnifying glass. When people say 'It is written', it is written *here*. [SG]

MAGICAL BOOKS

Magical books are more than just pulp and paper; their curly magical writing moves around the page, twisting and writhing in an attempt not to be read by a non-wizard.

All books of magic have a life of their own. In the LIBRARY of Unseen University some of the really energetic ones can't simply be chained to the bookshelves; they have to be nailed shut or kept between steel plates. Or – in the case of the volumes on tantric sex magic for the serious connoisseur – kept under very cold water to stop them bursting into flames and scorching their severely plain covers.

Things can happen to browsers in magical libraries that make having your face pulled off by tentacled monstrosities from the DUNGEON DIMENSIONS seem a mere light massage by comparison. No one in possession of a complete set of marbles would like to settle down with a book of magic, because even the individual words have a private and vindictive life of their own, and reading them, in short, is a kind of mental Indian wrestling. Many a young wizard has tried to read a grimoire that is too strong for him, and people who hear the screams find only his pointy shoes with a wisp of smoke coming out of them.

After the first Age of Magic the disposal of grimoires became a severe problem on the Discworld. A spell is still a spell even when imprisoned temporarily in parchment and ink. It has potency. This is not a problem while the book's owner still lives, but on his death the spell book becomes a source of uncontrolled power that cannot easily be defused. In short, spell books leak magic. Various solutions have been tried. Countries near the Rim simply took the books and threw them over the Edge. Near the Hub, less satisfactory alternatives were available. Inserting the offending books in canisters of negatively polarized OCTIRON and sinking them in the fathomless depths of the sea was one (burial in deep caves on land was ruled out after some districts complained of walking trees and five-headed cats), but before long the magic seeped out and eventually fishermen complained of shoals of invisible fish and psychic clams.

A temporary solution was the construction, in various centres of magical lore, of large rooms made of denatured octiron, which is impervious to most forms of magic. Here the more critical grimoires can be stored until their potency has attenuated. That was how there came to be, at the Library of Unseen University, the 'OCTAVO', greatest of all grimoires. At least one legend

suggests that it has always been there and that the university grew up around it.

Bookworm, .303. The fastest insect on the Discworld. It evolved in magical libraries, where it has to eat extremely quickly to avoid being affected by the thaumic radiations. An adult .303 bookworm can eat through a shelf of books so fast that it ricochets off the wall. [P]

Borass, Venter. Much of what is known about the deep history of the Discworld is the result of the work (some would say the imagination) of the wizard Venter Borass. He is buried in the private cemetery of UNSEEN UNIVERSITY but possibly hasn't noticed, since he spent most of his life at the bottom of some hole or other.

It was Borass who claimed that the fossilized magical fields in long-buried rocks indicated occasional reversal of the Discworld's direction of spin, and it is to him that we are indebted for a number of promising theories: that rocks underneath other rocks are likely to be older than the rocks on top (instead of being arranged in order of colour, the prevalent idea at the time), that the continents of the Discworld were once all one land mass, and that mountains gradually turn into grains of sand instead of, as common sense would dictate, the other way around.

After all – anyone who has ever tried to pick a vegetable garden clean of large stones will have observed how, after the briefest shower of rain, a fresh crop will have grown. And no matter how many are taken out over the years, more will still be found. A small garden will generate five large wheelbarrows of stones every year, for years. If they're not growing like truffles, what's the explanation, eh?

He would have been more highly regarded among the faculty were it not for his insistence that curious monsters had existed on the Discworld before the arrival of man, dwarf and troll. He extrapolated from fragments of what he called fossil bone, and one of his drawings, called 'Really Big Lizard', showed his idea of the creature that once possessed the tiny fragment of bone that he had found. It was later claimed that the bone was in fact an old spoon handle.

All this was too much even for his fellow wizards, who took the view that any god worth bothering, and who had something to say about Creation and all the rest of it, would write it all down fair and square somewhere, and would have too much respect for their creations to expect them to go grovelling around in some kind of cosmic game of hunt the slipper.

He was forced to go back and teach students, and mercifully died soon afterwards. [DM]

Borgle, Nodar. The Klatchian who ran a large canteen in Holy Wood, with a cuisine very nearly on a par with that of C.M.O.T DIBBLER himself. [MP]

Borogravia. In its own view, a peace-loving country in the midst of treacherous, devious, warlike enemies. Borogravia fights with everyone. It is ruled by the Grand Duchess ANNAGOVIA. Borogravia's capital (PrinceMarmadukePiotreAlbertHansJosephBerhardtWilhelmsberg) is 2300 miles from Ankh-Morpork by broomstick. Its principal river, the meandering Kneck, separates it from its warlike neighbour, Zlobenia. The Kneck wanders across a wide, rich, silty plain like a piece of dropped string. The country does have some tallow mines and Borogravians are not bad farmers, but the country has no great architecture, no big libraries, no famous composers, no very high mountains, no wonderful views. It has many small towns, mostly with names such as Lipz, Drok, Plotz, Crotz, Plün (a dump, allegedly) and Tübz (watch out for the troll bridge).

Its national anthem (in translation) runs:

'Awake, ye sons of the Motherland
Taste no more the wine of the sour apples
Woodsman, grasp your choppers!
Farmers, slaughter with the tool formerly used
for lifting beets the foe!
Frustrate the endless wiles of our enemies
We into the darkness march singing
Against the whole world in arms coming
But see the golden light upon the mountain
tops!
The new day is a great big fish!'

The last line, it seems, is a literal translation. It means something like 'an amazing opportunity' or 'a glittering prize'. [MR]

Borrowing. Magical technique employed by some witches to enter the mind of other living creatures. The witch reaches out to share a mind with a forest creature, while her body remains behind in a sleep so deep that it can be mistaken for death (which is why when Granny Weatherwax, a very skilled exponent of the craft, goes borrowing, her apparently lifeless hands hold a piece of card on which is written 'I ATE'NT DEAD'). The witch rides on the animal's mind, steering it gently; it is important not to upset the owner, who would undoubtedly panic if it realized that the witch's mind was there as well. There is a price for this skill: no one asks you to pay it, but the very absence of a demand is a moral obligation to a witch. The borrower's motto is: 'Leave nothing but memories, take nothing but experience'.

The more apparently complex a mind is, the harder it is to borrow. For the purposes of most witches the 'best' minds are those of small uncomplicated creatures, like rabbits and most birds. Humans, with their interweaving parallel streams of thought, are very hard. Hardest of all, though, is a hive mind; borrowing the mind of a swarm of bees, for example, when all its components might be travelling in various directions and at varying speeds, is the Everest of borrowing. It is known to have been achieved once.

A built-in danger is that a witch, by accident or design, will become so immersed in the mind of the 'borrowed' creature that she will not return. Indeed, it has sometimes been suggested that witches never die – they merely don't come back.

Borvorius. Imperiator of the Tsortean army. [SG]

Bottler, Violet. Tooth fairy. She lives in Shamlegger Street, Ankh-Morpork, and has a voice like a talking flute. [H]

Bottomley, Duke. Leather-skinned farm worker who also helps out with the harvest at Miss FLITWORTH's. Duke's parents have upwardly mobile, if rather simplistic, ideas about class structure – his brothers are called Squire, Earl and King. [RM]

Bounder, Makepeace Thomas. The Poet of the Cabbages. A bard of little repute who wrote over 2000 poems, mostly around the theme of winter vegetables, usually cabbages. A committed evangelist for vegetables, he invested – unsuccessfully – in several schemes to create vegetable-based clothing. He later died in a pickled cabbage explosion. [TDA]

Bradshaw, Georgina, Mrs. A widowed lady; her late husband, Archibald, was a lawyer. She studied at the Quirm College for Young Ladies. When we first encounter her, she is sporting a noticeable gold and diamond ring, and carrying an expensive-looking bag. She is employed by the new railway company to write a series of travel guides for the new tourism industry. [RS]

Brass Neck. Village in the RAMTOPS, under Leaping Mountain and in the next valley to BAD ASS. [ER]

Brattsley. Member of VITOLLER's troupe of players. [WS]

Bravd the Hublander. Big, strong barbarian. Thick as two short planks, if the planks are extremely thick (*see* STANDARDS). [COM]

Brazeneck University. Magical university in Pseudopolis. Once known as the Braseneck School of Conjuring. It is now seeking to acquire a status to match Unseen University and has, for example, a Higher Energy Magic Building. With the help of (Professor) Adrian TURNIPSEED, it has constructed Pex, a chicken powered version of HEX. However, much to the disappointment of its new Archchancellor, the one-time DEAN of Unseen University, banquets are in short supply due to government grant issues which limit their funding.

Brazeneck is keen to attract new students, and offers them a free crystal ball and a voucher for a free frog or frog-like creature.[UA]

Breccia. Troll actor in the clicks. Also the name of a troll encountered by RINCEWIND in *The Light Fantastic* and of an oft-alluded-to secret society of trolls, similar to the popular images of the Mafia or the Chinese Tongs or the Rotary Club. [MP]

Brian (1). A wizard who works at ZakZak Stronginthearm's. You could tell he was a wizard. Wizards never want you to have to guess. He has long flowing robes, with stars and magical symbols on them; there are even some sequins. His beard would have been long and flowing if indeed he'd been the kind of young man who could really grow a beard. Instead, it's ragged and wispy and not very clean. And the general effect is also spoiled by the fact that he is normally found smoking a cigarette, with a mug of tea in his hand and a face that looks a bit like something that lives under damp logs.

The mug is chipped and on it are the jolly words 'You Don't Have To Be Magic To Work Here But It Helps!!!!!'

He is actually not really a wizard – he just did the evening classes at Unseen University in fretwork. He read a few of the magic books and pinched the robes. [HFOS]

Brian (2). Brian Roberts. Sergeant of the Baron's guard over on the Chalk. Brian taught the Baron's son to ride a horse, and taught him how to hold a sword and how to hunt. He is married to Millie and he writes poetry, such as 'What Good Is The Sky Without Stars?' [ISWM]

Brick. A young troll in Ankh-Morpork. When we first meet him, he is over-fond of banned substances such as Scrape. He was a loser's loser – a troll without a clan or a gang. He was considered thick even by other trolls. He does not look very prepossessing – emaciated, with watery, fried-egg eyes and scarred, knobbly arms. He was called Brick because he had been born in the city and trolls, being made of metamorphorical rock, often take on the nature of the local rocks. His hide was a dirty orange, with a network of horizontal and vertical lines; if Brick stood up close to a wall, he was quite hard to see. But most people didn't see Brick anyway. He was the kind of person whose mere existence is an affront to the litter laws. [T!]

Broadman. Former landlord of the Broken DRUM, Ankh-Morpork. A fat little man with small black beady eyes. He was killed while setting fire to his own pub shortly after learning the strange new concept of 'insurance'. [COM]

Broken Drum. *See* DRUM.

Bronze Psepha. One of the dragons of the WYRMBERG. This dragon, with its long, equine head and bronze-gold wings, is ridden by K!SDRA. Like all the dragons of the Wyrmberg, he was imaginary and given solid existence by the very high level of ambient MAGIC in the area. [COM]

Brooks, Mr. Royal Beekeeper in LANCRE. Although most of the castle staff are known by their surname, Mr Brooks, like the cook and the butler, has the privilege of an honorific. He treats everyone as an equal – not *his* equal, but equal to everyone else and slightly inferior to him. This is perhaps because he deals with royalty in his hives every day. A truly skilled man, and proba-

bly as near to being a witch as you can be while wearing trousers. Hates wasps. [LL]

Broomfog. Author of '*Anima Unnaturale*'. [S]

Brothers of the Order of Midnight. The organization involved in the search for RINCEWIND and the Eighth Spell. [LF]

Brown, Mr. Locksmith in Ankh-Morpork. A neat, elderly, skinny man with a neat little voice and properly polished shoes. He was a very skilled locksmith – a skill which led inevitably to his unfortunate demise. [H]

Brown Islands. Land of big waves and men who surf, rumoured to be the place where bread grows on trees and young women find little white balls in oysters. Located somewhere between the CIRCLE SEA and the COUNTER-WEIGHT CONTINENT. Insofar as there is any trading official between the two continents, it takes place here. [COM]

Brunt, Ossie. A bit of a loner. Friends would have called him a quiet sort who kept himself to himself but they didn't because he didn't have any friends. Or relatives. He used to do odd jobs. He was implicated in the attempted assassination of the Prince KHUFURAH. He was described as 'a weird little twerp, as impressionable a wet clay'. [J]

Brutha. First seen as a loyal and devout novice in the Omnian church, wearing huge sandals and a grubby robe, tending the Temple garden. He was then about seventeen years old, with a big, round, red, honest face and ham-sized hands, a body like a barrel, and tree-trunk legs ending in splay-feet and knock-ankles.

Brutha didn't leave his small village until he was twelve. He was by nature kind, generous and therefore marked down by FATE as a natural target. The other novices called him the Big Dumb Ox. Brutha mastered neither reading nor writing, but he had an absolutely perfect memory, which more or less compensated; all he needed to do was glance at a text in order to be able to write it – or, from his point of

Brutha

view, draw it – in its entirety. When the Great God OM was trapped in the form of a tortoise, Brutha – whose quiet and unquestioning belief meant he was the only person left in the entire country who could hear the god speak – carried him round in a wickerwork box slung over his shoulder. After many adventures, both prospered in their chosen spheres.

Although Brutha was made a bishop by VORBIS, he was later personally appointed CENOBIARCH by the Great God Om. He died after having reached a great age.

Brutha's reinterpretation of the Omnian religion as one of peace and love almost immediately fractured it into a thousand different sects, who have subsequently spend their time arguing about what he said, what it meant, or if he really existed, or if any of them really existed, or if it meant anything, or if anything really meant anything when you got right down to it…thus leaving large parts of the world free to amble through history without being put to the sword every other week. [SG]

Bucket, Seldom. Proprietor and owner of the Ankh-Morpork Opera House. A self-made man, and proud of his handiwork. He confuses bluffness and honesty with merely being rude. He bought the Opera House with the assistance of money borrowed from CHRISTINE's father. He made his money in the cheese and milk derivatives business. His companies include Bucket's Cheese Factory, Bucket's Dairy Products, Bucket's Spreads and Bucket's Bovine, Ovine and Caprine-Based Drinks, ALC. [MA]

Bucket, the. A tavern, of sorts, in Gleam Street, Ankh-Morpork. The Bucket, which lacks charm, ambience or even many customers, is now the bar of choice for the City WATCH. Watchmen don't like to see things that'd put them back on duty when they just want a quiet drink. There's little passing trade in Gleam Steet. The street is, if not a dead end, then seriously wounded by the area's change of fortunes. [TT]

Bugarup. Major university city of XXXX. Famous for its Opera House, which looks like a box of tissues, its harbour and for its wizards' university. [TLC]

Bugarup University. The corrugated-iron XXXX equivalent of Unseen University, Ankh-Morpork. The iron sheets around its gates (also corrugated iron, nailed to bits of wood with second-hand nails) have been bent and hammered into the shape of a stone arch. Over it, burned into the thin metal, are the words 'Nullus Anxietas', the university's motto. The walls incorporate a loose sheet so students can get in after hours. Alongside this loose sheet is a chalked message, 'Nulli Sheilae Sanguineae', a wizardly philosophy. Inside the walls, there is a short, pleasant lawn illuminated at night by the light from a large, low building. In fact, all the buildings are low with wide roofs – like a lot of square mushrooms that've been stepped on, accord to the wizard Rincewind. There is also a tower, which is twenty feet high from the outside, although it is half a mile high at the top. The tower's base is stonework, but about halfway the builders got fed up and resorted to rusted tin sheets nailed onto a wooden framework, telling the Archchancellor of the time 'No worries, mate, she'll be right!' If you brave the rickety ladder leading to the top, you'll find a plank flooring surrounded by corrugated battlements. [TLC]

Bunty. A friend of Sybil Vimes in Ham-on-Koom. Berenice Waynesbury, née Mousefather. She has a daughter who lives outside Quirm and a son who had to go to Fourecks in a hurry. [T!]

Burleigh. President of the Guild of Armourers and, with Pors Stronginthearm, proprietor of Burleigh and Stronginthearm, crossbowmakers to the nobility. [J]

Bursar. *See* DINWIDDDIE, A. A., DR.

Bustle, Simplicity. Sensibility Bustle, D.M. Phil., B.El L., Patricius Professor of Magic. Author of 'Hivers: A Dissertation Upon a Device of Amazing Cunning'. All that could be found of Professor Bustle was buried in a jar in the old Rose Garden at Unseen University. UU advises all research students to spend some time there, and reflect upon the manner of his death. [HFOS]

Butch. A dog in Ankh-Morpork. His top and bottom set of fangs have grown so large that he appears to be looking at the world through bars, and he is bow-legged; this is what calling a dog 'Butch' does to it. A member of the DOG GUILD. [MAA]

Butcher. A carefully selected and extremely credulous jailer employed by Evil Harry DREAD. Carried his keys on a big, easy-to-lift-off hook on his belt. [TLH]

Butterfly, Quantum Weather. *Papilio tempestae.* So called because of its ability to create weather. The Quantum Weather Butterfly is an undistinguished yellow colour, with Mandelbrot patterns on its wings. The wings are slightly more ragged than those of the common fritillary; the ragged edges are infinite – therefore, if their edges are infinitely long, the wings must be infinitely big. They only *look* about the right size because human beings have always preferred common sense to logic. [IT]

Butts, Eulalie. Miss Butts co-founded and runs the QUIRM COLLEGE FOR YOUNG LADIES, a large boarding school which is single-sex, although Miss Butts would prefer it to be no sex whatsoever. She is short, but with a bearing and manner that make people think she is tall even while they're looking down at her. She is not unkind, despite a lifetime of being gently dried out on the stove of education. She is conscientious and a stickler for propriety, and did not deserve to have Susan STO HELIT as a pupil. [SM]

Bylaxis, Mrs. An Ephebian customer of DIDACTYLOS. [SG]

B'zugda-Hiara. Dwarfish insult. Means 'Lawn Ornament'. [WA]

It was something about Cohen. Maybe it was what they called charisma.
It overpowered even his normal smell of a goat that had just eaten
curried asparagus.

– Interesting Times

Cable Street Particulars. A plain-clothes branch of the police force re-introduced by Commander VIMES, although in practice it is merely a front for the occasional training and employment of specialists who have skills, talents or knowledge unavailable to the average copper. In old Ankh-Morpork, it was an unpleasant force, working for the patricians, using torture, coercion and subterfuge to manipulate the city. It almost certainly led to the young Sam Vimes's deep distrust of plain-clothes policemen. Unfortunately, though, secret crimes sometimes need secret policemen. [MA]

Cadram, Prince. Klatchian ruler. A far-sighted, widely read man, recognized as stict but fair. Unlike his younger brother, Prince KHUFU-RAH. [J]

Cake, Evadne, Mrs. A small medium, living in Elm Street, Ankh-Morpork. Squat and short-sighted, she is almost perfectly circular; in spite of this she looms tremendously, largely because of her hat, which she wears at all times. It is huge and black and covered with stuffed birds, wax fruit and other assorted decorative items, all painted black. Carrying an enormous handbag, she travels under her hat like a basket travels under a balloon, grumbling away to herself – her mouth is constantly moving.

Mrs Cake is a very religious woman: there isn't a temple, church, mosque or small group of standing stones anywhere in the city that she hasn't attended at one time or another. Straitlaced and intolerant, in most respects she is, in fact, exactly the kind of person who disapproves of people like her. Apart from church work, her main hobby is dressmaking.

She is not a bead-curtain-and-incense-medium. She is actually very good at her profession, with a lifetime of involvement in the spirit world, an involvement which – it must be said – the spirits feel they could well have done without. With her precognition switched on, she has a disconcerting tendency to respond to questions before they're asked.

Mrs Cake has a daughter, Ludmilla, who is a werewolf. It is because of this that she has a surprisingly understanding attitude to the undead and morphically challenged, and by the time of *Men At Arms* (when Ludmilla had left home) she had opened her home as a lodging house for those of a nocturnal and fur-growing persuasion.

It is very clear that Mrs Cake is, at least in practical terms, a witch. [RM]

Cake, Ludmilla. Daughter of Mrs Evadne CAKE. A werewolf. When in human form, Ludmilla is still built to a scale slightly larger than normal: she is the sort of person who goes through life crouching slightly and looking apologetic in case she inadvertently looms. She has magnificent hair, which crowns her head and flows out behind her like a cloak. She also has slightly pointed ears and teeth which, while white and beautiful, catch the light in a disturbing way. Like all werewolves, her habit of staring at people's throats while she talks to them tends to put a damper on conversation. [RM]

Cakebread. Person once cursed by Nanny OGG for kicking her cat. Since her cat is GREEBO, it is amazing that Cakebread survived long enough to be cursed. [WS]

Caleb (the Ripper). A member of the Silver Horde of COHEN the Barbarian. He killed more than 400 men with his bare hands, and

Mrs Cake & Ludmilla

two with *their* bare hands. Caleb was known to be over 85 years old at his death if, indeed, he died. [IT]

Calendars.

THE DISCWORLD YEAR

The calendar on a planet that is flat and revolves on the back of four giant elephants is always difficult to establish.

It can be derived, though, by starting with the fact that the spin year – defined as the time taken for a point on the Rim to turn one full circle – is about 800 days long. The tiny sun orbits in a fairly flat ellipse, being rather closer to the surface of the Disc at the Rim than at the Hub (thus making the Hub rather cooler than the rim). This ellipse is stable and stationary with respect to the Turtle – the sun passes between two of the elephants.

The effect of all this is that the 'spin year' contains two of each season – two summers, two winters and so on. The winters occur when our theoretical point is at 90° to the orbit of the sun, and the summers when it is directly under the orbit.

In theory this should mean that the point on the Rim should be extremely cold during the 'winters', whereas it has been established that the climate on the Rim is quite mild all year round. It has been suggested by wizards at Unseen University that this is caused by the scatter effect of the very high magical flux around the edge of the Disc, which tends to equalize temperatures all around the circumference.

In the days of the Ankh-Morpork Empire this was fully understood and the Great Year was divided into eight seasons: Winterprime, Spring Prime, Summer Prime, Autumn Prime, Winter Secundus, Spring Secundus and so on. But this was always a purist's view of the calendar, of interest only to wizards and astrologers. Most people – and certainly those in rural areas – really dealt quite sensibly in what were technically half-years, a little longer than a terrestrial year, but noted that in some years the sun rose on your left as you faced the Hub,

and in others it rose on your right. Apart from that, they followed the natural year. You plough, you sow, it grows, you harvest – that's a year, no matter what some daft old man in Ankh-Morpork says.

This has caused some confusion over the naming of various festivals. Hogswatchnight and Crueltide are, from the farmer's point of view, the 'same' festival, although in fact they are the middle and end of the year. Midsummer Eve and Small Gods Eve are also 'the same' for practical purposes. In rural areas Midsummer Eve and Hogswatchnight tend to be used to refer to both festivals, since they refer to natural, homely things (the beginning of summer and the killing of animals).

There are thirteen months in the year – Offle, February, March, April, May, June, Grune, August, Spune, Sektober, Ember, December and Ick. There are eight days in a week, Octeday being the eighth.

Centuries and years are given names, usually chosen by astrologers. The action in most of the Discworld books is set in the final years of the Century of the Fruitbat, which follows the Century of the Three Lice.

Ankh-Morpork also numbers its years for governmental purposes, although the numbering system has been tinkered with as the fortunes of the city have changed.

Initially, they dated from the founding of the city, but Ankh-Morpork has been burned, razed, rebuilt – lost and founded, as it were – many times, and various rulers with more pride than sense have started the numbering from 1 all over again, usually from some vitally important event such as their accession to power. But the recent calendar can be deduced as follows.

Unseen University is known to be two thousand years old in its present form (although in one form or another there has been some kind of magical presence on the site since the creation of Discworld). It was founded in what was then known as AM 1282 by Alberto Malich, during the closing days of the Ankh-Morpork Empire (this lasted from AM 1, the building of one of the first cities in what is now the Shades area, until shortly after the founding of UU).

The wizards began numbering their years from that date, since it didn't matter much to them what the year was called on the other side of the walls. And, as the civil calendar was tinkered with, and revised when people lost count, or found nineteen days that shouldn't have been there, or mislaid the whole of Grune, the city eventually took to using the University's Ankh-Morpork Years, which at least were reliable and happened one after the other, apart from 1256, which for some reason happened twice.

The fact that there are therefore at least two 'counts' has not really caused confusion – historians know their history and don't get confused, and most other people don't need to think much outside the present century.

The Century of the Fruitbat is therefore the twentieth century. The Ankh-Morpork Civil War, which took place in 432 by the city count at the time, took place in AM 1688 by the more reliable University calendar. Students should in any case be wary of references to 'the civil war'; there have been at least seven in the city's recorded history, besides a large number of uncivil or even downright impolite ones. That was, however, the last one, and marked the end of the lengthy monarchical period in the city's history. Since then the city has been ruled by a succession of oligarchies and self-elected dictators of varying degrees of sanity (see PATRICIANS, etc.).

Cambric, Miss. Long Tall Short Fat Sally (she suffers from tides). She is being trained as a witch, in Ankh-Morpork, by old Mrs Happenstance. [ISWM]

Camels, Joe. Mayor of Sto Lat. A short, bird-like man in an outsize robe and chain. By trade he is a parasol-maker. [GP]

Carbonaceous. A troll in LANCRE who climbed the Copperhead Mountain with the young RIDCULLY. [LL]

Carborundum. (Jade.) A troll. Looks like a builder who has spent centuries in the damp pine forests. Covered in lichen – with stringy grey moss hanging in curtains from its head and chin.

A bird's nest in one ear – and carries a genine troll club made from an uprooted sapling. [MR]

Also the name of a troll who works as 'Ead 'Itter for Goatberger the publisher [MA]

Carcer. A psychopath. A complete nut job, yet quite intelligent in many ways; he'd simply worked out that if you kill people who stand in your way, you move forward. Carcer smiled all the time, in a cheerful, chirpy sort of way, apparently convinced that he'd never done anything really wrong even while the blood was dripping from his hand. When he laughed, according to Sam VIMES, it was a sort of modulation to the voice, an irritatingly patronizing chortle that suggested that all this was somehow funny, but you hadn't got the joke. He also ate one hard-boiled egg too many. That was his undoing. [NW]

Carding, Marmaric. An eighth-level wizard. Head of the Hoodwinkers. This seventeen-stone wizard, with his beringed fingers and vein-crazed jowls, was killed by COIN's staff. [S]

Carlton, Alex. (Sane Alex.) He has a beard a dwarf would be proud of – no, one that two dwarfs would be proud of. When we first meet him, he is, with a couple of friends (Adrian Emery and Al Winton), renting an old pigeon loft on the roof of the Ankh-Morpork Post Office. He and his friends are members of the Smoking Gnu – a group of outlaw clacks signallers. [GP]

Carney, Ronald. Slight young man, not as cunning as he thought. Founder of the 'Ankh-Morpork Inquirer' and Chairman of the Guild of ENGRAVERS (AND PRINTERS). [TT]

Caroc cards. Distilled wisdom of the Ancients. Deck of cards used on the Discworld for fortune telling and for card games (see CRIPPLE MR ONION). Cards named in the Discworld canon include The Star, The Importance of Washing the Hands (Temperance), The Moon, The Dome of the Sky, The Pool of Night (the Moon), Death, the Eight of Octograms, the Four of Elephants, the Ace of Turtles. [LF]

Carpenter, Obidiah. Tailor in LANCRE. Also a general poacher, cess-pit cleaner and approximate carpenter (as in 'with a couple of nails it'll stay up all right'). A member of the Lancre Morris Men. [LL]

Carrot. (Carrot Ironfoundersson.) A dwarf (by adoption). His adoptive dwarf parents found him in the woods as a toddler, wandering near the bodies of his real parents, who had been victims of a bandit attack. Also in the wreckage of the cart was a sword, and a ring that was very similar to one recorded as having once been a part of the royal jewellery of Ankh.

When first encountered in the chronicles he was 6' 6" tall (6' 3" in his stockinged feet) and nearly sixteen years old, with a big, honest forehead, mighty neck and impressively pink skin, due to scrubbing. He became known as Carrot not because of his red hair, kept short for reasons of hygiene, but because of his shape – the kind of tapering shape a boy gets through clean living, healthy eating and good mountain air in huge lungfuls. His dwarfish name is Kzad-blat (Head Banger). When Carrot flexes his muscles, other muscles have to move out of the way first. He has a punch that even trolls have learned to respect. He walks with a habitual stoop, which comes from being six feet tall while living with dwarfs. Like all dwarfs, when

he's away he writes home at least once a week.

His adoptive parents, embarrassed at his size and by the fact that he reached puberty at what in dwarf terms is about playgroup age, realized that he needed to be among his own kind. They arranged for him to join the Night WATCH in Ankh-Morpork because, they had been told, it would make a man of him.

Being very literal-minded is a dwarfish trait. It is one which Carrot shares. In the whole of his life (prior to his arrival in Ankh-Morpork) no one ever really lied to him or gave him an instruction that he wasn't meant to take literally.

He is direct, honest, good-natured and honourable in all his dealings. Despite several years in the WATCH, where, as Captain, he is effectively the second-in-command, he still thinks everyone is decent underneath and would get along just fine if only they made the effort. He is genuinely, almost supernaturally, likeable. And he is astonishingly simple – which is not at all the same as 'stupid'. It is just that he sees the world shorn of all the little lies and prevarications that other people erect in order to sleep at night.

After a few initial setbacks, Carrot has had an exemplary career as a policeman, often helped by the fact that people confuse his simplicity with idiocy. In fact there are vast depths to Carrot, and many have wondered at what currents may run there; Carrot has a Destiny, and sometimes Destiny doesn't worry about the innocent bystanders.

For he has a crown-shaped birthmark at the top of his left arm. Coupled with his sword, his charisma, his natural leadership, and his deep and almost embarrassing love of Ankh-Morpork, this rather suggests that he is the long-lost rightful heir to the throne of the city. It is a subject that he avoids, to the point – it has been hinted – of destroying any written evidence to the fact. He seriously believes that to be a policeman is to be the guardian of civilization. He is, in fact, very happy in his job. Or so, without plumbing those depths, it appears.

This is just as well for Ankh-Morpork. Few civilizations can survive long under an honest, just and strong leader, which is why they generally take care never to elect them. [GG]

Carry, Arthur. A very successful candlemaker in Ankh-Morpork who, like a number of other craftsmen, paid to have a coat of arms created for them. His motto was 'Art gave birth to the candle' and was rather more than it seemed. [FOC]

Carter, Bestiality. LANCRE's only baker. Married to Eva. A member of the Lancre Morris Men. His parents, though of a logical turn of mind, got the wrong end of the stick when it came to naming their children. Their first four children (all girls) were called Hope, Chastity, Prudence and Charity; then the boys were, with a sort of misplaced recognition of the need for balance, called Anger, Jealousy, Bestiality and Covetousness. [LL]

Cartwright, Mr. One of the named lodgers at Mrs Arcanum's. He was (and, for all we know, may still be) a travelling seed salesman. [TT]

Casanunda, Giamo, Count. A dwarf. The most enthusiastic lover in the history of the Disc. He also claims to be the Disc's greatest liar – his card says 'World's 2nd Greatest Lover. Finest Swordsman. Outrageous Liar. Soldier of Fortune. Stepladders Repaired'. However, all this may be a lie.

Casanunda is 3' 9" tall, with a typically dwarfish bullet head. But he eschews dwarfish clothing and goes in for periwigs, satins and lace, being aware that big iron boots and great prickly beards attract only ladies of a specialized taste.

Everything his fellow dwarfs do very occasionally as nature demands he does all the time, sometimes in the back of a sedan chair and once upside down in a tree – but with care and attention to detail that is typically dwarfish. He received his title after performing a small service for Queen AGANTIA of Skund (details unknown).

He has done some service also as a highwayman…well, *lowwayman*, really.

He has a natural attraction for Nanny OGG, who is probably his female equivalent. [RM]

63

Catroaster. Disc philosopher. Found floating face down in the Ankh within hours of uttering the famous line 'When a man is tired of Ankh-Morpork, he is tired of ankle-deep slurry.' [M]

Catseye. One of a number of freelance criminals employed by Mr TEATIME. He could see very well in the dark but, as it turned out, this was no help. [H]

Cena. Prophet of the Omnian religion. A tall fellow with a full beard, whose eyes wobbled when he talked. His sandals are a religious artefact. [SG]

Cenobiarch. Head of the Omnian religion. The Superior Iam. After him come six archpriests, thirty lesser iams, hundreds of bishops, deacons, sub-deacons and priests, plus the inquisitors and exquisitors (see QUISITION). Then novices, bull breeders, torturers and Vestigial Virgins. [SG]

Cern. One of the sons of Gordo Smith, and brother of ESK. [ER]

Chair of Indefinite Studies, the. One of the faculty Unseen University. [MP]

Chalky. Troll who runs a wholesale building-supplies firm in Ankh-Morpork. He also does jobbing printing, cheap pottery and, in short, all those little jobs that need to be done to a budget, badly and quick. And, sometimes, with the Law finding out. [RM]

Champot. Past king of LANCRE, who built LANCRE CASTLE. As a ghost, he carries his head under his arm. Since he died of gout, this may take some explaining. [WS]

Chance. Broadly, the greater the odds against anything happening the more likely it is to happen on the Discworld. It's summed up by the saying – amounting to a scientific law – that million-to-one chances crop up nine times out of ten.

Changebasket, Skrelt. Wizard, and re-founder of the Ancient and Truly Original Sages of the Unbroken Circle. By dint of close study Skrelt learned that although a wizard's spells will say themselves when he dies, a Great Spell will simply take refuge in the nearest mind open and ready to receive it. [ER]

Charley. Barman at the Mended DRUM. A large, heavy-set man, whose face is a net of scars. [GG]

Charlie (1). Used to run a clothes shop in Pseudopolis. He, and his wife Henrietta, have two children – a daughter and a son (Rupert). Now a member of the Guild of Actors, he makes his living as a Lord VETINARI look-alike at children's parties, etc. He can stare at balloons until they twist *themselves* into strange shapes. [TT]

Charlie (2). For a nod towards completeness, we might also briefly note some other Charlies – Unlucky Charlie, the scarecrow target for Curses at the Witch Trials; Young Charlie, who, amazingly, had managed to be employed at the Mint while still too young to shave but definitely old enough to have spots; and Charlie, the skeleton who works in the Unseen University. Department of Post-Mortem Communications. [SALF, MM]

Charnel, Brother. A priest who stole the altar gold from the Temple of OFFLER and had it made into a horn, and played magical music until the gods caught up with him and... The story always ends with those terrible three dots, as if legend itself is too scared to continue. [SM]

Cheerysson, Maelog. A old cobbler, who lives at Copperhead with his son. And that's just about all there is to it. [RS]

Cheese, Mr. Owner of the BUCKET in Gleam Street, Ankh-Morpork. A thin, dry man who only smiles when he hears news of some serious murder. Traditionally, he has always sold short measure but, to make up for it, he short-changes as well. He also makes money by renting out the rat's nest of old sheds and cellars that back onto the pub. The Bucket, which lacks charm, ambience or even many customers, is now, as mentioned elsewhere, the bar of choice for the City WATCH. [MAA]

Cheesemongers, the. The Borogravian 10th Infantry Regiment, known as the Ins and Outs – first into battle, last out of the fray. The regiment has battle honours from Raladan, Sheep's Drift, Blunderberg, Ibblestarn and Slomp. [MR]

Cheesewaller, C. V. A very elderly wizard (D.M. (Unseen), B.Thau, B.F.) who lives in QUIRM. He has a talking brass plate outside his premises, a piece of stage magickery that is typical of jobbing wizards in small towns where the natives need to be impressed from the word go.
    The same thinking applies to his props, which happen to include a raven and a talking skull. The raven QUOTH has gone on to greater things; there is no news of the skull. [SM]

Cheesewright, G. Fellow student of TEPPIC at the ASSASSINS' GUILD in Ankh-Morpork. A skinny young man with red hair and a face that is one large freckle. [P]

Chelonauts. Men who journey – or at least intend to journey – below the Rim to explore the mysteries of the Great A'TUIN. Their suits are of fine white leather, hung about with straps and brass nozzles and other unfamiliar and suspicious contrivances. The leggings end in high, thick-soled boots, and the arms are shoved into big supple gauntlets. Topping it all is a big copper helmet designed to fit on the heavy collars around the neck of the suits. The helmet has a crest of white feathers on top and a little glass window in front. [COM]

Chert. Troll who runs a sawmill near Cutshade Forest in the Ramtops. He also sells coffins. [WA]

Chickenwire. One of a number of criminals employed by Mr TEATIME. He got his nickname from his habit of encasing bodies in chicken-wire before dumping them in the sea, to prevent bits floating to the surface. A small but considerate action, on the whole. [H]

Chidder. Classmate of TEPPIC at the ASSASSINS' GUILD in Ankh-Morpork. When first encountered he was wearing a plain black suit which looked as though it had been nailed on to him in bits. He ambles through life as though he's already worked it all out. Teppic calls him 'Chiddy'. His family are merchant venturers. They provide things that people want, using their boat, the *Unnamed*. [P]

Chillum, Millie. Servant at LANCRE CASTLE. A small, dark girl with a tendency to call her female superiors (i.e., everyone else) 'm'm'. [LL]

Chimera. A desert creature, with the legs of a mermaid, the hair of a tortoise, the teeth of a fowl, the wings of a snake, the breath of a furnace and the temperament of a rubber balloon in a hurricane. Clearly a magical remnant. It is not known whether chimeras breed and, if so, with what. [S]

Chimeria. Desert country, now invisible on any map. Original home of a hero called Codice (hero: very strong, beats people up, can't read if his index finger is removed, wears a leather loincloth whatever the weather. Straight from stock, in fact).

Chimeria is possibly a *brigadoon*, of which there are a number on the Disc. These are areas which, owing to a localized instability in reality, do not have a continuous existence in one place and may turn up for only one day every hundred years before once again being squeezed out of the local universe. They reappear either randomly or at lengthy fixed intervals, a common denominator being that no time passes inside the brigadoon between appearances. The lost city of EE is probably one of these, as is the village of Turnover in the RAMTOPS (a special case). In all likelihood there are also a large number of rural areas, or stretches of ocean, where the phenomenon passes unnoticed owing to the absence of anyone to notice it. For anyone interested in further research, a good place to begin looking is any area where sea-going vessels disappear or strange and theoretically extinct animals stroll out of the undergrowth.

Although most brigadoons do have a generalized geographical location to which they are anchored, occasionally one loses this point of contact and floats randomly across the worlds, coming to earth again in any time or place. Evidence suggests that the Wandering SHOPS use some kind of controlled version of this phenomenon on their travels.

Ching Aling. Method of divining used by the Hublandish. It involves the throwing of yarrow sticks into the air, observing the ensuing pattern, interpreting the results using a reference book and pretending you have the faintest idea what it's talking about. (Example: the Octogram 8887: Illegality, the Unatoning Goose.) [M]

Chinny, Clarence. The Ankh-Morpork Consul to Zlobenia. He used to work in the Patrician's Office, and he has been out of the city for five years at the time we meet him. At school, he was not a good fighter – but no one could beat him over the 100 yard dash. [MR]

Chriek, Otto. Vampire iconographer with the '*Ankh-Morpork Times*'. He is thin and pale with thin, blue-veined hands, a carefully cut widow's peak and skinny black-clad legs. He wears little, oval dark glasses, shiny black shoes and a red-lined opera cloak (with pockets for his gear), and also wears the only photographer's jacket with tails. He has a ridiculous accent which grows thicker or thinner depending on who he is talking to. Otto is a black ribboner – a member of the vampires' League of TEMPERANCE. He is quite an innovator in the world of Discworld photography and he is working on such new processes as colour printing and the obscurograph – a camera to take pictures with DARK LIGHT. His use of salamanders for flash pictures causes him some problems and he used to deal with this by carrying a card saying: 'DO NOT BE ALARMED. The former bearer of this card has suffered a minor accident. You will need a drop of blood from any species, and a dustpan and brush'. Later, he refined his recovery technique by carrying a small bottle of blood on a string around his neck – this breaks on the floor if he turns to dust as a result of a salamander flash. Otto suffers for his art. [TT]

Christine. A singer at the Ankh-Morpork OPERA HOUSE who, prior to joining the Opera, had spent three years with Mme Venturi at the Quirm Conservatory. If this had an improving effect on her voice, we can only speculate that beforehand it was used to frighten large animals. She is slightly built (and has gone to some pains to make herself look even thinner), has long, blond hair and a voice that seems to have an excited little squeak permanently attached to it. The impression she gives is that she simply cannot get a whole idea into her head in one go, but has to nibble it into manageable bits. Nevertheless, she really does look good on stage and has that quality to which mere talent comes a poor second. [MA]

Chrysoprase. (Also Krysoprase [LF] and Chrystophrase [WS].) Well, trolls were never good at spelling. A troll gang leader and extortionist; when he demands an arm and a leg in payment, he means it. Owns the Cavern, a troll nightclub, and wears jewellery made from the diamond teeth of other troll gangsters who have come second in their business dealings with him. Unlike most trolls he wears a suit – and a tie

with a diamond pin. He is said to be big in the BRECCIA, a rather inefficiently organized troll crime syndicate. [MAA]

Chubby. A swamp dragon. Rescued by Lady RAMKIN from a blacksmith in Easy Street. Exploded by Edward D'EATH. His blue collar was an important clue in one of the Night WATCH'S few real homicide cases. [MAA]

C'hulagen. Old dark god of the 'NECROTELICOMNICON'. [ER]

Chume. The Notorious Herring Thrower. [RM]

Churn, Ezrolith. Very old wizard and a former ARCHCHANCELLOR of Unseen University. He had been writing a treatise on 'Some Little Known Aspects of Kuian Rain-Making Rituals'. [E]

Circle Sea. A sizeable but almost landlocked sea approximately halfway between the Hub and the Rim, opening at its turnwise side into the Rim Ocean. Its principal trading ports are Ankh-Morpork, on the STO PLAINS coast, and AL KHALI and EPHEBE on the rimwards side. Discworld civilization, which can broadly be defined as those countries that have invented the fork as well as the knife, is found around its historic coasts.

Circumfence. A barrier built by the Kingdom of KRULL around almost a third of the Disc, to catch salvage. The biggest construction ever built on the Disc. Seven navies used to patrol it constantly to keep it in repair and bring its salvage back to Krull. However, the repair work now seems to have ceased.

Civil War. The Ankh-Morpork Civil War ran from 8.32 p.m., Grune 3, 432 to 10.45 a.m., Grune 4, 432 (but *see* the Discworld CALENDAR – by the calendar now commonly used, this would have been 1688). The origins of the war have always been the subject of heated debate among historians. There are two theories:

1. The common people, having been heavily taxed by a particularly stupid and unpleasant king, decided that enough was enough and that it was time to do away with the outmoded concept of monarchy and replace it with, as it turned out, a series of despotic overlords who still taxed heavily but at least had the decency not to pretend the gods had given them the right to do it, which made everyone feel a bit better. *Or*

2. One of the players in a game of CRIPPLE MR ONION in a tavern accused another of palming more than the usual number of aces, and knives were drawn, and then someone hit someone with a bench, and then someone else stabbed someone, and arrows started to fly, and someone swung on a chandelier, and a carelessly hurled axe hit someone in the street, and then the WATCH was called in, and someone set fire to the place, and someone hit a lot of people with a table, and then everyone lost their tempers and commenced fighting.

According to the history books, the decisive battle that ended the Ankh-Morpork Civil War was fought between two handfuls of bone-weary men in a swamp early one misty morning and, although one side claimed victory, it ended with a practical score of Humans 0, Ravens 1000, which is the case with most battles.

The famous fire during the Civil War is noteworthy simply because it was started by both sides at the same time in order to stop the city falling into enemy hands. It was not otherwise impressive; the ANKH had been particularly high that summer, and most of the city was too damp to burn. [MP]

Clacks. The semaphore system now taking over as the principal method of communicating over long distances on Discworld. There are now clacks towers all over Ankh-Morpork, the Sto Plains, and all the way to Lancre, Überwald and beyond. These are spaced at eight-mile intervals, each tower being 150 feet high. Watchmen in Ankh-Morpork now carry mini-clacks paddles to communicate with each other across the city whilst they are on the move. The roofs of Ankh-Morpork are now a forest of clacks towers, winking and twinking and twinkling in the sunlight. The big tower on the Tump is one end of the Grand Trunk that winds more than 2000 miles to Genua.

Clamp, Mrs. Making this brief appearance to announce that she was a cook at the Opera House. [MA]

Clancy, Sidney. Sidney Clancy & Son. Purveyors of the finest cat and dog meats to the gentry, from their premises at 11, Long Hogmeat, Ankh-Morpork. [TT]

Clarence. Palace Guard. That's it – but welcome back to the *Companion*, Clarence. [GG]

Cleph-ptah-re. Past queen of Djelibeybi. TEPPIC's aunt. [P]

Clete, Mr. Secretary of the MUSICIANS' GUILD. Had a pointed nose and a strange, mirthless laugh ('Hat. Hat. Hat.'). He looked like something you might get if you extracted fossilized genetic material from something in amber and then gave it a suit.

For some years he was very active in Ankh-Morpork's Guild system, into which he fitted like a moray eel fits into a reef.

Many people have sought power by great feats of arms or complex diplomatic negotiations, but Clete followed what we might call the Grand Vizier road to power. He did things. Trivial and thankless but essential things. Keeping Minutes, for example (after all, no one remembers what they decided until they read the Minutes). Making sure the membership roll is quite up to date. Filing. Organising. He worked hard on behalf of the THIEVES' GUILD, although he wasn't a thief (at least in the normal sense). Then there was a rather more senior vacancy in the FOOLS' GUILD, and Mr Clete was no fool and took it immediately. And finally there was the Secretaryship of the MUSICIANS' GUILD. Since technically he should have been a musician, he bought a comb and paper. Mr Clete believed in organization rather more than he believed in the people and things that needed organizing. [SM]

Clockson, Jeremy. He was left on the doorstep of the Guild of Clockmakers in a basket when he was a few days old and has been a member of the Guild since then, as a foundling. He was

(although past tense is somewhat problematical here) a thin lad who never laughed. He grew up healthy, in body at least, and with an absolute genius for clockmaking to the exclusion of everything else, such as proper human relationships, the ability to be sensibly untidy, intelligent conversation and so on. He also had a perfect, even pathologically accurate, sense of time. On the table by his bed he had a row of alarm clocks, currently under test; he'd set them for seven and then would wake up at 6.59 to check that they went off on time. Jeremy had an interesting relationship with TIME and with Lobsang LUDD and, in the problematical sense alluded to above, still does. [TOT]

Clogston, Major. An officer in the Borogravian Army Provost's Office. At first impression, the Major is a smart young man, with half-moon reading glasses and a blood sugar disorder which means he needs to eat regularly. Known, to some colleagues, as Christine. [MR]

Clubs and societies. Ankh-Morpork has a wide range of clubs catering for its vast population. These include:

Ankh Committee on Safety [UA]
Ankh-Morpork Trespassers' Society (was Explorers' Society) [UA]
BRECCIA [SM]
Caged Birds Society, Ankh-Morpork [TT]

Campaign for Dead Rights [TFE]

Campaign for Equal Heights – a pressure group to ensure and enforce equable treatment for dwarfs in Ankh-Morpork. And this is strange because, unlike trolls, dwarfs have never really been the subject of discrimination and are the city's largest ethnic group after humans themselves. Most of thoe on the Campaign's committee are human. [H]

Cavern Club – a sort of Kennel Club for the breeders of pedigree swamp dragons. Not to be confused with the Cavern, in Quarry Lane, which is a club for the cooler sort of human and the nastier sort of troll. [GG, SM]

Cockbill Boars (AM football club) [UA]

Country Landowners' Association [MAA]

Dimwell Old Pals (AM football club) (colours – pink & green) [UA]

Dolly Sisters' Baking & Flower Circle [TT]

Dolly Sisters Football Club (colours – white & black) [UA]

Dolly Sisters Players [UA]

ELUCIDATED BRETHREN OF THE EBON NIGHT [GG]

Fidgett's – exclusive gentlemen's club in Ankh-Morpork. [TOT]

Fine Art Appreciation Society (Ankh-Morpork) – believed by Sergeant Colon to be an excuse for men to 'paint pictures of women in the nudd'. [GG]

Floral Arranging Society, Ankh-Morpork [TT]

Folk-Dance & Song Club (Morpork) – not much is known except that one of its keenest members is Corporal 'Nobby' Nobbs of the City WATCH. This is like finding King Herod attending meetings of the Bethlehem Playgroup Association. [GG]

FRESH START CLUB

Friendly Flamethrowers' League – another dragon organization. Whereas the Cavern Club judges, however, would award points for pointiness of ear and healthiness of scale, the Flamethrowers are a much jollier bunch whose dragon shows include

categories like The Dragon Who the Judges Would Most Like To Cook On. [GG, MAA]

Funny Vegetable Society, Ankh-Morpork [TT]

Golem Trust, the [GP, MM]

Illuminated & Ancient Brethren of Ee – one of Ankh-Morpork's many well-known secret societies. [GG]

League of Decency (AM) [MM]

Little Sisters of Perpetual Velocity, FURIES (Ephebian) [UA]

Merry Pranksters, the [FGD]

Nap Hill Jolly Pals [TT]

Nap Hill United (AM football club) [UA]

Offler's League of Temperance (wear a blue ribbon) [H]

Peeled Nuts, The – The Ankh-Morpork Historical Re-Creation Society [FOC]

Pigsty Hill Pork Packers (AM football club) [UA]

Pink PussyCat Club (Ankh-Morpork) [T!]

Recovering Accordian Players Society, Ankh-Morpork [TT]

Royal Society for the Betterment of Mankind – founded by King VERENCE II. [CJ]

Silicon Anti-Defamation League (often considered, without any real evidence, to be a front organization for the Breccia). This is a troll organization, formed originally by working trolls in Ankh-Morpork who were fed up with the way trolls in general were stereotyped as big, slow, violent and stupid. Initially their response was to knuckle around to an offender's house and pull off his arms. Things have since settled down a bit, and the SADL is now just another one of Ankh-Morpork's numerous pressure groups. [MAA, MP, FOC]

Skunk Club, Brewer Street, SoSo. You can buy drinks and watch females of various species take their clothes off (in the case of trolls, put their clothes on; trolls are normally stone naked, in their natural surroundings, and the males find the idea of the females wearing fifteen overcoats strangely exciting. They've never understood why humans seem to see things the other way – after all, they say, it's not as if you don't know what to expect. Most troll *robers* get embarrassed and rush off after putting on no more than fourteen layers of clothing).

Smell Preservation Society, Ankh-Morpork [SN]

Überwald TEMPERANCE Movement. Also the Überwald League of Temperance. The Black Ribboners [TT, NW]

Unpleasantly Squeaky Animal Front [FGD]

White Hand Gang [FGD]

Young Men's Pagan Association [LF]

Young Men's Reformed Cultists of the Ichor God Bel-Shamharoth Association [P]

Coalface. A troll privy cleaner in Ankh-Morpork. Sometime right-hand troll for CHRYSOPRASE, but not a henchman on account of failing to understand how to hench; subsequently enlisted into the militia by Corporal, now Captain, CARROT. Considered stupid by other trolls. This is like being considered flat by other carpets. [MAA]

Coates, Ned. Constable in the Night Watch when Vimes was a new recruit. Promoted to lance-corporal by Sergeant Keel. A freethinker, probably a revolutionary at heart and better fighter than Keel in every respect except that of unscrupulous cunning. A hero of the Glorious Revolution of 24/25 May (it happened overnight). [NW]

Coaxes. An Ephebian philosopher. He wrote a book about dreams. [SG]

Cohen the Barbarian. Ghenghiz Cohen. The greatest hero the Disc has ever produced, with an uncanny ability to get close to money. His father drove him out of the tribe when he was eleven and he has been living on his wits and other people's nerves ever since. When first encountered, he was a skinny, little eighty-seven-year-old; totally bald, with a beard almost down to his knees and a pair of matchstick legs on which varicose veins have traced the street map of quite a large city.

Cohen had only one working eye – the other was covered by a black patch. He had so many scars that you could play noughts and crosses on him, although your hand would have been chopped off if you dared. His teeth quit long ago but, inspired by TWOFLOWER, he obtained a set of dentures made of troll's teeth, which are diamond. He also suffered from lumbago, arthritis, backache, piles and bad digestion, and smelled strongly of peppermints as an alternative to just smelling strongly.

Although he could read, after a fashion, he never really mastered the pen and he signed his name with an 'x', which he usually spelt wrong. He is, nevertheless, claimed as the author of '*INNE JUSTE 7 DAYES I WILLE MAKE YOU A BARBEARIAN HERO!*'

Cohen, in fact, just went on doing what he had always done. Many a younger opponent challenged him in the belief that he couldn't be any good because he was so old, whereas a moment's thought would suggest that since he'd managed to become old he must have been very good indeed. He was also something of a philosopher. His answer, when asked what are the greatest things in life, was: 'hot water, good dentishtry and shoft lavatory paper'.

Possibly it was in search of these that, towards the end of his life (and even closer to the end of the lives of anyone who stood in his way), Cohen put together his Silver Horde of equally elderly men and conquered the AGATEAN EMPIRE, where he effectively became the new Emperor. However, the soft life got them all down, and faced with the unthinkable prospect of dying in their beds the remnant of the Horde undertook one last, very final adventure. They climbed CORI CELESTI, the Disc's central mountains and the home of the gods, to – shall we say – get their own back.

What finally became of them is a little unclear. Cohen's life was just too big, it seems, for mere death to put an end to it.

Cohen the Barbarian

Coin. The eighth son of the wizard IPSLORE THE RED and a SOURCERER. When we encountered him, he looked about ten years old, with a slender, young face framed by a mass of blond hair, a thin mouth and two golden eyes that seemed to glow from within. He wore a simple white robe. He inherited his staff from his father; it was of black OCTIRON, so dark that it looked like a slit in the world, with a meshwork of silver and gold carvings that gave it a rich and sinister tastelessness. Most wizards have no taste, of course, but this staff had a very stylish kind of tastelessness.

While acting under the influence of the staff, Coin caused wholesale devastation in Ankh-Morpork and put at risk the continued existence of the Discworld itself. After his technical defeat by the wizard RINCEWIND, he retired to a better plane. [S]

Colette. A worker, if that is the term, at Rosemary PALM's House of Negotiable Affection. She would be described as a very handsome young woman in any language, particularly Braille. She is noted for her unusual ear-rings. [MA]

Collabone, Devious H. Unseen University's representative in Genua. He is studying Oyster Communications in a Low Intensity Magical Field for his B.Thau. His terrible halitosis means he is known as 'Dragonbreath' Collabone. [GP]

Collar, Mrs. Bedder at the Assassins' Guild. TEPPIC's bedder in the sixth form. (For those readers who have escaped the clutches of higher education, a bedder, well, makes the beds, cleans the rooms and so on. And nothing more.) [P]

Colon, Frederick. Sergeant in the Ankh-Morpork City WATCH. Age believed to be about sixty. A fat man with a huge red face like a harvest moon. He likes the peace and quiet of the night and owes thirty years of happy marriage to the fact that Mrs Colon works all day gutting fish and he works all night. There must have been occasions when they were in the same room, however, since he has three grown-up children and some grandchildren. He has looked retirement in the face and didn't like it.

Fred Colon used to be in an army or armies (including, at one time, the Duke of Eorle's First Heavy Infantry (the Pheasant Pluckers) and, prior to that, the Duke of Quirm's Middleweight Infantry) but has been in the City Watch for thirty years all told, and has known Commander VIMES for many years. Fred is now 'Head of Traffic' in the Watch. He smokes a pipe, and wears sandals with his Watch uniform, along with a breastplate with impressive pectoral muscles embossed on it, which his chest and stomach fit into in the same way that jelly fits into a mould.

In Vimes' opinion, Fred Colon is not the greatest gift to policing. He is slow, stolid and not very imaginative. But he's plodded his way around the streets for so long that he's left a groove and somewhere inside that stupid fat head is something very smart, that sniffs the wind and hears the buzz and reads the writing on the wall, admittedly doing the last bit with its lips moving.

When out on the streets, he has a habit of

Frederick Colon

loitering near large buildings – not in case they are stolen, but because he enjoys a quiet smoke out of the wind.

He is the sort of man who, in a military career, will automatically gravitate to the post of sergeant. As a civilian, his natural role would be something like a sausage butcher – some job where a big red face and a tendency to sweat even in frosty weather are practically part of the specification.

He looks like the sort of man who, if he fell off a cliff, would have to stop and ask directions on the way down.

He is currently the Watch Liaison Officer and the Custody Officer. He has an office in the Watch Training School (in the old lemonade factory) in the old Twaddle Room (named for the basic soft drink syrup).

It is known that, as a child, Sergeant Colon had a pink stuffed pig called Mr Dreadful. This sort of thing can come back to haunt you in later life. [GG]

Computers. The Disc's main known computer is now HEX, the computer at Unseen University. Although originally powered by ants ('Anthill Inside'), Hex now more or less redesigns itself to suit any problem it encounters, and the only thing preventing it from becoming a full member of the Faculty is that no one has yet perfected Artificial Stupidity.

In physical size the great computer of the skies on the Vortex Plains is much larger. It is an immense construction of grey and black slabs of stone, arranged in concentric circles and mystic avenues; a triumph of the silicon chunk, a miracle of modern masonic technology. Designed and built by druids, but, oh, *so* fifteen centuries ago. (*See also* RIKTOR.)

Confectionary School of Architecture. A style responsible for the house encountered by Rincewind and TWOFLOWER in *The Light Fantastic*; the style in which gingerbread houses are built.

Conina. One of the daughters of COHEN the Barbarian, and therefore genetically a barbarian heroine who, unfortunately, wants to be a hairdresser. A superb fighter, she carries a large number of concealed weapons, although absolutely anything she can get hold of – a hairgrip, a piece of paper, a hamster – is used as a deadly weapon.

Her hair is long and almost pure white, her skin tanned. She is a demure and surprisingly small figure. Although she inherits her looks from her mother, a temple dancer, she inherits from her father sinews you could moor a boat with, reflexes like a snake on hot tin, a terrible urge to steal things and a sensation that she should be throwing a knife at everyone she meets. [S]

Conjurers' Guild. Motto: NVNC ILLE EST MAGICVS. Coat of arms: a shield, decorated with a vierge, dévêtée on a field, azure et étoilé. The whole bisected by a bend, sinister et indented.

The Conjurers have a very small Guildhouse annoyingly close to Unseen University in Ankh-Morpork, but it's really more of a club house – there is no such thing as a professional conjurer, it being more of an evenings-and-weekends hobby for respectable men who do other jobs during the day. They tend to be jolly and fat and well balanced, and inclined to drop their aitches and drink beer and, besides the usual cries of 'hey presto!', pepper their normal conversation with terms like 'many moons ago' and 'for my sins'. They go around with sad, thin women in spangly tights and unsuitable feathers in their hair; it's impossible to imagine a conjurer without one (as in the Amazing Bonko and Doris). They infuriate wizards by not realizing how lowly they are in the magical pecking order and by telling them jokes and slapping them on the back. They are very popular in Ankh-Morpork – knowing that something is done by trickery and sleight-of-hand is somehow much more intriguing than boring old magic. (*See also* THAUMATURGISTS.) [ER]

Cool, Monks of. Tiny and exclusive monastery, hidden in a really cool and laid-back valley in the lower RAMTOPS. The Brothers of Cool are a reserved and secretive sect which believes that only through ultimate coolness can the universe be comprehended, that black works with everything and that chrome will never truly go out of style. They're so cool they sometimes never get out of bed. [LL]

Cooper, Ted. How can we fail to include a man who blew up a roast chicken at his mum's birthday party? [TSC]

Coplei, Bosun. Bosun of the Omnian ship, the *Fin of God*. [SG]

Copolymer. The greatest storyteller in the history of the world. It is only unfortunate that this basic skill is confounded by a very poor memory and a lack of any practical narrative ability, so that, for example, his actual stories tend to proceed on the lines of: 'It was a Thursday... No, I tell a lie, it was a Wednesday... When – what's his name, tip of my tongue, forget my own head next – set out...'. [P]

Copperhead Mountain. One of the more impressive mountains in the RAMTOP chain, on the edge of the Kingdom of LANCRE; the mountain and its lesser mountains and foothills are home to both dwarfs (in whose low mines CARROT Ironfoundersson grew to a slightly concussed manhood) and trolls.

Cori Celesti. A spire of grey stone and green ice ten miles high at the Disc's hub. It rises through the clouds and supports at its peak the realm of DUNMANIFESTIN, home of the Disc gods. As the AURORA CORIALIS discharges over it, it becomes a column of cold, coruscating fire. Other mountains cluster around it, and although these are no more mountains than termite mounds by comparison, in reality each one is a majestic assortment of cols, ridges, faces, cliffs, screes and glaciers that any normal mountain range would be happy to associate with.

Corksock. Proprietor of Corksock's Natty Clothing in Ankh-Morpork. [MAA]

Cornice Overlooking Broadway. A GARGOYLE on the Opera House, Ankh-Morpork. [MAA]

Cosmopilite, Marietta, Mrs. An elderly seamstress (a real one, with needles and everything; not the other sort) who lives at 3 Quirm Street, Ankh-Morpork with 'Rooms to Let, Very Reasonable'. During the HOLY WOOD times she became a wardrobe mistress, becoming Vice President in Charge of Wardrobe.

She is known occasionally to run a haberdashery shop and is also, much against her wishes, a religious icon (*see* COSMOPILITE, THE WAY OF MRS).

The History Monk LU-TZE has collected all her cosmically wise sayings (such as 'It'll end in tears') and finds them a pretty good guide to understanding the universe. Wisdom is where you find it. [MP]

Cosmopilite, The Way of Mrs. As you may just have read (above), Mrs COSMOPILITE, LU-TZE's former landlady and occasional seamstress is also, against her wishes, a religious icon.

It could have happened to anybody, but it happened to Mrs Cosmopilite, within minutes of meeting the Sweeper. She and the young Lu-Tze were having a discussion about the rent when she said, 'I was not born yesterday!'

This statement astonished the Sweeper, because it was a simple rephrasing of the words of WEN the Eternally Surprised when he discovered the true, ever-renewing nature of time: 'Truly, yesterday I was not born.'

Lu-Tze began to pay closer attention to Mrs Cosmopilite's everyday utterances, and quickly realized that – without any kind of training – the woman was speaking cosmic truths in practically every sentence; for example: 'You are so sharp you'll cut yourself one of these days', 'I'd forget my own head if it wasn't nailed on' and 'There is a time and a place for everything'. The latter showed a grasp of the eightfold nature of Time that even venerable scholars has failed to achieve.

Seldom, he realized, had so much wisdom been so openly imparted. He began to note these down, marvelling at how ancient wisdom was encapsulated so succinctly, and he spoke at length on this subject when he got back to Oi Dong Monastery.

As a result, the Way of Mrs Cosmopilite opened, and was soon thronged. This is because people always assume that wisdom is, well, *more* wise if it comes from a long way away. So, while impressionable people in Ankh-Morpork follow the path of distant religious teachers with names like Rinpo and Gompa, the orange-robed, bald young men from the high mountains now follow the Way of Mrs Cosmopllite (down to the shops, dropping in on her sister for a cup of tea, an appointment with the chiropodist, and then back home ('the Way').

It is considered a blessing to have her throw things at you. A signal honour is to be attacked with her broom, the broom being a symbol of Time. On very infrequent occasions, if she is in a rare good mood and has some heavy shopping, she might actually give one of them a bag to carry. Acolytes seeking the Way to true wisdom, peace and harmony have actually kicked, scratched and bitten one another, just for a moment's grip of a bag handle.

The Spiritual Way of Mrs Cosmopilite has been mostly gleaned by Lu-Tze himself from observations whilst staying with her and, subsequently, during his frequent travels among the Hzo-lym, or 'trouser-wearers', where the Way is followed extensively, usually by elderly ladies who don't know they are doing it.

Unusually among paths of enlightenment, 'the Way' doesn't involve detaching the individual from mundane reality. Following the path means one becomes as closely involved in mundane reality as possible, particularly with the lives of one's neighbours.

Lu-Tze called it transubstantialism, a path which engages the everyday in every possihle way. Followers will take an active interest in those around them, discussing them at length with other neighbours and friends, paying great attention to detail so that stuff may he passed on further, possibly with narratively satisfying additions.

Particular interest should be taken in the ailments of other people. A follower will always have some chronic ailment, such as: 'It is my leg', 'It is my elbow' or 'It is my foot' ...

It is vital that, when hearing of someone's ailment, followers should know of someone else who had that very same ailment, and it went away after a few days, or possibly they died of it. Death (or lack of same) plays a major role in these concerns, usually where the subject in question was 'Told by doctors when he was thirty that he "had a year to live" and is now ninety-five' or 'He looked as right as rain, and then next morning, bang! Dead as a doorknob!'

Followers will need extremely long memories to be able to recall in great detail who said

what about whom when, for example, 'At our Fran's wedding ...'

Mrs Cosmopilite's Way does not preclude attendance at a place of worship, traditionally one of the more austere and demanding sects. Indeed, an ideal church for Mrs C. would be one with commandments against the woman next door, young people, other people's cats in your garden, people who object to your cat in their garden, etc. Until that happy day, she is an Omnian, because of all the smiting.

Here is a, fairly basic, introduction to some elements of the Way:

MEDITATION AND THE WAY OF MRS COSMOPILITE

Buy mat, incense, wind chimes, book. Join class. Leave note for loved ones in case self gets stuck on astral plane.

There are then a number of stages to successful meditation:

Phase 1.
Unroll mat, cross legs. Let mind empty.
Phase 2.
Wonder if you've been meditating long enough. Also, slight concern over not being able to feel left leg. Try to dismiss mental picture of huge blood clot.
Phase 3.
Wonder if anyone will notice if you look at your watch.
Phase 4.
Wonder if perhaps you ought to have gone to the toilet before beginning meditation.
Phase 5.
Glance at watch. Find you have been meditating for forty-five seconds.
Phase 6.
Wonder if you have the right kind of robe for meditating. Probably cannot achieve Nirvana with huge red and gold Kung-fu fighter on back.
Phase 7.
Can't feel leg at all now.
Phase 8.
Wonder if should be wearing sandals at this point.

Phase 9.
Wonder what it is that's buzzing behind one's head.
Phase 10.
Wonder if allowed to slap buzzy thing away?
Phase 11.
If one kills buzzy thing, will one still acquire cosmic enlightenment?
Phase 12.
Wonder if absolutely forbidden from treading on an ant. Does that prohibition apply to elephants? Because if so, what's the position regarding the fact that the world turns on the back of four of them? That's like treading on them, surely?
Phase 13.
Wonder if should have bought more expensive robe.
Phase 14.
Really, really want to scratch.
Phase 15.
Search for inner self.
Phase 16.
Cannot find inner self.
Phase 17.
Go to pub.

FOOD AND THE WAY

The Megabiotic Diet

Much spiritual teaching about food, in the opinion of Lu-Tze, concentrates on the health of the body rather than the needs of the soul. The Diet of the Way redresses this imbalance.

There is no upper limit to the amount of tea and biscuits that may be consumed. Readily consume Baked Beans upon the toast, a celestial foodstuff. Eat cheerfully of Macaroni Cheese, Bubble and Squeak, Bread-and-Butter Pudding and other foods that nourish the soul, and do not go into the water for an hour afterwards. (Followers of the Black Cult of Mrs Dolly GOLIGHTLY hold that this means that water *must* be entered after an hour, but they always come up with that sort of thing.)

Diet and Meditation in the Way

Meditation should be undertaken after the consumption of one of the transubstantial foods, such as Boiled Beef and Carrot, or Toad-in-the-Hole.

For deep meditation, this should be followed by Prunes and Custard, or Spotted Dick and Custard.

Do not be afraid of exploding. In the same way the followers of the transcendental path look to the opening of the Third Eye, so the *transubstantial* student awaits the opening of the Second (or Pudding) Stomach. It is latent in all humans, as the following mantra, repeated somewhere every day, very clearly shows:

'*I couldn't eat another thing, honestly. I'm full up!*'

'*Well, it can't do any harm to look at the menu.*'

'*All right, but— Oooh, Sticky Toffee Pudding!*'

And the Second Stomach has opened.

Whatever the sacred meal of choice, the student should lie back, hands folded across the chest – feet, for preference, raised up upon a stool – and start to meditate on the nature of Being until you hear somebody getting the tea.

Fasting

When you decide you are going to fast, eat as much as you can first. This is vitally important for successful fasting.

If you begin to feel peckish, the following things do not count as breaking the fast:

Anything you didn't mean to eat
Food tasted while preparing food
Anything you don't like
Rice cakes
Slimming food (the more slimming food you eat, the slimmer you will become and the less you will have eaten. Homeopathic food works the other way.)
Food eaten while taking exercise

RULES OF THE WAY

Wear a woollen vest, summer and winter
Mind your own business
Speak as you find

Don't talk nonsense
Always wear clean underwear

Classically, the reason for this last is said to be: 'In case you are knocked down by a runaway horse and cart', which is puzzling, since the colour of anyone's underwear after being trampled by a horse and flattened by a cart is, firstly, likely to be taken for granted and, secondly, unlikely to be the biggest problem. [LTD]

Cotton, Corporal. Or is it Medium? or Hand-wash Only? Anyway, a corporal in the, er, KLAT-CHIAN FOREIGN LEGION, whose soldiers are so successful at joining to forget that they have to rely on the labels in their uniforms to remind themselves who they are. [SM]

Counterweight Continent. Almost a legend, although a real one. It is a small continent, but equal in weight to all the mighty land masses on its opposite hemicircle. It is said to be made of gold – the area is also known as the Aurient, or 'place where the gold comes from'. But sailors searching for it return empty-handed or not at all. In fact, although gold is very common there, most of the mass is made up of vast deposits of OCTIRON deep within the crust. There is a very small amount of surreptitious trading. (*See also* AGATEAN EMPIRE.)

Counterwise wine. *See* RE-ANNUAL PLANTS.

Counting pines. These grow right on the permanent snowline of the high RAMTOPS. They are one of the few known examples of borrowed evolution. The counting pines let other vegetables do their evolving for them, to save all the millions of years of trial and error. A pine seed coming to rest anywhere on the Disc immediately picks up the most effective local genetic code via morphic resonance and grows into whatever best suits the soil and climate, usually doing much better than the native trees themselves, which it usually usurps.

What makes them particularly noteworthy is the way they count. Being dimly aware that human beings learned to tell the age of a tree by counting the rings, the original counting pines decided that this was *why humans cut trees down.* Overnight every counting pine readjusted its genetic code to produce, at about eye-level on its trunk, in pale letters, its precise age. Within a year they were felled almost to extinction by the orna-mental house number-plate industry, and only a very few survive in hard-to-reach areas. [RM]

Cranberry, 'Professor'. A hired killer in the pay of Cosmo Lavish. Cranberry was a scholarship boy at the ASSASSINS' GUILD – a foundling. He is quietly spoken and modestly dressed, with a shiny bald head (in fact he has no body hair at all). [MM]

Crank, Arthur. Lives in Prattle Alley. A serial suicide jumper, or more correctly a serial threat-ener – he does it for the tobacco money, a cup of tea and the conversation. He was a steeplejack by trade and has been married for thirty-five years (though his wife can't cook cabbage to save her life or, presumably, his). [TT]

Crash. Son of a rich dealer in hay and feedstuffs. Also the leader of a would-be Music With Rocks In group, originally called Insanity. [SM]

Creator, the. A little rat-faced man, with a slightly put-upon voice made for complaining with. He created the Discworld while the main universe was being built, and it was obviously on a budget. It is clear that World Creation is a purely mechanical function and doesn't call for any godlike attributes. [E]

Creator of XXXX, the. A distinct entity from the CREATOR. An enigmatic man who carries the whole universe in a leather sack on his back. His modus operandi is sticking on extra bits to already-existing worlds, always adding his distinct signature – kangaroos. He is usually accompanied by the Trickster. [TLC]

Creosote. Seriph of AL KHALI. A rather fat, middle-aged man whose chief pleasure is in writing very bad poetry and indulging in the kind of simple life only the very rich can afford. His grandfather built up the family fortune by somewhat mysterious means, which left the family in possession of a magic carpet, lamp and ring, and a deep distrust of caves. Creosote, however, bears out the old Klatchian saying 'Going from very rich to quite poor in three generations' (Klatchian sayings lose something in the translation) and the money he did not squander on building an artificial Paradise around his palace was stolen from him by his evil Grand Vizier. Creosote is very fond of stories, and somehow manages to confuse the practice of narration with that of sex, and is given to accosting decent young women and asking them for a swift anecdote. The many trite comments that could be addended here will, out of decency, not be made. [S]

Cribbins. He was just Cribbins. No one knew his first name. He had a serious personal problem that made him smell of bananas.

The teeth! They were that man's pride and joy. He'd prised them out of the mouth of an old man he'd robbed, while the poor devil lay dying of fear! He'd joked that they had had a mind of their own! And they spluttered and popped and slurped and fitted so badly that they once turned around in his mouth and bit him in the throat! He used to take them out and talk to them! And they were so old – the stained teeth had been carved from walrus ivory and the spring was so strong that sometimes it'd force the top of his head back so that you could see right up his nose.

And he was a nasty piece of work. Cribbins didn't have style. He wasn't violent, unless there was absolutely no chance of retaliation, but there was some generalized, wretched, wheedling malice about the man that just gets on your soul. [MM]

Cripple Mr Onion. Very complex card game played with great intensity on the Disc. Winning combinations include: Two Card Onion, Broken Flush, Three Card Onion, Double Bagel, a Five Card Onion, a Double Onion, a Triple Onion (three kings and three aces) and a Great Onion, which is unbeatable except with a perfect nine-card run. If you are unable to tell 1 from 11 you may lose money playing Cripple Mr Onion. It is one of those games the learning of which costs a very great deal of money.

Cripslock, Sacharissa. Granddaughter of an engraver in the Street of Cunning Artificers. She wears a wedding ring, but is definitely a 'Miss'. She is not particularly attractive, but not particularly bad-looking either. In fact she is quite good-looking if considered over several centuries. Her eyes, chin, nose and ears were all classically beautiful, in different centuries. Mind you, she also has a well-crafted supply of features that never go out of fashion at all and are perfectly at home in any century. She believes that severe, old-fashioned dresses tone these down. They do not.

She suffers from misplaced gentility and the mistaken belief that etiquette meant good breeding. She mistakes, in fact, mannerisms for manners although, since becoming the first reporter on the '*Ankh-Morpork Times*', her approach to life has been a little more down-to-disc.

Sacharissa has blond hair, which she wears in a bag net, with a small and quietly fashionable hat perched on top of her head to no particular purpose. She often carries a large shoulder bag.

A member of the Cripslock family is also employed as a typesetter at Goatberger's publishing house. [TT]

Crisp. Gardener/handyman to Moist von LIPWIG and Adora Belle DEARHEART. Crisp (his only name) is a decent handyman and quite talkative, although Moist never understands a word he says. He came from somewhere in the Shires and speaks using a vocabulary that is theoretically Morporkian, but in reality has lots of straw in it with the syllable 'ahh' working hard in every conversation. He makes cider in his shed at the bottom of the garden, utilizing the apple trees that the previous owner had carefully cherished. He also, as a matter of course, cleans the windows and, with the help of an enormous box full of every type of hammer, saw, drill, screwdriver and chisel, bags of nails and a number of other items that Moist could not recognize, and moreover did not wish to, made Moist's life easy whilst making Crisp possibly the richest handyman in the neighbourhood. [RS]

Critchley, Master. Member of the Bakers' Guild. [GG]

Croissant Rouge Pursuivant. An official at the College of Arms, Ankh-Morpork. A little old man with thick glasses. [FOC]

Crossly. Butler to Moist von LIPWIG and Adora Belle DEARHEART. His wife is their cook. [RS]

Cruces, Dr. Head tutor at the ASSASSINS' GUILD in Ankh-Morpork in TEPPIC's day. Later became Master of Assassins. A lean figure, with a soft voice. Came to a bad end in complex circumstances. [P]

Crullet. A fisherman from Jowser Cover, who used to deliver fish to Deccan RIBOBE. [MP]

Crumley, Vernon. Proprietor of Crumley's Department Store. During the events of *Hogfather*, the store was located in the Maul. It was later relocated to Furtive Forth Street. [H]

Crundells. The Ramkin country home, just up the road from Ham on Rye. About twenty miles downriver from Hangnail, and Ankh-Morpork is a full day's coach journey away. The house is usually called Ramkin Hall. A well-appointed house or, as Vimes might style it, a freezing pile that could house a regiment. [SN]

Cuckoo, Clock-building. Lives in the RAMTOPS. It builds clocks to nest in, as a part of its courtship ritual. There is nothing very wonderful about this and it does not, emphatically, suggest that the universe was created according to any kind of Divine plan. After all, the clocks are not very good and some of them lose as many as five minutes a day. [RM]

Cuddy, Lance-Constable. First (genetic) dwarf member of the Ankh-Morpork City WATCH. One glass eye, the usual dwarfish steel-capped boots, and a tendency to use his battle-axe rather than the official truncheon. A keen dwarf, sorely missed. [MAA]

Cumber, Miss. Teaches Language at the Quirm College for Young Ladies. [SM]

Cumberbatch, Silas. Used to be a town crier in Ankh-Morpork. Now a member of the WATCH. Has a voice that can be heard three streets away, and no neighbours. [MAA]

Cumblethigh. A dwarf. Er, in ANKH-MORPORK. [MAA]

Cunning Man, the. He was a witchfinder, some 1000 years before the Discworld 'now'. He was an Omnian priest who was so mad that he wouldn't have been able to see sanity with a telescope. His rage lived on after his death – like an idea – whose time came during the events of *I Shall Wear Midnight*. When he appears, his face has empty eye holes... . He later takes over the body of a condemned prisoner called Mackintosh. [ISWM]

Cupidor, Mme. Mistress of Mad King Soup II of Lancre. Owner of one of the world's most complex wigs, which included a small takeaway linguini shop. [LL]

Curiosity, Cabinet of. It is kept in a room in Unseen University. The room is bigger than it ought to be. No room ought to be more than a mile across, especially when, outside in the corridor, it appears to have perfectly normal rooms on either side of it. It shouldn't have a ceiling so high that you can't see it, either. It simply should not fit. Technically it appears to be a classic Bag of Holding but with n mouths, where n is the number of items in an eleven-dimensional universe that are not currently alive, not pink and can fit in a cubical drawer 14.14 inches on a side, divided by P (unknown). The wizards don't know what it's for or who built it. Nothing in it is bigger than about fourteen inches square, but they don't know why this is or who it is who decides they are curious, or why,

and they certainly don't know why it contains nothing pink. Anything taken out of it has to be returned in 14.14 hours recurring. When it closes up, its drawers slam in on themselves far too fast for the human eye to follow as the edifice shrinks and folds and slides and rattles down into house size, shed size and, finally, in the middle of the huge space it becomes a small polished cabinet, about a foot and a half on a side, standing on four beautifully carved legs. [UA]

Curious Squid. These are found only in the seas around the drowned land of Leshp. Very small, harmless and difficult to find. It is their curiosity which is the curious thing about them; they seem to take a lot of interest in any new thing that enters their world. Since often the 'new things' are nets, hooks and tridents, this demonstrates that curiosity is only the handmaiden of intelligence, and does not work very well as its replacement. Curious Squid taste absolutely foul and therefore sell for quite high prices in certain eating-houses in Ankh-Morpork. Skilled chefs make dishes containing no squid at all. [CJ]

Currency. The 'hardest' currency on Discworld (outside the AGATEAN EMPIRE) is the Ankh-Morpork dollar (one hundred pennies equals one dollar; in addition, ancient tradition says that ten pence is one shilling, twenty-five pence is half a ton, fifty pence is a nob/a ton/half a bar/a knocker).

The sequin-sized dollars are theoretically made of gold but the metal has been adulterated so often over recent years that, technically, there is more gold in an equivalent weight of sea water. In a sense, then, Ankh-Morpork is on the gold standard in all respects except the one of actually having any gold to speak of.

But Ankh-Morpork is, despite superficialities, a stable city. It is also, despite more superficialities, a rich one. Its dollar is therefore the currency of choice throughout the lands washed by the CIRCLE SEA. Other city states have their own currencies but it is wise to ensure that these are firmly linked to the dollar, because

Ankh-Morpork is the only place with anything worth buying.

These trailing currencies include the Ephebian *derechmi* (fifty cercs equals one derechmi), the Klatchian *wol*, the Überwaldian *crown*, the XXXX'ian *squid*, the Djelibeybian *talent* (worth one Ankh-Morpork penny) and the Omnian *obol*. The smallest denomination coin is the Zchloty leaden quarter *iotum*, which is worth less than the lead it is made of.

In the Agatean Empire, where gold is as plentiful as copper, the basic unit of currency is the *rhinu*. The rate of exchange with the dollar has never been officially established, other than to say that a handful of *rhinu* would significantly increase the amount of gold in circulation in the whole of the STO PLAINS.

The unit of currency in LANCRE is the Lancre penny, which weighs more than an ounce. Money is not much used in that country; currency is, in any case, only a universally accepted IOU, and Lancre is small enough for everyone to remember what they owe and are owed. The fact that they choose not to, and spend much of their time in highly enjoyable rows, is just part of civic life and whiles away the long winter evenings.

Curry, Annabel. Nine-year-old orphan of Corporal Curry of the City WATCH, whose upbringing was secretly paid for by Captain VIMES. [MAA]

Curry Gardens. Klatchian eating house in Ankh-Morpork. On the corner of God Street and Blood Alley. The sign on the back door reads: 'Curry Gardens. Kitchren Entlance. Keep Out. Ris Means You'. Like immigrant restaurateurs the world over, the owners have found that if you can cause the customers to laugh at your spelling, they'll be too amused to examine your maths. [M]

Cusp, Deacon. Deacon Cusp was an Omnian Inquisitor. He reached his position, which was a place he wasn't sure that he wanted to be, because he liked hurting people. [SG]

Cutangle. Past ARCHCHANCELLOR of Unseen University and Archmage of the Silver Star. An eighth-level wizard. He was very fat, with waggly jowls and extensive stomach regions, although in all conscience we must admit that this could be just about any wizard. In his youth, he knew Esme Weatherwax, who lived in a neighbouring village. He was the first Archchancellor to admit a woman to Unseen University. [ER]

Cutangle, Acktur. Father of Cutangle, the Archchancellor. Used to live in a big house under Leaping Mountain. [ER]

Cutwell, Igneous. A young wizard in Wall Street, STO LAT. Cutwell is twenty years old when first encountered, with curly hair and no beard. He is basically good-humoured, with a round, rather plump face – pink and white like a pork pie.

When we first meet him he is wearing a grubby, hooded robe with frayed edges and a pointy hat that has seen better days. He lodges in a very untidy house with peeling plaster, and a blackened brass plaque by the door – 'Igneous Cutwell, D.M. (Unseen), Marster of the Infinit, Illuminartus, Wyzard to Princes, Gardian of the Sacred Portalls, If Out leave Maile with Mrs Nugent Next Door'. On the door is a heavy knocker that talks – a common bit of flammery used by a wizard to impress the customers.

Cutwell enjoys food, although not to the point of actually cooking any; he grazes, more or less on whatever seems to be available when the cupboards are rummaged at 3 a.m. When he was made Royal Recognizer, with a salary and a much better wardrobe, this tendency towards indiscriminate eating of anything vaguely organic and stationary meant his highly deco- rated clothing achieved even greater degrees of decoration.

He was later promoted, by Queen KELI, to Wizard First Grade of STO LAT, and Ipississi- muss. This is an important wizarding distinc- tion that is only ever written down and never said aloud owing to the trouble this can cause among non-swimmers. [M]

Cyril. Myopic cockerel with a poor memory and dyslexia ('Lock-a-doodle-flod!'). Lives on Miss FLITWORTH's farm. [RM]

There is nowhere Death will not go, no matter how distant and dangerous.
In fact the more dangerous it is, the more likely he is to be there already.

– Eric

Dactylos, Goldeneyes Silverhand. The world is divided into those who can, and those who can afford to employ those who can. Unfortunately, the latter category often gets very jealous of its employees. History is full of the tragic stories of craftsmen who are killed or disabled or imprisoned by their masters to stop them running off and making something even better for someone else – people like Daedalus, Wayland Smith and Hephaistos. Their Discworld cousin never knew when to give up. He made the Metal Warriors that guard the tomb of Pitchiu (for which he was given much gold and had his eyes put out and replaced with golden ones). He designed the Light Dams of the Great NEF (for which he was loaded with fine silks, and was then hamstrung so that he could not escape – but in fact he did escape, in a silk and bamboo flying machine). He built the Palace of the Seven Deserts (for which he was showered with silver and had his right hand cut off and replaced with a mechanical silver hand). He finally built the *POTENT VOYAGER*, the vessel intended for lowering over the Rim from KRULL (for which he was killed by the ARCH-ASTRONOMER). It would seem that his ingenuity lacked some vital facets in the area of self-preservation. [COM]

Dafe. One of VITOLLER's band of strolling players. [WS]

Daft Wullie. Member of the Nac Mac Feegle clan near Tiffany Aching's village, over on the Chalk. An affable clan member, though he often speaks before he thinks. [WFM]

Dahoney. A tall, thin man with hair like a dandelion. [LF]

Dancers, the. Eight stones in a circle in the RAMTOPS. Each stone is about man-height and barely thicker than a fat man. They are not shaped or positioned in any significant way; someone has just dragged eight rocks into a rough circle, wide enough to throw a stone across. Made of thunderbolt iron, they look as if long ago they were melted and formed into their current shapes. Three of the stones have names: the first two are the Piper and the Drummer; the third is the Leaper, and no one in Lancre has yet been unfortunate enough to find out why.

To find them you must follow an overgrown path up to the moorland, a few miles from the town of LANCRE. People say that when it starts to rain, the rain always falls inside the circle a few seconds after it falls outside, as if the rain were coming from further away. Also, when clouds cross the sun, the light inside the circle fades a moment or two after the light outside. It is apparent that the meteoric iron of the stones contains magnetism, a very minor and little-understood form of energy on the Discworld. Because of this, the stones form a barrier between the human world and the world of the lords and ladies. (*See* ELVES.) [LL]

Dances. Dancing is a popular pursuit across Discworld, but not many have been named. Apart from Devil-Among-the-Pictsies [TSC], only four are referred to in specific terms:

Gathering Peasecods and *Gathering Sweet Lilacs*. Both folk dances, but they are somewhat emasculated versions, since they are danced by the members of the Ankh-Morpork Folk Dance Society. Anything with 'folk' in it will refer, sooner or later, to sex.

Serpent Dance. A quaint Morporkian folk-way which consists of getting rather drunk, holding the waist of the person in front, and then wobbling and giggling uproariously in a long crocodile that winds through as many rooms as possible, preferably one with breakables, while kicking one leg vaguely in time with the beat, or at least in time with some beat.

The Lancre Stick and Bucket Dance. A folk dance, shrouded in ancient mystery. Shouldn't be done when there are women present (in case of sexual morrisment); it is danced to the folk tune 'Mrs Widgery's Lodger'.

Dangerous Beans. The *de facto* spiritual leader of the Clan, a tribe of rats who developed intelligence after, apparently, scavenging food off Unseen University's rubbish dump. He is an albino – snow-white and with pinky eyes – and is very short-sighted, although he can tell the difference between dark and light. [TAMAHER]

Dark Clerks. Mostly scholarship boys at the Assassins' Guild. A group of little men in black suits and bowler hats who work for Lord Vetinari.

Dark Light. This is the light absorbed by Überwaldean Deep Cave Land Eels, in the same way that Discworld salamanders absorb normal light. Dark light is not darkness, exactly, but the light within darkness. It is heavier than normal light, so most of it is under the sea or in really deep caves in Überwald. There is, however, always a little of it present even in normal darkness. It is said that dark light is the original light from which all other light evolved, and it is a light without time – what it illuminates may not necessarily be what is here now.

Darktan. Another rat clan member. A big, lean and tough rat with a scarred muzzle and a large red scar around his waist from a near-miss in a rat trap. As the leader of the Trap Disposal Squad, he spends his time taking traps apart to see how they work. He wears a network of belts with pockets, incorporating a range of tools and a sword, and is the undisputed expert on all makes of trap. A thoughtful rat, who wondered a lot about how the world works – especially those bits of it with springs. [TAMAHER]

D'Arrangement, Volentia, Lady. A thin, quite useless but good-natured high-born lady, who was fated to be a guest at a ball in Genua when Granny Weatherwax needed to borrow a dress and wig in a hurry. [WA]

Dat's Me. A troll employed as a cell guard by Evil Harry DREAD. He had no sense of direction and was unable to remember his own name, but was still cleverer than Evil Harry would have preferred. [TLH]

Daviss. A butcher in the Ramtops. Once cursed by Nanny OGG. [WS]

Dawe, Marjorie. A chief librarian for the borough of Four Farthings in London – and thus from Roundworld – accidentally brought to Discworld during the events of *Science of Discworld 4: Judgement Day*. She attended Roedean School and has a fondness for expensive and stylish footwear. She drives a very old Morris Minor bequeathed to her by her father. She finds that it can sometimes be persuaded to start by singing to it from a few verses of *Hymns Ancient and Modern*; she finds that a few bars of 'All Things Bright and Beautiful' does the trick even on frosty mornings. Her father was a vicar, who thought you could find a semblance of life

in the most unlikely things.

She has a gentleman friend, Jeffrey; the two of them have an understanding, and understood quite a lot. [TSOD4]

Dblah, Cut-Me-Own-Hand-Off. Purveyor in OMNIA of suspiciously new holy relics, suspiciously old rancid sweetmeats on a stick, gritty figs and long-past-the-sell-by dates. Sidling everywhere and wearing the *djellaba* of the desert tribes, Dblah's nickname comes from his catch phrase: 'And at that price, I'm cutting me own hand off'. It is clear that he is a distant cousin, alter ego, psychic double or somatype of the even more famous Cut-Me-Own-Throat DIBBLER. [SG]

Dean, the. One-time Dean of Unseen University, now known to be called Henry. He is now Archchancellor of BRAZENECK UNIVERSITY. He joined UU on the same day as Mustrum Ridcully. [MP]

Dearheart, Adora Belle. A tall young woman in a tight grey woollen dress, with coal-black hair – plastered down so that she looks like a peg doll and forced into a tight bun at the back. She smokes cigarettes as if she has a grudge aganst them, sucking the smoke down and blowing it out almost immediately. She holds her cigarettes at shoulder height, the elbow of her left arm cupped in her right hand.

There is a definite sense that she is barely holding down an entire woman-ful of anger.

Her father, Robert Dearheart, was Chairman of the original Grand Trunk (clacks) Company. She now runs the Grand Trunk – which she sees as her legacy, and woe betide anyone who gets between it and her – even if that someone is her husband (Moist von LIPWIG). That's a really tiny spoiler, yes? Her brother, John, was allegedly killed by a fall from a clacks tower. His nickname for her was Killer – though Moist von Lipwig now calls her Spike. Before she married, Adora Belle lived with her aunt in Dolly Sisters. They now live in Scoone Avenue. Fortunately for Moist, they employ Mrs Crossly as their Cook – Adora Belle is a creatively bad cook.

She used to work at the Cabbage Growers' Co-operative Bank in Sto Lat. She was fired for letting through four forged cheques which, we later learn, were passed by Lipwig. [GP]

Death. The Defeater of Empires, the Swallower of Oceans, the Thief of Years, the Ultimate Reality, the Harvester of Mankind, the Assassin against Whom No Lock Will Hold, the only friend of the poor and the best doctor for the mortally wounded. An anthropomorphic personification. Almost the oldest creature in the universe (obviously something had to die first).

He is a seven-foot-tall skeleton of polished bone, in whose eye sockets there are tiny points of light (usually blue). He normally wears a robe apparently woven of absolute darkness – and sometimes also a riding cloak fastened with a silver brooch bearing his own personal monogram, the Infinite Omega. He smells, not unpleasantly, of the air in old, forgotten rooms.

Death's scythe looks normal enough, except for the blade, which is so thin you can see through it – a pale blue shimmer that could slice flame and chop sound. His sword has the same ice-blue, shadow-thin blade, of the extreme thinness necessary to separate body from soul.

His face, of necessity, is frozen into a calcareous grin. His voice is felt rather than heard. He is seen only by cats, professional practitioners of magic, and those who are about to die or are already dead – although there is some evidence that he can be glimpsed by those in a heightened state of awareness, a not uncommon state given the Discworld's normal alarums. When he needs to communicate with the living (i.e. those who are going to continue living) he is perceived very vaguely by them in some form that does not disturb them. There was a period when he made an effort to appear in whatever form the client expected (scarab beetles, black dragons and so on). This foundered because it was usually impossible to know what the client was expecting until after they were dead. He decided that, since no one ever really expected to die anyway, he might as well please himself and he henceforth stuck to the familiar black-cowled robe.

His horse, though pale as per traditional specification, is entirely alive and called BINKY. Death once tried a skeleton horse after seeing

Death

a woodcut of himself on one – Death is easily influenced by that sort of thing – but he had to keep stopping to wire bits back on. The fiery steed that he tried next used to set fire to the stables.

Despite rumour, he is not cruel. He is just terribly, terribly good at his job. It is said that he doesn't get angry, because anger is an emotion, and for emotion you need glands; however, he does seem to be capable of a piece of intellectual disapproval which has a very similar effect. He is a traditionalist who prides himself on his personal service, and, despite the absence of glands, can become depressed when this is not appreciated.

Humanity intrigues Death. He is particularly fascinated by mankind's ability to complicate an existence which, from Death's point of view, is momentary. He appears to spend a lot of time trying to learn, by logical deduction, the things that humanity takes for granted. In the process, he seems to have developed what can only be called preferences and likings – for cats, for example, and curry. He has tried to take up the banjo, but lacks any skill with such a living thing as music.

Death has a property not locatable on any normal atlas, on which he has called into being a house and garden. There are no colours there except black, white and shades of grey; Death could use others but fails to see their significance. And, because he, almost by definition, lacks true creative ability – he can only copy what he has seen – no real time passes in his domain. Nor do things live or grow in the normal sense, unless they are brought in from outside, but they exist in an apparently unchanging, healthy state.

He appears to derive his opinion of how he should live by observing people, but the nuances consistently escape him. He has a bedroom, for example, because although Death never sleeps, it's right that houses have bedrooms. He also has a bathroom, although the ablutionary fixtures were supplied by a plumber from Ankh-Morpork because plumbing is among those activities where Death's constructive abilities find themselves cramped; he was not aware

that pipes were hollow inside, for example. On his dressing table he has a pair of silver-backed hairbrushes and a little glass tray for cufflinks, despite having neither hair nor cuffs. He thinks that's what he ought to have.

As with all creatures that have existence, Death has an hourglass/lifetimer that measures the length of his days. His is several times the size of normal people's glasses, and is black, thin and decorated with a complicated skull-and-bones motif. It has no sand in it.

There is a strong suggestion in the books that Death is somehow *on our side*, which is borne out by events in *Reaper Man* and *Thief of Time*.

Death and being dead. From the point of view of the recently dead, the world suddenly looks at one and the same time very complicated and very simple.

It is complicated because, while death frees the mind from the strait-jacket of three dimensions, it also cuts it away from TIME, which is only another dimension. So a cat can be seen as a tiny kitten and a fat, half-blind old moggy and every stage in between. All at once. Since it will have started off small it will look like a white, cat-shaped carrot – a description that will have to do until people invent proper four-dimensional adjectives (generally, however, the dead stick to normal temporal perception by force of habit, one of the strongest forces in the universe).

It is simple, on the other hand, because the self-delusion that attends the living is immediately stripped away. The dead see the world as real for the first time.

There appears on Discworld, as everywhere else, to be no general consensus about the afterlife. Some religions believe that the dead must journey across a vast empty desert, or sea, or range of metaphorical mountains, in order to receive some kind of judgement at the end. There are various heavens and hells, and it appears that the soul's ultimate destination is that place where its owner, shorn by death of all self-deception, believes he or she ought to go. Which suggests that they won't go to any kind of hell if they don't know about it, a depressing thought that should call for the instant cessation of all missionary activity.

Basically, everyone gets what they think is coming to them. This does not seem fair, but then no one ever said it would be.

d'Eath, Edward. The thirty-seventh Lord d'Eath. A trained and qualified assassin who was also the first person ever to pass the post-graduate course with full marks. Although the family were at one time very rich, the money was frittered away and Edward, dreaming of better days, was forced into cramped lodgings in Kingsway in Ankh-Morpork. As sometimes happens with people who don't mix with other humans often enough to have their mental clocks reset to 'sanity', he developed strange notions and became obsessed with Ankh-Morpork's royal heritage and its noble past, i.e. the time when the d'Eaths had money and power. He very foolishly set in motion the events of *Men At Arms* and shortly afterwards met his death (no relation). [MAA]

Death, House of. Mon Repos*. The Farewell Tour. The land on which DEATH's house rests floats in space. It can only be described as raw surface. Seen edge on, it has no apparent thickness. When walked on it appears quite solid. To get to the house we walk across the black moors, through a gate and up a little path lead-

ing to a small black house, backed by an extensive garden.

DEATH'S GARDEN

Deep in the garden is an apparently bottomless pit, through which souls travel to their next destination. There are extensive areas of topiary and an ornamental fish pond. In keeping with Death's erratic approach to matters of taste, there are also cheery little skeletal garden gnomes.

There is a bird table. One may speculate upon the nature of the birds.

There is an orchard, where black apple trees grow black fruit. Among the trees are Death's beehives; the bees are big, black and slow in their movements, storing glistening black honey in pure white combs. It's anyone's guess what it tastes like, or what would happen to any living person who ate it.

On the front lawn is a sundial. It has no gnomon, because no time passes here (*see* below) and in any case, there is no sun. The sky is night-black, with visible stars, although the landscape is quite brilliantly illuminated.

The back garden contains a large vegetable patch. Real plants grow here, from real seeds brought from the Discworld and fed with compost derived from the stables. There is a tendency, however, for all the plants to be black. It may be that at some genetic level they enter into the spirit of the thing. Surrounding the garden are rolling fields of corn, making a

---

* *Quirmian for 'My Place of Rest'.*

strange golden splash of colour in the otherwise sombre landscape. Elsewhere, within the house as well as in the garden, there is no colour other than that which has been imported from the Discworld by the human occupants.

DEATH'S HOUSE

To one side of the house, as we enter, is the courtyard leading to the stable block, from which a stone-flagged passageway leads into the main hall of the house. We, however, are going to use the front door.

Notice the mat with 'Welcome' on it. The hall beyond is obviously much bigger than the whole house appears to be from the outside. This is Death's domain; dimensions are entirely arbitrary and the size of rooms depends upon the degree of perception of the observer.

For example, this is Death's observation of his servant Albert (*see* MALICH, ALBERTO) bringing him a cup of tea:

Albert approached very carefully.

It had continually puzzled Death in his more introspective moments, and this was one of them, why his servant always walked the same path across the floor.

I MEAN, he thought, CONSIDER THE SIZE OF THE ROOM ...

... which went on to infinity, or as near infinity as makes no difference. In fact it was about a mile. That's big for a room, whereas infinity you can hardly see.

Death had got rather flustered when he'd created the house. Time and space were things to be manipulated, not obeyed. The internal dimensions had been a little too generous. He'd forgotten to make the outside bigger than the inside. It was the same with the garden. When he'd begun to take a little more interest in these things he'd realized the role people seemed to think that colour played in concepts like, for example, roses. But he'd made them black. He liked black. It went with anything. It went with everything, sooner or later.

The humans he'd known – and there had been a few – had responded to the impossible size of the rooms in a strange way, by simply ignoring them.

Take Albert, now. The big door had opened, Albert had stepped through, carefully balancing a cup and saucer...

...and a moment later had been well inside the room, on the edge of the relatively small square of carpet that surrounded Death's desk. Death gave up wondering how Albert covered the intervening space when it dawned on him that, to his servant, there was no intervening space...

At this point it should be added that, since all dimensions here have a certain subjective element, so also does the dimension of TIME. No time passes in the real sense. But *something* passes; a dropped cup will hit the floor and break, so there must be some 'time' in which this can happen and some framework in which the cup is *now* broken but was *once* whole. What there appears to be, in fact, is a sort of subjective recirculating time, very similar to that experienced in DJELIBEYBI owing to the temporal braking power of its many pyramids. It is as though, instead of proceeding in a straight line like a train, time spins gently in a circle like a carousel; people can talk and move about and even appear to travel, while in fact never actually going anywhere.

The hall is illuminated by tall, narrow

windows, is full of doors and is decorated with a lot of funereal drapes. The arched doorways are decorated with a skull-and-bones motif. To one side is an umbrella stand with a scythe in it. The floor is covered with black and white tiles.

Ahead of us are two curved wooden staircases, leading to a bare wooden corridor lined with yellow candles set in holders in the walls. This leads to the private area of the house – the bedrooms and other facilities. The staircases are covered with strange and disturbing carvings, which do not bear close examination, possibly because they are horrible but more probably because of general tastelessness. (No one on the Disc has yet sold paintings on black velvet, or pictures of jolly dogs sitting at the table having dinner, but if they did, and if by chance they sold them at Death's door, he would certainly buy several copies. Death, as has been intimated elsewhere, has no artistic taste. It is not simply that he cannot see the difference between, say, the *Mona Ogg* and a set of three plaster flying ducks – for him there is no difference. In fact, he would probably prefer the ducks, which are more cheerful. He likes a bit of life around the place.)

Occupying the space between the staircases is a large grandfather clock. Two things about the clock are worthy of notice: first, it has a very long pendulum, with a knife-edged and very sharp weight. Second, the clock has no hands because there is, strictly speaking, nothing here for it to measure.

Then there is the passageway leading to the stables. Another one leads eventually to Death's study. In real terms his study is probably more than a mile across, with shadows of what might be wheels and strange machinery in its distant recesses. The rest of the furniture, out of deference to the house's human occupants, is grouped on a square of carpet in what has to be called the 'conceptual' room.

Large hourglasses cover every flat surface – work in progress, as it were. There are also a lot of fat, yellow and runny candles. Apart from the imposing and ornate desk and large, leather swivel-chair, the room also contains bookcases, more shelves of hourglasses, a large lectern with a map on it and a black baize card table. In one

corner and dominating the room, however, is a large disc of the world. This magnificent feature is complete down to solid silver elephants standing on the back of a Great A'TUIN cast in bronze and more than a metre long. The rivers are picked out in veins of jade, the deserts are powdered diamonds and the most notable cities are picked out in precious stones.

On the scarred woodwork of the desk is a large ledger, an abacus, an inkwell and pen, a scythe-shaped paper-knife and a coffee mug – 'To The World's Greatest Granddad', with a picture of a teddy bear. There is also what can only be called an executive toy (you swing one ball against a small lead slab, where it stops). As we turn to leave the room we note the sword, Death's other working tool, in the rack by the door.

We turn left into the corridor and unlock the door into the long lifetimer room.

This tiled room is vast by any or all standards. In here are serried rows of hourglasses of all manner of designs, stretching away into the distance on row after row of shelves. Here and there the shelves are divided by stone pillars inscribed with angular markings. We can't show you this, but part of the shelving swings out to reveal a smaller room (about the size of a cathedral) which contains the lifetimers of the gods and of anthropomorphic personifications. The sound in the lifetimer room, of hissing sand, is deafening (but the discerning may hear the 'pop' and 'ping' as empty hourglasses vanish and new, full ones reappear elsewhere).

Leaving the roaring sand behind us we return to the main hallway and find, through another door, the extensive library of the house. As we open the door with its protesting creak (there is no rust; Death knows that some doors *should* creak) a gust of warm air drifts out. Entering the book-lined room, one is struck immediately by the sound of subdued scratching, as of a room full of clerks all writing away with quill pens. This is the library of the autobiographies – each book writing itself as its subject drifts through their life.

Lighting a candle to supplement the light from the high windows and moving aside the huge pedal-driven library ladder with considerable effort, we come to a little alcove and pass through another door which leads us down stone steps into the velvet gloom of the stack. In this vast space are stored biographies more than five hundred years old. The room is as dark and silent as a cave deep underground. The shelves are barely far enough apart for one person to walk between them and they tower up well beyond the dome of our candlelight. The dusty floor records our footprints.

Everyone who ever lived and died is recorded here. Go far enough through the book-lined darkness and the books become scrolls, the scrolls become wax tablets, the tablets become mere scratchy stones .

And now our tour takes us back, through the entrance hall and down a few steps into the kitchen. Again, this is a smaller room within a great black cavern, but the little square of light suggests a low, warm room, with copper pans hanging from the non-existent ceiling and a vast black iron stove – a Little Moloch, almost certainly imported from Ankh-Morpork – along the whole of one wall (or edge). In the centre of the floor is a white scrubbed table and some chairs. On another wall is a set of bells connecting with the rest of the house.

One of them jangles.

That's the back door over there. I should use it quickly, if I were you...

Death, New. A hooded figure, carrying a scythe and riding a burning skeletal steed. Taller even than DEATH himself, he had no face – smoke curled formlessly between the top of his robe and a golden crown. Called into existence as a result of Death's temporary retirement, and lacking any of the empathy resulting from thousands of years of close personal contact with humanity. [RM]

Death of Rats. About six inches high, the Death of Rats wears a black robe and holds a small scythe in one skeletal paw or, when he needs to hurry and wants to use all four legs, his mouth. He has a bone-white nose with brittle grey whiskers protruding from its shadowy hood. As his name suggests, he specializes in rats but also does gerbils, mice and hamsters if it is DEATH's busy time. In a sense he is a sub-Death, and it appears in the books that Death allows him to show those traits, like humour and mischievousness, that Death himself could not decently employ. [RM]

Death's Glory. Dry fly invented by DEATH when he was looking for ways of having Fun. He'd heard that fishing was fun. In fact fishing is like being dead, but with the additional disadvantage of being alive to experience it. [M]

Declivities. Ephebian philosopher. [SG]

Dee. A dwarf of the old school. The Low King's jar'ahk'haga, or ideas taster – a sort of personal assistant cum political adviser. Dee wore robes of thick overlapping leather plates and a pointed leather hat with more leather flaps around it – the one at the front being tied up to allow him to look out at the world... using thick, smoked glasses

when reading. Dee was involved in some intrigue relating to the coronation of the Low King. [TFE]

Dee, John. One of a few (one?) non-Discworlders to break into the *Companion*. He was a Roundworld astrologer to Mary Tudor and Elizabeth I, encountered by Unseen University's wizards during the events of *The Science of Discworld 2*. He never quite got over it. [TSOD2]

Dehydrated Ocean. Sited at the heart of the Great NEF. Water on the Disc has an uncommon fourth state, caused by intense heat combined with the strange desiccating effects of OCTARINE light; it dehydrates, leaving a silvery residue like free-flowing sand through which a well-designed hull can glide with ease. Said to have very strange fish. Dehydrated water can easily be reconstituted by adding water. [COM]

Deities and supernatural beings. There are 3000 known major gods on the Disc, and more are discovered by research theologians every week.

It is quite probable that some deities feature under many different names. In fact many gods, by means of false noses and other props, can appear in religious chronicles under anything up to a hundred different names and descriptions.

Since belief is the true life-force of the gods, this is a good way of getting as much of it as they can – rather like working in a fast-food joint or running a mini-cab in your spare time, although it is more on the level of fraudulently claiming a thousand different social security giros by means of forged IDs.

It seems likely that this is particularly prevalent in DJELIBEYBI, where the plethora of gods with short, explosive names, like Nat, Wat and Zak, suggests a particularly profitable scam by someone with a dictionary and little imagination.

Known gods and 'god-like entities' (i.e., not human, but immensely powerful, capricious, self-centred and generally amoral beings; unfortunately, this definition includes most monsters and demons as well, but there you go) include:

Alohura, Goddess of Lightning (beTrobi) [COM]

Aniger, Goddess of Squashed Animals [TLH]

ANOIA [MR, GP, UA]

Astoria, Goddess of Love (Ephebe) [SG]

AZRAEL

Bast, Cat-Headed God of Things Left on the Doorstep or Half-Digested Under the Bed (Djeli) [P]

BEL-SHAMHAROTH

Bibulous, God of Wine and Things on Sticks [H, TLH]

BILIOUS, Oh God of Hangovers [H]

Bin (Djeli) [P]

BLIND IO

Bogeyman, the

Bunu, Goat-Headed God of Goats (Djeli) [P]

Ceno [FOC]

Cephnet (Djeli) [P]

Cephut, God of Cutlery (Djeli) [P]

Chance [COM]

Cheerful Fairy, the [H]

Chefet, Dog-Headed God of Metalwork (Djeli) [P]

Chondrodite, God of Love (Troll) [MP]

Cubal, Fire God (Ephebe) [SG]

Czol (goddess) [GP]

DEATH

Destiny [COM, M]

Dhek (Djeli) [P]

Disgraces, Three, the (daughters of Blind Io). Nudicia, Pulchritudia, Voluptia [SN]

Eater of Socks [H]

Electric Drill Chuck Key Fairy [H]

Evolution, God of

EXPLETIVES [RM]

Famine [LF]

FATE

Fedecks, Messenger of the Gods (Ephebe) [SG]

Fhez, Crocodile-Headed God of the Lower Djel (Djeli) [P]

Flatulus, God of the Winds (Ephebe) [SG, TLH]

Fon (Djeli) [P]

Foorgol, God of Avalanches [SG]

F'rum [S]

Gigalith, God of Wisdom (Troll) [MP]

GLINGLEGLINGLEGLINGLE FAIRY [H]

Glipzo (goddess) [TLH]

God of Indigestion [H]

Grune, God of Unseasonal Fruit [RM]

Hast (Djeli) [P]

Hat, Vulture-Headed God of Unexpected Guests (Djeli) [P]

HERNE THE HUNTED

Herpentine Triskeles (Djeli) [P]

Hinki [RM]

HOGFATHER, the

HOKI of the Woods, Hoki the Jokester

Hotologa Andrews (Genua) [WA]

Hyperopia, Goddess of Shoes [RM]

Io (Djeli) [P]

Jack Frost [H]

Jeht, Boatman of the Solar Orb (Djeli) [P]

Jimi, God of Beggars [MAA]

Juf, Cobra-Headed God of Papyrus (Djeli) [P]

Ket, Ibis-Headed God of Justice (Djeli) [P]

Khefin, Two-Faced God of Gateways (Djeli) [P]

Lady Bon Anna (Genua) [WA]

Lela, the Volcano Goddess [GP]

Libertina, Goddess of the Sea, Apple Pie, Certain Types of Ice Cream and Short Lengths of String [TLH]

LUCK (the Lady)

Mister Safeway (Genua) [WA]

Moon Goddess (Druidic) [LF]

Nept (Djeli) [P]

Nesh (Djeli) [P]
Net (Djeli) [P]
Night [COM]
Noddi (Nothingfjord) [TSOD]
NUGGAN, God of Paperclips, Correct Things in the Right Place in Small Desk Stationery Sets and Unnecessary Paperwork (Borogravia) [TLH, MR]
OFFLER, Crocodile God
Old Man Trouble [H]
Olk-Kalath the Soul Sucker [TLH]
OM
Ordpor the Tasteless [RM]
Orexis-Nupt (Djeli) [P]
Orm, Great [P]
Patina, Goddess of Wisdom (Ephebe) [SG, TLH]
Pedestriana (Goddess of Football) [UA]
PESTILENCE [LF]
Petulia, Goddess of Negotiable Affection (Ephebe) [SG]
PIPPINA, the Lady with the Apple of Discord [RS]
P'tang P'tang, Newt God [SG]
Ptooie (Djeli) [P]
Put, Lion-Headed God of Justice (Djeli) [P]
QUEZOVERCOATL, the Feathered Boa (Tezuman)
Reg, God of Club Musicians [SM]
Sandelfon, God of Corridors [RM]
Sandman, the [H]
Sarduk, Goddess of Caves (Djeli) [P]
Scissor Man, the [H]
Scrab, Pusher of the Ball of the Sun (Djeli) [P]
Sea Queen, the [SG]
Sessifet, Goddess of the Afternoon (Djeli) [P, TLH]
Set (Djeli) [P]
Seven-Handed Sek [M]
Silicarous, God of Good Fortune (Troll) [MP]
Silur, Catfish-Headed God (Djeli) [P]
Skelde, Spirit of the Smoke [LF]
Sky God [LF]
Smimto, God of Wine (Tsort) [SG]
Sot (Djeli) [P]
SOUL CAKE DUCK [H]

Stealer of Pencils [H]
Steikhegel, God of Isolated Cow Byres [M]
Stride Wide Man (Genua) [WA]
Summer Lady, the [W]
Sweevo, God of Cut Timber [TLH]
Syncope (Djeli) [P]
TAK (wrote the dwarf laws, as annotated by Grag HAMCRUSHER) [T!]
Teg, Horse-Headed God of Agriculture (Djeli) [P]
Thrrp, Charioteer of the Sun (Djeli) [P]
Thrume [RM]
Tooth Fairy, the [SM, H]
Topaxi, God of Certain Mushrooms, Great Ideas You Forgot to Write Down & Will Never Remember Again, and of People Who Tell Other People That 'Dog' is 'God' Spelled Backwards and Think This is In Some Way Revelatory. Also called Topaxci, God of the Red Mushroom [LF]
Towel Wasps [H]
Tuvelpit, God of Wine (Ephebe) [SG]
Tzut, Snake-Headed God of the Upper Djel (Djeli) [P]
Ukli (god) [TLH]
Umcherrel, Soul of the Forest [LF]
Ur Gilash [SG]
Urika, Goddess of Saunas, Snow & Theatrical Performances for Fewer Than 120 People [TLH]
VERRUCA GNOME [H]
Virtues, the (Patience, Chastity, Silence, Charity, Hope, Tubso, Bissonomy, Fortitude) [MR]
Vometia, Goddess of Vomit (Ankh-Morpork) [TLH]
Vut, Dog-Headed God of the Evening (Djeli) [P]
WAR [LF]
What, Sky Goddess (Djeli) [P]
Wintersmith, the [W]
Wisdom Tooth Goblin [H]
Yay (Djeli) [P]
Zephyrus, God of Slight Breezes [COM]

Deja Fu. A discipline where the hands move in time as well as in space, the exponent twisting space behind his own back whilst doing so.

The only known Master of this martial art is LU-TZE.

Delcross, Miss. Co-founder, with Miss BUTTS, of the QUIRM COLLEGE FOR YOUNG LADIES. She teaches Biology and Hygiene, and is keen on eurythmics. [SM]

De Magpyr, Count & Countess. Family crest: two magpies on a black and white shield. Family motto: 'Carpe Jugulum'. The Count is a handsome, powerful vampyre (not vampire, a word which is *so* fifteen centuries ago). He looks like a gentleman of independent means and an enquiring mind, the kind of man who goes for long walks in the mornings and spends the afternoons improving his mind in his own private library or doing small interesting experiments on parsnips and never, ever worrying about money. There is something glossy about him, and an urgent, hungry enthusiasm – the kind you get when someone has just read a really interesting book and is determined to tell someone all about it. He is quite an advanced thinker and is determined that vampyres can adapt and shake off the old and unnecessary traditions, such as fear of garlic, light and religious symbols.[CJ]

De Magpyr, Lachrimosa. Daughter of the Count and Countess De Magpyr. She is a thin girl in a white dress, with very long black hair and far too much eye make-up. She is a chronic complainer and is a keen supporter of the more modern vampyre fashions, besides being the vampyre equivalent of a Goth – that is, she and her friends wear brightly coloured clothes, pretend to drink wine, and outrage their parents by going to bed early. [CJ]

De Magpyr, Old Count, the. Uncle of the Count. Tall, thin, grey-haired man in evening dress and a red-lined cloak. He also wears the star and sash of the Order of Gvot. Distinguished in a distant, aloof sort of way, with a glimmer of lengthened canine on his lower lip. He built the family home, Don'tgonearthe Castle. Rose from the dead so often he had a coffin with a revolving lid. [CJ]

De Magpyr, Vlad. Son of the Count and brother to Lachrimosa. A very attractive young-looking man (barely 200 years old) with an infectious grin and a ponytail. He favours the 'New Romantic' look, running to lacy shirts and embroidered waistcoats. Took a bit of a shine to Agnes NITT. [CJ]

Demonologists. Nature of: Surreptitious, pale men who get up to complicated things in darkened rooms and have damp, weak handshakes. Technically they are wizards, although Unseen University frowns on the practice. [E]

Demons. Demons have existed on the Disc for at least as long as the gods, who in many ways they closely resemble. Indeed, some – such as QUEZOVERCOATL – can be both at the same time. The difference is basically the same as that between terrorists and freedom fighters.

Demons don't breathe. They belong to the same space–time continuum, more or less, as humans, and have a deep and abiding interest in humanity's day-to-day affairs. Their home is a spacious dimension close to reality, traditionally decorated in shades of flame and maintained at roasting point. This isn't actually necessary, but if there is one thing that your average demon is, it is a traditionalist (in fact it's hard to think of many other things that it is; a demon is generally as capable of original thought as a parrot is capable of original swearwords).

In the centre of the inferno, rising majestically from a lake of lava substitute and with unparalleled views of the Eight Circles, lies the city of Pandemonium.

As has been indicated, demons are not great innovative thinkers and really need the spice of human ingenuity. They are strong believers in precedence and hierarchy. Numb and mindless stupidity is part of what being a demon is all about.

Smaller and more controllable varieties of demon may be employed in picture boxes, watches, doorknockers and hinges. After a few years, however, they invariably escape or simply evaporate.

Demons, names of.

ASTFGL
Azaremoth [E]
Beezlemoth, Earl [E]
Drazometh the Putrid, Duke [E]
QUEZOVERCOATL
Riinjswin [E]
Urglefloggah [E]
Vizzimuth [E]
Winswin [E]
WXRTHLTL-JWLPKLZ

Demurrage, Aliss. Black Aliss. A witch, so good at magic that there wasn't room for anything else. They said weapons couldn't pierce her, that swords bounced off her skin. They said you could hear her mad laughter a mile off. She turned people into gingerbread and lived in a house made of frogs.

She was, in fact, a very powerful witch, who lived near the forest of Skund (itself an area of strong residual magic). Some of her best-known exploits involved turning a pumpkin into a royal coach and sending a whole palace to sleep for a hundred years.

She was not called Black Aliss because of her exploits, which were the result of bad temper rather than actual malice. She was called Black Aliss because of her fingernails. And her teeth. She had a sweet tooth and as a result used to live in a real gingerbread cottage (similar to the one still standing when discovered by RINCEWIND and TWOFLOWER in *The Light Fantastic*); this followed early experiments with broccoli and bran cottages, which didn't seem to have the same frisson and smelled a lot worse. All the same, modern witches declare that she never really ate anyone. Well, perhaps a *few* people, but only rarely, and more or less by accident and short-sightedness, and that hardly made her a *cannibal*. A couple of kids shoved her into her own oven in the end.

She is generally spoken of by modern witches, who live in more democratic times when such ungoverned excesses of power are frowned upon, with a sort of wistful disapproval. [WS]

Derghart, Uncle. A relative of ESK's father. [ER]

Detritus. A troll. In many ways, *the* troll. He is the troll many people in Ankh-Morpork, particularly University students, think of when they hear the word, bringing back as it does vague memories of sudden concussion and extreme pain.

He is rangy rather than huge (for a troll) and is widely – and wrongly, on the whole – believed to have an IQ the size of a walnut. His knuckles drag on the ground, but that is not unusual among trolls, although his ability to touch the ground with his lower lip when moving fast is the envy of many. Like most of his fellows, when not employed in some office that requires a uniform he wears a ragged loincloth to cover whatever it is that trolls feel it is necessary to conceal.

Lacking any other skill and finding even unskilled labour mentally taxing, Detritus found work anywhere a hired fist was required. When first encountered, he was working as a splatter at the Mended DRUM in Ankh-Morpork (like a bouncer, but trolls use more force) but he has since become upwardly mobile, or at least horizontally portable. His career began to move when he found employment hitting people in the HOLY WOOD moving picture industry, where he met RUBY, a singer.

It is obvious that her influence caused him to rethink his life goals, because he later became an acting-constable and then a sergeant in the Ankh-Morpork City WATCH, a profession in which his unquestioning obedience to orders and a loud voice proved a major, or at least sergeant, advantage. His Watch armour gleams almost as brightly as that of Captain CARROT, although in Detritus' case this is because he often forgets to stop rubbing. He now carries a specially adapted 200lb siege crossbow, which he calls 'The Piecemaker', which is capable of blowing open the front and back doors of a house simultaneously. He built it himself, from a siege weapon. Within the Watch, Detritus has bloomed, and there are hints that although he is quite thick he is also, in many ways, not entirely stupid. [GG]

Devant-Molei, Rosie. Runs the Sunshine Sanctuary for Sick Dragons in Ankh-Morpork. Described as having the build of someone who could pick up carthorses in one hand and shoe them with the other. One of the particular type of high-born lady who is seldom seen not wearing rubber boots. [GG]

De Vere. Captain of the Genuan Palace Guard. [WA]

Devereaux. Innkeeper in Genua. Not fat or red-faced, and this was practically a hanging offence under Genua's strange laws. [WA]

DeVice, Amanita. One of DIAMANDA's coven in LANCRE. She had a dagger-and-skull tattoo on her arm (drawn in ink). [LL]

Device, the. (Cube.) A sort of dwarf machine. No one knows who made them. They might be older than the world. They have been found in volcanoes and the deepest rocks. The deep-down-dwarfs have most of them. They come in all sorts of shapes and sizes and are unbelievably valuable, especially the cubes. [T!]

de Worde, Lord. Father of William DE WORDE. One of those upper-class people who are 'never wrong'. His open-minded view is that people who hold opposing views to his are 'insane, dangerous, or not really people'. He manages to use words with a tone and volume that makes them as good as fists. [TT]

de Worde, William. A professional scribe. Ankh-Morpork has a number of these, who will write letters home for you, or draft a petition to the PATRICIAN. Son of Lord de Worde (a man with definite, and rather unpleasant, views on how Ankh-Morpork should be run) and the product, therefore, of a wealthy family who are used to getting their own way. The family motto is 'Le Mot Juste'. Their family's town house is at 50 Nonsuch Street. His elder brother, Rupert was killed in battle in Klatch.

William, who is the youngest son, was educated at HUGGLESTONES, where he enjoyed swordsmanship and merely survived everything else. He enjoys reading and writing and he loves words. William is less than typical of the great mass of scribes because of two personal inventions.

One is the Standard Letter. Movable type had not at the time been invented in Ankh-Morpork and most printing of things like playbills and posters was done by wood-block engravers. It occurred to William ('Thynges Written Downe') de Worde to make use of this facility, because so many of the letters he had to write were so similar.

William de Worde's related concept was his 'letter of thynges that have happened'. The basic idea wasn't new. Many nobles, foreign dignitaries and expatriate Ankh-Morporkians employ scribes to send them regular letters to keep them up to date with city affairs. But, again, William realized that all he needed do was write one letter with suitable spaces to allow for things like 'To my Noble Lord the...', trace it backwards on pieces of boxwood provided for him by the engraver, and then pay the said engraver twenty dollars to carefully remove the wood that wasn't letters and make twenty impressions on sheets of paper.

However, a chance encounter with Gunilla GOODMOUNTAIN, and coincidentally with an out-of-control cart full of lead, led William to found Ankh-Morpork's first newspaper, 'The Ankh-Morpork Times'. In fact it would be true to say that he didn't found it, it found him. His editorial style has been likened to someone with their bum stuffed with tweed. Without ever actually meaning to, William invented a primitive form of journalism (that is, one not yet so advanced as to consist entirely of things made up) and such associated ideas as the Public Interest and the Freedom of the Press. He appears to have survived despite this suicidal mind-set. No doubt Lord VETINARI thinks he will be useful. His lordship is quite happy for people to annoy him, provided they annoy other people even more. [TT]

Diamanda. Her real name is Lucy Tockley, but she felt that Diamanda was more witchy, and the mere fact that someone could think a phrase like that should tell us everything about them that we need to know. And, indeed, she does paint her nails black, and wears black lace and a floppy black velvet hat with a veil, and does all the other necro-nerdy things that people do when they are young and therefore immortal. This naturally skinny seventeen-year-old was the leader of the self-taught coven of young girls in LANCRE, up until Granny Weatherwax found out about it. [LL]

Dibbler, Cut-Me-Own-Throat. Claud Maximillian Overton Transpire Dibbler. Wheresoever two or three are gathered together, someone else will turn up and try to sell them something hot in a bun. This person will probably be C.M.O.T. Dibbler.

Dibbler is the purveyor of absolutely anything that can be sold hurriedly from an open suitcase in a busy street. He likes to describe himself as a merchant adventurer; everyone else likes to describe him as an itinerant pedlar whose money-making schemes are always let down by some small but vital flaw, such as trying to sell things he doesn't own or that don't work or, sometimes, don't even exist. Quite often they describe him as someone they would like to catch up with.

He is not, strictly speaking, a criminal.

In his natural state – i.e., when not inspired to take advantage of some passing fad or problem in Ankh-Morpork – Dibbler sells meat pies and sausages-in-a-bun from a tray around his neck or, when funds permit, a barrow. There is no need to describe these items, even as food. Dibbler takes the view that anything that has at any time been any part of a pig, or even near a pig, or possibly even within earshot of a pig, can be called pork. His guiding principle is that with enough mustard people will eat anything

(his brief foray into ethnic food for trolls, a siliceous species, proved that Dibbler was even capable of finding stale rock).

He is skinny, and when regarding him people are moved to recall that humans have some kind of small rodent somewhere in their ancestry. He speaks very quickly, with many a sidelong glance, and usually wears a huge overcoat, full of pockets, none of which have exact change. He is known to have premises in a cellar near the SHADES in Ankh-Morpork. No one knows where he actually lives. Since going to sleep might involve missing a wonderful business opportunity he possibly never does so.

Dibbler is also the seller of mail-order lessons on the Path of the Scorpion, a self-defence system, under the name of Grand Master Lobsang Dibbler. He also served short stints as moving pictures mogul and music industry promoter, two occupations that came as near to suiting his peculiar talents as any he has ever tried. When we last see him, he is the proprietor of 'CMOT Dibbler Practically Real Estate & Associates'.

He feels that it is not his fault that perfectly sound business propositions have a habit of exploding or tasting awful. [GG]

Dibblers have turned up in various parts of Discworld, which just shows the effects of parallel evolution. Wherever there are people prepared to eat terrible food, there will be someone there to sell it to them. These incarnations have included:

Al-Jiblah [J]
DBLAH, CUT-ME-OWN-HAND-OFF [SG]
Dib Diblossonson [TLC]
Disembowel-Meself-Honourably Dibhala (street trader in Hung-Hung) [IT]
Fair Go Dibbler [TLC]
May-I-Be-Kicked-In-My-Own-Ice-Hole Dibooki [TLC]
May-I-Never-Achieve-Enlightenment Dhiblang [TLC]
Swallow-Me-Own-Blowdart Dlang Dlang [TLC]

Dibbler, Solstice. ('Soll'.) C.M.O.T. DIBBLER's nephew. Was heavily involved in the moving picture industry, where he showed a business acumen very nearly equal to that of his uncle. But he has a more modern outlook. Should mobile phones ever be invented on the Discworld, one feels, then Soll will be the first to have one (although he will not have anyone to talk to, of course). [MP]

Dickins, Dai, Sergeant. Watch officer from Dimwell. At the time of the events of *Night Watch*, he was close to retirement age. He maintained a flourishing sergeant's moustache, waxed to points and clearly dyed, and the proper sergeant shape, occasioned by means of undisclosed corsetry. He came from Llamedos originally. He belonged to some druid religion so strict that they were strongly against swearing, which is a real handicap in a sergeant. Or would be, if sergeants weren't so good at improvising. [NW]

Didactylos. Ephebian philosopher. This short, bald, blind man in a grubby toga and with a petulant, reedy voice is nevertheless one of the most quoted and popular philosophers of all time. His wise sayings are quoted throughout the multiverse (and include such axioms as 'There'll be another one along in a minute', 'It's a funny old world', 'It'll all end in tears', 'You cannot trust the bastards an inch', and so on). At one time he carried a lantern, telling people that he was looking for an honest man, but this was probably just a pose and an attempt to get money. He lives in a barrel and would probably benefit from bathing rather more often, or at all.

He reasoned that if the Disc is 10,000 miles across and light travels at about the speed of sound, then the sun has to travel at least 35,000 miles in its orbit every day, or twice as fast as its own light. This means that it is, from the standpoint of modern physics, a tachyon (a scientific term meaning magical thing).

He was made a bishop of the Omnian church despite not believing in any gods, although this is perfectly OK for a modern bishop. [SG]

Dijabringabeeralong. Major town in XXXX, reached by a wooden bridge over the bone-dry Lassitude River. There is a huge windmill on a metal tower with the words: 'Dijabringabeeralong: Check Your Weapons' that is to say, check that they work. The sign is important, because otherwise you might be unaware that you'd ridden through a town. The architecture could be described as 'vernacular', which means 'made up, with a lot of swearing'. Dijabringabeeralong is famed for its Annual Regatta, cancelled on one famous occasion because the river filled up with water. [TLC]

Dil. Embalmer in the Kingdom of DJELIBEYBI. Thirty-five years' experience in the funeral business. A solid and thoughtful man, with that tranquillity of mind and philosophical outlook that comes from spending most of your working day up to the elbows in a dead king. [P]

Consequently he was a man of tradition and organization – indeed, he considered that there are no things more important.

Dios, although a devout priest, was not a naturally religious man. He felt that it was not a desirable quality in a high priest; it affected your judgement, and made you 'unsound'. He felt that the gods were necessary, but he required that they should keep out of the way and leave him to get on with things. [P]

Dinwiddie, A. A., Dr. DM (7th), D.Thau, B.Occ, M.Coll, BF. The Bursar at Unseen University, Ankh-Morpork. Aged 71. The Bursar is kept on the right side of apparent sanity by a regular dosage of dried frog pills, which make him hallucinate that he is sane.

Diome. Witch of the Night. An adventuress. [E]

Dios. High Priest in DJELIBEYBI. First Minister and High Priest among High Priests.

Dios was (or is, or will be – certain temporal uncertainties make the choice of tense very difficult) a tall, bald man with an impressive nose. In his role as general adviser to the ruler he spoke (speaks, etc.) softly but carried a big stick, in this case his staff of office – symbolic snakes wrapped round an allegorical camel prod.

He ate (we will settle on the past tense) no meat, believing that it diluted and tarnished the soul, and lived for 7000 years by regularly sleeping in a pyramid, which renewed him or, more accurately, recycled him. In fact it could be said that he was only 7000 years old from the point of view of an external calendar; more realistically, he had for most of that time been living the same day over and over again. Since the palace days on Djelibeybi were a complex network of rigidly observed ritual, this suited him quite well. There was never any *need* to do anything differently.

Discworld, the. As all will know, the Discworld is a flat planet – like a geological pizza, but without the anchovies. It offers sights far more impressive than those found in universes built by Creators with less imagination but more mechanical aptitude. It exists right on the edge of Reality; the least little things can break through from the other side. It is allowed to exist either because of some impossible blip on the curve of probability, or because the gods enjoy a joke as much as anyone else. More than most people, in fact.

It was the Ephebian philosopher EXPLETIUS who first proved that the Disc was 10,000 miles across. It is about thirty miles thick at the Rim, although it is believed to be considerably thicker towards the Hub, possibly to accommodate the internal layer of molten rock which powers the volcanoes and allows the continental plates to move. Exactly how this molten state is maintained, and how the water that pours ceaselessly over the rim from the Circle Sea is replaced, are but two of the unfathomable mysteries of the world. A tenable theory is that the heat is generated by vast masses of octiron under pressure. The octiron theory also accounts for the Disc's vast standing magical field.

Whatever the explanation, the fact is that the surface features of the Discworld uncannily mirror those of spherical rocky worlds, as though the Creator had seen one somewhere but had to go ahead without a chance to examine the works.

The continents certainly have moved around (possibly on wheels of some kind, if the molten rock theory is discounted). Discworld time is always a tricky thing to measure, but by inference it must have been several hundred million years ago that the supercontinent of Pangola was struck by a giant meteorite, which may have killed off those lifeforms not equipped by a neglectful Nature to survive impact with flaming rock travelling at several thousand miles a second, and also instigated the break-up which led eventually to the Discworld of today.

Inspection of residual magic in deep-sea rocks and very old trolls suggests that it was also around this time that the Discworld first changed its direction of spin, a phenomenon that appears to occur every hundred thousand years or so, possibly for the comfort of the elephants.

About one hundred million years before the present day, in the period described by the wizard and geologist BORASS as the Borassic era, the proto-continent had clearly split into two vast land masses – Howondaland (named after the continent where his researches were largely carried out) and Lauragatea (partly named after the empire that occupies much of the Counterweight Continent, and partly after his mother). A generally confused banging-about as the spin direction changed raised most of the mountain ranges visible today.

It was the second, smaller continent of Lauragatea which, some thirty million years before the present, lost the even smaller and deeply mysterious continent known only as XXXX, which wandered off by itself (according to Borass) in search of the geographical equivalent of a cool drink.

Of course, it is only a theory. The truth might be stranger (see, for example, ELEPHANT, THE FIFTH).

Of course, none of this explains the sheer beauty of the whole thing...

Viewers from space can appreciate in full the Discworld's vast, 30,000-mile circumference, garlanded by the long Rimfall, where the seas of the Disc drop endlessly into space. It gives the impression, with its continents, archipelagos, seas, deserts, mountain ranges, that the Creator designed it specifically to be looked at from above.

The Disc revolves at a rate of about once every 800 days. This means that, except at the Hub, a full astronomical year contains eight seasons, or two each of the classical four (see CALENDARS).

Its tiny orbiting sunlet, with prominences no bigger than croquet hoops, maintains a fixed elliptical orbit, while the Disc revolves beneath it. The little moon shines by its own light, owing to the cramped and rather inefficient astronomical arrangements.

The Hub, dominated by the spire of CORI CELESTI, is never closely warmed by the weak sun and the lands there are permanently locked in permafrost. The Rim, on the other hand, is a region of sunny islands and balmy days. From the RAMTOPS' highest peaks you can see all the way to the Rim Ocean that runs around the edge of the world, since the Discworld, being flat, has no horizon in the real sense of the word.

There appear to be at least four major continental masses:

The (unnamed) continent of which the STO PLAINS and the Ramtops are a major feature: this stretches all the way to the Hub and finishes, at least in the area of Ankh-Morpork, at the CIRCLE SEA. Less than half of it has been covered in the chronicles, and there must be far more land on the far side of the Ramtops. So far we know only of GENUA and some miscellaneous small countries.

KLATCH (the continent): this is detailed elsewhere, but here and now we might not be far wrong in thinking of Klatch as the Discworld's Africa, with a collection of 'Mediterranean' countries shading into the large, and more or less unexplored, plains of HERSHEBA and HOWONDALAND.

The COUNTERWEIGHT CONTINENT: smaller than either of the above, and occupied by an advanced civilization.

'XXXX': the name as it appears on maps of the mysterious fourth continent, once reached by people from Ankh-Morpork, then lost, found again and, now, fully a part of Discworld and performing a valuable role in the supply of opera singers, bartenders, backpackers and so on.

There have been other continents, which have sunk, blown up or simply disappeared. This sort of thing happens all the time, even on the best-regulated planets.

And there, below the mines and sea-ooze and fake fossil bones put there (most people believe) by a Creator with nothing better to do than upset archaeologists and give them silly ideas, is Great A'TUIN.

Chaotic as it sometimes appears, the Discworld clearly runs on a special set of natural laws, or at least on guidelines. There is gravity. There is cause-and-effect. There is eventuality – things happen after other things. After that, it becomes a little more confusing. The following theory can be gingerly advanced:

The Discworld should not exist. Flatness is not a natural state for a planet. Turtles should grow only so big. The fact that it *does* exist means that it occupies an area of space where reality is extremely thin, where 'should be' no longer has the veto it has in the rest of the universe. The Discworld creates an extremely deep well in Reality in much the same way as an incontinent Black Hole creates a huge gravity well in the notorious rubber sheet of the universe.

The resulting tension seems to have created a permanent flux which, for want of a better word, we can call magic. There are several secondary effects, because the pressure of reality is so weak. Things that might *nearly* exist in a 'real' world – back up there on the rubber sheet – have no difficulty at all in existing in quite a natural state in the Discworld universe; so here there *will* be dragons, unicorns, sea serpents and so on. The rules are relaxed.

But there are additional factors which make up Discworld 'physics'. These could be called:

a) Life force

b) The Power of Metaphor and Belief

c) Narrative Causality

Life, it has been said, has a tendency to exist. It has even been argued that the universe has been *designed* in order that this should happen, although of course it is hard for a life that does not exist to look around and declare that the universe has clearly been designed not to come into being. Certainly on the Discworld life is a very common commodity. Whatever obstacles there are to life elsewhere are that much weaker on Discworld. Almost anything can be alive and develop, if not intelligence at least a point of view. Rocks, thunderstorms and even entire buildings can, in the right circumstances, demonstrate their literal vitality.

Then there is metaphor. On Discworld, metaphor has a disturbing tendency to take itself seriously. Death as a robed skeleton is not just a metaphor for the process of mortality; he really *is* a robed skeleton, with a rich existence of his own. On Discworld, belief is a potent force. What is believed in strongly enough is real. (Conversely, what is not believed can't be real regardless of the fact of its existence. For example, the dog GASPODE can talk. But most people cannot hear him when he does because they know, in their soul, that dogs do *not* talk. Any dog that appears to be talking, says their brain, is a statistical fluke and can therefore safely be ignored.) Discworld gods exist because people believe in them, and their power waxes and wanes with the strength of that belief. There is nothing very magical in this. After all, half the power of witches – and wizards, too, for that matter – lies in the fact that they advertise what they are. The pointy hats are a kind of power-dressing; they're no different from the white coats worn by any actor hawking washing powder. If people believe you can do magic, you're halfway there already.

Finally, there is narrative causality, the power of stories. This is perhaps the strongest force of all and, again, weaker echoes of it are found in this world. Not for nothing do we say: History repeats. History does have patterns, clichés of time. People find themselves again and again in situations where they are playing roles as surely as if a script had been thrust into their hands: the Marital Row, the Job Interview, the Man Behind has Shunted You at the Traffic Lights, the Bastard. And there are the bigger patterns: the rise of empires, the spread of civilizations... Again and again humans tread the same dance through life, and with each dance the path becomes deeper and harder to leave.

The sense of predestination permeates Discworld. History Monks observe history to make sure that it happens 'according to the book' (although now, thanks to the discovery of quantum uncertainty, it's hard to know *which* book). When a princess is saved by MORT, History itself conspires to kill her. The process is focused in Lily WEATHERWAX, who forces the lives of people into stories – and also in DIOS, the high priest of DJELIBEYBI, who has been practising the same daily rituals for so long that he is incapable of dealing with anything new.

On Discworld, the future is written. The role of humans, thanks to bloody quantum, is to choose which book.

Dismass, Old Mother. Also called Gammer Dismass. Beryl Dismass's clothes have the disarray of someone who, because of a detached retina in her second sight, lives in a variety of times all at once. [WS]

Dis-Organizer, the. A little demon in a box which can be used to store information, appointments, record conversations and memos, etc. The more recent Mk 2 is advertised as the very latest in thaumaturgic design, although it is still guarded by an extremely carefully worded warranty.

The Mark V is known as the Gooseberry™. It is now cased in a smart brown box, with a pointy eared small green imp inside. The new version includes the handy-to-use Bluenose™ Integrated Messenger Service, the games of Splong™ and Guess My Weight in Pigs. iHum™ can remember up to 1500 of your all-time favourite tunes. [J]

Disuse. A corporal in the Tsortean army. A victim of the LUGGAGE. [E]

Djelibeybi. (The name means 'Child of the Djel', after the river which flows through this land.) Also called the Kingdom of the Sun and the Old Kingdom. Principal crops: melons, garlic and, since they are increasingly encroaching on the fertile agricultural land, pyramids.

Djelibeybi is two miles wide and 150 miles long and is on the CIRCLE SEA coast of KLATCH. Almost entirely under water during the flood season and both threatened and protected on either side by stronger neighbours (TSORT and EPHEBE). It was once great, but all that now remains is an expensive palace, a few dusty ruins in the desert, and the pyramids. The entire economic life of the country is, until after the events of *Pyramids*, devoted to building them. As a result, Djelibeybi is permanently bankrupt.

The kingdom is 7000 years old. In the Pyramid era, even the heat was old. The air was musty and lifeless, pressing like a vice. Time moved slowly in Djelibeybi, and even then only in circles.

And this was, once again, because of the pyramids. Pyramids slow down time and prevent decay, a fact known to ancient Egyptians and modern Southern Californians. So many had been built in the Old Kingdom, however, that their cumulative effect was to act as a temporal brake of major proportions. In fact (again until events chronicled in *Pyramids*) the thousands of pyramids in the necropolis, a city of the dead occupying some of the kingdom's best land and second only to Ankh-Morpork as the biggest city on the Disc, were actually preventing time from moving at all. The pyramids were acting as time accumulators, sucking in fresh time as it occurred and, around sunset, flaring it off from their tips. As a result the kingdom spent thousands of years re-using the same day.

Please note that it was not the same as repeating the same day. People were born, grew and died (and, if they were important enough, they were placed in a pyramid). It was similar to the 'time' in DEATH's domain. Plants grew and flowered. There was an ongoing history. But it took place, as it were, in the temporal equivalent of an unaired room – the stale time could be detected in the kingdom's obsessive reverence for the past and its resistance to, or even ignorance of, the possibility of doing things differently. The more things changed, the more they stayed the same...

This impasse was finally broken with the construction of the Great Pyramid, which put so much additional pressure on the local dimensions that the entire kingdom was temporarily removed from them.

The country has an enormous number of local gods, unknown to the world outside. Its ruler, the Pharaoh, is also a god, although in human form. He wears a gold mask (the Face of the Sun) and during his official functions carries the Flail of Mercy, the obsidian Reaping

Hook of Justice, the Honeycomb of Increase, the Asp of Wisdom, the Sheaf of Plenty, the Gourd of the Water of the Heavens, the Three-Pronged Spear of the Waters of the Earth, the Cabbage of Vegetative Increase and the Scapula of Hygiene. He may well lose points for dropping any of these.

Under the current ruler, Queen PTRACI I, it is quite likely that the mask has been sold and the money spent on plumbing.

Dog Guild. No motto; no coat of arms, not even a little tartan one. Led by the Chief Barker. The Guild consists of dogs who have all been 'bad dogs'; every dog has to have run away from his or her owner. It controls scavenging rights, night-time barking duties, breeding permissions and howling rotas. [MAA]

Dolly. Kitchen girl at the Unseen University. [SM]

Dolly Sisters. Once a separate village in Ankh-Morpork, but the city sprawl had rolled over it. Residents still consider themselves apart from the rest of the city, with their own customs – Dog Turd Monday, Up Needles All – and almost their own language.

Dongo. Barman in a pub in DIJABRINGABEER-ALONG, XXXX. He is a crocodile, though he wears a grubby shirt and a pair of shorts. He's called 'Crocodile' Crocodile, because of the fact of him being a crocodile. [TLC]

Door, Bill. Name adopted by DEATH while temporarily alive and working for Miss FLITWORTH. [RM]

Doorkeeper, Brother. A member of the ELUCIDATED BRETHREN OF THE EBON NIGHT. A baker by trade. [GG]

Dopplepunkt, Sgt. One half (the largest half), with Cpl KNOPF, of the Bad Blintz official Watch. Any narrativial physical resemblance to a certain sergeant and corporal in the Ankh-Morpork Watch is entirely coincidental, I'm sure. [TAMAHER]

Dorfl. A GOLEM by species, and a butcher by trade until the events recounted in *Feet of Clay* caused him to look for a new life as a Watchman. He lurches a little, because one leg is shorter than the other, and like most golems he wears no clothes because he has nothing to conceal. His surface is mottled where fresh clay has been added over the years. Originally, some attempt had been made to depict human musculature, but the endless repairs have nearly obscured these. Dorfl in fact looks hand-made and, by now, those hands have mainly been his

own. Incredibly strong, like all golems. And also the world's first ceramic atheist. The gods really hate that sort of thing. [SM]

Douglas. Captain of the Patrician's Guard. [RM]

Dove, Darling. This man with an unusual first name makes it into the *Companion* because, as the landlord of the Star Inn, he briefly encounters Geoffrey SWIVEL and his goat. He employs the former as a bar boy for a short while. [TSC]

Downey, Lord. White-haired Deputy Master, now Master, of the ASSASSINS' GUILD. He is an amiable-looking man whose speciality is poison, in particular (it is believed) poisoned peppermints. He was a large and unpleasant bully when he was a student at the Guild. [MAA]

Downspout. Constable in the Ankh-Morpork City WATCH. A gargoyle with huge pointy ears. Somewhat of a lonely soul, like all gargoyles, but an incredibly good officer on a stake-out. [FOC]

Doxie. Captain of the Ankh-Morpork City Guard Day Watch. [RM]

Dragon, the. *Draco nobilis* summoned by the ELUCIDATED BRETHREN. It was a large beast – 60 feet long and with a 80 foot wingspan, and weighing around 20 tons. Its face – with its craggy nostrils the size of drain covers, and red gleaming eyes – was taller than a man. It was the cause of the Dragon's Landing redevelopment site in Ankh-Morpork. [GG]

Dragon King of Arms. Manipulative vampiric head of the Ankh-Morpork Royal College of HERALDS. And we are not talking here about lah-di-dah modern vampires who wear ponytails, fancy waistcoats and agonize all the time about being forced to look cool and live for ever. We are talking about a vampire of the old school, where all the agonizing is done by other people. We are talking a voice from the crypt and not going out in daylight, no, not even in stylish shades. [FOC]

Dragons. Until recently, these were only thought to exist in two forms – *Draco nobilis* and *Draco vulgaris*, more commonly known as noble dragons and swamp dragons. There are a number of differences between the two forms, but they can all be summed up succinctly: noble dragons are dragons as they are imagined, and swamp dragons are dragons as they have to be. There have also been more recent new discoveries – *Draco lunaris* (moon dragons), a curious and striking branch of the genus, and *Draco stellaris nauticae* (star-voyaging dragons), but details of this breed are still very sketchy. Of these four species, this is what we do know:

NOBLE DRAGONS

Noble dragons, although obviously weighing up to 20 tons and with a wingspan of 80 feet, can fly and breathe very hot fire. There is considerable argument about this, but it is believed that they were transmuted from the common swamp dragons during the MAGE WARS, when the intense magical flux allowed the existence of many creatures quite unviable in normal conditions. Any flapping-winged creature weighing 20 tons would, even with the Discworld's amiable natural laws, leave a large hole if it ever tried to get airborne.

When favourable conditions ceased to exist, the theory runs, Draco nobilis used its magical nature to exploit an under-used ecological niche – the human imagination. In very exceptional circumstances the dragons can be recalled. They are intelligent, cunning and cruel. The DRAGON which, for a brief period, ruled Ankh-Morpork was entirely representative of the breed. They eat meat and do not physically need to eat people, but will do so for ceremonial purposes because such things are expected of them and they are sticklers for tradition, even if it means having clothing stuck in their teeth.

SWAMP DRAGONS

The swamp dragon, on the other hand, is totally real, although this state of affairs is often quite brief owing to the explosive nature of their digestive system, which is very unstable. Their internal plumbing can rearrange itself to make the best possible use of any raw materials available for flame-making (although there is at least one recorded case of a dragon being able to flame ventrally for ramjet propulsion). The drawback to this talent is that the swamp dragon is capable of exploding violently if excited, frightened, aroused, surprised or bored. It is prey to a whole host of diseases, including a number only otherwise contracted by the common household oil-fired boiler. Most of its body fluids are corrosive.

It is has been presumed that the explosive capability is a defence mechanism acting for the good of the species as a whole, since it certainly doesn't work for the individual concerned. Any general advantage is also in doubt. There are many creatures that use bitterness and poisons to discourage predators, but blowing them to pieces serves no useful purpose. A wolf cannot teach its young that 'these things are bad to eat' when it is an expanding cloud of fur.

More recently, observations during the orbital flight of the KITE suggest that dragons may originally have been space-dwelling, and their flame merely an evolution of their original propulsion system. Further research is clearly necessary, as people say when they are on the lookout for further grant money.

In the wild places where these dragons are

still found, incidentally, the occasional explosion is all part of the normal background noise (hence the Ankh-Morpork saying, used to mean 'Unquestionably': 'Is the High Priest an Offlian? Does a dragon explode in the woods?').

Nevertheless, there is an occasional vogue for the smaller varieties of swamp dragon as pets. And, as often happens when pets get too big, too difficult or, in this case, explosive, they are frequently abandoned on the streets of Ankh-Morpork. Others are cruelly used as paint-strippers or fire-lighters. The SUNSHINE SANCTUARY in Morphic Street endeavours to rescue and care for as many as possible of these unfortunates, but the occasional 'bang!' of a lost pet is still heard in the city. On at least one occasion a dragon has deliberately been used as an explosive [MAA] and a handgun [GG].

There are thirty-seven known varieties of swamp dragon:

Avery's 'Epolette' (miniature shoulder dragon)
Big-nosed Jolly (frightened of shovels)
Big-nosed Smut (seldom breeds true; attracted to mirrors)
Birbright's Lizard (rare mountain breed; flightless)
Birbright's Smut (morbidly afraid of spoons)
Brindisian Courser (not a very special dragon at all)
Broken-faced Cowper (seldom seen these days)
Classic Smut
Common Smut
Curly-maned Slottie (amiable, tendency to slimp, seldom explodes)
Flared Smut (good with cabbage)
Golden Deceiver (good watch dragon; should not be allowed near children)
Golden Rharn
Guttley's Leaper (flightless, but can exceed 30 mph running over open ground)
Horned Regal (largely nocturnal, flightless, well-coloured, short in the wouters)
Jessington's Blunt (rare and very stupid)
Jessington's Deceiver (small and better

behaved than the Golden; hoards pickle jars)
Lion-headed Cowper (large breed, easy to keep, but often afflicted with skiplets)
Narrow-eared Smut (nervous and, thus, short-lived)
Nothingfjord Blue (good scales, tendency to homesickness)
Pique (small, flightless, lives indoors; eats only chicken and furniture)
Pixy-faced Smut (many congenital problems; for experts only)
Porpoise-headed Cowper (a breed for aficionados)
Quirmian Long-ear (mild-natured, needs regular exercise)
Ramkin's Optimist (good natured, rarely explodes)
Retiring Smut (not often seen)
Rough-nosed Smut
Silver Regal (classic breed, popular in Sto Lat)
Smooth Courser
Smooth Deceiver (good-natured, suitable for the smaller home)
Smooth-nosed Smut
Spiked Oncer (rare; needs much attention)
Spike-nosed Regal (hates shoes)
Spouter (flies very badly; explodes in the presence of mint)
Tabby Cowper (best of the Cowpers, quite popular)
Tomkin's Neurovore (handsome, but highly explosive owing to nerves)
Wivelspiker (excitable, walks into windows)

A typical swamp dragon may reach a length of about 2 feet, tail excluded, although varieties and individuals down to 6 inches and up to more than a yard have been recorded. In the lexicon of dragon breeders a female dragon is a hen, and a male dragon is a pewmet (up to eight months), a cock (eight to fourteen months), a snood (fourteen months to two years) and then a cobb (two years to death). After death a swamp dragon is known as a crater.

MOON DRAGONS

A lineage of dragons discovered during the events of *The Last Hero*. These dragons are sleek and silver, and altogether well-adapted for their environment – that of Discworld's moon. It seems likely that swamp dragons are descended from moon dragons that have had to adapt to the heavy air and less-than-ideal food-stuffs available to them on the Disc.

STAR-VOYAGING DRAGONS

Records by Leonard of Quirm give us some details about these creatures. Adapted for life in the void, these dragons grow to immense proportions and convert stellar debris into gases which they use for propulsion. Smaller dragons may attach themselves to star-voyaging dragons to join them on their journeys.

Drapes, Miss. The very conscientious Senior Clerk at the Royal Bank of Ankh-Morpork. She is a skinny woman, sparse-bosom'd, in a white blouse and long black dress. She lodges in Welcome Soap and is a regular reader of the '*Tanty Bugle*' – full of 'orrible murders. [MM]

Dread, Evil Harry. A wholly professional, if unsuccessful, Dark Lord. When he was first encountered by COHEN the Barbarian, he was starting up with just two lads, his SHED OF DOOM and SLASHER, THE STEED OF TERROR (a donkey).

History has not been kind to Evil Harry. He is, in his way, a kind of mirror image of NIJEL the Destroyer, in that he has a deep, passionate desire to be a Dark Lord yet lacks absolutely any talent in that area.

This is unfair, because he has mastered all the essential elements (in his own mind, at least).

His stupid henchmen are *incredibly* stupid, his gaolers always sleep right up close to the cell bars with the keys hanging from an easy-to-reach hook on their belt, and his guards wouldn't stop a departing washerwoman even if she had a beard like a prophet. He installs big, wide ventilation ducts in every cell, has a white hamster in a diamante treadmill (he is allergic to cats), explains his plans in explicit detail, often with slides and numbered charts, to every hero who falls into his clutches…but, for some reason, it never quite comes together. On the rare occasions when he appears to be making any kind of progress, a larger Dark Lord sets up on an out-of-town site where the parking is better.

Yet Harry, in true Dark Lord tradition, never gives up. He has met most of the Discworld's great professional heroes, who make a point of calling whenever he sets up a new Dark Tower-lette and are very supportive. Heroes tend to be old-fashioned, and respect tradition. Harry may effectively be less evil than the average pensions salesman, but at least his heart is in the wrong place. [TLH]

D'regs. A desert tribe of Klatch. Very warlike, fierce and honourable. If a D'reg is your friend, he's your friend for life. If he is your enemy, then he is your enemy for life, which is now about twenty seconds. Their word is their bond (though they set no store at all by 'oaths'). When they attack, they attack at dawn – the whole tribe: women, children, camels, goats, sheep, chickens. Oh, and the men, of course. [J]

Drongo, Big Mad. A student wizard at Unseen University. His real name is Adrian Turnipseed. General assistant to Ponder STIBBONS. Now works at BRAZENECK's Higher Energy Magic Building, where he is the inventor of their version of Hex – Pex. [SM]

Druellae. Smooth-voiced Dryad encountered by RINCEWIND. She had green flesh and wore nothing but a medallion around her neck. Her long hair had a faintly mossy look about it; her eyes had no pupils and were a luminous green. [COM]

Druids. The Druids of the Disc pride themselves on their forward-looking approach to the discovery of the mysteries of the universe. Of course, they believe in the essential unity of all life, the healing power of plants, the natural rhythm of the seasons and the burning alive of anyone who doesn't approach all this in the right frame of mind.

Their theory of creation is that the universe depends for its operation on the balance of four forces, which they have identified as charm, persuasion, uncertainty and bloody-mindedness. Thus it is that the sun and moon orbit the Disc because they are persuaded not to fall down, but don't actually fly away because of uncertainty. Charm allows trees to grow and bloody-mindedness keeps them up, and

so on. Some druids suggest from time to time that there are certain flaws in this theory, but senior druids explain very pointedly that there is indeed room for informed argument and the cut and thrust of exciting scientific debate, and basically it lies on top of the next solstice bonfire.

The home of druidism is in the small, wet country of LLAMEDOS. Druids occupy themselves with the building of large stone circles for computing purposes; these seldom work properly, but the druids always take the view that the problems can be solved only by building a much larger and more expensive circle. Sixty-six-megalith circles are now commonplace.

On this basis, it can be tentatively suggested that the circle at Stonehenge in England, which is actually a number of circles and isolated stones, was originally commissioned by a local tribe who wanted nothing more than a simple circle, suitable for basic calendar use and possibly the occasional sacrifice. But within a year or two they were forced to upgrade. Everyone is. [LF]

Drull, Mrs. A ghoul, and a past member of the FRESH START CLUB. A vague, shy old lady in a shapeless grey dress. Resides at Mrs CAKE's. Now retired, she does children's party catering. It is best not to touch her food, although this is not because of her past. She just doesn't cook very well. [RM]

Drum, the Broken/Mended. Principal inn of Ankh-Morpork. Located in Filigree Street, at the junction with Short Street. A battered sign hangs over the door, showing a drum, not very well drawn.

The pub opens straight on to the street at the front (guarded by a troll), and its rear backs straight on to the river. The current landlord is Hibiscus DUNELM, but he probably won't last long – the Drum breaks men, or at least men who are not satisfied with the tavern as it is and have dreams of striped umbrellas and a better class of clientele. You have to take the Drum as you find it, which you do by following the noise of breaking glass...

...down the stairs into the beamed bar, with

its walls stained with smoke and its floor a compost of old rushes and nameless beetles. Its sour beer is not so much purchased as hired for a while (a comment so old that it probably postdates the invention of beer by an afternoon). But the Drum is famed not for its beer, which looks like maiden's water and tastes like battery acid, but for its clientele. It is said that if you sit long enough in the Drum, then sooner or later every major hero in the Disc will steal your horse.

The atmosphere inside is loud with talk and heavy with smoke. Thick coils of the stuff hang in the air, perhaps to avoid touching the walls. Nevertheless, it is a reputable disreputable tavern. Its customers have a certain rough-hewn respectability – they might murder each other in an easy-going way, as between equals, but they don't do it vindictively. A young woman could happily spend an evening in the Drum without being molested, unless that was her intention. A child could go in for a glass of lemonade and be certain of getting nothing worse than a clip round the ear when his mother heard his expanded vocabulary. On a quiet night, when he's certain that the LIBRARIAN isn't going to come in, the barman is even known to put bowls of peanuts on the bar.

The Drum is now conscious of its near-legendary status as the most famous tavern on the Discworld and is such a feature of the city that, after one bout of unavoidable redecorations, the then owner spent days recreating the original patina of dirt, soot and less identifiable substances on the walls and imported a ton of pre-rotted rushes for the floor.

Drumknott. Rufus Drumknott is Personal Secretary to Lord VETINARI. He is a little, pink-faced man with no discernible character, although later on he does start to take a keen interest in the steam railway. [MAA]

Drunah, Bishop. Secretary of the Congress of Iams in Omnia. [SG]

Dryad. *See* HAMADRYAD.

Duck Man, the. A beggar in Ankh-Morpork and member of the Canting Crew. He has a duck on his head. At least, everyone else thinks he has a duck on his head. The Duck Man knows he has no duck on his head. The duck's views on this are unrecorded. If it wasn't for the duck, he would be viewed as well-spoken and educated and as sane as the next man. Admittedly, the next man is probably Foul Old RON. [SM]

Duc of Genua, the. When first encountered, the Duc appeared to be a vain and stupid man with long and well-turned legs and a wide mouth. He wore black silk and smoked glasses, in order to conceal his eyes (a fundamental rule of magical change that even gods have to obey – you can alter your shape, age, sex and species, but the look of your eyes cannot be changed). His bedroom, in the castle in GENUA, was green and full of flies. There was no bed, just a big, wooden cover on the floor with a pond under it.

The Duc was a frog under enchantment, and he met an unfortunate and rather depressing end. He really served only to be on the throne behind which Lily WEATHERWAX was the power. [WA]

Duncan, Done-it. Skinny little thief in Ankh-Morpork. Not very bright, and with a matted beard. In his day, he was a good thief, but now he confesses to everything and anything. He calls the Watch every day – mainly to secure a hot meal and a bed for the night. [J]

Dunelm, Hibiscus. Current landlord of the Mended DRUM and, like many before him, full of ideas for attracting new customers. The idea of selling good beer cheaply is always the last one they think of. [SM]

Dungeon Dimensions, the. The endless wastelands outside space and time. The sad, mad things that dwell there have no understanding of the world but simply crave light and shape and try to warm themselves by the fires of reality, clustering around it with about the same effect – if they ever broke through – as an ocean trying to warm itself around a candle.

A few have managed to survive in the Discworld in very special circumstances, but for most of them the reality they desire is soon fatal. Insofar as they can be said to have any emotions, the guiding one is hatred of all 'real' creatures. They are jealous of life and all things alive.

They are lured by really heavy concentrations of magic, because these weigh heavily on the frail rubber sheet of reality and present a weak point at which to break through. They can even break through inside a mind, using its owner's voice and brain to further their own ends – and a mind with magic in it shines out for them like a beacon. The number eight is also said to have some attraction for them, which is why wizards are enjoined to avoid saying it.

Dunmanifestin. Abode of the Disc's gods, atop CORI CELESTI. The stuccoed Valhalla wherein the gods face eternity with the kind of minds that are elsewhere at a loss to know what to do to pass a wet afternoon. Your basic home of the gods, with marble pillars and huge, impossible-to-carpet floors.

Dunnykin, Brother. A member of the ELUCIDATED BRETHREN OF THE EBON NIGHT. Seemed to consist entirely of a little perambulatory black robe with halitosis. [GG]

Durance. Brother-in-law of Lance-Constable CUDDY. [MAA]

Dwarf bread. A dwarfish delicacy and battle weapon. Originally a sensible attempt to make a weapon that could also be eaten, it contains all you need to sustain you for days, mainly by causing you to perform miracles of endurance in order to get somewhere where you don't have to eat dwarf bread. Dwarf cake is similar, but thicker. A properly thrown slice of dwarf bread is a fearsome weapon, especially in view of its erratic aerodynamic properties.

Ingredients are often secret, since every dwarf baker has their own special recipe, but generally flour, water, grit, gravel and stone-ground stones are in there somewhere.

Dwarf Bread Museum. This is in Whirligig Alley, Ankh-Morpork, and experts in the history of aggressive baking concede that it is

A denizen of the Dungeon Dimensions

probably the most comprehensive display of battle bread yet assembled. There are many examples of classic cowpat-like shape, said to be an echo of their taste, but also to be seen are buns, close-combat crumpets, deadly throwing toast and several splendid specimens of the rare boomerang croissant.

The Museum was closed for a long time following the death by bread of its curator, Mr HOPKINSON. It is now intermittently open, and run by the Campaign for Equal Heights.

Despite its fame in specialized circles, the Museum (entrance: one penny) is largely unvisited.

Dwarfs. A race of humanoids approximately 4 feet tall. Stocky, bearded, long-lived (*c.* 300 years) and with a natural attraction for mountains and mineshafts, they provide the STO PLAINS area with most of its miners and 'heavy' engineers.

Unlike TROLLS, it appears that beyond the matter of build there are no major genetic differences between dwarfs and men, any more than there are genetic differences between bulldogs and poodles. Certainly the Discworld's second-greatest lover, CASANUNDA, seems to have met no insurmountable difficulties in his busy schedule.

A flaw in dwarfish nature from a human point of view is their tendency to take things literally. This is a result of their subterranean life. In an environment where there are things always ready to explode or collapse it is vitally important that information be passed on clearly and honestly. The human language, with its unthinking reliance on metaphor and simile, is a veritable minefi– a complete morass– a fog of incomprehensi– very difficult for dwarfs.

Dwarfs wear up to twelve layers of clothing, including the famous woolly dwarf's vest made from RAMTOPS sheep's wool, which is the closest thing possible to natural chain mail. All dwarfs have beards and this, together with the aforesaid clothing, makes gender more or less optional for everyday purposes.

Many of the more traditional dwarf tribes have no female pronouns like 'she' or 'her'. It should be pointed out that they have no male pronouns either – 'he' is considered by them to embrace both sexes equally, as it were, in the same sexless sense as the word mankind (or at least the same sexless sense as the word mankind is considered to have by men). They do, however, adopt a suitable pronoun when they are dealing with men, because of the embarrassment otherwise caused to humans.

A dwarf is not considered old enough to have the facts of life explained to him until he has reached the age of puberty (at about fifty-five). Dwarfs are very reticent about revealing their sex, which most of them don't consider to be very important compared to things like metallurgy and hydraulics. Dwarf courtship consists of finding out, in delicate and circumspect ways, what sex the other dwarf is.

Socially, when they meet, more old-fashioned dwarfs greet each other warmly in the traditional dwarf manner of butting helmets. This is a part of dwarf etiquette that outsiders find nearly impossible to master. The traditional helmet butt is a little less vigorous than the manoeuvre known on the tougher streets of Ankh-Morpork as the 'Shamlegger Kiss', but it must also not be so gentle as to imply that either the giver or the receiver is a sissy.

Copperhead dwarfs tend to be shorter and noisier than their Überwald fellows, and they are more at home among humans. The Überwald dwarfs are quiet and tend to scuttle around corners to avoid people and often don't speak Morporkian. These two factions, however, strongly dislike each other and their divisions give rise to vendettas and feuds that have their origins in two adjoining mine shafts five hundred miles away and a thousand years ago. The way you wear your helmet, the way you part your beard – all these speak volumes to dwarfs.

Politically, the dwarfs are ruled by a king, although again the word is shorn of most of its human connotations and really means 'chief mining engineer'. Most mines have a king.

There are, however, kings and kings. The senior king, perhaps better thought of as the first among equals, is the Low King of Überwald, who rules all those areas of Überwald that are below ground. As titular head of such an area, he is therefore accorded respect by all other dwarfs (in dwarf terms, that means they don't raise their voice when arguing with him). He is crowned on the 1500-year-old Scone of Stone, an ancient bun the size and shape of a well sat-on cushion, with a few fossilized currants visible on the surface. It weighs about 16lbs, and has represented the legitimacy of the Low King since the days of B'hrian Bloodaxe, who sat on it when it was still warm and left his impression, as it were.

The Low King is the final court of appeal for all matters relating to Dwarf Law. He sits on the Scone to give his judgements. It's the real thing, too. No matter what happens…

Large numbers of dwarfs have been drawn to Ankh-Morpork, where they are the biggest non-human ethnic group. Usually, they fit in well. All dwarfs are by nature dutiful, serious, obedient and thoughtful, and their only failing is a tendency, after one drink, to rush at enemies, screaming 'Aarrgh!' and axing off their legs at the knee. No one knows why it is that dwarfs, who at home in the mountains lead quiet, orderly lives, forget it all when they move to the big city. Something comes over even the most blameless iron-ore miner and prompts him to wear chain mail all the time, carry an axe, change his name to something like Grabthroat Shinkicker and drink himself into surly oblivion. It is noticeable that the dwarfs in Ankh-Morpork are far more 'dwarfish' (in the clichéd sense of being stroppy, gold-obsessed little buggers in iron helmets and chain mail) than they are in their natural envi-

ronment, but the same statement with minimal adjustments could be made about the Irish in New York, the Welsh in London and Australians everywhere.

Dwarfs and Marriage. The facts are these: a dwarf needs to get gold to get married. It costs a lot of money to raise a young dwarf to marriable age. Food, clothes, chain mail….endless expenses. And they need repaying. Two dwarfs getting married must each 'buy' the other dwarf off their parents. It's a sort of two-way dowry. And it has to be paid in gold or gems, because that's traditional. Hence the dwarf saying: 'worth his weight in gold' (dwarfs aren't big on metaphor – some mines priced dwarfs that way).

Of course, if a dwarf has been working for his parents then that will be taken into account on the other side of the ledger, and a dwarf who leaves off marrying until later in life may possibly be owed quite a tidy sum in wages.

All this appears rather chilly, but it is traditional and appears to work. Invariably, after being paid in full for the raising of their offspring, the parents will give the couple a huge wedding present – often much bigger than the dowry. But that is then between dwarf and dwarf, out of love and respect – not between people who are, in a sense, debtor and creditor. In many ways, it works rather better than the human system. Everybody seems to win.

Dykeri. Ephebian philosopher. Author of 'Principles of Navigation'. Got lost trying to find his way out of the bathroom. [SG]

Dysk. VITOLLER's theatre in Ankh-Morpork. Presumably rather similar to London's Globe Theatre, but possibly flatter. [WS]

'What's an elephant?'
'A kind of badger,' said Granny. She hadn't maintained forest-
credibility for forty years by ever admitting ignorance.

– *Equal Rites*

Earwig, Letice, Mrs. A tall, thin witch from the Ramtops, though she was not born locally. She pronounces her surname 'Ah-wij'. Mrs Earwig had been married for many years to a wizard (though he doesn't do any wizarding these days). She is, as I said, tall and thin, with a long, sharp face, set off with an expression that says you are slightly annoying her and she is being gracious enough not to let it show. She dresses in black, of course, but it's a very decorative, rich, deep black – all lacey and ruffled and set off with more silver jewellery than you might imagine. Some of her silver rings are like silver ring gloves – designed to look like claws. She has a very tall pointy hat, with stars on it and glittering silver hatpins. Every doorframe in her house has a tall pointy hat bit to accommodate her hat. She wears silver spectacles on a little chain. Her house has a five-pointed silver star on the door. Mrs Earwig *advertised*. [W]

Eateries. Prominent among Ankh-Morpork's most available places to eat are the CURRY GARDENS (a greasy stick), GIMLET's Hole Food delicatessen, HARGA'S HOUSE OF RIBS, Ron's Pizza Hovel, the Stab in the Back, Mundane Meals, the Laughing Falafel and Fat Sally's. The Three Jolly Luck Take-Away Fish Bar in Dagon Street did not make it beyond its opening night (*see* HONG, MR). For completion, we should also mention Fat Marie's which, although not in Ankh-Morpork (it's on the Quirmian turn-pike), does have the honour of being recommended in *Raising Steam*.

Ee. The Lost, or Forbidden, City of Ee was originally sited in the Great NEF, and it was the location of the miraculously preserved first pizza created on the Disc. It appears that Ee is not only a brigadoon but also one of the specialized ones that are not moored to one site but re-appear in different places.

Eight. A number of some considerable occult significance on the Disc. In theory it must never be spoken by a wizard, although in fact it is generally safe in and around the University, and wizards do seem to be able to get away with it elsewhere. However, outside of magically protected places, no sensible wizard will mention it if he can avoid it; the problem lies in finding the sensible wizard. After all, generations of young wizards have accepted, with a frisson of fear, the injunction 'never say the number that comes between seven and nine, otherwise you will be *ate alive*' without wondering how the terrible occult forces were able to distinguish between two identical-sounding syllables without seeing them written down. Nevertheless, there is something about the harmonics of the word that is attractive to the denizens of the DUNGEON DIMENSIONS, and it is the number of BEL-SHAMHAROTH, one of the most successful of them to have maintained form and vitality in the world of reality. There are eight days in a Disc week, and eight colours in a Disc spectrum. [COM]

Eightfold Seal of Stasis. Design on the floor of the room housing the 'OCTAVO'. Generally agreed in magical circles to have all the stopping power of a well-aimed brick. [LF]

Eightpanther. Maker of Captain Eightpanther's Traveller's Digestives. Claimed to have saved many a life at sea. They are rock-hard, and purchasers are not sure whether to use them as a raft or just throw them at the sharks and watch the wretched things sink. Although these biscuits originated on the Counterweight Continent, anecdotal evidence suggests they are very similar to Dwarf Bread. [COM]

Elenor of Tsort. (or is it of Crinix? or of Elharib?) Elenor was the cause of the Tsortean Wars. She was kidnapped from the Ephebians (or was it by the Ephebians? She has figured in legend so often that details have become obscured, or possibly she was just a very popular girl). What *is* known is that however legendarily beautiful she may have been at the start of the war, by its conclusion she was plump, good-looking in a slightly faded way, wearing a black dress and with a squint and the beginnings of a moustache. She also had at least seven children and seemed to have become somewhat attached to her captors. In fact she much preferred life there (wherever it was) to life back home (wherever that was). But it's the principle of the thing, isn't it? [P]

Elephant, the Fifth. Legend has it that the elephants who support the Discworld have bones of living rock and iron, and nerves of gold for better conductivity over long distances. It is said that once there was a fifth elephant. They say that the fifth elephant lost its footing, or got shaken loose and had drifted off into a curved orbit before eventually crashing down, screaming and trumpeting through the atmosphere of the young world and landed hard enough to split continents and raise mountains. They say a billion tons of enraged pachyderm hit with a force that rocked the entire world and split it up into the continents as they now exist. They say the rocks that fell back had covered and compressed the corpse, and the remains, after millennia of underground cooking and rendering, led to the seams of gold, iron, fat, etc. that are the source of Überwald's trading wealth. Anyway, that's what they say.

Elucidated Brethren of the Ebon Night. A group of rather inadequate men who summoned a dragon to help them to overthrow the government of Ankh-Morpork. Almost all of them ended up as little heaps of ash. The thing about Discworld karma is that it often happens real soon. [GG]

Elves. A humanoid race, extending through a number of worlds. They are vain, vapid, cruel and totally without any feeling or regard for any other creatures – but they are also beautiful, and it is a sad fact that the truly beautiful can get away with just about anything despite behaving in a way that would make the Marquis de Sade say, 'Ooo, what nasty people'.

Their power derives from the use of a mental ability that could be described as 'glamour' to confuse and over-awe people. They can also hypnotize humans with their singing (which is not, as such, musical; elves cannot make music or, indeed, anything else – they traditionally kidnap human musicians for this purpose).

Socially, elves somewhat resemble bees. They have a queen and a king, whose attitude towards one another is chilly contempt for most of the time. The sexuality of the rest of the elves is fairly obscure, and appears to be more or less a matter of personal choice at the time. Nor does there seem to be any great sense of the individual elf, except for the royal family and a few retainers.

They also resemble bees, and pigeons, in being very sensitive to weak magnetic fields, to the extent that the magnetic sense is as important to them as taste or smell, and gives them their acrobatic poise and their absolute sense of position and direction. Elves always know exactly where they are. It is also the cause of their traditional hatred of iron, because this distorts the local magnetic field and leaves them panicky and powerless. This explains the familiar horseshoes over cottage doors and the legendary power of blacksmiths, and is also the reason for the erection of Lancre's DANCERS, whose magnetic field forms a barrier between Discworld and one entrance to the elvish worlds.

Elves have in the past bred with humans and there are some Discworld families with an elvish taint to them. Elves do not seem to be sexually attracted to other elves, possibly because they know what they're really like.

Elves meddle with other people's worlds and mess with their heads. Beware.

Elves, King of. A tall, horned, man-like creature with heavily-lidded eyes, goat's legs and overlarge hooves and, er, other areas. For some reason, he is hugely attractive. In a way. He smells of lions' cages and leaf mould and has a rich, lazy, dark voice, like a voice-over for a chocolate advert. Unlike the Queen, who is constantly seeking new worlds to dominate, he is content to lie up in his sweat lodge and wait for the end of this temporary aberration which seems to have mankind in its grip, i.e. farming with ploughs, the use of metals, civilization and other gewgaws. [LL]

Elves, Queen of. Now known to be named Nightshade. Was usually seen as dark-haired, wearing a red dress, but she could make herself appear in whatever form she liked and no stated appearance is definitive. She wore a copper crown in her hair and had exquisitely thin hands. Her true face was almost triangular, with a tiny mouth, an almost non-existent nose and eyes larger than human eyes – but, again, this may not always have been the face that people saw. They also might not have seen the same individual; little is known about the elves outside their forays in the worlds of humanity, but it is reasonable to posit that there are many groups, and many queens, who tend to act in very similar ways because...well, they're elves, and not good at original thought.

The relative positions of the elven royalty were similar to those on the chess board; the queen was ostensibly the more powerful of the two, but ultimately fails without the king. [LL]

Embalmers' Guild. (Guild of Embalmers and Allied Trades.) Motto: *FARCIMINI*. Coat of arms: a shield, per bend sinister. On it, a seringue argent on a field gules et vert.

An ancient and international Guild, with fraternal links to other STO PLAINS cities and even to the countries of KLATCH. Guild histo-

rians trace their origins back to the very first shambling creature who dropped a mammoth thighbone and a bunch of flowers on a dead fellow shambling creature in a shallow grave and charged the descendants a big lump of bear.

As is so often the case, the Guild is now the official body for a large number of associated trades, such as undertaking and grave-digging. Unlike other Guilds, many of its members have their practices actually based in the building, so that the smells of camphor and formaldehyde make the Guild easily distinguishable on a dark night.

Embalming is still popular in the city, many inhabitants remaining firm in their belief that you might be able to take it with you. Since the Guild includes some highly skilled experts, many people in Ankh-Morpork are buried looking healthier than they did when they were alive, although this is not difficult to achieve.

The training school for gravediggers is worthy of note because it includes classes in cackling and graveyard repartee. In the crowded cemeteries of Ankh-Morpork, previous incumbents are often exhumed by the digging of new holes and, in the ancient traditions of their trade, the trainee gravediggers are taught morbid philosophy, humorous recitation and – in case they find a particularly well-preserved skull – ventriloquism.

Emery, Adrian. (Undecided Adrian.) A member, with Alex CARLTON and Mad Al Winton, of the SMOKING GNU. His eyes are always on the move, as if he's trying to see everything at once. [GP]

Empirical Crescent. (Ankh-Morpork.) Empirical Crescent is just off Park Lane, in what is generally a high-rent district. The rents would have been higher still were it not for the continued existence of Empirical Crescent itself, which, despite the best efforts of the Ankh-Morpork Historical Preservation Society, had still not been pulled down.

This was because it had been built by Bergholt Stuttley Johnson, better known to history as 'Bloody Stupid' Johnson, a man who

The Queen of the Elves

combined in one frail body such enthusiasm, self-delusion and *creative* lack of talent that he was, in many respects, one of the great heroes of architecture. Only Bloody Stupid Johnson could have invented the 13-inch foot and a triangle with three right angles in it. Only Bloody Stupid Johnson could have twisted common matter through dimensions it was not supposed to go.

This highly original approach to geometry was responsible for Empirical Crescent. On the outside it is a normal terraced crescent of the period, built of honey-coloured stone with the occasional pillar or cherub nailed on. Inside, the front door of No.1 opens into the back bedroom of No.15, the ground floor front window of No.3 shows the view appropriate to the second floor of No.9, smoke from the dining room fireplace of No. 2 comes out of the chimney of No.19 [T!]

Endless Street, Ghost of. Endless Street, Ankh-Morpork, is the name of the street running entirely around the city centre inside the city wall. It is said to be haunted by the ghost of one Gumler Vode, condemned for eternity to measure its length. Vode's unfortunate sentence began some three hundred years ago.

It is agreed in the city that, since Broad Way is in two sections, Short Street is the longest street in the city. Vode bet a wizard in the Broken DRUM that it was not, and then, with what was considered by bystanders to be a nasty, know-it-all smirk, claimed that the space behind the walls (then unnamed) was a street. The wizard, annoyed at the thought of losing $5, pointed a finger at him and said, simply, 'Measure it, then...'

The ghost of Vode, and the clink of his tape measure, can be heard on quiet nights. It is a reminder to everyone that, when dealing with wizards, it is always best to know when not to be right.

Endos. A skinny little man who takes payment for listening to Ephebian philosophers. He doesn't do anything else except listen. This

is why he is known as Endos the Listener. (Although for a small extra sum he may vouchsafe grace phrases like 'That is true', or 'A well-made point, if I may say so'.)

In EPHEBE, people who only listen are far rarer than people who only talk. This may be the case everywhere else. [P]

Engravers' (and Printers') Guild. Motto: NON QVOD MANEAT, SED QVOD ADIMIMVS (Not what remains, but what we take away).

Coat of arms: a shield, dimidiation. Sinister an 'I' capitale sable on a field argent. Dexter an 'I' capitale argent on a field sable.

A small, select and solemn bunch of men, whose Guildhouse is on the corner of Short Street and God Street, Ankh-Morpork. They prize practical engraving skills (on wood and metal) above all else, although candidates for membership are also expected to demonstrate lack of imagination, an anal-retentive attention to detail and the ability to think in reverse.

Because of the peculiar informal rules that used to relate to printing in Ankh-Morpork, which effectively used to ban movable type (*see* PRINTING), the engravers were responsible for all semi-mechanically printed output in the city, and their prices were high (although, in Ankh-Morpork's flourishing free market, there are a large number of non-Guild engravers). The events of *The Truth* have now changed all this, and the Guild, mindful of the need to keep in the vanguard of publishing, is now the Guild of Engravers *and Printers*.

Enid, Mrs. Laundress at Kneck Keep in Borogravia. Not a particularly large woman, but she has big forearms and a very mobile mouth. Her lips and tongue draw out every word like a big shape in the air. [MR]

Eorle, Duke of. Nobleman of Ankh. Appears to be a rather lazy and stupid man with a braying laugh and the mental powers of a mole. A dead mole. On the other hand, the Eorles have survived everything life could throw at them for hundreds of years, so it may be that the most intelligent thing they've ever done is to appear stupid on every occasion. [MAA]

Ephebe. Pop. (city and surrounding farmlands): 50,000.

Political system: tyranny (a form of democracy); slavery is a long-established tradition.

Major export: ideas.

General description: the white marble city lazes around its rock overlooking the blue CIRCLE SEA. Blindingly white houses coil all the way up to the top, where a wall runs around the peak like a headband. Beyond that is the famous and ancient labyrinth, full of one hundred and one amazing things you can do with hidden springs, razor-sharp knives and falling rocks. There are six guides – each one knows his way through one sixth of the labyrinth. Alongside the palace within the labyrinth are the remains of the famous library, which used to be the second biggest on the Discworld before it was burned by Omnian soldiery (or so legend has it; but there is a story that the first match was put to it by DIDACTYLOS the philosopher just seconds before the guard arrived, on the basis that setting fire to your own library is more philosophical).

This tiny but influential city state lies on the rimward coast of the Circle Sea, between DJELIBEYBI and OMNIA. It is the land of the bourzuki (a kind of dog) and retsina (a kind of paint-thinner) and, above all, the land of philosophy.

Ephebe has more philosophers per square yard than anywhere else on the Disc. It is impossible to throw a brick in Ephebe without hitting a philosopher and, owing to the heightened level of philosophical debate that rages in the city, this often happens. For it is unfortunate that a city whose inhabitants frequently storm the walls of paradox and smash the doors of perception is also beset with that particular dogged Discworld logic which would not recognize a metaphor if it was handed to it in a cornet with chocolate chips on top.

This certainly makes for briskness of thought. Any philosopher who suggests that, logically, an arrow cannot hit a running man (Xeno's Arrow Paradox) will be given a short head start before all the other philosophers reach for their bows. This experiment was actually performed and the philosopher did escape unscathed, but after some thought rewrote the statement so that it read that a running man cannot be hit by an arrow *providing it is fired by someone who has been in the pub since lunchtime.*

Which, rather neatly, leads on to the subject of Ephebian food and drink. In short, Ephebians make wine out of anything they can put in a bucket, and eat anything that can't climb out of one. They will drink wine which varnishes the inside of the throat, and sometimes their food will try to hold on to the plate. (Plate-smashing is a tradition at the end of an Ephebian meal, although it may be a better idea to smash them beforehand.)

Ephebe has been called 'the cradle of democracy', and it is true that Ephebian democracy could do with having its nappy changed. The Ephebians believe that every man should have the vote – providing he isn't poor or a slave or foreign or disqualified by reason of being mad, frivolous or a woman.

The voters (1300 of them) go to the polls every five years to elect the Tyrant, who is more or less the supreme ruler for his period of office. In order to be considered for election a candidate for Tyrant must prove beyond doubt that he is pure in thought, word and deed, with no stain whatsoever on his character. Once elected it is assumed by everyone that he is a criminal madman.

Candidates for Tyrantship are elected by the placing of black or white balls in various urns, thus giving rise to a well-known comment about politics.

A note on slavery: slaves make up more than half of Ephebe's population. Periodically someone suggests that they should be freed, but there is always a tremendous outcry. It comes from the slaves themselves, who have several times risen in revolt against the very idea. The reason lies in the particular status of slaves vs free men in Ephebian society. A free man is, clearly, free – free to sleep in the rain, free to starve, free to suffer whatever vicissitudes the world might drop upon his manumitted head.

No one is there to care for a free man. A free man is free to drop dead.

Whereas there are rules for slaves, established over a thousand years. Slaves get three meals a day, at least one with named meat in it. And one day off a week. And two weeks being-allowed-to-run-away every year (it is generally understood that a proper master will pay for his slave to come back from wherever it is he or she has run away to). A slave may not be beaten without a chance to appeal to the Tyrant, and the mistreatment of slaves is a grave crime. A slave is, after all, property. Respect for property is the cornerstone of democracy.

A slave does, of course, have to work, although not work like a slave.

After twenty years as a slave he can automatically become a free man, but most slaves take one look at what freedom entails and, despite the entreaties of a master who may well be living on olive pits in order to feed his household, sign up again for another twenty years.

Slavery would in fact be a huge drain on the economy of Ephebe were it not for the fact that it hasn't got one. The sun shines, ripening the olives and the grapes, there are fish in the sea, there doesn't seem to be any really pressing reason to do anything much except sit and think, and so Ephebe ambles amiably from day to day.

Special notes for the visitor to Ephebe: do not be surprised to see naked old men, dripping wet, trotting through the streets. Most of the really serious philosophizing in Ephebe is done in the bath, and the birth of a new idea will often lead the bather to spring away crying 'Eureka!' (literally, 'Give me a towel!') to start work on the theorem right away.

Barrels will be seen dotted around the streets. This is where the philosophers traditionally live, in order to show their disregard of matters in the mundane world. In order to show their love of comfort, however, the barrels are often very large, with enough room for a sauna.

Erasmus. Great-uncle of Mrs CAKE. Sometimes used to eat his meals under the table on account of werewolf blood. [RM]

Eric. *See* THURSLEY, ERIC.

Errol. Goodboy Bindle Featherstone of Quirm, and technically a pedigree dragon. His sire was Treebite Brightscale, a prizewinner bred by the then Lady Sybil RAMKIN. But it was clear right from the egg that Errol was something unusual. He had a pear-shaped body and a head like an anteater, with nostrils like jet intakes, two tiny spiky ears and a pair of eyebrows almost the same size as his stubby wings, which should never have supported him in the air. He was named Errol by Corporal NOBBS, because of a supposed resemblance to his brother (Corporal Nobbs's, not the dragon's). In fact Errol, dismissed as a whittle (or runt), turned out to be, according to the most modern thinking, a throwback to the original space-faring dragons; his genes remembered what could be done with a streamlined body, small wings and a very hot flame, if only the flames could be persuaded to, er, come out of the other end. [GG]

Errol

appeared in the moving pictures. Probably the most intelligent mind in Holy Wood. [MP]

Evil-Smelling Bugger. Renowned as the greatest camel mathematician of all time, who invented the maths of eight-dimensional space while lying down with his nostrils closed in a violent sandstorm. [P]

Expletius. Ephebian philosopher who proved that the Disc is 10,000 miles wide. A lucky guess. More than twenty other philosophers proved that the Disc varied in size from infinite to 'too small to see' and, since they turned out to be wrong, Expletius got the Top Brain award. [SG]

Esk. Eskarina Smith. Daughter of Gordo SMITH. Eight years old and four feet tall, she has long brown hair and a gap in her front teeth, and the sort of features that promise to become, if not beautiful, then at least attractively interesting. She is the eighth child of an eighth son, and was handed, at birth, the wizard's staff belonging to Drum BILLET. She was the first female to be admitted to Unseen University. And the last, so far as records show. Current whereabouts unknown for many years, until she emerged, with white hair in a ponytail, wrinkles and wearing heavy, stiff clothing and big boots, in the events of *I Shall Wear Midnight*. She lives in the UU Unreal Estate and can walk through time and make it take orders from her. [ER]

Esmerelda Margaret Note Spelling. Princess of LANCRE and daughter of MAGRAT GARLICK and KING VERENCE II. [CJ]

Evil-Minded Son of a Bitch. Camel who

Expletives. For a very brief period, during the events of *Reaper Man*, RIDCULLY's swear words gained a transitory existence as little creatures. For example, a random, and fortunately unde-fined, bout of swearing produced something small and striped red and yellow, with tiny dripping fangs and three pairs of wings, making a noise like a miniature buzzsaw. A further utterance, unfamiliar to those in the faculty unfamiliar with animal husbandry, yielded a fat, round, black and glossy creature, with horrible eyebrows. Others included:

'Bugger' – produced a slightly different
  variety of mad, waspy creature;
'Blasted' – materialized as a tiny, purple
  spider-like creature;
'Dammit' (combined with 'Blasted') –
  produced a long creature with four pairs
  of wings, two at each end, and three eyes.
[RM]

Ezeriel. One-time Queen of KLATCH. Every young student of history knows that Ezeriel had a lot of lovers, used to bathe in asses' milk and died when she sat on a snake (they seldom know any more than this). She is a distant ancestor of KELI, which suggests that royalty around the CIRCLE SEA, as in Europe, followed the mix'n'match approach to royal weddings. [M]

Forget you were ever Polly. Think young male, that was the
thing. Fart loudly and with self-satisfaction at a job well done.

— *Monstrous Regiment*

Fairies. As so often is the case on Discworld, any attempt at a precise description of the nature and role of fairies is bound to raise a crop of exceptions. They are *not* a species. The Tooth Fairies are human, although with *ex officio* special powers to enable them to remain unseen as they go about their essential business, but many other fairies appear to be dwarfs, gnomes, animals or even invisible.

Basically, they are a job description. A fairy is there to perform some specific, minor task – take away unwanted teeth, bring boils and warts, see that you never have enough paperclips, steal the last wafer-thin After Dinner Mint and so on. The mere act of belief will, in a sufficiently charged environment, summon one into existence. In fact, the strangest of them all is the GLINGLEG-LINGLEGLINGLE FAIRY, whose sole job it is to make, via some hand bells, the cheap and tinselly 'glingleglingleglingle' noise that precedes the appearance of a fairy or any act of fairy magic.

It is said that every time a bell rings a fairy gets a pair of wings, which means that there have been a lot more fairies since the invention of alarm clocks.

False, Praise & Salvation. False is a derivation of the original Klatchian name, Thalassa. He is a breeder of complicated chickens. [SN]

Famine. An anthropomorphic personification. One of the Four Horsemen of the APOCRALYPSE. Arrogant, and always hungry. Technically, Famine, like PESTILENCE, was a Horseman created by humanity; Death has always been around, and ants and apes wage War. There have always been droughts and locusts, but for a really good famine, for fertile land to be turned into a dustbowl by stupidity and avarice, you need humans.

Fantailler, Marquis of. The Marquis got into so many fights in his youth (mostly as a result of being called the Marquis of Fantailler) that he decided to write a set of rules for what he called the 'noble art of fisticuffs', which mostly consisted of a list of places where people weren't allowed to hit him. Many people were impressed with his work and later stood with noble chest outthrust and fists balled in a spirit of manly aggression against people who hadn't read the Marquis' book but *did* know how to knock people senseless with a chair. The last words of a surprisingly large number of people were, 'stuff the bloody Marquis of Fantailler....' [TFE]

Far-re-ptah. Past queen of DJELIBEYBI. Grandmother of TEPPICYMON XXVII. A strict and fearsome old woman who was, however, known as 'Grandma Pooney' to TEPPIC. [P]

Fasta Benj. A fisherman from a small nation of marsh-dwelling nomads near OMNIA, who were unknown to the world at large and entirely bypassed by history until by sheer chance his little boat was swept up by the multi-national fleet sent to destroy that country. His only recorded contribution to the very short Omnian war was a hopeful attempt to sell raw fish to all parties. Nevertheless, as a representative of a sovereign nation he went home with his own share of the spoils, which included the secret of fire and the use of metals. [SG]

Fate. Another anthropomorphic personification. A friendly looking man in late middle age, with greying hair brushed neatly around features that a maiden would confidently proffer a glass of small beer to, should they appear at her back door. It is a face a kindly youth would gladly help over a stile. Except for the eyes, of course... while at a mere glance they are simply dark, a closer look reveals that they are holes opening on to a blackness so remote, so deep that the watcher feels himself inexorably drawn into the twin pools of infinite night and their terrible, wheeling stars. [COM]

Febrius. Ephebian philosopher. He proved that light travels at about the same speed as sound, in his famous 'Give us a shout when you see it, OK?' experiment involving two hills, a lantern with a movable cover over it and an assistant with a very loud voice. [SG]

Feegles. *See* NAC MAC FEEGLE.

Felmet, Lady. Wife of Leonal, Duke FELMET. A powerful and impressive woman who could not abide slackness or weakness and regarded the whole universe as something to bully. She had a big red face with thick eyebrows and a stubbly chin, and wore red velvet dresses that matched her complexion. Possibly eaten to death by rabbits and other fluffy creatures in the forests of LANCRE. [WS]

Felmet, Leonal, Duke. Murdered his cousin, King VERENCE I of LANCRE. An insect of a man with a thin face and heavily beringed hands, he had a mind that ticked like a clock and, like a clock, it regularly went cuckoo.

He was married for twenty years to the massive Lady FELMET, whom he wed largely because he was fascinated by power, of which she was practically the embodiment. Fell to his death into the River Lancre. [WS]

Fergmen. Sergeant of the Palace Guard in Kom. [SG]

Fhem-pta-hem. A Djelibeybian lord with whom TEPPIC spent a summer. [P]

Fiddler's Riddle. An unpleasant inn in Ohulan Cutash. No self-respecting goat can endure the smell in the Fiddler's Riddle. It was here that Eskarina Smith (ESK) turned a barrel of plum brandy into milk. [ER]

Fido, Big. Chief Barker of the DOG GUILD. A small and rather dainty white poodle with the overgrown remains of a poodle cut and wearing a diamante collar. Big Fido was, to hijack a convenient phrase, barking mad – apparently driven to this state one day by the realization that everything around him (his bowl, his collar, his kennel, his blanket) had his name on it. He ate his blanket, savaged his owner and ran off. The madness seemed to tap some deep pit of primordial rage in his soul which enabled him to fight and kill dogs much larger and theoretically much stronger than him, and thus he became the acknowledged leader of the feral dogs of Ankh-Morpork. To them he expounded, at length and with much excited farting and foaming when he talked, his Dream: that all dogs were wolves at heart, and needed only to band together to overthrow humanity (the 'Master' race) and reclaim their ancient heritage. [MAA]

Fingers, Brother. Member of the ELUCIDATED BRETHREN OF THE EBON NIGHT. He used to work as an odd-job man at Unseen University, but was better known to the City WATCH as Bengy 'Lightfoot' BOGGIS, of the famous thieving family. [GG]

Duke and Lady Felmet

Fion. Nac Mac Feegle. Daughter of the Feegle clan that lives near Tiffany Aching's village. Eventually leaves to become Kelda of a clan near Copperhead Mountain. [WFM]

Firefighters' Guild. Not in existence long enough to develop a motto or a coat of arms. Outlawed by the PATRICIAN after many complaints. If you bought a contract from the Guild, your house would be protected against fire. Unfortunately, the general Ankh-Morpork ethos quickly came to the fore and firefighters would go to prospective clients' houses in groups, making loud comments like 'Very inflammable looking place, this,' and 'Probably go up like a firework with just one carelessly dropped match, know what I mean?' Since the disbanding of the Ankh-Morpork Guild of Firefighters the incidence of fires has gone down considerably. [GG]

First, Legitimate. Resident grave-digger at the Cemetery of Small Gods in Ankh-Morpork. Known as 'Leggie', he is a black-clad, skinny figure. He owes his rather unusual first name to a mother's natural pride. [NW]

Fizz. Cartoonist at the 'Ankh-Morpork Times'. [MR]

Flannelfoot, Zlorf. Past President of the ASSASSINS' GUILD, and of rather earthier origins than many of its later members. Broad, honest face, a welter of scar tissue, the result of many a close encounter. Said by some that he chose a profession in which dark hoods, cloaks and nocturnal prowlings predominated because there was a day-fearing trollish streak in his parentage. People who repeated this in earshot of Zlorf tended to carry their ears home in their hats. [COM]

Flead, Professor, the Late. A member of the Department of Post-Mortem Communications at Unseen University. He has been dead for 300 years, but willed his soul to the University. He appears as a robed, pointy-hatted, bearded, elderly wizard, with a silvery monochrome effect and some slight transparency. [MM]

Fliemoe. A student at the ASSASSINS' GUILD, and a bit of a bully. [P]

Flint, Constable. A troll conscripted into the City Watch during the events of *Men at Arms* and later promoted to Sergeant. [MAA]

Flitworth, Renata. Skinny, short-sighted, aged seventy-five, with a face the colour and texture of a walnut. Miss Flitworth never had the chance even to become a widow because of the death of her intended, Rufus, in an avalanche just before their wedding, but she overcame a tendency to mope about this and got on with life in a determined, no-nonsense sort of way. She owned a farm in the plains below the RAMTOPS, not far from SHEEPRIDGE.

Her main claim to fame was as the employer of Bill DOOR (DEATH), who was sufficiently impressed by her to allow her soul to remain in the world just long enough to attend the long-looked-forward-to harvest dance. [RM]

Floral Clock, the. A horticultural – and horological – curiosity created by Lu-Tze. Of course, in Oi Dong, time doesn't really pass, but the floral clock does a pretty good job of keeping time anyway. [LTD]

Flora of the Disc. The Discworld has a rich and unusual variety of plants. These include:

Achorion Purple [P]
Aphacia wood [SG]
Bindweed, Purple [TOT]
Bloodwater Lily [ER]
Choke apples [COM]
Climbing Elderberry [NOCB]
Climbing Henry & Twirling Betty [ISWM]
COUNTING PINES
Creeping Foxglove [NOCB]
Creeping Shrillflower [NOCB]
Devil's Bit Scabious [WA]
Devil's Crotch [LTD]
Dropley's Etiolated Bladderwrack [J]
Dum-dum [RM]
Earwort [ER]
Egregious Flytrap [RS]
False Gentian [HFOS]
Fellwort, Woolly [WS]
Field Sowthistle [TOT]
Floribunda Mrs Shover (a rose) [RM]
Forget-me-Lots (pretty red and white flower) [ISWM]
Gherkins, Water [ER]
Goat's Beard, Yellow [TOT]
Humming Tulip [LTD]
Ice Plant [TOT]
Jack-in-the-Alley [LTD]
Jack-Jump-Into-Bed [ISWM]
Kzak fruit [M]
Lancre Stinklily [LTD]
Love-in-a-Pickle [ISWM]
Love-Lies-Panting [NOCB]
Maiden's Puzzle [NOCB]
Maiden's Wish [ER]
Mandrake, Five-Leaved False [WS]

The Floral Clock

Maniac [RM]
Mouse Cress [NOCB]
Mustick [P]
Nervousa gloriosa [RM]
Nettle-Leaved Forthright [NOCB]
Nose Dropwort [HFOS]
Old Maids A-Plenty [NOCB]
Old Man's Frogbit [WS]
Old Man's Trousers [ER]
Peahane, Greater [ER]
Pines, Predicting [TSC]
Purple Bindweed (Love-in-a-Spin) [SM]
Pyramid Strangler Vine [TLC]
Ragged-Leaved Trefoil [NOCB]
Sago-Sago Tree [H]
Sandwort, Red [TOT]
SAPIENT PEARWOOD
Sapu tree (carnivorous tree of Sumtri) [TLC]
Scarlet Bellweed [NOCB]
Seven-leafed Clover [ISWM]
Sledgehammer Plant (Bhangbhangduc) [TLC]
Snake's Head [WA]
Spikkle [RM]
Stumbleweed (like tumbleweed, but less energetic) [RS]
Syphacia bush [P]
Three Times Charlie [ISWM]
Toad Spurge [NOCB]
Twisting Honeydew [RS]
Uloruaha bush [COM]
WAHOONIE
Wamwam Tree [TOT]
Wasp Agaric [P]
Water Dropwort [NOCB]
Wormseed, Treacle [WS]

Additionally, a large number of herbs are listed in *The Shepherd's Crown* as being in Granny WEATHERWAX's garden. These include:

Creepalong Minnie
Daisy-upsy-Daisy
Doubting Plums
Ginny Come Nether
Jack by Moonlight
Jack-go-to-bed-and-never-get-up
Jump in the Basin
Love Lies Oozing
Maiden's Respite
Merryday (Root)
Multitude (Root)
Old Man Root
Rotating Spinach
Tickle My Fancy (root)
Troubling Tony
Twirlabout

Flume, Odile, Lady. A pupil in the fifth form of the Quirm College for Young Ladies. Her great-great-grandmother was once seduced by the god Blind Io in the form of a vase of daisies. So she claims, anyway.[SM]

Flutter, Ted. A snotty bugger who used to work for young Lord Rust over at Hangnail. He's just a bloke. If someone needs help for something or other, he's the kind of bloke who'd be the lookout or be told to take away the bones. When not up to mischief, he hangs wallpaper and runs a turkey farm up on the road towards Overhang. It's a stinky place and he doesn't take care of his birds. In Feeney UPSHOT's opinion, he's not entirely all there. [SN]

Follett, Dr. Master of Assassins and ex-officio Headmaster of the Assassins' Guild School. Known, to the boys, as 'Old Folly'. There were rumours about whether or not his white hair was a wig, but nothing has ever been firmly established. He went missing very shortly after assisting Lord Snapcase to become Patrician of the city. All that can be usefully said is that Lord Snapcase was not a naturally grateful man. [NW]

Folsom, Jimmy. *See* JIMMY, DOUGHNUT.

Fondel. Composer. Wrote '*The Wedding March*' and '*Prelude in G Major*'. [MAA]

Food and drink. The Discworld is famed for its cuisine. A visitor would be able to eat for a year without needing to repeat a meal, and in most cases without wanting to.

Almonte (liqueur) [T!]

Amanita Liquor [M]

Antipasta. Created some hours *after* the meal, whereupon it exists *backwards in time* and, if properly prepared, should arrive on the tastebuds at exactly the same moment, thus creating a true taste explosion. It costs five thousand dollars a forkful, or a little more if you include the cost of cleaning the tomato sauce off the walls afterwards. [RM]

Apple Glazier (invented by Imposo for Dame Margyreen Glazier). [TLC]

Banged Grains. Made of corn heated in cooking oil with salt and butter added. Tastes of salt, butter and cardboard. [MP]

Bang Suck Duck [SN]

Barnacle canapés [COM]

Bearhugger's Whiskey Cream [T!]

Bentinck's Very Old Peculiar Brandy [RM]

Black Death Meringue [TFE]

Blowfish, Deep Sea. Safe to eat if every bit of stomach, liver and digestive tract is removed. Better still, to be on the safe side it is wise to remove every part of the fish. [P]

Boiled Eels [NW]

Brandy Pillows [MR]

Bung Ming Suck Dog [SN]

Cakes, Dwarfish (very solid and inedible – *see* DWARF BREAD)

Captain Horace Calumney's Patent Field Biscuits [MR]

Carrot and Oyster Pie. Nanny Ogg's recipe. Carrots so you can see in the dark, oysters so you've got something to look at. [LL]

Cheese (Lancre has the holes, Quirm is the one with the blue veins). [SM]

Chocolate (of course), notably made by Wienrich & Boettcher and by Higgs & Meakins. [TOT]

Clammer's Beefymite Spread [FOC]

Clooty Dumplings [MAA]

Cocktails – Angel's Tears, Just Sex, Pussy Galore, No Brainer, Screaming Orgasm, Pink, Big & Wobbly and (a troll one) Electrick Floorbanger. [MR, T!]

Dark Enchantments (chocolates) [RM]

Distressed Pudding [MAA]

Duck & Dirty Rice [TOT]

Englebert's Enhancer [H]

Farmhouse Nutty (cheese with the human touch since that...accident...at the vat). [MA]

Fatsup (soup with sausages) [TFE]

Fikkun Haddock [MAA]

Fluff (a mix of strong beer & scumble) [T!]

Ghlen Livid. Fermented vul nut drink distilled in the Agatean Empire. Also made in the Rehigreed Province using re-annual plants. It is believed that now some is being imported now into Ankh-Morpork. [COM]

Hang Suck Butt Dog [SN]

Jammy Devils [MAA]

Jellyfish, Crystallized [COM]

Jimkin BEARHUGGER's whiskey – quite strong, and often matured for hours at a time.

Klatchian Coffee. Very strong: goes through an untrained stomach like a hot ball-bearing through runny butter. This strange, thick brew is drunk in thimble-sized cups. It doesn't just sober you up; it takes you through sobriety and out the other side, so that you glimpse the real universe beyond the clouds of warm self-delusion that sapient life usually generates around itself to stop it turning into a nutcake. Coffee enthusiasts take the precaution of getting thoroughly drunk before touching the stuff. Varieties include Curly Mountain Straight and Red Desert Special. [S]

Klatchian Delight (doubles as a sweetmeat and flypaper). [SG]

Klatchian Hots (type of pizza) [GG]

Klatchian Migratory BOG TRUFFLE [RS]

Klatchian Rare Roasted ('When a Pickaxe is Not Enough!') [MR]

Knuckle Sandwich [MAA]

Lancre Blue Cheese [W] (see also HORACE)

Lancre Extra Strong (cheese) [MA]

Leftover Sandwiches Soup (invented by Nanny Ogg). [W]

Lob Scouse [NW]

Lord Green (tea) [TAMAHER]

Luglarr ('Big Hammer' – a strong troll drink) [MR]

MacAbre single malt [HFOS]

Merckle & Stingbat's Very Famous Brown Sauce [GG]

Mustard – Mrs Edith Leakall's Premium Reserve [GP]

Noggi (buckwheat dumplings stuffed with stuff). [TFE]

Nourishing Boiled Socks Surprise [W]

Old Blonk (Überwaldian beer) [RS]

Old Overcoat (another fine product from Jimkin Bearhugger's vats). [M]

Orakh. Made from cactus sap and scorpion venom. One of the most virulent alcoholic beverages in the universe. Not drunk for its intoxicating effects, but to mitigate the effects of Klatchian coffee (see above).

Orange Ormulu (invented by Charley's dad for Dame Janeen Ormulu). [TLC]

Peach Corniche. One of those sticky drinks no barman ever expects to take off the shelf. [M]

Peach Nellie (invented by Rincewind for Dame Nellie Butt). [TLC]

Pressed Seaweed biscuits [COM]

Sclot (bread made from parsnips). [TFE]

Scubbo (various forms of military stew). [MR]

SCUMBLE

Sea Grape wine [COM]

Sea Urchin, Candied [COM]

Shark's Fin soup [LF]

Sheergold's (Mrs) Lubricated Throat Lozenges [W]

Sklang [TOT]

Slumgullet [NW]

Slumpie [MAA]

Smitten Steak [TFE]

Soft Nellies (sheep cheese) [HFOS]

Soggy Mountain Dew, C.M.O.T. Dibbler's Genuine Authentic. Despite its name, it is not strong and may not even be alcoholic, its effects being caused by whatever Mr Dibbler thinks might give it some kind of kick – gunpowder, corroded copper, and so on. [MAA]

Special Sheep Liniment (not strictly a food, though). [WFM]

Spring Cordial [M]

Squid, Crystallized [COM]

Squishi (possibly like sushi, only older). [LF]

Stardrip (plum brandy, brewed in the Ramtops). [M]

Starfish, Baby, with Purée of Sea Cucumbers [COM]

Starfish, Candied [COM]

Strawberry Sackville (invented by Nunco for Dame Wendy Sackville). [TLC]

Three Wizards' Chardonnay [H]

Tracklement's Yums (dog biscuits) [MM]

Traveller's Digestives [LF]

Treacle Billy [NW]

Turbot's Really Odd (real ale) [SM]

Vole & Pork Sausages [TAMAHER]

Wahlulu (liqueur) [T!]

Walago (a kind of pastry made from curtains). [TFE]

Wet Nellies [NW]

Winkle's Old Peculiar (beer) (also Mage's Special) [FOC]

WOW-WOW SAUCE

Fool, the. See VERENCE II.

Fools' Guild. Guild of Fools and Joculators and College of Clowns. Motto: DICO, DICO, DICO. Coat of arms: a shield, bisected dancette. The upper half, sable with a roundel, gules. Each lower point decorated with a clochette d'or. The lower half is bisected vertically, the right half being azure, the left half, argent.

The Guildhouse is located on the corner of God Street and Widdershins Broadway. One of the more recent Ankh-Morpork Guilds, although like the ASSASSINS' GUILD and Unseen University it is a major exporter of its graduates and has ancient origins among the circus fraternity.

A BRIEF TOUR OF THE GUILD BUILDING

Little is known about the origins of the building which was to become the Guild House. It features in some early records of Unseen University as 'the Plague House', and the last known occupants before the mysterious fire and highly localized earthquake in 1547 were apparently The Brotherhood of Infernal Zoth the Undying Renderer, a contemplative order.

The ruins were bought by the Guild shortly afterwards and there have been many changes, although many areas of the property still have a certain monastic charm, particularly the Chamber of Spikes (although the mechanism no longer works).

Much of the current frontage, including the famous Red Nose, was designed by the great architect Bergholt Stuttley JOHNSON. His equally famous water cannon in the shape of a giant daisy is no longer in use following the unfortunate drowning incident and is now in the Guild Museum, as is the very humorous Custard Pie machine that originally greeted visitors. Its purpose was put them in the right mirthful frame of mind, but regrettably Mr Johnson underestimated the effects of even quite runny custard when accelerated instantly to 300 m.p.h.

The building is built around a circle, or ring, which is permanently in use for training purposes and is roofed with canvas in the winter. There is a Floral Buttonhole target range and, of course, the traditional pie butts (bulk custard and whitewash tanks have been installed on the roof for easy distribution throughout the building).

Visitors, once they have cleaned themselves off, should on no account miss the Office of Fun, where the Guild Council meets. There has been much hurtful talk suggesting that the Guild are behind the times, but these days as many as three new jokes a year are considered by the Council, and a good candidate joke or routine gets through the various stages and committees in as short a time as twenty years.

Some of the earliest jokes are on display here, including the meagre remains of the *actual* custard pie which, as any Fool knows, was inadvertently hurled by Gilbert the Stupid when he slipped on a mutton bone in the long house of Picric, Eorle of Nothingfjord, and delivered the custard full in Picric's face. The rest is history. Students of Foolish history still visit his graves which, owing to Picric's curious lack of a sense of humour, are dotted around Nothingfjord, some of them in quite inaccessible places.

Other exhibits include the *original* Dog with No Nose (which smells of formaldehyde, and is also shaggy), part of the cranium of what is believed to be one of the original trio of Three Men Who Went Into A Pub, and a genuine Alligator Sandwich.

Close by is the very heart of the Guild:

The Hall of Faces

Even outsiders have heard of the hall which contains, ranging in long lines, blown eggs on which have been carefully recorded the facial make-up of every Guild member (plus full documentation about dress, special routines and so on). Few, though, realize the full significance of this. A clown is the face; the face is the clown.

Using the face of another clown except under very special circumstances is an offence punishable by *eventual* death. For a clown's face is also his fortune. A dying clown may will it to a son, or it may be auctioned by the Guild, and the full make-up, dress and routines of a famous clown may change hands for many thousands of dollars. It is a kind of immortality. The Great Bazonko has been clowning now for over four hundred years. Doctor Whiteface has been head of the Guild for almost three hundred. He has worked in the same office, worn the same costume and certainly always worn the same make-up. He speaks in the same clipped tones. Men may come and go, but there is always a Doctor Whiteface.

From here it is but a short walk to:

The Bouncy Normo Library

Very little is known about Bouncy Normo. He seldom spoke. Shortly after his arrival in Ankh-Morpork he was given sanctuary in the Guild because no other premises in the city would allow him across the threshold.

There are people with perfect pitch, people with absolute rhythm, and even people with green fingers. Bouncy Normo had two strange talents. He had no sense of humour at all, and he was a natural funny man. A *really* funny man.

Official public performances were banned

when three people died laughing, even though Normo was standing with his back to the stage and did not utter a word. People would go purple and roll on the floor even while watching him shave.

Everything Bouncy Normo did was dangerously hilarious. Eventually, Doctor Whiteface insisted that he wear a bag over his head but this, strangely enough, only made things worse; people would collapse with laughter at the thought of Normo being so funny under there.

Eventually, after leaving a short note which contained his unwitting catch-phrase 'What is everyone laughing about?', Bouncy Normo leapt to his death from the top of the House of Mirth. He landed on the marquee over the custard pie butts, rebounded onto the trampoline used for Amusing Trouser practice, thence onto a seesaw being erected by The Three Incompetent Acrobats, was flipped through a window on the second floor, landed on a trolley laden with pastries which rolled down the stairs and out through the main doors, and was trampled to death by an escaped elephant. Seven people who witnessed this had to be treated for various self-inflicted traumas caused by laughing too much.

Bouncy Normo was a model clown. He told no illicit jokes, he kept his bed space scrupulously clean, and he would certainly had make friends if anyone had been able to stop laughing long enough to talk to him.

In his memory, the library of clowning, with its unrivalled collection of books on jokes, japes and routines, was renamed after him and a statue of Bouncy Normo was erected over the door. To honour the memory of a true clown's clown, all the library steps were replaced by trampolines. Visitors should not miss the library during revision period, but should wear protective clothing.

An Outline of Foolery

The Guild uses the term 'fool' to apply to all members, even though their chosen field may be clowning or juggling. Newcomers to the Guild, of any age, are expected to work alongside more experienced Fools and will, provided they are not foolish, progress through the various early grades of Muggins, Gull, Dupe and Butt within the first few years. It takes about five years to become a Fool, but it is then that the enthusiastic student will realize, even as his trousers fill with the official whitewash, that he is but setting foot on the very bottom rung of Foolishness. The senior ranks of Tomfool, Stupid Fool and Arch Fool beckon, and in the fullness of time he may even strive to become a Complete Fool.

The Guild does not admit women. It has been proved that women have no sense of humour whatsoever.

A History of the Fools' Guild

Monsieur Jean-Paul Pune founded the Guild in 1567, when he came to Ankh-Morpork from Quirm in search of people with a better sense of humour who didn't keep trying to drown him. It is quite probable that, before he gave his name to the classic 'play on words', people had already made crude, rural attempts in that direction, but Pune was the first to explore and codify the 'pun' in his work 'Essay on a Form of Wit', in which he spent 160,000 words defining the Five Great classes and seventy-three sub-classes of pun. Pune was the first man to perfect the art of pronouncing brackets, an invaluable aid to the punster faced with an audience lacking in intellect, as in 'Q. When is a door not a door? A. When it is ajar (a jar)' – one of his early puns for which he was tarred and feathered and left for dead.

There was already an ancient tradition of Foolery, of course. The first fools, according to earliest historical records, were actually skilled warriors who rode alongside the king and fought bravely and Foolishly, hacking their way through the melee with comments like 'Aha, you need to get ahead (a head)!' and so on. They were also confidants and advisers, whose role was tell the king things that he really needed to know, such as the fact that he ought to be taking more baths at this time or year and perhaps he should adjust his chain mail.*

Ankh-Morpork already had fools, too. The King had a fool, Will Centunculus, a man recognized throughout the city as someone to avoid. Most of the city nobles also had fools, imported from Quirm Société Joyeux, La Sorbumme (another slightly more sophisticated offering from M. Pune) and in fact there was already a loose association of fools extending throughout the Sto Plains and along the Ramtops.

M. Pune was a wealthy man. He felt that humour needed to be taken very seriously and he chose for his new school the recently vacated monastery (as already mentioned) which did not seem to be attracting new occupants despite being such a prime site.

The Assassins' Guild next door had just acquired its Guild status. M. Pune immediately saw the prestige value of this and applied to the city's elders for his as-yet nonexistent school also to be granted Guild status.

Curiously enough, they concurred and the Guild of Fools, Joculators, Minstrels, Buffoons and Mime Artists was created before the first student had been enrolled.

Over the years the Guild's influence on all sorts of foolery was such that there soon were very few fools in civilized countries who were not graduates. It has been suggested that the new Guild became nothing more than a vast spy network, sending back to the House of Mirth snippets of political information which were used by the Guild Council to become enormously rich.

We must make it CLEAR that the Guild's vast wealth accrues from PROWESS WITH THE CUSTARD PIE, CAREFUL CONTROL OVER EXPENDITURE and other Foolish activities. Dr Whiteface is no more than a hard-working administrator, and certainly NOT the cruel and devious international manipulator that UNSUBSTANTIATED RUMOUR makes him out to be.

---

* And, as every schoolboy knows, if only King Harold the Rampant had listened to that advice, or if one of the Pseudopolitan archers had not been such a good shot, the Battle of the Field of the Cloth of Ants would not have ended on such a piercingly high note.

Anyone suggesting otherwise can expect a visit from the Jolly Good Pals in VERY SHORT ORDER.

M. Pune toured the Discworld to recruit the most experienced Fools, Jesters, Idiots and other specialists to tutor his new Guild. He wanted the Guild run on very austere lines, with students having to work from dawn to dusk.

He promised a regime of cold baths, hard wooden beds, self-flagellation, awful food and hours spent meticulously copying the manuscripts containing the true basis of humour, punning, pratfalls and the full paraphernalia of stomach-churningly embarrassing humour. This brought to the school a collection of fooldom's bizarrest outsiders, misfits, sadists and sociopaths. In the early years, most students succumbed to malnutrition, exposure or poisoned book pages. The recruitment and selection of staff is still carried out to M. Pune's specification – a grand tradition which has been upheld to this day, although with Lord Vetinari's imposed health and safety guidelines, far more students now survive to graduate. Those who graduate in mime, however, generally don't last long after going down. In the early days, students were recruited from those who had failed to get entry to any of the city's other schools, colleges and Guilds. Although the Fools' Guild offered, and still offers, a high standard of general education, having a child who is to qualify as a bit of a prat still carries a certain social stigma and it is only very strange parents and, of course, Fools who send their children to the Guild.

Nevertheless, most of the Disc's fools, jesters, minstrels, idiots and mimes herald from Ankh-Morpork's Guild. Indeed, in 1788, it bought out La Sorbumme and now runs that as a summer school.

The Guild holds a strange position in city society. Most of the city's wealthy and nobility now avoid contact with the Guild and its officers, but, because of the enormous donations made by M. Pune, the Guild retains a high status on the City Council, though Doctor Whiteface tends to be treated like the leader of a political party that will never get to form a government.

THE JOLLY GOOD PALS (THE BLOODY FOOLS)

Comedy requires discipline, and discipline *is* the discipline of the Jolly Good Pals, the Guild's enforcers, who are universally known by their nickname of The Bloody Fools.

Not so long ago they would be required to police fooldom in vigilant search for tellers of unregistered jokes, lack of prescribed honking and unlicensed foolery of all kinds. Since they were often a long way from the Guild their response had to be swift and memorable, which it certainly was in the case of the Cement Down the Trousers, the 'Custard' Pie and, of course, the Seesaw of Jolly Japes. Very few clowns ever got on that a second time.

Captain Billy 'Clapstick Jack' Nodger and his men patrol the Guild buildings and major places of entertainment and will deal with transgressions in immediate and (to bystanders at least) amusing ways.

A FOOL'S DAY

When the Guild was first set up, a Fool's life was a very hard one. A typical summer regime was:

> 1.30 a.m.
> Rise

2.00 a.m.
Nocturnal Jocularity (pillow fights, 'apple pie' beds, buckets over doors)

3.30 a.m.
Puns

5.30 a.m.
Breaking of Wind

6.00 a.m.
Lectio (Recital of the Known Jokes)
Chapter Meeting
Specialist work and lectures

8.00 a.m.
Locus Publicus (Public Joking, in the quadrangle)
Reading

11.30 a.m.
Crusta et Bracae Laxae (slapstick humour, lit.: pies and loose trousers)
Dinner
Rest

2.30 p.m.
Vesicae et Tintinnabulae (bladders and bells)
The Merry Jests
Supper

6.00 p.m.
Liber Caerulus (Jokes for Adults)
The Eighteen Pratfalls

8.00 p.m.
Comploratus (wailing and honking)

8.15 p.m.
Retire to Bed

However, the Guild has moved with the times. Merry Jests are no longer compulsory, and clowns may go for a walk instead. Breaking of wind is allowable at any time. Nor are the rising and retiring times so rigid. Indeed, in the summer, students are often still copying out the Great Approved Jokes into their exercise books until well after nine in the evening and in winter the day's programme doesn't usually start until well after 5.30 a.m.

SLOSHI – THE FOOL'S MARTIAL ART

Even a cursory glance at a clowning routine will reveal the carefully moderated insane violence underneath it, and *Sloshi* is, in a nutshell, clowning without the moderation.

It had its origins in the travelling clowning companies of Überwäld, where competing troupes would duel for the choicer sites. Eventually this became formalized amongst student clowns in the mountain areas around Müning, where the scars of a *sloshi* fighter were worn with pride (only in very informal company, however, since *sloshi* garb involved protective padding everywhere but the buttocks; showing the proud scars of battle became known, after the area, as 'müning').

This was a highly stylized form of *sloshi*, making much use of the slapstick and pie, but battle *sloshi* is a different matter. Several Guild battalions have taken part in the defence of Ankh-Morpork during past wars, reaping a terrible revenge on enemies who literally died laughing. Indeed, the Guild Hall of Fame records that Uncle Bootsie, a *sloshi* master of the Seventh Nose, despatched seventeen Pseudopolitan mercenaries in one melee using nothing more than a ladder and two buckets of common wallpaper paste. In addition, forty-one mercenaries who witnessed the act were overpowered by the rest of the battalion while help-less with laughter.

It is strange but instructive to contrast the Guild with the ASSASSINS' GUILD next door. One is a pleasant, airy building, whose corridors echo with the laughter of students and hum with the quiet activity of people working hard in a job they love – the other is gaunt, forbidding and silent except for the occasional muffled sob. One leaves its gates open most of the time and its graduates are considered to brighten up any party – the other operates its wretched craft behind locked doors and its members are regarded with disdain by right-thinking people. One turns out people who, admittedly, must in the course of their duties sometimes stab, poison or otherwise inhume their patients, but at least they never ask them to believe that pouring whitewash down someone's trousers is funny.

Foot-the-ball. Also known as Poore boys' Funne, or football. The game became a key element of the events of *Unseen Academicals*.

At the time, the game seemed at first to be all about mobs in the streets, kicking and punching and yelling. And the spectators were nearly as bad. There were hundreds of men in a team and a game could go on for days.

In the general melee, it became almost impossible to score an actual goal – most people never managed one in their lives. In the old game, the most number of goals scored by one man in his whole life is four. That was Dave Likely.

The old game of football was about more than the rules and the nature of the play. The chanting and the food were an integral part of the game, as were the teams, such as the Pigsty Hill Pork Packers, Dimwell Old Pals and Naphill Untied, each of which had supporters' clubs. Clubs might seem to be a good thing, but, sadly, they used to hit one another over the head with them. It would be true to say that mindless violence was one of the cornerstones of the sport.

The chanting, also, had a certain power, coming, as it is now believed, from hymns to the goddess to grant her favours to the team of choice.

The nature and content of the game changed, however, when the original rules of foot-the-ball were apparently discovered, as laid down a thousand years previously, when the game was played in honour of the goddess Pedestriana. [UA]

Forefather, Edward. Purveyor of fine beers, stouts and ales in the Effing Forest. His whimsical location is the only reason he made it into this book. [RS]

Forest of Skund. Enchanted forest rimwards of the RAMTOPS. The only forest in the entire universe to be called 'Your finger, you fool', the literal meaning of the word *Skund*. When the first explorers from the warm lands around the CIRCLE SEA travelled into the chilly hinterland they filled in the blank spaces on their maps by grabbing the nearest native, pointing at some distant landmark, speaking very clearly in a loud voice and writing down whatever the bemused man told them. Thus were immortalized in generations of atlases such geographical oddities as Just a Mountain and I Don't Know, What? This is known as the 'surly native' technique of map-making. [LF]

Fornacite, Teasy-Weasy, Mr. A troll hairdresser in Ankh-Morpork. This renowned hair stylist is a lovely blue-green colour. He counts among his clients, Adora Belle DEARHEART. [RS]

Fox, Cassandra. Pupil at the Quirm College for Young Ladies. A rather horsey gel. [SM]

Frank, Mister. Card sharp on the Vieux River riverboats, until he played Cripple Mr Onion against Granny Weatherwax. [WA]

Fredor. Landlord of the Crimson Leech in Morpork. [COM]

Fresh Start Club. Motto: *UNDEAD, YES – UNPERSON, NO.* A club for those who are having difficulty in relating to being undead, founded by Reg SHOE, a zombie; it met at 668 Elm Street, Ankh-Morpork, on the first floor, above a tailor's shop. The entrance to the club was via an alleyway, at the end of which was a wooden door with a notice saying: 'Come In! Come In! The Fresh Start Club. Being Dead is only the Beginning!!!' Club slogans, all devised by Reg, include: 'Dead Yes! Gone No!', 'Spooks of the World Arise, You Have Nothing to Lose but your Chains', 'The Silent Majority want Dead Rights' and 'End Vitalism Now!' A sad place. Most of its members were embarrassed by the whole business but kept coming along so as not to upset Reg; the club is his whole life. As it were. Now that Reg has enthusiastically embraced a new life – as it were – in the WATCH, it is not known whether the club was still in existence. [RM]

Fresnel's Wonderful Concentrator. Spell used to create the flying lens on which RINCEWIND and TWOFLOWER are taken to KRULL. The spell calls for many rare and unstable ingredients, such as demon's breath, and it takes eight fourth-grade wizards to envision. The lens itself is 20 feet across and totally transparent, with

rings, onto which passengers and the twenty-four HYDROPHOBES strap themselves, and a stubby pillar dead centre. [COM]

Fri'it, Iam. Officer who ran most of the Omnian Divine Legion. He clicked his knuckles when worried, which was often. History remembers him as a fairly honest soldier who fell among priests and politicians. [SG]

Froc, Iam, General. Borogravian Army. Handsome, with a fine head of white hair and a scar down one side of his face, which just missed an eye and shows up clearly against the wrinkles. The General had the Frock coat and the Beef Froc named after him. Known, to some close friends, as Mildred. [MR]

Frord, Grisham. Leader of the Grisham Frord Close Harmony Singers, a cappella assassins and crack enforcers for the MUSICIANS' GUILD. [SM]

Frottidge, Violet. One of DIAMANDA's coven in LANCRE. (*See also* MAGENTA.) [LL]

Frostrip. Only in this book because he is a Guild Head. The Guild of Accountants and Usurers. [J]

Frout, Madam. Headmistress of the Frout Academy in Esoteric Street, Ankh-Morpork, and pioneer of the Frout Method of Learning Through Fun. Miss Frout, with her spectacles on a string around her neck, is not by any means a bad person and she is quite kind to children, in a haphazard way. However, she is rather silly and not a very good disciplinarian, which is a source of conflict with one of her teachers, Susan STO HELIT, who isn't and is. She had once been a good, if rather shy, teacher. [TOT]

Fruni. Prophet of the Omnian religion. [SG]

Fruntkin. Dwarf who worked as a short-order chef in Nodar Borgle the Klatchian's canteen in Holy Wood. [MP]

'*Fullomyth*'. An invaluable aid for all those whose business is with the arcane and hermetic. It contains lots of things that don't exist and, in a very significant way, aren't important. Some of its pages can be read only after midnight, or by strange and improbable illuminations. There are descriptions of underground constellations and wines as yet unfermented (*see* RE-ANNUAL PLANTS). For the really up-to-the-epoch occultist, who can afford the version bound in spider skin, there is even an insert showing the London Underground with three stations they never dare show on public maps. [S]

Furgle. Dwarf owner of a horn which sounded itself when danger was near, and also in the presence of, for some reason, horseradish. [SM]

Furies. An Ephebian species. Skinny women, winged – with claws and feathers. Their faces are really strange, as if someone has made a bird out of a woman. The ones encountered in *Unseen Academicals* are members of the Little Sisters of Perpetual Velocity. [UA]

Fusspot, Mr. A small, waddly, ugly dog with soulful eyes and a yappy bark, once owned by Topsy LAVISH. It reminds people of those goldfish with huge, bulging eyes that look as if they are about to explode. Its nose looks stoved in, it wheezes, and its legs are so bandy that it must sometimes trip over its own feet. Mrs Lavish left Mr Fusspot shares in the Royal Bank of Ankh-Morpork. She then left the dog himself to Moist von LIPWIG. Mr Fusspot was last seen in the company of Lord Vetinari. [MM]

In Mrs Whitlow's book, gods were socially very acceptable, at least if they had proper human heads and wore clothes...

– The Last Continent

Gaiter Family. Family for whom Susan STO HELIT worked as governess. Mr Gaiter was very successful in the wholesale boot and shoe business; Mrs Gaiter read books on etiquette and worried about whether a serviette should be called a napkin, especially since her husband persisted in not using either. Their children were Twyla and Gawain, which shows the damage that can be done when untrained people are let loose with a book of baby names. [H]

Gak. A really old zombie in the employ of Evil Harry DREAD. [TLH]

Galena. A troll who worked in the clicks in HOLY WOOD. His screen name was Rock Cliffe, although he had been considering calling himself Flint and having a cement nose-job. (In *Men At Arms*, a Flint was working in the armoury and later joined the WATCH, but there are not a great many troll names and it might well be a different Flint.) Galena has pointed ears, a nose that looks like Neanderthal Man's first attempt at an axe, and a fist the size and hardness of a foundation stone. [MP]

Gamblers' Guild. Motto: *EXCRETVS EX FORTVNA* (loosely speaking: 'Really Out of Luck'). Coat of arms: a shield, gyronny. On its panels, turnwise from upper sinister: a sabre or on a field sable; an octagon gules et argent on a field azure; a tortue vert on a field sable; an 'A'

couronnée on a field argent; a sceptre d'or on a field sable, a calice or on a field azure; a piece argent on a field gules; an elephant gris on a field argent. The arms represent the eight suits of the classic Ankh-Morpork pack of cards.

The Guildhouse is in the Street of Alchemists. Current President (chosen by the draw of a card) is Scrote Jones.

Guild membership is small, because it is restricted to professional gamblers. The Guild mainly exists to enforce rules about marked cards, loaded dice, shaved billiard balls and so on. Note that it does not *ban* them, it merely regularizes the size of marks and weight of dice and closeness of shave. (Since all professional gamblers use these items, a game between any two of them means that they are cancelled out and the contest becomes, perforce, a matter of skill and luck.) The Guild also controls very strictly the amount of money a member may take from a non-member (a 'mark') in any game; in the words of Scrote Jones, 'If you want to make money out of keeping sheep you don't rip their hides off all in one go'. There are plenty of customers in Ankh-Morpork, where the basic gambling survival rules appear to be unknown. (Never play Find the Lady; play cards against anyone named after a city or gamble in any game against anyone called Doc.)

Games. Disc games include:

Aargrooha. Troll game, played with obsidian boots and a human head. Not played any more, of course, except in remote mountain regions. [SM]

Aqueduct (or is it Fishing Line/Weir/ Dam?) Rules include mention of trumps, ruffs, trump return, trump lead, contract, psychic bids, rebiddable suit, double finesse, grand slam and rubbers. [LF]

Barbarian Invaders, see BARBARIAN INVADERS MACHINE

Chase My Neighbour Up the Passage. Details have never been given, but it appears to be a simple game like Old Maid or Happy Families. [WA, W]

Chess, and Stealth Chess (Assassins) [AGD]

Craps. Dice game played with three eight-sided dice, and probably similar in general rules and terminology to our craps, although since it is played on the cobbles of Ankh-Morpork the name may have a rather more honest origin. [M]

CRIPPLE MR ONION

Crockett. Invented by novice priest Jackson Fieldfair at St. Onan's Theological College. [SN]

Darts. Effectively the standard British game, although the Ankh-Morpork rules specifically ban leaning out over the oche and hammering the darts in with your fingertip while exclaiming 'Ook!' [RM]

Dead Rat Conkers [T!]

Exclusive Possession. Game once played by Death instead of the symbolic chess game. Reference is made to another player getting 'three streets and all the utilities'. One of the playing pieces is a boot. We can only guess at what the board looks like... [RM]

Floods and Droughts (played only by gods). [IT]

Foot-the-Ball (Poor Boys' Funne) [UA]

Grandmother's Footsteps [H]

Hooray Jolly Tinker [H]

Mad Kings (another god game) [IT]

Mighty Empires (yet another god game) [IT]

Pond. Game played on a table with holes and nets around the edge and, in rural areas, balls carved expertly out of wood. [RM]

Saddle Pork [SN]

Shibo Yangcong-san (Learned readers will instantly recognize that this appears to be the Agatean of Cripple Mr Onion.) [IT]

Significant Quest. Very popular among gods, demi-gods, demons and other supernatural creatures. [S]

Star-Crossed Lovers (these gods certainly like to play games!) [IT]

Thud!

Tiddley Rats [T!]

Turd Races (Poo Sticks) [T!]

Wallgame. Played at the Assassins' Guild, usually two or three storeys above street level. [P]

Gancia. Leader of the gang of mercenaries led by HERRENA on their mission to capture Rincewind for Ymper TRYMON. A fairly long explanatory note for someone whose job was, basically, to die at the right time. [LF]

Gander, Adab. Trail boss of the caravanserai which transported ESK from Zemphis to Ankh-Morpork. An impressive figure in a troll-hide jerkin, rakishly floppy hat and leather kilt. Trollhide as a type of very hard-wearing leather – in fact, a flexible type of stone – is certainly not polically correct wear in Ankh-Morpork these days. Or a survival suit, if it comes to that. [ER]

Gargoyles. An urban species of troll, which has evolved a symbiotic relationship with gutters, funnelling run-off water into their ears and out through fine sieves in their mouths. This means their mouths can never fully close and their speech is only intelligible to a trained ear. Gargoyles often spend years without moving from one spot and do not have names so much as locations or descriptions (see CORNICE OVERLOOKING BROADWAY). When they do move it is in a jerky fashion, like bad stop-motion photography. Few birds nest on buildings colonized by gargoyles, and bats also tend to fly around them.

Garhartra. Guestmaster of Krull. His job is to make sacrificial victims feel comfortable, at least up to the point just before they are sacrificed. A wizard, with a cracked yet cheerful voice. [COM]

Garlick, Magrat. A witch in LANCRE. The youngest member (comparatively speaking) of the coven that Granny Weatherwax swears she has not got. Magrat had a cottage in Mad Stoat, but she now lives in LANCRE CASTLE, as Queen to VERENCE II, after a romance which was always on the point of foundering because the principals were invariably too embarrassed to speak to each other. They must have said something, however, since now they have produced an heir – the Princess Esmerelda Margaret Note Spelling (don't ask). In becoming Queen, Nanny Ogg and Granny Weatherwax both feel she has settled for second prize.

Magrat is the daughter of Simplicity Garlick, now deceased. Her grandmother was Araminta Garlick, and her aunt Yolande Garlick. None of her relations was a witch, which is unusual. Although by tradition witches do not train their relations, witchcraft tends to run in families. Magrat is an original. Her unusual name is down to a misunderstanding over the spelling at her naming ceremony, presided over by

Brother Perdore; her own daughter's unusual name just goes to show that, despite everyone's best efforts, things tend to keep on going wrong.

Magrat was selected and trained by Goodie WHEMPER, a methodical and sympathetic witch with a rather greater regard for the written word than is common among the Lancre witches. Goodie was a research witch; she may have had some long-term aim in mind.

In a certain light, and from a carefully chosen angle, Magrat Garlick is not unattractive. Despite her tendency to squint when she's thinking, and her pointy nose, red from too much blowing. She is short, thin, decently plain, well scrubbed and has the watery-eyed expression of hopeless goodwill wedged between a body like a maypole and hair like a haystack after a gale. No matter what she does to that hair, it takes about three minutes to tangle itself up again, like a garden hosepipe left in a shed. She likes to wind flowers in it, because she thinks this is romantic. In some other kind of hair it might be.

Magrat has an open mind. It is as open as a field, as open as the sky. No mind could be more open without special surgical implements. As a result, it fills up with all sorts of things. For example, Magrat is one of those people who firmly believe that wisdom is wiser if it comes from a long way away (see WISDOM). A lot of what she believes in has the word 'folk' in it somewhere (folk wisdom, folk dance, folk song, folk medicine), as if 'folk' were other than the mundane people she sees every day. She plays a guitar badly and sings wobbly folk songs with her eyes shut in a way that suggests she really believes them. She thinks it would be nice if people could just be a bit kinder.

She is a relentless doer of good works, whether or not anyone needs them or wants them to be done. She rescues small lost baby birds and cries when they die; at various times, trying to get into the swing of it, she has attempted to keep a magical familiar – generally some small creature that wanders away or dies or just gets the hell out of it at the earliest opportunity.

She is, however, more practical than most

people believe. And latterly there is some evidence that marriage and motherhood are burning away some of the deeper layers of silliness. However, she still quite likes flowers in her hair. These days, she can afford slightly more expensive flowers. [WS]

Gaskin, Herbert 'Leggy'. A member of the City Watch. Killed in the line of duty. His widow lives in Mincing Street, Ankh-Morpork. [GG]

Gaspode (the Wonder Dog). Small, bow-legged and wiry; basically a rusty grey but with patches of brown, white and black in outlying areas. Gaspode has fleas, hardpad, scurf, crusted yellow eyes, arthritis, rotting teeth and horrible bad breath, and is probably the only dog to contract Licky End, which is usually restricted to sheep. In fact he is host to so many doggy diseases that he is surrounded by a cloud of dust and, all in all, smells like a privy carpet.

He is named after the original 'famous' Gaspode, who belonged to an old man in Ankh many years ago. When his owner died and was buried, the dog lay down on his grave and howled and howled for a couple of weeks, growling at everyone who came near. Then he died. He was considered a paragon of doggy faithfulness and loyalty until it was discovered that his tail had been trapped under the stone.

Gaspode was thrown into the river with a brick in a sack when he was a pup. Luckily, it was the ANKH, so he walked ashore inside the sack, forming for several days a certain confused relationship with the brick.

Gaspode encapsulates the essential schizophrenia of all dogs. On the one hand, he desires nothing more than to be owned, to have a master and in general have a very secure warm place in front of the fire of life; on the other hand, he rebels against the very idea of ownership and any restriction on his freedom to roam Ankh-Morpork, eating and rolling in whatever he likes. Gaspode's tragedy is that, unlike other dogs, he is aware of this conflict.

Oh, and he can talk. But not many people pay any attention, because everyone knows that dogs can't talk. [MP]

Gavin. A large wolf, and friend to ANGUA. Uncomplicated and well informed (he could understand over 800 words). [TFE]

Geas. A bird, with a head like a flamingo, a body like a turkey and legs like a Sumo wrestler. It walks in a jerky, bobbing fashion, as though its head were attached to its feet by elastic bands. Its prime means of defence is to cause a predator to laugh so much that it can run away before the predator recovers. *Geas* is also a word meaning curse or obligation. [S]

Genetics. The study of genetics on the Disc has never been very organized. The wizard Catbury (some 300 years before the present) is on record as having noticed, while strolling in his garden, that some plants were taller than other plants and, interestingly enough, that some plants were shorter than other plants. The response to his monograph on the subject can be summed up as 'Yes? Well? So what?', because Ankh-Morporkians have that logical and common-sense approach to life which means that Science is beaten before it starts.

Nevertheless, Catbury's writings remain in the LIBRARY and there were, later, some experiments based on his simple observations. These failed at an early stage, however, when wizards tried the experimental crossing of such well-known subjects as fruit flies and sweet peas. Unfortunately, they didn't quite grasp the fundamentals, and the resultant offspring – a sort of green thing that buzzed – led a short, sad life before being eaten by a passing vegetarian spider.

In any case a more dispassionate study of the evidence suggests that on the Discworld heredity is more mental than genetic, and certainly owes more to Lamarck than Mendel. The observation of the current ARCHCHANCELLOR, Mustrum RIDCULLY, that heredity means 'that if your father has a good brocade waistcoat you'll probably end up getting it' contains a certain amount of truth. In *Soul Music*, DEATH becomes encumbered with a granddaughter, Susan STO HELIT (daughter of his adopted daughter YSABELL and MORT), who has

Gaspode

certainly acquired his powers of invisibility and memory. On Discworld, cutting off the tails of mice might well lead to them having tail-less offspring. And probably vengeful ones, too.

Something that appears more like a high-speed conventional evolution, or at least like conventional evolution is commonly understood, has been engineered by the God of Evolution on an island near Fourecks. Plants there try to make themselves as useful as possible as quickly as possible in the hope of being taken off the island, and on at least one occasion a dinosaur evolved into a bird in a fraction of a second.

Genua. The Magical Kingdom, the Diamond City, the Fortunate Country. Genua was originally a pleasant and relaxed place in which to live but, under the iron rule of Lily WEATHER-WAX, it became a fairytale city; this meant that people had to smile and be joyful the livelong day – at spearpoint, if necessary.

Genua nestles on the delta of the Vieux river, surrounded by swamp. It is a wealthy kingdom, having once controlled the river mouth and taxed its traffic. It has always been rich, lazy and unthreatened. From a distance, it looks like a complicated white crystal growing out of the greens and browns of the swamp.

Close to, there is an outer ring of small buildings, an inner ring of large, impressive white houses and, at the centre, a palace – tall, pretty and multi-turreted, like a toy castle. Under Lily, everything was very clean. Even the cobblestones had a polished look. The city was guarded by tall soldiers in red and blue uniforms. The place looked, in fact, like a fairy-tale city ... with all the horrors that implies.

Both before, during and since the Weatherwax period Genua has also been a city of cooks. They don't have much to cook there, so they have learned to cook everything. A good Genuan cook can more or less take the squeezings of a handful of mud, a few dead leaves and a pinch or two of some unpronounceable herbs and produce a meal to make the gourmet burst into tears of gratitude and swear to be a better person for the rest of their entire life if they could just have one more plateful. [WA]

Geoffrey. One-time Secretary and Chief Butt of the Guild of Fools and Joculators. A Fool. He had eyes like two runny eggs and a very nervous disposition, as is often the case when you do not know where the next custard pie is coming from. [RM]

George, Sir. A nobleman in Ankh. [MAA]

Gern. Apprentice embalmer in DJELIBEYBI. A plump young man with a big, red, spotty face. He is fond of all the practical jokes you can play with the sad remnants of mortality, such as the disembodied handshake gag and all the other little delights so familiar to generations of medical students. [P]

Gibbsson. Apprentice guitar-maker in the employ of Blert WHEEDOWN. [SM]

Gilt, Reacher. Chairman and CEO of the Grand Trunk Company ('As Fast As Light'). A lot of rumours had begun concerning Reacher Gilt, just as soon as people had noticed him and started asking 'Who is Reacher Gilt? What kind of a name is Reacher, anyway?' He threw big parties, that was certain. They were the kind of parties that entered urban mythology (was it true about the chopped liver?). Some said he owned a gold mine, others swore that he was a pirate. And he certainly looked like a pirate, with his long, curly, black hair, pointed beard and eyepatch. He was even said to have a parrot (this is true – a cockatoo called Alphonse, who says '12½ per cent'). Certainly the piracy rumour might explain the apparently bottomless fortune and the fact that no one, absolutely no one, knew anything about him prior to his arrival in the city. Perhaps he'd sold his past, people joked, just like he'd bought himself a new one. He was certainly piratical in his business dealing,

With his big head, flowing black hair and beard, he also looked like a better class of pirate, a buccaneer maybe, but one who took the time to polish his plank. He was a great bear of a man, in a frock coat and striped waistcoat.

Later, briefly, styled himself 'Randolph Stippler'. [GP]

Gimick. One of the many cousins of Lance-Constable CUDDY. A manufacturer of pins. [MAA]

Gimlet. A dwarf with a famously penetrating gaze who runs a café and delicatessen in Cable Street, Ankh-Morpork, as well as another dwarf deli, and 'Yo Rat!' in Attic Bee Street. It used to be for dwarfs only but under the influence of civic decency, a sense of the brotherhood of all sapient species and a desire to get some of the 'troll dollar', it has subsequently catered for that species as well. Try their rat and cream cheese. For vegetarians, they do a soya rat.

By Ankh-Morpork standards, Gimlet's is a well-run and hygienic eatery, although he has been caught substituting 'rats' carved out of pork, beef and mutton when the real thing was in short supply. [RM]

Ginger. See WITHEL, THEDA.

Ginnungagap. The name given by the History MONKS for the darkness at the end of the world, before the new world takes its place. [RS]

Gladdybone, Mr. A resident of Sto Lat who caused a scandal when he used the language of flowers* to incense the local folkloreist, Miss Mellifera Buster, by the arrangement of his flowerbeds. After the scandal died down, there were rumours that Miss Buster had invented some of the lewder definitions herself. The two later married. [NOCB]

---

* *A system by which a gardener can use and combine the often obscure meanings of plants and flowers to convey complex messages.*

and its sole job is to the make the 'glingleglingleglingle' noise which heralds the arrival of any other fairy. It may also toss up the handful of chopped tinsel which makes those little twinkly glints in the air, you know the ones. Sometimes fairies have their work cut out to live up to human expectations.

Glod. A dwarf, the tangential victim of a curse placed on the Seriph of AL-YBI (everything he touched turned into Glod, which shows how important it is, when cursing, to check your spelling). His son, Glod GLODSSON, later found employment as a horn player in Ankh-Morpork. [WA]

Glodsson, Glod. A dwarf. Small, even for a dwarf. He has lodgings behind a tannery in Phedre Road and plays a large bronze horn. A member of the BAND WITH ROCKS IN who considers himself to be an extremely professional musician, in that money is always on his mind. [SM]

Glooper, the. The Glooper, as it is affectionately known, is an 'analogy machine'. It solves problems not by considering them as a numerical exercise but by actually duplicating them in a form that can be manipulated – in this case, the flow of money and its effects within society becomes water flowing though a glass matrix – the Glooper. The geometrical shape of certain vessels, the operation of valves and ingenious

Gladys. A seven foot tall, thousand-year-old golem. Named Gladys by Miss Maccalariat, so that it could clean the ladies' rest room at the Post Office. Miss Maccalariat, who ruled the Post Office counters with a rod of steel and lungs of brass, had objected to a male golem cleaning the ladies' privies. How Miss Maccalariat had arrived at the conclusion that they were male by nature rather than custom was a fascinating mystery, but there was no profit in arguing with such as her.

And thus, with the addition of one extremely large, blue gingham dress, a golem became female enough for Miss Maccalariat.

The odd thing is that Gladys *is* female now, somehow. It isn't just the dress. She tends to spend time around the counter girls, who seem to accept her into the sisterhood despite the fact that she weighs half a ton. They even pass on their fashion magazine to her, although it's hard to imagine what winter skin care tips would mean to someone a thousand years old with eyes that glow like holes into a furnace. [GP]

Gleet, Henry, Lord and Lady. Guests at the ball in Genua on Samedi Nuit Mort. [WA]

Glingleglingleglingle Fairy, the. While there are many FAIRIES, this one deserves a special mention as a sort of meta-fairy. It is generally a gnome or small goblin, with a set of handbells, tipping buckets and flow-rate propellers enable the Glooper to simulate quite complex transactions. It is also possible to change the starting conditions, too, to learn the rules inherent in the system. For example, one could find out what would happen if you halved the labour force in the city by the adjustment of a few valves, rather than going out into the streets and killing people! The Glooper had been worked on by glassblowing geniuses – and by their counterparts from the hypothetical Other Side, glassblowers who had sold their souls to some molten god for the skill to blow glass into spirals and intersecting bottles and shapes that seemed to be quite close but some distance away at the same time. Water gurgled, sloshed and, yes, glooped along glass tubing. There was a smell of salt. [MM]

Glwenda. The daughter of a garlic farmer in DJELIBEYBI. Romantically linked with GERN the apprentice embalmer. [P]

Gnolls. A softer-skinned variety of troll, but without the latter's intelligence and noble disposition. A few are now moving into Ankh-Morpork. They are scavengers, both as a means of eating and also for more complex, hard-to-understand reasons; they'll make careful collections of old spoons or dead seagulls, which appear to be extremely significant to both themselves and other gnolls. It is believed that the huge foetid heaps carried on the bent backs of gnolls are not, in fact, some kind of carapace but are their worldly goods. [ER]

Gnomes, goblins (and pictsies) A more or less interchangeable term (a gnome is merely a goblin found underground, a goblin is merely a gnome coming up for air, a pictsie is a gnome fighting) for the Discworld's smallest (4" to 2') humanoid species.

Seldom encountered, not because of their rarity but because of their speed and natural desire to keep out of the way of creatures to whom they would merely be something sticky on the sole of the boot – although a well-trained gnome, with that strength so often found in small creatures, can in fact lift a human being. They are generally hunters and gatherers, usually of property belonging to someone else.

This entry is left here for completeness; since the first *Companion*, GOBLINS have been specifically identified as a separate species and they began to play a bigger part in the later stories – *see* separate entry below.

Gnomon. An Ehebian philosopher, and author of 'Ectopia'. [SG]

Goatberger, Mr. Publisher in Ankh-Morpork. Responsible for publishing, among other books, Nanny OGG's 'The Joye of Snacks'. An honest, helpful man, who cares nothing for profit and seeks only to enrich the cultural environment of his fellow men. A typical publisher in every way, in fact. [MA]

Goatfounder, Hilta. A witch in OHULAN CUTASH, where she sells thunderdrops and penny wishes at a small, covered, market stall. Small and fat, Hilta wears an enormous hat with fruit on it and gives the impression of a mass of lace and shawls and colours and earrings and ordinary rings, and so many bangles that a mere movement of her arms sounds like a percussion section falling off a cliff. She laughs like someone who has thought about life for a long time and has now seen the joke.

Her lodgings are over a herbalist and behind a tannery, offering splendid views over the rooftops of Ohulan. Among her 'back of the stall' preparations are: Tiger Oil, Maiden's Prayer, Husband's Helper, ShoNuff Ointment, Stay

Long Ointment and Madame Goatfounder's Pennyroyal Preventatives. She performs an important function in the town, although no one talks very much about what that actually is. The only clue is that, if Hilta wasn't there, the town would be a good deal larger. [ER]

Goblins. The first thing people notice about goblins is the smell. Once you get over the shock, it actually isn't too bad. The compensation for the odour, and goblins' less than lovely appearance, is that they are great workers. They don't just like their work, they love it – and they have taken the clacks system to their scrawny hearts. The wheels and levers fascinate them. They have improved the efficiency of the clacks across the Sto Plains by threefold. They are, in fact, the reason why clacks traffic is now so much faster, more accurate and streamlined. They also take care of the rat and mouse infestations.

The villains of storybooks have found their place in society at last; all it needed – was technology.

With all goblins, the male ones especially, you get the impression of sinews, but they mostly consist of sinews tied together with other sinews. Surely, the mind protests, there must be muscles in there somewhere, but quite possibly they had to fight to find some room among all the damn sinews.

Goblins value their complex names, and they must always be addressed using the full name – Of the Twilight the Darkness, Of the Chimney the Bones, Of the Lathe the Swarf, Of the Happiness the Heart. Using a part, or half, name is shame for them, and is seen as the challenge for a fight.

The correct name for a group of goblins is a malignity. Perhaps this will change as they take their place in society.

Godmothers, Fairy. A specialized form of witch with particular responsibility for the life of one individual or a number of individuals. They use wands – probably a modification of the wizard's staff – and tend to have an interest in travel. Fairy godmothers develop a very deep understanding of human nature, which makes the good ones kind and the bad ones powerful. [WA]

Gods, the. The Discworld has gods in the same way that other worlds have bacteria. There are billions of them, tiny bundles containing nothing more than a pinch of pure ego and some hunger.

Most of them never get worshipped. They are the small gods – the spirits of lonely trees, places where two ant-trails cross – and most of them stay that way. Because what they lack is belief. A handful, though, go on to greater things. Anything may trigger this. A shepherd, seeking a lost lamb, for example, may find it among the briars and take a minute or two to build a small cairn of stones in general thanks to whatever spirit might be around the place.

Despite the splendour of the world below them, the Disc gods are seldom satisfied. It is embarrassing to know that one is a god of a world that only exists because every improbability curve must have its far end; especially when one can peer into other dimensions at worlds whose Creators had more mechanical aptitude than imagination. No wonder, then, that the Disc gods spend more time bickering than in omnicognisance.

They are quarrelsome and somewhat bourgeois gods, who live in a palace of marble, alabaster and uncut moquette three-piece suites they choose to call DUNMANIFESTIN. It is always a considerable annoyance to any Disc citizen with pretensions to culture that they are ruled by gods whose idea of an uplifting artistic experience is a musical doorbell.

The gods don't play chess, they haven't got the imagination. They prefer simple, vicious games, where you 'Do Not Pass Transcendence but Go Straight to Oblivion'; a key to the understanding of all religion is that a god's idea of amusement is Snakes and Ladders with greased rungs.

They are great believers in justice, at least as far as it extends to humans, and have been known to dispense it so enthusiastically that people miles away are turned into a cruet.

The trouble with gods is that, if enough people start believing in them, they begin to exist. People think the sequence is: first object, then belief. In fact it works the other way. Belief sloshes around in the firmament like lumps of clay spiralling into a potter's wheel. That's how gods get created. They clearly must be created by their own believers, because a brief résumé of the lives of most gods suggests that their origins certainly couldn't be divine. They tend to do exactly the things people would do if only they could, especially when it comes to nymphs, golden showers and the smiting of your enemies.

Gods and humans are inseparable. Because what gods need is belief, and what humans want is gods. (*See also* DEITIES.)

Gogol, Erzulie, Mrs. A voodoo woman in GENUA, who smokes a pipe and is known to have made use of zombies when household chores need doing. She is tall, handsome, middle-aged, and wears heavy gold earrings, a white blouse and a full red skirt with flounces. She has a black cockerel, Legba, as her familiar. She used to be linked romantically with Baron SATURDAY, who was later a zombie, and is the mother of Ella SATURDAY.

For practical purposes she can be consid-

ered a witch, although perhaps with a slightly different moral sense from that of the classic RAMTOPS craftswomen.

She foretells the future ostensibly by staring into bowls of jambalaya (but probably by relying on close observation and a deep study of human nature – all witches understand the need for a little magic in people's lives).

She lives in a house in the swamps close to Genua. From the river it looks like a simple affair of driftwood, roofed with moss and built over the swamp itself on four stout poles. They end in four large duck feet on which the house can, when necessary, move around the country. [WA]

Golems. One of the rarest of Ankh-Morpork's minority groups, and unique in that for years it had not been found anywhere outside the city. The original golem builders are now known to have come from the ancient city of UM.

They can hardly be called a 'species', since golems are created by priests or holy men from clay animated by a spell (or holy word). The word or spell is carved on their forehead or inserted in their hollow head and is, in effect, their life force. Highly moral creatures.

No such creation has been attempted by humans for a thousand years, it being held to be a little tasteless, but the events recounted in *Feet of Clay* reveal that there is a third group that can create golems, and that is golems themselves. All they need is some more clay, an oven and a Word. There are no such things as golem children, merely golems who are younger than other golems.

Traditionally, even trolls have looked

down on golems, who tend to be (physically) larger and more shapeless even than computer programmers, and (mentally) withdrawn and rather sad, yet very alert creatures, doomed to do the jobs that men disdain and trolls don't want; not for nothing are they called 'horny-handed tons of soil'. A golem is not legally a living creature, merely property...

But now, the golems are freeing themselves. It's the quietest, most socially responsible revolution in history. Legally they are tools – property – and so, often supported by the GOLEM TRUST, they save up and *buy* themselves.

A golem must not harm a human being or allow a human being to come to harm – unless ordered to do so by a Duly Constituted Authority.

Golem Trust, the. Motto: *by our own hand, or none.* A charitable foundation set up by Adora Belle Dearheart to help to free golems. What happens is that the free golems support the Trust, the Trust buys golems whenever it can, and the new golems then buy themselves from the Trust at cost. The free golems earn 24/8 and there are more and more of them. They don't eat, sleep, wear clothes or understand the concept of leisure. The occasional tube of ceramic cement doesn't cost much. They buy more golems every month now, and pay Adora Belle's wages, and the iniquitous rent the landlord charges her for their offices because he knows he's renting to golems.

Due to the pace of change in Ankh-Morpork, the golems are now quite happily trusting themselves. [GP]

Golightly, Dolly, Mrs. Mrs Dolly Golightly, the neighbour of Mrs COSMOPILITE, is Darkness Incarnate and the embodiment of all evil. Her sins are thicker than the stars in the sky, but largely consist of:

> Letting her cat scratch up Mrs Cosmopilite's flowerbed;
> Allowing her demonic henchman, Alfred, her lodger, to keep pigeons, which do their doo-dahs on Mrs Cosmopilite's washing;[*]
> Being no better than she should be;[**]
> Wearing a fur coat, because you know what that means;[***]
> Looking like mutton dressed as lamb;
> Acting all la–di-dah.

In the little mountain kingdom of Mutaran, which has adopted the Way as its state religion, there has been considerable debate about the nature of 'Acting all la-di-dah'. In the annual procession, various groups dance their own interpretations of 'Acting all la-di-dah', a sight that, once seen, is never forgotten. Mutaran is also the home of the Black Cult, who believe that, because of the universe's natu-

---

[*] *According to the scrolls in the Mrs Cosmopilitetist temple in Mutaran: 'So she says, but I've only ever seen one pair of sheets on their line, and I call that disgusting when her poor husband's hardly been dead the past nine years!'*

[**] *The sage Wy-won has written an 8000-word treatise on the implications of this statement.*

[***] *No Seeker has yet managed to find out what this means.*

ral tendency to balance, Mrs Dolly Golightly is equally worth of esteem and study. [LTD]

Gonnagle (Feegle). A gonnagle is the Feegle clan's bard and battle poet, but they don't spend all their lives in the same clan. In fact, they're a sort of clan all by themselves.

Gonnagles move around among the other clans, making sure the songs and stories get spread around all the Feegles. They are skilled (usually) at the mousepipes. They recite poems that frighten the enemy; when a well-trained gonnagle starts to recite, the enemy's ears explode.

The rage of a gonnagle is a dreadful thing to see. A gonnagle can use words like swords.

Two notable gonnagles are AWF'LY WEE BILLY BIGCHIN Mac Feegle and, of course, WILLIAM THE GONNAGLE.

Goodmountain, Gunilla. A dwarf, who opened a 'word smithy' at the sign of the Bucket in Gleam Street, Ankh-Morpork. Co-founder, with William DE WORDE, of 'The Ankh-Morpork Times'. Gunilla was later on husband ... er, wife ... er, *partner* to BODDONY. [TT]

Goom, 'Wazzer'. A volunteer, with Polly PERKS, to the Borogravian Army. When first encountered, he appears to be a small, nineteen-year-old, stick-thin lad with round eyes, a bad haircut and a reedy little voice. Wazzer is very religious and says grace loudly before meals. Stands just slightly too close to you and stares slightly to the left of your face – very disconcerting – as is the fact that Wazzer hears voices – in particular the Duchess ANNAGOVIA. Some friends call Wazzer 'Alice'. [MR]

Gordon, Ariadne. Friend of Sybil VIMES (nee Ramkin). She is keen to find suitable husbands for her girls. She had sextuplets: Mavis (very devout), Emily (excellent cook), Hermione (a lumberjack!), erm... Amanda (quite interested in frogs?), Fleur (loves bonnets – creates a range of them called... Gordon Bonnets), and Jane, who has aspirations to become a writer. [SN]

Gordo of Tsort. Philosopher who said that

sand was worn-down mountains. [SG]

Gorper. Male member of the FRESH START CLUB. [RM]

Gorphal. A bearded, elderly diplomat in Ankh-Morpork. Famed as a student of Agatean Empire affairs. [COM]

Gorrin the Cat. A thief in Ankh-Morpork. B12 was his code identification from YMOR. Called 'the Cat' because of his tendency to sleep a lot and not do much work. [COM]

Gortlick. A writer of dwarf songs with HAMMERJUG. Songs are important to the dwarf community and new ones are commissioned for birthdays, weddings and so on. Cynics say that the word 'gold' will inevitably turn up somewhere. It rhymes so easily with other words. Well, in fact it rhymes most easily with 'gold', but that's fine for dwarfs, who know what they like and like lots of it. [SM]

Gorunna Trench. An undersea chasm in the Disc's surface that is so black, so deep and so reputedly evil that even the krakens go there fearfully, and in pairs. In less reputedly evil chasms the fish go about with natural lights on their heads . In Gorunna they leave them unlit and, insofar as it is possible for something without legs to creep, they creep. No living thing knows what lies down there; those who have found out have not been in a position to tell. [COM]

Granny's Cottage. Home to Granny Weatherwax. A witch's cottage so typical that, if there were any kind of tourist organization in the RAMTOPS, it would be given a grant. The description can be taken to apply to a greater or lesser extent to all rural witch cottages, although, as indicated, this one can be considered a witch's cottage *par eldritche*.

It nestles in the woods. It leans against itself for support. It's of the architectural style known as 'the vernacular', i.e. somebody swearing, and by now it gives the impression of having grown

Granny's Cottage

in place rather than having been built. Granny's cottage pulses with the force of Granny's personality.

Access to the cottage is exclusively via the back door, but it is first worth taking some time to look at the garden. In the front of the building is a bit of lawn, with a forlorn windsock on a pole, although the cottage is largely surrounded by unruly beds of herbs which seem to move, even on windless days. At the far end of the 'herb garden' is an apple tree, given to her by old Mr Parsons. There are also some leggy soft fruit bushes and, in front of the rimward wall, a bleached wooden bench to catch the sun. Such shrubs and flowers as are otherwise found are all cuttings or spare clumps given to Granny Weatherwax by neighbours. A witch would never dream of *buying* anything for the garden. Around the side is a water butt and a walled paddock for her goats when they are not turned loose in the forest (witches prefer goats to cows). In a corner are half a dozen beehives and an old goat shed.

Marking a boundary of the herb garden is a tree stump, beyond which is Granny Weatherwax's privy. Apart from the usual offices, the privy also contains the key to the cottage (on a nail), half a copy of an '*Almanack and Booke of Dayes*' (also on a nail), a stump of candle on a shelf and a chrysalis (this shelf tends to be a repository of things Granny Weatherwax has found on her walks and which appear to be interesting: oddly shaped stones, strange roots, fossils and so on). Next to the privy is a large beech tree.

A key sign that this is the garden of a witch is the lack of a wall. Creatures of the forest could wander across it at any time. They very seldom do.

And now, the cottage...

Through the back door is the hall, with Miss Weatherwax's official witching hat hanging on a hook. This leads through into the stone-flagged kitchen, dominated by its wide chimney and inglenook fireplace, with its firedogs and hook over the fire for a big, black kettle. Over the mantelpiece hang a small key and a clock, kept mainly for its tick; in front of it are a rag rug and a rocking chair.

The room is otherwise furnished with a kitchen table and chairs, a dresser (which contains Granny's box of memorabilia) and an old chest, with a pair of pewter candlesticks. There is also a small speckled mirror. None of the furniture is new. None of it even looks as though it could ever have *been* new. In a drawer on the dresser is a clean bandage and on top of the dresser is a box of dried herbs: medicinal herbs, because people will even seek out Granny Weatherwax when whatever ailment they have got gets too bad. The room is grey-walled – the colour plaster gets from age, not from dirt. There is not a thing in it that isn't useful – except perhaps a green glass ball, a present from Magrat GARLICK.

Off the kitchen is the dank little scullery, which contains the walk-in pantry, a well (topped with a stone slab and a pump), a copper washpot, washboard, scrubbing brushes, slop bucket and a big copper still. Shelves containing bottles and jars of ingredients suggest quite correctly that this is where some of the more physical, take-one-spoonful-at-night-and-an-other-if-you-wake-up-in-the-morning aspects of witchcraft are carried out. This includes a bottle of triple-distilled peach brandy (for medicinal use only). A door in the scullery leads to the lean-to where the goats are bedded down in bad weather.

Back in the kitchen is a small door opening on to the cramped corkscrew staircase, the tiny steps of which lead to the bedroom. The plaster on the bedroom ceiling is cracked, and bulges like a tent. On the wash stand are a jug and a basin with a fetching rosebud pattern, which also matches another china item under the bed. Alongside the basin is a bar of home-made soap which, like Granny's advice, is strong and sharp, stings a bit at the time, but it works.

There is a small wardrobe with a few well-worn and serviceable dresses hanging in it along with a cloak. Tucked away on a shelf is the Zephyr Billow Cloak given to her by Tiffany ACHING.

On the bed itself is a patchwork quilt which looks like a flat tortoise. It was made by Gordo SMITH and was given to Miss Weatherwax by ESK's mother one HOGSWATCHNIGHT. On the quilt is Granny Weatherwax, lying very still and holding (at the time this visit was recorded) a card saying 'I ATE'NT DEAD'.

Er...

Don't all rush for the stairs...

Granny Weatherwax. *See* WEATHERWAX, ESMERELDA.

Grateful, Sara, Lady. A pupil at the QUIRM COLLEGE FOR YOUNG LADIES. Another horsey gel and an INTERCHANGEABLE EMMA. [SM]

Great Pyramid of Tsort. A now-derelict ancient wonder of the Discworld. Made of 1,003,010 limestone blocks, ten thousand slaves were worked to death in its construction. It is a maze of secret passages, their walls reputedly decorated with the distilled wisdom of ancient TSORT. In the circumstances the most important of these wise sayings must have been: Don't be a Slave.

It took sixty years to build. Its height plus its length divided by half its width equalled exactly 1.67563, or precisely 1,237.98712567 times the difference between the distance to the sun and the weight of a small orange. [LF]

Greebo. Nanny OGG's cat. A huge, one-eyed tom who divides his time between sleeping, eating and fathering the most incestuous feline tribe. He is technically a mottled grey but is covered with so much scar tissue that he looks like a fist with fur on it. He can only be said to have ears because there's no other word for the things left on top of his head.

Greebo's good eye, his left one, is yellow. The other one is pearly-white. He radiates genuine intelligence. He also radiates a smell that could knock over a wall and cause sinus trouble in a dead fox. Although he is addressed by virtually everyone as 'Yarrgeroffoutofityahbarstard', to Nanny Ogg he is still a cute little kitten and still sleeps on her bed when not out at night looking for something to fight, rape, eat (or all three). The way he affectionately tries to claw her eyeballs out in the morning is as good as an alarm clock.

However, a residual effect of a hasty spell on

Greebo

the part of his owner has now left Greebo with the ability, not always controllable, to turn into human form. As a human, he is 6 feet tall, broad shouldered and leather clad, with rippling muscles under his shirt. He has long sideburns, a mane of black hair, a broken nose and a black patch over his bad eye. And, it should be added, a worried expression for much of the time. A lot of the things which, as a cat, he would do quite naturally, present him with all kinds of problems when he attempts them in human form.

Greebo tends of flip into his alternate shape when he finds a situation he can't deal with in the current one. On top of all his other problems, this means that people occasionally find a naked human running around meowing. [WS]

Green-Teeth, Jenny. A water-dwelling monster with big teeth and claws and eyes like soup plates. Jenny attempted to abduct Wentworth until Tiffany ACHING intervened. Jenny acted in service to the Queen of the ELVES and, as a fairytale creature, shares the elves' aversion to iron. [WFM]

Greenyham. Treasurer of the Grand Trunk Company, also of Ankh Sto Associates. [GP]

Greetling. Master Greetling is the Head of the Teachers' Guild, and allergic to loud noises, chalk and anyone under the age of 16. [GG]

Greggs, Miss. Teaches History at the Quirm College for Young Ladies. [SM]

Greicha the First. Lord of the WYRMBERG. He was killed by his daughter LIESSA but, because he was also a powerful wizard, he resolved to remain alive unofficially until only one of his children was left to conduct the funeral. [COM]

Gretelina. *See* MELLIUS.

Grido. Ephebian philosopher and author of 'Mechanics'. [SG]

Grillos. A cobbler in EPHEBE. [SG]

Grim, Agoniza and Eviscera. The Sisters Grim are the authors of *real* fairy tales – you know, the ones with blood and bones and bats and rats in. Their stories include such uplifting tales as 'How The Wicked Queen Danced in Red Hot Shoes', 'The Old Lady in the Oven', 'The Glass Clock of Bad Schuschein', 'The Seventh Wife of Greenbeard'. [TOT]

Grim, Malicia. Daughter of the mayor of Bad Blintz. Her grandmother was Agoniza Grim and her great aunt was Eviscera Grim. As a result, she has inherited a fascination with stories and her life is dominated by fairy tales. She wears a long, black dress with black lace fringing and sometimes she bundles her rather-too-red hair up under a black head scarf. Not unattractive, although she can glare better than a cat and her nose is perhaps a shade too long. She carries a bag that contains absolutely everything anyone might need when on 'an adventure'. [TAMAHER]

Grim, Mayor. Mayor of Bad Blintz. A small, thin, worried-looking man, with a bald spot inadequately disguised by the three strands of hair he combs over it. [TAMAHER] and wants to be a midwife for humans as well as pigs when she 'grows up'. She has three brothers.

Petulia is a specialist pig-borer – indeed she has been the local champion in the noble art of boring. She can sit down with a pig and talk to it gently and calmly about extremely boring things until some strange pig mechanism takes over, whereupon it gives a happy little yawn and falls over, no longer a living pig and ready to become a very important contribution to the family's diet for the following year. This might not appear the best of outcomes for the pig, but given the messy and, above all, noisy way pigs died before the invention of pig boring, it is definitely, in the great scheme of things, a much better deal all round. [HFOS]

Gritz. A troll hotel in Ankh-Morpork. Considered very high-class by trolls, since water is piped to every room and there are carpets, or at least something soft, on the floor. The dining room, with its fine selection of clays, is particularly noted. [SM]

Grimnir. Queen Grimnir the Impaler (1514–53, 1553–7, 1557–62, 1562–7, 1568–73). A vampire Queen of Lancre. The phrase 'the Queen is dead, long live the Queen' is particularly apposite in her case. [WS]

Grineldi. A clown in the FOOLS' GUILD. [MAA]

Grinjer. Maker of grave models in DJELIBEYBI. He is twenty-six, acne'd and still lives with his mother because he cannot find a girl who shares his interest in glue. [P]

Grinjo. One of the Assassins who accompanied Zlorf FLANNELFOOT into the Broken DRUM. [COM]

Gristle, Petulia. A young witch, and a friend to Tiffany Aching. Petulia is short, plump and permanently red-faced and worried-looking. She wears lots of jewellery – she can't resist occult jewellery such as her necklace of silver bats and her amulet of owls. She is a very honest girl and a good friend. Petulia is afraid of pins and she hates to disagree with anyone about anything – she's the sort of person who apologizes if you tread on her foot. She used to work for Old Mother (Gwinifer) Blackcap over in Sidling Without; she specializes in animals

Groat, Tolliver, Junior Postman. A very elderly postman at the Ankh-Morpork Post Office. A bent, elderly man with a wheezy voice and a bad cough like a wall being hit repeatedly with a bag of rocks. His short bristly beard suggests to the casual viewer that its owner has been interrupted halfway through eating a hedgehog.

Groatie wears a toupee – not a good one.

It's chestnut brown, the wrong size, the wrong shape, the wrong style and – all in all – wrong.

He has an odd smell – vaguely chemical, coupled with the eye-stinging aroma of every type of throat medicine invented, with just a hint of old potatoes. He is a great believer in natural medicine, opting for 'cures' such as his poultice of goose grease, flannelette and hot bread pudding. He also puts sulphur in his socks – and takes tincture of rhubarb and cayenne pepper – to keep his tubes open.

Mr Groat also wears a dead mole around his neck, to ward off any sudden attack of doctors. Everyone knows doctors make you ill, it stands to reason. Nature's remedies are the trick every time, not some hellish potion made of gods knew what.

He is a strict follower of the old Post Office Regulations. Despite, or because of, that, he ends up being promoted, initially to Probationary Senior Postman and, later, to Postal Inspector. [GP]

Grodley, Sister. A witch from the Skund area. Drops her aitches and sticks her little finger out when she drinks her tea. [WS]

Gruneberry the Good. A past king of LANCRE (906–967). [WS]

Gruneweld. A past king of LANCRE. [WS]

Gryle. A 'colleague' of Reacher GILT. A banshee – a humanoid race who evolved the ability to fly in some high jungle somewhere. He is a tall figure, in a black cloak and wide, flat-brimmed hat, with a voice which is more of a breath than a voice. He is very thin – there is nothing spare about him – no spare flesh, spare words or spare time. He is as light as a child – and he is not strong as such, but he has sinews like cables. He has a long, pale face and a thin-lipped mouth with rows of pointy teeth. Mr Gryle's special talents came as a package with some funny little ways. He was trustworthy – he'd never blackmail you, because such an attempt would be the first move in a game that would almost certainly end in death for *somebody*; if

Mr Gryle found himself in such a game he'd kill right now, without further thought, in order to save time, Presumably he was insane, by the usual human standards, but it was hard to tell; the phrase 'differently normal' might do instead. After all, Gryle could probably defeat a vampire within ten seconds, and had none of a vampire's vulnerabilities, except perhaps an inordinate fondness for pigeons. [GP]

Guilds. Ankh-Morpork is the home of many of the Disc's oldest and most respected Guilds, the largest and most senior of which are micro-societies in their own right. A Guild may well, in return for a tithe, oversee all aspects of a member's life practically from the cradle to the grave (particularly in the case of the ASSASSINS' GUILD) and possibly beyond (in the case of the Guild of Priests, Sacerdotes and Occult Intermediaries). The oldest and richest Guild is the Beggars'; the most stylish, the Assassins'; and the largest, the Thieves' (although there is popularly supposed to be a Rat Guild).

The smallest Guild is, most people are surprised to learn, the Guild of C.M.O.T. Dibblers, membership one. It nevertheless qualifies, under ancient rules that were changed almost immediately after Mr Dibbler discovered them, for full Guild status.

Almost all the schools and most of the hospices in Ankh-Morpork are Guild-run. The 300-odd Guilds to be found in the city include:

Accountants' and Usurers' Guild [J, AGD]
Actors' Guild [TT]
ALCHEMISTS' GUILD
Architects' Guild [NOCB]
Armourers' Guild [J]
ASSASSINS' GUILD
Bakers' Guild [GG]
Bandits' Guild [LL]
Barber-Surgeons' Guild (motto: *shave & a haircut, no legs*) [CJ]
BEGGARS' GUILD (Fellowship of Beggars)
Butchers' Guild
Butlers' Guild [AGD]
Carters' and Drovers' Guild [TFE]
Chefs' Guild [AGD]

Confectioners' Guild [TOT]
CONJURERS' GUILD
Cunning Artificers' Guild (headed by Mr
   Pony) [RS]
Dibblers, C.M.O.T., Guild of
DOG GUILD [MAA]
Dunnikin Divers' Guild [FOC]
EMBALMERS' GUILD (Guild of Embalmers
   and Allied Trades)
ENGRAVERS' (AND PRINTERS') GUILD
FIREFIGHTERS' GUILD
FOOLS' GUILD (Guild of Fools and Jocula-
   tors and College of Clowns)
GAMBLERS' GUILD
Glassblowers' Guild [FOC]
Haberdashers' Guild [P]
Handlemen's Guild [MP]
Historians Guild [J, TOT]
Lags' Guild (Professional Prisoners)
   (Chairman – Joe 'Lifer' Bushyhead) [TGD]
Lawyers' Guild [WS]
MERCHANTS' GUILD
PLUMBERS' GUILD (Guild of Plumbers and
   Dunnikin divers) [P]
Priests', Sacerdotes' and Occult Intermedi-
   aries' Guild
Rat-Catchers' Guild [FOC]
SEAMSTRESSES' GUILD
Shoemakers', Cobblers' and Leatherworkers'
   Guild [TT]
Smugglers' Guild [P]
STRIPPERS' GUILD
Tailors' Guild [TFE]
Teachers' Guild [GG]
THIEVES' GUILD (Guild of Thieves,
   Burglars and Allied Trades)
Towncriers' Guild [TT]
Victims' Guild (sole member – Mr Echi-
   noid Blacksly) [TGD]
Watch and Clockmakers' Guild [TT]
Watchmens' Guild [TFE]

Gulta. One of the sons of Gordo Smith, and
brother of Esk. [ER]

Gumption, Bewilderforce. Proprietor of a
tobacconist emporium on the corner of Cheap-
side and Rhyme Street, Ankh-Morpork [SN]

Gumridge. One of VITOLLER's band of strolling players. [WS]

Gurnt the Stupid. A past king of Lancre. He
had a plan for an aerial attack force of armoured
ravens. It never got off the ground. [LL]

Things just happen, one after another. They don't care who knows. But history
… ah, history is different. History has to be observed. Otherwise it's not history.
It's just … well, things happening one after another.

– *Small Gods*

Haddock, Constable. Member of the Ankh-Morpork City Watch – known, unsurprisingly, as 'Kipper' to his colleagues. Serves as an Acting Captain while seconded to the Quirmian Watch. [UA]

Hakardly, Ovin. A seventh-level wizard and once a lecturer in Lore at the Unseen University. He was an elderly wizard, who gave the impression of being as fragile as a cheese straw. [S]

Halter, 'Tonker'. A volunteer to the Borogravian Army. Tonker is big, red-haired and with an air of nervousness not quite concealing some bubbling anger. Also known, to close friends, as Magda. [MR]

Hamadryad. Tree-dwelling species. The females have green skin and long, mossy hair. The males are tall and have skins the colour of walnut husks, with muscles bulging like sacks of melons. Their eyes are luminous green and have no pupils. Hamadryads do not wear clothes. They live not exactly in the tree, as squirrels do, but inside what can only be called the psyche of the tree. [COM]

Hamcrusher, Grag. A deep-downer dwarf and as fundamental as the bedrock. Hamcrusher occupies, with other deep-downers, a house in Treacle Street, Ankh-Morpork. As a Grag, he is a renowned master of dwarfish lore; he preaches the superiority of dwarfs over trolls and that it is the duty of every dwarf to follow in the footsteps of their forefathers and remove trollkind from the face of the earth. He is a little figure (of course), dressed in heavy black leather robes and hooded so that he cannot commit the sin of seeing daylight. [T!]

Hamesh. A farmer. Brother to LEZEK and thus MORT'S uncle. [M]

Hamish. Aviator feegle in the Nac Mac Feegle clan near the village of Tiffany Aching, over on the Chalk. He wears leggings instead of a kilt, and usually has a pair of goggles over his eyes. He summons his buzzard using a pipe, which he keeps in his waistcoat. Some people might ask, 'How can a man six inches high train a bird that big?'. The answer is that all it takes is a 'wee drop o' kindness'. Oh, and a big dollop of cruelty. Hamish trains them by running around in a rabbit skin until a bird pounces on him. He then knocks it out with his head, and then he blows a special oil that he makes their beak. When it wakes up, it thinks he's its mother and will do what he asks. [WFM]

Hamish, Mad. Member of the Silver Horde. Wizened, bearded, 105-year-old little man with false teeth. He still wore a horned helmet and didn't let being wheelchair-bound get in the way of barbarian heroing. Deaf as a post, but barbarian heroes don't usually listen to people in any case. [IT]

Hammerhock, Bjorn. A dwarf craftsman in Ankh-Morpork, with a workshop in Rime Street. Killed by the march of weapons technology. [MAA]

Hammerjug. He is a writer of dwarf songs with his partner, Gortlick. [SM]

Hamnpork. An old, greying, big, fierce and scabby rat who was the head rat in the group travelling with the Amazing MAURICE. [TAMA-HER]

Hamslinger. Another of the early books' 'walk-ons'. A dwarf in Ankh-Morpork. [MAA]

Hamstring, Goodie Ammeline. Address unknown, but almost certainly the RAMTOPS. A witch, bent with age, like a bow. White hair, and a cracked and quavery voice, but her eyes were bright and small as blackcurrants.

After death, her soul was no longer bound by the body's morphic field and her hair unwound itself from its tight bun, changing colour and lengthening. Her body straightened up, her wrinkles dwindled and vanished, and her grey dress changed to something leaf-green and clingy. Her voice became suggestive of musk and maple syrup. A prime example of the Discworld truth that what you look like isn't who you are. [M]

Hancock, Andy. 'Two Swords'. A member of the SPECIALS. An amiable, bearded man, with an amiable smile, and more cutlery about his person than Vimes thinks is quite appropriate. Amongst his cutlery are two curved Agatean swords strapped across his back. [T!]

Handisides, Rambut. A History monk, who looked after the oak, and stone, Procrastinators at the Monastery of Oi Dong. The monks of the Procrastinator floor are not among the temple's great political thinkers. Their job is to tend and grease, and strip down and rebuild, and follow the directions of the man on the platform. [TOT]

Hangovers, Oh God of. *See* BILIOUS.

Harebut the Provision Merchant. Father of NIJEL the Destroyer. [S]

Harga, Sham. Owner of HARGA'S HOUSE OF RIBS in Ankh-Morpork. Sham, with his beefy hands and well-padded vest, is an expansive, if grubby, advert for his own carbohydrate merchandise. He has run a successful eatery for many years by always smiling, never extending credit and realizing that most of his customers want meals properly balanced between the four food groups: sugar, starch, grease and burnt crunchy bits. [M]

Harga's House of Ribs. An eatery down by the docks in Ankh-Morpork. It is probably not numbered among the city's leading eateries, catering as it does for the type of clientele that prefers quantity and breaks up the tables if it doesn't get it. HARGA's All-You-Can-Gobble-For-a-Dollar menu is famous wherever huge appetites gather and mountainous stomachs rumble.

The fat in the pan has a geological history all of its own. Bits of ancient sausage and nodules of bacon from pig varieties long extinct are still in it somewhere. Nor does the coffee jug ever get cleaned out – the coffee is like molten lead, but it has this in its favour: when you've drunk it, you have an overwhelming feeling of relief that you've got to the bottom of the cup. Normally the only decoration in the cafe is on Harga's vest, which also acts as a sort of unofficial menu.

The city's dogs have also noted that Sham Harga puts out his rubbish at midnight. This would come as a surprise to his clientele, who thought he cooked it.

Hashimi. A prophet of the Omnian church. It is said that he was given the '*Book of Creation*' by the Great God OM. They all say this. [SG]

Hashishim. The original assassins. A band of mad killers, who were feared throughout hubward KLATCH, and were led by the first CREOSOTE, Seriph of AL KHALI. They derived their name from the huge quantities of hashish they consumed. They were unique among killers in being both deadly and, at the same time, inclined to giggle, groove to interesting patterns of light and shade on their terrible knife blades and, in extreme cases, fall over. [S]

Hawkin, Annagramma. A trainee witch from Tiffany's part of the Disc. She is taller than Tiffany, with a face that seems to have been built backwards from her nose, which she constantly holds slightly in the air. She works for, *with*, Mrs EARWIG and she has the kind of voice you obey.

It's an annoying voice – it can make even 'hello' sound like an accusation.

Like Mrs Earwig, she wears stylish black and a lot of silver jewellery. Annagramma has an air about her as though she's taking notes about the world in order to draw up a list of suggestions for improvements.

She ran the coven of Tiffany, Lucy Warbeck, Petulia Gristle, Dimity Hubbub, Lulu Darling and Gertruder Tiring. She ran it because she invented it, she had the tallest hat – and the sharpest voice. [HFOS]

Heddwyn, Sulien. An elderly dwarf fat-miner; also a random entry to this book. [RS]

Hedge wizards. Hedge wizardry is a very honoured and specialized form of magic that attracts silent, thoughtful men of the druidical persuasion and topiaric inclinations. If you invite a hedge wizard to a party he will spend half the evening talking to your potted plant. And he will spend the other half listening to it. These wizards do not have anything to do with Unseen University, where they would be considered in dire need of dried frog products. [ER]

Heinrich, Prince of Zlobenia. A 'friend to Ankh-Morpork'. He is over six feet tall, with a pretty smile, good teeth, a duelling scar, a monocle – and a well-trimmed moustache, waxed to points. He has a local reputation for cunning, and inherited the throne in a country where the chief export is the hand-painted clog. He is an educated man, who has great plans for Zlobenia and has banned the worship of Nuggan. At one point, he disguised himself as Captain Horentz of the First Heavy Dragoons. [MR]

Heliodeliphilodelphiboschromenos. Disc town mentioned in the song 'The Ball of Philodelphus'. A sort of architectural equivalent of 'Colonel Bogey'. [E]

Hell. There are, almost by definition, an unlimited number of Hells – potentially at least a personal one for every living sapient being.

However, humans are impressionable, gregarious creatures (one famous definition of Hell, after all, is that it is other people). Hell tends to look like what they have come to expect and what they expect is often conditioned by what they've read and seen, so that for people around the CIRCLE SEA there is a kind of general, consensus Hell. This is the one described quite fully in *Eric*, where rather dull demons mindlessly apply physical torture to non-physical bodies and there is a general wailing and gnashing of teeth subsequent to a handout of free, badly fitting false teeth for those who die toothless.

The unremarkable horror of the place is somewhat ameliorated by the lack of imagination of the demons who run it. For example, a forbidding door leads to it, with a sign on it saying, 'You Don't Have To Be "Damned" To Work Here, But It Helps!!!', and the three exclamation marks and quote marks around a word that patently does not need it suggest a type of dreadfulness all their own. It also has a door-knocker – black, horrible and tied up so that it can't be used. There is a doorbell next to it, which plays a jolly little chime. For anyone with any interest in music, Hell starts right there.

As you might expect – in fact, precisely because you would expect – the broad steps leading up to Hell are made of good intentions, carved in stone. (*See also* DEMONS.) [E]

Helmclever. A novice dwarf Grag, related to the Helmclevers of Tallow Lane, Ankh-Morpork. He was born in Ankh-Morpork, and went off to study in the mountains – against his parents' wishes. He is a junior official (orders the groceries, relays orders, pays the miners, etc.). He dresses as a standard city dwarf – helmet, leather, chain mail, battleaxe/mining pick, and a black sash. [T!]

Henchance thee Unsatysfactory. The author of the 'Demonylogie Malyfycorum'. [ER]

Henderson, Fred 'Mr Harpsichord'. Musician and council member of the Musicians' Guild. [SM]

Henri, Big. A regular at the Mended DRUM. Has probably drunk a beer at a table near to RINCEWIND. [GG]

Henry, Coffin. A professional beggar in Ankh-Morpork and the leader of the Canting Crew. He is paid money not to attend important social occasions. If people don't take this small but essential precaution, he sidles ingratiatingly into the party and invites guests to inspect his remarkable collection of skin diseases. He also has a cough, which sounds almost solid, and is known for his volcanic spitting. Apart from this, he can be recognized by his signs on which are chalked: 'For sum muny I wunt follo you home. Coff Coff' or 'Will Threaten For Food'. He would be the city's champion expectorator if anyone else had wanted the title. [SM]

Henry, Scrubado. A beggar on the streets of Ankh-Morpork.

Heralds, Ankh-Morpork Royal College of. The Royal College is, or was, the repository of the only record of the heraldic ancestry of the all the oldest and most noble families in Ankh-Morpork and the Discworld as a whole. It maintains itself behind a green gate in a wall in Mollymog Street – just head towards the sound of the heraldic beasts waiting to be fed.

The Ankh-Morpork College of Heralds is headed by Dragon King of Arms, who is traditionally responsible for proclamations of war and peace, for carrying the King's challenges to battle and messages between sovereigns. He is also responsible for all matters relating to heraldry affecting the Cities of Ankh & Morpork and has overall responsibility for his deputies, Hubward King of Arms (responsible for heraldry affecting cities and states to the hubward of Ankh-Morpork) and Rimward King of Arms (responsible for the lands to the rimward of Ankh-Morpork).

Working for them are six heralds, each representing a major city state: Chirm Herald, Al Khali Herald and Genua Herald (for the rimward states) and Pseudopolis Herald, Lancre Herald and Sto Lat Herald (for the hubward states).

The Heralds attendants are called pursuivants: Pardessus Châtain Pursuivant, Croissant Rouge Pursuivant, Garderobe Pursuivant and Rouge Dragon de Marais Pursuivant. Two additional officers, whose duties are unclear, are Scrote Pursuivant Extraordinary and Ankh Pursuivant Extraordinary.

All this is, however, more or less irrelevant since practically none of the above posts are in fact occupied and all the practical business of the College is now carried out by the last two remaining pursuivants, Croissant Vert (Green Crescent) and Pardessus Châtain (Brown Overcoat), or Sid and Frank as they are known to outsiders. They still do jobbing heraldry work for those members of the rising merchant class of Ankh-Morpork which believes that having lots of dough makes you upper-crust, but spend most of their time tending the decrepit collection of heraldic animals still kept on the premises (the heraldic creatures used on shields and so on are always painted from life; one reason why so many of them are such a strange shape – legs of a lion, body of a weasel, head of an eagle and so on – may lie in the fact that in the cramped quarters of the College yard the beasts are allowed to run free and seem to get along quite well, as it were).

Most of the College records were destroyed during the events of *Feet of Clay* but, given the average human's persistent desire for bits of paper proving his or her superiority over the neighbours, Sid and Frank seem to be kept busy.

Herapath, Mrs. Glass-blower's wife, who was provided with a potion by Granny WEATHERWAX. ESK thinks the glassblower doesn't blow much glass, because his wife calls him Old Mister Once A Fortnight. [ER]

Here'n'Now. An unlicensed thief and stool pigeon in Ankh-Morpork. The worst thief in the world (worst as in not good at it). A very small, raggedy man, whose beard and hair are so overgrown and matted together that he looks like a ferret peering out of a bush. Called Here'n'Now because of his nervous inability to master anything but the present tense, so that his speech is therefore on these lines: 'So I'm standing outside the Mended Drum when who is coming up to me but Flannelfoot Boggis who tells me he is seeing where the De Bris gang are robbing the jewellers' shop in Gleam Street, but I am reticent because I know this to be nothing but an untruth...'. [MAA]

Heretofore. Secretary to Cosmo LAVISH. He is a pale young man in an old-fashioned clerk's robe. Heretofore *had* told Cosmo that he had been employed at the Patrician's Palace. Indeed, he had been employed for a while at the palace, but he did not let Cosmo find out that it had been as a gardener. He *had* been a minor secretary at the Amourers' Guild before that, which was why he'd felt confident in saying 'I was a minor secretary and I was employed at the palace', a phrase that readers will recognize that Lord Vetinari would have examined with more care than the delighted Cosmo had done. [MM]

Herne the Hunted. God of all small, furry creatures whose destiny it is to end life with a brief, crunchy squeak. Herne is about three

Hex

feet high with long, floppy, rabbit ears and very small horns. He has an extremely good turn of speed. Found in the mountains and forests of LANCRE, moving extremely fast. [WS]

Heroes and Heroines. Most of the Disc's classic heroes – and heroines – are from the barbaric tribes nearer the frozen Hub, which have a sort of export trade in heroes, which shows that the leaders of these tribes are by no means stupid, because their sons are usually suicidally gloomy when sober and homicidally insane when drunk. They tend to acquire magic swords, a forthright attitude to women and a complete disrespect for other people's property. Some of the Disc's best-known heroes include COHEN the Barbarian, HRUN the Barbarian, Erig Stronginthearm [COM], Black Zenell [COM], Codice of Chimeria [COM] and Cimbar the Assassin [LF]. Stronginthearm is a dwarf name, but presumably they have heroes just like everybody else. Other heroic types, of the female persuasion, include: HERRENA the

Henna-Haired Harridan; Red SCHARRON; VENA the Raven-Haired; DIOME; Witch of the Night; and CONINA.

Herrena the Henna-Haired Harridan. An adventuress. A good swordswoman who has amassed a modest fortune for a future that will certainly include a bidet if she has anything to do with it. She is usually sensibly dressed in light chain mail, soft boots and a short sword, and would look quite stunning after a good bath, a heavy-duty manicure and the pick of the leather goods in Woo Hun Ling's Oriental Exotica and Martial Aids on Heroes Street, Ankh-Morpork. [LF]

Hersheba. Small desert kingdom rimwards of KLATCH, practically on the more-or-less vague boundary with HOWONDALAND. Said to be ruled by a queen who lives for ever.

Hex. It was, perhaps, inevitable that the combination of enthusiastic students and a disinterested faculty would lead to the creation of a machine to explore the unknown and to advance the search for knowledge. Such is the case in Unseen University and Hex, although the underlying reason for Hex's construction is probably the same as the one that has inspired so many other technological advances: we can build this, so let's see what it does if we do.

The *official* reason was the speeding up of the University's magical throughput. There are more than 500 known spells to secure the love of another person. Enquiring minds wondered whether an analysis of all these spells might reveal some small, powerful common denominator, some meta-spell, some simple little equation which would achieve the required end far more quickly.

To answer both these questions, Hex was built. Part of it is clockwork. A lot of it is a giant ant farm (the interface, where the ants ride up and down on a little paternoster that turns a significant cogwheel, is a little masterpiece). The intricately controlled rushing of the ants through their maze of glass tubing (which looks like it had been made by a glass-blower with hiccoughs) is the most important part of the whole thing. Stuff that just seemed to have accumulated included the Phase of the Moon Generator, the aquarium and the wind chimes, that now seemed to be essential. A mouse has built a nest in the middle of it all and has now been allowed to remain – indeed, Hex stopped working when the mouse had been removed.

Hex redesigns itself and, although the students assert that it was they who constructed the Unreal Time Clock (a strange wobbly thing with a cuckoo), other features now form integral parts of the machine without anyone being quite sure how they accumulated. These include: a device a bit like a wind-speed measurer, blocks with occult symbols that dropped into a hopper (although these now seem to have been replaced by a quill pen in the middle of a network of pulleys and levers, and Hex communicates in handwriting), a clothes wringer, a thing like a broken umbrella with herrings on it, some small religious pictures, a large hourglass on a spring (which shows when

the machine is thinking) and a thing that goes 'parp'. Long-term memory storage is achieved by using beehives and, apparently, some kind of telepathic contact between the ants and the bees – placement of pollen and honey in the wax cells indicates a kind of code and, unlike more traditional forms of computer equipment, can be eaten when obsolete. Hex has now also been enhanced with a white carnival mask on one wall of its room – so that users have someone to talk to.

Hex weighs around ten tons and its gnomic bulk is operated by an enormous keyboard – almost as big as the rest of Hex. It now also houses a ram's skull at its core, and its two most technical features are the GBL and FTB. Oh, sorry, the Great Big Lever and the Fluffy Teddy Bear – without the latter, it refuses to work at all. On its outer surface it has a sticker – 'Anthill Inside'. No one knows why it is there, but it turned up one day. [IT]

Hicks, John, Professor. Head of the Department of Post-Mortem Comunications at Unseen University.

He has a widow's peak, a skull ring, a sinister staff, a black robe – and a coffee mug with the legend – 'Necromancers Do It All Night'. He is tolerated as a slightly useful, if irritating, member of the College Council. He looks as though he's tried to grow a proper goatee beard, but owing to some basic lack of malevolence it has turned out a bit sheepish.

Now spells his name 'Hix' – a man who

wears a black robe with nasty symbols on it would be mad, or let us say even madder, to pass up the chance to have an 'X' in his name. [UA]

Hierarch. Ephebian philosopher and author of 'Theologies'. [SG]

Hipwood, Millie. Young girl whose baby was delivered by Nanny OGG. [WS]

History, nature of. See MONKS, HISTORY.

Hiver, the. A form of demon. Hivers were formed in the first seconds of Creation. They are not alive but they have, as it were, the *shape* of life. They have no body, brain or thoughts of their own, and a naked hiver is a sluggish thing indeed, tumbling gently though the endless night between the worlds. Most end up at the bottom of deep seas, or in the bellies of volcanoes, or drifting through the hearts of stars. [HFOS]

Hix. See HICKS.

Hobson, Willie. Willie is a thickset man and owner of Hobson's Livery Stable in Creek Alley, Ankh-Morpork. A huge, multi-storey building. Hobson found a niche and occupied it. Many people in Ankh-Morpork occasionally needed a horse, but hardly anyone has somewhere to park one, or the money for the stable, groom, hayloft…. To hire a horse from Willie you just needed a few dollars. Lots of people rent space to keep their own horses there, too. Hobson's Livery Stable is at once the most famous and notorious such establishment in the city. It is probably not the hive of criminal activity that popular rumour suggests, although the huge establishment often seems to contain grubby-looking men with not much to do apart from sit around and squint at people. And Willie now employs an Igor, which *of course* is sensible when you have such a high veterinary overhead, but you hear stories – such as, for example, stolen horses got dismantled at dead of night and might well turn up with a dye job and two different legs. And it was said that

there was one horse in Ankh-Morpork that had a longitudinal seam from head to tail, being sewn together from what was left of two horses that had been involved in a particularly nasty accident. [TT]

Hodgesaargh. Castle falconer at LANCRE. Hodgesaargh is not his original name, but he is regularly attacked by his birds just as you speak to him, and this has led to a common misunderstanding. An amiable, good-natured man, whose love and care for his charges is only surpassed by their own fervent desire to eat his eyeballs. He is not a bad falconer, in fact he's one of the best trainers in the mountains. His personality tends towards the one-man feudal system; he doesn't disagree with his betters and he doesn't mind who runs the castle as long as they don't tamper with his birds.

Currently, his favourite gyrefalcon is the Lady Elizabeth – a descendant of LADY JANE.

As the official Royal Falconer he is entitled to wear a ceremonial costume, which was designed hundreds of years previously by someone with a lyrical view of the countryside. It includes a lot of red and gold, with a big, red floppy hat with a feather in it. The whole outfit would look much better on someone two feet taller and who has the legs for red stockings. Usually, however, he wears working leathers and about three sticking plasters. [LL]

Hogfather, the. Now, at least, the Hogfather is a kind old gentleman with whiskers and boots who arrives, to the sound of hog bells, with a sack of toys on HOGSWATCHNIGHT. Children leave out a glass of wine and a pork pie for him, and they decorate their houses with an oak tree in a pot and strings of paper sausages; on Hogswatchday they wear paper hats while they eat their pork dinner.

However, this is a light modern version of a darker myth. The original Hogfather is a winter god who was associated with the pig-killing that is customary in country districts in the month before Hogswatchnight. According to legend – at least in those areas where pigs are a vital part of the household economy – the Hogfather spends the year in his secret palace of giant pig bones, emerging on Hogswatchnight to gallop from house to house on a crude sledge drawn by four tusked wild boars to deliver presents of sausages, black puddings, pork scratchings and ham to all the children who have been good. He says 'Ho Ho Ho' a lot. Children who have been bad get a bag full of bloody bones (it's these little details that tell you it's a tale for children). There is a song about him, which includes the line: 'You'd Better Watch Out...'.

The kinder version of the Hogfather is said to have originated in the legend of a local king who, one winter's night, happened to be passing, or so he said, the home of three young women and heard them sobbing because they had no food to celebrate the midwinter feast. He took pity on them and threw a packet of sausages through the window – badly concussing one of them, but there's no point in spoiling a good legend.

However, it is clear that the root of the story goes back much, much further, to those bloody and often abrupt ceremonies that were once thought necessary to give the sun a nudge in the darkest times of the year.

The Hogfather's sledge is drawn by his four boars: Gouger, Rooter, Tusker and Snouter. They are not your average cuddly piggies.

Hogswatchnight. The one night of the Disc's long year when witches are expected to stay at home. Occurs at the turn of the Disc year. By tradition, shops do not open on Hogswatchday. It's generally the occasion for festivities of a let's-get-the-whole-family-together-and-have-a-row nature, at which otherwise sane people may occasionally blow squeakers.

Hoki (Hoki the Jokester). A nature god in the RAMTOPS. He manifests himself as an oak tree, or as half-man and half-goat, or in his most common aspect as a bloody nuisance. He is found only in deep woods and likes to haunt the Ramtops. Hoki was banished from DUNMANIFESTIN for pulling the old exploding mistletoe joke on BLIND IO.

Holland, Mistress. She is the wife of the miller of the Chalk and is here because she used the wrong herb on her husband's skin condition. She used Love Lies Oozing instead of...? Yes, you're right, she should have used Merryday Root. [TSC]

Hollow, Desiderata. A fairy godmother, which is a very specialized form of witch. A kindly and intelligent soul, who lived in LANCRE. Although blind for thirty years, she was blessed, or possibly cursed, with second sight and always saw what she was doing just before she did it.

Her cottage was stuffed with old books, maps and curios from Foreign Parts. Her friendship with Magrat GARLICK, who has rather more respect for book learning than her fellow witches, led to Magrat inheriting her magic wand and, directly, to the confrontation between the Weatherwax sisters (*see* WEATHERWAX, LILY). [WA]

Holy Wood. A wind-blown old forest, a temple and some sand dunes about thirty miles turnwise of Ankh-Morpork, on a sun-drenched spit of land where the CIRCLE SEA meets the Rim Ocean. There is a legend that a city on the site was destroyed by the gods for some unspeakable crime against them or mankind, and, given what the gods (and mankind) get up to all the time without any kind of punishment at all, it must have been something pretty awful.

For a while, Holy Wood was the focus for creatures from the DUNGEON DIMENSIONS, who tried to use the magic of the area to break into the real world during the time that moving pictures were being made there. [MP]

Hong, Lord. Grand Vizier of the Agatean Empire until his death at the age of twenty-six. He rose to the leadership of one of the most influential families of the Agatean Empire by relentless application, total focusing of his mental powers and six well-executed deaths (including that of his own father). Like all Grand Viziers he was power-obsessed and pathologically intelligent. There just seems to be something about the job. [IT]

Hong, Mr. (No relation, as far as is known.) Owner of the short-lived Three Jolly Luck Take-Away Fish Bar, which was built on the site of an old temple on Dagon Street and opened at the time of the full moon. No one really knows what happened to him in that terrible five minutes just after he opened for business, but he was certainly removed from the world so quickly that he had to leave some things behind. They were things you wouldn't expect to leave behind. [MAA]

Hoodwinkers. The Brotherhood of the Hoodwink were involved in the search for RINCEWIND and the Eighth Spell during the events of *The Light Fantastic.* [LF]

Hopcroft, Percy. A premier grower of fruit and vegetables in LANCRE. Despite his awful wig, he is a keen man when it comes to sexual antics with a camel-hair brush among the horticulture. He named an apple after Nanny OGG. [SALF]

Hopkins, Chickenwire. A farmer in the Ramtops who once threw a rock at Granny Weatherwax just after she'd helped a local troll. Soon afterwards his barns were mysteriously flattened one night. [WA]

Hopkins, Dr. Secretary of the Clockmakers' Guild. He is a middle-aged, bespectacled, sheep-faced man who likes to see the best in everybody. Although apparently as mild-mannered as milk, he *has* survived several years as Guild Secretary, so he must have hidden depths. He has a workshop several streets away from Jeremy CLOCKSON's, where he makes novelty watches for a rather strange kind of discerning customer. [TOT]

Hopkinson. One-time Curator of the Ankh-Morpork Dwarf Bread Museum in Whirligig Alley. He was not himself a dwarf, being a tall man with a white beard and a squeaky voice. He wore his spectacles on a length of black tape – the sure sign of a dangerously tidy mind. He wrote the definitive work on offensive bakery and was himself, ironically enough and much to his subsequent annoyance, beaten to death with a loaf of bread. [FOC]

Horace (1). *See* SENIOR WRANGLER, THE.

Horace (2). A Lancre Blue Cheese made, and owned, by Tiffany ACHING. Horace is probably the only cheese in the multiverse who moves around, mutters and eats mice. He is now an honorary Nac Mac Feegle. [W]

Hornett, Lieutenant. Equerry to Lord Rust. That's it. [J]

Horsefry, Crispin. Of the Ankh-Morpork Credit Bank, and once on the board of the Grand Trunk Company. He acquired other people's money in a safe, secret and not very clever way.

He is a youngish man, who favours pink shirts. He is not simply running to fat, but vaulting, leaping and diving towards obesity. Even at the young age of thirty, he had acquired an impressive selection of chins. It is wrong, though, to judge by appearances. Despite his

expression, which was of a piglet having a bright idea, and his mode of speech, which might put you in mind of a small, breathless, neurotic but ridiculously expensive dog, Mr Horsefry might well have been a kind, generous and pious man. In the same way, the man climbing out of your window in a stripy jumper, a mask and a great hurry might merely be lost on the way to a fancy-dress party, and the man in the wig and robes at the focus of the courtroom might only be a transvestite who wandered in out of the rain. Snap judgements can be so unfair. [GP]

Horse People. The Horse Tribes of the Hubland steppes are born in the saddle, despite the inconvenience, and are particularly adept at natural or witch magic. They live in yurts heated by burning horse dung; this makes good fuel, but the Horse People have a lot to learn about air-conditioning – starting with what it means. They eat horse cheese, horse meat, horse soup, horse black pudding, horse d'oeuvres and drink a thin beer you wouldn't want to speculate about. When he's not working elsewhere they tend to be joined by COHEN the Barbarian, who enjoys their easygoing attitude to life, or at least to other people's lives. [LF]

Hoskins, Grabber. A criminal in Ankh-Morpork. It seems he may be a bit of a recidivist, as the Watch is aware of his proclivity for getting a bit lairy when he's had a celebratory drink. [MAA]

Houser, Berenice. In charge of the back numbers department at the 'Ankh-Morpork Times'. A plump lady, with a slightly wistful hungry look so many women of a certain age wear when they've decided to trust in gods because of the absolute impossibility of continuing to trust in men. [MM]

Howondaland. When people talk of the 'dark and mysterious continent of KLATCH' it is Howondaland they are referring to. Its borders are imprecise, since they begin where those of the other countries on the hubwards coast of Klatch fade away (that is to say, where surveyors don't come back and map-makers are found nailed upside down to a tree). Indeed, it is hardly correct to call it a country – it has a name simply because cartographers don't like vast expanses of empty paper. A few hardy souls trade there, but it remains one of the biggest genuinely unexplored areas of the Disc, and is widely believed to be even more dangerous for the unwary traveller than Shamlegger Street, Ankh-Morpork, on a Saturday night.

Hron. A guard in Lancre Castle. [WS]

Hrun the Barbarian. Hrun of CHIMERIA. One of the CIRCLE SEA's more durable heroes. Not exceptionally bright, but exceptionally unimaginative. Nevertheless, practically an academic by Hub standards in that he can think without moving his lips.

Hrun has the statutory wide chest and neck like a tree trunk, but a surprisingly small head, with bushy eyebrows and stubbly chin under its wild thatch of black hair – the effect is like putting a tomato on an upright coffin. His skin has a coppery gleam and there is much gold about his person in the shape of anklets and wristlets that once belonged to someone else, although he is otherwise naked apart from the usual leopardskin loincloth. (He killed the leopard with his teeth, according to legend, or his breath, according to likelihood.) For a while, at least, he carried the magical sword KRING.

He is believed to be working somewhere for wages these days. Sigh. [COM]

Hub, the. The centre of the Disc and site of CORI CELESTI. [COM]

Hubbub, Dimity. A trainee witch, along with others such as Tiffany Aching. [HFOS]

Hugglestones. A bleak, spartan boarding school, it is housed in a granite building on a rain-soaked moor, and its stated purpose is to make men from boys using methods such as playing very simple and violent games in the healthy outdoor sleet. A good way to survive on the playing fields of Hugglestones is to run very

fast and shout a lot while inexplicably always being a long way from the ball. The staff at Hugglestones believe that, in sufficient quantities, 'being keen' can take the place of lesser attributes like intelligence, foresight and training. One of its old boys is William DE WORDE. [TT]

Hummock, Sergeant. A member of the Ankh-Morpork City Day Watch. [GG]

Humptemper. Author of 'Names of the Ants'. A strange book, half magical treatise and half autobiography. The title apparently derives from an account of the time Humptemper, who was highly skilled in the discipline witches call 'borrowing' and wizards called *psychoproicio* (lit. 'throwing away the mind'), spent inside the group mind of a nest of ants in the University's walls. [E]

Humptulip. Author of the 2000-page 'Howe to Kille Insects'. Frequently confused with HUMPTEMPER, although the former lived several centuries before. [MAA]

Hurker. A poacher in the Ramtops. [WA]

Hwel. A dwarf, banished from his tribe, not only because of his claustrophobia but also because of his tendency to daydream (both undesirable, not to say fatal, traits if you work in a mine). He has a very receptive mind for raw inspirations and is still one of the Discworld's premier playwrights, writing for VITOLLER's troupe of players. He has a hairy bullet head and stubby legs and, at the time of *Wyrd Sisters*, was 102 years old – the prime of life for a dwarf. [WS]

Hydrophobes. Also known as Loathers. Wizards who loathe water; the very idea of it revolts them. A really good hydrophobe has to be trained on dehydrated water from birth. Although they make great weather magicians (rain clouds just give up and go away), they are mainly used in the kingdom of KRULL to power the flying lens means of transport, which can be suspended over water by the sheer power of revulsion from the hydrophobes strapped to the lens' rim. They wear distinctive black and dark-blue robes and all wear ingrained expressions of self-revulsion at their own body fluids. They die young; they just can't live with themselves. [COM]

People in drought-stricken areas would have paid good money to have Igor
pronounce 'sausages'.

– *The Fifth Elephant*

Ibid. Ephebian philosopher and author of *'Discourses'* and *'Civics'*. Tall and willowy, with an indefinable air of authority, he is a well-known expert on everything except geometry, interior decorating and elementary logic. [P]

Ice Giants. The size of large houses, craggy and faceted, glinting green and blue in the light. Their eyes are tiny and black and deep-set, like lumps of coal (although this is the only way in which they resemble the idols built, in response to ancient and unacknowledged memories, by children in snowy weather).

The Ice Giants have been engaged in an eons-old battle with the gods and are currently imprisoned inside a wall of mountains at the Hub. They probably began as a metaphor for glaciers, but we know what happens to metaphors on the Disc.

Technically, the Ice Giants are probably a type of troll. [LF]

Ichlos, Dervi. A 38-year-old private in the Omnian Army. [SG]

Iconoscope/iconograph. The iconograph is a picture-making box. It operates via a small demon with a good eye for colour and a speedy hand with a paintbrush, imprisoned inside.

Introduced to the STO PLAINS by TWOFLOWER the tourist, it was subsequently developed in Ankh-Morpork. By the time of the moving picture craze in HOLY WOOD it was possible to achieve motion pictures by using a lot of demons and getting them to paint very fast, by means of a handle attached to a lot of tiny whips. And by the time of *Men At Arms*,

CARROT – even on a Watch corporal's salary – was able to buy a small iconograph, by then known, because of the demon inside, as a 'brownie'. [COM]

Iesope. An Ephebian, and another contender for 'Greatest Teller of Stories in the World'. The one about the fox and the grapes went down very well among the farmers who know how important it is to lock up their grapes every night. [P]

Igneous. The not-very-law-abiding troll owner of a pottery in Ankh-Morpork, and one of the city's most established troll residents His foetid production line is often the first place of employment for trolls who have arrived rather hurriedly in Ankh-Morpork because they are wanted for various crimes in the mountains, and Igneous has long been suspected of occasionally working for the Breccia, which sometimes needs things to be moved around surreptitiously. It was his registering the name of the Hollow Statue Export Company that first made the Watch suspicious. [GG]

Igor. Everyone who is (or was) anyone in Über-wald has an Igor as a servant. Überwald's servant class is heavily populated with extremely similar-looking assistants, all of whom are called Igor, to save confusion. At least, to save confusion amongst Igors.

They are, in fact, a clan which, instead of myths and legends, passes on the secrets of incredibly skilled surgery (except in the area of cosmetics), plus various associated hints and tips, often to do with weird chemistry and lightning rods. The Igors effectively treat their own bodies as the common property of all Igors and they would hope that any useful bits they have will be passed on to their relatives; Igors do not so much die as get broken down for spares.

For reasons that have never satisfactorily been explained, Igors seem very popular with the ladies and, bizarrely perhaps, their daughters (Igorinas) tend to be very pretty. Igorinas sometimes learn the skills, although they refrain from the lisping and the very visible stitching; they are not necessary in any case, but are the Igor equivalent of tribal markings. One of the better known Igorinas played a main role in the events of *Monstrous Regiment*.

Although, classically, Igors are to be found working for insane geniuses living in draughty castles, they give freely of their time and talent to anyone in need. Many a life or livelihood has been saved by a carefully grafted-on foot, arm or head. However, the Igors are firm believers in the principle of 'what goes around, comes around' and, whenever possible, they assume and expect that anyone helped by them will, when the time finally comes, see their way clear to letting any local Igor have a quick rummage to see if there are any organs worth recovering. Thus, Igors are very respected in Überwald; they may look like a road accident, but a good Igor could probably get an uncooked sausage to grunt and hunt truffles.

The Igors have now formed an agency – We R Igors 'A Spare Hand When Needed' – based at the Old Rathaus, Bad Schuschein (c-mail: Yethmarthter Überwald). The code of the Igors is very strict – Never Contradict. Never Complain. Never Make Personal Remarks. Never, Ever Ask Questions. Never Oil Doors.

Igors are loyal, but they are not stupid. A job is a job. When an employer has no further use for your services, for example because he's just been staked through the heart by a crowd of angry villagers, it's time to move on before they decide that you ought to be on the next stake. An Igor soon learns a secret way out of any castle and where to stash an overnight bag. In the words of one of the founding Igors: 'We belong dead? Ecthuthe me? Where doeth it thay "we"?'

In the course of the books, we have met a variety of Igors (including the one who worked for Reacher GILT):

Igor, Jeremy Clockson's. He has the traditional blackened fingernails and was sent to work for Jeremy by Lady LEJEAN. His grandfather, with Demented Doctor Wingle, built the first Glass Clock of Bad Schuschein. Before working for Jeremy, he had worked for Mad Doctor Scoop, Crazed Baron Haha, Screaming Doctor Berserk, Nipsie the Impaler, Dribbling Doctor Vibes and Baron Finkelstein. This is a fairly normal résumé for an Igor, and rather than indicate a footloose nature it merely recognizes that, quite often, the mob wins.

Igor, Lady Margolotta's. As he says himself, he is Igor, son of Igor, nephew of several Igors, brother of Igors and cousin of more Igors.

Although he wears the traditional shabby black tailcoat, he has both eyes the same colour, which suggests a young Igor just starting out.

Igor, The de Magpyr. Like most Igors, he has a lisp and walks with a limp. His hand is a mass of scars and stitches and he has a geometrical smile because of the row of stitches right across his face. He has two thumbs on his right hand and two hearts (one, it is thought, a bequest from a Mr Swines; installing his own second heart is something an Igor does early in his career). His feet were a bequest from a Mikhail Zwenitz. He has installed a metal plate in his head, wired down to his boots in case of lightning strikes. [CJ]

Igor, The Embassy. *His* eyes are different colours, unlike those of his cousin, at Lady Margolotta's.

Igor, The Watch. Nephew of the Embassy Igor and constable in the City Watch, although strictly speaking he is a forensics specialist and Watch medic. He's quite young-looking. Like many Igors, he has his eyes on different levels. One ear is larger than the other and his face is a network of scars. He has a deformed hairstyle – greasy black hair brushed forward into an overhanging quiff of excessive length and with a 'ducktail' at the back. He enhances his Igor clothing with a pair of crêpe-soled shoes. He has two thumbs on his right hand and two hearts. He thinks of himself as quite modern and every so often forgets to lisp. Being at the forefront of Igoring, he is keen on genetic experimentation and his gloomy cellar generally has an angry tomato or enraged experimental leek in it somewhere.

Igorina. The Igorina in *Monstrous Regiment* wears dusty black, with cobwebs all over it – the kind of suit people get buried in. Aged around eighteen, with a homely face (the kind of home that has a burned-out vehicle on the lawn). Quiet and neat – with her hair kept initially in a jar – she sometimes forgets to lisp.

Illuminated & Ancient Brethren of Ee. Secret society in Ankh-Morpork. You never hear about all the charity work they do because they don't do any. [GG]

Illuminated Mages of the Unbroken Circle. One of the organizations involved in the search for RINCEWIND and the Eighth Spell during the events of *The Light Fantastic*. [LF]

Imbetos. A prince, who was a plaintiff before TEPPIC in the Djelibeybian supreme court. [P]

Imp y Celyn. A bard from LLAMEDOS. A tall, eighteen-year-old harpist with dark, curly hair, who went to Ankh-Morpork to seek his fortune after falling out with his father, a strong-minded druid. Until the city and certain other things worked their magic on him, he had been a good, circle-going boy from the valleys, who didn't drink, didn't swear and played the harp at every druidic sacrifice.

He became a member of the pop music group, The BAND WITH ROCKS IN, adopting the stage name 'Buddy' because his real name, 'Imp', means 'small shoot' or 'bud'. 'y Celyn' means 'of the holly'; it was obvious that anyone with a name like 'Bud of the Holly' would find this a drawback in the music business. [SM]

Incessant, the Hon. Douglas. An assassin, a guest at the ball in GENUA on Samedi Nuit Mort. [WA]

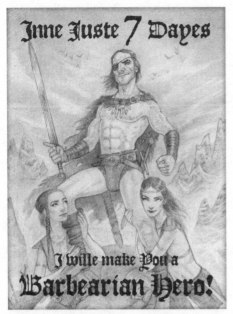

Inne Juste 7 Days I Wille Make You a Barbearian Hero! A guide for the aspiring adventurer, allegedly penned by COHEN THE BARBARIAN. There is some evidence that C.M.O.T. DIBBLER was involved in this publication. NIJEL the Destroyer owned a signed copy. [S]

Inns. Known drinking-houses on the Disc include:

Baron's Arms (John Parsley, landlord) [TSC]

BIERS (used to be the Crown and Dagger) [FOC]

Blue Lias (Holy Wood) [MP]

BUCKET (Ankh-Morpork) [MAA]

Bunch of Grapes (Ankh-Morpork) [GG]

Butcher's Eagle [MM]

Crimson Leech (Ankh-Morpork) [COM]

Duchess, the (Borogravia) [MR]

Fiddler's Riddle (Ohulan Cutash)

Fifth Elephant, the (Wilinus Pass) [TFE]

Goat & Bush (Lancre) [LL]

Goat & Spirit Level [GP]

Goblin's Head [SN]

Grosszügig Stein (Herr Muckenfuss, owner) [TSC]

King's Back, the [ISWM]

King's Head [FOC]

King's Legs, the [HFOS]

Mended DRUM (Ankh-Morpork)

Quene's Hed/Duke's Head (Sto Helit) [M]

Stab in the Back (near the Opera) [MA]

Thank Gods It's Open [T!]

Treacle Miner (a dwarf pub also called the Sticky Head) [RS]

Troll's Head (Ankh-Morpork, in the Shades) [S]

Turkey and Vegetables [UA]

Inn-sewer-ants. An Agatean concept: people pay money against the odds of a disaster occurring. The importation of this idea is allegedly the reason behind the most recent fire to have destroyed much of Ankh-Morpork. [COM]

Insider, the. An old dark god of the 'NECRO-TELICOMNICON'. As the name suggests, probably yet another Dungeon Dimension inhabitant who managed to enter Reality and stay there. [ER]

Inspirations. A fundamental particle in the Discworld universe. It is harder to describe them than it is to describe their effect, which is to create ideas – or, more accurately, sudden insights – in the human brain.

It has been postulated that untold millions of inspirations constantly sleet through the universe. They can pass through absolutely anything and also seem to be able to travel, tachyon-like, through time. However, the human or near-human brain contains a receptor which, while it doesn't stop an inspiration, can be fired up by the passage of one (causing, in that telling phrase, 'a flash of inspiration' – and not for nothing do we say 'I was struck by an idea').

This causes the throwing out of an idea. It may be for a play, an invention or something insubstantial, such as a theory of genetics. Since inspirations are not restricted in time, it may also be for something quite anachronistic. Presumably, the brighter proto-hominids went to sleep in their trees and were occasionally awakened and mystified by the idea of pre-sliced bread or cold fusion for hundreds of years before the more immediately useful one, involving the idea of hanging on more tightly, happened to be shooting past.

According to Ponder STIBBONS of Unseen University, inspirations also *originate* in the human brain. In some rare individuals, an inspiration may excite the inspiration node, causing it to throw off new inspirations. There is certainly anecdotal evidence for this. Everyone knows people who are not only brilliant in themselves but also generate ideas in other people around them.

Which, given the Discworld's love of opposites, must also mean that there are people who are an 'ideas *sink*'. And, again, common observation suggests that this is the case. There are certainly people who, humdrum in themselves, cause humdrumity in others as well. It is as if they act as a lightning rod for any originality around them, diverting it to earth.

For some reason, these people quite often end up in positions of power.

Interchangeable Emmas. Commander VIMES's name for the well-bred young women who muck out, dose, worm and exercise the dragons at Ankh-Morpork's SUNSHINE SANCTUARY – and, by extension, that large army of Alice-banded sisters who do much the same job at stables and kennels all over the universe. It's a strange fact that the more highly born the family, the more likely the young female members are to be doing something smelly with a big fork.

Invisible writings. The study of invisible writings is a new discipline in Unseen University, made available by the discovery of the bi-directional nature of Library-Space. The thaumic mathematics are complex, but boil down to the fact that all books, everywhere, affect all other books. This is obvious: books inspire other books written in the future, and cite books written in the past (as is the case at this very moment). The General Theory of L-Space suggests that, consequently, the contents of books as yet unwritten can be deduced from

books now in existence.

The Reader in Invisible Writings is currently Ponder STIBBONS. [LL]

Iodine. Fourth-former at the Quirm College for Young Ladies. Her father liked the sound of the word. [SM]

Ipslore the Red. A wizard. Eighth son of an eighth son – powerful and, of course, wearing a pointy hat. He fled the halls of magic and fell in love and got married (not necessarily in that order). He had eight sons: the first seven were at least as powerful as any wizard in the world; the eighth was a sourcerer. (*See* COIN and MAGIC.) [S]

Irexes. Ephebian philosopher who found that sandstone is stone pressed out of sand, which suggested to him that grains are the fathers of mountains. [SG]

Ironcrust, Setha. Proprietor of a dwarf bakery in Ankh-Morpork, the motto of which is 'T'Bread Wi'T'Edge'. This is, of course, dwarf bread, the meal that is also a weapon. Ironcrust's slightly industrialized process apparently produces quite a reasonable loaf, although most dwarfs say that it does not have the taste or destructive power of the traditional hand-forged stuff, quite a lot of which is still imported from the mountains. This takes some time, but dwarf bread is said to improve with age. [FOC]

Ironfoundersson, Mr. 'King' Ironfoundersson, of COPPERHEAD in LANCRE. CARROT's adoptive father. He made the crown for the Queen of Lancre. As is usual among dwarfs, the royal title is merely a technical term and has few of the connotations that it carries among humans, where being treated like 'royalty' means that people are likely to try to take sneaky pictures of you with your clothes off. [LL]

Iron Girder. First seen as a 'pro-to-type' steam engine, constructed by Dick SIMNEL, to use the expansion or rapid condensation of steam to generate power. Power for locomotion.

Many years previously, an Ephebian philosopher had built an engine that was scarily powerful. If they had persevered with the engine powered by steam, then the nature of life on the Disc might have been very different. But, as Lord VETINARI says: 'When it's steam engine time, steam engines will come.'

Iron Girder (also known as Engine One) progresses in technology as the events of *Raising Steam* unfold, and Dick Simnel seeks to keep her ahead of the game.

She is the initial mainstay of the Ankh-Morpork and Sto Plains Railway, soon being joined by other 'flyers', such as the Spirit of Scrote and King of Pseudopolis.

Iron Girder seems, though, to be more than a mere engine. At one point she seems to have spoken to Moist von Lipwig, in a voice soft and warm and somehow damp, saying 'I am Iron Girder. But all it takes is for people to believe and I am no longer just an artefact put together by clever engineers. I am an idea, a something made of nothing, whose time has come to be.' [RS]

Ishkible. Prophet of the Omnian religion. [SG]

Ivy, John. A farmer from Slice. His wife, Florence, was kicked by a cow when she was pregnant, which led Granny WEATHERWAX to have to make a difficult choice. [CJ]

Ixolite. The last surviving banshee. A member of the FRESH START CLUB, who stays at Mrs CAKE's lodging house. Tall, with a long, sad face, he is usually seen wrapped in something which may be a long cloak but could possibly be wings. He has a speech impediment and is shy of meeting people, so instead of sitting on rooftops screaming when people are about to die he just writes them a suitable note ('OooeeeOooeeeOoooeee') and slips it under the door and runs away. Technically, banshees should be female; this might be one of the reasons for his sadness. [RM]

'... there has to be some justice in the world, you see, not necessarily law
justice but justice justice, and that's why I'm going to kill you.'

– Snuff

Jabbar. A D'reg wise man, who offers hospitality and advice to VIMES in the events of *Jingo*. [J]

Jackrum, Sergeant (Jack). Later Sergeant-Major. A big, fat sergeant in the Borogravian army – Tenth Infantry – the 'Ins & Outs' (also, the 'Cheesemongers'). The word 'fat' could not honestly be applied to Jackrum, not when the word 'gross' is lumbering forward to catch your attention. One of those people who don't have a waist – instead, Jackrum has an equator. A gravity. If Jackrum fell over, in any direction, he would rock. Sun and drink have dried his face red – his small, dark eyes twinkle in the redness like the sparkle on the edge of a knife. In his shirtsleeves, he is still almost spherical – from his neck, folds of skin lap their way down to the tropical regions.

Has had a long career in the army – over forty years. He has been court-martialled twice (got off both times), saved the life of General FROC and is believed to have killed at least one officer.

Around his neck he wears his official King's Shilling and a locket with a picture of a dark-haired girl and a young man (William), who was killed at Sepple. Jackrum used to run a pig farm and looked after his three brothers. He has a son, William, who is an armourer in Scritz. [MR]

Jackson, 'Tonker'. An old army pal of Sergeant Fred COLON. [MAA]

Jade, Princess. A troll schoolfriend of Susan STO HELIT at the QUIRM COLLEGE FOR YOUNG LADIES. She had bad eyesight, knitted chain mail in handicraft class and had a note excusing her from unnecessary sunshine. Comes from the COPPERHEAD area of LANCRE. Anti-siliconism is still a feature of Discworld affairs and she was probably accepted because snobbery beat speciesism; the headmistress said a princess, even a troll one, would add *ton* to the school. In Jade's case she was right to within a few pounds. [SM]

Jahmet. A royal servant in DJELIBEYBI. [P]

Jaims. A son of Gordo Smith, and another brother of ESK. [ER]

Jape, Brother. Lecturer at the Fools' Guild. He has a soul like cold, boiled string and teaches juggling. [WS]

Jasper. A troll encountered by RINCEWIND during the events of *The Light Fantastic*. [LF]

Jeannie. The kelda of Tiffany's local Nac Mac Feegle clan and wife to Rob ANYBODY. As round as a tiny football. Very wise and kind, she is an educating and calming influence on the Feegles. In her first brood, she produced a daughter, MAGGIE. Jeannie is a modern kelda, and she has encouraged literacy among her sons and brothers. [ISWM]

Jefferies, Bowden. A purveyor of the very best in seafood in Ankh-Morpork. He also owns an ice house in Ankh-Morpork, built by his own two hands, and another halfway on the Quirm to Ankh-Morpork road. His cousin, Relief Jefferies, is a market gardener. Bowden's challenges in securing fresh seafood to sell in the city may be resolved by the arrival of steam railways. [RS]

Jefferson, Jethro. Village blacksmith near to Ramkin Hall. He lives, with his old mum, near the centre of the village, overlooking the village green. [SN]

Jenkins, Captain. He is the master of the *Milka*; his first officer is Mr Scoplett. Jenkins is a trader in, mostly, dried fish offal and condemned meat. Nom, nom. [J]

Jenkins, Owlswick. An expert engraver (and stamp forger). He is a little man, clean shaven apart from a little pointy beard. He used to live in Short Alley, Ankh-Morpork – no house number because Short Alley is only big enough for one door. Has also been known as Exorbit Clamp and Owlswick Clamp. He *is*, by certain standards, very sane. Faced with a world too busy, complex and incomprehensible to deal with, he's reduced it to a small bubble just big enough to hold him and his palette. It's nice and quiet in there. All the noises are far away, and They can't spy on him. [MM]

Jerakeen. One of the four giant elephants supporting the Discworld. [COM]

Jim. A coachman in Ankh-Morpork. [LL]

Jimbo. Best friend to CRASH. Plays the bass guitar, or at least moves his hands on one, in Crash's musical group – originally called Insanity. [SM]

Jimi. God of beggars. Panhandles prayers. [MAA]

Jiminy. Landlord of the Goblin's Head, close to Ramkin Hall. He lives there with his wife and his daughter, who is a maid up at Ramkin Hall. He used to be a copper in the Pseudopolis City Watch, and he still keeps his rosewood truncheon under the bar at the pub. [SN]

Jimmy. Underfootman at the palace in GENUA. [WA]

Jimmy, Doughnut. Full name: James Folsom. A horse doctor in Ankh-Morpork, who can usually be found up at the stables on King's Down. He has bandy legs, hence his name, but the second thing people notice about him is his teeth – the colour of the inside of an unwashed teapot and arranged like an explosion in a graveyard. Oddly enough, in a city where people have to die as best they can without doctors to help them, Doughnut is a handy man to have around in a medical emergency. After all, he usually works with racehorses, which are worth a lot of money, rather than people, who generally aren't worth very much. So he has to get results, because the kind of people who race and bet on horses can get very, very angry if none are forthcoming. However, if you call him in, you must remember that he won't ask you questions, may well prescribe bran and, if you have a broken leg, will shoot you. [FOC]

Johnson, Bergholt Stuttley. 'Bloody Stupid Johnson'. A broadly incompetent landscape gardener, but also considerably unskilled in the fields of civic statuary and large musical instruments.

Also known as 'Bloody Stupid "It Might Look A Bit Messy Now But Just You Come Back in Five Hundred Years' Time" Johnson', or 'Bloody Stupid "Look, The Plans Were the Right Way Round When I Drew Them" Johnson'.

It would be wrong to call him completely unskilled, because some of the creations for which he'll be remembered must surely have taken considerable skill. It was just not the right skill.

Fundamental to his approach was blindness to the significance of, and more importantly the difference between, such things as feet and inches and ounces and pounds. He never let this get him down, however, and was relentlessly cheerful in the face of endless disappointment.

Among his achievements were an artificial hillock built from 2000 tons of earth in front of Quirm Manor because 'It'd drive me mad to have to look at a bunch of trees and mountains all day long, how about you?'; he also designed the commemorative arch celebrating the Battle of Crumhorn, which is kept in a small cardboard box, the Collapsed Tower of Quirm, the huge beehive in the Palace gardens, the Quirm Memorial, the Hanging Gardens of Ankh and the Colossus of Morpork (the last three are pocket-sized), and the ornamental cruet set for Mad Lord SNAPCASE. Four families live in the salt shaker, and the pepper pot is used for storing grain (both in Upper Broadway, souvenir guidebook 2p). The less said of his Great Fruit Pie, the better; buildings some distance away still bear scars from the explosion.

Johnson was never a man to let inexperience or incompetence in any field stand in his way and, with his near-godlike ineptitude, often achieved effects that a genius might find hard to accomplish. For example, he built the organ in the Ankh-Morpork OPERA HOUSE as well as the great organ of Unseen University, which has the widest range of any musical instrument known to man, god or devil. The organ is also linked by some means (to Johnson all pipes are pretty much the same) to the UU's Patent 'Typhoon' Superior Indoor Ablutorium with Automatic Soap Dish, recently re-opened. However, only Archchancellor RIDCULLY was brave or foolish enough to have a shower in it. No one has ever got to the bottom of what happened, but he had it sealed up again very soon afterwards.

He also designed the Sorting Machine at the Ankh-Morpork Post Office. (It had started life as an organ, but ended up as a machine for sorting letters.)

Strangely enough, Johnson's renowned lack of aptitude brought him considerable fame and quite a few commissions in later life. There are always very rich people looking for fashionable and amusing ways of spending their money, and Johnson was, for a while, much in demand by those who found that oversized ornamental temples at the bottom of small lakes, or tree-lined avenues four feet long, brightened up their day. It became quite the thing 'to have been Johnsoned'.

Johnson can be summed up as being on the opposite end of the scale which, at the other end, contains people like LEONARD OF QUIRM. The high spot of his career is thought to be the PATRICIAN'S PALACE grounds (do not go at noon, when the chiming sundial tends to explode).

Johnson, Noodle. Co-student at Unseen University with Rincewind. Everyone wanted to be friends with him but somehow, if you were in his gang, you found yourself being trodden on, or chased by the Watch, or being hit in fights you didn't start, while Noodle was somewhere on the edge of things, laughing. [IT]

Jolson, All. A huge man who owns a restaurant close to Broad Way (as you can see from his lard-stained calling card). He is Ankh-Morpork's best chef and keenest eater. He is a man who'd show up on an atlas and could change the orbit of small planets. His full height is, in fact, slightly less than his full girth. Therefore, no one seeing him for the first time could believe it was *all* Jolson. He has a daughter, Precious.

His interest in supplying food ensures that he is an early franchisee in the area of railway catering. [TFE]

Jolson, Precious. Daughter of All Jolson, and a constable in the Ankh-Morpork City Watch. She is a large – family-sized – good-natured lady. A fountainhead of jolliness. [SN]

Jones, Llamedos. No chronicle of exploration would be complete without its quota of semi-mythical religious explorers, who could cross seas on millstones or, in extreme cases, on foot. The most notorious of these on the Disc was Llamedos Jones.

Legend says that he set out one day in his leather coracle, armed with no more than a holy sickle, a sack of mistletoe, a small portable stone circle and a harmonium, in an inspired effort to bring the advantages of Strict Druidism to the heathen (that is to say, everyone else).

His evangelical endeavours were, for some years, hampered by his inability to travel more than three days in any direction, since he felt it necessary to return to Llamedos for druidic sacrifices and male-voice choir practice once a week.

He was finally given dispensation by the circle elders to miss services, and is believed to have discovered the Brown Islands in the Rim Ocean by the very practical technique of continuing in a straight line until he hit something.

Evidence for this popular claim is sketchy. The natives of the Brown Islands are generally a friendly, easy-going race, who spend a lot of time on the beach.

However, there is one island where it rains a lot, choral singing has been elevated to the status of a martial art, and the most noticeable religious ceremony involves two teams of fifteen men who ritually maim one another in pursuit of a small ball which isn't even properly round – just as is in Llamedos. [DM]

Jorgen. A cousin of Lance-Constable CUDDY. A dwarf, and a watchmaker. [MAA]

Judy. A gnome. Works, reluctantly, with Chas SLUMBER. [TOC]

Jupe, Father. A priest of Nuggan. [MR]

*Mustrum Ridcully believed that knowledge could be acquired by
shouting at people ...*

– Hogfather

Kabona, Lagro te. Innkeeper in the village that used to have a festival called the Thing with the Bulls. After they were visited by three witches, they decided to hold a flower festival in future. [WA]

Kaos. An anthropomorphic personification. The Fifth Horseman of the APOCRALYPSE, although he left before they got famous, and always said he didn't begrudged them their later success. He embodies apparently complicated, apparently patternless behaviour that nevertheless has a simple, deterministic explanation and is a key to new levels of understanding of the multidimensional universe (or so LU TZE says). He rides out on a chariot drawn by a black horse which shines as though illuminated by a red light – redness spangles off its shoulders and flanks. Kaos' eyes are black – shiny and black without any whites at all. Carrying his sword of burning cold, he wears a full-face helmet with eyeholes that look slightly like the wings of a butterfly, and rather more like the eyes of some strange, alien creature. See also SOAK, RONALD. [TOT]

Keeble, Liona. A job broker in Ankh-Morpork. [M]

Keel, John. Past sergeant of the Night Watch. He used to be with the Watch in Pseudopolis. Notable for his eyepatch and a scar on his face, Keel was the sergeant who taught young Sam Vimes all he needed to know about proper policing. His grave is in the Cemetery of Small Gods. [NW]

Keepsake, Duchess of. Turkey-necked mother of Letitia. When we first meet her she is a bully, holding a shiny black stick with a silver knob at the end. She always travels in funeral clothes because, she says, you never know when someone is going to drop dead. She lives at Keepsake Hall, at the far end of the Chalk. Before she married the Duke, she was a dancer in the music hall, and was called Deirdre Parsley. [ISWM]

Keepsake, Letitia. *See* LETITIA.

Keith. A fair-haired young man, called 'Kid' and 'Stupid-looking Kid' by MAURICE. He was found in a doorstep at the MUSICIANS' GUILD. He is good at playing musical instruments and has been earning his own living since the age of six. With Maurice, and some educated rodents, he was part of the 'Pied Piper' scam in Überwald. [TAMAHER]

Keli. Princess Kelirehenna of STO LAT. When

first encountered, she was a slim, red-haired girl of fifteen with a strong jawline; not beautiful, being over-endowed in the freckle department and, frankly, rather on the skinny side. Her role in life was to fail to be killed by an assassin, owing to the gland-led incompetence of MORT.

She eventually became Her Supreme Majesty, Queen Kelirehenna I, Lord of Sto Lat, Protector of the Eight Protectorates, and Empress of the Long Thin Debated Piece Hubwards of Sto Kerrig. [M]

Ken, Stalling. A beggar on the streets of Ankh-Morpork. He had the privilege of supping with Death, or at least of supping with Death and getting up the next morning. [SM]

Kepple. A past sergeant of the Night Watch in Ankh-Morpork. He was head of the Watch when Sam Vimes was a recruit. [MAA]

Kerible the Enchanter. Owner of a workshop in Morpork. [COM]

Khaphut, Queen. Past monarch of DJELIBEYBI. [P]

Khat-leon-ra-pta, Queen. A past monarch of DJELIBEYBI, during the 2nd Empire. She conquered Howandaland, but it was subsequently sold back to its inhabitants to pay for yet more pyramids. [P]

Kheneth XIV. Past monarch of DJELIBEYBI. [P]

Khuft. Accidental discoverer of the subsequently mighty land of DJELIBEYBI. A small, dark man in a loincloth and with two blackened stumps of teeth. He fled into the desert to escape disgruntled purchasers of his sub-standard camels, and founded a huge dynasty. [P]

Khufurah, Prince. Younger brother of Prince CADRAM of Klatch. A tall, bearded man, with disconcertingly intelligent eyes, who had once been athletic until all the big dinners associated with his class took their effect. [J]

King, Euphemia ('Effie'), Lady. Wife of Sir Harry KING; she says she was 'born in the next-door gutter' to him. At times, her language would make a barrow-boy blush – so be warned. [TT]

King, Harry, Sir. Now Lord King of the Permanent Way. Also known as 'King of the Golden River', and less politely as Piss Harry. Harry can't read or write, but that has been no drawback to his career, because he employs people who can. He is an enormous man, pink and shiny-faced, with a few strands of hair teased across his head. He is usually cheerful and has a good digestion. It's hard not to imagine him in shirtsleeves and braces, or to imagine him not smoking a cigar. He is married to Effie and they have two daughters, Daphne and Hermione. He also has a niece, Emily, who is training to be a lawyer.

He has a persistent, but not particularly bad, odour of old potatoes and abandoned tunnels. Except for the pinky of his left hand, he has a heavy gold ring on each finger spelling H.A.R.R.Y.K.I.N.G.

Harry King had made his fortune by the careful application of the old adage: where there's muck there's brass. There was *money* to be made out of things that people threw away. Especially the very *human* things that people threw away. In other words, he made a fortune minding other people's 'business'.

The real foundations of his fortune came when he started leaving empty buckets at various hostelries around the city centre, especially those that were more than a gutter's length from the river. He charged a very modest fee to take them away when they were full. It became part of the life of every pub landlord; they'd hear a *clank* in the middle of the night and turn over in their sleep content in the knowledge that one of Piss Harry's men was, in a small way, making the world a better-smelling place.

They didn't wonder what happened to the full buckets, but Harry King had learned something that can be the key to great riches: there is very little, however disgusting, that isn't used somewhere in some industry. There are people out there who *want* large quantities of ammonia and saltpetre. If you can't sell it to the alchemists then the farmers probably want it. If even the farmers don't want it, then there is nothing, *nothing*, however gross, that you can't sell to the tanners.

Harry felt like the only man in a mining camp who knows what gold looks like.

He started taking on a whole street at a time, and branched out. In the well-to-do areas the householders paid him, *paid him* to take away night soil, the by-now established buckets, the horse manure, the dustbins and even the dog muck. Dog muck? Did they have any *idea* how much the tanners paid for the finest white dog muck? It was like being paid to take away squishy diamonds.

Harry couldn't help becoming rich. The world fell over itself to give him money. Someone, somewhere, would *pay* him for a dead horse or two tons of prawns so far beyond their best-before date it couldn't be seen with a telescope, and the most wonderful part of all was that *someone had already paid him to take them away*. If anything absolutely failed to find a buyer, not even from the cats'-meat men, not even from the tanners, not even from Mr Dibbler himself, there were the mighty compost heaps downstream of the city, where the volcanic heat of decomposition made fertile soil ('10p a bag, bring your own bag...') out of everything that was left, including – according to rumour – various shadowy businessmen who had come second in a takeover battle ('...brings your dahlias up a treat').

He'd kept the woodpulp-and-rags business closer to home though, along with the huge vats that contained the golden foundations of his fortune, because it was the only part of his business that his wife Effie would talk about. Rumour had it that she had also been behind the removal of the much-admired sign over the entrance to his yard, which said: H. King – Taking the Piss Since 1961. Now it reads: H. King – Recycling Nature's Bounty.

Sir Harry, sorry, Lord King, is now a major mover and shaker in the Ankh-Morpork and Sto Plains Hygienic Railway. [TT]

Kings of Ankh-Morpork. The named ones have included:

- Aguinna IV (Queen) [MAA]
- ARTOROLLO
- Cirone IV [MAA]
- Coanna (Queen) [MAA]
- LORENZO THE KIND
- Mad King Ludwig, the Tree [CWD]
- Paragore [MAA]
- Tyrril [MAA]
- Veltrick III [MAA]
- Webblethorpe the Unconscious [MAA]

***Kite*, the.** Flying machine devised by LEONARD OF QUIRM to transport him, Captain CARROT and RINCEWIND (oh, and the LIBRARIAN) into orbit around the Disc in order to travel to CORI CELESTI during the events of *The Last Hero*. It resembled a huge, wooden eagle and had functional wooden wings so that it could glide or swoop, given appropriate winds and thermals. Its main power to achieve its amazing journey, however, came from the segmented Salmon of Thunder it carries in its claws; this fish-shaped construction contained arrays of dragons, facing moveable mirror mechanisms to get them to flame on demand and provide the motive force to get the *Kite* into orbit around the Disc. [TLH]

Kittens, the torture. The 'feared kitten torture' was actually one improbably dreamed up by Moist von LIPWIG and, amazingly, it seems VETINARI had been impressed.

In the dungeons of the palace there was a large iron maiden, seldom used. In these modern times the kitten torture regime was the punishment that would cause the miscreant to 'paws' before doing anything that would place them in the dungeon again. The mechanism and the kittens were presided over by Cedric. The kittens would be placed in the iron maiden in large numbers, along with the miscreant, who could just about sit. Every time a kitten was in distress, and made its distress noticeable, Cedric would open up the maiden and give the victim a whack with his cudgel. There were some idiots (including me) who thought this laughable, but we are told it worked and, after a certain amount of cudgelling, visitors were said to be amazed at the general atmosphere of happiness inside the iron maiden, where the purring was so loud it resonated throughout the dungeon. Personally, I still think the traditional scorpion pit provides a more improving punishment. [RS]

Klatch. The name of both an individual country and the great mysterious continent, between the CIRCLE SEA and the Rim Ocean, which is its hinterland. Once Klatch, too, had an empire and ruled, more or less, the greater part of the continent. Hence the name has lingered on, at least as far as the people of Ankh-Morpork are concerned.

It has to be said that the words 'Klatch' and 'Klatchian' are used by people of the STO PLAINS as practically interchangeable with 'foreign', in the same way that the fierce D'reg nomads in the Klatchian desert use the words 'foreigner' and 'traveller' interchangeably with the word 'target'.

The sovereign countries of TSORT, DJELIBEYBI, EPHEBE and even OMNIA are all on the Klatchian coast.

Klatch the country is the centre of a prosperous and expanding empire, whose capital city is now AL KHALI, and has a proud and venerable civilization. Its tongue is said to have all the subtlety of a language so ancient and sophisticated that it had fifteen words meaning 'assassination' before the rest of the world caught on to the idea of bashing one another over the head with rocks. Klatch has a big trading fleet, and is also known for its 'bhong' music, its blue-black-skinned people and its cuisine (curry, boiled fish, dark green sauce, rice, etc.).

Klatch is the nearest 'foreign' nation to Ankh-Morpork. Technically, of course, Pseudopolis and QUIRM and Sto Helit are all independent city states and much closer, but they are really, for all their protestations, economic and social satellite states of Ankh-Morpork. Klatch, however, is clearly a rival and is also obviously foreign, and there is therefore that strange love–hate relationship that always exists between two nations whose fortunes are historically intertwined (cf. England and France, the United States North and South, Western Australia and the rest of Australia, Scotland and Scotland, etc., etc.). Traditionally, this means that Klatchians are regarded as being at one and the same time incredibly cunning and irredeemably stupid, bone-idle and deviously industrious, highly cultured and obstinately backward.

The continental hinterland consists of deserts, jungles and rain forests. It also contains lost kingdoms of Amazonian princesses, volcanoes, elephants' graveyards, lost diamond mines, strange ruins covered in hieroglyphics and hidden plateaux where reptilian monsters of a bygone era romp and play. On any reasonable map of the area there's barely room for the trees.

Klatchian Foreign Legion, the. A special force set up by KLATCH (the country) to defend its rather vague desert borders against predatory neighbours and also against the D'regs, a desert tribe. It is, however, open to recruits from any country and traditionally is a refuge for the disgraced, the fugitive and the lovelorn.

It is well known that people join the Klatchian Foreign Legion to forget (everything except sand) and this seems to work, because no one in the Klatchian Foreign Legion can remember why they are there.

Or their name. Or their rank.

The Klatchian Foreign Legion has a famed drinking and marching song, which goes 'Er...'.

Klopstock. Mr Klopstock is the proprietor of the Bull Pit in Pseudopolis, a crude theatre. [SM]

Knibbs, Lettuce. Lady's maid to Queen MOLLY of the BEGGARS' GUILD. Killed in error for Queen Molly. As was remarked by Lance-Constable ANGUA, she was one of those people whose chief role in life is to die. [MAA]

Knock, Sergeant. Sergeant Winsborough 'Knocker' Knock of the Ankh-Morpork City Night Watch. A man with little weaselly eyes. He taught policing to Sergeant COLON. [NW]

Knopf, Corporal. The smaller half (with Sergeant Doppelpunkt) of thr Bad Blintz official Watch. He used to be a trombonist in the army. Any narrativial physical resemblance to a certain sergeant and corporal in the Ankh-Morpork Watch is entirely coincidental, I'm sure. [TAMAHER]

Knurd. Knurd is the opposite of drunk. It should not be mistaken for sobriety. Sobriety is merely the median state; knurdness is a sort of super-sobriety. By comparison, sobriety is like having a bath in warm cotton wool.

Knurdness strips away all the illusion, all the comforting pink fog in which people normally spend their lives, and lets them see and think clearly for the first time ever. Then, after they've screamed a bit, they make sure they never get knurd again.

Klatchian coffee makes you knurd.

Koble, Miskin. Owner of a jellied starfish and clam stall in Sator Square, Ankh-Morpork. [S]

Kom. City in the lands between the deserts of Klatch and the plains and jungles of Howondaland. Its citadel extends for miles – temples, churches, schools, dormitories, gardens and towers. The doors of its central temple are 100 feet tall and made of bronze. They weigh 40 tons each and on them, in letters of gold, are the Commandments – 512 of them so far. [SG]

Koomi. Koomi of Smale. A religious philosopher and author of 'Ego-Video Liber Deorum'. [SG]

Koomi, Hoot. Bald-headed Djelibeybian High Priest of Khefin, the Two-Faced God of Gateways. [P]

Koom Valley. Koom Valley, the site of the most famous battle between the dwarfs and the trolls, is basically a drain. Nearly thirty miles of soft limestone rock edged by mountains of harder rock, so it would have been a canyon if it wasn't so wide. One end was almost on the snowline, the other merged into the plains.

It was said that even clouds kept away from the desolation that was Koom Valley. Maybe they did, but that didn't matter. The valley got the water anyway, from meltwater and the hundreds of waterfalls that poured over its walls from the mountains that cupped it. One of those falls, The Tears of the King, was half a mile high.

The Koom River doesn't just rise in this valley. It leaps and dances in this valley. By the time it is halfway down this valley, it is a criss-crossing of thundering waters, forever merging and parting. They carry and hurl great rocks, and play with whole fallen trees from the dripping forests, colonizing the scree that has built up against the walls. They gurgle into holes and rise again, miles away, as fountains. They have no mappable course – a good storm higher up the valley could bring house-sized rocks and half a stricken woodland down in the flood, blocking the sinkholes and piling up dams. Some of these could survive for years, becoming little islands in the leaping waters, growing little forests and little meadows and colonies of big birds. Then some key rock would be shifted by a random river, and within an hour it would all be gone.

Nothing that couldn't fly lived in the valley, at least for long. The dwarfs had tried to tame it, back before the first battle. They'd never tried again. Hundreds of dwarfs and trolls had been swept up in the famous flood, and barely a few had ever been found again. Koom Valley had taken them all into its sinkholes and chambers and caverns, and had kept them.

There are places in the valley where a man could drop a coloured cork into a swirling sink and could count for twenty minutes before it bobbed up on a fountain less than a dozen yards away.

The valley has guides who tell the history of the place. They'd tell you how the wind in the rocks, and the roaring of the waters, still carry the sounds of ancient battle, continuing in death. They say, maybe all those trolls and dwarves the valley took are still fighting, down there in the dark.

Kreeblephor. Bishop of the Omnian religion. [SG]

Kring. A magical, talking, black sword. Forged from thunderbolt (meteoric) iron. It has highly ornate runic inscriptions running up the blade, a couple of rubies set in its pommel, a slight nick two-thirds of the way up the blade and what it would really like to be is a ploughshare.

Kring speaks in a voice like the scrape of a blade over a stone. Once owned by HRUN the Barbarian, but present whereabouts unknown. [COM]

Krona, Heme. The owner of the Camels-R-Us livery stable in DJELIBEYBI. [P]

Krull. A secretive island kingdom. Geographically, it is a large island, quite mountainous and heavily wooded, with pleasant white buildings visible among the trees. The land slopes gradually up towards the Rim, so that the highest point in Krull slightly overhangs the Edge.

The island not only gets higher as it nears the Edge, it gets narrower, too. Here at the very lip is its major city, also called Krull. At the very edge of the city is a large amphitheatre, with seating for several tens of thousands of people. Its rimmost mountains project over the RIMFALL. In fact, a large part of its coastline sticks out over the Edge, so native Krullians need to look where they are going and avoid sleepwalking at all costs.

Since building materials on Krull are largely salvaged from the CIRCUMFENCE, their houses have a distinctly nautical look. Entire ships are morticed together and converted into buildings.

The city rises, tier upon tier, between the blue-green ocean of the Disc and the soft cloud sea of the Edge, the eight colours of the RIMBOW reflecting in every window and in the many telescope lenses of the city's multitude of astronomers.

Krull is known to the rest of the Discworld, but it generates little commerce or trade. It does have a magical university, far smaller than Unseen University. Krullians have a far more practical attitude to magic, and it is frequently employed for everyday purposes.

The Krullians once had plans to lower a vessel over the Edge to ascertain the sex of the Great A'TUIN. [COM]

Krysoprase. A troll encountered by RINCE-WIND during the events of *The Light Fantastic*. [LF]

Ksandra. A young woman, employed at the Unseen University on laundry duties and dusting. [ER]

K!sdra. A dragonrider from WYRMBERG. His steed is Bronze Psepha. He wears general dragonriders' clothing: a pair of high boots, a tiny leather holdall in the region of his groin and a high-crested helmet. [COM]

Ktoffle. A plaintiff before TEPPIC in the DJELIBEYBI supreme court. [P]

Ku. A continent that slipped into the ocean several thousand years ago. It took thirty years to subside; the inhabitants spent a lot of time wading. It went down in history as the multiverse's most embarrassing continental catastrophe. [E]

Kwartz. A troll encountered by RINCEWIND. He has a wife, Beryl, and, we think, a son called Jasper. [LF]

There was always this trouble with the Librarian. Everyone had got so accustomed to him it was hard to remember a time when the Library was not run by a yellow-fanged ape with the strength of three men.

— *Moving Pictures*

Lackjaw. Dwarf jeweller. He made COHEN the Barbarian's dentures. Current whereabouts unknown, but he is probably a floating piece of onion in the great melting-pot that is Ankh-Morpork. [LF]

Laddie. A pure-bred RAMTOP hunting dog who found fame in HOLY WOOD as Laddie the Wonder Dog. A friendly personality, but in the opinion of his manager (GASPODE) he was as dim as a ha'penny candle. [MP]

Lady, the. *See* LUCK.

Lady Jane. An ancient and evil-tempered gyrfalcon in LANCRE. Trained by HODGE-SAARGH as only he knows how. [LL]

Lancrastian Army Knife, the. Created by Shawn OGG. It was obvious to King VERENCE that even if every adult were put under arms, the kingdom of Lancre would still have a very small and insignificant army, and he'd therefore looked for other ways to put it on the military map. Shawn had come up with the idea of the Lancrastrian Army Knife, containing a few essential tools and utensils for the soldier in the field, and research and development work had been going on for some time. One reason for the slow progress was that the king himself takes an active interest in the country's only defence project, and Shawn is used to receiving little notes up to three times every day with further suggestions for improvement. Generally they are on the lines of: 'A device, possibly quite small, for finding things that are lost' or 'A curiously shaped hook-like thing of many uses'. Shawn diplomatically adds some of them but loses as many notes as he dares, lest he design the only pocket knife on wheels.

Nevertheless, the current knife includes, among more normal devices such as nose-hair tweezers and a folding saw, the following rather more existential attachments:

Adjustable Device for Winning Ontological Arguments
Tool for Extracting the Essential Truth from a Given Statement
Device for Dissecting Paradoxes
Appliance for Detecting Small Grains of Hope
Spiral Thing for Ascertaining the Reality of Being
Instrument for Ending Arguments Very Quickly. [CJ]

Lancre. A kingdom on the STO PLAINS side of the RAMTOP mountains. Coat of arms: two bears on a black and gold shield.

Pop. (including humans, trolls, dwarfs and miscellaneous): approx. 600. (Dwarfs and trolls do not formally acknowledge the Crown of Lancre, but the three species get along quite amicably, or at least seldom practise open warfare within shouting distance of the border.)

Pop. for tax purposes: 27.

Size: technically it has a border some 100 miles in length. The actual acreage of the kingdom is hard to calculate because of its mountainous nature and, in any case, it backs on to the Ramtops themselves and areas that are claimed by no man, troll or dwarf. The fact that there are at least two gateways into other dimensions in the country could also be held to give it a possibly infinite area.

Imports: none, except for various minor items (rare herbs, some manufactured goods). The people of Lancre are smugly self-sufficient.

Exports: iron ore and gold (from the dwarfs) and people (from mothers and fathers). People are Lancre's greatest export; the tiny kingdom has produced many wizards, at least one ARCHCHANCELLOR of Unseen University, one possible king of Ankh-Morpork and a vast number of industrious dwarfs and humans who have gone off to seek their fortune and send some of it back to their mum every week, regular. Lancre is one of those places, like A-Town-You've-Probably-Never-Heard-Of, Iowa, in which are generated people who go off somewhere and become famous.

Geography: Lancre occupies little more than a ledge cut into the side of the Ramtop mountains. Behind it, towering peaks and dark, winding valleys climb to the massive backbone of the central ranges. In front, the land drops to the Sto Plains. Most of Lancre is thus cruel mountainside with ice-green slopes and knife-edge crests, or dense, huddled forests. As has been indicated, it gives visitors the feeling that it contains far too much geography. There are few places in the kingdom where you could drop a football and not have it roll away.

On the hubward side of the country are glacier lakes and alpine meadows. This end of the kingdom is dominated by COPPERHEAD – by no means the biggest of the Ramtops, but an impressive mountain whose slopes and foothills are home to many dwarfs and trolls.

The kingdom has a number of human habitations: Lancre Town, where most human inhabitants live, and the villages of BAD ASS, Slippery Hollow, Razorback and, of course, Slice.

Slice is in a deep, forested cleft in the mountains, and contains both the original Rock and a Hard Place, and the Place Where the Sun Does Not Shine. The inhabitants of Slice are considered strange even by the lax standards of the rest of Lancre. We are talking twenty-toe country here; we are talking the kind of place where you may have to learn to play the banjo to survive and marrying your cousin is considered posh.

Other features of note include the DANCERS, a circle of standing stones on a small area of moorland not far from the town, and the LONG MAN, an assemblage of one long and two round barrows, now badly overgrown. Both of these features contain secret entrances to the world of the ELVES and, in the case of the Long Man, also to Lancre Caves.

The caves are rumoured to run everywhere in the kingdom; it is widely believed that there is a secret entrance in the castle. But they are also one of those features that are not bound by the laws of time and space. Travel far enough in the caves and you will find mythical kings, asleep with their warriors; you will hear the roar of the Minotaur and the sheep of the Cyclops. Walk far enough and you will meet yourself, coming the other way.

Politics: in theory, under VERENCE II, a constitutional monarchy. This is not running smoothly because the citizens of Lancre, bloody-minded monarchists to the bone, feel that if someone is supposed to be king he should damn well get on with it. They don't expect the king to tell them how to farm or thatch, and so don't see why he should expect them to tell him how to king.

Verence and his queen, Magrat (Magrat GARLICK), have devoted themselves to the well-being of their subjects, instituting a number of social, agricultural and educational improvements, which the people of Lancre seem to be surviving by dint of ignoring them all as politely as possible.

State religion: none. However, various wandering monks and priests tour the mountains for those who need them. The Nine Day Wonderers and the Priests of Small Gods are generally welcome, if only because their religions hinge on the uncertainty of knowing anything at all.

Lancrastians, however, do instinctively practise a kind of civil religion. It is felt right and proper to have some kind of religious service to mark births, marriages and deaths, without much attention being paid to which god or goddess is actually involved, and a regular feature of the Lancre calendar is the harvest festival, when the people give thanks – not to anyone, exactly, but in general terms.

Another peculiarly Lancrastian custom is that new-born children are formally named at midnight, so that they start a day with a new name.

Lancre operates on a feudal system – everyone feuds all the time and hands on the fight to their descendants. The chips on some shoulders have been handed down for generations. Some had antique value. A bloody good grudge, Lancre reckons, was like a fine old wine; you looked after it carefully and left it to your children.

Lancrastians never throw away anything that works. The trouble is, they seldom *change* anything that works, either. They wouldn't dream of living in anything other than a monarchy. They've done it for thousands of years and they know it works. In any case, you don't need to pay too much attention to what the king wants, because there is bound to be another king along in forty years or so and he'll be certain to want something different, and so you'd have gone to all that trouble for nothing. In the meantime, his job, as they see it, is to mostly stay in the palace, practise the waving, have enough sense to face the right way on coins and let them get on with the ploughing, sowing, growing and harvesting. It is a social contract. They do what they always do, and he lets them.

Lancre Castle. The most striking thing about the castle is that it is much bigger than it needs to be. This may be a relic of the time when elves made more incursions than they do now – as has been said, Lancre contains at least two dimensional doorways into their worlds.

It is built on an outcrop of rock, leaning vertiginously over the River Lancre and immediately overlooking the town square. It is in very bad repair, and one of the first jobs of the staff in the morning is to see what parts of the castle have fallen down during the night.

Under the present monarch the staff have been reduced somewhat, and now consist of Mrs SCORBIC the cook, SPRIGGINS the butler, Millie CHILLUM the maid and Shawn OGG (Commander-in-Chief of the Army, the rest of the army, Captain of the Guard, the guard, the seneschal, the kitchen boy, the armourer, the odd-job man, the herald, the gardener, Chief Constable, the gatekeeper and Lord Privy of the Privy).

Other outside staff, who in many ways pursue their own jobs with only a mild interest in whosoever is actually running the place, consist of HODGESAARGH the falconer and Mr BROOKS the beekeeper.

Lancre River. A shallow and very fast-flowing river, a tributary of the Ankh. As it curves around the town it foams over a series of rapids and weirs, but further into the mountains there are occasional hidden water meadows and quiet pools. Lancre Bridge, over which travels the road to the Plains, is three miles from the castle, upstream of the town of Lancre Gorge. The road from the bridge to the town curves between high banks, with the forest crowding in on either side.

Lancre Town. The town is a stone's drop from the river. Technically it would barely pass anywhere else as a village, but, by dint of being that much bigger than anywhere else in Lancre, it acts as though it were a city. A town rule is that all mummers, mountebanks, etc., must be outside the gates by sundown. This is not a problem as the town has no walls to speak of, and after sundown they just come back again. It boasts a tavern (the Goat & Bush) on the main square, plus an old forge and a lodging house.

Langas, Pilotus and. The legend of Pilotus and Langas, who wanted to fly like the birds, is known by every well-educated boy (editor's note – or, presumably, girl). They did indeed build themselves wings by sewing together feathers and thistledown. The boy, at least, flew a little way, but his elderly and portly father crashed. The moral of this story is: understand what you are doing before you do it. [TSC]

Lankin. An elf. High cheekbones, a perfect nose and a ponytail. He wears odds and ends of rags and lace and fur, confident in the knowledge that anything looks good on an elf. Like all elves, totally self-confident and immensely cruel – but with style, so that's OK. [LL]

Laolith. LIESSA's dragon. Described as having a great, horsey head with a leathery neck and jowls greasy with pork fat. [COM]

Larsnephew, Lars. 'Father of Exploration'. Little is known of the life of Lars Larsnephew except that he never travelled further than ten miles from the village of NoThing, in NoThingfjord, where he was born. Yet he inspired one of the most sustained periods of exploration in the history of the Disc. He was not so much an explorer as the cause of exploration in other people.

This is thought to be because of his mastery of ancient sagas, some of which could last for several years. It was rumoured that the standing stones in the area were merely people who had sat through his complete repertoire, which was mainly to do with snow. The mere sight of Lars looking thoughtful was enough to send local people dashing to their longboats and rowing desperately for the open sea; most of them later grounded on islands which, while often inhospitable, had the major advantage of not containing Lars Larsnephew.

Many of them returned when he'd finished, but left no foreign settlements or very precise navigational records, owing to being almost permanently drunk on a form of beer made from herrings.

As sea-borne, longboat-rowing, fair-haired explorers went, the villagers were not a great success. They possessed the tendency of some Hubland peoples to be very meticulous on matters of etiquette, and their forages to rape, loot and pillage along the wintry rimward coastline of the Vortex Plains were consequently marred by their attempts to do so by appointment.

The occupants of many far-flung hamlets never pointed out to them the essential flaw in this approach and got quite used to returning home from their temporary hide-out in the hills to find a reproachful note saying: 'We called today a.m./p.m. but you were out.' [DM]

Lasgere. A former prince of Tsort. Killed by a slave during an experiment in 'learning while you sleep'; the slave's duty was to read to him all night. What Lasgere presumably did learn was that it is not a good idea for the slave to be armed with a knife. [SG]

Launch Controller. Official of KRULL who was responsible for the planning of the launch of the *Potent Voyager* from Krul. He was a practical magician, rather than a diplomat. [COM]

Lavaeolus. The finest military mind on the continent of KLATCH. When first seen, he was wearing tarnished armour and a grubby cloak. The helmet plume looked as though it had been used as a paintbrush. He was skinny, with all the military bearing of a deckchair.

His genius consisted of realizing that, if there has to be a war, the aim should be to defeat the enemy as quickly and with as little bloodshed as possible – a concept so breathtaking in its originality that few other military minds have been able to grasp it, and it shows what happens when you take the conduct of a war away from skilled soldiers.

He was a hero of the Tsortean Wars, which he ended by bribing a cleaner to show him a secret passage into the citadel of TSORT. So not many people actually died during its capture, which means it couldn't have been that much of a victory, really.

It is possible that he is an ancestor of RINCE-WIND. [P]

Lavatory, Charles, Sir. Owner of C. H. Lavatory & Son, Mollymog Street, Ankh-Morpork, and president of the PLUMBERS' GUILD. Invented the first really efficient flushing toilet, which was therefore named after him. Of course, flushing a lavatory in Ankh-Morpork is not likely to make things any better.

A remarkable parallel with Thomas Crapper, the Victorian sanitary engineer who also lent his name to the more modern version of the privy, although the term 'crapper' in that sense dates back at least to the sixteenth century. Perhaps Thomas got teased a lot at school and decided that if he was going to bear this name through life, then he'd damn well see to it that it was one to be proud of. [SM]

Lavish, Cosmo. Stepson of Topsy Lavish and brother to Pucci Lavish (from whom he was forbidden, by court injunction, from coming within twenty yards). He has made a detailed study of Lord Vetinari and is one of his biggest admirers.

Cosmo Lavish is cool, or at least makes a spirited effort to be so. He wears black, of course, as people do to show how rich they are, but the real giveaway is the beard. It is, technically, a goatee, but so exotic that it would have to be a very rare sort of goat, that maybe lived on high vertical cliff and had wool so fine that you'd have to shave five of them before you could knit a scarf. A thin line of black hair comes down each cheek, makes a detour to loop equally thinly under the nose and meets in a black triangle just below the lip, thus giving what Cosmo must have thought was a look of menacing elegance, but in fact creates the effect of a pubic chin.

It is a high maintenance beard, even so. It isn't the beard of a man who has to get to work in a hurry. Some master barber has to deal with it hair by hair every day, and his job isn't made any easier by the fact that Cosmo has inflated somewhat since the day he adopted the style. There is a time in a thoughtless young man's life when his six-pack becomes a keg, and now the elegant facial topiary floats unhappily on a layer of fat. Cosmo is heavy bearded, too, so his jowls are usually blue. And yes, little tiny beads of sweat glint amongst the stubble.

And then you see the eyes, and they make up for everything. They have the faraway look of a man who can already see you dead... [MM]

Lavish, Pucci. Stepdaughter of Topsy Lavish and sister to Cosmo Lavish – who views her as a fiend in technically human shape. She is forbidden, by court injunction, from coming within fifteen yards of Cosmo. Pucci has a voice like a saw encountering a nail, with a slight additional touch of foghorn, and is always referred to as 'a society beauty', which shows just how rich the Lavishes are. Cut in half, she might make two society beauties but not, at that point, very beautiful ones. While it is said that men she had spurned jumped off bridges in despair, the only person known to have said this is Pucci herself.

She is a 'large girl' and is blessed with beady, suspicious little eyes and a generous upper lip, which combine with the long neck to put the honest observer in mind of a duck who's just been offended by a passing trout.

Someone should have told her that black is not her colour, that the expensive fur could had looked better on its original owners, that if you are going to wear high heels then this week's fashion tip is *don't wear sunglasses at the same time*, because when you walk out of the bright sunlight into to the relative gloom of, say, a bank, you will lose all sense of direction and impale the foot of one of your own bodyguards. Someone should have told her, in fact, that true style comes from within. You can't buy it. Pucci can flounce better than a fat turkey on a trampoline. [MM]

Lavish, Topsy, Mrs. (Née Turvy.) Widow of Sir Joshua Lavish and stepmother to Pucci and Cosmo. She was a very small, very elderly, grey-haired woman with thin little hands. Moist von LIPWIG classes her as a 'Mark I Feisty Old Lady'; turkey neck, embarrassing sense of humour, a gleeful pleasure in mild cruelty, direct way of speaking that flirts with rudeness and, more importantly, also flirts with flirting. Game for anything that doesn't carry the risk of falling over and with a look in her eye that says 'I can do what I like, because I am old.' She used to own or control 51 per cent of the shares in the Royal Bank of Ankh-Morpork and she was the original owner of Mr FUSSPOT. [MM]

Lawn, Mossy, Dr. Doctor Lawn lived in Twinkle Street, Ankh-Morpork but has moved to premises in Goose Gate, now the Lady Sybil Free Hospital. He is a large, expansive man, who looks as though he played many rough, competitive games when he was younger and wishes he could do so now, if only his belly were smaller and the legs still willing.

He wears the tradtional long black robe and silly floppy hat, but has some radical new ideas about washing hands and keeping patients alive even *beyond* the time needed to get paid. Lawn's customers are at the bottom end of Ankh-Morpork society, in several senses. He is the unofficial doctor to the SEAMSTRESSES' GUILD and, now, to Her Grace the Duchess of Ankh-Morpork. It's amazing how rich you can become if you're in the right place with the right skills at the right time. [NW]

Law of Unequal Returns. A growing cause of friction in Ankh-Morpork. Let us say the rate for a job is five dollars a day. To a dwarf, the five dollars is worth rather more because, although dwarfs have much the same appetites as humans, they have much reduced accommodation expenses. This has always been noticed but has not led to much trouble; it is the recent influx of gnomes and goblins that has really brought the problem to light.

In trades like watchmaking and rat-catching, for example, very small people are not only at an advantage but in practical terms their wages are worth a lot more.

A dollar buys a man a big loaf. To him it is a meal. The same loaf at the same price is, to a gnome, bread for a week and can also be hollowed out to make temporary accommodation for his family. In occupations where small size and tiny fingers are a positive advantage (engraving, fine lace-making and so on) gnomes can both undercut human competition and yet live very stylishly.

There is clearly going to be trouble.

Laws of Ankh-Morpork. There aren't any.

Well...

Not entirely true. There aren't any now, except in the almost iconographic memory of Captain CARROT of the City WATCH. There are Guild laws, administered by the various Guilds and often the cause of friction between them (*see* VETINARI, LORD), but laws in the modern sense have gone out of fashion in the last several hundred years. The city is not, however, lawless. It more or less runs on the 'Patrician's Rules'. Lord Vetinari takes the unvoiced view that most citizens are guilty of something, or just generally guilty in a low-grade way. If there is a crime, then there ought to be seen to be a punishment; if the punishment can involve the actual perpetrator of the crime then this is a happy state of affairs, but it is not essential. Anything that threatens the city in any way – be it a man, a philosophy or a device – is 'against the law'.

Beyond that, Lord Vetinari believes in a common or natural law; if a man can sell short-weight bread and get away with it, then get away with it he does. If, however, his defrauded customers decide to nail him to his own ceiling, then that is fine, too.

The known and somewhat fossilized laws of Ankh-Morpork are:

Being Bloody Stupid Act, 1581
Decency Ordinances, 1389
Dignity of Man (Civil Rights) Act, 1341
Domestic & Domesticated Animals (Care
    & Protection) Act, 1673
Gambling (Regulations) Acts

General Felonies Act, 1678

Industrial Processes Act, 1508

Licensed Premises (Hygiene) Acts, 1433, 1456, 1463, 1465 and 1470–1690

Privacy Act, 1467

Projectile Weapons (Civil Safety) Act, 1634

Public Ale Houses (Opening) Act, 1678

Public Forgatherings (Gambling) Act, 1567

Public Order Act, 1457

They are listed merely for completeness.

THE SYSTEM OF JUSTICE

1. Criminal Justice

As explained, there is none.

Although the current system in Ankh-Morpork consists almost entirely of 'Guild Justice' enforced by the city's Guilds, it is still the case that criminals taken by the Watch may opt to stand for trial before the PATRICIAN.

The accused may, if they have money, employ a member of the Guild of Lawyers (motto: LVCRE SERMAT [Money Talks]) to speak on their behalf. If they wish to be found not guilty, they will often need large reserves of money. The long-held principle is very clear – the more money you have, the more likely you are to be innocent. This is considered right and proper by the Guild, because rich people are an asset to society and there are far too many poor people around in any case, and they're probably all criminals.

If the accused has no money, then their only hope is if the Patrician decides in their favour. He quite often does so, because he finds it instructive to all concerned.

As indicated elsewhere, there is no formal system of criminal law in the city. Nor is there any recognized scale of punishment. Imprisonment is viewed as a school for criminals and a drain on the state, and so therefore most punishments are a fine or a flogging. There are a number of specialized punishments, of which the scorpion pit is the best known, but for offences of a sexual nature, particularly against minors, the usual recourse is the traditional tree, jar of honey and herd of cows.

Occasionally – but rarely – other ancient punishments are resurrected for deserving cases. A classic one is tying the offender to one of the pillars of the Brass Bridge at low tide and untying him twenty-four hours later, at which point he is free to go.

The death penalty is usually reserved for treachery to the city, continuing to commit murder after being told not to, irredeemable stupidity while not being a troll, and persistent street theatre.

2. Civil Justice

A state whose citizens are as perennially indignant and argumentative as are Ankh-Morpork's is bound to have a thriving Civil bench, and this is where the Guild of Lawyers make their real money. Cases are usually heard before a Court of Magisters (for poor people) or before a senior member of the Guild who has been appointed by the Patrician to serve as a judge.

(Since this is a fixed-salary post, this means that the appointee suffers an effective drop in income, barring bribes, of course. Thus appointment to the role of judge is usually used by the Patrician as a form of mild rebuke to lawyers who have failed him in one way or another.)

3. The Historical System

In the very early days of Ankh-Morpork, justice was dispensed by the Archchancellor's Court (see UNSEEN UNIVERSITY). There then followed a system set up under the city's monarchy, and many of today's traditions and titles date from that period. A three-tier system of justice prevailed:

 i. Small cases, involving the common citizens, would be heard by the Court of Magisters (or Justices of the King's Peace), made up of men of the city's ruling classes. These JKPs would carry a nosegay into court, to ward off the offensive smell of the lower orders. As Ankh-Morpork got bigger, sometimes three or four people were needed to carry the flowers.

 ii. Larger cases, involving the wealthier members of society, would be pleaded on their behalf by trained legal experts from the Guild of Lawyers. These experts, known as pleaders (who wore robes with a purse sewn into the upper-left back, so that their fee could be dropped in without them having to be seen handling filthy lucre), carried the title of Serjeant (a corruption of their old title of *servientes Regis ad legem*). They were the only people entitled to plead cases before one of the King's Judges. The King's Judges were reputed to be the finest judges that money could buy and they were often employed by other kings and queens in the STO PLAINS.

   iii. Ultimate recourse was to the king, who would hear their pleadings in the Rats Chamber (so called because of the fresco of dancing rats painted on its ceiling). A vestige of this system still prevails in that the Patrician is the last court of appeal.

Reference is still made to the 'Inns of Court'. These were the ale-houses surrounding the Court House from which accused people would try to entice drunken lawyers with offers of hard cash.

COURTS AND PRISONS

The old and derelict Ankh-Morpork Court House was taken over by the THIEVES' GUILD as their headquarters in the time of Lord Vetinari. Large, and probably profitable, court cases are now heard in a courtroom within the Guild of Lawyers.

   There used to be a large prison (now private houses) around Sybil Lane near Hen and Chickens Field. The field got its name from the frequent processions to the gallows there, when the priest of choice would walk ahead of the gaggle of warders and accused, like 'a hen and her chicks'. This is how proper old cities name their places; they wouldn't *dream* of calling something First Avenue just because they'd got a lot of avenues and it was the first.

   For the few individuals it is necessary to lock up, the modern prison, originally a royal palace called Tintement but now known as The Tanty, is on the Rim Bank. Its current head warder is

an enlightened man who practises an intensive counselling and caring approach, subsequent to which many prisoners apply briskly for the cow and honey cure.

Lawsy Family. Mrs Angeline is the widow of a Mr Lawsy, an eel juggler. Their offspring, Henry, who works as a clerk in the firm of Morecombe, Slant and Honeyplace, is actually the result of a *liaison* with Henry SLUGG. [MA]

Laziman, Timo. A member of the Thieves' Guild who, rather audaciously, mugged Alberto Malich. [SM]

Leakall, Edith. Champion pig borer, who verbally euthanized a pig in only nine minutes with an anecdote about the problems her friend, Mrs Insufflator, had with her knee. [TDA]

Legba. A large, black cockerel. Familiar of Mrs GOGOL. [WA]

Legibus. An Ephebian philosopher and author of 'Geometries'. A little man with a beard you could camp out in. He is quite old, and resembles a frog that has been dried out for some time. Something about him generally makes people think of the word 'spry'. [SG]

LeJean, Myria, Lady. Originally an AUDITOR OF REALITY, she adopted human form to undertake a task for the Auditors. She was later named 'Unity' by Susan STO HELIT. In human form, she has long, black hair cascading over her shoulders and she is quite attractive, in a monochromatic sort of way. Strictly speaking, she was an Auditor sent to learn more about being human; what she learned, in summary, was that she never wanted to go back to being an Auditor. Oh…and that there was such a thing as chocolate. [TOT]

Lemon, Satchelmouth. The recruiting and enforcement officer for the Musicians' Guild, Ankh-Morpork. [SM]

Leonard of Quirm. (Aka Leonard da Quirm.) A painter and inventor; the greatest Discworld technological genius of all time. He had a house in the Street of Cunning Artificers, Ankh-Morpork, but currently resides in an attic in the PATRICIAN'S PALACE.

This may be considered cruel, but in many ways it is quite impossible to imprison someone like Leonard. Give him enough wood, wire, paints, drawing materials, food, a potty and a window through which he can watch the birds and it's unlikely that he will even notice. It's a large attic, airy and bright and cheerful, with sunlight from windows in the roof. It's a sort of cross between a workshop and a store room. Several bird skeletons hang from the ceiling; there are other bones on the work tables, along with coils of wire and metal springs, and tubes of paint and more tools – many probably unique – than you normally see in any one place. There is also a narrow bed, wedged between a thing like a loom with wings and a large bronze statue.

In appearance, he is clearly one of those people who started to look old around the age of thirty. He is not exactly bald. He has a lot of hair, long and curly and reaching almost to his shoulders. And he has a beard large enough to conceal a small chicken. His head has just grown up through his hair.

One of his achievements is the well-known painting the MONA OGG (her teeth are said to follow you round the room).

Leonard's genius lies in seeing inherent in the common world the obvious things that men have never seen before. He is obsessively interested in *everything*. Yet within the vast amber of his genius is locked the tiny insect of what would be called, in a lesser man, stupidity. He watches the swirl of water over weirs, the intricate movements of musculature, the gliding of birds and the play of light through prisms and, then, fills up notebook after notebook with ingenious devices for killing whole cities by means of hot oil, explosions, etc. He has never in his life harmed a living creature, and would be greatly surprised and terribly shocked to think that anyone would take these doodles (with their carefully numbered components and cutaway diagrams) seriously. Inventions of his, lying unnoticed in obscure places or drawn as idle sketches in the margins of otherwise unremarkable books, lie around Ankh-Morpork like razor blades in a ham sandwich.

It has to be added that one reason why Leonard's inventions have not totally changed the face of the world is, probably, that he finds it hard to deal with the relative importance of things. He will expend as much time on designing a new hinge as he will on some vast scheme for extracting sunlight from oranges.

He also has a strange attention span. He does not quickly lose interest in things. In fact, he remains greatly interested in all sorts of things, all the time, which leads him down all kinds of side alleys while the ostensible main invention gets neglected. For him there is, as it were, no difference between designing the *Titanic* and designing the deckchairs.

For example, Leonard's invention of the internal combustion engine has been delayed for some years while he works on the problem of how to make dice fluffy. But when a flying machine capable of reaching the highest mountain on the Disc was urgently needed, he designed it in a day, and that included two hours developing the Frying-Pan-that-Sticks-to-Everything.

Leonid. A past king of EPHEBE. [MP]

Leonard of Quirm

Leshp, Brass Gongs of. The legendary Brass Gongs can be heard far out in the CIRCLE SEA on stormy nights, as the currents stir the drowned towers of the city of Leshp, three hundred fathoms below. The kingdom briefly reappeared for the events of *Jingo*. [M]

Letitia. Letitia Keepsake. Daughter of the Duchess of Keepsake and one-time fiancée, now wife of ROLAND (and thus a Baroness). A colourless, fragile girl, with very blond hair and blue eyes. She wears a silly lacy dress and seriously impractical tiny white shoes. She has definite magical skills. Her family live at Keepsake Hall, at the far end of the Chalk. She is so good at being a Baroness that Tiffany ACHING wonders if Being a Baroness might come to win over Being a Witch in the end. [ISWM]

Level, Miss. A witch, who lives in 'the Cottage in the Woods, Near the Dead Oak Tree in Lost Man's Lane, High Overhang, If Out Leave Letters In Old Boot By Door'. Her garden is full of ornaments – sad, cheap ones – bunny rabbits with mad grins, pottery deer with big eyes, gnomes with pointy red hats and expressions that suggest they are on bad medication.

She is a research witch, who tries to find new spells by learning how old ones were really done. There are, were, two of her – she is/was one person in two bodies. She has/had a right right hand and a right left hand and a left right hand and a left left hand. She could go shopping and stay home at the same time. She is like one person with four arms and four legs and four eyes. And two noses. Her right body was slightly clumsier than her left body, but she had better eyesight in her right pair of eyes. If there's a gap of more than twenty miles or so between her two bodies, she gets rather clumsy.

She has long, grey hair, and she is quite tall, just slightly overweight and she wears lots of necklaces – and her glasses on a chain. She wears all black, with black jewellery and surprisingly high-heeled boots. Her trick broom is disguised as a bundle of firewood. Her pointy hat is only 9" high, to avoid having to duck in low-ceilinged rooms.

Her mother died shortly after she was born, and her father was at sea and never came back. She ran away to join the circus as Topsy & Tipsy, The Astounding Mind-Reading Act (also the Stupendous Bokunkus Sisters). At one time, she walked out with Marco & Falco, the Flying Pastrami Brothers (really called Sidney & Frank Cartwright). [HFOS]

Lezek. MORT's father. Bearded, shorter than his son, he made a haphazard living as a farmer. [M]

Liartes. Brother of LIO!RT Dragonlord and LIESSA Dragonlady, and son of GREICHA THE FIRST, Lord of the WYRMBERG. [COM]

Librarian. The Librarian of Unseen University is an orang-utan. This was not always the case. He was magically transformed by the events chronicled in *The Light Fantastic* – but since then no member of the University staff can remember who he was beforehand. In addition, a page was torn out of the relevant year book; no one knows why, or why the place was marked with a banana skin. There is a rumour that the Librarian was once Dr Horace WORBLEHAT, B.Thau, D.M.

It is clear that, whoever and whatever he once was, the Librarian is now blissfully happy in himself, reckoning that the prehensile toes and extra-long arms are very helpful in his role. In a sense, say the wizards, it is as though he always was the Librarian and whatever inoffensive human shape he had for the first several decades of his life, he was merely marking time until he could become his own self.

In looks he has the red-haired-rubber-sack-filled-with-water look of a very well-grown (300lb) male, although he has not developed the overlarge cheek pads that are a feature of a dominant male orang. This is because he is not, strictly, a dominant male – he is an ex-officio member of the college council and a member of the faculty, and he therefore, quite rightly, regards the ARCHCHANCELLOR as the dominant male, even though the Archchancellor does not often sit high up in trees with a large

The Librarian

leaf on his head.

Habits and habitat: he has a book-lined nest in a cubby-hole under the desk in the middle of the Library. He hides there under his tattered blanket when he is worried. He appears to want nothing more than soft fruit, a regular supply of index cards and the opportunity, every month or so, to hop over the wall of the PATRICIAN's private menagerie. (This is a puzzle. There are no orangs in the menagerie. Nor are there any other kinds of ape.) He is generally naked but he does wear an old green robe when he's had a bath or modesty really requires it.

The Librarian is, of course, very much in favour of reading in general, but readers in particular get on his nerves. There is something sacrilegious about the way people keep taking books off the shelves and wearing out the words by reading them. He likes people who love and respect books, and the best way to do that, in the Librarian's opinion, is to leave them on the shelves where Nature intended them to be.

In short, he is a useful and well-respected member of the University staff, his only failing being a tendency to educative violence if referred to as a 'monkey'. During the evenings he can often be found enjoying a quiet pint and, if the landlord is not wary, every single bowl of peanuts in the Mended DRUM, where his iron grip and ability to swing from the rafters adds an extra dimension of terror to bar-room brawls. [COM]

Libraries, nature of. Even big collections of ordinary books distort space and time, as can readily be proved by anyone who has been around a really old-fashioned second-hand bookshop, one of those that has more staircases than storeys and those rows of shelves that end in little doors that are surely too small for a full-sized human to enter.

The relevant equation is: Knowledge = Power = Energy = Matter = Mass; a good bookshop is just a genteel Black Hole that knows how to read. Mass distorts space into polyfractal L-space, in which Everywhere is also Everywhere Else.

All libraries everywhere are connected in L-space by the bookwormholes created by the strong space–time distortions found in any large collection of books. Only a very few librarians learn the secret, and there are inflexible rules about making use of the fact – because it amounts to time travel.

The three rules of the Librarians of Time and Space are: 1) Silence; 2) Books must be returned no later than the last date shown; and 3) the nature of causality must not be interfered with. (*See also* BOOKS and INVISIBLE WRITINGS.)

Library, the. Books play a major role in the Discworld. In Discworld reality, as well as in general magical theory, the Name is often nearly identical to the Thing itself; to know the Name is to control the Thing. Books on the Discworld often do far more than merely record its history and the concerns of its inhabitants; they often are the script on which the unfolding drama is based.

Books can also be affected by their contents, and a book containing powerful magic spells can become, for all practical purposes, alive.

The Library at Unseen University therefore has to deal with problems rather greater than readers writing 'Rubbish!' in the margins and using slices of bacon as a bookmark.

From the outside, the Library of Unseen University is a low, brooding building, with high, narrow, barred windows and a glass dome high above its centre. There clearly is a centre, because it is quite possible for someone to walk from the door to the middle of the floor.

However, all four of the standard dimensions are, in this place, plaited like soft clay by the presence of the very high thaumic field generated by the magic in the books coupled with the pressure on space–time from the books themselves. Because of the distortions caused by the vast amount of assembled knowledge, the Library has a diameter of about 100 yards but an infinite radius. The interior is a topographical nightmare; the sheer presence of so much stored magic twisting dimensions and gravity into the kind of spaghetti that would make M. C. Escher go for a good lie down, or possibly sideways. The floor seems to become the wall in the distance, shelves play tricks on the eyes and seem to twist through more dimensions than the usual three. There are even some shelves up on the ceiling.

The Library is the greatest assemblage of magical texts anywhere in the multiverse; over 90,000 volumes weigh down its shelves. (This may not sound like many, but it should be borne in mind that most of the books are fully two feet high and six inches thick and some are much larger. And these are merely the *magical* books. The Library also houses an uncounted number of less volatile texts, in the occult sense at any rate; indeed, if the L-space theories are correct, the Library contains every book everywhere, including the ones that never actually got written.)

Magic is volatile. A spell may be pinned to the page like a butterfly, but it still tries to escape, to have form, to take control, to be said. In a sense, the books in UU's library are semi-alive. At UU, your homework could eat the dog.

Great care has to be taken to ensure that this magic causes no harm. As the raw magic crackles from the spines of the magical books, it earths itself harmlessly in the copper rails nailed to every shelf for that very purpose.

In most old libraries the books are chained to the shelves to prevent them being damaged by people; in the Library of Unseen University, of course, it's more or less the other way around.

Faint traceries of blue fire crawl across the bookcases and there is a sound, a papery whispering, such as might come from a colony of roosting starlings. In the silence of the night, the books talk to one another.

It is always warm in the Library, because the magic that produces the OCTARINE glow also gently cooks the air.

In the lower levels are the maximum security shelves where the rogue books are kept – the books whose behaviour or mere contents demand a whole shelf, a whole room, to themselves. Cannibal books. Books which will read you rather than the other way about. Books which, if left on a shelf with their weaker brethren, would be found in a 'Revised, Enlarged and Smug Edition' in the morning.

Down in these dark tunnels, behind heavily barred doors, are also kept the, er, erotic books, in vats of crushed ice. Also kept in the Library of Unseen University is the 'OCTAVO', originally in the possession of the CREATOR of the Discworld.

And, as indicated before, there is L-space. Somewhere beyond the common shelves lies an entire library universe, peopled by creatures that have evolved in the immense biobibliographical field, such as kickstool crabs and the wild thesaurus. It should be possible eventually to find your way into any other library at any point in time, and it is known that the LIBRARIAN made use of this feature to rescue some of the more interesting works from the burning library of EPHEBE (in *Small Gods*).

New readers are required to make the following declaration.

Declaration to be Read Aloud When Asked

'I, Speak Your Name, hereby undertake not to remove without permission from the Library, or to mark, deface, or injure in any way, any volume, document, or other object belonging to it or use inappropriate force in fighting back any such volumes as may from time to time attack me; not to bring into the Library or kindle therein any fire or flame be it magical or otherwise, and not to smoke or expectorate or explode or levitate above 2' in the Library; to refrain, to the best of my abilities, from spontaneously combusting in the Library; and I promise to obey all rules of the Library and any which may, from time to time, be added by the Librarian, whose judgement on all matters relating to the operation of the Library is final and if necessary terminal. I further promise to read and inwardly digest any documents that are drawn to my attention attesting to the difference between those creatures commonly referred to as "monkeys" and the higher apes, accepting further that being allowed to do so is a concession on the part of the Librarian and that holding my head two inches from the page is an aid to reading and then repeatedly banging it on the table is a valuable aid to memory.'

Various legends are linked to UU's library. There is the persistent story of the Lost Reading Room, for example. Wise students in search of more distant volumes take care to leave chalk marks on the shelves, and tell friends to come looking for them if they're not back for supper.

Even wiser students don't go in at all.

Liessa. Dragonlady, Liessa Wyrmbidder. Lady of the WYRMBERG. Sister to LIO!RT and LIARTES and daughter of GREICHA THE FIRST. She is a magnificent sight, with waist-length red hair, flecked with gold. She is almost naked, apart from a couple of mere scraps of the lightest chain mail, and riding boots of iridescent dragonhide. In one boot is thrust a riding crop – unusual in that it is as long as a spear and topped with tiny steel barbs. She has a slim, black dagger in her belt. She is heavily into jewellery, with a diamond spangle in her navel, tiger-rubies adorning her toe-rings, and large, incredibly rare blue-milk diamonds adorning the rings on her fingers. They just don't make heroines like her any more. For one thing, they force them to wear more clothes. [COM]

Lifton. The landlord of the inn in the village close to Miss FLITWORTH's farm. [RM]

Light, nature of. As far as can be determined, there are now four distinct types of light on the Disc. For the sake of discussion they could be called common light, meta-light, dark light and 'the light fantastic'.

Meta-light is almost an idea rather than a phenomenon. It is the light by which darkness can be seen, and therefore is always available, everywhere. If it didn't exist, darkness could not be visible. It is widely used in the film industry for shots in caves and mines.

Common light undergoes some important changes in the Discworld's vast and ancient magical field. It slows down considerably (and variably, but generally to about the speed of sound) and, at the same time, becomes very slightly heavier than air and also – by assump-

tion – soluble. (It pools in deep valleys but has gone by midnight, so it either sinks into the ground or is soluble in darkness.)

The speed of common light was established by FEBRIUS, the Ephebian philosopher.

The combined effect of these changes can be seen by watching a Discworld day from a convenient point in space. The disc is 10,000 miles across. The sunlight strikes point A and proceeds towards point B at about 600 mph, producing a rather pleasing effect similar to an incoming tide. When it strikes a mountain range (C) it piles up on the dawn side, so that dawn will be postponed in the 'light shadow' of the mountain until either the light flows over the top or around the sides.

The light fantastic is perhaps best evidenced by the dull, sullen light which fills the room where the 'OCTAVO' is kept. Not strictly light at all, but the opposite of light. Darkness is not the opposite of light, it is simply its absence. The light fantastic is the light that lies on the far side of darkness.

Ordinary light passing through a strong magical field is split into not seven but eight colours, and the eighth – OCTARINE – is generally associated with things magical. It can be described in terms of other colours about as readily as red can be described in terms of green, yellow and blue, but if some description is really insisted on then octarine is a rather disappointing greeny-purple-yellow colour.

Light Dams. Some of the tribes in the Great NEF region construct mirror walls in the desert mountains to collect the Disc sunlight, which they then use as a currency. This is possible because of the strange nature of light in the Discworld's magical field. [M]

Likely, Dave. Big Dave Likely. Regarded as one of Ankh-Morpork's best football players, having scored a record four goals during his lifetime. [UA]

Likely, Trevor. Son of Dave 'Big Dave' Likely – a legendary Ankh-Morpork footballer. Trevor is congenitally lazy – he can sleep anywhere – and does. He is keen on football, and is very skilled at kicking tin cans. He runs the cande vats at Unseen University. He is not a bad lad – not a

gentleman, of course, and if he did not take life so easily he could make something of himself, if he had reason to put his mind to it. [UA]

Lilith, Lady. Lady Lilith de Tempscire. (*See* WEATHERWAX, LILY.)

Lily, Iron. Nickname for the woman who teaches games at the Quirm College for Young Ladies. The girls say that she shaves, and lifts weights with her teeth. She is well known for her hearty bellows from the touchline during sports matches: 'Get some ball, you bunch of soft nellies!' and so on. [SM]

Lilywhite, Medium Dave. Thoughtful, patient criminal in Ankh-Morpork, who was considered something of an intellectual because his tattoos were spelled correctly. He was, in his own way, honest, in that he dealt fairly with other criminals, and that counts for a lot in any underworld. If he had a fault, it was a tendency to deal out terminal and definitive retribution to anyone who said anything about his brother, Banjo.

Both brothers lived in terror of their mother, Ma Lilywhite, who was clearly a woman who cherished old-fashioned values and thought that being thrashed senseless never did anyone any harm. [H]

Lio!rt. Dragonlord. Brother of LIESSA and LIARTES, and son of GREICHA THE FIRST. A lord of the WYRMBERG. [COM]

Lipwig, Moist von. Appointed by Lord Vetinari as Postmaster General of the Ankh-Morpork Post Office and then as Master of the Royal Mint.

Moist is, by nature, an experienced and skilled con man. A natural-born criminal, an habitual liar, a fraudster and a totally untrustworthy perverted genius. He has used a variety of aliases – Albert Spanger, Edwin Streep, Mondo Smith, etc. He has stolen, embezzled, defrauded and swindled without discrimination. He has ruined businesses and destroyed jobs. When banks fail, it is seldom bankers who starve. Moist's actions in the past had taken money from those who had little enough to begin with. In a myriad of small ways he had hastened the deaths of many. For sport. For the joy of the game.

Moist did not mean anyone any harm. There is a saying 'you can't fool an honest man' which is much quoted by people who make a profitable living by fooling honest men. Moist never knowingly tried it, anyway. If you did fool an honest man, he tended to complain to the local Watch. Fooling dishonest men was a lot safer and, somehow, more sporting. And, of course, there are so many more of them.

Half an hour after arriving in a town he would be sitting outside an inn, downcast, with nothing in the world but a genuine diamond ring worth a hundred dollars and a pressing need to get home, where his poor, aged mother was dying. Eleven minutes later he would be standing patiently in a jeweller's shop, where the jeweller was telling a sympathetic citizen that the ring the stranger was prepared to sell for twenty dollars was worth seventy-five (even jewellers have to make a living). And thirty-five minutes later he was riding out of town on a better horse, with ten dollars in his pocket, leaving behind a gloating sympathetic citizen who, despite having been bright enough to watch Moist's hands carefully, was about to go back to the jeweller to try to sell for seventy-five dollars a shiny brass ring with a glass stone that was worth fifty pence of anybody's money.

The world was blessedly free of honest men, and wonderfully full of people who believed they could tell the difference between an honest man and a crook.

Moist had a talent. He'd also acquired a lot of skills so completely that they were second natures. He'd *learned* to be personable, but something in his genetics made him unmemorable. He has a talent for not being noticed, for being a face in the crowd. People have difficulty describing him. He was...He was 'about'. He was about twenty, or about thirty. On Watch reports across the continent he was anywhere between, oh, about six feet two inches and five feet nine inches tall, hair all shades from mid-brown to blond, and his lack of distinguishing features included his entire face. He was about...average. What people *remembered* was the furniture, things like spectacles and moustaches, so he always carried a selection of both. They remembered names and mannerisms, too. He had hundreds of those.

Oh, and people remembered that they'd been richer before they met him.

He now runs the Ankh-Morpork Post Office, Bank and Mint. He is a likeable boss. He chats to people. He talks to them about their work, asks how their wives and husbands are, having memorized the names of the family members of the person he's talking to. A knack, a wonderful knack and it works a treat. His goblin workers know him as 'Mister Slightly Damp'.

He nows lives in Scoone Avenue with Adora Belle Dearheart and eschews the concept that there are two 7 o'clocks in every day. [GP]

Listeners, the. Also Listening Monks. The oldest of the Disc's religious sects – although even the Gods are divided as to whether Listening is really a proper religion.

The Listeners are trying to work out precisely what it was the CREATOR said when he made the universe: clearly nothing the Creator makes can ever be destroyed, so those first syllables must still be around somewhere, bouncing and re-bouncing off all the matter in the cosmos but still audible to a really good listener.

The monks dwell in a temple shaped like a great white ammonite at the end of a funnel-shaped valley. Eons ago the Listeners found that ice and chance had carved this one valley into the perfect acoustic opposite of an echo valley, and built their multi-chambered temple in the exact position that the comfy chair always occupies in the home of a rabid hi-fi fanatic. Complex baffles catch and amplify the sound that is funnelled up the chilly valley, steering it ever inwards to the central chamber where, at any hour of the day or night, three monks always sit.

This hidden valley is accessible only by a narrow staircase. There is a village in a lower valley a few miles from the temple. [M]

Littlebottom, Cheery. A dwarf corporal, now a sergeant, in the Ankh-Morpork City Watch, and its forensics expert. Cheery's father was Jolly Littlebottom and his (though see below for a new pronoun) father was Beaky Littlebottom, both from the Überwald mountain regions, where the naming of dwarfs follows a very famous tradition. His brother, Snorey, died in an explosion somewhere under Borogravia.

Cheery originally studied as an alchemist, until an unfortunate accident blew up the Guild Council. Unusual as a dwarf, not for having no eyebrows and a frizzled beard (fairly common amongst alchemists and people who undertake this type of forensics work), but for an inability to hold an axe, a fear of fighting, a hatred of beer, an inability to drink dwarfishly and a belief that songs about gold are stupid.

Socially, of course, Cheery is notable for being the first dwarf to come out and admit that he, OK, *she* is female. Her initial attempts at portraying this outwardly have had a mixed reception, since the only suitable role-models around are human females, who generally do not wear beards and are less attached to the wearing of iron helmets. She now sports a heavy leather skirt, for example, when on duty, plus slightly raised heels to her iron boots. However, she is learning as she goes along. Her early attempts have been met with horror by most of the dwarf population. A small minority have asked her for a date, and are probably male. An even smaller minority sidles up and asks timidly where they can buy lipstick like hers. They are probably female, but who knows in these changing times? This is the Century of the Fruitbat, after all. [TFE]

Llamedos. A small, mountainous country, where it rains continuously except for brief periods of drizzle and snow. Rain is the country's main export. It has rain mines. Only holly grows there – everything else just rots. Its principal town is Pant-y-Girdl.

It styles itself as 'sensibly dwarfish'. There are, in fact, as many humans as dwarfs in Llamedos, but they are mostly miners and either small or almost permanently concussed.

The Llamedese are a musical but quite strict people of the druidical persuasion. They are, in fact, the centre of druidical expertise, and stone-circle builders from Llamedos are found wherever megalithic circles are not quite working properly. The Llamedese are also famed and feared for their singing, and in more warlike times their massed male-voice choirs and reinforced harps laid waste the land wherever they appeared. The bardic tradition is now a little less warlike. Central to it is the annual Eisteddfod: three days of poetry, singing and superb bladder control.

Lobsang, Abbot. Leader of the LISTENERS. A small and totally bald man, with more wrinkles than a sackful of prunes. Currently he is the eighty-ninth Abbot, but he is the victim of reincarnation. He is constantly reincarnated in a child conceived at the moment of his death. Each time an Abbot dies, the monks go down to the village to look for a boy child conceived

at the hour that the old Abbot died. That boy is then made the new Abbot, and so it goes on. Only in the brief time between death and conception is Lobsang allowed to be aware of the true situation: that he is, in fact, in a kind of karmic loop. [M]

Lofthouse. An uncle of Lady Sybil VIMES, née Ramkin. [MAA]

Long Man, the. A collection of three burial mounds in a very old part of the forest in LANCRE. They comprise two round mounds at the foot of a long one.

In the old days, the men of Lancre would come up to the Long Man for strange rites. They used to build sweat lodges and drink SCUMBLE and dance around the fires with horns on their heads, and so on. This may have been a very ancient rite, or possibly just a response to man's age-old desire to get out of the house and have a jar and a few laughs.

At the foot of the long mound three large irregular stones form a cave, inside which is a flat rock carved with the symbol of a horned man and an inscription in Oggham (a runic alphabet). The inscription as translated by Nanny OGG reads: 'I've got a great big tonker' although this may be her idiosyncratic spin on one central theme of all fertility and Nature cults.

Below the stone is one entrance to the Lancre Caves, which run all through Lancre and also lead to one world of the elves. [LL]

Longshaft, Mr. A dwarf lodger at Mrs ARCANUM's. He is 'something in the jewellery business'. [TT]

Longstaff, Ardrothy. Purveyor of Pies Full of Personality. Owner of a stall in Sator Square, Ankh-Morpork. We're told he has a touch of magic in his genetic make-up. It's not known if any other make-up requirements were fulfilled by Grabpot THUNDERGUST. [S]

Loremaster. An hereditary official of the WYRMBERG. [COM]

Lorenzo the Kind. The last king of Ankh-Morpork. A fat and elderly man with unspecified, and possibly unspeakable, predilections. He was beheaded by 'Old Stoneface' VIMES, who didn't say much. [MAA]

Lotus Blossom. Young female member of the Agatean Red Army, Hung-Hung cadre. She is also a daughter of TWOFLOWER. [IT]

Luck (the Lady). The Goddess Who Must Not Be Named. She appears beautiful, with bright green eyes – the green of fresh emeralds and iridescent as a dragonfly. Like all gods and goddesses she can change her appearance at will, but cannot change the look of her eyes.

Those who seek her never find her, yet she is known to come to the aid of those in greatest need. Then again, sometimes she doesn't. She does, it may be gathered, have a soft spot for last, desperate million-to-one chances, but it would be unwise to depend upon this.

Although she is arguably the most powerful goddess in the entire history of Creation, there are no temples to her. She doesn't like the clicking of rosaries, but is attracted to the sound of dice. [COM]

Ludd, Lobsang. Originally called Newgate Ludd when he was a foundling at the THIEVES' GUILD – one of 'Ludd's Lads and Lasses', as the foundlings were known, in memory of one of the founders of the Guild. When we first met him, he was aged about sixteen or seventeen and weighed a bit over 110 lb. He was recruited to the History MONKS by SOTO. He could move *very* fast. The monks observed that, around him, things went missing; they seemed simply to vanish. He was always late for his lessons but he was *smart*. He thought he knew more than his tutors, he answered back and he interrupted. He never paid attention in class but he always knew the answers to questions posed by his teachers, though he could never say *how* he knew. Lobsang has an interesting relationship with TIME and with Jeremy CLOCKSON. [TOT]

Ludorum, Arthur. A fellow student of TEPPIC's at the ASSASSINS' GUILD. One of only two worshippers of the Great Orm (a god who, therefore, must no longer be that great) and a son of Johan Ludorum – one of the greatest assassins in the history of the Guild. Arthur's innocent, friendly smile and boyish complexion are frequently the last thing some people see. [P]

Luggage, the. In appearance: a largish, metal-bound chest, which is capable of extruding a large number of little legs, ending in horny-nailed, calloused feet, to help it move about. It is made of SAPIENT PEARWOOD, a magical timber that can cause its constructs to portray characteristics similar to that set of characteristics known as 'life'.

Pearwood constructions can be set to do small tasks, such as carry water or guard property. Since it is a magical substance, sapient pearwood is impervious to magic, and in the STO PLAINS is much sought after for the manufacture of wizards' staffs, since its capacity for storing magic is up to ten times greater than that of other leading timbers.

In the case of the Luggage, built to serve as a self-propelled travel accessory and bodyguard, one of the set of characteristics known as 'life' is a particular characteristic known as 'faithfulness' and another is one known as 'murderous intent'.

When it opens its lid – often in order to snap it hard on something it considers to be threatening its owner – the luggage may reveal clean laundry, or a king's ransom in gold. As often as not, though, it displays teeth like bleached beechwood and a tongue as large as a palm leaf and red as mahogany.

Although it has a keyhole, it cannot be opened when it is in a locked mood.

The Luggage will follow its owner everywhere. The word is an absolute – *everywhere*. One use for sapient pearwood in the AGATEAN EMPIRE – where it is quite common – used to be the manufacture of grave goods that the dead could be certain of taking with them.

The Luggage is currently owned, or at least chooses to follow, the wizard RINCEWIND. Its progress across the Disc is marked by debris, people who get nervous at the sound of hurrying footsteps, and communities who are unusually polite to strangers.

No other item in the entire chronicle of travel accessories has quite such a history of mystery and grievous bodily harm. So best not to mention that it was briefly named 'Trunkie' when he travelled with PETUNIA, The Desert Princess, during the events of *The Last Continent*. [COM]

Lully. A thin, hesitant alchemist. [MP]

Lully I. A past king of LANCRE. A bit of an historian and a romantic, which is a polite way of saying that he invented most of Lancre's history and several of its monarchs and almost all of its printable folklore. Of course, this does not mean that the history he invented was untrue, only that it did not, in actual fact, happen. In fact this is generally the case everywhere. History is what people believe; therefore, what people believe is history. [LL]

Lupine. A wereman. That is to say, the exact opposite of a werewolf. He is a seven-foot-tall, muscular, hairy, young man with long canines, pointy ears and yellow eyes – during full moon. The rest of the time he is a real wolf. Last seen leaving Ankh-Morpork in the company of Ludmilla CAKE, a female werewolf. They appeared to have worked out a satisfactory *liaison* despite being the same shape for only one week per month. [RM]

Lu-Tze. A senior History Monk, also known as Sweeper. Because he is a ... well, sweeper. Although he is generally acknowledged to be 800 years old, there are some who claim he is 6000 years old, because for History MONKS time is a resource to manipulate rather than an amber in which they are imprisoned. There is no doubt that he encourages every conflicting

Lu-Tze

rumour about himself.

Lu-Tze is a little, bald, yellow-toothed man with a wispy beard and a faintly amiable grin, as if he is constantly waiting for something amusing to happen. He wears a robe which was once white before it fell prey to a variety stains and patches. He uses just a piece of old string to keep his robe closed, and string, too, plays an important part in keeping his sandals repaired. He smokes foul roll-ups (which probably accounts for at least some of the stains on his robe – and his teeth). In Oi Dong monastery, at least, he eats nothing but brown rice and drinks nothing but green tea with a knob of rancid butter in it. However, this is simply because he likes the stuff. There's nothing particularly holy about rancid butter.

In his life he has done just about everything, and his past deeds are legend among the History Monks. He is Master of every martial art ever conceived; indeed, he conceived most of them himself. However, he prefers to avoid fighting, as such, and can usually find another way, frequently by taking advantage of Rule One: Do Not Act Incautiously When Confronting Little Bald Wrinkly Smiling Men. Everyone *knows* what happens to people who forget this easy-to-understand piece of guidance (and possibly Lu-Tze, when there has been no alternative, has been the reason for the Rule).

His actual position at Oi Dong is uncertain. He is clearly the most accomplished of the History Monks, but works as a lowly servant. He seems to enjoy sweeping, but it also means that he has entry into all kinds of places (dust gets everywhere) and, since no one notices humble old sweepers, he overhears much that he shouldn't. He is an expert listener, having worked out years ago that if you listen hard and long enough people would tell you more than they think they know.

He appears to acknowledge no authority but that of the ABBOT, who appears to get him to undertake the most difficult of tasks by very specifically forbidding him to do so. He deals with the other monks, all of whom outrank him, by cheerfully ignoring them – and gets away with it. Remember Rule One, particularly

around Lu-Tze.

Lu-Tze is a follower of the Way of Mrs Marietta COSMOPILITE, with whom he stayed when, as a younger man, he travelled to Ankh-Morpork in search of Perplexity. Lu-Tze soon found that her home-spun wisdom neatly dove-tailed into the teaching of WEN the Eternally Surprised, and that Mrs Cosmopilite had an apt saying for every occasion, such as 'There Is A Time and a Place for Everything', 'I Have Only One Pair of Hands' and 'It Never Rains But it Pours'. Seldom, he realized, had so much wisdom been confined in so small a space.

Lu-Tze also grows BONSAI MOUNTAINS. [SG]

Ly Tin Wheedle. Arguably the Disc's greatest philosopher (well, he always argued that he was). Someone once asked him at a party 'Why are you here?' and the reply took three years. Wheedle is a citizen of the AGATEAN EMPIRE on the COUNTERWEIGHT CONTINENT, where he is regarded as a great sage because of his peculiar smell. His many sayings about respect for the old and the virtues of poverty are often quoted by the rich and elderly. Among Ly Tin Wheedle's oft-quoted homilies are: 'When many expect a mighty stallion they will find hooves on an ant' and 'An ass may do the work of an ox in a time of no horses'. Once you get the hang of it, you make these up at the rate of ten or more a minute. [LF]

'What's magic, eh? Just wavin' a stick an' sayin' a few wee magical words. An' what's so clever aboot that, eh? But lookin' at things, really lookin' at 'em, and then workin' 'em oout, now, that's a real skill.'

– The Wee Free Men

Macarona, Bengo, Professor. D.Thau (Bug), D.Maus (Chubb), Magistaludorum (QIS), Octavium (Hons), PHGK (Blit), DMSK, Mack, D.Thau (Bra), Visiting Professor in Chickens (Jahn the Conqueror University, Floor 2, Shrimp Packers Building, Genua), Primo Octo (Deux), Visiting Professor of Blit/Slood Exchanges (Al Khali), KCbfJ, Reciprocating Professor of Blit Theory (Unki), D.Thau (Unki), Didimus Supremuis (Unki), Emeritus Professor in Blit Substrate Determinations (Chubb), Chair of Blit and Music Studies (Quirm College for Young Ladies), He is the holder of thirteen doctorates, a visiting professorship at BUGARUP UNIVERSITY and has been cited in 236 papers and one divorce petition. Professor Macarona is from Genua, where his family owns a huge ranch and the biggest coffee plantation outside Klatch – his grandmother owns the Macarona Shipping Company. RIDCULLY describes him as 'tall feller with a tan and a dinky beard'. His lengthy list of qualifications led to a challenging bit of text for the reader who recorded the unabridged novel… he's convinced this was an example of Terry's puckish humour. [UA]

Maccalariat, Miss. She works at the Ankh-Morpork Post Office and is a force to be reckoned with. She is a very prim and proper lady, who has kept her maiden name for professional purposes – she is the fifth generation of Maccalariats, a very old Post Office family. Sensible shoes, thick black stockings that are slightly hairy, baggy cardigan and glasses – oh,

and an expression like an early frost. She has a bit of a moustache, and a withering voice. Her hair is plaited and coiled up on either side of her head in those discs that in Überwald are called 'snails' but in Ankh-Morpork put people in mind of a woman with a curly iced bun clamped to each ear. Oh, and it's decorated with a little pink hairgrip with tiny hand-painted violets on it. [GP]

Mackleduff, Mr. The longest-serving lodger at Mrs Acanum's. He works as the nightshift foreman at a bakery. He is one of those large men who is instantly an expert on anything. [TT]

Mad. Dwarf encountered by Rincewind in *The Last Continent*. His family blew into XXXX from Nothingfjord when he was a kid, and now his Dad has a chain of bakeries in BUGARUP. Although Mad is bullet-headed, like most dwarfs, he doesn't wear a beard or a helmet – though he does have a chin you could break coconuts on. He is very heavily weaponed and, in his leather suit with metal rivets all over it, he travels around XXXX in an armoured cart. [TLC]

Magazines (and Newspapers). If you're reading this book in order, you'll already know that the Disc has a wide variety of book titles. Magazines are a newer phenomenon, but already they include:

Acuphile Digest [GP]
Ankh-Morpork Inquirer, The [TT]
Ankh-Morpork Times, The [TT]

Back Alley Pins [GP]
Battle Call [FOC]
Beaks & Talons [LL]
Beginning Pins [GP]
Big Cabbage Gazette [RS]
Bows & Ammo [LL, J]
Bu-Bubble [UA]
Extreme Pins [GP]
Fang and Fire [SN]
Fretwork Today [UA]
Girls, Giggles and Garters! [T!]
Golem Spotter Weekly [UA]
Journal of Irreducible Research (BRAZENECK
    UNIVERSITY)[CCDD]
Ladies' Own Magazine, the [MM]
Modern Pins [GP]
New Pins [GP]
Pins & Pinneries [GP]
Pins Extra [GP]
Pins International [GP]
Pins Monthly [GP]
Pins World [GP]
Pin Times [GP]
Popular Armour [LL]
Popular Needles [GP]
Practical Pins [GP]
Practical Siege Weapons [J]
Pseudopolis Daily Press [RS]
Pseudopolis Herald [GP]
Satblatt (dwarf newspaper) [UA]
St Plains Dealer [GP]
Stanley Howler's Stamp Monthly [UA]
Stifte! [GP]
Talking Pins [GP]
Tanty Bugle [MM]
Total Pins [GP]
Unadorned Facts [FOC]
Warrior of Fortune [J]
What Gallows? [GP]
What Novelty? [MM]
World of Pins [GP]
World Pin [GP]

Apart from 'The Inquirer' and 'The Times', many of the magazines that are produced in Ankh-Morpork are crudely printed wood-block broadsheets – all produced at the same address. Nothing is known about the company concerned, but there is a distinct possibility that the name C.M.O.T. DIBBLER is not far away.

Magenta. One of DIAMANDA's coven in Lancre. [LL]

Mage Wars. Took place shortly after the Creation. In those days magic in its raw state was widely available, and was eagerly grasped by the first men in their battle against the GODS.

The precise origins of the Mage Wars, as this period was known, are lost in the fogs of time, but Disc philosophers agree that the first men took one look at their situation and understandably lost their temper. And great and pyrotechnic were the battles that followed – the sun wheeled across the sky, the seas boiled, weird storms ravaged the land, small white pigeons mysteriously appeared in people's clothing and the very stability of the Disc was threatened. This resulted in stern action by the OLD HIGH ONES, to whom even the gods themselves are answerable. The gods were banished to high and deserted places, men were re-created a good deal smaller and much of the old, wild magic was sucked out of the earth.

In those places on the Disc that had suffered a direct hit by a spell, the magic faded away very slowly over the millennia, releasing as it decayed a myriad sub-astral particles that severely distracted the reality around it.

Maggie. Nac Mac Feegle. Daughter of JEANNIE and Rob ANYBODY. As a young Feegle, Maggie decided to eschew tradition and become a warrior, rather than leaving home and becoming kelda of a different clan. [TSC]

Magic. Including wizards and witches.

INTRINSIC MAGIC

This is the magic that derives from the very nature of the Discworld universe, and has a certain similarity to some of the matters discussed in quantum physics (physicists who seriously postulate extra dimensions that are curled up on themselves and are too small to see would be right at home in Unseen University). It is the intrinsic magic of Discworld which, for example, is responsible for the slowing down of light but at the same time makes it possible to see light coming. Intrinsic magic is the equivalent of God, thinking.

RESIDUAL MAGIC

A powerful force, which needs some background explanation.

Most magic as used by wizards and witches is a simple channelling of the intrinsic magic of the world. It can be stored – in accumulators such as staffs, carpets, spells and broomsticks – and can be thought of as a slowly renewing resource, like geothermal energy. It is subject to certain laws similar to those of the conservation of energy. A wizard can, for example, cause fires and apparitions and coloured lights quite easily, because these require very little energy. In the same way, a person may quite easily be turned into a frog by causing their brain to reprogram their own morphogenetic field. The effect is temporary but embarrassing.

But a wizard can rise vertically in the air only by locating a large solid object of similar weight in a high place that can be dislodged without much force, so that the descent of the object largely propels the rise of the wizard.

No common magic is powerful enough to cause, for example, a pork pie to come into complete, permanent existence. This would require quite a large amount of new energy to be created within the universe – as much energy, in fact, as would be necessary to create a one-hundredth of a pig, one-ten-thousandth of a baker, one hundred-thousandth of a cleaver, several pounds of flour, salt and pepper to taste, and a couple of hours of baking.

All this can, however, be easily achieved by a sourcerer, who can channel raw creative force and may be thought of as the human equivalent of a white hole. A sourcerer, in fact, pretty much conforms to the classic picture of a wizard – he can create and destroy by a mere thought.

Fortunately sourcerers are now very rare on Discworld and only one is known to have arisen during the entire period of the chronicles (in *Sourcery*). But they were far more common in much earlier times. And, since power corrupts, and sourcerers were as naturally sociable as cats in a sinking sack, they engaged in vast magical wars which left whole areas (for example, the FOREST OF SKUND and the WYRMBERG) so lousy with magic that the Discworld's fairly lax laws of cause and effect no longer apply even today. Many of the Disc's stranger species, and some of its most potent magical artefacts, probably derive from that period. While such residual magic can be discovered and exploited, in the same way as other worlds exploit the deposits of coal and oil which are similarly stored forms of the energy of earlier periods, the results are likely to be unpredictable, i.e., predictably fatal.

INDUCED MAGIC

An often neglected but very powerful form, and available for use even by non-practitioners. It is the magic potential created in an object, or even a living creature, by usage and belief.

Take, in its simplest form, royalty. It needs but a royal marriage to turn a perfectly ordinary girl that no one would look at twice into a Radiant Right Royal Princess and fashion icon. Similarly, the ARCHCHANCELLOR'S HAT actually became quite magical in itself simply from having been worn on the heads of generations of Archchancellors and thus being only inches away from brains buzzing with magic.

The armour of the warrior Queen YNCI of Lancre had clearly absorbed enough potency to stiffen the resolve of Magrat GARLICK when she wore it (the fact that the armour was a complete fake is quite beside the point – it is association and belief that are important). Mirror magic, as exemplified by the practices of Lily WEATH-ERWAX, also comes into this category. Witches believe that if they stand between two mirrors their personal power is multiplied by their reflections. This is clearly a primitive folk superstition, which by sheer luck happens to be true.

Possibly the most interesting example was the sword of CARROT Ironfoundersson of the Ankh-Morpork City WATCH. It was not a magic sword. It had no mystic runes. It quite failed to light up in the presence of enemies or anything else. But it had clearly been used by

the royal heirs of the city's throne for generations and had become magical in a very subtle way – it had become more and more sword-like, until it was both a thing and the symbol of a thing.

WIZARD MAGIC (AND WIZARDS)

Largely, these days, the province of graduates of Unseen University, Ankh-Morpork. There are eight orders of wizardry and eight grades associated with UU. In practical terms the affairs of academic wizardry as a whole are run by the ARCHCHANCELLOR and faculty.

There are many other schools of wizardry on the Disc, some considered arcane even by wizard standards, and there is nothing to stop anyone calling themselves a wizard of the ninth grade, except the fact that if they meet a real wizard they're likely to end up sitting sadly by the pond waiting for a short-sighted princess with a thing about the colour green.

Grades of up to twenty-one have been reported, but this is considered to be just foreigners being excitable, and they impress the Unseen wizards as much as the porcupine-sized epaulettes on the shoulders of a shifty-eyed banana republic generalissimo impress a battle-hardened soldier.

Wizard magic generally consists of illusion, a little weather-making, fireballs and the occasional darning of the Fabric of Reality. Fundamental to its use is the wizard's staff, usually about six feet long with the proverbial knob on the end. Daily rituals with the staff accumulate magical power which can be discharged very quickly at need, or stored in spell books and triggered by the syllables of the spell. People often make jokes about the knob on the end and wizards never understand why. It is a truism that the more senior the wizard, the less likely he is to do any showy or practical magic. Senior wizards' time in the University is taken up with sleeping, eating at least four large meals a day, University administration and generally, well, just existing and being a wizard just as hard as they can. Since UU and its LIBRARY probably hold enough accumulated magic to end the universe, it is just as well that they are run by large, contented and stable personalities (with the exception of the Bursar, who is as mad as a spoon, and the Dean, and the Senior Wrangler, and the Lecturer in Recent Runes).

A sourcerer is the eighth son of an eighth son, and his father must be a wizard. Unlike wizardry which, shorn of the coloured lights and fireballs, largely consists of persuading the universe to do it your way, sourcery is the immensely powerful magic of the storybook wizard – he can stop the sun, make the sea boil and all the other things such wizards feel they have to do. He is a channel through which magic flows into the universe, and the human equivalent of a white hole. Much that is strange on the Discworld (*see* Residual magic) is the result of wars fought between sourcerers long before the present age; they are absolutely incapable of united effort.

It was fears of the occurrence of sourcerers that led to the practice of, and then the insistence on, celibacy among UU wizards, although most of them are quite old and find even celibacy is a bit too exciting. Celibacy has no physical effect on magic ability. Gravity doesn't care if you're good or bad and, likewise, celibacy *per se* has no relevance to the magical act, otherwise Nanny OGG would be a washerwoman.

A sourcerer can only be beaten by another sourcerer. This belief held sway for hundreds of years and it was only when the first sourcerer for millennia appeared on the Disc (in *Sourcery*) that it was realized that this only applied where direct magical contest is involved. A half-brick wielded in a sock is otherwise perfect for the job. (*See also* RINCEWIND.)

WITCH MAGIC (AND WITCHES)

Unlike wizards, witches are solitary creatures. They stand on the edge, where the decisions have to be made. They make them, so others didn't have to, so that others can even pretend to themselves that there *were* no decisions to be made. They enrol in no schools and have no formal system of regulation.

The informal coven of Granny WEATH-ERWAX, Nanny OGG and Magrat GARLICK in LANCRE was extremely unusual – witches generally get together only rarely, on sites such as Lancre's Bear Mountain, to exchange gossip and discuss the affairs of the region, and once a year – in the Ramtops at least – for the Witch Trials.

Wherever they met there was, contrary to salacious popular belief, absolutely no question of them doing anything without their clothes on, with the possible exception of Nanny Ogg. Most serious witches are elderly and keep several layers of flannelette between themselves and the outside world at all times, except Nanny Ogg. Witches have, in fact, a very strict and ancient moral code, although Nanny Ogg's is rather more ancient than the others'.

Witches are trained by other witches, one to one, with one of the trainees taking over the area when her teacher either dies or quits the world in some other definite way. This means that over time an area may see a succession of witches of a roughly similar strain. The basic unit of witchcraft is the cottage, which may be inhabited by witches for several centuries. Magrat's cottage (now occupied by new informal coven-member, Agnes NITT) is traditionally the home of research witches. Another significant difference between wizards and witches lies in the attitude to books. Most witches can read and write but place no particular value on books; wizards without a library would just be fat men in pointy hats.

The three main Lancre witches at the time of *Wyrd Sisters*, *Lords and Ladies* and *Witches Abroad* exemplified aspects of Discworld witchcraft. Granny Weatherwax's personal power is built on a considerable practical knowledge of psychology ('headology'), an iron will, an unshakeable conviction that she is right and some genuine psychic powers, which she distrusts. She is respected, but not liked. She would prefer to look like a crone, because ugliness engenders fear in the beholder and someone who is frightened of you is already in your power (Granny Weatherwax has never claimed to be nice). Unfortunately, she has a clear skin and excellent teeth, which despite her deliberate consumption of sugar show no signs of falling out. She is a traditionalist; she believes that progress is an excuse for making bad things happen faster.

Nanny Ogg is amiable and broad-minded to the point where she could pull it out of her ears and knot it under her chin. Of the three, she seldom does any magic in the normally accepted sense – her role is more one of a highly informal social worker and jobbing wise woman.

Magrat Garlick has a soul of hopeless niceness and welcomes new ideas. Occult candles, cards, mystic philosophies from distant regions – she approached all these things with an open mind which, unfortunately, then filled up. She does, however, have a natural talent for herbal remedies and, like many small harmless animals, a vicious streak when cornered.

All three of course fulfil (or, in Magrat's case, *used* to fulfil) the usual daily functions expected of a rural witch: midwifery, the laying out of the dead (and sitting up with them at night, possibly playing cards with the more unusual cases) and folk medicine. Their approach to this last again used to represent three aspects of witchcraft:

Magrat: would give patients a specific remedy which careful observation over the years had suggested is most efficacious for that complaint;

Nanny Ogg: will give patients a stiff drink and tell them to stay in bed if they want to;

Granny Weatherwax: will give them the first bottle of coloured water that comes to hand and tell them it can't possibly fail. Her success rate is notable.

Their magical philosophies could be summed up as variations on the traditional sour mantra, Do What Thou Will:

Magrat: If it harms no one, and doesn't make, you know, too much noise or unnecessary stickiness or a mess or anything, do what you will, if you really want to. Um.

Granny Weatherwax: Don't do what you will, do what I tells you.

Nanny Ogg: A little bit of what you fancy does you good.

Witches are nominally matrilinear, but in areas around the RAMTOPS, where people are fairly rare and therefore recognized and understood as individuals in their isolated communities, even this system is a bit haphazard and has more to do with an individual's perceived standing than any hard and fast rule. It is certainly the case that all the children of Nanny Ogg and her various husbands are Oggs. Strictly speaking, the children of her sons should not be Oggs but should take their mother's surname. However, this would mean that a daughter-in-law would have to explain this to Nanny Ogg, a woman who once coined the phrase: 'Over your dead body.'

There is no Discworld concept of white/black magic. There is simply magic, in whatever form, which may be used in whatever way the user decides. Suggesting that there is any type of magic that is intrinsically good or bad would make as much sense to a Discworld wizard as suggesting that there is good and bad gravity. (Of course, from a subjective point of view there are such things as good and bad gravity; the gravity which causes an aircraft to crash is obviously different from the gravity which stops everything flying off into space.) (*See also* RESEARCH WITCHCRAFT.)

Magicians. The term is sometimes used interchangeably with 'wizards', but strictly speaking true magicians are mere magical technologists with defiant beards and leather patches on their elbows, who congregate in small groups at parties. Mostly they are failed students of Unseen University, who have nevertheless opted to stay on the fringes of the profession, where they perform menial but essential tasks such as setting up equipment, obtaining magical supplies and so on. They carry out pretty much the same 'lab tech' functions for wizards as people called Igor do for pioneering brain surgeons.

But even magicians can look down on conjurers (*see* CONJURERS' GUILD). [ER]

Magnusson, Magnus. A young dwarf in Ankh-Morpork. He is keen on Scouting, and is a member of the Ankh-Morpork Rat Pack. He is a speedy runner, which he needed to be during his first hours in the city. [RS]

Makepeace, Charles Augustus, Colonel. Late of the Light Dragoons, and married to Letitia for fifty-five years. Lives close by Ramkin Hall. Chas (as his friends know him) had long ago, with the expertise of a lifelong strategist, decided to let Letitia have her way in all things. It saved so much trouble and left him able to potter around in his garden, take care of his dragons and to occasionally go trout fishing, a pastime that he loved. He rented half a mile of stream, but was sadly now finding it difficult to keep running fast enough. Nowadays he spends a lot of time in his library, working on the second volume of his memoirs, keeping from under his wife's feet and not getting involved. [SN]

Malachite, Tubal de. A wizard, and a great student of dragon lore. Author of 'THE SUMMONING OF DRAGONS'. Died in a mysterious fire which left half his workshop completely melted. There were the tracks of something like a large wading bird in the ashes, and on the charred wall someone had apparently painted an outline of a wizard with his hands upraised protectively. This was put down to sunspot activity. [GG]

Maladict. A volunteer to the Borogravian army, who ends up being promoted to Corporal. Maladict is a vampire (a black ribboner), with long canine teeth; short and quite slim, and dressed in black – expensively, like an aristocrat. He carries a small sword. Maladict's vampiric energy is now focused on caffeine and he is very fond of coffee! Close friends also call him Maladica. [MR]

Malich, Alberto. Albert. DEATH's manservant, but also Alberto Malich the Wise, the founder of Unseen University (1222–89 by the city count of that time).

Although in real years he is only about sixty-seven, he has been alive while two thousand years have passed on the Disc.

The generally held belief is that Alberto, one of the most powerful wizards alive at the time, tried to outwit Death by performing the Rite of ASHKENTE backwards. Insofar as his charred notebooks hold any clue, he seemed to believe that he could obtain another sixty-seven years of life.

In fact he disappeared, apart from his hat. Unseen University tradition is that he blew himself into the DUNGEON DIMENSION, which is the usual destination of those whose magic gets out of control; in reality, he ended up alive in Death's own country. The price of immortality, it turns out, was immortality. As explained elsewhere, real time does not pass in Death's house; there is, instead, a sort of endlessly recycled day.

It seems, however, that this entirely suits someone like Albert. Endless days filled with the same routine are something that makes a university wizard feel entirely at home. And he is, after all, a hierarchical creature. Wizards usually are.

Back on the Disc, Albert would have had only 91 days, 3 hours and 5 minutes left to live. That is now down to a handful of seconds, since most of it has been frittered away on shopping trips and holidays back in the world. When in Ankh-Morpork, Albert stays at the Young Men's Reformed Cultists of the Ichor God Bel-Shamharoth Association, where he nicks the soap and towels (Death has not got the knack of making towels, or soap, or anything to do with plumbing).

In appearance, Albert is a small hunched old man. This merely shows that first impressions can be wrong. Second impressions suggest quite a tall, wiry man who merely walks like the third illustration along in the usual How Man Evolved diagram. He has a red nose which drips so much that people talking to him blow their own noses out of sympathy. [M]

Malik, Nudger. A late member of the Klatchian Foreign Legion. [SM]

Maltoon, Skully. (Sometimes known as Muldoon; spelling is not an exact science in

Alberto Malich

A partial map of Discworld

Ankh-Morpork.) A member of the Palace guard. He used to live in Mincing Street with his mother, who made cough sweets. She died one day in a freak accident involving a wet floor, the cat, and a vat of the basic mixture for Mrs M.'s Expectorant Lozenges ('Don't They Make You Want to Spit'). Although she was subsequently pulled out, there were nasty rumours that the family didn't want to waste the mixture and sold the lozenges anyway, so Skully grew up under cruel street taunts like 'Hey, these sweets have got some body in them' and 'There's a button in mine'. Lives in Easy Street. [GG]

Manickle, 'Shufti'. A volunteer to the Borogravian army. Stocky, running to plump. One of those people who bustle about being helpful in a mildly annoying way, taking over small jobs that you wouldn't have minded doing yourself. She is aso known as Betty, is quite a good cook and she joined the army to find her fiancé, Johnny. [MR]

Mante, Bay of. Scene of a famous shipwreck. [M]

Maps. Map-making has never been a precise art on the Discworld. People tend to start off with good intentions and then get so carried away with the spouting whales, monsters, waves and other twiddly bits of cartographic furniture that they often forget to put the boring mountains and rivers in at all.

Ankh-Morpork has, of course, been mapped. It is a mercantile city, after all, and people getting lost wastes time and money.

Marchesa. A fifth-level (female) wizard who commanded the flying lens which transported RINCEWIND and TWOFLOWER to KRULL. She is a woman with skin as black as the deep black of midnight at the bottom of a cave. Her hair and eyebrows are the colour of moonlight, with the same pale sheen about her lips. A graduate of Krull's own college of wizards. [COM]

Margolotta, Lady. Lady Margolotta Amaya Katerina Assumpta Crassina von Überwald. Referred to, by the dwarfs, as 'the Dark Lady'. Governess of Überwald. A rich vampire, who occupies four pages in the 'Almanack de Gothicke'. She lives in a castle that looks as though it could be taken by a small squad of not very intelligent soldiers. The builder was clearly influenced by fairy tales and, possibly, by some of the more ornamental sorts of cake. It is a castle for looking at. In the chintzy sitting room, with patterns on the furniture which have a bit of a bat look about them, we find Lady Margolotta.

She is not particularly tall, quite pleasant and with a slightly fussy air. She looks like someone's mother – someone with an expensive education, that is, and she moves like someone who's grown used to her body. She wears pearls, a pink jumper and sensible flat shoes. Admittedly, there are bats embroidered on the jumper. At her feet, lying on a cushion, is a little dog with a bow at its neck. It looks more like a rat.

Lady Margolotta does not drink human blood. She has persuaded Überwald's vampires to at least tone down their nocturnal activities. She herself has been 'teetotal' for almost four years when we meet her and she is a member of the Überwald League of TEMPERANCE – the black ribboners. She introduced coffee to Überwald, exchanging one craving with another.

She was the person who, by diplomacy, and probably more direct means, had got things moving again in Überwald and she had some sort of . . . . relationship with Vetinari. Everyone knew it, and, that was all everyone knew. A dot dot dot dot relationship. One of those. And nobody had been able to join up the dots. She had been to the city on diplomatic visits, and not even the well-practised dowagers of Ankh-Morpork had been able to detect a whisper of anything other than a businesslike amiability and international co-operation between the two of them. And they play endless and complex games via the clacks system, and that apart from that, that was, well that. [TFE]

Maroon, Mrs. The widow of a Watchman, Sergeant Maroon. Secretly the recipient of a small pension paid personally by Captain Vimes. [MAA]

Marrowleaf. Wizard and author of the 'Theory of Thaumic Imponderability'. This says that it is impossible to know exactly what any magical

spell will do until afterwards, when it will be too late, although the Theory itself takes ninety closely written pages. [SM]

Maurice. 'The Amazing Maurice and His Educated Rodents' are first referred to during the events of *Reaper Man*. We then knew of him that he ran a very remunerative operation by infesting a city with rats and then charging the city a large sum to get rid of them. We now know that he is a talking cat. A mucky yellow-eyed tabby, in fact. Before the magical events that gave him self-awareness and a speaking voice, he had lived on the streets of Ankh-Morpork for four years and as a result had barely any ears left and scars all over his face. He has a cat's self-assurance in spades. He swaggers so much that if he doesn't slow down he flips himself over, and when he fluffs his tail up, people have to step around it. His money-making scam is aided by a stupid-looking kid called KEITH, who plays the pipes, and by a band of intelligent, talking rats, whose numbers include:

Additives
Bestbefore
Big Savings
Bitesize
DANGEROUS BEANS
DARKTAN
Delicious
Farmhouse
Feedsfour
Finest
Fresh
HAMNPORK

Inbrine
Kidney
NOURISHING
PEACHES
SARDINES
Sellby
Specialoffer
Tomato
Toxie
[RM, though, of course, mainly TAMAHER]

Mausoleum. A King of Tsort. [E]

Mayhap Street. A street in Ankh-Morpork which, at the time of writing, still remains … temporarily displaced … as a result of incautious activities at Unseen University. [CCDD]

Mazda, Fingers. A sort of mythic hero to thieves everywhere. He was the first thief in the world; he stole fire from the gods. He was unable to fence it. It was too hot. [MAA]

M'Bu. Twelve-year old assistant to Azhural N'choate, a Howondaland livestock exporter. He also had one of the best organizational brains in the world, which was entirely necessary to get one thousand elephants all the way to Ankh-Morpork (a trek which at one point included sledging them down mountains). [MP]

McAbre. Head BLEDLOW at UNSEEN UNIVERSITY. [TLC]

McTavish. Stable lad to Lord Swivel. He smokes an enormous pipe and is as old as the hills, but he is nevertheless still known as 'lad'. He knows, and can imitate, the songs of every bird on Discworld. [TSC]

Medicine. Discworld medicine is occasionally sophisticated but always erratic.

It might be thought that the practice of medicine would be simple in a world where magic is commonplace, and in purely diagnostic terms this is often the case. But Unseen University wizards, certainly, are expressly forbidden to use magic to cure. Magic is tricky stuff and can have a mind of its own – using it to perform a complex operation might solve the immediate problem but it might also present the patient with a range of new, and probably worse, ones. An analogy would be bringing in a wolf to keep the foxes away from your sheep. It *would* work, but...

Putting back an arm by magic would not be difficult, but getting it to do what its new owner wanted – since it would now be a creature of magic – would be hard and would involve a lot of embarrassment and the probable wearing of a boxing glove at night.

So in Ankh-Morpork, for example, the term 'surgical precision' still means 'to within an inch or two, with a lot of sawdust about, and a bucket of hot pitch in the corner'. However, wizards can be used as anaesthetists in preference to the usual large hammer.

Outside the cities of the STO PLAINS the stricken usually resort to witches. Techniques vary, ranging from Keep the Patient Amused While Nature Takes Its Course (since people often get better from things that don't actually kill them) to serious if haphazard knowledge of the genuine healing properties of herbs.

Chiropracty in particular is a witch art – many a witch knows the amazing healing properties of a good prod in the right place. Few other people understand this; throughout the history of the universe people gained an inconvenient reputation for messiahdom merely by demonstrating a useful knowledge of the common slipped disc. (*See also* RETROPHRE-NOLOGY.)

Meggelin. Keeper of Para Mountain before Tento and Deccan RIBOBE. [MP]

Mellius and Gretelina. The Disc's greatest lovers, whose pure, passionate and soul-searing affair would have scorched the pages of History had they not been born 200 years apart on different continents. [M]

Mended Drum, the. *See* DRUM.

Mephistopheles. Geoffrey SWIVEL's goat. A runt from a litter produced on the Swivel family estate. Mephistopheles grew into a strong young goat with a devilish kick. He is a very intelligent animal – and can even use a toilet. Nanny OGG calls him 'The Mince of Darkness'. [TSC]

Merchants' Guild. Motto: *VILIS AD BIS PRETII.* Coat of arms: a shield, quartered. In the top-right quarter, a jeune coq, gules, on a field d'or; in the bottom-left quarter, a tête de boeuf, gules on a field d'or. In the top-left quarter, a vaisseau d'or on a field, azure; in the bottom right quarter, a bourse d'or on a field, azure. Superimposed on the shield, a morpork holding an ankh.

The youngest of Ankh-Morpork Guilds,

founded in self-defence by the city's traders and shopkeepers when they realized that their role in the great scheme of things was to be robbed. 'Robbing fat merchants', it seemed, was a perfectly socially acceptable thing for even *heroic* heroes to do. 'Ah, yonder lies a fat merchant,' they'd cry, using the special Land-lord-a-flagon-of-your-finest-ale hero talk, 'let us relieve him of some of his ill-gotten gains, 'pon my scalliard!' And *this* to a man who'd been up all night carefully mixing sand with the sugar, and who regularly gave small sums to the less smelly beggars.

The Guild was thus formed to further the aims of its members peacefully, advertise the civic charms of Ankh-Morpork and beat seven kinds of hell out of anyone with a leather loin-cloth. It is now one of the city's more talkative pressure groups.

It is particularly hot in pursuit of those misguided people who publicly fail to recognize the many attractive points of their fine city. The merchants now hire large gangs of men with ears like fists and fists like bags of walnuts to point out that Ankh-Morpork is, on the contrary, a marvellously clean and decent city in which to live, the ongoing neature of which might be swiftly curtailed if that person does not shut up right now.

The Guild has an annual knife-and-fork supper, held in the upper room of the Mended DRUM. [M]

Merco. Merco the Ephebian is a building materials supplier. [P]

Mericet. A tutor and examiner at the Assassins' Guild. He lectures about Strategy and Poison Theory every Thursday afternoon. An old, bald man with a tiny, dried-up smile that had all the warmth boiled out of it long ago. And one of the city's most skilled assassins. [P]

Meserole, Lady. Lady (Madam) Roberta (Bobbi) Meserole is a wealthy lady, with business interests in Genua and ÜBERWALD, who lives on the corner of Easy Street and Treacle Mine Road, close to the old Watch House. She has brown eyes, brown hair, intricately painted fingernails and she wears an expensive-looking vivid purple dress. She has the trace of a Genuan accent. She owns a cat with a diamond collar, but the effect is somewhat spoiled because the cat is an elderly, ginger street tom with irregular bouts of flatulence. She is, it seems, Lord VETINARI's aunt. [NW]

M'Guk, Hummok. A small, flat-faced man from one of the Hublands tribes, who literally diced with DEATH. [M]

Mica. A bridge troll encountered by COHEN the Barbarian. [TB]

Michael, Cumbling. A member of the BEGGARS' GUILD. [MAA]

Mimpsey, Gritoller. One-time vice-president of the THIEVES' GUILD. [S]

Mims, Terpsic. An angler in KRULL, rescued from drowning in the Hakrull river by Death because he had fallen in too soon. [M]

Mint, Royal, Ankh-Morpork. It would be hard to imagine an uglier building that hadn't won a major architectural award. The Mint is a gaunt brick and stone block, its windows high, small, many and barred, its doors protected by portcullises. Its whole construction says to the world: Don't Even Think About It.

Poking out of the roof is a sort of disc-shaped device which makes it look like a money box with a big coin stuck in the slot. This did, indeed, used to be known as the Bad Penny. It is a large treadmill to provide power for the coin stamps. It used to be powered by prisoners, back in the days when 'community service' wasn't just a word. Or even two.

Its main hall is three storeys high, and picks up a fair amount of daylight from the rows of barred windows, which send shafts of dusty sunlight slanting to the floor. Everything else is sheds.

Sheds have been built onto the walls and even hang like swallows' nests up near the ceiling, accessed by unsafe-looking wooden stairs. The uneven floor itself is a small village of sheds, placed any old how, no two alike, each one carefully roofed against the non-existent prospect of rain. Wisps of smoke spiral gently through the thick air. Against one wall a forge provides the dark orange glow that gives the place the right stygian atmosphere. The place looks like the after-death destination for people who have committed small and rather dull sins.

This is, however, just the background. What dominates the hall is the Bad Penny. This treadmill is strange. There is one in the Tanty, wherein inmates can invigorate their cardiovascular systems whether they want to or not. The Bad Penny is much larger, but hardly seems to be there at all. There is a metal rim that looks frighteningly thin. It's hard to see the spokes at all, until you realize that there are no spokes as such, just hundreds of thin wires. [MM]

Modo. The dwarf gardener at Unseen University. He used to be the assistant gardener at the Palace. He smokes a pipe, and is often found in a secluded area behind the High Energy Magic building, where he lights his bonfires, keeps his compost heaps, his pile of leaf mould and the little shed where he sits when it rains. He is a great believer in compost – his compost heaps heave and glow faintly in the dark, perhaps because of the possibly illegal ingredients Modo feeds them. ARCHCHANCELLORs have come and gone, UU has been destroyed and rebuilt, various dire horrors have visited the city, and Modo has still managed to mow the lawns every Friday. [RM]

Moghedron. Wine Butler in the castle of Sto Lat. [M]

Molly. Kitchen girl at UNSEEN UNIVERSITY. Originally edited from earlier *Companions*. Now back. [SM]

Molly, Queen. Head of the BEGGARS' GUILD. She walks with a stick and wears layers and layers of rags. Her hair looks as though it has been permed by a hurricane and her face is a mass of sores and warts (which have sub-warts, and they have their own hair). A very sharp woman. [MAA]

Mona Ogg, the. A painting by LEONARD OF QUIRM. The Mona Ogg's teeth are said to follow you round the room. The painting is currently in the PATRICIAN's collection. It is believed that Nanny OGG had not as yet visited Ankh-Morpork when this work was first brought to our attention; this may be some other Ogg, which, considering the fecundity of the Ogg tribe, is quite likely. However, there have also been hints that the young Leonard went on sketching holidays in the mountains during his youth, and there is no doubt that if he had ever been within ten miles of the young Gytha Ogg he would have heard about her.

Monarchy, Ankh-Morporkian. For most of its history Ankh-Morpork has been a monarchy. An important distinction, however, must be made between the kings of Ankh-Morpork and the kings of Ankh. The original kings of Ankh are enshrined in city mythology as 'real' kings (i.e., wise, powerful, charismatic, etc.), while the later kings of Ankh-Morpork are remembered as, well, real kings (i.e., power-mad, unjust and inventively evil).

Little is really known of the line of the kings of Ankh. It came to an end approximately 2000 years ago and its period is generally thought of as a 'golden age' – i.e., a time so long ago that no one can remember how wretched it was. Its physical remains are few: there are the ancient sewers, the ruins of what was possibly a castle on the hillock known as The Tump, a throne so worm-eaten that it would become a cloud of dust if sat upon and – according to legend – a sword.

There followed seventeen centuries of monarchy of a sort, where the crown was available to anyone with enough soldiers and a strong stomach; the history of the Ankh-Morpork monarchy is a litany of betrayals, massacres, ambushes, poisonings, imprisonments in towers, wars, people staggering around battlefields looking for their horse, family feuds and assassinations and wars. Of these last, the longest continued on a low-key basis for two centuries and the shortest, between the followers of Blad, Scourge of Dolly Sisters, and those of Mad Eric the Peaceful, is known as the .002 Years War.

Compared to the legendary kings of Ankh, all the later kings of Ankh-Morpork were pretenders. Most of them had as much interest in good government as the Borgia popes had in divinity, and most of the big families in Ankh-Morpork were 'royal' for a time. Not many lines survived for more than two or three generations and a number did not make it to the end of the coronation feast (in fact the shortest reign on record was that of Loyala the Aaargh, at 1.13 seconds). For a week, Ankh-Morpork was technically ruled by a wasp, and for several days by the left foot of the then High Priest of Io, who'd dropped the crown on it during the crucial point of the ceremony.

The legend of the sword figured very largely in the whole business. It was vaguely understood by the general population that possession of 'the sword' was the badge of the true king, and over the years any amount of 'true swords' were produced. In the case of Blad, it was two bits of wood hurriedly nailed together but for some reason, possibly to do with spikes and things, no one pointed this out for fifty-one years. It is now assumed (if not actually believed) that the 'true' sword is lost.

The last civil war, and execution and revelation of the personal habits of LORENZO THE KIND in 1688, marked the final end of any kind of monarchy in the city. The citizens did not object to rulers, even to cruel ones, but they did draw the line at being told that the various imbeciles and bloody-handed tyrants were there by the will of the gods.

And so the rule of kings gave way to the rule of the PATRICIANS. In a kind of mirror image of democracy, they have tended to get into power by lies, trickery and deceit, but remain in power only by a very crude democratic process; if they make too many enemies, they'll be out of office, power and probably their corporeal form. It seems to have worked, possibly for the reason advanced by the current Patrician in his treatise on the art of government, 'The Servant': 'If it continues for long enough, even a reign of terror may become a fondly remembered period. People believe they want justice and wise government but, in fact, what they really want is an assurance that tomorrow will be very much like today.'

Monflathers, Lord. The first Duke led 600 men to a glorious and epic defeat at the Battle of Quirm, which somehow therefore has managed to become one of the great and proud moments of Ankh-Morpork's military history. [MAA]

Monks, Balancing. Little has been revealed of this rather strange order, although the monks do run a charity hospital in Ankh-Morpork.

Central to their faith is a belief that the Discworld will wobble if things aren't perfectly balanced, and the monks spend much of their time moving small weights around according to rituals in one of their holy books. The weights can sometimes be found in the most inaccessible places, the monks travelling thousands of miles to put just one rather small weight in one place on some otherwise insignificant mountain. The weights seldom exceed a pound or two and it is possible – although not necessarily wise – to assume that the whole thing is merely ceremonial.

Monks, History. Also called The Men in Saffron, but they have many names. An order of humans, but with attributes that almost put them in the realm of anthropomorphic personifications. Founded by WEN the Eternally Surprised.

They perform a number of functions, which have changed over the years because of all the QUANTUM going on these days.

Traditionally, the monks also guard the History Books – huge, lead-bound volumes held in a secret cave in their hidden valley near the Hub at the Monastery of Oi Dong (also known as No Such Monastery). It is located in the highest, greenest, airiest valley of all, where apricots are grown and the streams have floating ice in them even on the hottest day. It is always a spring day in the little valley and the cherry trees are *always* in bloom, which is tough if you actually want cherries.

The key to understanding the function of the monks is the fact that these books are not chronicles of history, but instructions for it – they are, as it were, the script. Every significant fact – and from the point of view of the historical narrative, many quite small events can have tremendous significance – is written down. It is now believed that the books were written as a gift to his followers by Wen who, because of his special 'relationship' with TIME, knew everything that was going to happen.

Classically, the role of the monks lay in the very important distinction between History and what might be called sequential events.

History, in order to happen, has to be observed *by people who know they are observing History*. Skilled people, in fact. It's no good just anyone being there. It is well known that vast areas of the planet Earth had no history whatsoever until explorers turned up and brought History with them. Geography is similar in this respect; the fact that some lake, waterfall or continent is known to millions of people who live there is really of no significance compared to the arrival of an explorer who knows what Geography is.

History on the Discworld generally unfolds according to the patterns laid down in the books and has a natural tendency to spring back into shape, and for most of the time the monks merely have to observe. However, quantum uncertainty means that occasionally they have to intervene, usually in the most subtle of ways. In the same way that the placing of a 2oz weight can (possibly) affect the balance of the Discworld (*see* MONKS, BALANCING), the course of history can be changed by the mere misplacing of a pebble in a stream. These apparently trivial actions can send the whole world rushing down a different leg of the TROUSERS OF TIME.

At least, this is how the role is traditionally seen. Novices who rise through the ranks, however, learn that the truth is different, and can be summarized thusly: *For anything to happen, everything else has to happen, so everything happens anyway. Hang on, and try to steer with your knees.*

This means, for example, that intervening to prevent an unwanted historical outcome may well stop it happening in this universe, but won't prevent it happening in all the other, infinite number of universes. On that basis, what is the point of doing anything about anything?

The current ABBOT of Oi Dong has been considering this over many lifetimes, and has advised the monks thusly:

Do your job. Do not worry about the other universes. We are there, too. Do not let the fact that you cannot lift a mountain prevent you from seeking to raise a man. Or, as summarized by Lu-Tze: 'Get on with it! What'd happen to business if everyone took the day off!' Nevertheless, the historical role has now perforce taken a back seat to the simple task of making sure that there is enough time for *anything* to happen. Humans, with their unique ability to manipulate time – to save it, waste it, lose it and kill it, but seldom to make it or save it – are seriously reducing the amount available, and the monks have so far been able to make up the shortfall by moving time around – collecting it from where it is wasted or underused, such as the deep abyssal plains or the average classroom, and pumping it to those areas that use it fast. This is done using the ancient technology of the PROCRASTINATORS, which can wind and unwind time.

Since they are, by definition and training, outside History, the monks are invisible to normal people except when they are performing some role in the unfolding drama (it is sometimes necessary to go into History in order to steer it). They experience time on a continual basis but age only when taking on these roles.

They are also skilled in martial arts such as oki doki, upsidazi and – rarely– déjà-fu, where the hands move in time as well as space. Some of them, at least, possess the secret of being able to walk for many hours in the sub-zero temperatures of the high mountains (known as the Double-Knit Woollen Combinations with the Reinforced Gusset and Trapdoor).

Monks, Listening. *See* LISTENERS, THE.

Monolith. A troll folk-hero, who first wrested the secret of rocks from the GODS. Believed to have been the first-ever troll. Apparently, the secret of rock is that if you pick one up you can throw it at someone. This knowledge was jealously guarded by the gods. [MP]

Mooner, Dr. The owner of Dr Mooner's Travelling Take Your Breath Away Emporium. [P]

Mooty, Zebbo. A thief, third class, in Ankh-Morpork. The first person for hundreds of years to have been killed by a dragon. But not the last. [GG]

Morecombe. A vampire, although obviously housetrained. He is the solicitor of the Ramkin family, and senior member of the firm Morecombe, Slant and Honeyplace. Scrawny around the neck, like a tortoise; very pale, with pearly, dead eyes. [MAA]

Morraine. A troll who acted in moving pictures. (After the collapse of the industry a Morraine is known to have worked at the Armoury, and later joined the Ankh-Morpork militia.) [MP]

Morris Dancing. Morris dancing is common to all inhabited worlds in the multiverse, though only on Discworld is it danced properly.

The Lancre Morris Men are six times winners of the Fifteen Mountains All-Comers Morris Championship.[*] The Lancre tradition seems to favour a combative style, the Stick and Bucket dance, in particular, is considered too dangerous to perform, and whilst technically legal, shouldn't be performed when women are present.[**]

On the Chalk, the Morris men traditionally come to Tiffany Aching's village sometime in May. You can never be sure when, because they have to call at lots of villages along the Chalk, and every village has a pub, which slows them down.

They carry sticks and wear white clothes with bells on them, to stop them creeping up on people. No one likes an unexpected Morris dancer. For the same reason, before they start, the drummer beats the drum a few times and the accordionist plays a long drawn-out chord; the legal signal that a Morris Dance is about to began and people who hang around have only got themselves to blame.

They dance on the village green to the beat of a drum, banging their sticks together in the air, and then everyone would go to the pub and summer would come. The dancers danced, and then summer came, that was all anybody seemed to know. Mr Aching said that there had once been a year when the dancers hadn't turned up, and a cold, wet spring had turned into a chilly autumn, with the months between being filled with mists and rain and frosts in August.

That is why up on the Chalk they also dance the Dark Morris, to balance things. The Dark Morris welcomes the winter because of the new summer deep inside it.

Among the white-clad men there is the seventh dancer, the one they call the Fool. He is generally a small man, wearing a battered top hat and bright rags sewn all over his clothes. Mostly he wanders around holding out the hat and grinning at people until they give him money for beer. But sometimes he will put the hat down and whirl off into the dancers, always managing to be where the other dancers weren't.

Morris dancing is also known in Sto Helit, Ankh-Morpork (the Folk-Dance & Song Club counts Nobby NOBBS among its members) and New Ankh, which is home to the renowned Ninja Morris Men, who dance ruthlessly and can do strange and terrible things with a simple handkerchief and a bell.

Mort. Mortimer. Youngest son of LEZEK. Tall, red-haired and freckled, thin, white face, with the sort of body that seemed to be only marginally under its owner's control; it appeared to have been built out of knees. He had the kind of vague, cheerful helpfulness that serious men soon learned to dread. Despite these drawbacks Mort was chosen by DEATH to be his apprentice, and during that time became considerably less undirected and considerably more serious. Mort married YSABELL and became Duke of STO HELIT. They had a daughter, Susan STO HELIT, and were later killed in a coach crash.

As duke, his coat of arms was faux croisé on a sablier rampant against a sable field. His motto: *NON TIMETIS MESSOR.* [M]

---

[*]   *Three times outright, once after eleven hours extra time, and twice when the other finalists ran away.*

[**] *Even Nanny Ogg, no prude, considers it 'sexual morrisment'.*

Mort

Mountjoy-Standfast, Clive, Major. A cavalry officer during the events of *Night Watch*. Much to his chagrin he was born in Quirm because his mother was visiting her aunt and the coach was late. The major was not a fool, even though he looked like one. He was idealistic, and thought of his men as 'jolly good chaps' despite the occasional evidence to the contrary, and on the whole did the best he could with the moderate intelligence at his disposal. When he was a boy he'd read books about great military campaigns, and visited the museums and had looked with patriotic pride at the paintings of famous cavalry charges, last stands and glorious victories. It came as rather a shock, when he later began to participate in some of these, to find that the painters had unaccountably left out the intestines. Perhaps they just weren't very good at them. [NW]

Moutarde, Colonel. A guest at the Samedi Nuit Mort ball in Genua. [WA]

Moving Pictures, Production Companies.

Century of the Fruitbat Moving Pictures
Fir Wood Studios
Floating Bladder Pictures
Microlithic Pictures
Untied Alchemists

Moving Pictures, Titles of.

Bad Menace of Troll Valley
Beyond the Valley of the Trolls
Blown Away
Bolde Adventurer, A
Burninge Passiones
Dark Forest
Exciting Study of Pottery Making, An
Golde Diggers of 1457
Golde Rushe, The
High Jinks at the Store
King's Ransom, A
Mystery Mountain
Night at the Arena, A
Pelias and Melisande
Shadowe of the Dessert
Sons of the Dessert

Sword of Passione (or *The Interesting and Curious Adventures of Cohen the Barbarian*)
Tales of the Dwarfes
Third Gnome, The
Turkey Legs
Valley of the Trolls

Muckloe. Pig breeder in Slice. [LL]

Muldoon, Skully. A sergeant in the Ankh-Morpork City Day WATCH. Has a little house in Easy Street. [MAA]

Muluccai. Animal dealer in KLATCH. [MP]

Murderer, Captain. Highly respected in the coast around Quirm. Captain of the *Queen of Quirm* – and a smuggler. [SN]

Murduck, Brother. A missionary member of the brethren in the Citadel in OMNIA. His death was used to incite conflict between EPHEBE and Omnia. [SG]

Murune. A past King of LANCRE (709–745). He met a terrible fate involving a red-hot poker, ten pounds of live eels, a three-mile stretch of frozen river, a butt of wine, a couple of tulip bulbs, a number of poisoned eardrops, an oyster and a large man with a mallet. Some people just don't seem to get along with others. [WS]

Muscara. Née Susan. A member of DIAMANDA's coven. [LL]

Musicians' Guild. Motto: ID MVRMVRATIS, ID LVDAMVS. Coat of arms: a shield, azure, bisected by a band wavy, argent et melodieux. Sinister a trousseau des clés, or. Dexter a cor, or.

The Guild has a very small office in Tin Lid Alley, Ankh-Morpork (a couple of poky rooms above a barber shop). On the wall of its poky, brown-walled waiting room is a sign: 'For Your Comfort and Convenience YOU WILL NOT SMOKE'. Unlike most of the other Guilds, it does not involve itself in education or social work, but does involve itself very deeply and sincerely in collecting very high membership fees and imposing very high performance rates to pay for them. It is not compulsory for a musician to belong to the GoM. On the other hand, it is not *compulsory* for a musician to breathe and see out of both eyes. Although most members of its senior council were once practising musicians, their contact with the Muse these days is generally limited to the notes you can obtain by hitting the human skull quite hard.

Mustardseed. An elf lord, coincidentally sharing a name with one of Shakespeare's fairies. [TSC]

Mwnyy, Owen. Owner of a legendary harp which, according to Llamedese legend, sang when danger threatened. [SM]

Nature abhors dimensional abnormalities, and seals them neatly away so that they don't upset people. Nature, in fact, abhors a lot of things, including vacuums, ships called the Marie Celeste, and the chuck keys for electric drills.

– *Pyramids*

Nac Mac Feegle. Also called Pictsies and, among themselves, The Wee Free Men; The Little Men and 'Person or Persons Unknown, Believed to be Armed'). Small, red-haired, blue men and, infrequently, women. They always smell like slightly drunk potatoes.

From 'Fairies and How To Avoid Them' by Miss Perspicacia Tick:

'The Nac Mac Feegle are the most dangerous of the fairy races, particularly when drunk. They love drinking, fighting and stealing, and will in fact steal anything that is not nailed down. If it *is* nailed down, they will steal the nails as well.'
'Nevertheless, those who have managed to get to know them, and survive, say that they are also amazingly loyal, strong, dogged, brave and, in their own way, quite moral. (For example, they won't steal from people who don't have anything.)'
'The average Feegle man (Feegle women are rare – *see later*) is about six inches high, red-haired, has skin turned blue with tattoos and the dye called woad and, since you're this close, he's probably about to hit you. He'll wear a kilt made of any old material, because amongst the Feegles the clan allegiance is shown by the tattoos. He may wear a rabbit-skull helmet, and Feegles often decorate their beards and hair with feathers, beads and anything else that takes their fancy. He will almost certainly carry a sword, although it is mainly for show, the Feegles' preferred method of fighting being with the boot and the head.'

They often have very descriptive names, such as Wee Honeymouth Jock, Wee Jock O'the White Head and Slightly-Thinner-Than-Fat-Jock-Jock. There are many feegles named in the books. They're not keen on having their names written down but we'll also risk including, for interest, Slightly-more-wee-than-Wee-Jock-Jock, and – a wee list of 'Wees' – Wee: Duggie Bignose, Clonker, Slogum, Fungus and Gimmie Jimmie.

HISTORY AND RELIGION

The origin of the Nac Mac Feegle is lost in the famous Mists of Time. They say that they were thrown out of Fairyland by the Queen of the Fairies because they objected to her spiteful and tyrannical rule. Others say they were just thrown out for being drunk.

Little is known about their religion, if any, save for one fact: they think they are dead. They like our world, with its sunshine and mountains and blue skies and things to fight. An amazing world like this couldn't be open to just *anybody*, they say. It must be some kind of a heaven or Valhalla, where brave warriors go when they are dead. So, they reason, they have already been alive somewhere else, and then died and were allowed to come here because they have been so *good*.

This is a *quite* incorrect and fanciful notion because, as we know, the truth is exactly the other way around.

There is not a great deal of mourning when a Feegle dies, and it's only because his brothers are sad that he's not spent more time with them before going back to the land of the living, which they also call 'The Last World'.

HABITS AND HABITAT

For choice, the clans of the Nac Mac Feegle live in the burial mounds of ancient kings, where they hollow out a cosy cavern amongst the gold. Generally there will be one or two thorn or elder trees growing on it – the Feegles particularly like old, hollow elder trees, which become chimneys for their fire. And there will, of course, be a rabbit hole. It will look just like a rabbit hole. There will be rabbit droppings around it, and maybe even a few bits of rabbit fur if the Feegles are feeling particularly creative.

Down below, the world of the Feegle is a bit like a beehive, but with a lot less honey and a lot more sting.

The reason for this is that females are very rare among the Feegle. And, perhaps because of this, Feegle women give birth to lots of babies, very often and very quickly – usually about seven at a time. They're about the size of peas

The Nac Mac Feegle

when born but grow extremely fast if they're fed well. (Feegles like to live near humans so that they can steal milk from cows and sheep for this purpose.)

The 'queen' of the clan is called the kelda, who, as she gets older, becomes the mother of most of it. Her husband is known as The Big Man. When a girl child is born – and it doesn't often happen – she stays with her mother to learn the *hiddlins*, which are the secrets of keldaring. When she is old enough to be married, *she must leave the clan*, taking a few of her brothers with her as a bodyguard on her long journey.

Often she'll travel to a clan which has no kelda. Very, very rarely, if there is no clan without a kelda, she'll meet with Feegles from several clans and form a completely new clan, with a new name and a mound of its own. She will also choose her husband. And, from then on, while her word is absolute law among her clan and must be obeyed, she'll seldom go more than a little distance from the mound. She is both its queen and its prisoner.

But, once, for a few days, there was a kelda who was a human girl…

FEEGLE GLOSSARY

Adjusted for those of a delicate disposition ('*A Work in Progress*' by Miss Perspicacia Tick).

Bigjobs: human beings.

Big Man: chief of the clan (usually the husband of the kelda).

Blethers: rubbish, nonsense.

Boggin': to be desperate, as in 'I'm boggin' for a cup of tea.'

Bogle: *see* Schemie.

Brose: porridge with a drop of strong drink added – or more than a drop. Be warned: it will put hairs on your chest.

Bunty: a weak person.

Carlin: old woman.

Cludgie: the privy.

Corbies: big, black burdies known by most people as crows.

Crivens!: a general exclamation that can mean anything from 'My goodness!' to 'I've just lost my temper and there is going to be trouble.'

Dree your/my/his/her weird: facing the fate that is in Store for you/me/him/her.

Een: eyes.

Eldritch: weird, strange; sometimes means oblong too, for some reason.

Fash: worry, upset.

Geas: a very important obligation, backed up by tradition and magic. Not a bird.

Gonnagle: the bard of the clan, skilled in musical instruments, poems, stories and songs.

Hag: a witch, of any age.

Hag o' hags: a very important witch.

Hagging/Haggling: anything a witch does.

Hiddlins: secrets.

Kelda: the female head of the clan, and eventually the mother of most of it. Feegle babies are very small, and a kelda will have hundreds in her lifetime.

Lang syne: long ago.

Last World: the place where Feegles believe they live before death, and the place to which they return when they 'appear' to die on Discworld. *See* History and Religion, above.

Mowpie: furry animals with white tufts as tails, making them easy to spot. Sometimes called rabbits. Good to eat, especially with a dab of snail relish on the side.

Mudlin: useless person.

Pished: I am assured that this means 'tired'.

Schemie: an unpleasant person.

Scuggan: a really unpleasant person.

Scunner: a generally unpleasant person.

Ships: woolly things that eat grass and go baa. Easily confused with the other kind.

Spavie: *see* Mudlin.

Special Sheep Liniment: probably moonshine whiskey, I am very sorry to say. A favourite of the Feegles. Do not try to make this at home.

Spog: a small leather bag at the front of a Feegle's kilt, which covers whatever he presumably thinks needs to be hidden and generally holds things like something he is halfway through eating, something he'd found that now therefore belongs to him, and quite often – because even a Feegle can catch a cold – it might hold whatever he was using as a handkerchief, which might not necessarily be dead.

Steamie: only found in the big Feegle mounds in the mountains, where there's enough water to allow regular bathing; it's a kind of sauna. Feegles on the Chalk tend to rely on the fact that you can only get so much dirt on you before it starts to fall off of its own accord.

Waily: a general cry of despair. [TSC]

Nancyball, Horace. A very tall Watchman, brought up by his gran. He was a participant in the events of *Night Watch*. He did the job he had to do. [NW]

Nanny Ogg. *See* OGG, GYTHA.

N'choate, Azhural. A Klatchian stock dealer. [MP]

Necrotelicomnicon. (Also known as the '*Liber Paginarum Fulvarum*'.) A book, written by ACHMED THE MAD, which lists all of the old, dark gods of the Disc. The first edition is kept in the LIBRARY of Unseen University, between iron plates, behind a balanced stone door, with its name hacked on to the lintel over the door. The page headed 'About the Author' combusted shortly after his death. Legend says that any mortal man who reads more than a few lines of the original copy will die insane; it is also said that it contains illustrations that could make a strong man's brain dribble out of his ears. Usually, people only read tenth or twelfth-hand copies.

There was once a wizard who started to read it and let his mind wander. Next morning they found all his clothes on the chair and his hat on top of them and the book had... a lot more pages. [ER]

Nef, Great. An incredibly dry desert region of the Disc, rimwards of KLATCH, at the heart of which is the DEHYDRATED OCEAN. It is so dry that it has a negative rainfall. It is the site of the Lost City of EE and the Light Dams of the Sorca people. [COM]

Nesheley. An inhabitant of Inkcap, in the Ramtops. His claim to fame is that he once nearly ran over Granny Weatherwax in his cart and is still alive. [WS]

Nesmith, Edith. Almost caused a railway disaster in her attempts, with her siblings, to look like heroes and save a train from derailing. [RS]

Netherglades, the. The swamps of the Netherglades are famous for their birdlife but also notorious, because they move constantly and quickly. Dry land is hard to find. The human inhabitants live on large rafts that serve as both shelters and gardens. The older generations have splayed feet, which they try to encourage in their offspring because the webs show that the owner is a great hunter of the swamps. They have no known enemies, probably because most people don't want to step into a swamp. They are in fact helpful to travellers, and they distil extremely useful medications from the floating flora and fauna of the swamps, which include the twisting honeydew and the egregious flytrap, whose venom can be used in the making of delicate ironwork etchings, and which must be approached with extreme caution as the venom can be spat over several yards.

There clearly has been magic at work in the Netherglades, and its future as the pharmacopoeia of the world is being tested by Professor Rincewind of Unseen University. A dispatch from him reveals that the juice pressed from a certain little yellow flower induces certainty in the patient for up to fifteen minutes. About what they are certain they cannot specify, but the patient is, in that short time, completely certain about everything. And further research has found that a floating water hyacinth yields in its juices total uncertainty about anything for half an hour.

Philosophers are excited about the uses of these potions, and the search continues for a plant that combines the qualities of both, thereby being of great use to theologians. [RS]

Nhumrod, Brother. Novice Master in OMNIA. A kindly (by the standards of Omnia, anyway) old man, waxy-skinned, with thin, blue-veined hands. He walked with a cane and was also a mass of nervous tics, but perhaps this was due to the fact that he survived in the Omnian citadel for fifty years and spent every night wrestling with the evil temptations of the flesh. [SG]

Nijel. Nijel the Destroyer, son of HAREBUT THE PROVISION MERCHANT. To say that he is lean would be to miss a perfect opportunity to use the word 'emaciated' – he looks as though toast racks and deckchairs have figured in his ancestry. He has a shock of lank, ginger hair, eyes like boiled grapes and a face that is a battleground for its native freckles and the dreadful invading forces of acne.

Short-sighted, with quite a good brain and a tendency to asthma attacks, Nijel does not conform to the normal perception of a classic hero. He does, however, dress like one: a few studded leather thongs, big furry boots, a little leather 'holdall' and goose pimples. The woolly underwear doesn't really work, but he promised his mother.

And, indeed, he acts like a hero, too. In fact Nijel has every necessary attribute for the classical hero except strength, charisma and skill. [S]

Ninereeds. The rather unpleasant Agatean Master Accountant to whom TWOFLOWER was once apprenticed. It was also the name given by Twoflower to the dragon he conjured from his mind at the WYRMBERG. [COM]

Nine Turning Mirrors. Grand Vizier of the AGATEAN EMPIRE. Grew old in the service of several Emperors, whom he regarded as being a necessary but tiresome ingredient in the successful running of the Empire. He did not like things out of place – his view was that the Empire was not built by allowing things to get out of place. He had very clear views about who should run the country – e.g. that it should be him. Met his end during his attempt to poison a young Emperor who was handier with a pair of chopsticks. [COM]

Nitt, Agnes. *See* NITT, PERDITA X.

Nitt, Perdita X. The inner name of Agnes Nitt, daughter of Terminal Thomas 'Threepenny' Nitt (his parents, usually well if not wisely educated by Lancre standards, called their three sons Primal, Medial and Terminal.)

Agnes was a member of DIAMANDA's

amateur coven in LANCRE when first encountered in the canon, and was a small, fat seventeen-year-old with a naturally rosy complexion; the sort of girl who would love to be a Goth but was cut out by nature to be two Goths.

Easily swayed by her more imaginative friends, Agnes/Perdita wore black, had a black hat with a veil, and even a black lace hanky, all this conspiring to give the effect of a small, low-flying thunderstorm. Despite her love of black, she had two shelves of soft toys. According to Nanny OGG, who is seldom wrong in these matters, Agnes actually did have some useful magical talent. Perdita X Nitt is the thin person who is supposed to be trying to get out of every fat person, although Perdita makes no attempt to leave and merely stays inside and dreams ridiculous daydreams.

As so often happens, magical talent given no vent finds an outlet in other forms of expression, and it turned out that Agnes had an incredible singing voice – she could, in fact, reproduce practically any pitch or sound, and could sing in harmony with herself (Perdita had a rather reedy voice). She took this talent to Ankh-Morpork's Opera house just before Granny WEATHERWAX and Nanny Ogg decided that she would make a good third witch for their coven (they were tired of making their own tea). Events, as they say, eventuated (described in *Maskerade*) and as a result, to no one's surprise, Agnes found that when witchcraft calls you there's no point in hanging up. And that when it comes to choosing between, on the one hand, someone with talent, good hair and a wonderful personality and, on the other, someone who merely looks stunning, the world doesn't hesitate either.

Agnes is splay-footed, wears too much eye liner and has big hair... well, not simply big hair, it is enormous hair, as if it's trying to counterbalance her body. It is glossy, never splits and is extremely well behaved, except for a tendency to eat combs. Her hair obeys the rule. Perdita doesn't. Perdita is vain, selfish and vicious. She thinks Agnes is a fat, pathetic, weak-willed blob that people would walk over if she weren't so steep.

Agnes is now back in Lancre, still with Perdita's beguiling inner voice. She's also realizing, after her experience, is that she is probably more intelligent than other people, that most people don't think straight, and that the world needs sorting out. It seems that Granny Weatherwax has won again. [MA]

Nivor, Grunworth. A tutor at the Assassins' Guild. Fat, jolly and fond of his food. He was TEPPIC's housemaster, and lectured about traps and deadfalls on Tuesdays. [P]

No'-as-big-as-Medium-Sized-Jock-but-bigger-than-Wee-Jock-Jock. Member of the Nac Mac Feegle clan near the Tiffany Aching's village, over on the Chalk. Makes it here just because of his delightful name. [WFM]

Nobbs, Alphonse. Alf. A BLEDLOW at UNSEEN UNIVERSITY. Played Foot-the-ball for UU Most definitely not related to Corporal NOBBS of the City Watch. [UA]

Nobbs, C. W. St J., Corporal. (Cecil Wormsborough St John.) Generally known as Nobby, he is a corporal in the Ankh-Morpork Night WATCH. A four-foot-tall, pigeon-chested, bandy-legged man, with the muscle tone of an elastic band and a certain resemblance to a chimpanzee, Nobby is actually smaller than many dwarfs and carries at all times a tattered affidavit attesting to his species, and possibly his genus as well. He gives his age as 'probably thirty-four', but he's been 'probably thirty-four' for years. He is the son of Sconner and Maisie

'Nobby' Nobbs

Nobbs of Old Cobblers, where he was brought up in a cellar, and he is either their youngest or the only child, since it is beyond belief that any parents could look into the cradle containing the young Nobby and still be prepared to have another go. (Mind you, Nobby *did* name the swamp dragon ERROL, in *Guards! Guards!*, after his brother!)

He is the grandson of Slope Nobbes, who was *possibly* the illegitimate son of Edward St John de Nobbes, Earl of Ankh, although the link is suspect.

When he was a boy, Nobby dressed in an oversized evening dress jacket, shiny with grease and greenish with age, and a top hat that must once have been trodden on by a horse. No single feature on his childish, pinched-up face was more than passably ugly, but the combination was greater than the sum of the parts. He was streetwise and, frankly, a street urchin – that is, ugly, prickly and smelling strangely of fish.

He is rumoured to have terrible personal habits, although these appear to be no more than a penchant for petty theft (usually from people too unconscious or, for preference, too dead to argue), an ability to do tricks with his facial boils, and a liking for folk-dancing.

Men like Nobby can be found in any armed force. Although their grasp of the minutiae of the Regulations is usually encyclopaedic, they take good care never to be promoted beyond, perhaps, corporal. He smokes incessantly, but the weird thing is that any cigarette smoked by Nobby becomes a dog-end almost instantly and remains a dog-end indefinitely or until lodged behind his ear, which is a sort of nicotine elephants' graveyard.

Nobby's normal method of locomotion is a species of sidle; in times of danger he has a way of propelling himself from place to place without apparently moving through the intervening space. And he tends to speak out of the corner of his mouth. In fact there is something altogether very cornery about Corporal Nobbs.

Nobby is known to have served as a quartermaster in the army of the Duke of Pseudopolis. There are rumours that he had to join the Watch after items missing from the stores

were found in his kit. Since the items were the entirety of the store inventory, Nobby's kit at the time consisted of two warehouses.

He lives in the New Watch House in Pseudopolis Yard, Ankh-Morpork, moving from room to room as he fills them up. He is, or rather was, the founder of the Guild of Watchmen, which appears to have lasted for just as long as it took Commander Vimes to find out about it.

He is currently understood to have a girlfriend – a goblin called Shine of the Rainbow.

He is not, repeat not, related to Bledlow Alf (Alphonse) Nobbs from UU. [GG]

Noddy. A friend to Crash and a member of his music group, originally called Insanity. He was the Other One – you know, the one who isn't the lead guitarist, the bass guitarist or the drummer. The one who jumps around on the stage, sweating and drinking beer. [SM]

Nooni, Lady. Noblewoman of DJELIBEYBI. [P]

Norbut. Owner of a cow alleged to have stopped giving milk after Granny WEATHERWAX looked at it. [WS]

Nork the Impaler. A regular at the Mended Drum. No one has even dared ask how he got the nickname. [GG]

Notfaroutoe, Count and Countess. Arthur and Doreen Winkings. Members of the FRESH START CLUB, and vampires, by inheritance.

Arthur had been in the wholesale fruit and vegetable business before he inherited the title and, with it, a ruined castle and vampirism. At least, so he believes. And that is the important thing.

Vampirism sits uneasily on the middle class. The difficulty the couple face is that they feel there are established ways vampires should look and behave, and they do their best to behave that way. The snag is that these details – the wearing of evening dress at all times, and so on – were designed for people a good deal taller, thinner and, well, more inherently stylish than Arthur and Doreen. But since the only vampires they've ever heard of wear posh clothes and live in castles, they set out with a sort of resigned and dogged unimaginativeness to fit the stereotype.

The Countess (born to a washerwoman in Cockbill Street, Ankh-Morpork), for example, is basically a pear-shaped, amiable woman who is trying to look like a consumptive and mysterious lady two feet taller. She wears a figure-hugging black dress, long dark hair cut into a widow's peak and very pallid make-up. Nature, however, designed her to have frizzy hair and a hearty complexion. She speaks with an affected foreign accent except when she forgets. Vampires are always foreign, she believes. She is now the Treasurer of the AM Mission of the Überwald League of Temperance.

The only vampire trait not embraced by Arthur is the one involving climbing into the bedrooms of young women and sucking their necks. Doreen put her foot down about this. He has to have rare steak and black pudding and like it. This disappointment is on top of his shaving problem; his face is a mass of small cuts, because it's very hard to shave when you can't see yourself in the mirror.

Their four-roomed terraced house at 14 Masons Road, Ankh-Morpork, boasted a crypt, a vault (the Winkings haven't worked out that these could be the same thing), a torture chamberette, a dining room with dribbly candles and a painting whose eyes moved, a secret passage, an organ that was so big that a hole had to be knocked in the parlour ceiling for it, a laboratory and a moat. The house fell down shortly after Arthur knocked down the last load-bearing wall in order to install an Iron Maidenette, and the Winkings subsequently lodged with the understanding Mrs CAKE. It is believed that the Count's gravel-filled coffin is the first attempt to meet the orthopaedic needs of the vampire with a bad back. [RM]

Nougat Knights. Famed in dwarfish mythology as the ancestors who, at the beginning of the world, created the treacle mines and other subterranean sweets. [RS]

Nourishing. A young female rat involved in MAURICE's 'Pied Piper' scam. She had been in the Light Widdlers but transferred to the Trap Disposal Squad, under DARKTAN's leadership. Worships Darktan. [TAMAHER]

N'tuitif. On the veldt of Howondaland live the N'tuitif people, the only tribe in the world to have *no imagination whatsoever.*

For example, their story about the thunder runs something like this: 'Thunder is a loud noise in the sky, resulting from the disturbance of the air masses by the passage of lightning.' And their legend 'How the Giraffe Got his Long Neck' runs: 'In the old days the ancestors of Old Man Giraffe had slightly longer necks than other grassland creatures, and their access to the high leaves was so advantageous that it was mostly long-necked giraffes that survived, passing on the long neck in their blood just as a man might inherit his grandfather's spear. Some say, however, that it is all a lot more complicated and this explanation only applies to the shorter neck of the okapi. And so it is.' The N'tuitif are a peaceful people, and have been hunted almost to extinction by neighbouring tribes, who have lots of imagination, and therefore plenty of gods, superstitions and ideas about how much better life would be if they had a bigger hunting ground.

Nugent, Mrs. Housekeeper to Igneous CUTWELL. [M]

Nuggan. A god of Borogravia. He is a tetchy god, whose laws are enforced by informal citizen committees. His *'Book of Nuggan'* is in a ringbinder to accommodate new Abominations, which turn up in it magically. These are many and wide-ranging and include, for example, Chocolate, Garlic, Cats, Dwarfs, the Colour Blue, Oysters, Babies, the Theatre, Barking Dogs, Shirts with Six Buttons, Cheese, Women Wearing Men's Clothes, Rocks, Ears, Accordion Players – and Beating Your Wife with a Stick greater than an Inch Across. Quite tricky to keep up. [MR]

Nutmeg. An officer of Sto Plains Holdings and on the Board of Reacher Gilt's Grand Trunk Company. [MM]

Nutt, 'Gobbo', Mr. An orc. When we first meet him, he is a Temporary Apprentice Candle Dribbler at Unseen University. He is young, with a grey, round, guileless face – he has an unshakeably amiable look about him. He is very untidily dressed; he looks like a scarecrow. Although he looks like a bag of second-hand clothes, he talks like a retired theologian – he speaks three dead languages, and twelve living ones. He appears quite slight (his fingers look like cheese straws) but he is not as little as he first appears. Partly, he weighs himself down with humility, but – as an orc, from Überwald – he looks smaller when he is upset; it's a product of his morphic field contracting and expanding. He has a natural skill at football and he works with Trevor LIKELY at UU (another football fan).

He becomes close friends with Glenda SUGARBEAN. [UA]

N'vectif, Banana. Cunningest hunter in the great yellow plains of Klatch. He designed a better mousetrap shortly before being trampled by 1000 elephants. [MP]

It was octarine, the colour of magic. It was alive and glowing and vibrant and it was the undisputed pigment of the imagination, because wherever it appeared it was a sign that mere matter was a servant of the powers of the magical mind. It was enchantment itself. But Rincewind always thought it looked a sort of greenish-purple.

– *The Colour of Magic*

Oats, Quite Reverend. His full name is Mightily-Praiseworthy-Are-Ye-Who-Exalteth-Om Oats, but this is often shortened to Mightily. At the time of the events of *Carpe Jugulum*, he is a priest of the Omnian religion who trained at the Ohulan mission. He is a quite young, skinny man with a ripe boil beside his nose, and a smile that appears on his face as if someone has operated a shutter. There is something *damp* about him, the kind of helpless hopelessness that makes people angry rather than charitable. He is in two minds about almost everything since he always tries to see both sides of every question. He wears a black robe which ends at his knees and a razor-sharp starched collar. His legs are encased in grey socks and his feet are encased in sandals.

He also wore a holy turtle pendant and carried a finely printed graduation copy of the 'Book of Om', which he unfortunately mislaid during the events of *Carpe Jugulum*. Indeed, during the events of that book he embraced a more muscular form of Omnianism and might by now be doing or wearing *anything*. [CJ]

Ocean Waltzer. The boat used by RINCEWIND, the LUGGAGE and CONINA to travel from ANKH-MORPORK to KLATCH. Almost a whole entry in small caps. [S]

Octarine. The eighth colour of the Disc spectrum. The basic colour of which other colours are merely pale shadows impinging on normal four-dimensional space. It is a sort of fluorescent greenish-yellow-purple. (*See also* LIGHT, NATURE OF.)

Octarines. Gemstones which glow in a strong magical field. Otherwise they look like rather inferior diamonds. [S]

Octavo, the. The CREATOR's own grimoire. Reputedly left behind by the Creator – with characteristic absent-mindedness – shortly after completing his major work.

The Eight Spells are imprisoned on its pages.

For the whole of recorded time – except for a brief spell inside the LUGGAGE – it has been kept in a little room off the main LIBRARY, in the cellars of Unseen University. The walls are covered with occult symbols and protective lead pentagrams, and most of the floor is taken up with the Eightfold Seal of Stasis. The only furnishing is a lectern in the shape of a bird – or at least in the shape of a winged thing, it is probably best not to examine too closely – and on the lectern, fastened to it by a heavy chain covered in eight padlocks (one key for each of the Heads of the Eight Orders of Wizardry), is a book, so full of magic that it has its own keen sentience.

It is a large, but not particularly impressive book. The rather tatty leather cover has a representation of BEL-SHAMHAROTH and could be described in a library catalogue as 'slightly foxed', although it would be more honest to admit it looks as though it has been badgered, wolved and possibly beared as well. Metal clasps hold it shut. They aren't decorated, they're just very heavy – like the chain, which doesn't so much attach the book to the lectern as tether it. They look like the work of someone who had a pretty definite aim in mind, and who has spent most of his life making training harnesses for elephants.

No one is allowed to stay in the room for more than 4 minutes and 32 seconds (a figure arrived at after 200 years of cautious experimentation).

Octiron. A strange, iridescent metal, almost as highly valued in the lands around the CIRCLE SEA as SAPIENT PEARWOOD, and about as rare.

A needle of octiron will always point to the Hub of the Discworld, being acutely sensitive to the Disc's magical field; it will also miraculously darn socks. Octiron radiates a dangerous amount of raw enchantment and is a metal so unstable that it can exist only in a universe saturated with raw magic.

Octogen. A gas that radiates dangerous amounts of raw magic.

Odium. A moving-picture pit in Ankh-Morpork. Owned by Bezam PLANTER. Destroyed by fire. [MP]

Offler. Great Offler of the Bird-Haunted Mouth. Six-armed Crocodile God of Klatch, but also the default god of any place with a big river and warm climate. He has a flock of holy birds that bring him news of his worshippers and also keep his teeth clean. The teeth in his fanged snout cause him to speak with a marked lisp. [M]

Of the Twilight the Darkness. First seen as a tower goblin on the clacks. He has a face that would take a frantic battalion of mothers to love. He believes in the need for goblins to acclimatize to new challenges – 'Don't acclimatize, don't live!' Adora Belle employs him on the personal clacks on her house, telling Moist, 'He's punctual, fast, reliable and codes more accurately even than me and all he wants from us is to be allowed to live with his family on the roof.' He goes on to work closely with Moist, supporting his endeavors in the events of *Raising Steam*. He makes great coffee.

Of the Wheel the Spike. Goblin inventor of the first velocipede/bicycle. Another little bit of technology follows the steam railway onto Discworld. As Lord VETINARI says, 'The world is subtly changing and it needs its shepherds and sometimes its butchers. And in this case, I'm its shepherd. And all that anyone can say now is: What next? What little thing will change the world because the little tinkers carried on tinkering?' [RS]

Of the Wind Regretfully Blown. Goblin name of Billy SLICK. [SN]

Ogg, Gytha. Nanny Ogg. – most Ramtop witches of any note have some suitable grandmotherly honorific (Granny, Nanny, Gammer, Old Mother, etc.), regardless of actual marital status, but Nanny Ogg is *definitely* a grandmother.

Age: uncertain, even to her. Probably in her seventies, which means she was still capable of bearing children in her early fifties (this is by no means unusual for a healthy LANCRE woman, especially a witch, and certainly for an Ogg). There is a large population of long-lived dwarfs on the mountainous fringes of the country, and the Oggs are a remarkably ancient family with traditional skills in magic and iron-working; it may be, as CASANUNDA has claimed, that she has some dwarf in her, although this is probably an expression of his hopes rather than any genetic expertise.

After an adventurous girlhood – always chaste, as she says, and often caught – and a period as a maid at Lancre Castle, Gytha Ogg was accepted by a Biddy Spective as her successor to the cottage in Lancre town, where she brought to the craft of witchery an honest, earthy outlook, a non-judgemental understanding of human nature, and the ability to crack walnuts with her knees.

Nanny Ogg's family arrangements are cosy but haphazard. She has been formally married three times, to Albert Ogg, Winston Ogg and Sobriety Ogg (witches are matrilinear and in any case a man would be expected to accept the family name when marrying into such an ancient lineage as the Oggs). All three have passed happily, if somewhat energetically, to their well-earned rest. When asked how many husbands she's had, she says, 'Three of my own,

Gytha 'Nanny' Ogg

and let's say I've run out of fingers on the rest.'

She has fifteen living children: Jason, Grame, Tracie, Shirl, Daff, Dreen, Nev, Trev, Kev, Wane, Sharleen, Darron, Karen, Reet and Shawn. Many of them, Shawn, for example, live and work around Lancre; others have sought their fortune in far-flung foreign parts. There are innumerable grandchildren and great-grandchildren. Only two grandchildren have appeared in the chronicles – Shane, a bold sailor lad, and Pewsey, the stickiest child in the world. Contrary to the rules of traditional witchcraft, Nanny Ogg now lives in quite a modern cottage in the centre of Lancre ('Tir Nani Ogg' – Nanny Ogg's Place), with up-to-date conveniences like a modern wash copper and a tin bath a mere garden's walk away on a nail at the back of the privy. The cottage is between those of Shawn and Jason. She likes to have all her family around her in case of an emergency, such as when she needs a cup of tea (which she takes with three lumps of sugar) or the floor washed. [WS]

Nanny's Cottage. Nanny's cottage tends towards jolly clashing colours and smells of polish. The outside is spanking new with a gleaming thatch and manicured front lawn with gnomes, toadstools, pink bunnies and big-eyed deer around a tiny pond. On the edge of the pond, a tiny gnome is fishing ... oh, no, er, that isn't a *rod* he's holding. Let's move swiftly inside, which is a shrine to bad but enthusiastically painted ornaments.

There are no skulls or strange candles – apart from a pink novelty one she bought in Ankh-Morpork. There are *lots* of tables – mainly in order to display the vast number of drawings and iconographs of the huge Ogg clan. These pictures are carefully advanced or retarded around the room as various family members temporarily fall in or out of favour. What space is not taken up by pictures is taken up by ornaments, because no Ogg who travelled more than ten miles from Lancre would dream of returning without a present. Usually, these are cheapjack stuff bought from fairs, but Nanny Ogg doesn't mind, so long as they're colourful and shiny. There are lots of cross-eyed dogs, pink shepherdesses and mugs with badly spelled slogans like: 'To The World's Best Mum' and 'We Luove Our Nanny'. There is a huge china beer stein in a glass-fronted locked cabinet (a present from Shirl Ogg) and a blue clockwork ballerina which pirouettes to 'Three Blind Mice'. Oh, and a little hourglass with the legend, 'Tempus Redux'. That might come in useful one day.

Ogg, Jason. Eldest son of Gytha Ogg. Master blacksmith and farrier, and a member of the LANCRE Morris Men, for whom he plays the fiddle.

With his hairy brow, cheese-grater chin and fifteen-stone body, Jason looks as though he was not born but constructed. In a shipyard. He is a man with an essentially slow and gentle nature that should have gone to a couple of bullocks, arms like tree trunks and legs like beer barrels stacked in twos.

The smith in Lancre is a very powerful smith indeed. The Lancre smiths have an ancient bargain – if they shoe anything brought to them, their reward is the *ability* to shoe anything. It is not clear who the pact is with, but it may have something to do with Lancre's proximity to the worlds of the ELVES, against whom iron is a sovereign defence. Or it may be because, every so often, *someone* comes at the appropriately named dead of night to have his horse re-shod. Whatever the reason, Jason can put a shoe on anything with feet.

They brought him an ant once, for a joke. He sat up all night with a magnifying glass and an anvil made out of the head of a pin.

Jason also knows the mystic secret of the Lancre Horseman's Word, used by smiths to calm the wildest stallion. It broadly consists of a whispered explanation into the animal's ear of what all those hammers and pliers will be used for if the horse doesn't stop kicking and present a docile hoof *right now*. [WS]

Ogg, Mona. See MONA OGG, THE.

Ogg, Shawn. Private/Corporal/Sergeant/ Commander-in-Chief Ogg, S. is Gytha Ogg's youngest son: a short, red-faced youth in his early twenties. He is guard and general odd-job man at LANCRE CASTLE, where he dreams of a glorious military career. He empties the palace privies, delivers its mail, operates the Royal Mint, balances the budget, helps out the Royal gardener in his spare time and butles when Spriggs the butler is not on duty. He is also the Royal Historian (on Wednesday evenings), Lord Chamberlain and Conductor of the Lancre Light Symphony Orchestra. He is also the creator of the LANCRASTIAN ARMY KNIFE. Many days spent guarding Lancre Castle on a repetitive carbohydrate diet have given him an inner self-reliance and an ability to fart in tune. [WS]

Oggham. Ancient runic alphabet, still used by dwarfs throughout the RAMTOPS. There is some suggestion that this has something to do with the Ogg family – a suggestion which Nanny OGG is careful to foster.

Ohulan Cutash. Described by Moist von LIPWIG as '… a likeable kind of place: a little market town with the usual hinterland of farmers and lumberjacks. Some mining too, dwarfs and human quite often these days working on the same mine and even the same seams. It was big enough to have a mayor and sensible enough to have a very good tavern called the Fiddler's Riddle.'

A more widely-held view is that it is a quite barbaric and uncivilized sprawl of a hundred or so houses about fifteen miles from LANCRE and considered by Lancrastians to be a big city. It has one suburb. It's too small to have more than one, and this is just an inn and a handful of cottages for people who can't stand the pressure of urban life. There is a cobbled main square and on one side are the temples of the Disc's more demanding deities.

It has a tiny river dock, on the upper ANKH, with broad, flat-bottomed barges bobbing gently against the wharves. [ER]

Old High Ones, the. Only very obliquely referred to in the Discworld religions. Such piecemeal references as have been discovered suggest that there are eight 'entities' that oversee the universe, although 'oversee' is far too strong a word. There is no single word that really does explain their role, which seems to be to observe in a dynamic way, in order for the observed events to be able to happen. It might be simpler to say that the universe exists because they believe in it. They are not gods – from their point of view, gods are only a slightly more troublesome version of human beings. They are far above the AUDITORS OF REALITY, who are their executive arm. The names of seven of them, if they have names, have not been revealed. The eighth is AZRAEL.

Old Man Trouble. One of a large number of 'anthropomorphic personifications' brought into existence by the low reality quotient of the Discworld universe, which means in essence that anything believed in strongly enough will eventually come into existence.

Old Man Trouble wears a long mac and a large, raggedy, broad-brimmed hat. All that can be seen between the two are his dreadful glowing eyes. He is a personification variously of Murphy's Law, the general intractability of the universe, and the darkness in the cellar. He is easily summoned by failing to have 1) rhythm or 2) music or even 3) your girl. In which case, if you hear a soft knocking at your door – don't open it.

Olerve the Bastard. King of STO LAT and father of KELI. A tall, heavily built man with a golden beard and the kind of stolid, patient face you'd confidently buy a used horse from. No sense of humour, but kings don't need it, since people will laugh at their jokes anyway. [M]

Om. The Great God Om. When he is first encountered, he is a small tortoise with one beady eye and a badly chipped shell. When at full strength, he is an enormous, shimmering, golden figure (the appearance of a god when manifest is directly proportional to the amount of belief they command). Om is omnipotent, omnipresent, and many other omnis, but only within the boundaries of the Omnian church. Strangely enough, since the events of *Small Gods*, and his covenant with BRUTHA, Om worship has increased enormously, largely because *he doesn't do anything, but might.* Since the rest of the Discworld gods tend to thunder, rant and bicker in public, people find a quiet god curiously reassuring. [SG]

Om, Book of. Principal book of the Omnian religion. In its original Second Omnian IV text, it is known to contain, amongst other things, the following books:

> Testament of Mezerek
> Letter to the Omish, Brutha's First
> Letter to the Omish, Brutha's Second
> Letter to the Simonites, Brutha's
> Cena, Book of
> Riddles, II
> Gospel According to the Miscreants
> Prophecies of Tobrun

Omnia. A dry country on the Klatchian coast between the deserts of KLATCH and the plains and jungles of HOWONDALAND. There are two million people in the Omnian empire. Its principal city is Kom.

The Citadel in Kom extends for miles – temples, churches, schools, dormitories, gardens and towers. It also has a lot of under-ground cellars and sewers, forgotten rooms, dead ends, spaces behind walls and natural caves. There are very few steps in the Citadel – the progress of the many processions demands long, gentle slopes. What stairs there are are shallow enough to allow for the faltering steps of very old men.

One of the main thoroughfares leads to the Place of Lamentations – a square 200 yards across. On one side of the square is the Great Temple, its roof adorned with the golden horns of OM. The doors in the central temple are 100 feet tall, weigh 40 tons each and are said to be made of bronze, reinforced with Klatchian steel. They open only outwards. On them, in letters of gold set in lead, are the Commandments (512 of them by the time the doors were melted, during the events of *Small Gods*).

Until those events, Omnia and the Church of Om were more or less synonymous; there was no civil authority. The entire country was ruled by the priesthood. Since the Reformation, however (which happened more or less instantaneously), there is a government that perforce is made up of laymen, since the priests are now too busy arguing amongst themselves.

Since the accession of the prophet BRUTHA, whose genius lay in taking one of the most objectionable and blood-thirsty religions in the world and turning it into a huge debating shop, Omnia has become internationally known for its output of door-to-door evangelists and religious tracts. These are annoying, but so much better than the merciless armies they have replaced. You couldn't put *them* off by shouting 'Not interested!' through the letterbox. (*See* QUISITION.) [SG]

Omnius, Lady. A noblewoman of Ankh. [MAA]

One Big River. Guard in the Forbidden City, who failed the intelligence test to be a tsimo wrestler, because he'd eaten the table. He's called One Big River because he's the same size and moves at the same speed as the River Hung. [IT]

One Favourite Pearl. Young member of the Agatean Red Army, Hung-Hung cadre. Very small – she looks about seven and carries a toy rabbit. [IT]

One-Man-Bucket. Spirit guide of Mrs CAKE. A member (once) of a HOWONDALAND tribe who was killed when he was run over by a cart in Treacle Street, Ankh-Morpork, while drunk. He is a ghost, with a reedy and petulant voice. Called One-Man-Bucket because of his tribe's tradition of naming a child after the first thing its mother saw after giving birth. The first thing his mother saw was a man pouring a bucket of water over two dogs causing a, um, a disturbance outside the tent. One-Man-Bucket's marginally older brother, who slid into the world a few seconds earlier, was not so fortunate in his name. [RM]

One Sun Mirror. A past emperor of the AGATEAN EMPIRE. He has two claims to fame: 1) he had the stone garden of Universal Peace and Simplicity laid out, and 2) his habit of cutting off his enemies' lips and legs and then promising them their freedom if they could run through the city playing a trumpet.

He also led the terracotta army to unite Agatea and become its first emperor. That might make it 'three claims to fame'. [M]

Opera House, Ankh-Morpork. This is located in Pseudopolis Yard, one of the city's largest open spaces. The Opera is almost as big as the Patrician's Palace, but is far more, well, palatial, and covers three acres. It is basically a cube, covered in a riot of friezes, pillars, corybants and curly bits glued on the architecture afterwards. Gargoyles have colonized the higher reaches. The effect, seen from the front, was of a huge wall of tortured stone. Round the back, of course, the usual drab mess of windows, pipes and damp stone walls, and the roof is a forest of skylights and airshafts. Public entry to the Opera is via the Big Foyer, with its marble-banistered grand staircase.

The building includes stabling for twenty horses and two elephants in the cellar. Rooms behind the stage are so large that entire sets are stored there. The building is almost a town in its own right, and includes a whole ballet school with a mirrored practice room, canteens for the staff and artistes, and a warren of little rooms for the chorus, approached by multiple flights of back stairs. Young female members are encouraged to reside in the Opera House, to avoid the dangers inherent in returning to possibly distant lodgings late at night, although this does make them easy prey for any crazed masked musical geniuses with good tenor voices that happen to be lurking around. Ahahahah!!!!! Ahem...

The auditorium is huge and cherub-infested – an explosion of plush velvet and rococo carving. Within all this the stage itself is comparatively small – almost an afterthought. [MA]

Operas. The Discworld has an excellent history of the arts and this history features opera quite prominently. Better-known works include:
> *Barber of Pseudopolis, The*
> *Bloodaxe and Ironhammer* (a dwarf opera)
> *Cosi Fan Hita*
> *Enchanted Piccolo, The*
> *Flederleiv, Die*
> *Lohenschaak*
> *Meistersinger von Scrote, Die*
> *Ring of the Nibelungingung, The*
> *Triviata, La*
> *Truccatore, Il*

There has also been a trend towards new, profit-making operas, including:
> *Guys and Trolls*
> *Hubwards Side Story*
> *Miserable Les*
> *Seven Dwarfs for Seven Other Dwarfs* [MA]
> *Student Horse, The* [CJ]

Orang-Utan/Human Dictionary, The. A major project being undertaken by the LIBRARIAN of Unseen University, who is himself of the orang persuasion. Since he was also, once, a human being, he feels himself in a position to advance the understanding between the two species. This may be a problem since one of the species consists of mankind, but he is persevering.

A flavour of the work, which already runs

to more than 500 closely written pages, may further illustrate the difficulties:

Ook: Oh, I do beg your pardon, I didn't realize there was a dominant male in this group.

Ook: I'll just go and sit over here very quietly, shall I?

Ook: You're out of your tree. This is *my* tree.

Ook: Yes.

Ook: No.

Ook: Banana.

Ook: It may be vital oxygenating biomass to you, but it's home to me.

Ook: Did you see a rainforest around here a moment ago?

Orcs. According to '*Bows & Ammo*' magazine, orcs were big, horrible monsters that wouldn't stop fighting and were quite happy to tear off their own arms to use them as weapons. They were last recorded as having been deployed in conflict at the battle of Orc Deep. Fighters you cannot stop. There *are* ways to kill an orc, but there are not many of them, and anyone trying them out on a living orc is not going to have very much time to get it right.

Surprisingly for readers of that journal, Mr Nutt has said that, in fact, tactical thinking and combat analysis is part of the orc make-up. He is an orc who knows how to put his hands down a man's throat and pull his stomach out. But he is also an orc who knows how not to. A new future for orcdom beckons. [UA]

Orinjcrates. Ephebian philosopher and author of '*On the Nature of Plants*'. [SG]

Orohai Peninsula. (On the Rim coast of KLATCH.) Home to the sponge-eating pygmies, who live in little coral houses. For further information, see General Sir Roderick Purdeigh's book '*My Life Among the Sponge-Eating Coral-House-Dwelling Pygmies*', in which he discusses at length the twin problems of daily indigestion and concussion. [COM]

Osric. Victor Tugelbend's uncle. Victor thought that the Holy Wood statue of a golden knight resembled him. [MP]

Ossory. One of the Great Prophets of the Omnian church. The 193-chapter '*Book of Ossory*' was dictated to him by the Great God OM, it is said. It was certainly said by Ossory, and no one was going to argue with anyone who came out of the desert just after the mushroom season with his eyeballs spinning in different directions.

The Book contains the Directions, the Gateways, the Abjurations and the Precepts. Ossory's staff is a religious artefact. [SG]

Oswald. An ondergeist who lives with Miss Level. He is a sort of anti-poltergeist, and he is obsessive about tidiness and keeps putting things away. He is shy and usually hides if anyone new comes to the cottage. [HFOS]

Ottomy, Frankly, Mr. A BLEDLOW (sort of policeman) at Unseen University. Ottomy has a red Adam's apple and is a hefty man, seemingly carved out of bacon. He is good at shouting in public but, strangely, less happy at public speaking. It is in the way of Ottomies all around the worlds to look as if they have been built out of the worst parts of two men and to be annoyingly hushen footed on thick red rubber soles, all the better to peep and pry. And they always assume that a free cup of tea is theirs by right. [UA]

If the specific criminal should be involved in the punishment process then this was a happy accident, but if not then any criminal would do, and since everyone was undoubtedly guilty of something, the net result was that, in general terms, justice was done.

– Men at Arms

Pablo the Thieving Monkey. An accomplice, or possibly member, of the THIEVES' GUILD. [TGD]

Palm, Rosemary. 'Rosie', although not to her face these days. Mrs Palm is a stout and refined lady with a no-nonsense chin, who lives with a lot of younger ladies in a house in the SHADES, and whose occupation is broadly understood. It has been said that she keeps a house of ill-repute but, on the contrary, a lot of people have spoken very highly of it.

A lonely man may while away many an hour playing dominoes and Chase My Neighbour Up the Passage with Mrs Palm and her girls with no fear that he will end up naked in an alley with all his money gone (unless of course his tastes run that way).

Mrs Palm is president of the SEAM-STRESSES' GUILD. [ER]

Panter, Lemuel. A wizard, one of RINCE-WIND's old tutors and a Member of the Order of Midnight. [LF]

Pantries. One universal manifestation of raw, natural magic throughout the universe is this: that any domestic food store, raided furtively in the middle of the night, always contains, no matter what its daytime inventory, half a jar of elderly mayonnaise, a piece of very old cheese, and a tomato with white mould growing on it. [M]

Pantweed. Manufacturer of the slim panatellas smoked by VIMES. [FOC]

Paps of Scilla. An eight-peaked mountain range, visible on the route from ZEMPHIS to Ankh-Morpork. Many have speculated about the lady concerned. [ER]

Pardessus Chatain Pursuivant. An official at the College of Arms, Ankh-Morpork. A very short man, with a wooden leg, who paints coats of arms – from life. [FOC]

Parker, Robert, Mr. Chairman of the Merchants' Guild. As (also) a member of the Ancient and Venerable Order of Greengrocers', Mr Parker is honour bound never to put his punctuation in the right place. Example: 'As chairman of the, Merchant's' Guild gentlemen may, I point out that these thing's represent a valuable labour force in this city–' [MM]

Parrot. Eric THURSLEY's pet. It spoke, but utilized a somewhat limited vocabulary based around one metasyntactic variable. It had one evil but intelligent red eye; most of the rest of it was pink and purple skin, studded with fag-ends of feathers, so that the net effect was of an oven-ready hairbrush. It was given to PONCE DA QUIRM. [E]

Parsley, John. Hereditary landlord and bartender at the Baron's Arms in Tiffany ACHING's village. He runs a relaxed house, where he's happy for the locals to mind the pumps when there's a rush, or if he has to answer a call of nature. Smoking is allowed in the pub, but spitting is most definitely not. The only woman seen in the Baron's Arms is Mrs Parsley. Darts and shove ha'penny were commonly played, though the former is now banned, after Shake Gently almost lost an eye. [TSC]

Pasha of Re'Durat. A past owner of the magical sword Kring. Re'Durat has never been identified, but is presumed to be in Hersheba. [COM]

Patrician, Office of. The Patrician is the ruler of Ankh-Morpork. There have been no monarchs in Ankh-Morpork for 300 years, since the death of the last and possibly nastiest (*see* LORENZO THE KIND). The only real qualification to rule Ankh-Morpork is the ability to stay alive for more than five minutes, because the great merchant families of Ankh have been ruling the city as kings or Patricians for the past twenty centuries and are as about to relinquish power as the average limpet is to let go of its rock. Past Patricians have included:

Hargarth, Frenzied Earl [GG]
Harmoni, Deranged Lord [MAA]
Nersch the Lunatic [GG]
Olaf QUIMBY II
Scapula, Laughing Lord
Smince, Lord [GG]
SNAPCASE, Mad/Psychoneurotic Lord [GG]
WINDER, Homicidal Lord

The holder of the office throughout the Discworld chronicles (apart from some of the events in *Night Watch*) is Lord Havelock VETINARI. (*See also* MONARCHY.)

Patrician, the. *See* VETINARI, Lord Havelock.

Patrician's Palace. The old Royal Winter Palace of the Kings of Ankh. The most famous room in the Palace is the Oblong Office, which is the personal sanctum of the current PATRICIAN. Although much of the Palace is given over to the Patrician's clerks, collating and updating the information gathered by his exquisitely organized spy system, it still contains the public rooms left over from the city's royal heritage – in particular the Throne Room, which houses the magnificent Golden Throne of the Kings of Ankh. This throne is not used by the current Patrician; he prefers to sit on a plain wooden chair at the foot of the steps leading to the throne. Also of note are the Palace dungeons, which include all the usual equipment, together with the scorpion pit.

It is, however, the Palace Grounds that are the crowning glory. These include a bird garden, a little zoo, a racehorse stable – and gardens laid out by Bergholt Stuttley (Bloody Stupid) JOHNSON. Of particular note are the ornamental trout lake, the fountain, lawn, maze, ornamental chiming sundial and the hoho. (A haha is a cunningly concealed dip in the land enabling one to enjoy the view without being nibbled by inconvenient cows – it is, in fact, a sort of negative fence. A hoho is merely a much deeper version.)

The trout lake has room for one long, thin trout, the fountain only operated once, when it blew a small stone cherub right outside the city, and the maze, far from being big enough to get lost in, is so small that people get lost looking for it. All in all, the gardens represent Bloody Stupid's erratic genius in full flower.

Patricio. Twenty-three-stone Despot of Quirm. He was the largest victim/client of the Assassins' Guild; they had to break for lunch. [P]

Peaches. A sleek, female rat in the Clan, and the devoted scribe and personal assistant of the philosopher DANGEROUS BEANS. She has a small, squeaky but clear voice and she tends to clear her throat before speaking. In the rat troop she is also the official carrier of the copy of their holy book, 'Mr Bunnsy Has an Adventure'. [TAMAHER]

Peaseblossom. An elf lord with an unfortunately unimpressive name (goblins refer to him as Mr Pee-pee Flower). He argued with the Queen of the ELVES, because he wanted a showdown with the world of humans, dwarfs and goblins, and all the other peoples. He wanted elves to run free and fierce through the world again. [TSC]

Peason, Mother. A resident of LANCRE who keeps bees. [LL]

Peavie. Treasurer of the ALCHEMISTS' GUILD. A nervous man whose contribution to the development of moving pictures was the invention of banged grains. This may have done nothing for his nerves. [MP]

Pediment. A gargoyle and constable in the Watch. [J]

Peedbury, Iago. A farmer, neighbour of Miss Flitworth. The first man to use a Combination Harvester. [RM]

Pelc, Ladislav. D.M.Phil. Prehumous Professor of Morbid Bibliomancy at Unseen University. Professor Pelc works in a room full of books, and made of books – even his desk and chairs are shaped out of books. He keeps his beard on a hook on his door. When in use, that beard slots nicely over his very large ears. He works with Professor Goitre, who is the *Post*humous Professor of Morbid Bibiomancy (he took early death as a part of a very good package, but he can come back at a week's notice). [GP]

Pencillium, Osric. Discoverer of the pencil bush in the graphite-rich sands of Sumtri. So it is widely believed, in any case; and as so often happens, what everyone 'knows' is wrong. The idea is ridiculous. What he discovered was probably the bush *Plumbago sribens officianalis*, which has a very thick lead and a mere veneer of wood-like casing and was used by the Sumtrians only for crude sketching purposes. It wasn't until ten years of careful cross-breeding that Osric produced the reliable HB varieties found today. [H]

Pepe. He is, in his own estimation, a fashionista, working with Madame SHARM. Pepe is a dwarf, but he is a willowy dwarf – willowy like someone made from sinews. He was originally from Lobbin Clout in Ankh-Morpork (Old Cheese Alley) but he now moves in more stylish circles. He is not just someone who makes clothes – he creates gorgeous works of art that just happen to require a body to show them off. Keen on the occasional glass of strong liquor. [UA]

Perdita. The witching name of old Threepenny's little, fat daughter. She was seventeen at the time of the 'dancing' at the DANCERS in *Lords and Ladies*. [LL]

Perdore, Brother. A member of the Nine Day Wonderers, a religious order in the RAMTOPS. He is an amiable old man, which is just as well given that his flexible parish contains so many witches. [LL]

Peripatetic Teachers Self-employed teachers who, usually in ragged bands, travel from village to village in remote districts offering small amounts of education in exchange for food, a night's shelter or clean used clothing. A child might be excused from general homestead chores and given some spare vegetables and maybe an egg or two to 'get some learning'. Teachers are encouraged to move on before nightfall lest they steal chickens. Don't buy clothes pegs from them.

Perks, Polly. 'Ozzer'. A volunteer to the Borogravian Army. She used to have long hair, long golden curls, worn in a net when she was working in her father's inn. Now that her mother's dead, she runs the inn, in fact. The inn has a picture of the Duchess ANNAGOVIA as its sign. Polly is not conventionally beautiful, and that, plus her small bosom, is useful when she decides to enlist in the army as Oliver Perks. She performs well, becoming batman to Lieutenant BLOUSE at one stage, and gains promotion by the end of her adventures, to sergeant. [MR]

Persifleur, Mrs. Runs a lodging house on the main square in LANCRE. [LL]

Pessimal, A.E., Mr. A government inspector. Mr Pessimal is neat. Beyond neat. He is a folding person His suit is cheap but very clean, his little boots sparkle. His hair gleams, too, even more than the boots. It has a centre parting and has been plastered down so severely that it looks as though it's been painted on his head. He twinkles as he walks – every move is neat. He's the sort of person you'd bet would have a shovel purse and spectacles on a ribbon. He joins the City Watch as an acting constable. Later he become Vimes' adjutant and achieves the rank of lance-constable. He was also later appointed by Lord Vetinari to the post of Inspector of Universities. [T!]

Pestilence. Anthropomorphic personification. A member of the Four Horsemen of the APOCRALYPSE. He has a breathy, wet voice, which is practically contagious in itself. He likes hospitals because there is always something for him to do there. Humans created Pestilence, just as they created FAMINE. They have a genius for crowding together, for poking around in jungles, and for siting the midden so handily next to the well. [LF]

Petty, Amber. Daughter of Seth Petty, who did not treat her kindly, and suffered for it. Amber was helped by Tiffany and, more importantly, by the Nac Mac Feegles. She now has a young man, William, who is a very skilled tailor. [ISWM]

Petunia, The Desert Princess. A purple cart, decorated with huge swathes of pink and lavender, and what look like roses made out of paper. Boxes, also covered in cloth, have been set up in the centre to give a sort of raised dais. On this wonderful conveyance travel a group of XXXX-ian entertainers – all gayly clad in sequinned evening gowns, long gloves and high heels. They comprise Letitia, a … lady with large hands who is adept at changing cart wheels; Darleen, with sparkly hair, robust language and a fist that can floor a man; and Neilette, whose hair seems slightly drab, when compared with that of her colleagues. She doesn't wear as much make-up. She seems, in short, slightly out of place. She joined the group when her brother, Noelene, had to drop out. Luckily, they were around the same height, though Neilette's hands were much smaller... [TLC]

Philo. An Ephebian philosopher and author of 'Bestiary'. [SG]

Philosophy. EPHEBE is the home of philosophy, but other lands have also produced famous philosophers, most notably, of course, LY TIN WHEEDLE. There are almost as many systems of philosophy as there are philosophers. They include: Sumtin, Zen, Stoicism, Cynicism, Epicureanism, Stochaticism, Anamaxandritism, Epistemologism, Peripateticism, Synopticism and Ismism.

Astro-philosophers of KRULL once succeeded in proving conclusively that all places are one place and that the distance between them is an illusion. This news was an embarrassment to all thinking philosophers because it did not explain, among other things, signposts. After years of wrangling, the whole thing was then turned over to Ly Tin Wheedle who, after some thought, proclaimed that although it was indeed true that all places were one place, that place was very large.

Xenoists say that the world is basically complex and random. Ibidians say the world is basically simple and follows certain fundamental rules. DIDACTYLOS says basically it's a funny old world – and it doesn't contain enough to drink.

Phoenix. Also called the firebird. This bird *nearly* always hatches in the burning deserts of Klatch. It has found a way of making incubation work very, very fast: it lays a silvery grey egg with a very light shell and then burns itself up to hatch the new bird. In theory, you only ever get one phoenix at a time. Its cry is described as 'like unto the cry of a buzzard yet of lower pitch'. The phoenix is able, more or less, to disguise itself as other birds. Phoenixes share their minds and their memories. They don't tolerate evil and it is said that firebird feathers burn in the presence of evil. [CJ]

Pigeon, Sid. Younger of the two Pigeon brothers. He was a small boy, but he has now acquired a peaked cap, a whistle and a job on the railway, where he earns good money. [TSC]

Pilgarlic. Thief who encounters MORT in the SHADES. [M]

Pills, Dried Frog. The wizards of Unseen University are right at the forefront of modern medical thinking when it comes to the therapeutic use of frog products, and make up these pills for the current Bursar, who is mentally as stable as a tapdancer in a ballbearing factory.

Pilotus and Langas. *See* LANGAS.

Piloxi. An Ephebian farmer. [SG]

Pin, Mr. Also known, for a very short while, as Brother Upon-Which-The-Angels-Dance Pin. He, with Mr TULIP, comprised the New Firm, which arrived in Ankh-Morpork ready to make the town their own.

They didn't see themselves as thugs. Nor were they thieves… at least, they never thought of themselves as thieves. They didn't think of themselves as assassins (assassins are posh and have rules). They thought of themselves as *facilitators.* Men who made things happen; men who were going places. He and Mr Tulip were the sort of people who would call you 'friend'. People like that aren't friendly.

Mr Pin was the brains of the outfit only in comparison to Mr Tulip. His one vice was smoking (at least, it was the one vice that he thought of as a vice). He was small, slim and, like his namesake, slightly larger in the head than ought to be the case. He drank little, watched what he ate and considered his body, malformed as it was, as a temple, albeit one of those strange ones without windows. He carried a wallet with a legend burned on it in pokerwork: 'Not A Very Nice Person At All'. He wasn't so much killed as spiked. [TT]

Pine Dressers. A village high in the RAMTOPS and 500 miles from the sea, which nevertheless has managed to develop a thriving fish-gutting, smoking and canning industry, based on the very frequent rains of fish that occur in the area.

The townsfolk see no reason to object to strange phenomena if they can make a decent kipper out of them.

Pin Exchange, the. The 'Home of Acuphilia!' in Dolly Sisters, in an alley between a house of negotiable affection and a massage parlour. It is run by Big Dave – a huge, bearded man with dreadlocks, a pin through his nose, a beer belly belonging to three other people and the words 'Death or Pins' tattooed on a bicep. [GP]

Pippina. The Lady with the Apple of Discord. She is the deity who knows that the universe, whilst it requires rules and stability, also needs just a tincture of chaos, the unexpected and the surprising. [RS]

Pivey, Mrs. Neighbour of Count and Countess NOTFAROUTOE. Known to be unsympathetic to things like moats and crypts in a next-door context. [RM]

Pizza. The first pizza was created on the Disc by the Klatchian mystic Ronron 'Revelation Joe' SHUWADHI, who claimed to have been given the recipe in a dream by the CREATOR of the Discworld Himself, who had apparently added that it was what He had intended, all along. Those desert travellers who have seen the original, which is reputedly miraculously preserved in the Forbidden City of EE, say that what the Creator had in mind then was a fairly small cheese and pepperoni affair with a few black olives, and things like mountains and seas got added out of last-minute enthusiasm, as so often happens.

After the Schism of the Turnwise Ones and the deaths of some 25,000 people in the ensuing jihad, the faithful were allowed to add one small bayleaf to the recipe.

Pizzas are highly adaptable to the multi-species community in Ankh-Morpork, as attested by the Quatra-rodenti (for dwarfs) and Four Strata (for trolls).

Planter, Bezam. The owner of the ODIUM, a moving-picture pit in ANKH-MORPORK. His daughter, Calliope, plays the organ there. [MP]

Plasterer, Brother. A member of the ELUCIDATED BRETHREN OF THE EBON NIGHT. [GG]

Plays, etc.

> *Bloodaxe and Ironhammer* (dwarf opera) [TFE]
> *Blood-Soaked Tragedy of the Mad Monk of Quirm, The* [LL]
> *Chicken Lake* (a ballet) [TFE]
> *Comedy of Cuckolds, A* [MR]
> *Dragon of the Plains, The* [WS]
> *Gretalina and Mellias* [WS]
> *King of Ankh, The* [WS]
> *King Under the Mountain* [WS]
> *King's Brides, The* [WS]
> *Mage Wars, The* [WS]
> *Mallo, the Tyrant of Klatch* [WS]
> *Much Ado About Everybody* (by Stackpole) [TSC]
> *Night of Kings, A* (also called *The Lancre Play*) [WS]
> *Starcrossed* (by Hwel) [UA]
> *Swan on a Hot Tin Lake* (a ballet) [ISWM]
> *Taming of the Vole, The* [LL]
> *'Tis Pity She's a Tree* [MR]
> *'Tis Pity She's an Instructor in Unarmed Combat* [MM]
> *Troll's Tale, The* [WS]
> *Tyrant, The* [WS]
> *Wizard of Ankh, A* [WS]
> *Wizard of Sorts, A,* or *Please Yourself* [WS]

Many of these appear to have flowed from the quill of HWEL, the dwarf playwright attached to VITOLLER's men.

Pleasant, Mrs. A fat, naturally jolly, black lady who is a cook at the palace in GENUA (and this is just as well, in a period when failing to be fat and jolly while being a cook was punishable by death). A very superior cook, with the Genuan talent for making a gourmet meal out of things found under a damp rock. She is a close personal friend of Mrs GOGOL. [WA]

Plinge, Mrs. Works at the Ankh-Morpork

Opera House; amongst other things, she serves interval drinks to the boxes. She is an old woman with arthritic knees and thin, red hands, who worked very long hours for very little money. Lived in the Shades. Mother to Walter Plinge. [MA]

Plinge, Walter. Originally, and possibly still, the odd-job man at the Ankh-Morpork OPERA HOUSE. A scarecrow with spiky, black, greasy hair, clammy hands and pale, rubbery features. What most people noticed first of all, though, was his unique walk, which looked as though his body was being dragged forward and his legs were being left to flail around underneath it, landing wherever they could find room. Not so much a walk, in fact, as a collapse, infinitely postponed. Walter, the aforesaid most people considered, was clearly several ariettas short of a full opera. But others might speculate that, as in opera, what the scenery shows is not always what is actually there. [MA]

Plugger. A shoemaker with premises in New Cobblers, Ankh-Morpork. The first to take advertising space on C.M.O.T. DIBBLER's invention, the short-sleeved-singlet-made-of-cheap-cotton. [SM]

Plumbers' Guild. (Guild of Plumbers and Dunnikin divers). Motto: NON ANTE SEPTEM DIES PROXIMA, SQVIRI. Coat of arms: a shield, per pairle reversed. Top right, appaum e, argent on a field, gules. Top left, a bezant on a field, vert. Below them a coq, gules on a field, bouse.

The Guild House is in Pleaders Row, Ankh-Morpork.

Ankh-Morpork does not, currently, have a functioning sewerage system, and fresh water, once brought from distant hills by aqueduct, is now generally pumped from shallow wells. No one knows why this has not resulted in the city being a soup of diseases; it has been suggested that the centuries have bred a very high resistance among the population, and also that germs don't attack Ankh-Morpork citizens out of fellow feeling.

The Guild digs wells, plumbs houses and empties cesspits (the dunnykin, or dunnikin, divers – a small, select but lonely group of men who are always incredibly well-scrubbed and neatly dressed when off duty but never seem to attract many friends).

It is believed that the plumbers possess a specialized form of time travel which means they have no grasp of the concept of 'today', since 'immediately' to a plumber is identical with 'next week, maybe the week after'.

The president of the Guild is Sir Charles LAVATORY, of Mollymog Street. He, in fact, invented the device which bears his name (and is fast replacing the somewhat primitive invention of William de Privy). This marvellous device cleans and flushes beautifully, but not to anywhere in particular. The people of Ankh-Morpork have a cat-like approach to sanitation and waste disposal: if you can't see it, it isn't there, and if it's next door then it's their problem.

The Guild has no training school as such, being a prime exponent of the apprentice system. Boys are taught to carry bags, tell a three/eights Gripley from a 0.3 Cosworth, and never, ever, to do today what you could do next week, maybe the week after.

Pointer & Pickles. Co-owners of a rock emporium on 10th Egg Street. Two people with one body – one young, one old. Apparently, it's a sort of illness.[T!]

Poldy, Champett. A sentry at LANCRE castle, lightly terrorized by Granny WEATHERWAX. [WS]

Pole, Druto. A florist. Sells flowers one assumes. [RM]

Polly. A kitchen girl at UNSEEN UNIVERSITY. Edited from earlier *Companions*, but she's made it back for this one. [SM]

Ponce da Quirm. A Discworld explorer from the famous da Quirm family. He sought the Fountain of Youth for most of his life and in fact found it, dying shortly afterwards, having failed to remember to boil the water before drinking it. [E]

Pony, George, Mr. The fifty-eight-year-old Chief Engineer of the Grand Trunk Company. Mr Pony is a methodical craftsman, with a sick wife at home, twinges in his knuckles and a bad back. He is a member of the Artificers' Guild. [GP]

Poons, Windle. Deaf, toothless, 130-year-old wizard.

In the closing years of his life Windle moved, and was moved, around in an iron-wheeled wheelchair; a wide and long construction, steered by means of a little front wheel and a long, cast-iron handle. Bits of baroque iron-work adorned its frame; there were various dread levers of mysterious function and a huge oilskin hood. The front lever of this very heavy machine was adorned with a selection of trumpets, hooters and whistles.

At the time of his death, Windle was the oldest wizard in the world – born in the year of the Significant Triangle in the Century of the Three Lice, he died in the year of the Notional Serpent in the Century of the Fruitbat. He was an expert on ancient magical writings, although his expertise was somewhat suspect in his later years.

Windle was the first person to reach the end of his life after DEATH was (briefly) pensioned off, and he spent a short, but on the whole enjoyable, time as a zombie, which he seemed to feel made up for the numbing boredom of the previous century or so. [MP]

Poorchick. A resident of LANCRE who keeps a cow. [LL]

Poppley. He and his wife run a grocery business in ANKH-MORPORK. [MAA]

Pork Futures. Probably no other world in the multiverse has warehouses for things which only exist *in potentia*, but the pork futures warehouse in Ankh-Morpork is a product of the Olaf QUIMBY II rules about baseless metaphors (thoroughly enforced by the current PATRICIAN), the literal-mindedness of citizens who assume that everything must exist somewhere, and the general thinness of the fabric of reality around Ankh. The net result is that trading in pork futures – in pork that doesn't exist yet – led to the building of the warehouse to store it until it does. The extremely low temperatures are caused by the imbalance in the temporal energy flow. [MAA]

Postalute, Granny. A witch who went out borrowing one day and never came back. Nanny Ogg thinks she lived out the rest of her life as a bluetit. [LL]

Post-Mortem Communications, Department of. Minor department of Unseen University. The current Head is Professor HICKS. Well, I say Head, but that is the trouble with working in the DPMC, you can never exactly be the boss. In an ordinary job people retire, wander back to the ol' workplace a few times while there are people who remember them, and then fade in to the ever-swelling past. But the former staff here never seem to go... There is a saying: 'Old Necromancers never die'. When people then ask '...and?' department members just reply, 'That's all of it, I'm afraid. Just "Old Necromancers never die".'

POST OFFICE, ANKH-MORPORK

Post Office, Ankh-Morpork. The Ankh-Morpork Central Post Office has a gaunt frontage. It is a building designed for a purpose. It is, therefore, more or less, a big box to employ people in, with two wings at the rear which enclose the big stable yard. Some cheap pillars had been sliced in half and stuck on the outside, some niches had been carved for some miscellaneous stone nymphs, some stone urns had been ranged along the parapet and thus Architecture had been created.

In appreciation of the thought that had gone into this, the good citizens, or more probably their kids, had covered the walls to a height of six feet with graffiti in many exciting colours.

In a band all along the top of the frontage, staining the stone in greens and browns, some words had been set in letters of bronze, which, for many years, read:

NEITHER RAIN NOR SNOW NOR GLO M OF NI T CAN STAY THESE MES ENGERS ABO T THEIR DUTY

The missing letters have now been recovered and replaced by Moist von Lipwig.

On a board much further down the building, in peeling paint, were the less heroic words:

DONT ARSK US ABOUT:
rocks troll's with sticks All sorts of dragons Mrs Cake Huje green things with teeth Any kinds of black dogs with orange eyebrows Rains of spaniel's. fog. Mrs Cake

THE HISTORY OF THE POST OFFICE

In days of yore (about 100 years before olden days, but about 50 years later than ancient times), the kings of Ankh used messengers to take orders and other messages to all parts of the Sto Plains and beyond.

The fastest messengers could achieve 200 miles in one day with frequent changes of horse at commercial staging, or relay, posts along the route. These relay points were known as Royal Messenger Posts and this soon gave its name to the service itself.

Only the king and certain approved officials and royal relatives were permitted to send letters via the Royal Messenger Service. Unauthorized mail could lead to the sender being nailed to one of the Royal Posts as a gentle reminder to other potential unofficial users of the service.

In those days, the ordinary people of Ankh-Morpork had to rely on the good offices of traders and merchants to carry their mail for them as they journeyed around the Disc. This service was fairly reliable but letters could take months to arrive, depending on the merchant's trade route.

The Next 'Stage'

Unseen University and the Guilds soon set up their own postal services to handle their own mail within the city and beyond. Initially, though, these services were restricted either to faculty members of UU, or to students and officers of the Guilds.

In AM1530, King Cirone II established a formal network of messengers and horses along important routes and he appointed the first 'Master of the Posts' to administer the system and to ensure that it worked to maximum efficiency. The first Master of the Posts was Sir Rolande de Colline, who had been a warrior knight alongside the ASSASSINS' GUILD founder, Sir Gyles de Murforte. This high-profile link helped to ensure that the Royal Mail Posts were not subject to attacks from licensed thieves.

By AM1635, King Lorenzo I (father of Lorenzo the Kind) had decided that the general public could also use the King's Letter Office of Ankh-Morpork and the Sto Plains. This building, sited as it still is on Broad Way, was already commonly known as the Post Office and its chief administrator was now called the 'Post Master'. King Lorenzo dictated at the same time that all houses and properties in Ankh-Morpork should display a number, to facilitate the delivery of the post. There was some initial confusion when people thought they could choose their own number, and it transpired that – after an evening's drinking in a local ale house – every house in Brewer Street was wittily numbered 346. This was soon sorted out after the king helpfully arranged for the owner of every second house in that street to be placed in the stocks in Hide Park, under a sign reading 'DON'T MESS WITH THE POST OFFICE'.

As the system established itself, all mail on the Sto Plains, using the Royal Mail, had to travel via Ankh-Morpork. This meant that, say, a letter going from Sto Helit to Sto Lat (a distance of only about five miles) would have to journey twenty miles into Ankh-Morpork, and a similar distance back again to Sto Lat. The Post Master at the time, Mr Jedediah Palmer, set up a system of new postal routes – called Cross Posts – which meant mail did not have to travel via Ankh-Morpork. He also introduced the first mail coach service.

Mail Coaches

Highway robbery was (and still is) a major problem on the Sto Plains and the old system of Post Boys left the mail, and its carriers, very vulnerable to attack. The passenger stage coaches fared little better and travellers rarely arrived at their destinations with all their possessions, or even their clothes. So Palmer set up a system of mail coaches, with a driver and an armed guard on each coach. In the first week of operation, four highwaymen were shot on sight by guards on the mail coaches. After that, the mail was left alone and, as a result, the mail coaches became much more popular with passengers, too.

Post Marks

It was during the reign of Lorenzo the Kind that the Postmaster General, Sir Henri d'Évêque, came up with the postmark to enable him to time the progress of the mail through the city and beyond – he could then detect inefficient postal stages and slow-moving postal carriers. Lorenzo the Kind embraced this management tool and, during the following ten months, the service improved tremendously, although some fifty-eight Post Boys and seventeen Sub Post Masters were hung, drawn and quartered for the amusement of citizens and, as Sir Henri said, 'Pour encourager les autres'. Word of mouth had transformed this to 'pour encourager les autruches' (ostriches) by the time it had reached Quirm, where the local postal staff immediately started to train these flightless birds to deliver the post in that city. This worked surprisingly well, although the new Post Birds did have a tendency to swallow any amusingly-shaped packages. The Quirm Sub Post Master met with resistance when he tried to encourage his fellow Sub Post Masters to use exotic birds as delivery tools. He resented their reactionary attitude and accused them of burying their heads in the sand.

HOURS OF BUSINESS

Weekdays

Offices in Ankh-Morpork. At the larger post offices the hours of business are, as a rule, from 8.30 a.m. to 6 .p.m., or 6.30 p.m., except on public holidays. Exceptionally, some sub offices close earlier on Saturdays. All classes of postal and clacks business are transacted at the Broad Way headquarter building between the hours of 8 a.m. and 8 p.m.

Offices outside Ankh-Morpork. Larger post offices will be open from 9 a.m. until 6 p.m. Smaller local offices may operate shorter hours – 9 a.m. until 5.30 p.m.. All those excepting public holidays. Local small offices may also close early on one day of the week, generally on the local half-holiday.

Hogswatch, Patrician's Day and Other Public Holidays

Offices in Ankh-Morpork. The Broad Way office will be open from 9.30 a.m. until 12.30 p.m. for all normal services, except for the sales of stamps of a face value of 2 dollars or more and for the acceptance of mail addressed to the Shades, to Borogravia, to Tezuman or to 36 Chitterling Street.

On Hogswatch Day, there is one house-to-house delivery of letters and other postal packets within the city walls of Ankh-Morpork (excepting the Shades and 36 Chitterling Street).

Offices outside Ankh-Morpork. Local offices may open by local arrangement. There will be no deliveries on Hogswatch Day except in those areas where there is only usually one delivery per day.

EXCLUSIVE RIGHTS OF THE POST MASTER GENERAL

Subject to certain exceptions, the Post Master General has the exclusive privilege of carrying letters from place to place, and of performing all incidental services such as those of collecting and delivering letters. The principal exceptions are:

Letters sent by a private friend, on his journey, to be delivered to the person to whom they are directed;

Letters sent by the personal servant of the sender;

Letters concerning goods sent by a carrier, such letters being carried gratuitously and delivered with the goods to which they relate;

Packets containing news intelligence, that is, matter or pictures for publication in a newspaper.

Carriers are specifically prohibited from carrying letters.

LETTERS: WEIGHT AND SIZE

There is no limit of weight. The limits of size are:

Maximum: Two feet in length, 18 inches in width and 18 inches in depth; or if made up in a roll, 3 feet 3 inches for the length and twice the diameter combined, and 2 feet 6 inches for the greatest dimension.

Minimum: Envelopes less than four inches in length by two and three quarter inches in width must not be used.

INADMISSIBLE ARTICLES

Eggs, fish, poultry, game, rabbits, meat, fruit and vegetables are not transmissible by letter post and certain articles may be sent only if specially packed.

Coupons, forms, cards and so on, bearing written answers to acrostics and guessing competitions. Written communications indicating, whether by means of words, marks, letters or numbers, moves in a game of chess, are inadmissible.

Stationery, when sent not filled up to a person who is subsequently to use it, is inadmissible. However, not more than three blank forms of a kind, or three of each kind of dissimilar forms may be included in a packet with a covering document which is itself admissible.

Yearly diaries are admitted, but diaries for shorter periods are inadmissible.

Blotting paper and similar substances are not regarded as ordinarily used for writing or printing and are inadmissible, but a single unfolded flat sheet of blotting paper and not sent as a sample, or having affixed to it such an advertisement printed on ordinary paper or cardboard, is admitted in a suitable open cover.

PROHIBITED ARTICLES

Prohibited articles will be refused or detained. These may include:

  Certain Circulars
  Fortune-telling advertisements
  Lottery tickets
  Unsolicited circulars from money lenders

Dangerous Articles

Inflammable, noxious, corrosive, deleterious or otherwise harmful articles. Sharp instruments not properly packed. Matches of all kinds. Hogswatch crackers are, however, permitted.

Any packet which is likely to injure either other postal packets in the course of conveyance, or an officer of the Post Office, or any other person who may deal with that packet.

Embarrassing Packets

Packets embarrassing to the Post Office staff are also prohibited. Embarrassment may be caused by the method of addressing and the affixing of the stamp; the colour, type, shape and dimensions of the envelope. Examples would be:

Addresses. A packet having its address parallel to the breadth instead of to the length of the envelope.

Addresses mis-spelled so as to give rise to a humorous double entendre.

Stamps. A packet bearing on its address side an adhesive label or printed design resembling a postage stamp in shape or size.

Shape. Any packet wrapped in such a way as it resembles certain private portions of the male human anatomy.

CARRIAGE OF PRIVATE PARCELS BY OFFICERS OF THE POST OFFICE

With the following exceptions, no post man, post golem or other officer of the post office may act as a carrier of packages of any kind or weight which have not passed through the post, whether or not he receives payment for the carriage. However:

Contractors for the carriage of mails by passenger conveyance are not subject to any restrictions as to the parcels they convey;

Mail contract drivers and postmen in rural districts are allowed to carry light packets of medicine sent from a doctor or chemist to a patient.

PACKING REGULATIONS FOR CERTAIN ARTICLES

Any fragile article must be packed in a container of sufficient strength, and surrounded in that container with sufficient soft material or wadding, to protect the article from the effects of concussion, pressure and knocks to which postal packets are ordinarily exposed. The packet must bear the words 'Fragile With Care' written conspicuously on the face of the cover above the address, so that postal officers will know which packages will need to be tested to ensure that they can withstand dropping from great heights, stamping on, kicking, hitting with lump hammers and any other normal treatment that would be given to such a package.

Eggs

These are a challenge to the postal worker, and their safe transit cannot be guaranteed. If you want to risk it, you might try using a wooden box with suitable partitions and a well-fitting lid, wrapping each egg separately in newspaper or other soft material, placing the eggs on end, each in a separate partition, and filling up the vacant spaces in the box with newspaper or cotton waste. The parcel should be marked 'Eggs' so that we don't waste time trying to damage a parcel containing, say, rock samples.

Fish and other meat, including body parts travelling by mail between Igors

These should be sewn into rush baskets, straw matting, sacking, or similar material, with sufficient internal waterproof wrapping or absorbent packing to prevent the contents from damaging or tainting the outer covering and thus making the parcels objectionable to handle for human officers of the post office. The boxes must be marked clearly: 'Meat Products', or 'Igor2Igor – Pathological Specimen'.

Soil of the homeland being shipped to certain citizens of Überwald

To be accepted in the post, this must be enclosed in a secure wooden box, screwed down at no fewer than twelve inch intervals and transported in such a way as it will only be in transit during the normal hours of daylight. Under no circumstances will such crates be accepted for transit by ship. Such crates must be marked clearly: 'Not to be Handled in Hours of Darkness'.

ADDRESSES AND PETITIONS TO THE PATRICIAN

Addresses and petitions forwarded to Lord Vetinari as Patrician of Ankh-Morpork are exempt from postage. This exemption applies only to an original petition or address and not to any copy thereof.

POSTMASTERS

A Post Master shall reside within the delivery limits of his own post office. Post Masters at Main Post Offices shall be appointed by the Patrician; all other Post Masters shall be appointed by the Post Master General.

Commissions

A commission shall be issued to every person appointed Post Master upon the filing and acceptance of his bond and oath of office. The amount of the bond will be established by the Patrician of Ankh-Morpork on each occasion that a Post Master is appointed.

Oath of Office

'I (name of appointee), having been appointed (designate office of appointment), do solemnly swear that I will support and defend the Rules and Regulations of the Ankh-Morpork Post Office against all enemies, foreign and domestic; that I take this obligation freely, without any mental reservation or purpose or evasion; and that I will well and faithfully discharge the duties of this office on which I am about to enter.

I do solemnly swear that I will faithfully perform all the duties required of me and abstain from everything forbidden by the laws in relation to the establishment of post offices and post roads and that I will honestly and truly account for and pay over any money belonging to the city state of Ankh-Morpork as may come into my possession or control; and I also swear that I have not paid or offered or promised to pay any money or any other thing of value to any person, firm or corporation for the use of influence to procure my appointment. So help me (deity of choice).'

Duties

Post Masters are responsible for proper organization of their offices, for proper and efficient conduct of the employees and for courteous and efficient postal service to their patrons.

The attitude of Post Masters to the public should be helpful, and enquiries regarding postal matters should be given prompt attention.

Post Masters will be held personally responsible for unnecessary expenditures, whether they are for excess auxiliary staff or extravagance in the use of supplies or equipment.

Other Business of Post Masters

Post Masters should not engage in any business or activity which in any way interferes with the proper discharge of their duties, nor which involves canvassing, soliciting or threatening their patrons.

Sub Post Masters may conduct other, approved business in the same room in which the post office is located; but such business must be approved in advance and must be kept distinct and separate from that of the post office.

Absence from Office

In an emergency, a Post Master may absent himself for not longer than two days without first securing written authority. Such emergencies might include, for example, and not exclusively, death (of self, of an immediate blood relative or of a favourite dog. Deaths of cats do not count for this purpose.)

Death of Post Master

When a Post Master dies, a report thereof should be made by the Assistant Post Master or senior employee of that office to the Patrician, by clacks.

Acting and Assistant Post Masters

The Authorized Assistant Post Master shall in all cases manage the business of the post office in the absence of the Post Master.

When there is no Authorized Assistant Post Master then, upon the death , dismissal and/or resignation of the Post Master, and Acting Post Master will be designated.

CARE AND CONDUCT OF POST OFFICES

Post offices shall not be allowed to become resorts for loungers or disorderly persons, or the scene of disputes or controversies. If necessary, the Post Master should call upon the City Watch (or its equivalent if the post office is not in Ankh-Morpork) to preserve order and, if they refuse or are unable to do so, the office may be closed – even if it is proper opening hours.

Post offices shall at all times be kept in a clean and orderly condition. No post office shall be located in a room where intoxicating liquor is stored , sold or consumed.

Unauthorized persons shall not be allowed access to the workroom floor (the Sorting Room) of any post office. Employees of the post office, while off duty, are unauthorized persons within the meaning of this requirement and they shall not be allowed to loiter in post offices after their tour of duty has ended, or before the start of their tour of duty.

REPORT OF VIOLATION OF POSTAL LAWS

Post Masters and all others in the postal service shall report immediately to the proper inspector in charge any violation of the postal laws. If the Post Master has reason to believe that a postal law violator can be arrested by speedy action, he shall at once report all the facts and evidence to the City Watch (or other similar responsible local officer of the law). [POD]

Potent Voyager. Vessel constructed by DACTYLOS to take two chelonauts out over the Rim to determine the sex of the Great A'TUIN. A huge, bronze space ship, without any motive power other than the ability to drop. [COM]

Pounder, Mr. Ratcatcher at the OPERA HOUSE. An elderly man who'd worked with rats so long there was something rat-like about him. His face, for example, seemed merely a rearward extension of his nose. This, combined with his bristly moustache and prominent front teeth, made people find themselves looking for his tail.

His trademark was a battered top hat, the brim of which was thick with wax and old candle ends, which he used to light his way through the darker cellars of the Opera House. He was a Member of the Inner Circle of the Guild of Ratcatchers, having won the Golden Mallet for most rats caught five years in a row. 'Was' is the operative word. Presumably someone else has it now. [MA]

Prankster, Brother. Lecturer at the FOOLS' GUILD. [WS]

Pratchett, Professor Sir Terry. Kt, OBE. Yes, OK, he isn't strictly speaking a character in the books, but he was the true Creator, right?

Terry was intelligent, irascible, witty and loyal, wryly observing the world around him, taking inspiration from everyone and everything he encountered and pouring wit and imagination into every word he wrote. He had a driven sense of fairness and justice, and was a staunch supporter of the conservation of orang-utans, of research into Alzheimer's disease and of the right of people with a terminal illness to die with dignity.

He loved the natural world and fought to preserve the nation's wildlife. He and his wife Lyn owned (if that is the right word!) many cats. He was a keen amateur astronomer and built his own observatory in the garden of his home.

Terry was also an inveterate collector of unconsidered trifles. He adored the strange and quirky things that happen in 'real life', and was fascinated by just about everything. Terry was an entertaining companion, an avid player of computer games and, oh yes, he also wrote books...

His first story was published in 1963 when he was 15 – he used the proceeds to buy a sturdy typewriter – and the rest is history. More than 50 novels followed, selling over 85 million copies worldwide – in 37 languages.
[All the books]

Preptil, Brother. Master of the Music in the Citadel, KOM. [SG]

Preston. A guard at the Baron's Castle. He is an intelligent Lance-Private, who is also a skilled amateur veterinary surgeon. He becomes close to Tiffany ACHING. He now works at the Lady Sybil Free Hospital, where he has been training as a doctor. He was promoted to surgeon by Dr. LAWN. [ISWM]

Pretty Butterfly. A member of the Agatean Red Army, Hung-Hung cadre. A round-faced, snub-nosed young woman, who looks as fragile as a flower (whilst keeping a serviceable knife in her robe). She is a daughter of TWOFLOWER. [IT]

Prime. A modern, logical and efficient measure of magical strength propounded by the wizard Augustus Prime to replace the traditional Thaum. The Prime was to be based on a very careful observation of the amount of magic it took to move one pound of lead one foot, and it was to be broken down into milli-, nano- and micro-Primes.

The system never really caught on, however, with old wizards traditionally saying to a student using the 'Prime' system – 'But what's that in old money?'

The Prime/Thaum business is very similar to Centigrade/Fahrenheit.

Everyone knows that freezing at 0 degrees and boiling at 100 degrees is logical, but it doesn't stop them believing in their hearts that 70 degrees should be a nice comfortable temperature.

Printing. Until quite recently, movable type had not been utilized in Ankh-Morpork and, surprisingly enough, the printing industry was basic in the extreme. Books were either copied by hand in the numerous copying shops around Gleam Street or, increasingly, engraved and printed one whole page at a time by the engravers in the alleys around the Street of Cunning Artificers.

The reason for this was the tremendous power Unseen University wields over the whole business, as the biggest customer for copying services in the city. It was this demand for cheap copies which led the wizards to change their views on movable type during the events of *The Truth*.

The wizards used to say that books weren't there to be read by just anyone. A large print run would seriously dilute the power of the words. And, they added, it was one thing for a magical book to be copied by the human hand in controlled circumstances, and quite another for it to be 'printed' by type that might then be broken up and used to print a book about household management, or squirrels. The metal might *remember*...

All this became rather academic when, quite suddenly, movable type entered Ankh-Morpork, with the arrival of its first two newspapers, 'The Ankh-Morpork Times' (editor: William DE WORDE) and 'The Ankh-Morpork Inquirer' (editor: Ronald CARNEY). Who knows where it will lead? (*See also* ENGRAVERS' (AND PRINTERS') GUILD.)

Procrastinators. Huge, spinning, columnar devices for the movement and storage of time, found at Oi Dong, the monastery of the History MONKS, and also in their secret temples elsewhere (it is known that one is installed in the privy at the temple in Ankh-Morpork, turning waste disposal into history's problem). Small, portable ones have been developed for field operations.

Prone, Mr. A lodger at Mrs ARCANUM's. He is a traveller in wholesale boots and shoes. [TT]

Proust, Eunice, Mrs. The proprietor of the Boffo Novelty & Joke Emporium in Ankh-Morpork (4, Tenth Egg Street), which she runs with her son, Derek, her husband having died some twenty-five years ago. She looks like the evil witch of fairy tales – her face is a curse, her voice the sound of the oven door slamming on children. She has a fearsome hooked, wart-encrusted nose, claw-like hands and blackened teeth. She uses her own face as the mould for the masks she sells in the shop. She wears big black boots and a battered hat. [ISWM]

Prung, Bundo. He was expelled from the THIEVES' GUILD for unnecessary enthusiasm and conduct unbecoming in a mugger. After seeing ANGUA 'change', he ran away to sea. [MAA]

Psam-nut-kha. A past king of DJELIBEYBI. [P]

Ptaclusp. An architect and jobbing pyramid builder in DJELIBEYBI. Owner of Ptaclusp Associates, Necropolitan Builders to the Dynasties. He has twin sons – Ptaclusp IIa (interested in accounts/finance) and Ptaclusp IIb (an inveterate architect and designer). [P]

Pta-ka-ba. A past king of DJELIBEYBI. [P]

Pthagonal. Ephebian philosopher, specializing in geometry. A glum-looking heavy drinker, because of his discovery of the irrational value of pi. [P]

Ptorne. A Djelibeybian farmer who was a

plaintiff before TEPPIC in the Supreme Court. [P]

Ptraci. Favourite handmaiden (and daughter) of King TEPPICYMON XXVII. Long, dark hair; small, pretty jaw; painted toenails. She uses scent like a battering ram. Not a great singer, despite the traditional requirement of handmaidens to be skilled in music; in fact she sounds like a flock of vultures who've just found a dead donkey. Ptraci became Queen of DJELIBEYBI when TEPPIC renounced the throne, whereupon the priests and courtiers found that sweet young handmaidens can be far tougher to deal with than amiable old pharaohs. [P]

Pump, Mr. An eight-foot-tall golem, who we first encounter as Moist von LIPWIG's parole officer. He was originally Pump No.19, and stood at the bottom of a 100-foot-deep hole and pumped water. He was at the bottom of that hole for 240 years, but is now a government official with perfect recall (he can replicate anyone's voice). Lord Vetinari selected him as Moist's parole officer because Mr Pump does not sleep, Mr Pump does not eat, Mr Pump does not *stop*. [GP]

Purdeigh, Roderick, Gen. Sir. Son of Major-General Sir Ruthven Purdeigh, Royal Sto Plains RIFLERS (d.1858), of Grunefair, Ankh-Morpork, and Margaret, née Burberry (d. 1856); b.14 Spune 1842 (disappeared on or around 25 Sektober 1898); Educ.: Thrasher's School, Pseudopolis – and Sto Lat Military Academy.

Career: joined Quirm Lancers as ADC to CIC; transferred on promotion to the 35th Llamedosian Foot, serving as platoon commander under General Lord Rust; promoted (in error) to Colonel in the field of battle (at the expense of Captain the Honourable Rupert Purdey, hero of Lawke's Drain); then transferred to the Royal Sto Plains Riflers where he served for 5 years at GHQ before gaining promotion to General upon the death of General the Duke of Eorle. Subsequently left the army and took up a career as an explorer. Publications: 'The Use of Pliers in Warfare', 'Boots and Teeth: A Soldier's Life', 'The Old Man of the Woods', etc., etc.

His life's goal was to rediscover the 'mythical' continent of XXXX and its companion islands ('Foggy Islands', reputedly the place where XXXX kept the lawnmower).

This obsessed him, and he devoted a large part of his life to a meticulous search of the ocean in its rumoured position, proving to his satisfaction that there was no such place. He made three important voyages during which he entirely failed to discover it; they were longer than expected owing to his inability, once he determined to return home, to discover Ankh-Morpork again. Or, indeed, any land of any consequence at all.

At one point towards the end of his first odyssey he wrote a short monograph claiming that the Circle Sea was in fact one million miles across. His erratic six-month voyage on it, during which he never once sighted land, has long been considered one of the most difficult ever achieved (akin to turning an elephant around inside a phone booth without touching the sides). It was curtailed only by thick fog, which prevented him from seeing where he was going, and thus allowed him to collide with a shrimp boat five miles from Ankh-Morpork.

Navigators have speculated upon the secret of Sir Roderick's technique. It is known that he eschewed the use of compasses, sextants, measuring ropes and other aids as unworthy of the true explorer, and chose instead to just sail around until he could find someone to stop and ask the way.

This was his first mistake. It has been established that this never works. Firstly, whoever is stopped and asked, whether at the bottom of a mineshaft, in the heart of a trackless jungle or high on a distant glacier, never knows where they are ('sorry, dunno, 'm not from round here'), despite the fact that they are walking a dog. Or, much worse, they know it so intensively that they are quite unable to pass on any worthwhile information to the traveller ('turn where you get to where the boot factory used to be, no, tell you what, it'll save you some time, go along where the viaduct was, you can't miss it, then turn

right, only it's really straight ahead, and kind of jiggle past the main road and … No. I tell a lie, what you do is, you go back down here till you get to where you can see where the old hospital was, only you can't no more cos they've taken the Sign away, and...')

His second mistake was to assume implicitly that anyone he met was fully capable of understanding him if he shouted loudly enough, and that failure to do so was a sign of wilfulness, to be punished by a sharp prod with Sir Roderick's walking stick and an exhortation to smarten up, pay attention and stop slouching.

As far as Sir Roderick was concerned, being foreign was like catching some minor but embarrassing sexual disease – it could be avoided by decent living, and if you happened to contract it, it was your fault.

This was to prove his undoing. His final voyage took him to the large island of Bhang-bhangduc which, with his intuitive grasp of geography, he declared to be about thirty miles from Ankh-Morpork. While his crew made repairs, he busied himself in the study of rain-forest fauna and flora, as detailed in his short and unfinished work 'The Man of the Woods'. In particular, he was incensed by the behaviour of the local people:

>...a Red-haired, Ruffianly but well–toothed crewe, who seem to be entirely unwilling to conduct their lives in a proper manner and, instead, hang by their feet in the trees all day, eating fruit and sleeping and engaging upon Further Activities which I will not detail lest this document be read by those of an Unmarried persuasion. That they are quite capable of rational thought is evinced by the fact that, when I made one of them the gift of an old pair of Trousers, these he instantly donned, although on his head; yet he persisted in saying no more than 'ook' even when questioned in a slow, clear voice, another example of the discourtesy so prevalent, I fear, in this part of the world. I am determined to put a stop to this Folly and if it means a sharp prod with my walking stick then the cause of proper civilized behaviour will not find me wanting...

The walking stick was found in a tree some days later. [DM]

Pushpram, Verity. 'Queen of the Sea'. A trader in fish in Ankh-Morpork's fish market. She is a self-made woman – although she could have used some help when it came to her eyes, which are set so far apart that she resembles a turbot. She initially made enough from her stall to buy a boat, then another boat, and then a whole aisle in the fish market. [UA]

Puzuma, Ambiguous. The fastest animal on the Disc, the puzuma is extremely neurotic and moves so fast that it can actually achieve near light-speed in the Disc's magical field. This means that, if you can see one, it isn't there. Most male puzumas die young of acute ankle failure caused by running very fast after females which aren't there and, of course, achieving suicidal mass in accordance with relativistic theory. The rest of them die of Heisenberg's Uncertainty Principle, since it is impossible for them to know who they are and where they are at the same time, and the see-sawing loss of concentration this engenders means that the puzuma achieves a sense of identity only when it is at rest – usually about fifty feet into the rubble of what remains of the mountain it just ran into at near light-speed. The puzuma is rumoured to be about the size of a leopard with a rather unique black and white chequered coat, although those specimens discovered by the Disc's sages and philosophers have inclined them to declare that in its natural state the puzuma is flat, very thin and dead. [P]

Pyjama, Hrolf. A dwarf enlisted into the Ankh-Morpork city militia by Carrot.[MAA]

Pyramids. Dams in the stream of time. Correctly shaped and oriented, with proper paracosmic measurements correctly plumbed in, the temporal potential of the great mass of stone can be diverted to accelerate or reverse time over a very small area, in the same way that a hydraulic ram can be induced to pump water against the flow.

The whole point of a correctly built pyramid is to achieve absolute null time in the central chamber so that a dying king, tucked up there, will indeed live for ever – or at least never actually die. The time that should have passed in the chamber is stored in the bulk of the pyramid and allowed to flare off once every twenty-four hours.

Many of the Klatchian countries have built pyramids at some stage in their history, but in Djelibeybi they became a national obsession. [P]

'And then there's quantum, of course.' The monk
sighed. 'There's always bloody quantum.'

– Night Watch

Qu. Master of Devices for the History MONKS. He is tall and rather heavily built, with white hair and a straw hat. He has the look of a good-natured bank manager. Qu invented the Portable PROCRASTINATOR, a device for adjusting time in the immediate vicinity of the wearer. In fact, most of his devices, in theory created to aid agents in the field, are achieved by taking the ancient technology of the Procrastinators and harnessing it to practical, everyday purposes such as blowing people's heads off. [TOT]

Quantum. In a nutshell, a word used on Discworld to summarize any complex scientific explanation, in the pretty much the same way as 'magic', here, is used to summarize any complex occult one. A kind of cosmic 'get out of half-understood explanation free' card, in other words.

Quarney. The only shopkeeper in LANCRE. Mrs Quarney also helps him to run the store. [LL]

Quezovercoatl. The Feathered Boa. God of Human Sacrifices. Half-man, half-chicken, half-jaguar, half-serpent, half-scorpion and half-mad. Quezovercoatl was both a god of the Tezuman Empire and a demon. He was also six inches high. Or *was*. He got trampled to death. The Tezumen now worship a metal-bound chest with hundreds of little legs. [E]

Quimby II, Olaf. A PATRICIAN of Ankh-Morpork. He passed some legislation to put a stop to excessive exaggeration in descriptive writing, and to introduce some honesty into reporting. Thus, if a legend said of a hero that 'all men spoke of his prowess', any bard who valued his life would add hastily 'except for a couple of people in his home village who thought he was a liar and quite a lot of other people who had never really heard of him'. Poetic simile was strictly limited and any loose talk about a beloved having a face that launched a thousand ships would have to be backed by evidence that the object of desire did indeed look like a bottle of champagne. Quimby was eventually killed by a disgruntled poet during an experiment conducted in the palace grounds to prove the disputed accuracy of the proverb 'The pen is mightier than the sword.' In his memory it was amended to include the phrase 'only if the sword is very small and the pen is very sharp'.

Quire, the. Major river, which drains most of the Octarine grass country and comes out in Quirm. Known, because of its challenging nature, as 'Old Treachery'. The violent surges of water on Old Treachery are named, in technical manuals, as a Dam Slam. It's a river that has moods. [SN]

Quirke, 'Mayonnaise'. He started out in the Night Watch, where he rose to the rank of corporal and where he was thought to have a private income from bribes. He was a bully, a brown-noser and a delighter in small evils. After being booted out by Sergeant Keel he found a niche in the Day Watch, where he eventually rose to the rank of captain. Called 'Mayonnaise' because he's thick, oily and smells faintly of eggs. Quirke is not actually a bad man in the classic sense, but only because he doesn't have the necessary imagination. He deals more in that sort of generalized low-grade unpleasantness which slightly tarnishes the soul of all who come into contact with it. [NW]

Quirm. A pleasant little city in a wine-growing area overlooking the Rim Ocean. Wild geraniums fill its sloping, cobbled streets. It has a famous floral clock. And that really says it all about Quirm. It is a dull place. Most of its inhabitants have lived elsewhere during times of considerable excitement and have sworn mighty oaths that it won't happen here. The current Quirmian Ambassador to Ankh-Morpork is Monsieur Cravat.

Quirm, Ponce da. *See* PONCE DA QUIRM.

Quirm College for Young Ladies. School attended by, among others, DEATH's grand-daughter, Susan STO HELIT, Lady Sybil VIMES (nee Ramkin), and also by Miss Perspicacia TICK. It is surrounded by high, spike-topped walls whose aim is to protect its young inmates from the wicked world and whose effect is to cause them to have a keen curiosity about it.

The school uniform is a loose, navy-blue woollen smock that stretches from neck to just above the ankle, with a waistline somewhere around knee level (practical, healthy and as attractive as a plank). The girls also have to wear their hair in two plaits; if they are dwarfs they may keep their iron helmets on but they have to plait their beards instead.

Riddled with a kind of genteel wrong-headedness though it is, the College is one of the very few establishments in the STO PLAINS where a girl can get other than the most simple vocational education. Its alumni are women who know their own minds, even if no one else does. [SM]

Quisition. The sharp end of the religious system in OMNIA. It comprised the inquisitors – torturers who extracted confessions and bodily parts from heretics – and the exquisitors, who just... arranged matters. By and large the inquisitors were simple, burly men who just had a job to do. It was they who would busy themselves about your person with knives and needles and hammers; it was the exquisitor who would talk to you afterwards. Some people who have survived both have said that half an hour with an inquisitor and his complete kit was

preferable to a pleasant chat over a cup of tea with an exquisitor.

The Quisition felt they could act without possibility of error. Suspicion was proof. How could it be anything else, it was argued? The Great God OM would not have seen fit to put the suspicion in the minds of his exquisitors unless it was right that it should be there. Some people pointed out the essential flaw in this argument, but not very loudly and they were often running while they said it.

The Quisition's unwritten motto was: *CVIVS TESTICVLOS HABES, HABEAS CARDIA ET CEREBELLVM*, which, loosely translated, means that when you have people's full attention, you have their hearts and minds. The organization has now been abolished. [SG]

Quizzing device. A three-ton, water-driven monstrosity based on a recently discovered design by LEONARD OF QUIRM. It is a games machine once used in the Mended DRUM but removed when Captain CARROT of the WATCH found it a useful way of picking up criminal intelligence. [SM]

Quoom, Ishmale. Inquisitor First Class Ishmale 'Pop' Quoom. A retired inquisitor in OMNIA. Handed in his knives and corkscrew-shaped things after fifty years, shortly before the Quisition itself was forcibly retired. Remembered as an amiable, good-hearted sort, with plenty of time for everyone, and a man always ready to show apprentice torturers how to break every bone in the human body (including the little ones in the fingers, which are quite hard to do). Breeds canaries in his spare time. [SG]

Quoth. A talking raven owned by C.V. CHEESEWALLER. Originally from the unkindness of ravens in the forever crumbling, ivy-clad TOWER OF ART overlooking Unseen University, whose innate intelligence has been amplified by the magical radiation from the buildings below. Quoth is not his actual name; ravens have never felt the need for such things. Despite his intelligence, however, he has yet to understand that not every small, round, glittery thing is an eyeball, or why human beings will cheerfully put out crumbs for robins but stop short of entrails for corvids, no matter how intelligent they are. He has now attached himself to Death's household as the DEATH OF RATS' personal transport and crony. He is only in it for the eyeballs, he says. [SM]

He didn't make a very good revolutionary. People as meticulously fervent as
Reg got real revolutionaries worried.

– *Night Watch*

Ramkin, 'Black Jack'. Also 'Mad Jack' Ramkin. He was regrettably mistaken when he made an enormous drunken wager with one of his equally drunk drinking pals that he could see the smoke of the city from his estate. He was told by a surveyor, who had tested the hypothesis, that Hangman's Hill was thirty feet too short. Pausing only to attempt to bribe the surveyor, and when unsuccessful to subsequently horse-whip the same, he rallied all the menfolk from his estate and all the others round about and set them to raise the hill by the aforesaid thirty feet, a most ambitious project. It cost a fortune, of course, but every family in the district probably got warm winter clothes and new boots out of it. It made him very popular, and of course he won his bet. Two gallons of brandy. Which he drank in one go, at the top of the Hill, to the cheers of the assembled workforce, and then, according to legend, rolled all the way down to the bottom, to more cheers. [SN]

Ramkin, Sybil Deirdre Olgivanna, Lady. *See* VIMES, SYBIL DEIRDRE OLGIVANNA, LADY.

Ramkin, Woolsthorpe. Brother to Mad Jack, the 3rd Earl. He was something of a scholar and would have been sent to the university to become a wizard were it not for the fact that his brother let it be known that any male sibling of his who took up a profession that involved wearing a dress would be disinherited with a cleaver.

Nevertheless, young Woolsthorpe perse-vered in his studies of natural philosophy in the way a gentleman should, by digging into any suspicious-looking burial mounds he could find in the neighbourhood, filling up his lizard press with as many rare species as he could collect, and drying samples of any flowers he could find before they became extinct.

The story runs that, on one warm summer day, he dozed off under an apple tree and was awakened when an apple fell on his head. A lesser man, as his biographer put it, would have seen nothing untoward about this, but Wools-thorpe surmised that, since apples and practi-cally everything else always fell down, then the world would eventually become dangerously unbalanced – unless there was another agency involved that natural philosophy had yet to discover. He lost no time in dragging one of the footmen to the orchard and ordering him, on pain of dismissal, to lie under the tree until an apple hit him on the head! The possibility of this happening was increased by another footman who had been told by Woolsthorpe to shake the tree vigorously until the required apple fell. Woolsthorpe was ready to observe this from a distance.

Who can imagine his joy when the inevita-ble apple fell and a second apple was seen rising from the tree and disappearing at speed into the vaults of heaven, proving the hypothesis that what goes up must come down, provided that what goes down must come up, thus safeguard-ing the equilibrium of the Universe. Regretta-bly, this only works with apples and, amazingly, only the apples on this one tree, *Malus equi-libria*! Someone has now worked out that the apples at the top of the tree fill with gas and fly up when the tree is disturbed so that it can set its seeds some way off. Wonderful thing, nature, shame the fruit tastes like dog's business. [SN]

Ramtops. A range of jagged peaks, upland lakes, dense forests and little river valleys so deep that the daylight has no sooner reached the bottom than it is time to leave again. The Ramtop Mountains stretch from the frozen lands near the Hub all the way, via a lengthy archipelago, to the warm seas that flow into space over the Rim.

Raw magic crackles invisibly from peak to peak and earths itself in the mountains, because the range lies across the Disc's vast magical standing wave like an iron bar on a pair of subway rails. It is so saturated with magic that it is constantly discharging itself into the environment. In the Ramtops the leaves on the trees move even when there is no breeze; rocks go for a stroll of an evening. Even the land, at times, seems alive. It is not surprising that the Ramtops have given the world so many of its famous witches and wizards.

There is plenty of flat land in the Ramtops:

the trouble is, it's nearly all flat in the vertical plane. There are little kingdoms all over the place. Every narrow valley, every ledge that something other than a goat could stand on, is a kingdom; LANCRE is one of the biggest.

On the turnwise slopes, leading towards the STO PLAINS, are the rolling uplands known as the OCTARINE grass country, from the distinctive colour imparted to its vegetation by the ambient local magic. From the highest points in the Lancre area – the High Tops – you can see all the way to the Rim Ocean. In the other direction, wrapped in eternal winter, the mountains march all the way to the Hub.

The Ramtops have very definite weather. Winter in the Ramtops doesn't mess about; it's a gateway straight through to the primeval coldness that lived before the creation of the world. Winter in the Ramtops is several yards of snow, the forests a mere collection of shadowy green tunnels under the drifts. Winter means the coming of the lazy wind, which can't be bothered to blow around people and blows right through them instead. Ramtoppers have eighteen different words for snow (all of them, unfortunately, unprintable). No dweller in the Ramtops would dream of starting a winter without a log pile on three sides of the house – no one in the Ramtops lets their fire go out, as a matter of pride and, in the winter, survival.

And after the snow melts, there's the rain. Ramtop rain has a curiously penetrative quality that makes ordinary rain seem almost dry. It rains a lot in the spring. The weather is full of shrapnel rain and whiplash winds and permanent thunder storms.

The summer and autumn are hot, dry and pleasant. They are also quite brief. The Ramtops breed a phlegmatic, insular type of person.

Rascal, Methodia. Born, painted famous picture, thought he was a chicken, died. He's believed to have painted around Discworld year 1802. Mad as a spoon. He used to write notes he wanted to keep secret from 'the chicken'. His last note is believed to be 'Awk! Awk! It comes! IT COMES!' He is best known as the creator of 'The Battle of Koom Valley' a ten-foot high,

fifty-foot long masterpiece which took him years to complete and which was, for a while, owned by the Ramkin family. [T!]

Rat Catchers, the. The two rat catchers encountered during the events of The Amazing Maurice were called Ron Blunkett and Bill Spears. Both wore long, dusty overcoats and battered, black top hats, with large, shiny, black boots. They had a small terrier. One was big and fat, one was thin – in fact they made some effort to comply with all the narrative stereotypes for comic thugs. [TAMAHER]

Rat Traps. Several manufacturers are referenced in The Amazing Maurice. For a random impression of completeness, these include:

Jenkins & Jenkins (makers of the Big Snapper)
Nugent Brothers, the (makers of the Breakback series)
Prattle & Johnson
Snippet & Polson (makers of the Ratsnapper series).

Re-annual plants. Plants on the Disc, while including the categories known commonly as annuals (which are sown this year to come up later this year), biennials (sown this year to grow next year) and perennials (sown this year to grow until further notice), also include a few rare re-annuals which, because of an unusual four-dimensional twist in their genes, can be planted this year to come up last year. They can be grown only in excessively high magical fields, such as are found in the RAMTOPS.

Re-annual grapes produce wine much sought after by fortune tellers since it enables them to see the future. Although re-annual wine causes inebriation in the normal way, the action of the digestive system on its molecules causes an unusual reaction, the net effect of which is to thrust the ensuing hangover backwards in time, to a point some hours before the wine is drunk. A hangunder, in fact. These tend to be very bad, because people feel so dreadful with the effect of the alcohol they have not yet consumed that they drink a lot to get over it. Hence the saying: 'Have a hair of the dog that's going to bite you'.

Re-annual crop-growing is an art in itself. It does have some advantages, in that the grower can raise enough on the crop to afford to buy the seed and rent the field, but there are concomitant drawbacks. A farmer who neglects to sow his seed loses his crop, whereas anyone who forgets to sow seeds of a crop that was harvested twelve months before risks disturbing the entire fabric of causality, not to mention acute embarrassment.

Recent Runes, Lecturer in. One of the senior faculty at Unseen University. Like many of the senior wizards, he is referred to only by title, leading to some uncertainty about his true moniker. His name is not Arnold. [MP]

Reet. A lady of the streets rescued from some robbers by CARROT. She was apparently a girlfriend of his for a while, but the relationship foundered quite quickly because Carrot's idea of an exciting time was to walk to some distant part of the city to view an interesting example of iron bollard. [GG]

Reforgule (of Krull). A scientist who theorized that the Disc revolves once in every 800 days in order to distribute the weight fairly upon its supportive pachyderms. [COM]

Remitt. An armourer in Ankh-Morpork. Generally used by the Night Watch when their amour needs repairing. [MAA]

Rerpf. Ran the Groaning Platter, down by the Brass Bridge, Ankh-Morpork. A short, fat man, very richly dressed. With beringed hands. He was a founder member of the Merchants' Guild. [COM]

Research witchcraft. Or whichcraft. A small but very valuable side of the Craft. Eye of what kind of toad? Maw of which sea-ravin'd shark? The Granny Weatherwax view of whichcraft is that it simply doesn't matter, but many witches of an enquiring mind have, down the centuries, experimented with thousands of different ingredients. One of the results is the – presumably – penicillin-encrusted mouldy bread poultice used by Magrat in *Lords and Ladies*. The patient was quite lucky. Stretching down the ages must have been considerable experimentation with the antibiotic effects of mouldy cheese, mouldy apples, mouldy sheep and so on.

Retrophrenology. Phrenology, as everyone knows, is a way of reading someone's character, aptitude and abilities by examining the bumps and hollows on their head. Therefore – according to the kind of logical thinking that characterizes the Ankh-Morporkian mind – it should be possible to mould someone's character by giving them carefully graded bumps in all the right places. You can go into a shop and order an artistic temperament with a tendency to introspection and a side order of hysteria. What you actually get is hit on the head with a selection of different sized mallets, but it creates employment and keeps the money in circulation, and that's the main thing. [MAA]

Rham-ap-efan. Admiral of the Djelibeybian navy. [SG]

Rhoxie, The. Palace of the Seriph of AL KHALI. Famed in myth and legend for its splendour. Said to have been built in one night by a genie, and therefore known colloquially as the Djinn Palace. [P]

Rhumusphut. A plaintiff before TEPPIC in the Djelibeybian supreme court. [P]

Rhysson, Rhys. The new Low King of the Überwald dwarfs. He is a dwarf with vision, an astute politician, a new thinker, although he doesn't like Ankh-Morpork very much (he visited the city when he was much younger), and he is considered to be pretty clever. People have described him (though not to his face) as a 'fairytale dwarf with a Hogfather beard'. He is short, even by dwarf standards and he wears leather and home-forged chain mail. He looks quite old, as dwarfs do, and he speaks with the musical cadences of those from Llamedos – he comes from a little coal-mining clan near there. Events in *Raising Steam* resulted in her changing her name to Blodwen and her title to Low Queen of the Dwarfs. [TFE]

Ribobe, Deccan. The last Keeper of the Door in Holy Wood. He took over from old Tento, who himself had taken over from Meggelin – people known only from their entries in the logbook kept by the keepers. He wore a frayed ceremonial robe of dark red plush with gold frogging. [MP]

Ridcully, Hughnon. Chief Priest of Blind Io and brother of Mustrum. He is married, but otherwise sensible and solid. Solid as a rock and, sometimes, as sensible. [TT]

Ridcully, Mustrum. Ridcully the Brown. ARCHCHANCELLOR of Unseen University.

He became a seventh-level mage at the incredibly young age of twenty-seven. He then quit the University in order to look after his family's estates deep in the country.

He had not set foot in UU for forty years when he was made Archchancellor, and his surprising elevation came only because the faculty wanted a bit of a breather after several rather hectic years in which Archchancellors (never a job with long-term prospects) were dying off so fast that they were getting buried with their inaugural dinner only half-eaten. What was needed was someone quiet and easy to manipulate. It was known that Ridcully was an inveterate countryman and it was assumed that a wizard so close to nature would fit the bill and, if he became a nuisance, could easily be disposed of.

Ridcully in the flesh therefore came as a breath of fresh air in a wind-chime factory.

He has a huge personality. He is quite capable of getting drunk and playing darts all night, but then he'll leave at five in the morning to swim, or at least clamber, in the frozen Ankh or to go duck hunting; at one time he had a pack of hunting dragons installed in the butler's pantry at UU.

He likes beer with his breakfast of kidneys and black pudding, and especially likes those sausages, you know the ones, with a transparent skin through which can be seen the occasional green fleck which you can only hope is sage; he is a shameless AUTOCONDIMENTOR and makes his own version of the infamous WOW-WOW SAUCE.

Intellectually, Ridcully maintains his position for two reasons. One is that he never, ever, changes his mind about anything. The other is that it takes him several minutes to understand any new idea put to him – this is an invaluable trait in a leader, because anything anyone is still trying to explain to you after two minutes is probably important, and anything they give up after a mere minute or so is almost certainly something they shouldn't have been bothering you with in the first place. By the same token, he never reads any paperwork put on his desk, reasoning that he'll find out about anything *really* important when the shouting starts.

Nevertheless, Ridcully isn't stupid; he has quite a powerful intellect but it is powerful like a locomotive, and runs on rails and is therefore almost impossible to steer. He shouts at people and tries to jolly them along. He is brusque and rude to absolutely everyone and he never wastes time on small talk. It's always large talk or nothing. Economy of emotion is one of his strong points.

A key to understanding him is that, like Granny Weatherwax, he sees himself as quite outside the rules which he nevertheless imposes on everyone else. He is quite incapable of understanding any reasonably intelligent joke and therefore frowns upon them; nevertheless he prides himself on his sense of humour, which is rudimentary, and he himself often tells jokes – long, dull ones, often with the punch line incorrectly remembered. And, while he is a stickler for his staff to be dressed in proper wizarding robes, he himself avoids wearing them on all but the most formal occasions, although he does of course retain the wizarding hat.

Mrs WHITLOW has made him up a sort of baggy trouser suit in garish blue and red, which he wears for his early morning jog, with his pointy hat tied on to his head with string.

The hat is quite a work of art, and he made it himself. It has fishing flies stuck in it. A very small pistol crossbow is shoved in the hatband and a small bottle of Bentinck's Very Peculiar Old Brandy is stored in the pointy bit. The very tip unscrews to become a cup. It also has small cupboards in it. Four telescopic legs and a roll of oiled silk in the brim extend downwards to make a small but serviceable tent, with a patent spirit stove just above it and inner pockets containing three days' iron rations.

His study is dominated by a full-sized snooker table, piled high with papers. Stuffed heads of a number of surprised animals hang on the walls. From one of the antlers hang a pair of corroded boots worn by Ridcully as a Rowing Brown. In one corner of the room is a large model of the Discworld on four wooden elephants.

He is now about seventy. About fifty or more years ago he had a romantic fling with young Esmerelda Weatherwax.

His brother, Hughnon, is the Chief Priest of BLIND IO in Ankh-Morpork, and his uncle lives near LANCRE.

Depending on your point of view, Ridcully is either the best or the worst Archchancellor that UU has had for a hundred years. He is certainly the most long-lived, having survived dragons, monsters, rogue shopping trolleys and, most importantly, his fellow wizards. The unkillability of Mustrum Ridcully has had an amazing knock-on effect through university wizardry, because it has effectively slowed to a halt the practice of rising through the magical ranks by killing wizards of a superior grade.

Some of the fun goes out of this when the man at the top is not only very good at the game, but tends to creep up behind ambitious would-be murderers, shout at them very loudly, and then slam their heads repeatedly in the door. [MP]

Riflers, Royal Sto Plains. The Royal Sto Plains Riflers were so named because of their habit of collecting weapons, boots, gold teeth and jewellery off the stricken enemy, and the idiotic bravery necessary to see that there were as many of the stricken as possible. So keen was the average riflingman that many would go into battle armed only with pliers and armoured shoehorn, and would often manage, in the press of battle, to get teeth and footwear from enemies who were not only alive but actively fighting back. [DM]

Riktor. 'Numbers' Riktor. Riktor the Tinkerer. A wizard at Unseen University. A man with a one-track mind; he was convinced that the universe could be entirely understood in terms of numbers and, indeed, *was* numbers. He invented the reso-graph (a 'thingness-writer'), a device for detecting and measuring disturbances in the fabric of reality. Also the Star Enumerator, Mouse Counter, Swamp Meter and Rev Counter for Use in Ecclesiastical Areas. [MP]

Rimbow. The eight-coloured, world-girdling rainbow that hovers in the mist-laden air over the RIMFALL. A double rainbow. Close to the lip of the Rimfall are the seven lesser colours, sparkling and dancing in the spray of the dying seas. But they are pale in comparison to the wider band that floats beyond them, not deigning to share the same spectrum.

The Rimbow hangs in the mists just beyond the edge of the world, appearing only at morning and evening, when the light of the Disc's little orbiting sun shines past the massive bulk of the Great A'TUIN and strikes the Disc's magical field at exactly the right angle.

Rimfall. The long waterfall at the vast circumference of the Discworld, where the seas of the Disc boil ceaselessly over the Edge into space.

People ask how the water gets back on to the Disc.

Arrangements are made.

Rimfisher. A small bird with a tuft of blue and green feathers, iridescent as jewels. It lives on the Rim, feeding off whatever raw fish plummet past its perch. [COM]

Rincewind. A wizard. At least, generally referred to as a wizard. Strange to tell, it is also the name of the Archchancellor of BUGARUP UNIVERSITY (RINCEWIND, BILL).

Our Rincewind is tall, thin and scrawny, with a raggedy beard that looks like the kind of beard worn by people who aren't cut out by Nature to be beard-wearers. He is a non-smoker (unusual in a wizard). He is a survivor. There are scars all over him . Mostly on his back.

He traditionally wears a dark red, hooded, frayed plush robe on which a few mystic sigils are embroidered in tarnished sequins. The robe has been made darker by constant wear and irregular washing. Under his robe he wears britches and sandals. Around his neck is a chain bearing the bronze octagon which marks him as an alumnus of Unseen University (quite wrongly, it must be pointed out, since he has never passed any kind of magical exam. Indeed, he never scored more than 2 per cent in his exams (and that was for spelling his name almost right).) On his head is a battered pointy hat with a floppy brim, which has the word 'WIZZARD' embroidered on it in big, silver letters by someone whose needlework is even worse than their spelling. There's a star on top. It has lost most of its sequins. Interestingly, a reference in Sourcery mentions that Rincewind's headgear is a 'battered grey hat', although

Rincewind

it's usually depicted as red.

He was born under the sign of the Small Boring Group of Faint Stars – a sign associated with chess board makers, sellers of onions, manufacturers of plaster images of small religious significance and people allergic to pewter. His mother ran away before he was born, and the young Rincewind grew up in Morpork.

He does have an innate gift for languages, which enables him to shout 'Don't kill me!' and be understood in a hundred different countries. He is also good at practical geography, which means that he always knows exactly where it is he is running away from. He has a razor-sharp instinct for survival equalled only by an uncanny ability to end up in situations where every bit of it is required.

Rincewind's room number as a student at UU was 7a (wizards avoid the number eight). Later, during his spell as Deputy Librarian (an ape's Number Two, as the Dean nastily remarked), he lived in a room close to the LIBRARY used mainly to store old furniture. It contained a large wardrobe (on top of which the LUGGAGE hibernated) and a banana crate which he used as a dressing table. It also housed a wicker chair with no bottom and three legs, and a mattress so full of life that it occasionally moved sluggishly around the floor, bumping into things. The rest of the room was a litter of objects dragged from the street – old crates, bits of planking, sacks, etc.

There are eight levels of wizardry on the Disc; after all these years, Rincewind has failed to even achieve level one. It was in fact the opinion of some of his tutors that he was incapable of even achieving level zero, which most normal people are born at. It has been contended that when Rincewind dies the average occult ability of the human race will actually go up a fraction. 'To call his understanding of magical theory

"abysmal" is to leave no suitable word to describe his grasp of its practice,' said one of his tutors. He is also not very good at precognition: he can scarcely see into the present.

Some of this is unfair. For a bet, the young Rincewind dared to open the pages of the last remaining copy of the CREATOR's own grimoire, the 'OCTAVO'. A spell leapt out of the page and instantly burrowed deeply into his mind, whence even the combined talents of the Faculty of Medicine were unable to coax it. No one knew which spell it was, except that it was one of the Eight Great Spells that were intricately interwoven with the very fabric of time and space itself. Since then, no other spell dared stay in the same head. For that prank, he was expelled from UU.

Subsequently, he has been an unwilling travel guide, has been through Hell, has visited most of the countries of the Disc, has travelled extensively in time as well as in space, has been present at the creation of the Discworld where he caused the origin of life by dropping an egg-and-cress sandwich into the sea, has defeated the greatest magic-user on the Disc while armed with nothing more than a half-brick in a sock,* aided the rebels in the Counterweight Continent, visited XXXX (where he was called Rinso) and flown to the Moon. He is believed to have been one of only nine people to have visited the country of DEATH while mortal.

But what Rincewind has always sought is some secure, safe position somewhere, and seemed to get this when he was appointed as Egregious Professor of Cruel and Unusual Geography (even though the previous incumbent was probably eaten by a giant lizard). The post has no salary and total insecurity of tenure, but he does get his laundry done for free, a place at mealtimes and, because of a quirk of the coal

---

* There has been much discussion about this, but UU wizards do reluctantly concede that this is the historical state of affairs. Rincewind certainly challenged Coin with said sock, and as a result Coin ceased his troublesome reign (admittedly because being challenged by the most ineffective wizard in the world with such a primitive weapon amused him, caught his imagination and persuaded him to defy the power of his father). There are other ways to defeat someone than by bashing their head in with a brick (although this does remain the means of choice in many of Ankh-Morpork's shadier streets).

porter, seven bucketfuls of coal every day. He also gets his own (superheated) office, and no one chases him much. Despite the fact that he is the least senior member of the UU faculty, he is also, now, Chair of Experimental Serendipity, Reader in Slood Dynamics, Fretwork Teacher, Chair for the Public Misunderstanding of Magic, Professor of Virtual Anthropology and Lecturer in Approximate Accuracy. He has, in fact, accumulated all those jobs that require absolutely nothing more than that something in theory is doing them. [COM]

Rincewind, Bill. Archchancellor of Bugarup University and, possibly, a distant cousin of RINCEWIND. [TLC]

Rinpo. A History MONK. Chief acolyte to the ABBOT at the Monastery of Oi Dong. [TOT]

Rjinswand, Dr. This is the name assumed by RINCEWIND when he and TWOFLOWER appeared briefly on an aircraft in *The Colour of Magic*. He was then thirty-three, a bachelor, born in Sweden, raised in New Jersey, a specialist in the breakaway oxidation phenomena of certain nuclear reactors. It is believed that, while falling off a dragon in a field of high magical energy, he desperately wished to remain airborne – and was re-arranged in the nearest available dimension where this could be possible. [COM]

Robinson, Milly. *See* STANDISH, MILLY. [TSC]

Rock. *See* GALENA. Rock is a perfectly good name for a silicaceous troll, but it has also become a term of abuse used by the more speciesist humans in Ankh-Morpork.

Rocksmacker, Minty. CARROT's childhood sweetheart. A dwarf. It was partly in order to get him out of her life that Carrot was originally sent to Ankh-Morpork. After all, as his parents pointed out, when he was 6'6" she would still be only 4'2". [GG]

Rodley, Brenda, Lady. The Dowager Duchess

of Quirm. A small, white-haired, wiry woman with a face like old saddle leather. She owns Treebite Brightscale (a swamp dragon) and is a friend of Sybil Ramkin. She lives at the Dower House, Quirm Castle, Quirm. [GG]

Rodley, Lord (of Quirm). Heir to the fabulous Quirm estates. A rather stupid and fat young man who once danced with Death at a party. [M]

Rodney. Brother-in-law to Brother WATCHTOWER. It was his undeserved success (in the view of his brother-in-law) which was one of the motives behind the Elucidated Bretherne's search for a better social order, i.e., one where they got more of the cake. [GG]

Roger. One of Duke FELMET's guards. He isn't allowed fruit, on account of his trouble. [WS]

Roland. Roland de Chumsfanleigh (pronounced chuffley – it's not his fault). He is now the Baron of the area around the Chalk. He is handsome, in his way, but also so stiff in his way that you could iron sheets on him. His encounters with Tiffany Aching have helped to make him a less starchy person.

He has now met, fallen for and married Letitia Keepsake. [WFM]

Ron, Foul Ole. A member of the BEGGARS' GUILD and of the Canting Crew. He is a

Mutterer – he seems unable to move without a sort of low-key, random mumbling, and is capable of keeping a pretty good conversation going all by himself. He walks behind people muttering in his own private language until they give him money not to. His familiar phrases included 'Bug'r'em', 'Bugrit' and 'Millennium hand and shrimp'. People assume that Foul Ole Ron has no grasp on reality but this is not true. He holds very tightly indeed on to reality, but it is not the one shared by most of the rest of the world.

Ron wears a huge overcoat several sizes too big and a felt hat that has been reshaped by time and weather into a soft cone that overhangs the wearer's head. The grubby coat stretches from the pavement almost to the brim of the hat above it. There is a suggestion of grey hair around the join.

Foul Ole Ron is often, but not always, accompanied by his Smell, which has become so powerful over the years that it has developed a life of its own and often goes about its own occasions in the city without its theoretical owner. It is in fact rather more socially aware than Ron, and has been known to attend the opera while Ron is enjoying a meal of old boiled boots several streets away. [TT]

Ronald the Third. A past king of LANCRE. He is believed to have been an extremely unpleasant monarch, and is remembered by posterity only in an obscure bit of rhyming slang. Roland the Third =... er... manure. [WA]

Roundworld Project, The. When an experiment in fundamental thaumaturgy on the squash court of UNSEEN UNIVERSITY ran wild and threatened to destroy the universe, the computer HEX had to use up a huge quantity of magic in an instant. The only option was to activate the Roundworld Project, a magical force that – paradoxically – keeps magic out. When the DEAN poked his finger in to see what would happen, Roundworld switched on.

Roundworld isn't entirely sure which bit of itself its name applies to. Sometimes the name refers to the planet (our planet), sometimes

The Roundworld Project

to the entire universe. There have been a few mishaps along the way, but our Roundworld universe has now been running fairly successfully for thirteen and a half billion years; all of it started by an old man with a beard.

In the absence of magic, and lacking natural narrativium, the Roundworld universe runs on rules. Not rules made by people, but rules made by the Roundworld itself; which is weird, because Roundworld has no idea what its rules should be. It seems to make them up as it goes along, but it's hard to be sure.

Certainly, it doesn't know what size it ought to be. From outside, as it gathers dust on a shelf in Rincewind's office, the Roundworld universe – a globe about 20cm in diameter – resembles a cross between a foot-the-ball and a child's snowstorm toy.

From inside, it appears to be somewhat larger: a sphere whose radius is about 400 sextillion kilometres. As far as its only known inhabitants can tell, it may be much larger still; perhaps even infinite. [TSOD4]

Rouster, Dean. One-time faculty member at UNSEEN UNIVERSITY. Used to set traps to stop students attending his lectures. 'I'll tap talent from all backgrounds', he used to say, 'but a lad who can't spot a tripwire is no good to me!' He reckoned any student who didn't open a door very carefully and look where he was putting his feet would only be a burden to the profession. [CCDD]

Rthur. A fresco painter in DJELIBEYBI. His small claim to fame is that the dead kings and queens in his paintings all look identical, and beautiful. Perhaps this is why he has survived to paint so many. [P]

Ruby. A troll. She looks slightly like the statues cavemen used to carve of fertility goddesses thousands of years ago, but mostly she looks like a foothill. She is nearly 140 (not a great age for a troll, considering that in some respects they never actually die, but it is around the time a male troll decides to settle down and a female troll tends to think about the biological, or possibly geological, clock).

She and DETRITUS are romantically linked, and it is thought that her influence caused him to apply to become the Ankh-Morpork City WATCH's first troll guard. Ruby is, at least intellectually, a modern troll and felt it would be demeaning to be married to someone who hits people all the time without wearing some kind of uniform. [MP]

Rust, Lord. Ronald (Ronnie) is a tall, blue-eyed, ridiculously curly-moustached, apparently languid, definitely stupid nobleman of Ankh. In years gone by, he replaced Captain TILDEN as head of the Night Watch for a brief period, and did his very best to turn a small public protest into a full bloody revolution. His ancestor was created a baron after single-handedly killing thirty-seven Klatchians while armed with nothing more than a pin, and since then the Rusts have always been to the fore whenever pig-headed military incompetence (which may, by sheer luck, turn out to be bravery) is required.

S

There was this to be said about the Smell of Foul Ole Ron, an odour so intense
that it took on a personality of its own and fully justified the capital letter: after the
initial shock the organs of smell just gave up and shut down, as if no more able to
comprehend the thing than an oyster can comprehend the ocean.

– The Truth

Sal. Daughter of LIFTON, an innkeeper in SHEEPRIDGE. A small child, with a small child's way of speaking loudly whatever thought is occupying its mind at the time, such as 'You have a big nose.' Rescued from a fire by Bill DOOR (DEATH). [RM]

Salamanders. Magical creatures. They have no mouths, since they subsist entirely on the nourishing quality of the OCTARINE wavelength in the Discworld's sunlight, which they absorb through their skins. They absorb the rest of the sunlight as well, storing it in a special sac until it is excreted in the normal way. This allows them to be used as torches or, if surprised, as flashbulbs. A desert inhabited by salamanders is a veritable lighthouse at night. [COM]

Salami. The Ankh-Morpork composer of 'Prelude to a Nocturne on a Theme by Bubbla'. [SM]

Sally. Salacia Deloresista Amanita Trigestatra Zeldana Malifee (this goes on for quite some time) von Humpeding. A lance constable in the City Watch, and a vampire. She is fifty-one years old – no age at all for a vampire, of course. She could easily pass for sixteen. She has short hair – and looks, if not like a boy, then like a girl who wouldn't mind passing for one. Unusually, she plays the cello. [T!]

Salzella. Musical Director at the Ankh-Morpork OPERA HOUSE. An imposing figure, with flowing black hair, carefully brushed to give it a carefree alfresco look. His face was the face of an organizer and he was certainly the eminence grise at the Opera House. [MA]

Sandman. A fairly recent anthropomorphic personification in the Ankh-Morpork area, where he travels nightly from house to house sending children to sleep by means of his magic sand. Unlike sandmen on other worlds, he doesn't bother to take it out of the sack first. [SM]

Sapient pearwood. A plant so magical that it has nearly died out on the Disc and survives in only one or two places outside the AGATEAN EMPIRE, where it is still quite common; it is a magical equivalent of rosebay willowherb, a plant that traditionally colonizes bomb sites and areas devastated by fire. Sapient pearwood, in a similar way, sprouts in areas that have seen vast expenditures of magic. It owes its origins to the MAGE WARS; this has left it ingrained with a bad temper. It is totally impervious to all forms of magic.

Traditionally it is used to make wizards' staffs, and many of these still survive. But since no trees are now found within 500 miles of Unseen University, most modern staffs are made of oak or ash.

The LUGGAGE is made of it. Be warned.

Sardines. Plump little white rat who was one of of MAURICE's associates (he saw the name on a rusty tin and thought it sounded stylish). He wears a battered home-made straw hat and carries a small walking stick. He is one of the older rats in Maurice's group, but he dances and jokes and never gets into fights; in short, he wisely makes himself too harmless and useful to be a threat to the ambitions of any other male rat. He used to live in a theatre and once ate a whole box of greasepaint. This seems to have got the theatre into his blood. His feet move all the time, nervously – tippity-tap. [TAMAHER]

Sasho, Brother. One-time secretary to VORBIS in the Citadel of KOM. [SG]

Sator Square. The famous square in Ankh-Morpork's rather upmarket mercantile district is the traditional home of the Sator market, held weekly at considerable inconvenience to the traffic of the city. The market charter dates right back to the days when what is now the Square was a mere patch of ground outside Unseen University; traders were

encouraged to set up stalls there for the convenience of the wizards, since the alternative was shopping in what is now the SHADES, where the merchandise, even then, included assault and grievous bodily harm.

Saturday, Baron. One-time ruler of GENUA. Now a zombie. When alive, he was a wicked man, albeit tall and handsome (as if that excuses it, but alas it often does). He was murdered by the DUC OF GENUA, and as a result of being dead seemed to develop a more reflective attitude to things. As a zombie, he had burning eyes, grey skin, a resonant voice and he smelled of river mud. He looked as though he had just walked through a room full of cobwebs.

The Baron, with the assistance of Mrs GOGOL and to some extent also of Granny Weatherwax, invaded the Samedi Nuit Mort Ball at Genua to wreak a long-awaited revenge on his murderer. [WA]

Saturday, Ella. Daughter of Baron SATURDAY and Mrs GOGOL. A very attractive girl, with skin as brown as a nut and hair so blond as to be almost white. Because she works as a skivvy she is known as Emberella, or Young Embers. [WA]

Saveloy, Ronald. An honorary member of the Silver Horde and, for the most part, all of its brains. A tall, stick-like man with an amiably absent-minded expression and a fringe of white hair, so that, when viewed from above, he looked like a daisy. He wore a chain-mail vest slightly too big for him and a huge scabbard strapped across his back containing, instead of a sword, a variety of scrolls and brushes. The chain-mail shirt had a breast pocket with three different coloured pens in a leather pocket protector. This outfit was set off with a pair of orthopaedic sandals. Mr Saveloy used to teach geography and it is to this that he owes his soubriquet – Teach. On the whole, he found that membership of a gang of elderly cut-throats offered a quieter life than teaching. [IT]

Scalbie. A seabird; a member of the crow family. It seldom flies, walking everywhere in a sort of lurching hop. Its distinctive call is similar to that of a malfunctioning digestive system.

The scalbie has very greasy feathers and looks like other birds do after an oil slick. Nothing eats scalbies, except other scalbies. Scalbies eat things that would make a vulture sick. Scalbies would *eat* vulture sick. [SG]

Scallot, Corporal. 'Threeparts'. Quartermaster in the Borogravian army. A small, leathery old man, one of his arms ends in a hook, he has a patch over one eye and two peg legs. Hence the nickname. [MR]

Scant, William. Official Hereditary Keeper of the Monuments in Ankh-Morpork. An old man, and one of a number of people in Ankh-Morpork still doing jobs no longer appropriate to its modern civic life. According to ancient tradition, his pay is one dollar a year and a new vest every Hogswatchday. (For details of the monuments, *see* JOHNSON, BERGHOLT STUTTLEY.) [MAA]

Scharron, Red. A Discworld adventuress. [E]

Schleppel. A bogeyman, and a member of the FRESH START CLUB. A large, hairy creature with hands the size of wheelbarrows. He is also very, very shy, which is why he tends to be found under beds and behind doors. [RM]

Sconner, Benado. Led a group intent on setting fire to the LIBRARY. [S]

Scorbic, Mrs. The cook at LANCRE CASTLE. Huge pink arms, three chins and a whiskery face (the kind where the warts have whiskers, like a lot of little hills with woods on them). A power in her own kitchen. The kind of woman who thinks that cabbage isn't cooked until it is yellow, and who can't be having with this vitamin nonsense. She believes that the proper colour of meat is grey. [LL]

Scouting. Scouting for trolls, dwarfs and humans was brought in shortly after the Koom Valley Accord had been signed, on the suggestion of Lord VETINARI, to allow the young of the three dominant species to meet and hopefully get along together.

Naturally the young of all species, when thrown together, instead of turning against one another would join forces against the real enemy, that is to say their parents, teachers and miscellaneous authority which was so old-fashioned.

And up to a point, and amazingly, it had worked and that was Ankh-Morpork, wasn't it? Mostly, nobody cared what shape you were, although they might be very interested in how much money you had.

Scrappy. A talking, and magical kangaroo which 'befriends' Rincewind in *The Last Continent*. [TLC]

Scraps. A dog, built – there is no other way of putting it – and owned by IGOR. He has a spaniel's brain and is nine thirty-eighths Rottweiler – two legs, one ear, lots of tubes and his lower jaw, in fact. Although his four legs are nearly all the same length, they're not the same colour. He has just the one head, but his left ear is black and pointed and the right ear is brown and white and floppy. He does have two tails, though. Scraps is seventy-eight years old – some of him. He is a very enthusiastic animal in the department of slobber – he has a lot of lick to share. And he never dies, at least for long [CJ]

Scree. Son of Mica the Bridge Troll and Beryl. [TB]

Scrofula. A rather worried demon. Has been known to stand in for Death when he is busy. However, since Death has on every other occasion shown a most commendable dedication to duty, this must have been a unique occasion. [COM]

Scrope, Tuttle. Son of Tuskin Scrope and President of the Guild of Cobblers and Leatherworkers. Mr Scrope is a family man, with an old established leather-working shop in Wixon's Alley. He does *not* sell shoes, but caters to a rather more exotic clientele. [TT]

Scrope, William. A deer hunter, killed by a unicorn. He was a tall man, with a beard and one leg longer than the other (a common feature in LANCRE, and possibly a genetic adaptation to its lack of flat ground; a slightly smaller number of people have one leg shorter than the other). One of three brothers from the village of Slice, in Lancre. [LL]

Scrote. Tiny agricultural town about a day's slow ride from Ankh-Morpork. The usual shape – a crossroads around which is a seed merchant, a tavern, a livery stable. There are three old men sitting outside the tavern, and three young men lounging outside the livery stable saying what a hole this is and how they're going to up and leave as soon as they've got the money from the cabbage harvest, and don't you just know that in fifty years' time there'll be three old men outside the tavern...

Scrote is notable only for its mayor, Late Jim Cloop. Jim Cloop became Mayor of Scrote about 150 years ago, but died in office very soon after. There was no time or money for another election so soon after the first; after a year the townsfolk realized that Jim's period in office had been marked by a time of general prosperity: he hadn't raised taxes, embezzled the road-repair fund or taken any bribe. They voted him in again. They have voted him in ever since.

Scum. A friend to CRASH and the drummer in his musical band, first called Insanity. Considered to be without equal among drummers since he often entirely failed to make contact with the drums. [SM]

Scumble. A drink made, mainly, from apples and served in thimble-sized glasses. It tastes something like apples, something like autumn mornings, and quite a lot like the bottom of a log pile. You could clean spoons with it.

Many stories are told about scumble – how it is made out of the damp marshes according to ancient recipes handed down rather unsteadily from father to son; how the only apples that make good scumble are the Lancre Blackheart, the Golden Disagreeable and Green Billets...

It is not true about the rats, or the snake heads, or the lead shot. The one about the dead sheep is a complete fabrication, as are all the variations of the one about the trouser button. The one about not letting it come into contact with metal is true. So is the one about the drowned soldier.

It is also dangerous to let water touch scumble. It is, all in all, safer not to let scumble touch lips.

Scummidge. One-time porter at the ASSASSINS' GUILD. [MP]

Scurrick, Mrs. Widow of an Ankh-Morpork City Watchman, and the object of Captain Vimes' surreptitious charity. [MAA]

Seamstresses' Guild. Motto: NIL VOLVPTI, SINE LVCRE (this is possibly a play on the similar motto of the ASSASSINS' GUILD, whose members also work strictly for money). Coat of arms: aiguilles croisé over a lanterne, gules, on a field sable et etoilé.

One of the youngest Guilds in the city, despite the fact that its members practise the second-oldest profession in the world (the oldest profession is that of flint-knapper, a confusion that has caused many an embarrassed misunderstanding in quarries everywhere).

For it has to be said that the Guild is not there to support hard-working women who make what living they can through their skills with needle and thread. It is simply that 'seam-

stress' is considered a more polite term than otherwise might be used for young women whose affection is, not to put too fine a point on it, negotiable.

An Ankh-Morpork MERCHANTS' GUILD survey of tradespeople in the dock areas of Morpork found 987 women who gave their profession as 'seamstress', and two needles. As one of the researchers put it: 'They say they're seamstresses...hem, hem!'

The Guild House in Sheer Street is, like the MUSICIANS' GUILD, purely an administrative centre; there is no Guild school as such, most training being on the job. The Guild's concerns are with professional standards, certain specialized areas of preventive medicine, and particularly with investment finance. (*See also* AGONY AUNTS.)

The current Guild president is Mrs Rosemary PALM. 'Mrs', by the way, is an honorific acquired by all ladies of the Guild by the time they run their own establishment.

Selachii, Lady. A noblewoman of Ankh; the family are traditionally associated with the ASSASSINS' GUILD. [MAA]

Selachii, Lord Robert. A senior assassin. A Lord *Albert* Selachii is also mentioned during the events of *Night Watch*. [SM]

Sendivoge. Secretary of the Alchemists' Guild. [MP]

Senior Wrangler, the. Horace. One of the senior faculty at Unseen University. Looks rather like a horse. [RM]

Sestina, Sister. Sister Sestina of Quirm. She defied the wrath of the local king and walked unharmed across a bed of coals, and propounded a philosophy of sensible ethics on behalf of a goddess whose only real interest was in hairstyles. [SG]

Seth. Owner of the livery stable in Scrote. [SM]

Seven-league boots. A classic component of fairy stories that was the subject of a brief experiment at Unseen University. It soon became clear, however, that an unacceptable amount of groinal strain was involved in wearing boots that periodically caused your feet to be twenty-one miles apart.

Shades, the. The original and ancient part of the city of Ankh-Morpork whose inhabitants are largely nocturnal and never enquire about one another's business, because curiosity crept up on the cat in a dark alley and gave it a quick burst of skull percussion with a length of lead pipe. It is an abode of discredited gods and unlicensed thieves, ladies of the night and pedlars in exotic goods, alchemists of the mind and strolling mummers; in short, the grease on civilization's axle and the unidentified sticky stuff on the sole of its boots.

It is an inner city area sorely in need of either government help or, for preference, a flame thrower. It can't be called squalid, because that would be stretching the word to breaking point. It is beyond squalor and out the other side where, by a sort of Einsteinian reversal, it achieves a magnificent horribleness that it wears like an architectural award. It is noisy and sultry and smells like a cowshed floor.

The Shades is about ten minutes' slow stroll from Unseen University. If you drew a relief map of immorality, then even in Ankh-Morpork the Shades would be represented by a deep shaft. The Shades is as thronged as a rookery and as fragrant as a cesspit, and vice versa.

In the MERCHANTS' GUILD publication, '*Wellcome to Ankh-Morporke, Citie of One Thousand Surprises*', the Shades is described as: 'a folklorique network of old alleys and picturesque streets, wherre excitement and romans lurke arounde everry corner and much may be heard the traditional street cries of old time also the laughing visages of the denuizens as they goe about their business private'. (In other words, you have been warned.)

The Shades is also a pub in Skegness, England, which is probably very nice.

Shady, Mr, the Eighteenth. The hereditary foreman at the Ankh-Morpork Mint. [MM]

Shakespeare, William. (1564–1616) Roundworld playwright from the days of Queen Elizabeth I and King James I, who was involved in the events of *The Science of Discworld 2: The Globe*. One of his plays was called *A Midsummer Night's Dream*. [TSOD2]

Shamble. A shamble can be used as a simple

magic detector and amplifier. It's actually very crude, but it's always useful to make one in times of distress and confusion. It is something a witch makes from items she finds on her person and which she can use to be magical. Rather in the same way that spectacles help you see but don't see for you. Similarly, a telescope is not magical, it's just glass in a tube, but with one you could count the dragons on the moon. And a shamble can act like a bow, too. A bow stores up muscle power as the archer draws it, and sends a heavy arrow much further than the archer could actually *throw* it. In fact a witch can make one out of anything, so long as it… looks right.

With a shamble, for example, you can tell if magic is happening, if that's what you're looking for. When you're good at it you can use it to help you do magic yourself, to really focus on what you have to do. You can use it for protection, like a curse-net, or to send a spell. All young witches should learn how to make a shamble.

Shank, Andy. Son of the Captain of Dimwell Football Club, Ankh-Morpork, and a stone-cold psychopath. He could be quite charming when the frantically oscillating mood swing took him. Often carries a short sword in his calloused hands as he leads his gang, the Massive Posse – Maxie, Jumbo and Carter the Farter (the Fartmeister). [UA]

Sharn, Madame. A dwarf couturier and proprietor of Shatta, in the Maul, Ankh-Morpork. She is also looking to open a shop in Schmaltzberg. Shatta means 'a wonderful surprise'. She is extremely expansive around the waist, and she wears a breastplate so beautifully hammered and ornamented that taking it into battle would be an act of artistic vandalism. She has a voice that sounds like the darkest and most expensive type of dark chocolate, possibly smoked. She has so many rings on each finger you need to look with care to realize that he/she is not wearing a gauntlet. [UA]

Shatter of the Icicle. Lead goblin on a clacks tower in Sto Kerrig. I liked his name – so,

randomly and arbitrarily, he made it into the *Companion*. Also works with Shine on the Moon, who didn't get their own entry. [RS]

Shed of Doom, the. Evil Harry DREAD's modest first fortress, constructed on his allotment when he was just getting started in the Evil Dark Lord business. [TLH]

Sheds. The importance of sheds was first noted in the events of *Making Money*, with those constructed in the Royal MINT. In *The Shepherd's Crown*, though, Geoffrey SWIVEL is taken with the range of sheds he sees as he visits local people. Each one is different, expressing the personality of the occupant, unfettered by female intervention. Some were chaotic, with piles of scrap and half-made objects scattered about; others were tidier, like Captain Makepeace's shed, which was full of paints, brushes and canvases, but still had a clear sense of order. Most had evidence of a work in progress, whether it was a half-made bird table, or a stripped-down wheelbarrow with a new shaft. A notable exception to this was the shed of Laughing Boy SIDEWAYS. [TSC]

Sheepridge. A town in the RAMTOPS, and scene of the annual hiring fair on Hogswatch Eve. Very small – not much more than four sides to a cobbled square, including an ornamental clock tower, lined with shops that provide the service industry of the farming community. [M]

Shep, Three-Legged. Member of the Ankh-Morpork DOG GUILD. [MAA]

Shine, Mr. Troll king – a creature with an analytical mind, made entirely from diamond. He has to wear a black cloak and hood in normal light for fear of blinding people with the reflection from his crystalline body. [T!]

The Shed of Doom

Shoe, Reg. A zombie, former mortuary worker, currently a member of the WATCH, but perhaps most famously the founder of the FRESH START CLUB, whose premises are at 668 Elm Street, Ankh-Morpork. He lodges with Mrs CAKE. It doesn't matter what you say when talking to Reg Shoe, because Reg supplies your side of the conversation from somewhere inside his head.

He has a pallid skin, big protruding eyes and he wears a 'Glad To Be Grey' badge. His clothes look as if they've been washed in razor blades and smell as though someone has not only died in them but is still in them. This is, of course, the case.

Before his death, Reg used to live in Whalebone Lane. In those days, his clothing tended towards the more romantic black trousers, frilly shirt, sash and long, curly hair look, since he was a revolutionary or, rather would have been a revolutionary if any real revolutionary cadre had been insane enough to let him know where they met. Apart from his involvement in the events of *Night Watch*, not much is known about what Reg did when he was alive, but his tireless activities on behalf of the Dead – his Campaign for Dead Rights, his enthusiasm for the Fresh Start Club, his impressive sense of civic responsibility, his loyalty and his endless protest songs played on a guitar (he used to crawl around on the floor looking for his fingers afterwards) – suggest that life for Reg began around the time of death. [RM]

Shops, Wandering. *Tabernae vagrantes.* No one knows why, but all the most truly mysterious and magical items are bought from shops that appear and, after a trading life even briefer than a double-glazing company's, vanish like smoke. They can turn up wherever there is a suitable stretch of blank wall, but once there they *have always been there*; dust and grime and a general worn look instantly dispel any doubts in the minds of people who may have walked down that same street every day for a year without noticing them.

There are three general theories to explain the phenomenon of wandering shops:

1. Many thousands of years ago there evolved somewhere in the multiverse a race whose single talent was to buy cheap and sell dear. Soon they controlled a vast galactic empire or, as they put it, Emporium, and the more advanced members of the species found a way to equip their very shops with unique propulsion units that could break the dark walls of space itself and open up vast new markets. Long after the worlds of the Emporium perished in the heat death of their particular universe (after one defiant fire sale), the wandering star shops still ply their trade, eating their way through the pages of space–time like a worm through a three-volume novel.

2. They are the creation of a sympathetic Fate, charged with the role of supplying exactly the right thing at the right time.

3. They are simply a very clever way of getting around the various Sunday Closing Acts.

All these theories have two things in common: they explain the known facts and they are completely and utterly wrong. (*See also* SKILLET, WANG, YRXLE!YT, BUNGLESTIFF, CWMLAD AND PATEL.) [LF]

Shrucker & Dave. Long-established broomstick business in Ankh-Morpork. Their premises was one of the first ones to relocate into one of the city's new railway arches. [TSC]

Shuwadhi, Ronron. Ronron 'Revelation Joe' Shuwadhi. A Klatchian mystic and creator of the first pizza on the Disc. [M]

Sideney, Mr. A wizard, down on his luck, who ends up doing some work for Mr TEATIME. He attended Gammer Wimblestone's Dame School, where he was mercilessly bullied for having ringlets. [H]

Sideways, Arnold. A beggar in Ankh-Morpork, and member of the Canting Crew. He has no legs, and gets around on a small four-wheeled cart. His lack of legs only serves to give him an extra advantage in any pub fights, where a man with good teeth at groin height has it all his own way. His particular begging technique is to grab people by the knees and say, 'Have you got change for a penny?' – invariably profiting by the ensuing cerebral confusion. [SM]

Sideways, Laughing Boy. An old man once treated for a boil by Tiffany ACHING and Geoffrey SWIVEL. He has lived, for as long as anyone can remember, on his own in a small cottage with a rickety barn that is full of weaponry – souvenirs from many conflicts, and all lovingly oiled and meticulously labelled. He is, indeed, himself a very tidy man – always smartly turned out and dapper. His cottage, too, is immaculately tidy. He has a shed adjacent to his barn. You won't be surprised to read that it, too, is neat; shelves neatly stacked with carefully labelled tobacco jars and tins, and with tools hung on the walls, clean and sharp and neatly ranked by size. [TSC]

Sidney, Dribbling. Member of the BEGGARS' GUILD. [MAA]

Sillitoe, Gastric, Captain. Captain of the *Wonderful Fanny*. His wife is the daughter of Commandant Fournier of the Quirm Watch. This huge man is a first-class river pilot, having a detailed knowledge of one of the Disc's most treacherous rivers, the Quire (Old Treachery). [SN]

Silverfish, Thomas. President of the ALCHEMISTS' GUILD. He also dabbled briefly in the world of moving pictures. Despite being an alchemist, he is a very practical man who prides himself on being far more level-headed and down-to-earth than wizards. He believes that the function of the alchemist is to pursue those goals laid down by the wisdom of antiquity, and whose realization would make human existence so much more bearable – such as immortality and endless supplies of gold. The bane of his life are the Guild apprentices, who fritter away their time playing with lemons and bits of metal and lengths of wire, which can have no possible practical application. [MP]

Simmons, Grabber. A regular at the Mended DRUM. As such, he may have had a drink near RINCEWIND. Possibly. [GG]

Simnel, Dick. Now Sir Dick Simnel. He was brought up at the family smithy in Sheepridge. His father (*see*, possibly, SIMNEL, NED) died in a steam-related accident when Dick was only 10, but this did nothing to reduce the lad's interest in steam and engineering. After his father's death, Dick and his mum, Elsie (who worked as a midwife), moved back to her family home near Sto Lat. Using family money earned from 'fishing', his mum paid for young Dick to have a 'better learning'. Dick constructs the Discworld's first steam railway engine – IRON GIRDER – and this launches him into a successful career as a principal founder of the rail industry. [RS]

Simnel, Ned. Blacksmith in the village near Miss FLITWORTH's farm. He is a young man with black, curly hair, and a face, shirt and apron all black with soot and dirt.

He is by inclination an engineer rather than a farrier, and built the only working Combination Harvester on the Disc. The goal of his life is to find a way of making machines work without the need for horses. However, so far (i.e., up to the end of *Reaper Man*) he has watched a kettle lift its lid and boil over 147 times with no other thought in his head than 'that's a nuisance'. But *see*, potentially, SIMNEL, DICK. [RM]

Simon. An apprentice wizard, but with very good magical potential and an amazing grasp of magical theory.

He was a thin, gangling boy, with a xylophone chest – one of those tall lads apparently made out of knees, thumbs and elbows. He was also in dire need of a decent haircut, subject to hay fever (which gave him a red nose) and he also suffered from a stammer. Nevertheless, even as a first-year student, he amazed his seniors by pushing back the narrow boundaries of ignorance to reveal the wide, rolling vistas of fresh ignorance beyond. Has not been seen for some time. [ER]

Simony, Sergeant. Sergeant in the Divine Legion in OMNIA and a follower of the Turtle Movement. Born in Istanzia. A muscular young man with the deadpan expression of the truly professional soldier. He was, according to BRUTHA, a good man with only one flaw in his nature: he wished to overthrow a corrupt religion that ruled by fire and the sword by even greater fiery sword applications.

Sergeant Simony was made head of the reformed QUISITION by Brutha, with the express remit to wind it up. [SG]

Sisters, the. Two snakes transmogrified by Lily WEATHERWAX into women. As women they are taller than Granny Weatherwax, slender as sticks and wear broad hats with veils and shimmery dresses. Although beautiful, they have no voices and can sit for hours without blinking. Last seen fighting Magrat GARLICK; it was their misfortune that, when cornered like a rat, Magrat fights like a mongoose. [WA]

Six Beneficent Winds. One-time Deputy District Commissioner for the Langtang district. A Collector of Revenues. He is not a wicked man. He has no sense of humour – he plays the accordion for amusement and dislikes cats intensely. He has some irritating habits that annoy Mrs Beneficent Winds. He keeps his money in a small, leather, shovel purse, counting it out thoroughly whenever he makes a purchase, especially if there's a queue behind him. On the other hand, he is kind to animals and makes small but regular donations to charity. He frequently gives modest sums to beggars in the street – though he also makes a note in his little notebook to remind him to visit them in his official capacity later on. He never takes more money than they actually had. [IT]

Size 15. Legionary in the KLATCHIAN FOREIGN LEGION. (For an explanation of his name, *see* COTTON, CORPORAL.) [SM]

Skater, Viscount. A nobleman of Ankh. [MAA]

Skazz. A student wizard at the Unseen University. He looks about seven stone and has a shoulder-length fringe of hair all round his head – it's only the tip of his nose poking out that tells the world which way he's facing. [SM]

Skiller. Landlord of the Fiddler's Riddle in Ohulan Cutash. Too stupid to be really cruel, too lazy to be really mean. He and his thin wife sell only beer, which customers say he gets out of cats. [ER]

Skillet, Wang, Yrxle!yt, Bunglestiff, Cwmlad and Patel. A wandering shop, encountered by RINCEWIND, BETHAN and TWOFLOWER. The proprietor was believed to have given poor service to a sourcerer, and was thus condemned to run a shop for ever. (*See also* SHOPS, WANDERING.) [LF]

Skrp. Large, grey, red-eyed rat. Lives in the Patrician's Palace. [GG]

Slang, Dimwell Arrhythmic Rhyming. Various rhyming slangs are known, and have given the universe such terms as 'apples and pears' (stairs) and 'rubbity-dub' (pub). The Dimwell Street rhyming slang is pretty unique in that it does not, in fact, rhyme. Example – prunes, as in 'syrup of prunes': wig. No one knows why, but some theories so far advanced are: 1) that it is quite complex and in fact follows hidden rules; or 2) Dimwell is well named; or 3) it's made up to annoy strangers – which is the case with most such slangs.

Skimmer, Inigo. A small, neat man in neat but threadbare clothes. His over-large head gave him the appearance of a lolly nearing the last suck. It's not merely that his head was big; it's simply that someone appeared to have squeezed the bottom half of it and forced everything into the top. To make matters look worse, he was also going bald and had carefully teased the remaining strands of hair across the pink dome. He carried his black bowler hat in the way a soldier carries his helmet, and walked like a man who has something wrong with his knees. It was hard to judge his age – he could have been twenty-five and a big worrier, or a fresh-faced forty. He had the look of a man who had spent the whole of his life watching the world over the top of a book. His voice was unremarkable, except for a nervous throat noise which punctuated anything he said. Mr Skimmer worked in Lord VETINARI's offices and was a skilled graduate of the ASSASSINS' GUILD and, effectively, a secret agent. [TFE]

Skindle, Mr. Mr Skindle looked after Granny WEATHERWAX's goats when she was away from home. The Skindles live just up the hill from Nanny OGG. [LL]

Skipps, Henry, Lord. Led the army that defeated the trolls at the Battle of Pseudopolis. [MP]

Slant, Mr. President of the Guild of Lawyers, and a partner in Morecombe, Slant and Honeyplace. A 351-year-old zombie. The most renowned, and certainly the oldest, lawyer in Ankh-Morpork. When he sighs, it is like the wind from an ancient tomb. When he stands, he stands as zombies do, by using pairs of muscles in turn; not so much standing as unfolding upwards. Slant, with his grey pallor and stitched-on head, has spent centuries in courtrooms and is the undisputed expert on Ankh-Morpork law and a hidden hand in many of its affairs. [J] peeling potatoes or plucking geese. She often had a mint in her pocket for a boy who knew his alphabet and could say it backwards. And you had to be grateful to someone who taught you how not to be afraid. [SN]

Slasher, the Steed of Terror. A donkey. Evil Harry DREAD's first mount. Despite his unassuming appearance, he reputedly had a nasty bite and a predilection for fingers. [TLH]

Slick, Billy. A goblin. His real name is Of the Wind Regretfully Blown. He works for Harry King and lives with his granny (Regret of the Falling Leaf) in Ankh-Morpork's shanty town. [SN]

Slightly, Mistress. Sam Vimes was educated at the Dame School run by Mistress Slightly.

Mistress Slightly was everything a dame should be. She was fat, and gave the impression of being made of marshmallows, had a gentle understanding of the fact that the bladders of small boys are almost as treacherous as the bladders of old men, and, in general, taught the basics of the alphabet with a minimum of cruelty and a maximum of marshmallow.

She kept geese, as any self-respecting dame should do. Mistress Slightly certainly had a mob cap and a laugh like rainwater going down a drain. She may even – underneath the endless layers of petticoats – have worn red-and-white spotted drawers,

Invariably, while she took lessons, she was

Slime (1). A lizard man in the employ of Evil Harry DREAD (*see also* SLIME (II)*). [TLH]

Slime (2). A lizard man in the employ of Evil Harry DREAD. [TLH]

Slopes, Snowy. Also called Daceyville Slopes. Slopes was a heavy-set man (a bit bulky for his height), and wore a green coat and new boots. He couldn't read or write and he lodged in rooms over the sweet shop in Money Trap Lane. He didn't wash much, but he used expensive shampoos on his long, dry hair. He suffered mightily from dandruff, hence the nickname 'Snowy'. [J]

---

* *No relation.*

Slugg, Henry. Also known as Enrico Basilica. An operatic tenor of almost wizardly proportions, with a friendly, bearded, small face and a squeaky speaking voice. Henry Slugg grew up in Rookery Yard in the Shades, but he changed his name to Enrico Basilica and his origins from the Shades to Brindisi in order to gain credibility for his stunning singing voice. Frankly, no one is going to pay good money to listen to a tenor called Henry Slugg. [MA]

Slumber, Chas. Children's entertainer in Ankh-Morpork. [TOC]

Small Gods' Eve. Falls on the occasion of first midsummer. [COM]

Smeems, Natchbull. A candle knave at Unseen University. He has the never-ending job of keeping the candlesticks, sconces and candelabra of UU filled. People do not like Mr Smeems. A man could be dogmatic, and that was all right, or he could be stupid, and no harm done, but stupid and dogmatic at the same time was too much, especially fluxed with body odour. [UA]

Smith, Eskarina. *See* ESK.

Smith, Gordo. Blacksmith in BAD ASS. Not very tall (blacksmiths often aren't; it's amazing how many are short, wiry men). The father of ESK. Also father of Jaims, Cern and Gulta. [ER]

Smith, Howondaland. A balgrog hunter. No one knows what a balgrog is, perhaps because he has never actually caught one. During the great day of the Discworld moving picture industry, it was generally accepted as looking like Morry the troll painted green with wings stuck on. [MP]

Smith, John. Count Vargo St Gruet von Vilinus. President of the Ankh-Morpork Mission of the Überwald League of Temperance. He now collects bananas and makes models of human organs out of matchsticks, because he thinks hobbies make you more human. He smokes a pipe and wears a badly hand-knitted pullover – in a queasy zig-zag pattern of strange, unhappy colours. The sort of thing knitted as a present by a colour-blind aunt. The sort of thing you wouldn't dare throw away in case the rubbish collectors laughed at you and kicked your bins over. [T!]

Smith, Thomas. Owner of Stronginthearm's Iron Founders, Beaters and General Forging in Five And Seven Yard, Ankh-Morpork. Not a dwarf by birth, but he has changed his name, grown a beard and taken to wearing an iron helmet in an effort to capitalize on all dwarf craftsmen's reputation for quality. To his scornful delight, the Campaign for Equal Heights (which is run by humans, most dwarfs being too busy to bother with that sort of thing) have fallen out over his case. Some members consider that since he is clearly posing as a dwarf for commercial gain this is an affront to dwarfs worldwide, while others point out that actual height was never mentioned among the definitions of a dwarf in the Campaign's charter, because it was considered sizeist. In the meantime, Thomas Strongintheary is making an extra twenty pence on the dollar. [FOC]

Smoking Gnu. A secret society of three clacks nerds – Mad Al WINTON, Sane Alex CARLTON, Undecided Adrian EMERY. They were a group of outlaw signallers who rented space on the roof of the Ankh-Morpork Post Office. They designed 'The Woodpecker' – a plan to knock out every tower on the Grand Trunk system.

Alex and Al were old men in the clacks business. When Reacher GILT's consortium had taken over, they'd been fired from the Grand Trunk on the same day that Adrian had been fired from the Alchemists' Guild chimney; in their case because they'd spoken their mind about the new management and in his case because he hadn't moved fast enough when the beaker started to bubble.

The trio had done the kind of aimless jobs available to new square pegs in a world of old round holes, but every night, high above, the clacks flashed its messages. It was so close, so inviting, so...*accessible*. Everyone knew, in some vague, half understood way, that the Grand Trunk had been stolen in all but name. So they'd started an informal little company of their own, which used the Grand Trunk without the Grand Trunk knowing.

It was a little like stealing. It was exactly like stealing. It was, in fact, stealing. But there was no law against it because no one knew the crime existed, so is it really stealing if what's stolen isn't missed? And is it stealing if you're stealing from thieves Anyway, all property is theft, except mine. [GP]

Smother, Dolores. Madam of a tent of ill repute on a military encampment in Borogravia. A lumpy, crowlike woman with little beady eyes, wearing black bombazine. [MR]

Snackes, The Joye of. Written by a Lancre Witch (no, not Granny Weatherwax). Well, all right, it was written by Nanny OGG. This tome rapidly became a best-seller due to its, erm, well, *unusual* recipes, which seemed to be able

to achieve improvements in even the dullest of sex-lives. Better-known recipes include:

Banana Soup Surprise
Celery Astonishment
Chocolate Delight with Special Secret Sauce
Cinnamon and Marshmallow Fingers
Famous Carrot and Oyster Pie
Maids of Honour (although they generally end up Tarts)
Nibbles with Special Party Dip
Porridge (with Honey Mixture)
Spotted Dick
Strawberry Wobbler

Fortunately, we are unable to include the illustrations... [MA]

Snapcase, Mad Lord. A past Patrician of Ankh-Morpork. In fact, Lord Snapcase took over from Lord WINDER, and he was from much the same mould, although with fancier waistcoats, and more chins and a snuffbox. [NW]

Snapes, Daisy. Miss Daisy Snapes was officially the first person to be born on a moving train, thanks to a midwife who rushed the mother to the guard's van. Young Daisy was born at thirty miles an hour, and her doting parents named her Locomotion Snapes, until Moist von LIPWIG got to hear about it and gave her and her parents a free season ticket on the railway, along with the suggestion that Locomotion might sound better as a *middle* name. [RS]

Snell, Rebecca. Schoolfriend of Susan STO HELIT, one of whose earliest intimations of immortality was seeing a TOOTH FAIRY by Rebecca's bed. [SM]

Sniddin. An actor in the clicks. [MP]

Snoriscousin, Snori. Leader of Snori Snoriscousin and His Brass Idiots – a traditional dwarf band. [SM]

Snouty. Cecil 'Snouty' Clapman. Past Watchman in Ankh-Morpork. He was the jailer at the Treacle Mine Road Watch House. Snouty was a breathy little man, who survived by keeping his eye on which way the political wind was blowing and by being able to lay his hands on just about anything (there is someone like that in most nicks). He once had his nose broken in a fight, and it was spread all over his face. This incident has left him with permanently watery eyes and with a habit of making a sort of nose-clearing noise when he talks... a bit like 'hnah'. It is very possible that the blow also scrambled his brain. [NW]

Snoxall. A fellow student of TEPPIC's at the ASSASSINS' GUILD. [P]

Soak, Ronald. 'Ronald Soak, Hygienic Dairyman. Established' is painted on the side of his cart. Ronnie is quite short, and his regulation blue-and-white striped apron almost touches the floor. *See also* KAOS. [TOT]

Sock, Gerhardt. A member of the Butchers' Guild, and a master butcher. [MAA]

Soll. See DIBBLER, SOLSTICE.

Songs and Music of the Disc. The nations of the Disc – at least, in those areas so far chronicled – are musically inclined, although their taste is not necessarily commendable. Songs are either traditional folk melodies ('The Hedgehog Song'), cheap popular music of the blow-your-nose-ain't-it-so variety ('Carry Me Away From Old Ankh-Morpork'), or religious songs ('Claws of Iron Shall Rend the Ungodly' and, arguably, anything about gold sung by dwarfs). There are hints of a classic and baroque tradition in Ankh-Morpork, and presumably the opera house must have some raw material, but so far the hints allow no conclusions to be drawn.

Titles recorded are:

All the Little Angels (How Do They Rise Up?) [NW]
Amber & Jasper [MP]
Ankh-Morpork! Ankh-Morpork! So Good They Named it Ankh-Morpork! [RM]
Ankh-Morpork Malady [RM]
Ball of Philodelphus, The [E]
Ballad of Amber and Jasper, The [MP]
Bells of St Ungulant's, The [H]
Bonny Flowers, The [HFOS]
Carry Me Away from Old Ankh-Morpork [RM]
Cavern Deep, Mountain High [SM]
Claws of Iron Shall Rend the Ungodly [SG]
Colonel Crapski [MR]
Columbine Lament, the [TSC]
Devil Shall Be My Sergeant, the [MR]
Dingdong, Dingdong [WA]
Don't Cry for me, Genua [MA]
Don't Tread On My New Blue Boots [SM]
Express Mail Coming Through (Sir Arthur Brady) [POD]
Gathering Rhubarb [SM]
Girl I Left Behind Me, The [MR]
Give Me that Music with Rocks in [SM]
Gold [MAA]
Good Gracious, Miss Polly [SM]
He is Trampling the Unrighteous with Hooves of Hot Iron [SG]
Hedgehog Cakewalk [CJ]
Hedgehog Can Never Be Buggered At All, The [WS]
Hiho Song, The [MP]
Ich Bin Ein Rattarsedschwein (from The

Song Sung Lo, General. Author of 'The Craft of War'. He once moved his army disguised as a field of sunflowers. [MR]

Sonky, Wallace. Ankh-Morpork tradesman and maker of rubber boots and other … goods. Shonky's shop smells of incontinent cats and sulphur, an unfortunate aspect of the chemicals used in his trade. Sonky has a brother in Überwald, who is likely to continue the family business which must, after all, be very profitable. Mr Sonky gave his name to the street term for his 'Penny-a-Packet Preventatives' – a packet of sonkies. These come in an extensive range, including Sonky's Eversure Dependables and Sonky's Ribbed Magical Delights. [TFE]

Soon, Shine Sun. Runs the Shonky Shop in Clay Lane, Ankh-Morpork (a shonky shop being, more or less, the second-hand clothes shop of last resort). He is a small, glossy little man, totally bald, and wears some vague clothing that presumably even a shonky shop hadn't been able to sell. He is, besides, a History MONK of the secret Ankh-Morpork section. [NW]

Soto, Marco. A member of the Ankh-Morpork section of the History MONKS. A heavy young man in a grubby yellow robe and with very long, black hair. Actually, to say that it's black and bound up in a ponytail is to miss the chance to use the word 'elephantine'. It is hair with personality. Master Soto is a hard-working and friendly monk... provided you don't touch his hair. History Monks are supposed to have shaved heads, but Soto argues that, underneath his hair, he is bald. He is the man who found Lobsang LUDD for the Order. [NW]

Soul Cake Days. The first Tuesday, Wednesday and Thursday after the first half-moon in Sektober.

A STO PLAINS/RAMTOPS festival roughly corresponding to the traditional European/North American festivals of Hallowe'en and Bonfire Night. Celebrated both by dwarfs (Bobbing for Trout, Toffee Rats on a Stick) and humans (Trickle-Treating, All-Comers Morris Dancing, and a rather mysterious custom involving the rolling of boiled eggs down the Tump in Ankh-Morpork). In short, a three-day feast and celebration whose origins are lost in the mists of alcohol.

Soul Cake Tuesday Duck, The. A species of magical fauna in the Easter Bunny/Reynard the Fox league, possibly associated with the fact that Soul Cake Tuesday is the opening of the duck-hunting season. The sighting of the first duck on Soul Cake Tuesday is considered very lucky, except, of course, for the duck.

Sound of the Rain on Hard Ground. An old goblin from the mound close to Ramkin Hall. Widower of The Pleasant Contrast of the Orange and Yellow Petals in the Flower of the Gorse. Names such as hers are one of the many reasons why goblins don't wear identity badges. [SN]

Soup II. Mad King Soup II. Past king of Lancre. He had a mistress, Mme Cupidor. [LL]

Sourcerer. A type of super-wizard; one who can create magic rather than simply utilize it. *See* MAGIC.

Specials, the. Technically, the Citizens' Militia. Made up of men who could be coppers at times of dire need but who are generally disqualified from formal Watch membership by reason of shape, profession, age or – sometimes – brain. [T!]

Spells. A spell can be thought of as a kind of mental pill, containing all the ingredients necessary for achieving its purpose. Spells are short cuts, the results of tireless experimentation by wizards in the past. A wizard wishing to change the shape of some living thing could, of course, start from first principles and carefully work out how to do it; but he will generally use Stacklady's Morphic Resonator, for example, simply because it is tried and tested.

A spell, once memorized, will remain in the wizard's head until it gets said or he dies, in which case it auto-casts itself, with unpredictable results.

A spell takes up quite a lot of mental space. For instance, RINCEWIND, in possession of one of the Great Spells, was unable to memorize any others at all. The fact that he had never been able to do so before this happened is beside the point.

Many deceased wizards are remembered by the spells they have added to Unseen University's grimoire.

Spelter. Fifth-level wizard and former bursar of Unseen University. A tall and wiry man, he looked as though he'd been a horse in previous lives and only just avoided it in this one. Killed for trying to prevent the LIBRARY's destruction during the brief reign of COIN. [S]

Spent, Mrs. Landlady of the boarding house in Market Street where Ossie BRUNT stayed during the events of *Jingo*. [J]

Sphinx, The. An unreal and therefore chronically bad-tempered creature, with the body of a lion, the bosom of a woman and the wings of an eagle. It lurks on the dimensional borders of DJELIBEYBI. [P]

Spigot, William. An old farm worker with skin like leather. He helps out with the harvest at Miss Flitworth's. He is also known for his folk singing and fiddle-playing. [RM]

Spircle. A low-value chameleon gemstone that can take on the hue of real gemstones when put in a bag with them. Spircles are mined from the mountains near BAD ASS. [ER]

Spold, Greyhald. A wizard of the Ancient and Truly Original Sages of the Unbroken Circle. In his day, he was the oldest wizard and determined to remain so. He tried, unsuccessfully, to find a place impregnable by DEATH, and built a dense and magically protected box that nothing whatsoever could penetrate. This included, as he became briefly aware, any air molecules (the last words he ever heard were DARK IN HERE, ISN'T IT...?). [LF]

Spolwhittle. Author of the Trans-Congruency Theory. [UA]

Spools. The kind, and enthusiastic, proprietor of Teemer & Spools in Ankh-Morpork. The company is a quality printer who produced the Discworld's first postage stamps. Teemer & Spools have gone up in the world because of the big stamp contract. They've always done the best printing work in any case, but now they

have the men and muscle to bid for all the big contracts. [GP]

Spriggins. Mr Spriggins is the butler at Lancre Castle. He has a bad memory, a nervous twitch and a rubber knee. [LL]

Spudding, Mrs. Lives in New Cobblers, Ankh-Morpork, is seventy-five years old and has a fine set of wooden teeth. She's the cleaner at the Pink Pussycat Club. [T!]

Spuds, Hoggy. An old army pal of Sergeant COLON. [MAA]

Staffs, wizards'. Wizards in foreign parts may think they can get away with a crystal ball and some magic scarves, but what an Unseen University wizard expects to find in his hand is six feet of good solid oak or ash – or even SAPIENT PEARWOOD, if he is lucky – as a repository and storehouse of personal magic, a walking aid and, if necessary, a weapon. As the current ARCHCHANCELLOR of UU has pointed out in his robust way, what cannot be stopped by the magic in a staff can often be brought short by a good poke in any available soft bits with a length of heavy timber.

Most staffs in use today are quite venerable, having been handed down from wizard to wizard for perhaps hundreds of years, and in very extreme cases – the staff possessed by Drum BILLET and subsequently by Eskarina Smith (*see* ESK), for example – can be so imbued with magic as to have lives of their own.

A wizard will treat his staff with respect, taking care to top up its power every day and then give it a good polish, paying particular attention to the knob on the end. The fact that there is a popular song about said knob is deeply puzzling to wizards. 'So what?' they say, 'staffs have always had knobs on. What's funny about that? It's just the tool of our trade. It's nothing to joke about.'

The knobs may be ornate jewellery, a complicated piece of sculpture, a music box or even a small, polished container handy for some matches and a packet of fags. Sometimes, such artificial additions are not required because the staff grows its own knob, a growth rather like the 'knees' grown by the American swamp cypress. Because this gall is the wood's response to the magic within it, it can take many forms – the face of the wizard himself, or an object dear to him, or even stranger things...

Staffs made of metal are occasionally tried. They are efficient, but somehow the magic always seems to change for the worse.

Stamp, Miss. Teaches maths at the Quirm College for the Young Ladies. [SM]

Standards, Ankh-Morporkian. Obviously, any civilization needs some way of standardizing weights and measures and time. In modern times, for example, an official unit of measurement is likely to be a length of metal bar kept at a precise temperature, or some reproducible count based on atomic decay or the speed of light.

The old Ankh-Morpork Bureau of Measures in the Barbican still performs this role for a large part of the Discworld, but less so for its common units of measurement (which in any case have been filed down, soldered on to, drilled and had bits of chewing gum stuck to them on too many occasions) than for its more esoteric ones, a legacy of the precise-minded Patrician Olaf QUIMBY.

Here, for example, may be found the *exact* Blunt Stick, a crude but effective measurement of the acceptability of just about anything; it is *this* Blunt Stick* that the test object may, or may not, be better than. Although the official Pie that that the test object may even be as nice as is not maintained here, there is a standardized recipe readily available. Also, kept in a glass cabinet, are the original Two Short Planks and the stone used in the original Moss-Gathering trials.

Bureau officials still maintain a small programme of tests of, for instance, the degree of similarity of any two peas or the alcoholic tendencies of newts. It is vital, as the current PATRICIAN has noted, that something like this is found for people with minds like that to do, otherwise they might do *anything*.

Standing Stone, The. Stands on the crest of the moor in the RAMTOPS. It is the same height as a tall man and is made of bluish tinted rock. It is considered to be intensely magical because, although there is only one of it, no one has ever been able to count it. If it sees anyone looking at it speculatively, it shuffles behind them and, in extreme cases, goes and hides in the peat bogs. It is also one of the numerous discharge points for the magic that accumulates in the Ramtops. [WS]

Standish, Milly, Miss. Soon to be Mrs Robinson. A young girl, who gave birth to triplets, assisted by Tiffany Aching. They were two boys, and a girl – named Tiffany. She was briefly stolen by elves – but that's another tale. [TSC]

Stank. A mountain village. You might think that a name like Stank would put people off. But, in fact, it had once been a very popular place for tourists. They liked to send messages home saying, 'We're stinking in Stank'. And then go home with presents for their loved ones like tunics with 'I've been to Stank and all I've brought home is this stinking tunic' written on them.

Alas for them, with the coming of the railways – or in the case of Stank, the not coming of the railways – tourists began to go elsewhere, and Stank was now gradually disappearing into the mud, surviving mostly by taking in washing. [TSC]

---

* *Originally a Sharp Stick was installed, but extensive tests found that few things were worse than a poke in the eye with it.*

Stanley, Apprentice Postman. Later, Head of Stamps. Young man who works at the Ankh-Morpork Post Office. He is an orphan from the Siblings of Offler Charity Home, both his parents having died of Gnats on their farm out in the wilds. He was raised by peas until the home took him in. He is a good lad, if he doesn't get upset, and he once was quite obsessional about pins – he even edited 'Total Pins'. When we first meet him, he has a blue cotton shirt with the legend 'Ask Me About Pins'.

When he stands to attention, his right side stands considerably more to attention than his left side. He stands like a banana, with a huge nervous grin and big, gleaming eyes – he radiates keenness, quite probably beyond the bounds of sanity.

When he later becomes Head of Stamps, he then sports a T-shirt with 'Ask Me About Stamps' on it. [GP]

Stibbings, Reginald. A reporter for the 'Ankh-Morpork TIMES'. He lives at Loose Chippings, Dolly Sisters, Ankh-Morpork. He has a very young mistress who formally worked at the Pink PussyCat Club. [RS]

Stibbons, Ponder. Originally a fellow student wizard with Victor TUGELBEND at Unseen University and also known, to his UU colleagues, as Poncy Stibbons and Stibbo. He graduated by getting Victor's rigged exam paper in error (which had one question – Name?). Originally rather lazy by nature, he seems to have blossomed to become the youngest and most depressingly keen member of the UU faculty. He is now the Head of Inadvisably Applied Magic, as well as Reader in Invisible Writings and Praelector of UU. However, as one of the few wizards at the University with his head screwed on in any fashion, he now seems, quite against his will, to be in the front line. He has discovered too late that he has the unfortunate defect of a logical mind and an incipient desire to understand the Universe. He is in some way the creator of HEX, the UU computer, although now Hex appears to be self-creating.

Every organization needs at least one person who knows what's going on and why it's happening and who's doing it, and at UU this role was filled by Stibbons, who often wished it wasn't. He does all the jobs that involve paperwork, everything that requires even a modicum of effort and responsibility. Ponder now sees it as his mission in life to stoke the fires that keep Mustrum Ridcully bubbling and make the University a happy place. As a dog reflects the mood of its owner, so a university reflects its Master. As the University's sole self-confessed entirely sensible person, his job is to steer things as best he can, and to find ways of keeping the Archchancellor too occupied to get under his feet.

He now has twelve jobs at UU, including the posts of Master of the Traditions and Camerlengo. This means that if the Archchancellor drops dead, from any cause other than legitimate succession under the Dead Man's Pointy Shoes tradition, he runs UU until a successor is elected which, given the nature of wizardry, could mean a job for life.

Ponder once played third goblin in his school play. [MP]

Stinky. A goblin from the caves close to Ramkin Hall. He is as skinny as a skeleton and, like most goblins, looks like a cross between a wolf and an ape, sounds like a bag of walnuts being jumped on, and smells like... Well, it's more a sensation like your dental enamel is being evaporated and any armour you have is rusting at some speed. [SN]

Stitched, Reynold, Sir. Curator of Fine Art at the Royal Art Museum, Ankh-Morpork. A tall, thin figure, with the attitude of a preoccupied chicken. [T!]

Sto Helit, Duke of. Original motto: 'Faber Est Qvisqve Fortvnae Svae'. Original coat of arms: a boar's head, sable, on a field, argent.

A man with a little moustache and a grin like a lizard. Not the nicest of people, since he was quite capable of killing all who stood between him and the throne of Sto Helit, or even between him and the drinks cabinet. He murdered his way close to the throne of STO LAT and was only prevented from killing Princess KELI, the last barrier to his accession, by the actions of MORT. [M]

Sto Helit, Susan. Daughter of MORT and YSABELL, and granddaughter of DEATH, from whom she has inherited a number of traits (this should be impossible, since Ysabell was adopted, but *see* GENETICS).

A self-possessed and somewhat chilly young woman. As a pupil at the QUIRM COLLEGE FOR YOUNG LADIES, she was good at those sports that involved swinging some sort of stick (hockey, lacrosse, rounders) and she was academically brilliant at the things she liked doing. But brilliant, though, like a diamond – all edges and coldness, as it were. It is noteworthy that the only other pupils she even vaguely considered friends were a dwarf and a troll, both in some way 'outcasts' from normal school society. She had – and has – the ability to make herself so inconspicuous as to be invisible to non-magical minds (a definite family attribute).

She is attractive, in a skinny way, and while still quite young has an indefinable air of age about her. Her hair is pure white apart from a black streak. Initially it was uncontrollable, but now it tends to follow her mood, re-styling itself into a tight bun or a ponytail or whatever other shape suits the occasion (this is clearly a by-product of all the other talents she has 'inherited' from her grandfather, although Death himself needs few tonsorial attentions other than the occasional moment with a duster). She moves like a tiger and she has a most disconcerting Look – cool and calm but

Susan Sto Helit

not something you'd want to see twice.

On Susan's face is a birthmark, which shows up only when she blushes, or when she is angry, and these days she is angry far more frequently than she is embarrassed. It takes the form of three pale lines across her cheek (Discworld students will recall that her father was once slapped across the face by Death, leaving just such a mark – Discworld 'inheritance' at work again, it seems).

When she is covering for her grandfather she wears a black lace dress of the sort worn by healthy yet necronerdic young women who want to look consumptive. She currently works as a schoolteacher and is a remarkably effective one. Because of her own rather special upbringing (her parents, although very caring, avoided the whole 'magical childhood fantasy' business in an ultimately useless effort to shield her from the influence of her grandfather) she tends to treat children as inconveniently small adults and to her amazement this works very well.

Unlucky with boys (or, perhaps, lucky, depending on your point of view – in any case, relationships don't seem to last). [SM]

Sto Lat. A walled city kingdom, twenty miles hubwards of Ankh-Morpork, clustered around a castle built on a rock outcrop that pokes up out of the STO PLAINS like a geological pimple. It is a huge stone from the distant RAMTOPS, which was left there by retreating glaciers.

Its younger citizens consider it to be boring and, indeed, its night life is not as colourful and full of incident as that of Ankh-Morpork, in the same way that a wastepaper basket cannot compete with a municipal tip. On fire. In the rain. [M]

Stollop, Juliet. Daughter of the Captain of the Dollies Football Club, Ankh-Morpork. She lives in Dolly Sisters (of course), with her father and her brothers Billy and Algernon. Her mother is dead. Juliet (Jools) is very short, but she is so beautiful that boys get nervous and occasionally faint as she passes. Although she is beautiful, with milky blue eyes, and she doesn't

have a nasty bone in her body, she is not very bright – her head is not exactly overcrowded. She is dumb about everything. She is, however, (sadly) the brains of the Stollop family. [UA]

Stoner, William. A solicitor and Clerk to the Magistrates in the village close by Ramkin Hall. Bit of a country dresser in his fantailer hat and jodhpurs. [SN]

Sto Plains. A rich country, full of silt and rolling cabbage fields, and neat little kingdoms whose boundaries wriggle like snakes as small, formal wars, marriage pacts, complex alliances and the occasional bit of sloppy cartography change the political shape of the land.

The thick, black loam of the Sto Plains has been constructed over aeons by the periodic flooding of the great, slow ANKH, and every bit of it has at some time travelled along someone's alimentary canal. [M]

Stowley. A financial adviser from Ankh Futures. He was also on the Board of the Grand Trunk Company. [GP]

Strappi, Corporal. A greasy little corporal in the Borogravian army. The sort of person who puts a damper on everything. Described by one of his colleagues as a 'cross-grained little bugger'. He later rises, for a while, to the rank of captain in the political division. [MR]

Stratford. A nutjob and a knife cove. Worked for the young Lord Rust. What does he look like? Well, he's sort of average height. To tell you the truth, he sort of looks like everyone else. Until he gets angry. And *that* is when he looks like Stratford. Mr Stratford is the kind of maniac who will keep going in suicidal circumstances. [SN]

Street Theatre (prohibition of). Street theatre and mime artistry are banned in Ankh-Morpork under one of the strictest city ordinances (fire-eaters and jugglers are considered acceptable, provided they are good at it and can pass the exam; in the case of jugglers, this consists of juggling six razor-sharp knives and a live cat. It is seldom necessary to take the exam a second time.)

The unusually inflexible rule has led to the development of street theatre as a criminal activity, and those who feel inexorably drawn to looking like a dumb tit in white make-up or hectoring people while doing something dull with a diabolo live a desperate existence outside the law. Many of them have more mundane jobs as a cover, but they can be spotted by their tendency to unicycle when they think no one is looking.

If caught, they are imprisoned and tortured, usually by being put in a cell with one another (although scorpions also often feature). No one is certain why the PATRICIAN, who has a relaxed approach to assassins and thieves, has this particular quirk, but the citizens of Ankh-Morpork seem quite happy to accept it.

Strewth. An opal miner in XXXX who found the LUGGAGE in a mine. [TLC]

Strippers' Guild. Motto: *NVMQVAM VESTIMVS.* Coat of arms: enlevé.

Officially, the Guild of Ecdysiasts, Nautchers, Cancanières and Exponents of Exotic Dance. This small, all-female and mainly human guild is located in SoSo Street, SoSo. Its members are hard-working women, especially at lunchtimes; Ankh-Morpork is in many respects an unreconstructed society and removing one's clothes for money is considered perfectly acceptable, although doing it for nothing would be considered immoral.

Dwarfs have no grasp of the basic idea, since removing any item of clothing except in the direst emergency is quite foreign to them, and there are no dwarf members. Trolls, however, form a small but vital part of the membership, although the troll outlook on life, their habit of going around more or less naked in any case and their unusual grasp of the nature of time all mean that a troll stripper actually dons more clothes as the dance progresses, often causing a riot as the fourth overcoat goes on.

The Guild president for life – and, indeed, the entire committee – is Miss Dixie 'VaVa' Voom, now officially retired from the stage, along with Edward the snake, but still taking a very active part in the Guild's training programme. Her farewell performance in the Skunk Club, Brewer Street, resulted in three heart attacks, a riot and five separate fires; as she tells her trainees, 'It's not what you've got but what you do with it that counts.'

Stronginthearm, Abba. Enlisted into the city militia by CARROT. [MAA]

Stronginthearm, Bjorn. A dwarf. Carrot Ironfoundersson's great-uncle. [GG]

Stronginthearm, Zakzak. Dwarf proprietor of a magical emporium in Sallet Without – he sells everything for the modern witch from his low-ceilinged, dark shop. [HFOS]

Stygium. It's called a metal, but it's thought to be a magically constructed alloy. The dwarfs sometimes find it in the Loko region, and it is extremely expensive. It is usually only of interest to those who, by inclination or lifestyle, move in darkness –and also, of course, to those who find a life without danger hardly worth living. It can kill, you see. In direct sunshine it heats within a few seconds to a temperature that will melt iron. No one know why.

Occasionally there is a fad among young assassins for stygium rings. Classically, they wear an ornate black glove over the ring during the day. [MM]

Sugarbean, Glenda. Head of the Night Kitchen at Unseen University. She is an excellent cook, famed for her pies, and is the legendary inventor of the famous Ploughman's Pie. She lives up Dolly Sisters and has a generous nature – she cooks breakfast every day for a neighbour, the Widow Crowdy, for example. In her spare time she sells cosmetics. She has a soft spot, indicated by her love of romantic novels, and by her elderly (three-eyed) teddy bear, Mr Wobble.

She is not very tall, and a homely woman – but quite a nice home, clean and decent and with roses round the door and a welcome on the mat and an apple pie in the oven. She is pleasant-looking, but she has a bosom intended for a girl two feet taller. [UA]

Summoning of Dragons, The. A dangerous book by Tubal de MALACHITE. It was kept in the LIBRARY of Unseen University until it was stolen and used by LUPINE WONSE to unleash a noble dragon upon Ankh-Morpork. Upon its recovery, the book was returned to the archives of UU, slightly foxed and extremely dragoned. [GG]

Sumpkins. Nanny OGG's grandma's lodger. [WA]

Sumtin. A philosophical system from Klatch. A sub-sect of Sumtin is Zen. [WA]

Sun, Place Where It Does Not Shine. This has been firmly located near Slice, LANCRE, where it is coincidentally between a rock and a hard place.

It is, as its name suggests, a deep, dark hole under an overhang so that even heavy Discworld light cannot find its way into it. The people of Slice, considered crazed even by Lancre standards, occasionally lower one of their number to prospect for the items that turn up there – usually workmen's tools, musical instruments and unpopular jobs.

This geographical anomaly serves to illustrate the unusual role of metaphor and colourful language on the Discworld. As another example, the curiobiological museum in Unseen University contains, among even stranger things, The One That Has Bells On (preserved in formaldehyde) and the original Horse You Rode In On (stuffed).

Sunshine Sanctuary for Sick Dragons. Located in Morphic Street, Ankh-Morpork. Outside is a small and hollow and pathetic papier mâché dragon, holding a collection box, chained very heavily to the wall and bearing the sign 'Don't Let My Flame Go Out'.

There is a big sign scrawled over the big double gates: 'Here Be Dragons'. A brass plaque besides the gates reads: 'The Ankh-Morpork Sunshine Sanctuary for Sick Dragons'.

There is also yet another, smaller sign: 'Please Leave Donations of Coal by Side Door'.

The building has very, very thick walls and a very, very lightweight roof, a method of construction found elsewhere only in firework factories.

All these things are clues, you might say, to

the fact that the Sanctuary is a home for lost or strayed or abandoned swamp dragons. There tend to be more of the latter every day. There is occasionally a vogue for keeping young swamp dragons as pets, or even as cigarette lighters, but the charm wears off as the creatures grow and their essential dragonishness manifests itself in corroded carpets and big burn marks on the walls. Many are simply abandoned, and if they are lucky, end up at the Sanctuary.

This charity is run by Rosie Devant-Molie, with the very regular help of Lady Sybil Ramkin (now VIMES). Much of the actual work is done by a group of betrousered upper-class young women, described by that class warrior His Grace Commander Sir Samuel VIMES, Duke of Ankh, as 'the INTERCHANGEABLE EMMAS'.

Supreme Grand Master. Leader of the Unique and Supreme Lodge of the ELUCIDATED BRETHREN OF THE EBON NIGHT. (*See also* WONSE, LUPINE.) [GG]

Swine Town. A place on the outskirts of Sto Lat, named for the large numbers of pigs in the area. Location for Dick SIMNEL's railway workshops in the events of *Raising Steam*. [RS]

Swing, Findthee, Captain. Principal officer of the original CABLE STREET PARTICULARS. He was a small, thin, pale man with the screwed-up eyes of a pet rat. He looks like a clerk, a look reinforced by his lank hair – thick black strands plastered across a central bald spot. He is rumoured to have a weak chest. He moved as he talked, in a curious mix of speeds, as if he had no sense of timing.

Captain Swing trained at the ASSASSINS' GUILD and had too much brain to be a copper – at least, too much of the wrong kind of brain. However, he had impressed the then Patrician, Lord WINDER, was allowed into the WATCH as a sergeant and was promoted immediately to captain. His attitude was not: 'This is how people are, how do we deal with it?' He went instead for: 'This is how people ought to be, how do we change them?' Captain Swing invented craniometrics – the science of judging whether people do or do not have criminal tendencies by taking detailed measurements of the shape and conformation of the heads and faces. He usually carried a sword cane, steel ruler and steel callipers, the latter two to allow him to measure people he met. [NW]

Swires, Buggy, Corporal. A gnome, first met during the events of *The Light Fantastic*. He lived in a mushroom with a red-and-white spotted cap and little doors and windows. He is barely six inches high, picks his nose and looks like someone who smells like someone who lives in a mushroom. He is now a corporal in the Ankh-Morpork City WATCH. He is the Head, and only member, of its Airborne Division, flying with the aid of his buzzard, Morag, who was trained by pictsies and bought for him, by the Watch, for a crate of whisky. He has an inbuilt resistance to rules – not just the law, but also to those invisible rules such as 'Do not attempt to eat this giraffe'. [LF]

Swivel, Geoffrey. Third son of Lord Swivel, to whom he was a big disappointment. He is a vegetarian, who is not at all keen on blood sports. He further fails to match up to the standards expected of an offspring of the Swivel family by being keen on learning and reading, and by his love of watching wildlife and observing people.

Geoffrey travels with his highly intelligent goat, MEPHISTOPHELES.

Geoffrey has a knack for resolving conflicts. He wants to be a witch and he works, briefly, for Tiffany ACHING as back-house boy, and she recognizes his natural skill as a 'calm weaver'.

He assists Tiffany greatly in her burgeoning career, and becomes intrigued by the concept, and benefits, of SHEDS for men – the man shed. [TSC]

Swivel, Harold, Lord. An intolerant and bigoted nobleman, who lives in a mansion in the Shires, surrounded by acres of parkland, and accessed by a long drive. His father inherited money, and the title, from his father – a great master builder. But Harold's father was a great drunkard, who wasted almost all of it.

Harold, the current Lord Swivel, wheeled and dealed to restore the family fortune, adding two wings to the mansion. He has three sons – Harry, the eldest (who deals with the estate), Hugh (a clergyman in the Church of Om) and Geoffrey (*see* SWIVEL, GEOFFREY). [TSC]

'The Nac Mac Feegles feel the truth is so precious that it shouldn't be waved
about too much…'

– I Shall Wear Midnight

Tacticus, General. His intelligent campaigning was so successful that he has given his name to the detailed prosecution of martial endeavour. [CJ]

Tailor. A weaver in Lancre. Member of the Lancre Morris Men. [LL]

Tak. Dwarf deity and writer of the dwarf laws. To quote from dwarf writings:
The first thing Tak did, he wrote himself.
The second thing Tak did, he wrote the Laws.
The third thing Tak did, he wrote the World.
The fourth thing Tak did, he wrote a cave.
The fifth thing Tak did, he wrote a geode, an egg of stone.
And in the twilight of the mouth of the cave, the geode hatched and the Brothers were born.
The first Brother walked towards the dark, and stood under the open sky. Thus he became too tall. He was the first Man. He found no Laws, and he was enlightened.
The second Brother walked towards the darkness, and stood under a roof of stone. Thus he achieved the correct height. He was the first Dwarf. He found the Laws Tak had written, and he was endarkened.
Then Tak looked upon the stone and it was tryng to come alive, and Tak smiled and wrote: all things strive. And for the service the stone had given he fashioned it into the first Troll, and delighted in the life that came unbidden.
These are the things that Tak Wrote. [T!]

Tantony, Captain. Captain of the Bonk City Watch, in his uniform of shiny breast plate, 'silly' helmet and un-nicked sword. He is an agonizingly logical young man but also fair and ethical. [TFE]

Tanty, The. Ankh-Morpork's principal, and oldest, prison building, whose very mention chilled the blood of criminals throughout and beyond Ankh-Morpork. It was at one time the Palace de Tintement, ancestral home of the Duc de Tintement.
It is a dark, damp edifice with no fresh air,

food or water, and so will probably remind you of home. Everything has to be bought from the warders, including the lice (which must be handed back when you leave).
Convicted criminals will probably spend most of their time in the Sallydancy, the huge communal cell, where they will meet friends old and new. It's a tough life, but they will have an opportunity to improve their skills, and in fact the THIEVES' GUILD runs extensive courses there.
Those with extra cash can hire a cell in the Crush Yard, where for little more than the price of mansion in Park Lane they can enjoy a warm fire, clean sheets and food that has not been spat in. [TGD]

Tawnee. Betty. A pole dancer at the Pink Pussycat Club, Ankh-Morpork, and one-time girlfriend of Nobby Nobbs. She is almost six feet tall, with a prominent chest. While Tawneee has a body that every other woman should hate her for, she is actually very likeable. This is because she has the self-esteem of a caterpillar and, as you found after any kind of conversation with her, about the same amount of brain. Perhaps it all balances out, perhaps some kindly god had said to her: 'Sorry, kid, you are going to be thicker than a yard of lard, but the good news is, that's not going to matter.'
And she has a stomach made of iron. Alcohol doesn't seem to go to her head at all. Maybe it can't find it. But she is pleasant, easygoing company, if you avoid allusion, irony, sarcasm, repartee, satire and words longer than 'chicken'. [T!]

Tazikel. A Klatchian animal dealer. [MP]

Tear of Offler. The biggest diamond in the world, weighing 850 carats. Used to be kept in the innermost sanctuary of the Lost Jewelled Temple of Doom of OFFLER the Crocodile God in darkest HOWONDALAND. All Offlian temples have a Tear of greater or lesser size, and they are stolen on a regular basis. This particular one was picked up after the Harvest Dance at SHEEPRIDGE and given to his daughter by William SPIGOT, who reasoned that any gem that big had to be glass. [RM]

Tears of the Mushroom. A young teenage goblin girl, and star pupil of Miss Felicity BEEDLE. Despite her prognathous jaw, she is a handsome girl. Not exactly pretty, with her odd, fat, pale face – but she looks like a piece of fragile porcelain. She plays the harp exquisitely. [SN]

Teatime, Jonathan. Student at the ASSASSINS' GUILD. He preferred his surname to be pronounced Teh-ah-tim-eh. He was a very thin young man, with a friendly, pink and white face topped by curly hair. He was quite pretty, in a boyish sort of way, although this effect was spoiled by his eyes: one was a ball of grey glass, as a result of some childhood accident, and the real one had a small, sharp pupil. Mr Teatime saw things differently from other people, in that he saw other people as things. He lost both his parents at an early age, in a tragic accident that occurred while they were leaning over his playpen. In a student assassin, this might have been considered prescient.

He had a truly brilliant mind, but brilliant like a fractured mirror – all marvellous facets and rainbows but, ultimately, something that is broken. [H]

Temperance, Überwald League of. This new society for reformed vampires (Black Ribboners) exists to further the cause of temperance and of total abstinence from drinking human blood ('zer Old Vays'), to provide recreation and means of social intercourse for its members, and to assist members, by means of meetings, lectures, discussions, sing-songs and healthy refreshing cocoa, to help one another refrain from the Old Vays. Branches first opened in Überwald, but have quickly spread to Ankh-Morpork.

Tento. Keeper of ParaMountain before Deccan RIBOBE. [MP]

Teppic. Pteppic. Son of King TEPPICYMON XXVII and 1,398th monarch of DJELIBEYBI.

His father shocked the country's priesthood by sending his son away to be trained at the Assassins' School in Ankh-Morpork, since he had heard that it gave a very good education; the priesthood were very much against any kind of secular education for someone who would one day be a god.

After many adventures, Teppic returned to his own country and acceded to the throne and then abdicated in favour of the handmaiden PTRACI. [P]

Teppicymon XXVII. 1,397th monarch of DJELIBEYBI. TEPPIC's father. Also known as Pootle (by his grandmother). A pleasant and intelligent man who was therefore entirely unsuited to be king of that sombre kingdom.

Teppic

He died in an accident when he thought he could fly. It is a well-known fact that too much intelligence in a monarch is a bad thing for all concerned. [P]

Terton. A lengthman on the Circumfence. Lived in a hut built on wooden piles driven into the sea bed. He collected salvage for Krull along the 45th length of their Circumfence. As a result of his encounter with the LUGGAGE, he developed hydrophobia and went to live in the Great Nef. [COM]

Tethis. A sea troll. A lengthman for KRULL. He originally came from the water world of Bathys, but was first encountered in a driftwood shanty on a crag on the Rim of the world. Through the shanty passed a rope leading to the 10,000-mile-long net that runs along the CIRCUMFENCE to catch the salvage arriving at the Rim.

Tethis was a rather squat (although his height altered with the tides) but not entirely ugly old troll composed of water and little else. He was a pleasant translucent blue colour, with cold, fishy breath and a voice that made people think of submarine chasms and things lurking in coral reefs.

He briefly left the Disc with TWOFLOWER and RINCEWIND and has not been heard of since. The POTENT VOYAGER, the ship on which

they reluctantly travelled, eventually landed in a lake near Skund. Presumably he is still there. [COM]

Tewt, 'Lofty'. A volunteer to the Borogravian army. Tewt is short (petite), dark and dark haired, and with a strange, self-absorbed look. Very close to 'Tonker' Manickle. A bit of a pyromaniac and is good with explosives. Was treated very badly when younger. A past pupil at the Girls Working School, where he/she was known as Tilda. [MR]

Tez. Tez the Terrible. A student wizard at the Unseen University. [SM]

Tezuman Empire. (Kingdom of Tezuma.) The people are renowned for being the most suicidally gloomy, irritable and pessimistic you could ever hope to avoid meeting.

The Tezumen invented the wheel, but didn't put it to its right use. As a result, their chariots, which are pulled by llamas, have two people running along each side, holding up the axles. The wheel itself is used as headgear and jewellery.

Nor have the Tezumen discovered paper, or even wax tablets. Their pictographic language is chiselled into blocks of granite, allowing the more depressed members of the tribe to beat themselves to death with their own suicide notes.

The country is known for its organic market gardens, exquisite craftsmanship in obsidian, feathers and jade, and its mass sacrifices in honour of QUEZOVERCOATL. Their music sounds like someone clearing a particularly difficult nostril. [E]

Thargum I. Red-bearded past king of LANCRE. When he was killed (poisoned by the father of VERENCE I) they stuck his head on a pole and carried it around the village to show that he was dead, an exercise that everyone thought was very convincing. Then they had a big bonfire and everyone in the palace got drunk for a week. No one remembers now whether Thargum was particularly good or bad. Lancre people are traditionalists and aren't choosy about their monarchs, but the greatest sin an incumbent of the throne can commit is not acting like a proper king. [WS]

Thaum. The basic and traditional unit of magical strength. It has been universally established as the amount of magic needed to create one small white pigeon or three normal-sized billiard balls (a smaller measure for purposes of calculation is the millithaum). A thaumometer is used to measure the density of a magical field. It is a dark blue glass cube, with a dial on the front and a button on the side.

In Unseen University's High Energy Magic building the thaum has been successfully demonstrated to be made up of resons (lit: 'thing-ies') or reality fragments. Current research indicates that each reson is itself made up of a combination of at least five 'flavours', known as 'up', 'down', 'sideways', 'sex appeal' and 'peppermint'.

Students at UU have discussed the possibility of the power to be gained from splitting the thaum on an industrial basis, but were dissuaded by their superiors on the grounds that this would make the place untidy. In the event, wizards being wizards, it was just this sort of experimentation which led unwittingly to the ROUNDWORLD PROJECT. (*See also* PRIME.)

Thaumaturgists. Many spells require things like mould from a corpse dead of crushing, or the semen of a living tiger, or the root of a plant that gives an ultrasonic scream when it is uprooted. Who is sent to get them? Right.

Thaumaturgists receive no magical schooling. They can just about be trusted to wash out an alembic. They are the lowest rung of the hierarchy of magical practitioners – apart from witches, of course. That's the wizards' view. [ER]

Thieves' Guild. Motto: *ACVTVS ID VERBERAT* ('Whip it quick'). Coat of arms: a shield with alternate bars of sable and argent. On it a bourse, coupé.

Originally known as the Guild of Thieves, and then the Guild of Thieves, Cutpurses, Housebreakers and Allied Trades, and latterly the Guild of Thieves, Burglars and Allied Trades, purse-cutting having fallen out of favour.

Despite its pretensions to ghastly brigandage and claims to venerable antiquity – based on a perceived descent from the ancient gangs that roamed the city – the Guild is a young and very respectable body which, in a practical sense, represents the major law enforcement agency in Ankh-Morpork.

The Guild is given an annual quota which represents a socially acceptable level of thefts and muggings, and in return sees to it in very definite and final ways that unofficial crime is not only stamped out but also knifed, garrotted, dismembered and left around the city in an assortment of paper bags. In keeping the lid on unofficial crime they have turned out to be far more efficient than the WATCH, who could only cut crime by working harder – the Guild, on the other hand, has only to work less. All of this works so effectively that when, in the Year of the Engaging Sloth, the Guild declared a General Strike, the level of crime actually doubled.

This formal system, introduced by Lord VETINARI, is held to be a cheap and enlightened arrangement (except by those malcontents who are actually mugged or robbed and refuse to see it as their social duty). It enables the thieves to plan a decent career structure, entrance examinations and codes of conduct similar to those adopted by the city's other professions – which, the gap not being very wide in any case, they have rapidly come to resemble. The Guild has also introduced a complex system of annual budgeting, licensing, chits and allowances to see that (a) the members can make a reasonable living, and (b) no citizen is robbed or assaulted more than an agreed number of times. Many farsighted citizens in fact arrange to get an acceptable minimum amount of theft, assault, etc., over at the beginning of the year, often in the privacy of their own homes, and are therefore able to walk the streets quite safely for the rest of the year. A number of small firms operate under the auspices of the Guild, offering attentive and personal service to this end.

It is probably unnecessary to point out that the system is less advantageous to the thieves than at first seems to be the case. Firstly, an awful lot of energy is expended on internal Guild politics. Secondly, almost all the crime in the city is controlled by the Guild Council, who therefore have themselves to stamp out non-Guild criminals. Thirdly, if there is any trouble Lord Vetinari now knows where they all live.

TOUR OF THE GUILD BUILDING

The casual visitor to Ankh-Morpork can hardly fail to be impressed by the curious facade, or indeed facades, of the Thieves' Guild, sited at one of the most prestigious locations in the city.

It occupies the formerly derelict Ankh-Morpork Court House on the corner of the Street of Alchemists and Lower Broad Way, and many have remarked how good it is to see this fine building back once more in the hands of what, broadly speaking, is a part of the legal profession.

The frontage is still very much that of the Court House, a heavily crenellated and portcullis'd facade in Century of the Cheesemite style. The city coat of arms is of course over the entrance and the dome above, designed by Sir Cranleigh Stamp, is topped by the figure of Justice, holding a bag of gold in one hand and a set of scales in the other. (Once upon a time, for about the first twelve hours of its existence, the figure was gilded; now it is plated in brass.)

Moving up the stone steps past the mock Tsortean pillars, the visitor should take the time to admire the magnificent carved wooden doors, the work of the renowned artist Ralph 'Grumbling' Gibbons. Gibbons, although an exquisite wood carver, was not a happy man and, five days after completing the doors, he killed himself rather messily using a spokeshave.

The marbled entrance hall of the Guild is lit in daylight hours by sunlight filtering through the ornate dome above. The dome's stained glass depicts famous moments in the history of thieving – most notably, of course, the theft of fire from the gods by the legendary Fingers MAZDA, whose statue stands in the centre of the hall.

The statue holds aloft the Undying Flame, which never goes out except on Tuesday afternoons when the janitor tops up the oil.

Ahead of the visitor, beyond the statue, is the magnificent doubled-curved staircase leading to the galleried upper floors, containing the main hall and the offices of the Guild's principal officers and lecturers. The main hall, three storeys high, has been constructed using wood panelling from the original Ankh-Morpork High Court of Justice. It is used for balls, banquets and examinations. At the end of the main hall is an impressive dais housing an accurate replica of the Throne of Justice on which, it is said, the kings of Ankh would sit to hear appeals against the judgements of lesser courts. It is now used when the Guild Council sits in judgement on recalcitrant members, or against unlicensed thieves. A lever to one side of the throne operates the complicated mechanism which causes the throne to slide back into the wall behind it and be replaced by the Guild gallows – its woodwork another riot of rococo carving by

Grumbling Gibbons.

Off to one side is the Council chamber. Note how some of the chairs appear to be fixed to the floor, each of them with what appears to be a closed trapdoor behind it? Note the array of buttons arranged unobtrusively by the chairman's chair? Shortly after its formation the Guild often had to entertain the leaders of gangs who did not wish to affiliate. Shortly after *that*, affiliations climbed quickly.

These, then, with the usual offices, dormitories, storerooms and so on, comprise the main part of the original building. The rear of the premises was entirely rebuilt with the peculiar needs of the Guild in mind.

Pride of place, abutting immediately onto the rear of the courthouse, is a genuine brick-built Thieves' Kitchen. Tiny windowed, multi-chimneyed, its bottle shape almost dwarfs the original building. The Kitchen is now, in fact, the social and political centre of the Guild, with the Courthouse building now used primarily for official and civic purposes, and anything that requires a tilting chair.

Within the Kitchen are the Schools of Theft: Burglary, Cutpursing, Pickpocketing, Robbery and Language. Each of these rooms has been designed as an airy and well-equipped lecture hall, with every modern visual aid, including blackboards and... Well, blackboards is about it, actually. Oh, and chalk. A multi-media room (with coloured chalk, *and* crayons) is being built.

In addition, there are many rag-hung alcoves wherein all aspects of traditional and modern thievery are taught by visiting lecturers, including Acceptable Cheekiness, Jaunty Repartee and Tap-Dancing. There is also a School of Deportment for Gentleman Thieves and, owing to the Patrician's various decrees that insist that Guild members in most of the disciplines should look the part, there is also a extensive tailoring shop in the basement.

Outside, and effectively constituting the entire rest of the site, are the Practical Science Laboratories – where there are climbing walls with drainpipes and ivy (and with and without protective spikes), mock-up windows in a variety of styles, and doors and skylights to test the skill of even the most accomplished thief. There are also street scenes that include dummy passers-by with booby-trapped pockets, fake stagecoaches, etc., etc. This area is always crowded on the Guild's special Sports Days, where the Long Drop, the 100-yard Scarper, the Nick, Skip and Sidle and, of course, the free-style Nonchalant Walk are all very popular, if unusual, events.

Down some suitable grimy steps are the Guild cellars. Here is the Guild museum, with artefacts from many famous crimes and criminals. The visitor can admire such milestones in the history of theft as the jewel-encrusted jemmy belonging to Claude Tombola who, it is generally accepted, established the genre of Gentlemanly Theft. Here also is the torn, bloodstained tunic once worn by Subaltern Archibald 'Barmy' Postillion, the army officer who stole the Green Eye of the Little Yellow Dog in Klatchistan. The dog itself (stuffed) is also on display.

You will also see, down a further, shorter and narrower flight of stone steps, the dank and uninviting cells used to incarcerate any fortunate individuals whose crimes against the Guild were not so severe as to require the standard death penalty that is the reward for most unlicensed theft. Do not go down that corridor. It is a bad corridor.

WHY IS THERE STILL A GUILD?

(An Extract from a Guild Leaflet)

There has been some grumbling about Guild activities and changes in the Budget, and some people have been saying the perhaps the city can do without the Thieves' Guild at all. We have the Watch, they say.

Crime is always with us – well, not with *us*, as such, obviously, but with civilization in general – and we owe it to Lord Vetinari for pointing out that, since this is the case, it could be done better.

And we do it better. And we do it *reliably*. And we do it *traditionally*.

Look at the situation in those cities that do not have Guilds. People don't know when they are going to be robbed. They don't know how much will be taken. They live in fear of crime, rather than, as in Ankh-Morpork, accepting it as a kind of goods-and-services tax. Why is this? Because they are in the hands of *amateurs*.

Take your non-Guild burglar, for example. What does he know about skilled lock picking? Or casing the joint? About being quiet? Nothing. He smashes a window, turns out all the drawers, rummages around where he shouldn't... And that's only the start of your problems.

How often have you heard people say 'I wouldn't've minded, they didn't take much, but the *mess!*' That's not the work of a Guild burglar! Usually people will not find out they've been robbed until the lady next looks for her necklace and finds only our receipt in the box. A Guild burglar takes a pride in his work. In fact, some of our clients have been so kind as to inform us that the only reason they suspected a break-in was when they saw that the dressing table had been dusted and the cat had been fed.

The same applies to street crime. Your non-Guild mugger, now, what does he know about anatomy? Has he been trained to cause the maximum of unconsciousness with the minimum of damage? Will his assistant thoughtfully place a cushion under the client's head as they sink to the ground? Will the client's purse, bag or wallet be delivery promptly to their home address minus only the usual Guild fee? We think not!

And then it should be remembered that a high proportion of Guild income finds its way back to the city treasury in the form of taxes, and a prudent citizen who has carefully kept their Guild receipts will receive a modest reduction in their own personal taxes.

Of course, we are aware that a number of people are taking advantage of this and trying do-it-yourself crime, in order to cut out the Guild and save a bit of money There is no law against this. It is the right of everyone to hit themselves over their own head. But I must say that the Guild is now often being called in to sort out DIY crimes that have gone wrong, and we are forced to make a special charge for this service.

This year we are revising our suite of contracts to offer something for every householder or businessman, whatever their circumstances. All come with a suitable wall badge and personal certificate:

Special $100 Platinum Badge

Subject to status, location and availability: Complete immunity from *all* Guild activities for a full twelve months for a family of up to five people! Our premier service for the busy professional. Comes complete with a handsome gilt badge for the property. People will know you have 'made it' as a member of our exclusive Platinum Club.

The 'Fortune' Badge

A tried and trusted favourite of many citizens. A mere $50 gives a family of five entry to the Guild lottery. This year's odds against a burglary are twelve to one, mugging nineteen to one (outside the Shades) and a list of the other current odds is available upon application. In addition, there are upper limits to the value of goods taken. It may not be you! Comes with a set of steak knives.

The 'Steadfast' Badge

Good value at $15. Guild operations will be limited to one break-in or street theft without violence per eighteen months. Comes with musical dog ornament.

The 'Fearnaught' Badge

A budget bargain at $10. Not more than one mugging (not too hard) or one walk-in theft per year. Comes with free First Aid kit.

And remember – the Guild badge on the wall of a property is a signal to all non-Guild thieves to Keep Away. The City Watch have rules about what they can do to arrested non-Guild thieves. We don't. [TGD]

Thighbiter, Jethrod. Author of 'The Ankh-Morpork Succession', the definitive history of the Ankh-Morpork monarchy. [MAA]

Thogsdaughter, Gloria. A schoolfriend of

Susan Sto Helit. A dwarf. She has a beard a foot long, which is plaited and tied in ribbons in the school colours. [SM]

Thog the Butcher. A one-time member of the Silver Horde, athough no longer with them when they attacked the Agatean Empire. Somewhat troubled by a prostate problem. [IT]

Thrum. A member of the Lancre Morris Men team. Not a participant in the events of *Lords and Ladies*, however, having been injured during an attempt at the notorious Stick and Bucket Dance. [LL]

Thud. A game of tactics and skill played with eight troll pieces and thirty-two dwarf pieces.

Thunderaxe, Mr. The archetypal bit part that Terry and I loved. He was sold a sausage in a bun by C.M.O.T. DIBBLER. [TT]

Thunderbolt, Mr. A nephew of Diamond King of Trolls and a member of the Ankh-Morpork Guild of Lawyers, who served his articles under Mr SLANT.

His voice is that of a professor, but one who has chosen to speak in an echoing cave. The features are more or less like those of all trolls, unless you look for the giveaway signs and recognize the careful masonry work, the richness of the plant life in the visible cavities and, not least, that elusive shine, and possibly shimmer, which catches the light so delicately; not boldly in your face, but irresistibly there. [RS]

Thunderfoot. Actor in the clicks. [MP]

Thundergust, Grabpot. Proprietor of a cosmetics mill in Hobfast Street, Ankh-Morpork. His products are labelled 'The Halls of Elven Perfume & Rouge Co.', and he has a new range called 'Ladies' Secrets'. A fine example of the dwarfish tendency to project a tough, hard-drinking outer image while quietly getting on with making corsetry or whatever. [WS]

Thursley, Eric. A self-styled demonologist, of Midden Lane, Pseudopolis. He is nearly fourteen when RINCEWIND encounters him: slim, quite short, dark-haired, with glasses. His face would be a lot better if his acne cleared up, and his general aura would improve with more frequent washing. [E]

Tiddles, Mr. Large, black and white cat at the Ankh-Morpork Post Office. He is twenty years old and very set in his ways – he cannot tolerate furniture being moved and often grinds to a standstill if things are not where he expects them to be. Tiddles is not so much his name, more of a description. [GP]

Tick, Perspicacia, Miss. Absolutely not a teacher of witchcraft, but pretty close; her role is to tour out-of-the-way districts for girls whose destinies clearly have a tick against the box marked 'witch'. She travels alone (she has no 'beau' – 'they get in the way') in a little caravan pulled by her mule, Joseph. Everything in the caravan is ship-shape; racks of little things, all annotated and in alphabetical order.

So, her role is a sort of 'witch finder'; she keeps a magical look-out for girls who show promise and finds them an older witch to help them along. She certainly possesses some of those attributes – sharpness, irony, two pens with different coloured inks – traditionally associated with teaching. A known method she adopts is to attach herself to a wandering group of PERIPATETIC TEACHERS and pitch her small black tent amongst their gaudy stalls.

Any girl who enters after reading the notice on the flap, which says 'I can teach you a lesson you won't forget in a hurry', is probably halfway to being a witch already. She has a stealth hat (it's only pointy when it's safe to point), hates broomsticks and – fortuitously, since she must often visit areas where witches are not popular and tend to be thrown into ponds with their hands and feet tied together – has a small book of escapology and a Gold Swimming Certificate from Quirm College for Young Ladies. [WFM]

Tilden, Captain. One-time head of the Ankh-Morpork City WATCH. Had a brass ear and a wooden leg. At the time of the events of *Night Watch*, he was a man of seventy, with a skinny face, faded blue eyes and a bristling moustache. He was an ex-military man, having served with Lord Venturi's Medium Dragoons, and he was given the Night Watch post as a kind of pension. He set a lot of store by shiny breast plates and smartness on parade. As a copper he was useless, but is fondly remembered by those who knew him as a man who did his best. [NW]

Time. The idea that time is something that passes uniformly at every point in the universe has long been discredited, but humans persist in believing that it is so at a local level; yet most people have encountered days that pass very quickly or hours that trudge past (random time variations, like lumps or bubbles in custard) and have been to places where time flows faster/slower than at home.

Time is one of the Discworld's most secretive anthropomorphic personifications. It is hazarded that Time is female (she waits for no man) but she has never been seen in the mundane world, having always gone somewhere else just a moment before. In her chronphonic castle, made up of endless glass rooms, she does at, er, time materialize as a tall woman with dark hair and wearing a long red-and-black dress. She has a relationship with Lobsang LUDD and Jeremy CLOCKSON. [TOT]

Times, Ankh-Morpork. Ankh-Morpork's first real newspaper, started by Gunilla GOOD-MOUNTAIN and William DE WORDE and located behind the BUCKET in Gleam Street. Key staff of the newspaper are Sacharissa CRIPSLOCK (reporter), Otto CHRIEK (iconographer) and Berenice HOUSER (Backnumbers Department). Another reporter is Raymond Shuttle. Its banner motto was (usually) 'The Truth Shall Make Ye Free'. [TT]

Tinker. A tinker in Lancre. A member of the Lancre Morris Men. [LL]

T'malia, Lady. A tutor at the ASSASSINS' GUILD. She lectures in Political Expediency on Octeday afternoons and is one of the few women to have achieved high office in the Guild.

The jewellery of one hand alone carries enough poison to inhume a small town. She is stunningly beautiful, but with the calculated beauty that is achieved by a team of skilled artists, manicurists, plasterers, corsetières and dressmakers, and three hours' solid work every morning. [P]

Toad. This toad had once been a lawyer (a human lawyer; toads manage without them) who'd been turned into a toad by a fairy godmother who'd *intended* to turn him into a frog but had been a bit hazy on the difference. Now he lives in the Feegle mound, where he eats worms and helps them out with the difficult thinking.

A source of sadness for him, for many years, is the fact that most princesses *never* try to kiss toads. [HFOS]

Toby. A goblin dog, previously owned by Chas SLUMBER. [TOC]

Tockley, Lucy. *See* DIAMANDA.

Tomjon. Adopted son of Olwen and Mrs VITOLLER; half brother to the Fool (*see* VERENCE II). Tomjon's real mother was the Queen of Lancre but his real father was also the Fool's father (a fact known only to the LANCRE witches and, one assumes, his mother).

He was given three gifts by Granny WEATHERWAX, Nanny OGG and Magrat GARLICK: to make friends well, to always remember the words and to be whoever he thinks he is. With the benefit of these three gifts he carved out a career as a very successful actor. It was so successful and personally fulfilling that he later turned down the crown of Lancre on the grounds that he could wear a different crown on stage every night. [WS]

Tooth Fairy. The Tooth Fairy lives in the highest room of the Tower of Teeth in 'her' own land (although the sex of the Tooth Fairy is uncertain and perhaps even irrelevant).

The country itself is similar to that of Death, whose gloomy surroundings were initially defined by the expectations of the people he deals with. Death's land, therefore, tends to look funereal. That of the Tooth Fairy, on the other hand, was defined by children and is all primary colours and rather inexpertly drawn. If you ever visit, try not to look at the gap between the ground and the sky.

The Fairy herself has origins that go back a lot further than any pleasant little custom about paying children for their lost milk teeth. Like most pleasant little customs involving children, it is a fossil of something a lot more serious and undoubtedly nastier.

The Tooth Fairy herself does not do the collecting, but has set up a self-sustaining system involving humans, with an investment portfolio to provide cash for tooth purchase. For most of the people concerned, it is just a job. Human 'tooth fairies' collect the teeth and replace them with money, and a network of middlemen get the teeth to the Tower.

Typically, a working 'tooth fairy' is a young woman looking for a better job. The pay is not high. While at work she is invisible to anyone with normal human vision, and must be strong enough to carry a ladder and reach difficult windows. Pliers are a less obvious tool, but are necessary because the books must balance; if, at the end of a busy night, she can no longer make change for a tooth, she must remove another one. [SM]

Towering, Sergeant. A member of the 1st Battalion of the Zlobenian 59th Bowmen. Dark green uniform. [MR]

Tower of Art. The oldest building on the Disc. Older than Unseen University in whose grounds it stands, older than the city which formed about it like scree around a mountain. Maybe even older than geography. There was a time when the continents were different... Perhaps the tower was washed up on the waves of rock, from somewhere else. Maybe it was even there before the Disc itself. It is useless to speculate. It was certainly the original University.

It is 800 feet tall and now totally without windows. Time, weather and indifferent repairs have given it a gnarled appearance, like a tree that has seen too many thunderstorms. It is topped by a forest of little turrets and crenellations. Its crumbling stones support thriving miniature forests high above the city's rooftops. Entire species of beetles and small mammals have evolved up there and, aided by the emanations of magic from the University, have evolved very strangely indeed.

The small door in its base leads to the foot of the famous spiral staircase of 8888 very tiny steps. The interior smells of antiquity, with a slight suspicion of raven droppings. The tower is not now used for anything – the internal floors have rotted away so that all that is left inside is the staircase. From the top a wizard might see the edge of the Disc (after spending ten minutes or so coughing horribly, of course).

T'Phon, Great. One of the four giant elephants that support the Discworld. [COM]

Traitor, Miss. Teaches Logic at the Quirm College for Young Ladies. [SM]

Travis, Mr. Senior coachman at the palace in GENUA. [WA]

Treacle Mine Road, Ankh-Morpork. A major road separating the SHADES from the largely dwarfish community in the Cable Street – Easy Street area. Named after the treacle mines once found in the area, now abandoned.

It has always been assumed that the treacle (note to Americans and other rare and strange creatures: a thickly sweet syrupy substance) is the remains of thickets of sugar cane crushed by mud at about the same time as coal measures were being laid down. It was – and still is, in some parts of the Disc – mined either as a solid, which has to be cleaned and refined and cast in slabs ('pig treacle' or 'hokey-pokey') and, very rarely, as a liquid. In the area around GENUA, liquid treacle lakes near the surface have absorbed enough moisture to ferment naturally, giving rise to occasional springs of rum as the

results burst forth under pressure.

Lest it be thought this is far-fetched, treacle mines have been reported in a number of places in England (including Binsey, near Oxford, and Bisham, near Marlow).

Treason, Eumenides, Miss. A very elderly witch – 113 years old (actually 111, but she thinks it sounds adolescent). She went blind when she was sixty, and has bandages over her pearly grey eyes. She uses Borrowing to see, using the eyes of animals. She went deaf at the age of seventy-five, and uses Borrowing to the same effect to overcome this. Her knees click when she walks – which she does very fast, with her black cloak billowing around her, with the aid of two sticks. She has long, white hair, no hooked nose and all her own teeth; she smells like old locked wardrobes. Miss Treason is a big believer in the power of rumour, advertising and 'show'. She owns a heavy, rusty iron clock which she wears on a belt and which locals believe is her 'real' heart. She is also a big customer of the Boffo Joke Emporium and owns two of their skull candleholders amongst other artifacts. [W]

Treatle. A wizard. Once Vice-Chancellor (a post now in abeyance) of Unseen University and a mage of the Ancient and Truly Original Brothers of the Silver Star. He has bushy eyebrows and a nicotine-stained patriarchal beard; these, combined with his nice green waterproof tobacco pouch, curly boots and spangled robe, make Treatle a wizard's wizard. Generally considered as self-centred as a tornado. He is also regarded as being stupid in the particular way that very clever people can be stupid. [ER]

Treehallet, Ganmack. A member of the Venerable Council of Seers at UNSEEN UNIVERSITY. [LF]

Treem, Bishop. Archivist at the Citadel in KOM. [SG]

Troglodyte Wanderer. A rather sad and bewildered ghost who haunted LANCRE CASTLE

Miss Treason

because it was built on his burial mound and he hadn't got the faintest idea where he was. [WS]

Trolls. Trolls are a (usually) silicaceous but humanoid life-form, largely found in the RAMTOPS but increasingly migrating to Ankh-Morpork and other cities of the STO PLAINS. They are traditionally a strong, hardy and incredibly long-lived race. And proverbially, and quite unfairly, considered to be as thick as two short thick wooden things.

In the cold air of the mountains, trolls are in fact quite bright, almost cunning; only in the lowlands are they a byword for stupidity. In fact the slowness of thought is induced by the effect of heat on the silicon troll brain. If sufficiently deep frozen, a troll is astonishingly intelligent.

It is widely believed that trolls turn to stone in daylight. In fact they are stone all the time. But many trolls have brains that are so close to the heat tolerance level for operation that even the slight heating effect of early-morning light is sufficient to cause them to shut down.

Conception and birth roughly parallel the same occupations among humans, but trolls do not die except by accident or design. Left to themselves, trolls get bigger and slower and tend to settle in one place and think, very slowly and deliberately, about Things. They become more and more rock-like, a process that may take thousands of years. At some point they stop thinking, possibly because they have reached a kind of conclusion, but by then their thoughts are so slow that they are taking place against a geological timescale.

Even so, there is nothing subtle about trolls. While they cannot digest a human being, they have traditionally been very reluctant to accept this fact. And hitting another troll over the head with a rock is about equivalent to two humans exchanging the time of day. Troll courtship consists of a male troll, after consulting the intended's father, hitting her as hard as he can. This is in order to demonstrate the strength necessary to support a growing family. In deference to trollish femininity, he will normally select a pretty rock to do this with.

Their relationship with rural humans is generally on the rob-the-henhouse, jump-out-and-stomp, one-to-one basis. Between trolls and dwarfs, however, possibly because they tend to occupy the same landscape, there is a chronic state of low-grade warfare. The reason is possibly that dwarfs, who are miners and masons, sometimes use as their raw material trolls who have settled down for the long think. It is a tolerant troll indeed who can contemplate with equanimity his grandfather functioning as someone else's fireplace. Like the very best feuds, however, it really continues because it has always continued and its origins are lost in the dawn of time.

Or the sunset of time. Trolls believe that they move through time *backwards*. You can see the past, they say, therefore it must be in front of you. The future is invisible and therefore behind you.

Trolls have a socio-political system based on the concept of the troll with the biggest rock. They have some difficulty in adjusting to city conditions, because what is a quiet discussion to them is a riot to humans. Unlike dwarfs, who have a far more established civic culture, they don't fit easily into human houses or eat the same food. They tend to get the messy jobs. But recent experience in the great melting pot of Ankh-Morpork indicates that, with a little understanding on both sides, trolls and dwarfs can put aside their differences and settle down to trade, commerce, theft, usury (theft from bears), tax avoidance and other human pastimes.

Although the term 'troll' is, strictly speaking, reserved for silicon-based bipeds of the I've-got-dis-big-club-wid-a-nail-in-it persuasion, there are also other life forms of sufficiently troll-like characteristics to be considered as trolls. Sea trolls are animate sea water. The ICE GIANTS of the Hub must also be considered as a kind of troll, as must the artificially created GOLEMS.

It would be perverse of Nature to allow only the evolution of humanoid trolls and, while Nature is indeed perverse, there are other non-sapient (allowing for the moment that humanoid trolls *are* sapient) creatures that come under the broad stone umbrella of trolldom, although these are rare. There are troll dogs, and something roughly equivalent to a horse is used in the deep fastnesses of the mountains. There are also, surprisingly enough, troll ducks. They sink a lot.

Troll's Head, The. A tavern in the SHADES, Ankh-Morpork. Not a nice place. The Mended DRUM is also not a nice place, but it is a lot nicer than the Troll's Head, which isn't nice at all. It still has, nailed on a pole over the door, the original genuine troll head. Here may be found the kind of people too nasty even to be tolerated in the Mended Drum. Think about *that*.

Trooper, Daniel, 'One Drop'. Ankh-Morpork City Hangman. [GP]

Trouble. One of Harry King's giant-sized heavies – a security guard. He looks human. Or at least, *humanoid*. [RS]

Trousers of Time, the. There is probably a law, or at least a pretty strict guideline, that says that every book with the word 'Chaos', 'Time' or 'Fractal' in the title must, on some page, include an illustration of the Trousers of Time, viz.:

The trousers are used to demonstrate for very slow people the bifurcating nature of Time – how, for example, one simple choice can cause the universe to branch off into two separate realities (This One, and the One You Should Have Been In Where the Bus Wasn't About To Hit You).

On the Discworld, where metaphor can become interchangeable with reality, the Trousers of Time may actually exist. Where they are, and who will eventually wear them, and whether this has anything to do with the phrase 'Time Flies', may one day be revealed. Or not.

Truckle the Uncivil. Member of the Silver Horde. Had 'LOVE' and 'HATE' written on his walking sticks, and had yet to master the art of uttering a sentence without at least one *%$*! expletive in it. [IT]

Trymon, Ymper. A wizard. One-time second in command to the ARCHCHANCELLOR. Became Head of the Order of the Silver Star on the death of Galder WEATHERWAX, but had quite a short reign. A tall, nervous young man, whose personal habits are recalled only to the extent that he fussed about his hair and used all manner of magical spells and potions to get it to grow properly. He did not smoke – quite against the fashion among wizards at the time – and found solace instead in organizational charts that showed lots of squares with arrows pointing to lots of other squares. He was the sort of man who could use the word 'personnel' and mean it. [LF]

Tshup Aklathep. The Infernal Star Toad with A Million Young. Tortures its victims to death by holding them down and showing them pictures of its children until their brains implode. Probably an escapee from the Dungeon Dimensions who maintains a precarious existence on this plane. [MP]

Tsort. A desert kingdom on the continent of KLATCH. A neighbour of DJELIBEYBI and an historical enemy of EPHEBE. Tsort is known for the silent marshes of the River Tsort and the Great Pyramids (*see* GREAT PYRAMID OF TSORT), although it has to be pointed out that pyramid building belonged to a much earlier phase of the country's history and – no doubt because of the example of nearby Djelibeybi – modern Tsorteans scorn the things. The ancient city of Tsort was put to the torch by, it is thought, the armies of Ephebe under LAVAEOLUS. The people of Tsort worship all manner of gods, some of which seem to have been built of all the bits the creators of other gods had left over. Tsortean food relies heavily on garlic.

Tsort, River. The chocolate brown, slow-moving waters of the River Tsort bisect the desert rimwards of AL KHALI. Famed in myth and lies, it insinuates its way through the brown landscapes like a long, damp descriptive passage punctuated with sandbanks. And every sandbank is covered with sunbaked logs, most of which have teeth. [S]

Tubelcek, Father. A very thin, very decrepit priest who lived in an old house on Misbegot Bridge, and a harmless student who, unfortunately, died a horrible death. [FOC]

Tubul. One of the four giant elephants that support the Discworld. [COM]

Tugelbend, Victor. A student wizard at Unseen University, and possibly the laziest person in the history of the world. Originally, Victor chose to remain a student as a means of avoiding the realities of life and of securing an inheritance. (An uncle left him an annuity to allow him to study as a wizard but, being no fool, stipulated in his will that the annuity would cease if Victor ever got less than eighty in the examinations, the pass mark being eighty-eight. Victor therefore devoted tremendous effort to studying, in order to ensure that in every exam he achieved exactly eighty-four; on one occasion he successfully appealed when a mistake in the marking awarded him ninety-one points.)

Despite his aversion to anything that appeared to resemble work, Victor was the most athletically inclined student in UU. He had a thin moustache and smiled a lot, in a faintly puzzled way, which gave the impression that he was more intelligent than he really was. He seemed to amble everywhere, even when running.

He went on to make a short career in moving pictures, using the stage name Victor Maraschino. His current whereabouts are unknown, except that he is certain to be doing something he likes and devoting tremendous physical and mental effort to the pursuit of laziness. [MP]

Tulip, Mr. Member of the New Firm, with Mr PIN. Also, briefly, known as Sister Jennifer. He lived his life on that thin line most people occupy just before they haul off and hit someone with a spanner. For Mr Tulip, anger was the ground state of his being.

Mr Tulip, possibly from Überwald, did not have an intellect so much as a rage. Despite years of trying, he had not managed to acquire a drugs habit because he had not, in fact, managed to acquire any real drugs, although the various horse pills, bath salts, powdered moth balls and other fakes sold to him by chancy dealers probably did, in combination, make him see things. He was also, despite a vocabulary in which the word '—ing' was made to shoulder most of the load, one of the worlds' finest connoisseurs of fine art.

He was a huge man with a lot of self-inflicted scar tissue. It was hard to see his eyes, due to a certain puffiness, probably caused by too much enthusiasm for chemicals, which might also explain the general blotchiness and the thick veins that stood out on his forehead.

He was the sort of heavy-set man who was on the verge of bursting out of his clothes and, despite his interest in and knowledge of fine art, projected the image of a would-be wrestler who had failed the intelligence test.

He probably didn't like hitting people. It was just something he did. According to the dictates of an obscure potato-venerating religion, vaguely remembered from a troubled childhood, it would all be all right in the end if he still had a potato and was sorry for everything bad that he'd done. It may have worked. [TT]

Tumult, Gammer. A witch who taught Granny Weatherwax. But Granny also claims to have been taught by Nanny Gripes. Given the impatient nature of Esme Weatherwax, the truth of the matter is that she probably pumped *all* the local witches for as much instruction as they could give her. [ER]

Turnipseed, Adrian, Professor. *See* DRONGO, BIG MAD. [SM]

Turtle, the Great. *See* A'TUIN, GREAT.

Turtle Movement. A secret society in OMNIA which believes that the Disc is flat and is carried through space on the backs of four elephants and a giant turtle. Their secret recognition saying is 'The Turtle Moves'. Their secret sign is a left-hand fist with the right hand, palm extended, brought down on it. Most of the senior officials of the Omnian church are members of the 'movement', but since they all wear hoods and are sworn to absolute secrecy each thinks he is the only one. [SG]

Turvey, Hubert. Nephew of Topsy LAVISH

and inventor of the Glooper. Rightly or wrongly, Hubert is one of those names you put a shape to. There may well be tall, slim Huberts, but this Hubert is shaped like a proper Hubert, which is to say, stubby and plump. He has red hair, unusual in the standard-model Hubert. It grows thickly, straight up from his head, like the bristles of a brush; about five inches up, some-one has apparently cut it short with the aid of shears and a spirit level. You could stand a cup and saucer on it. Hubert wears a long, white coat, with a breast pocket full of pencils. [MM]

Twoflower. The Disc's first tourist. Originally, he was a small, bald and skinny man, but he soon put on weight, if not hair, under the influence of Ankh-Morpork's robust cuisine. He had false teeth and wore glasses, which led many of the Disc's inhabitants to assume that he had four eyes (both of these innovations were subsequently very popular in Ankh-Morpork).

He came from BES PELARGIC, the major seaport of the AGATEAN EMPIRE on the COUNTERWEIGHT CONTINENT, where he used to work at a desk job.

Twoflower was oddly dressed in knee-length breeches and a shirt in a violent and vivid conflict of colours. Central to his personal philosophy was the very strong belief that no harm could come to him because he was a visitor. A likeable, friendly and innocent man, his travels around the continent were marked by mayhem and sudden death. The fact that he was the original owner of the LUGGAGE has much to do with this. By the time he was encountered in *Interesting Times*, he had matured a little and grown a wispy beard, but still had that big, beaming, trusting smile. His wife was killed by soldiers, leaving him with their two daughters, Lotus Blossom and Pretty Butterfly. [COM]

Twoshirts. A small town with growing aspirations of being a bit more than one store, a coaching inn and a blacksmith's shop. [TSC]

Tyrant, The. The elected ruler of EPHEBE. The current ruler is a little, fat man with skinny legs, which gives the impression that an egg is hatching upside down. [SG]

You didn't get anywhere at Unseen University without being able to understand the vast number of meanings that can be carried by the word ook.

– Unseen Academicals

Überwald

Überwald. Large kingdom, some five or six times the size of the Sto Plains. Its florid crest incorporates the Überwaldian double-headed bat.

Überwald stretches all the way to the Hub. It is so thickly forested, so creased by little mountain ranges and beset by rivers that it is largely unmapped and unexplored.

Historically, Überwald was dominated by warring factions of werewolves, and vampires. In recent times, since the Diet of Bugs, dwarfs and humans play a much bigger part in the country's organization.

By and large, however, it is still a series of fortified towns and fiefdoms with no real boundaries and a lot of forest in between. Historically, there has always been a great deal of feuding and no laws, apart from whatever the local lords chose to enforce. Banditry is rife, and large areas are still controlled by feuding vampire and werewolf clans. In many areas, dwarfs and trolls have still not resolved their old grievances. There are huge tracts of Überwald with much higher than normal background magic.

Überwald, Angua von. *See* ANGUA.

Überwald, Guye von. The Baron is ANGUA's father and he is a werewolf. In human form,

he is enormous – not fat, not tall, just built to perhaps one tenth over scale. He doesn't so much have a face with a beard as a beard with, peeking over the top of the narrow gap between the moustache and the huge eyebrows, small remnants of a face. He makes therefore an imposing figure in his tattered dressing gown, smelling vaguely of old carpets. He has a strong handshake and a tendency to speak in short, sharp sentences. In wolf form (wolf name Silvertail) he is also large and heavy-set. The von Überwalds live in a rugged castle just outside Bonk. The family crest incorporates the Überwaldian double-headed bat and their motto is 'Homo Homini Lupus' – 'Every Man is a Wolf to Another Man'. [TFE]

Überwald, Serafine von. The Baroness is ANGUA's mother and she is a werewolf. She looks a little like Angua, but padded somewhat by the years. During the events of *The Fifth Elephant*, she wears a long, loose, green gown which, is very old-fashioned by Ankh-Morpork standards. She is a bit of a snob and, as Mme Serafine Soxe-Bloonberg of Genua, she went to finishing school with Lady Sybil Ramkin (now VIMES). Her wolf name is Yellowfang. [TFE]

Überwald, Wolfgang von. Wolf was Angua's brother. He was a strong werewolf. In wolf form, he had pale gold hair like a sort of mane – he looked a little like ANGUA, but heavier set. As a human, he was a heavily-built man with long, blond hair growing thickly on his head and down his shoulders, too. He liked to be naked, and to exercise regularly to demonstrate his fitness. When he did wear clothes, he favoured black uniforms with nickel insignia depicting wolf heads biting lightning. Wolf was a murderous idiot who believed that werewolves were born to rule. He led a movement with these beliefs, and their banner was a red flag with, in the middle, a wolf's head, its mouth full of stylized flashes of lightning. Even his father was afraid of him and he was known to have killed one sister (Elsa) and driven his brother Andrei away because they were not classic biomorph werewolves but YENNORKs.

He was a head-butting, eye-gouging, down-and-dirty bastard, who was good at thinking ahead and delighted in ambushes. He was a traditionalist when it came to nastiness. [TFE]

Ug. Ug and Zog are names on a couple of DEATH's oldest biographies. [M]

Um. Ancient city. Very ancient, dating back about sixty thousand years. Back in the Clay Age. The Umnians were the first golem makers. They invented some form of ceramic; no-one now knows how they made it. The Umnians even baked *boats* of the stuff. They worked. Up to a point. The city was totally destroyed in the first war with the ice giants. [MM]

Underdale, Lord. Earns his place in this book by being an entrepreneurial peer in the development of the new railway. He has long, white hair and a beard. [RS]

Underschaft, Dr. Chorus Master at the Ankh-Morpork OPERA HOUSE. A single-minded old man in half-moon spectacles, who believed that music is all that matters in opera, not the acting, or the shape of the singers. Had a fairly final encounter with the Opera Ghost. [MA]

Unggue. Goblin religion. The goblin experience of the world is the cult, or perhaps religion, of Unggue. In short, it is a remarkably complex resurrection-based religion founded on the sanctity of bodily secretions. Its central tenet runs as follows: everything that is expelled from a goblin's body was clearly once part of them and should, therefore, be treated with reverence and stored properly so that it can be entombed with its owner in the fullness of time. In the meantime the material is stored in Unggue pots, remarkable creations of which I shall speak later.

A moment's distasteful thought will tell us that this could not be achieved by any creature, unless in possession of great wealth, considerable storage space and compliant neighbours.

Therefore, in reality, most goblins observe the Unggue Had – what one might term the common and lax form of Unggue – which encompasses earwax, finger- and toenail clippings, and snot. Water, generally speaking, is reckoned not Unggue, but something which goes through the body without ever being part of it: they reason that there is no apparent difference in the water before and after, as it were (which, sadly, shines a light on the freshness of the water they encounter in their underground lairs). Similarly, faeces are considered to be food that has merely undergone a change of state. Surprisingly, teeth are of no interest to the goblins, who look on them as a type of fungus, and they appear to attach no importance to hair, of which, it has to be said, they seldom have very much.

The Unggue is stored in Unggue pots. These are traditionally crafted by the goblin itself, out of anything from precious minerals to leather, wood or bone. Among the former are some of the finest eggshell-thin containers ever found in the world. The plundering of goblin settlements by treasure-hunters in search of these, and the retaliation by the goblins themselves, has coloured human–goblin relationships even to the present day.

Goblins live on the edge, often because they have been driven there. When nothing else can survive, they do. Their universal greeting is, apparently, 'Hang', which means 'Survive'. Sometimes dreadful crimes are laid at their door. Those who live their lives where life hangs by less than a thread understand the dreadful algebra of necessity, which has no mercy. That is the time when the women make the Unggue pot called the 'soul of tears', the most beautiful of all the pots, carved with little flowers and washed with tears. [SN]

Ungulant, S. T. Ungulant the Anchorite. Sevrian Thaddeus Ungulant – hence 'St'. A saint, possibly of the Omnian church but probably just a generic saint. He lives on a cartwheel nailed to the top of a slim pole in the desert between EPHEBE and OM.

S. T. Ungulant is a very thin man with long hair and beard, and skin almost blackened by the desert sun. He wears a loincloth, and he has an imaginary friend called Angus. He is in fact almost completely and utterly mad, due to the sun and a continuous diet of the strange desert mushrooms. But the tiny core of reason left within him is aware that being completely insane is the only way to survive the desert existence. Besides, it means that he can enjoy the nebulous sumptuous meals and insubstantial carnal delights put before him by the small gods that swarm in the desert. His belief in all of them is possibly the only thing that keeps him alive. [SG]

Unseen University. Motto: *NVNV ID VIDES, NVNC NE VIDES*. Coat of arms: a livre des sortilèges, attaché en cuivre, sur un chapeau pointu, on a field, azure.

There is a UU scarf, basically burgundy and midnight blue with some tasteless thin yellow and purple stripes. The stripes are extremely symbolic, although not of anything very specific. The University likes to pretend that their eye-watering clash is an attempt to portray OCTARINE,* but in reality it graphically illustrates the importance of not letting someone like the current Bursar choose a colour scheme after eating half a bottle of dried frog pills. The stripes have been retained anyway, because of Tradition.

UU is the Disc's premier college of magic, whose campus is the occult, if no longer the actual, centre of Ankh-Morpork.

The University was founded in AM 1282 (the city count at the time) by Alberto MALICH, but Ankh-Morpork dating is always suspect; suffice to say that it was some 2000 years before the present. The aim was to force some sort of regulation on wizardry, which at that time was quite chaotic, and to permit the existence of an

---

* *Although octarine is the most important colour as far as wizards are concerned, it is not one that lends itself well to paint pigmentation. It quickly fades in sunlight and, in extreme cases, walks away.*

institution that would allow one wizard to meet another without immediately endeavouring to blow his head off with magical fire, as was then the case.

Like all really old universities, it is hard to tell where the University begins and the city ends, and in any case the size of UU can only be determined by reference to the kind of physics that you have to be a drunken physicist to understand.

In a purely mundane sense, the main buildings occupy a large part of the river frontage between the ANKH and SATOR SQUARE, with various outbuildings stretching out as far as Esoteric Street. But a mere floor plan would be quite misleading; UU has rooms and floors where logic says they simply could not exist. It has been a home of magic for so long that this is now part of the architectural inventory, like cement.

There are two ways of getting admitted to UU: achieve some great work of benefit to magic, such as the recovery of an ancient and powerful relic or the invention of a totally new spell, or be sponsored by a senior and respected wizard, after a suitable period of apprenticeship. The eighth son of an eighth son has a right to demand and receive a place.

Er...

All right, three ways – actual *entry* can be achieved by anyone of either sex willing to scrub and cook and make beds.

Er...

Four ways, in fact – possibly the most famous entrance to UU is via the alleyway between the observatory and the Backs, where a few loose bricks in the wall can be removed to make an informal ladder that has been used by students for hundreds of years. Whatever its original name, the alley has been known for years as Scholars' Entry, which in the hands of those inclined to the obvious is always good for a snigger.

With one exception (during the Archchancellorship of CUTANGLE), UU has never admitted women. Usually this is said to be on the grounds of plumbing problems, but probably the real reason is an unspoken dread that women, if allowed to mess around with wizardry, would probably be embarrassingly good at it. And less likely to do what they're told.

There is theoretically no age limit on students, since obviously it is better to have anyone with magical talent under the aegis of the University than, er, not under it. The normal age of entrants is around sixteen, although in earlier days it was a lot younger and undergraduates as young as four were enrolled. These days, however, few people at UU undertake magical practice clutching a woolly lamb.

WEALTH

UU is immensely wealthy, in a nebulous and threadbare kind of way. It owns large sections of Ankh-Morpork, particularly around Sator Square and also in the SHADES, which grew up as a service centre for the new university (a safe distance downstream). However, most of the rents are fixed and tend to be of the half-a-groat-every-Hogswatchnight variety, and the leases are either no longer decipherable or have long since mouldered away.

Generally speaking, the University survives from day to day by voluntary donations, usually in kind. (If you were a greengrocer, living a few streets away from what you perceive as a group of fat and slightly deranged old men sitting on enough raw magic to blow a hole right through Reality and out the other side, then wouldn't you see they got the occasional cartload of potatoes?)

TOWN AND GOWN: UNSEEN UNIVERSITY AND ANKH-MORPORK

As the University is well aware, Ankh-Morpork owes its entire existence to the presence of Unseen. The Shades were the core of the original city but, as the city began to develop its own momentum, the urban sprawl soon encompassed the villages now known as Dolly Sisters and Nap Hill.

Not unnaturally, the early ARCHCHANCELLORs resented any suggestion of control by the growing civil power and there were various trials of strength in the first few centuries, which usually ended with someone being turned into some kind of amphibian. Eventually an understanding was reached: UU would be left in peace to manage its affairs on the transtemporal level, and citizens would be allowed to go to bed the same shape as they were when they woke up that morning, whatever shape that had been.

Strictly speaking, the laws of Ankh-Morpork do not apply within the walls of the University even now, but this is nothing remarkable since they seldom apply outside the walls either. Wizards misbehaving in the city might be locked up by the WATCH for the night, but will then be handed over to the Archchancellors' Court upon payment of a small fine.

A list of offences under the rules of the Court, and their attendant punishments, includes:

Acceptable Waggishness 50p
High Spirits 60p
Being a Young Rip 75p
Having a Fling 75p
Sowing Wild Oats 33p per oat
Being found Drunk 80p
Being found Rascally Drunk 90p
Being found Objectionably Sober $1.00

Of course, where there is law there has to be crime, and where there is a court there must be policemen.

So it is at UU. Although these days they are really little more than porters, the University does have its 'policemen', known as the BLEDLOWS (origin unknown) or 'lobsters'.

UNIVERSITY ORGANIZATION

Despite appearances, UU is not simply a college of magic. There are faculties of medicine, minor religions and lore (history), for example. But these are very small and, in any case, University rules require that faculty members must have trained initially as wizards.

UU government is headed by the Archchancellor, who also chairs the College Council, or Hebdomadal Board (from the Latatian

hebes – sluggish or stupid, and domo – to tame or conquer. Hence the purpose of the College Council is to conquer stupidity. It is, say critics, beginning this activity by making a very careful and personal study of the enemy – really getting under its skin, as it were.)

The Council traditionally consisted of the heads of the eight orders of wizardry. However, since the events chronicled at the end of The Light Fantastic (when the University lost all eight heads but gained some incredibly life-like statues, most of them now decorating the wall overlooking Sator Square), the ex-officio membership of the heads of orders has ceased and the Council is now directly appointed by the Archchancellor.

The eight orders, each in theory headed by an eighth-level wizard, are:

The Ancient and Truly Original Sages of the Unbroken Circle
The Hoodwinkers
Mrs Widgery's Lodgers
The Ancient and Truly Original Brothers of the Silver Star
The Venerable Council of Seers
The Sages of the Unknown Shadow
The Order of Midnight
The Last Order, also known as The Other Order

A new student may apply to join any one of these orders, which combine the functions of 'houses' in English public schools with something of the 'fraternities' in American colleges. Despite their names, most of them are not at all ancient – there have always been orders, but their names have been lost or mislaid or muddled by wars and time. The current crop are the result of a deliberate 're-creation' of the orders less than a century ago. Apart, that is, from Mrs Widgery's Lodgers, which is as old as the University; in the very early days of UU the TOWER OF ART (then the only building on campus) was not big enough to hold all the students and they were boarded at the house of Mrs Widgery, on the site of what is now New Hall.

Once accepted, the student may study for

any one of the University's degrees:

Bachelor of Thaumatology (B.Thau.)
Bachelor of Magic (B.Mgc)
Bachelor of Sortilège (B.S.)
Bachelor of Magianism (B.Mn.)
Bachelor of Divination (B.D.)
Bachelor of Civil Lore (B.C.L.)
Bachelor of Applied Theurgy (B.Ap.Th.)
Bachelor of Impractical Necromancy
(B.Im.N.)
Bachelor of Fluencing (B.F.)*
Bachelor of Amulets and Talismen (B.Am.
Ta.)
Bachelor of Cabbalistic Rites (B.C.R.)
Bachelor of Hyperphysical Chiromancy
(B.H.Ch.)
Bachelor of Esoteric Occultism (B.Es.O.)
Bachelor of Eldritch Lacemaking (B.El.L.)**
Master of Thaumatology (M.Thau.)
Master of Magic (M.M.)
Master of Sortilège (M.S.)
Master of Magianism (M.Mn.)
Master of Divination (M.D.)
Master of Civil Lore (M.C.L.)
Doctor of Thaumatology (D.Thau.)
Doctor of Magic (D.M.)
Doctor of Sortilège (D.S.)
Doctor of Magianism (D.Mn.)
Doctor of Gramarye (D.G.)
Doctor of Divination (D.D.)
Doctor of Civil Lore (D.C.L.)
Doctor of Magical Philosophy (D.M.Phil.)
Doctor of Morbid Spellbinding (D.M.S.)
Doctor of Condensed Metaphysics
(D.C.M.)
Doctor of Wizardry (D.W.)

In addition to the above, the University also tolerates guest lecturers on 'fringe' aspects of magic (at least, fringe from the point of view of established wizardry) such as shamanism, witchcraft, voodoo and plumbing.

Progression through the eight levels of wizardry is determined in part by the acquisi-tion of degree qualifications and, particularly towards the top of the tree where the number of available places become few and far between (there are only eight eighth-level wizards, at least officially), by a policy of 'dead men's pointy boots', no questions being asked about the manner of their emptying.

(We suppose at this point that it must be admitted, with extreme reluctance, that the formal level is not necessarily an indication of a wizard's actual power. Like the whole struc-ture of UU, the levels and degree system is there to *control* the power of wizardry rather than further it. It has to be pointed out, for example, that by the University's own rules the wizard RINCEWIND, having defeated a sourcerer (in *Sourcery*), is therefore at the very least an eighth-level wizard. No one at UU seems to have worked this out, and it is just as well for their temper that this remains the case.)

Many of the faculties also support a spon-sored Professorship, which, although carrying a sturdy stipend, also carries with it the stigma of actually being expected to teach the students. The current Professorships are:

Egregious Professor of Cruel and Unusual
Geography
Egregious Professor of Grammar and
Usage
Professor of Recondite Architecture and
Origami Map-Folding
Patricius Professor of Magic
Magus Professor of Wizardry
Invisus Professor of Condensed Metaphys-
ics
Octavus Professor of Civil Lore
Haudmeritus Professor of Divination
Superbus Professor of Astrology
Infandus Professor of Morbid Spellbinding
Fluxus Professor of Sortilège
Professor of Recondite Phenomena
Professor of Logic
Professor of Illiberal Studies

* *A very popular degree and comparatively easy to obtain; a bit like sociology. Most wizards manage to get a B.F. after their name, to the quiet amusement of the citizenry in general.*

** *This one is a bit of a puzzler.*

STAFF

Identified members of the University's staff include:

Archchancellor
Bursar
Chair of Indefinite Studies
Dean of College
Dean of Liberal Studies
Dean of Pentacles
Lecturer in Applied Astrology
Lecturer in Recent Runes
Lecturer in Vindictive Astronomy
Lecturer in Creative Uncertainty
Librarian
Professor of Anthropics
Professor of Astrology
Reader in Esoteric Studies (also known as 'the Reader in the Lavatory')
Reader in Invisible Writings
Reader in Woolly Thinking
Senior Wrangler
Praelector

Again, the fact is that a university that has existed for two thousand years, and is as rambling as UU, develops all sorts of quirks. There are professors in distant parts of the building engaged in their own pursuits and hardly ever seen; there are lecturers who don't lecture, and research students who are older than most of the faculty. Mustrum RIDCULLY, Archchancellor at the time of writing, is resigned to the fact that there are plenty of wizards in outlying areas of UU who don't even know who he is. Once in UU, a wizard need never leave. Tenure is automatic. There is always a spare study somewhere, always room in the Great Hall. It is, in short, academic heaven – and a perfect way to ensure that the most potentially dangerous men on the Disc spend their time squabbling amongst themselves and, of course, eating big dinners.

TERMS

The University year is split into eight terms, each of which is approximately one week long in order to minimize the amount of time that the faculty needs to spend in any room with the student body.

The students, however, continue to live in the University throughout much of the calendar year, undertaking their own research and generally absorbing magic from the fabric of the building and adding to its storehouse of knowledge. (The theory runs thusly: it is very well known that students arriving fresh at any university know all there is to know about absolutely everything. But when they leave, after many years of study, they're usually only too ready to admit that there is a lot they don't know. Raw knowledge must therefore have been passing from the students into the University, where it accumulates.)

The University terms follow the Great or true astronomical Disc year, despite the fact that most of the world lives by the 'agricultural' year (see CALENDARS). All really old and important universities have terms linked to some temporal scheme now quite opaque to the mass of the population, to show them what they're missing by being so stupid.

The UU terms are: Octinity; Rotation; Backspindle; Hogswatch; Evelyn; Micklemote; Candlerent (Candlerent is rent from a house which continually deteriorates – this presumably has something to do with the Shades, where many of the buildings have deteriorated to the point at which flat ground would be urban improvement); Soul Cakes.

CEREMONIES AND FESTIVALS

The Convivium

The UU degree ceremony. The University's Archchancellor, Council, eighth-level wizards, doctors and masters process through the city from the University to the opera house, led by (traditionally) the Commander of the City Watch or, in those recent years when there has been no Commander, by a man carrying a cushion on which is a small pot of mustard and a quill pen (because of Tradition). The procession is extremely colourful and popular, and has put at least one nautical observer in mind of an entire fleet of galleons running in front of the wind.

In the opera house, new graduates are awarded their degrees in the presence of the PATRICIAN. After the ceremony, the procession proceeds rather more quickly back to the University for a large meal.

Until two hundred years ago the Convivium was held within the University grounds; it appears to have been moved outside as an exercise in impressing the masses; a very similar exercise, in fact, to the Moscow May Day parades in the great days of Soviet power. Look at us, the wizards seem to be saying as they proceed with robes astream – we've all got big staffs, and *they've* all got knobs on the end. We don't want to have to use them.

Gaudy Night

When graduate wizards attend a grand banquet in the Great Hall, with each wizard making a greater effort than usual to outdo his fellows in the splendour of his robes. The winner is carried shoulder-high out of the University and thrown on to the Ankh.

The Ceremony of Keys

This is an old custom, centuries old, and in the summer a few tourists hang around to watch it, but the Ceremony of the Keys goes on every night in every season. Mere ice, wind and snow have never stopped it. Bledlows in times gone past had clambered over tentacled monstrosities to do the Ceremony; they'd waded through floodwater, flailed with their bowler hats at errant pigeons, harpies and dragons, and ignored mere faculty members who'd thrown open their bedroom windows and screamed imprecations on the lines of 'Stop that damn racket, will you? What's the point!' They'd never stopped, or even thought of stopping. You can't stop Tradition. You can only add to it.

The Ceremony has a specific, and formal, set of dialogue to accompany it. The Head Bledlow, The Duty Keeper of the Other Jacket, and the Duty Gatekeeper deliver this dialogue in loud, clear voices:

Gatekeeper: Halt! Who Goes There?

Head Bledlow: *(saluting)* The Archchancellor's Keys!

Gatekeeper: Pass, The Archchancellor's Keys!

Head Bledlow: *(extends both arms in front of him with his palms bent back towards him, and pats his chest at the place where some bledlow long buried had once had two breast pockets. Then he extends his arms by his sides and stiffly pats the sides of his jacket.)* Damn! Could Have Sworn I Had Them A Moment Ago!

(Gatekeeper and Head Bledlow exchange salutes)

Gatekeeper: Have You Looked In All Your Pockets?

(Gatekeeper and Head Bledlow exchange salutes)

Head Bledlow: I Think I Must Have Left Them On The Dresser. It's Always The Same, Isn't It?

Gatekeeper: You Should Remember Where You Put Them Down.!

Head Bledlow: Hang On, Perhaps They're In My Other Jacket!

Keeper of the Other Jacket: *(exchanging salutes with the other participants)* No, I Looked In There This Morning!

Head Bledlow: *(pats his pockets again)* Hold On, Stone The Crows, They Were In This Pocket After All! What A Muggins I Am!

Gatekeeper: Don't Worry, I Do The Same Myself!

Head Bledlow: Is My Face Red! Forget My Own Head Next! Here's The Keys, Then!

Gatekeeper: *(handing the keys back)* Much Obliged! All Safe And Secure!

Head Bledlow: Gods Bless All Present!

Gatekeeper: Careful Where You Put Them This Time. Ha! Ha! Ha!

Head Bledlow: Ho! Ho! Ho!
(salutes, and returns to the Bledlows' Lodge)

Boy Archchancellor

This ceremony occurs around the turn of the year, at Hogswatch. A first-year student is selected to be Archchancellor for a whole day, from dawn until dusk. For that period he can exert the full power of the Archchancellorship and there are many tales of japes played on senior members of the College Council (hence the expression 'a wizard wheeze'). For this reason the student selected for this honour is usually the most unpopular boy in the University, and his life expectancy the following day is brief.

Head of the River

Like all riverside universities, Unseen is keen to promote its water sports. Because of the nature of the Ankh, rowing is tricky except in times of serious flood, and races consist of teams of eight student wizards chasing each other on foot up the Ankh while carrying a racing skiff (a similar practice, for different reasons, is found in the Alice Springs Regatta in Australia, which takes place on the dry river bed).

The race itself is known as the Bumps, because of the nature of the surface of the Ankh. The competing crews race from the University boathouses to the Brass Bridge. The winning crew is then awarded a 'brown' (pairs of brown pointy boots to replace the ones destroyed by close contact with the Ankh during the race), and becomes Head of the River, an earthy reference to the state of the members' boots and clothing.

May Morning

Every Mayday morning at dawn, the UU choir sing an anthem from the top of the Tower of Art, while the faculty and students (or as many of them as are awake at dawn) stand in the University gardens and listen. Since the Tower is 800 feet high, the listeners cannot hear the singing but, since the anthem takes five minutes to sing, they all applaud five minutes after dawn.

On a number of occasions the choir itself has failed to get up in time but the 'listeners' still clap anyway. To sneer at this is to misunderstand the Value of Tradition. If you don't understand this, you are nothing but a foreigner.

The Wizards' Excuse Me

Quite a new function, held on the last day of Backspindle term. It has been said that wizards don't have balls, but the Excuse Me belies this. It is a large dance to which the cream of Ankh-Morpork society (or, as they say, at least the stuff which is floating on the top) is invited. There are two bands and, most importantly, a buffet with eighteen different kinds of meat and, of course, cheese cubes and pineapple lumps on a stick.

The Excuse Me is particularly favoured by the current LIBRARIAN, as a result of which sales of hair oil soar in the preceding week. He is the only person in Ankh-Morpork who can achieve a parting down his entire body.

Rag Week

The entire Backspindle term. Wise citizens know enough to be on their guard around this time. The Week has all the normal perils of student humour with the additional seasoning of magic; these are viewed by the University authorities with the amused acceptance that is generally employed vis à vis student activities when baton rounds and tear gas have been found ineffective.

Citizens may encounter, for example, the Short Street Climb, in which wizards armed with crampons and pitons and ropes 'climb', in all seriousness, the length of the street. Many lose their grip and plunge helplessly through the door of the Mended DRUM where, in an attempt to revive themselves, much alcohol is consumed.

Another regular feature is the 'borrowing' of certain civic items and taking them to the Mended Drum, where much alcohol is consumed. Such items typically include street signs, potted plants and, on one occasion, the Brass Bridge.

An event often featured in the Week, but liable to break out at any other time, is 'tobogganing'. Traditionally, this took place inside the Tower of Art, when students on tea trays – after consuming much alcohol – would slide down the 8888 steps on the spiral staircase, with many death-defying plunges over the missing ones. By the time they were halfway down, in any case, centrifugal force was pinning them to the walls, and wizards often shot from the doorway at the bottom with enough speed to skim them across the Ankh.

These days Rag Week is more normally held inside the University buildings themselves, where the many curving staircases and polished corridors offer endless opportunity for impressively sudden death.

Beating the Bounds

(Also known as 'Plunkers'.) At dawn on 22 Grune the entire faculty, led by the choir and with the student body trailing behind, walk the ancient boundaries of the University (approximately the Backs, the Maul, Esoteric Street and the river frontage). They walk through or, if necessary, climb over any buildings that have since been built on the line of progress, while ceremonially striking any members of the public with live ferrets (in memory of Archchancellor Buckleby). Any red-headed men encountered are seized by several strong young wizards and given 'a plunking'; this tradition has, most unusually – and subsequent to an incident that left three wizards hanging precariously from a nearby gutter – been amended to read 'any red-haired men except of course for Captain CARROT Ironfoundersson of the Watch'. After the progress, the entire membership of the University heads back to the Great Hall for a huge breakfast at which duck must be served.

Scrawn Money

('Archchancellor Scrawn's Bequest'.) One of the oldest ceremonies in the University calendar, held in Sator Square. All tenants of University property are required to attend, whereupon they are given two pennies, a pair of long socks and a loaf of bread baked the previous morning. They then file into the University where they are allowed to watch the wizards having lunch.

The Poor Scholars

When UU was first established, a class of students was accepted without the benefit of financial backing or formal seconding by a University graduate. These were the 'Poor Scholars', young men with magical potential. It was felt that it would be in the interests of all concerned if the young men were educated in the ways of UU (in the words of Alberto Malich, the founder: 'We'd better keep the bright young buggers where we can see 'em').

They were not given rooms in the Tower of Art, and many had to live in lean-tos constructed against the walls. Once a month, in recognition of these stoics' determination not to be put off from their studies, the faculty would appear at the upper windows of the Tower and throw food to the 'Poor Scholars'. It was a popular event among the staff because it was quite possible to achieve a knockout blow with a well-gnawed cutlet from 200 feet.

This tradition lives on, even though the University is now physically much bigger and takes no 'Poor Scholars'. Once a year, the entire student body forgathers in Sator Square, where the faculty pelts them with stale bread rolls. Thrown with some force.

'Sity and Guilds

When the Guilds began to set up their own academic establishments there was a lot of rivalry between their various students, and lone UU students would frequently be set on by gangs from colleges. Ankh-Morpork has a relaxed attitude to sudden death, and many faculty members prefer dead students as being easier to teach, but the more pragmatic Guild Presidents, and the then current Archchancellor, decided that enough was enough because all those bodies around the place made it hard to open doors, and so on.

They decided to channel the rivalry into

an annual sporting contest, to be called the 'Sity and Guilds Match (although A. J. Loop, in the '*Ankh-Morpork Almanack and Booke of Dayes*', claims that this was merely a slightly modernized form of a much older and rather sinister contest known as the Ankh-Morpork Poor Boys' Fun, which involved teams of up to five hundred; certainly the old Laws and Ordinances of Ankh-Morpork contain several prohibitions mentioning the term).

The principle was to kick or carry a football from the outskirts of the Shades (the oldest part of the city) to the Tower of Art (the oldest building on the Disc). The game involved teams of fifty students from each of the principal Guilds, plus UU. Goals were scored by kicking the ball through the door (or, more often, the window) of landmarks along the way, many of them having names like the Mended Drum, Bunch of Grapes, etc. The scoring team had then to be bought drinks by the other teams. After a few years, the Archchancellor ruled that only one goal could be scored in each pub since the match had, three years running, gone on for a month.

UU records suggest that students from the University have not participated recently, but street football with various rules is still an Ankh-Morpork tradition. (In troll areas of the city the troll version of football is still occasionally played, although out of deference to modern sensibilities the 'football' of choice is no longer a human head, and a dwarf is substituted.)

Hunting the Megapode

A recently discovered tradition. The original Megapode (believed by some to be a sort of bird) was found in the under-butler's pantry many centuries ago. It escaped in the middle of dinner and caused, so we are now told, a veritable heyhoe-rumbelow as all the Fellows pursued it through the college buildings with much mirth and good spirits. For unknown reasons, this chase has been re-enacted every hundred years since then. Once every hundred years is quite enough.

UNSEEN UNIVERSITY: A GUIDED TOUR

The University's main gates open on to Sator Square. They are big and plated with solid OCTIRON. There is no doorknocker, and at sunset each day the gates are locked by magic (in actual fact by MODO, the University's dwarf gardener, but it pays to advertise).

Take a moment to inspect the interesting frontage, which is an amazing juxtaposition of architectural styles, although it may be that the word 'confectionery' is more appropriate. From various niches the statues of former Archchancellors, of which UU has a more than adequate supply, stare down over the city.

We may at this point draw the attention of gentlemen in the party to the statue of Archchancellor Bewdley, just over to the window to the right of the gates. If they are in a position to do so (i.e., alive), Archchancellors like to influence the style of their commemorative statues; Archchancellor Bewdley always disliked Ankh-Morpork intensely and I think you will agree, when you notice the position of his hands, that this is abundantly clear posthumously.

Note that the various architectural styles suggest that the roof and upper floor of the University were constructed several hundred years before the other storeys.

Now the massive gates open rather jerkily to admit us to the main octangle of the University's campus. UU has never satisfactorily been mapped. It is much bigger on the inside than on the outside and those maps that have been attempted look like a chrysanthemum exploding.

We enter a wide courtyard surrounded by lawns and dominated by some ancient chestnut trees. There are benches under the trees. Around the octangle is a great rambling building or buildings, looking not so much an architectural design as a lot of buttresses, arches, towers, bridges, domes, cupolas, etc., huddling together for warmth. Wizards like *quantity*. Visitors are asked particularly to note the cunning and disconcertingly alert gargoyles, a range of beaks, manes, wings, claws and pigeon droppings. Avoid feeding them if possible. They are at least as intelligent as trolls, by the way. You are being watched.

Behind us now is the University Clock Tower, with its ancient cracked bell (rumoured to be of octiron rather than bronze), Old Tom. The clapper dropped out shortly after it was cast, but the bell still tolls out some tremendously sonorous silences every hour.

Crossing the octangle, we proceed up a broad flight of steps to an impressive pair of doors, again made of octiron. Note the heavy locks, curly hinges and brass studs on the door itself and the intricate carvings on the archway. Passing through this entrance, we notice the University's keys on their huge iron ring. Not all of them are metal, not all are visible; some look very strange indeed, as if they are not entirely in this world.

We will go straight to the Great Hall. Around its walls hang or stand portraits or statues of past Archchancellors – full-bearded and pointy-hatted, clutching ornamental scrolls or holding mysterious symbolic bits of astrological equipment. They stare down at us with ferocious self-importance or, possibly, chronic constipation. In many cases they are unfinished, the subject having prematurely expired during the sitting.

However, it is worth seeking out the niche containing not the likeness but the actual body of Archchancellor 'Trouter' Hopkins, whose will stipulated that upon his death the University should continue his own work and pickle his body in alcohol. It sits beautifully preserved in its niche gazing happily at the festivities below, and is occasionally purloined by students and left around the University in a variety of humorous poses (sitting at the High Table with a bib on, wearing a night-cap in the Bursar's bed, etc.).

The floor is decorated with a worrying pattern of black and white tiles, and covered with long tables and benches. There is a big fireplace at the turnwise end and a big clock at the other. A third wall is largely occupied by the Mighty Organ. This magnificent instru-

ment, recently restored, was the work of Bloody Stupid Johnson (*see* JOHNSON, BERGHOLT STUTTLEY), famed wherever buildings are constructed back to front.

Genius knows no limitations. Leonardo da Vinci would design lock gates and new ways of soldering lead just as happily as he would paint pictures. In the same way, the reverse genius of people like Johnson also likes to dabble a bit. As he said, 'It's only air going through pipes, it can't be that difficult.'

And, indeed, the resulting construction must be one of the most versatile instruments known to pre-electronic mankind, with its three giant keyboards and range of additional controls seldom before encountered, including the one that floods all the pipes with poisonous gas to kill the mice. Dextrous use of resin, strips of metal, rubber tubing and special pipes allows a whole range of surprising effects, permitting composers to explore whole new areas of music-making (one has only to cite Bubbla's 'Variations On a Man Taking His Foot Out of a Pile of Mud', say, or Fondel's 'Double Top Overture', on the first playing of which the audience were mystified that they could hear nothing but were being stunned by falling bats).

No one is now allowed to use the *Terraemotus pedal*, which opens up the 128-foot pipe known as Earthquake. On the first occasion when it was used the sixteen students doing the pumping were sucked into the machinery, the population of a quarter of the city experienced acute bowel discomfort, and the building moved a quarter of an inch sideways.

To supplement the light from the small high windows, with their gentle patina of antique grease, the Great Hall is lit by a massive, heavy, black, tallow-encrusted chandelier which hangs from the Hall's dark, owl-haunted rafters like a threatening overdraft. It can hold one thousand candles.

The Great Hall is the scene of all major magical activities in the University, and it also hosts the four main meals of the day. The senior members of the faculty used to sit at the High Table which was indeed high, since it could float several yards up in the air, and landed only between courses. It now remains grounded as a result of what is referred to only as the Incident at Dinner.

Also in the main building are the Uncommon Room, with its roaring log fire, summer or winter, the University's small chapel and modest sanatorium (wizards tend to be either in rude health or dead), and of course the classrooms designed on the funnel principle, with their benches sloping precipitously over the central teaching areas.

Also worthy of note, for visitors who are interested in this subject, is the senior wizards' lavatory, which has real running water, interesting tiles and two big silver mirrors placed on opposite walls.

One room, amongst the more than 5000 known rooms in UU, which we may experience trouble visiting is 3B. It is not locatable on any floor plan of UU – but all *virtual* lectures take place there. That is to say, those lectures that neither the students nor the lecturers wish to attend, but which must have some type of existence since they are down on the timetable, are therefore held in this room which, in fact, does not exist. There are other rooms which contain rooms which, if you enter them, turn out to contain the room you started with.

In the cellars are a maze of cold-rooms, still-rooms, kitchens, sculleries, bakeries and taprooms that together form the driving engine of the University. It will be noted that while most of the University is in a permanent state of happy decay, the kitchens are quite modern and also in a permanent state of bustle. An army, it has been said, marches on its stomach; wizards sit holding theirs. Also in the cellars is the curiobiological museum, probably best not visited after a meal, particularly since it is situated next to the pickle pantry. You will also find the Museum of Quite Unusual Things down there, although this is now more or less abandoned. The cellars also contain a privy built by Archchancellor WEATHERWAX on a black hole into another dimension. It was found to discharge into another hole in one of the attics.

The cellars also house the washing engines. Each is two storeys high. A huge treadmill connects to a couple of bleached wooden paddles in each vat, heated by fireboxes underneath. In full production, they need half-a-dozen people at least to manhandle the loads, maintain the fires and oil the scrubbing arms. Were it not for the fact that they are very efficient at getting clothes clean they may have been designed by the Bloody Stupid Johnson, although if this really was the case he undoubtedly intended for them to do something else.

Passing through the main building we come to the University Gardens. Dominating these, as it dominates the entire city, is the Tower of Art, 800 feet tall, and the subject of a separate tour. To our left is the main Observatory, with its broad mosaic floor inlaid with the sixty-four signs of the Disc ZODIAC* and the gym, a large room lined with lead and rowan wood, where neophytes can work at High Magic without seriously unbalancing the universe. In that building is also the University squash court.

To our immediate right is the LIBRARY; access to this glass-domed building is via the inside of the University but is only with the permission of the Librarian.

There is, incidentally, a second observatory in the deepest cellars. It is lined with lead, and it is used for viewing... the *other* stars.

Further to our right is the tiny-windowed High Energy Magic Building, the only building on the campus less than a thousand years old. The senior wizards have never bothered much about what the younger, skinnier and more bespectacled wizards get up to in there, treating their endless requests for funding for thaumic particle accelerators and radiation shielding as one treats pleas for more pocket money, and listening with amusement to their breathless accounts of the search for ever more elementary particles of magic itself. They are, though, nervous of the fact that the students there seem to be engrossed in their work and, in fact,

---

* *At the time of the floor being relaid that is. This is done every few decades, during which time many of the constellations will have changed or been renamed.*

apparently enjoy it. This is always a dangerous thing in a student.

The grounds, with their rose beds and ancient velvet lawns, their neat patterns of gravel paths and hedges, stretch right down to the river, where some of the University's boats are moored to the jetties. A small bridge leads over the Ankh to WIZARDS' PLEASAUNCE.

The grounds, which incorporate the Archchancellor's garden and verandah, are protected by walls twenty feet high, lined with spikes. To our left are the ornamental drain covers, bearing a likeness of Archchancellor William Badger, not a popular man.

And now we should just make our way into this mossy courtyard, criss-crossed with washing lines. Yes, that is what wizards wear *under* their robes... What did you expect?

And now here is the University's back door, made of normal wood and with a knocker shaped like a dragon's head.

If you would just follow me through this door, which is used by most of the University's 'normal' visitors, we should find ourselves back in the streets of Ankh-Morpork.

Ah... It would seem that the party now includes an extra person, and he smells very strongly of embalming fluid and alcohol... Those students, eh?

Upshot, Feeney. Chief Constable of the local village near Ramkin Hall, in the Overhangs area. Upshot is seventeen years old and smells of pigs – due to Masher, an enormous boar who used to live in the village lock-up. Feeney's granddad used to work on the tall ships and he sailed to Bhangbhangduc, coming back with Ming Chang, the lady who would become Feeney's granny. [SN]

Upspire, Gurning. Famous, and historical, furniture maker. [UA]

Upwright. Big Jim 'Still Standing' Upwright became, at one time, the owner of the Ankh-Morpork Post Office coaches by buying out the other coach drivers. That business was then taken over and run by his sons – Harry

'Slugger' and Little Jim 'Leadpipe' – both huge men, made practically spherical by multiple layers of waistcoats and overcoats. They look like twins, built out of pork fat and bacon. [GP]

Urglefloggah. A demon. Spawn of the Pit and Loathly Guardian of the Dread Portal. He is over 30,000 years old, has various mouths and has more tentacles than legs, but fewer arms than heads. He bears a certain resemblance to QUEZOVERCOATL. Like most demons, he is irredeemably stupid. [E]

Urmond. One of the assassins who accompanied Zlorf FLANNELFOOT into the Broken DRUM. [COM]

Urn. A young man with a paintbrush hairstyle. Nephew to DIDACTYLOS the Ephebian philosopher. Urn built the Disc's first known steam-powered boat, and it is perhaps typical of his approach to life that he never thought it worth naming. [SG]

... the only thing more dangerous than a vampire crazed with blood
lust was a vampire crazed with anything else.

– The Truth

Valkyries. Anthropomorphic personifications, appearing as women dressed in chain mail, with shiny 46D-cup breastplates and helmets with horns on. They are normally associated with BLIND IO and other gods of the thick-necked, celestial rugby-playing persuasion, and their function is to carry off the souls of warriors who have died in battle. These apparently go to some huge hall somewhere and carouse for ever. ('Carouse' belongs to the same vocabulary as 'quaff'; there's a strong suggestion that bread rolls are thrown and a lot of good food ends up on the floor. 'Carouse' offers no possibility of a vegetarian option.) [SM]

Vampires. Or, Vampyres. It is said that there are as many vampires as there are types of disease and it is certainly true that there are more ways to kill vampires than you could shake a sharpened stick at. They are now attempting to work

their way into normal society and the Über-wald League of TEMPERANCE is attempting to distance itself from past crimes.

Van Pew, Urdo. President of the Guild of Thieves, Burglars and Allied Trades. [GG]

Vard, Rhunlet. A wizard. Once seen as the natural successor to GREYHALD SPOLD at UNSEEN UNIVERSITY. [LF]

Varneshi. Ox-cart driver in the Ramtops. A trader in metals. The only regular contact Carrot's adoptive father had with the outside world, and therefore responsible for some of his old-fashioned views. [GG]

Vassenego, Duke. A demon. One of the oldest demons – if he didn't actually invent original sin, at least he made one of the first copies. He generally takes the form of an old, rather sad lawyer, with an eagle somewhere in his ancestry. [E]

Va Va Voom, Miss. A feather dancer at the Skunk Club, Ankh-Morpork. [SM]

Vena the Raven-Haired. An elderly barbarian heroine, later encountered as a mother and grandmother then called Mrs McGarry, running an inn. Her raven hair was now grey and the only armour she wore was an armoured corset. She was attractive, or had been conventionally so about thirty years ago. Now she looked like the teacher you wished you'd had in your first year at school. She knits, but still has her large sword to hand. [TLH]

Venerable Council of Seers. An organization involved in the search for RINCEWIND and the Eighth Spell in *The Light Fantastic*.

Venturi, Alice, Lady. Eldest daughter of Viscount Venturi (d. 1864) of Pseudopolis, and Wilhelmina, née Higgins (d. 1828); b. 5 March 1799, d. 12 Ick 1897. Privately educated. Recreations: embroidery, ethnography, corsetry, anthropology, writing, public speaking. Books: '*The Harem Frescoes of Old KIatch*', '*Interesting Customs among the N'Kouf*', '*Travels in the Dark Hinterland*' and numerous pamphlets.

Lady Alice, the eldest of four daughters, took to travel late in life when she had at last got access to the family fortune. She wandered widely throughout rimward KIatch and Howondaland, usually by elephant or camel, and researchers are indebted to her for the very large collection of watercolours, sketches, maps, notes, dried flowers and pressed reptiles accumulated on her extensive journeys.

Those who have studied these works in detail have concluded that Lady Alice must have been either unshockable or almost terminally dense. The few copies of '*The Harem Frescoes of Old KIatch*' and '*Interesting Customs among the N'Kouf*' which did not spontaneously combust shortly after printing are now much sought after by discerning gentlemen; her collection of tribal fetishes and ceremonial objects of Howondaland had to be bricked up in a vault, especially the one with the painstakingly-written label in Lady Alice's own handwriting, which read: 'Personal ornament of T'etse Males Over the Age of 13'.

Her public recital of 'Folk Songs of Old Al-Ybi' caused a near riot, less because of the words – which the audience couldn't translate – but because the accompanying traditional hand gestures made this fact quite superfluous.

Lady Alice herself seemed quite oblivious to the effects of all this, and regularly returned for further journeys in what she referred to as 'the Dark Hinterland'.

Natives of Klatch and Howondaland grew accustomed to her camel hoving into view at every fertility dance or ceremonial circumcision, although the rumour that some of the more interesting rites were devised especially for her visits, amidst much hilarity, has never been substantiated.

Given that in her own home she was quite capable of banning a visitor from the house for yawning without covering their mouth, it would seem that Lady Alice adopted the traditional Explorer's viewpoint: that activities that would lead one to summon the Watch if they happened on your doorstep are intriguing folkways when they occur two thousand miles away with a feather stuck in them.

Her grave in the cemetery of Small Gods, Ankh-Morpork, is decorated with traditional Al-Ybian symbols, and can be viewed (by arrangement) by parties that include no unmarried women under the age of 30. [DM]

Venturii, Charles, Lord. A nobleman in Ankh. [MAA]

Verence I. A past king of LANCRE. Coat of arms: a shield bisected vertically; on the right side an ours, d'or on a field, sable; on the left an ours, sable on a field, or. Seen in the chronicles only as a ghost. Verence I, whose death at the age of forty only marginally slowed him down, was a big, well-muscled man with a moustache and flowing hair. His enviable physical condition meant that he was one of the very few ghosts ever able to manipulate physical objects. [WS]

Verence II. Current King of Lancre. Used to be the court Fool. An apparently short man, with permanently harassed expression, runny eyes, ears that stick out a bit and clothes that never seem to fit right, he is the most amiable monarch in the history of LANCRE. He has, of course, a weak chest. He is a great believer in the usefulness of knowledge derived from books and is using them to teach himself kinging.

Entered the oeuvre (in *Wyrd Sisters*) as the jester at the Lancre court, and a very loyal servant to his master. He was then seventeen years old and wore a red and yellow costume with silver bells on his hat and a red and yellow hankie, also decorated with bells. Although he looked short, he was in fact of at least average height, but he made himself look small by hunching his shoulders, bandying his legs and walking in a half-crouch.

He was a Fool like his father and grandfather before him, and was raised by his stern grandfather following his father's abrupt departure from Lancre. He was soon sent away to the FOOLS' GUILD in Ankh-Morpork, where he had the traditional education and, by employing application and hard work to make up for lack of talent, actually passed out as a very respected Fool.

He was half-brother to and slightly older than TOMJON, who was acknowledged as the son and heir of King VERENCE I. It is believed in Lancre that the Fool's father was also King Verence I, who had a somewhat old-fashioned approach to the young women of the kingdom, and that he had been christened Verence by his late mother in memory of that royal, er, connection.

However, the witches of Lancre have a slightly different, if unspoken, view of events. King Verence I was indeed a ladies' man, but so was the Fool's official father, who achieved with kind words and a fetching manner what the King achieved by hammering on the door with his sword. They also recall that the man left town hurriedly shortly after the birth of Tomjon, and that the Queen was a rather lonely lady who may well have appreciated a little gentle attention on those long nights when her husband was exercising his droit de seigneur around the kingdom. The witches are also midwives, and can count rather better than the Queen could. They're quite certain that Tomjon and the Fool are half-brothers.

Further evidence that Verence is the son of a commoner and has no genetic tradition of kingship in his bones may be gathered from the fact that he is hardworking, intelligent, conscientious, humble and kind. His only failings, if such they be, are a tendency to try to better the lot of his fellow men even if they are happy with the lot they've got – and he has no sense of humour whatsoever, and a strong aversion to custard. There is something about the regime at the Fools' Guild that can do that to a man. [WS]

Vermine. A small, black-and-white relative of the lemming, found in the cold Hublandish regions, particularly the RAMTOPS. Its pelt is rare and highly valued, especially by the vermine itself; the selfish little bastard will do anything rather than let go of it. The fur is used primarily for trimming robes, especially those of wizards.

It is a more careful relative of the lemming; it only throws itself over small pebbles. The point is that dead animals don't breed and over the

millennia more and more vermine are descendants of those who, when faced with a cliff edge,
squeal the rodent equivalent of 'Blow that for a
Game of Soldiers'. Vermine now abseil down
the cliffs and build small boats to cross lakes.
When their rush leads them to the seashore
they sit around avoiding one another's gaze for
a while and then leave early to get home before
the rush. [S]

Vernissage. A hat-maker in Slice, in the
Ramtops. [WA]

Verruca Gnome. A being accidentally brought
into existence during the events of *Hogfather*
by Ridcully as a result of an excess of belief on
the Disc. Presumably disappeared when events
returned to normal. [H]

Vestigial virgins. Found in the temples of a
number of Discworld religions, most particularly in those belonging to OM. A vestigial virgin
is more easily pictured than described. There is
a certain good-natured rumpledness about her,
a suggestion that whatever the body has done
the mind has remained more or less uninflu-
enced by it.

Vetinari, Havelock, Lord. A graduate of, and
now Provost of, Assassins at the ASSASSINS'
GUILD. Supreme ruler of the city of Ankh-Morpork, to which he is totally devoted. Tall, thin,
bearded and generally to be seen wearing black.
He has (mostly) walked with a stick since the
events of *Men at Arms*, although this may be a
bit of an affectation, to mislead potential attack-
ers. He is believed to be about the same age as
Commander VIMES.

He is the most recent of a line of unelected
heads (*see* PATRICIAN, OFFICE OF). As their
names suggest, these were not wholly pleasant
or well-balanced men and soon met their ends,
as did a red-hot poker in the case of one particularly unpopular ruler. Lord Vetinari, on the
other hand, is very, very sane. And still alive.

He appears to have survived by being equally
distrusted and disliked by all interest groups
in the city, but also by carefully not being as
unpopular as every interest group is to all the
others.

A popular form of punishment and mass
entertainment in the reign of Mad Lord SNAP-
CASE was the tearing to pieces of criminals by
teams of wild horses. Lord Vetinari appeared to
be like the man in the middle of the arena who
had managed somehow to chain all the wild
horses to one another and is groaning theat-
rically while watching them drag one another
to their knees. The result, in political terms, is
stability achieved by equal tension in all directions.

His genius lies in the realization that everyone craves stability even more than they hunger
after justice or truth. Even revolutionary anar-
chists want stability, so that they have breathing space to fight their real enemies, i.e., those
higher than themselves in the revolutionary
anarchist council, and those heretics whose
definition of revolutionary anarchy differs from
their own by about half a sentence in paragraph
97 of the charter.

This policy is dimly perceived by the more
intelligent Guild leaders in the city. Yet when
an assassination attempt was last made (*Men
at Arms*), the Assassins' Guild themselves were
prominent in the search for the perpetrator.
Annoying as the Patrician is, it is so easy to
think of someone worse. Technically, Vetinari
seems to have given in to every demand of every
Guild for years, so the Guilds are driving themselves mad wondering why he is therefore still
in charge.

It has been remarked that if the Patrician
were thrown to a pack of wolves he would, after
chatting to them for a few minutes, have them
tearing one another to shreds. It is certainly

Lord Havelock Vetinari

the case that when he was thrown into one of his own rat-infested, scorpion-filled dungeons (*Guards! Guards!*) he organized the rats to eat the scorpions and then to bring him food and reading matter. He'd also, years before, secreted a key to the dungeon behind a secret slab. As he wrote in his unpublished manuscript entitled '*The Servant*', a sort of handbook for the politically ambitious: 'Never build a dungeon that you cannot get out of.'

Politics is the ocean in which he swims. He had long ago perfected the art of giving way with a smile when engaged in complex negotiations, but Lord Vetinari's smile is that of a man who knows that his opponents have yet to find, metaphorically speaking, and despite their cleverness, that their underpants are now down around their ankles and their backsides are on show for all to see.

He is entirely without vices in any normal sense of the word. If he had any, we can be sure some Guild or other would have made use of them by now.

It is true that he has banned street theatre and hangs mime artists upside down in a scorpion pit opposite a sign that says 'Learn The Words', but this may be considered an excusable peccadillo or possibly an amusing character trait. He does have a small and very old terrier, called Wuffles, to which he is said to be quite attached (although it has not been seen in recent volumes and presumably even despotic rulers have a sad pile of earth behind the tool-shed).

Probably his greatest enemy is Commander Sir Samuel VIMES of the City WATCH but, strangely, the person with whom he gets on best – or least badly – is Captain CARROT Ironfoundersson of the same Watch. They share the same obsessive interest in the city itself.

Lord Vetinari lives in what was once the royal family's Winter Palace in Morpork (the summer palace is a long way from the city, and the reason will easily be appreciated by anyone who has spent a summer near the river). He manages the city either from a wooden seat at the foot of the steps on which is the ancient golden throne of the city, or more usually from the Oblong Office, high in the palace.

This is where he gathers information. People tell him things, for all sorts of reasons. He has a bedroom. He presumably sleeps.

Lord Vetinari has expressed a wish that, one day, he could retire and cultivate a garden. It will probably never happen. It is impossible to imagine him as a mere civilian. But if he did indeed take up horticulture, the roses would grow in lines, the garden would bloom on command – and the slugs would eat the caterpillars. [S]

Vimes, 'Old Stoneface'. Suffer-Not-Injustice Vimes. Commander of the City WATCH who beheaded – because no one else would do it – the last King of Ankh-Morpork, LORENZO THE KIND 'and led the city's militia in a revolt against the rule of a tyrannical monarch'. Sam VIMES secretly cherishes the fact this 'Old Stoneface' was his ancestor and that the nickname is sometimes applied to *him* by his men.

The act of regicide was followed by six months under the rule of Stoneface and his efficient if unimaginative soldiers, known colloquially as the 'Ironheads'. He was later hanged, dismembered and buried in five graves by a grateful city. Samuel Vimes embraces the cynical belief that Old Stoneface tried to introduce democracy to the city, and that the people voted against it. Certainly for much of the chronicles he has been a footnote to history, and not talked about in polite historical circles; when the 'Peeled Nuts' (the Ankh-Morpork Historical Re-creation Society) staged episodes from the Civil War, no one ever wanted to play him. However, as yet another incentive for Vimes to accept promotion, Lord Vetinari has arranged for the role of Old Stoneface in the city's history to be 'reassessed' by the Guild of Historians, who rewrite history all the time in any case.

There was something else… Oh, yes. He had warts and all. [MAA]

Vimes, Samuel, His Grace Commander Sir. Duke of Ankh and head of the Ankh-Morpork City WATCH. Badge No.177. An upright and honest man whose appointment as head of the

His Grace Commander Sir Samuel Vimes

despised Night Watch – regarded by all sensible people as a completely useless appendage to the running of the city – may have been the cause of his drinking problem. But it has also been suggested that he is in fact naturally more sober than other people (to put it technically, he is slightly KNURD).

It is known that he was born in Cockbill Street in the SHADES, that his father was Thomas Vimes and his grandfather was Gwillaim Vimes. In his younger years, he was a member of the Cockbill Street Roaring Lads. Membership of the Watch was a family tradition and Samuel claims to have joined the Watch shortly after leaving school. However, since he was in his late teens when he joined the Watch this means he was either a very slow learner or is delicately avoiding the subject of juvenile streets gangs, where he is believed to have picked up some of his fighting techniques.

Initially, Vimes never got the hang of ambition and worked his way sideways rather than up, and his promotion to captain was simply the result of the sheer unthinkability of promoting any other watchman.

By his own account he was a skinny, balding, unshaven collection of bad habits marinated in alcohol, although these days he is better shaved and doesn't drink. Partly as a result of this latter fact, he is morose, cynical and ridiculously – and to his own embarrassment – soft-hearted in certain circumstances. He is almost certainly one of Nature's policemen; it has been said of him that his soul burns to arrest the Creator of the universe for getting it wrong.

He loathes kings and aristocrats in general, despite the fact that he is, now, one of them. In fact, in his earlier life, Vimes was almost defined by what he disliked, and that included the undead, Assassins, trolls, dwarfs and the human race. These days, with undead, dwarfs and trolls all working well in the Watch, he seems to have mellowed considerably and may even have come to terms with the human race. He still draws the line at vampires, however.

Recent years have seen the universe play a huge joke on Vimes. He was promoted to Commander, knighted against his will and made a Duke by Lord VETINARI; in most cases his acceleration up the ranks of privilege has been part of a package to improve the standing of the Watch as a whole, but he still resents it. He also married Lady Sybil Ramkin, who is part of no package at all, and is now so rich he doesn't know how rich he is. He nevertheless likes to shave himself using his granddad's cut-throat razor.

For several years, he had a price on his head with the ASSASSINS' GUILD (getting as high as $600,000) but this has now been put into abeyance. It is suspected that this is because, like Vetinari, he is considered more useful to the city alive than he would be dead. (The Assassins' Guild don't mind rocking the boat but draw the line at drilling holes in the hull, as it were.)

He was once blackboard monitor at school for a whole term. This fact seems to really impress dwarfs. [GG]

Vimes, Sybil Deirdre Olgivanna, Lady. Maiden name: Ramkin; family motto: 'What We Have We Keep', although Lady Sybil prefers her personal motto: 'Non Svmet Nvllvs Pro Responso'. Coat of arms: a dragon vert, guardant passant, on a field, gules. The whole encaged by bars, sable.

Lady Sybil Ramkin is the richest woman in Ankh-Morpork.

The estate is worth seven million dollars a year. The Ramkin family own about a tenth of Ankh and extensive properties in Morpork, plus other considerable farm lands.

Although there are a few gaga old uncles and some distant cousins so far removed as to be confiscated, she is, for practical purposes, the last survivor of one of the oldest families in Ankh.

Sybil is a toweringly big lady, with a mass of chestnut hair (a wig – no one who has much to do with dragons keeps their own hair for long). The Ramkins have never bred for beauty, they've bred for healthy solidity and big bones, and Lady Sybil is the shining result. Her ballgowns are usually light blue – to combine the maximum of quiet style with the minimum of

Lady Sybil Vimes née Ramkin

visibility. She is large and kind, and she's can't lie – she goes red when she tries. However, she can refrain from telling the truth with clear-eyed honestly that can fool experts.

Until quite recently, she has apparently confined her own personal breeding to swamp dragons, which she keeps in pens behind the house, and she is the tower of strength behind the SUNSHINE SANCTUARY FOR SICK DRAGONS. For dragon handling, she wears huge and fearsomely padded armour. She is the author of several self-published volumes on the diseases of the dragon, which is a fruitful and probably endless field of study. This activity may well take second place since she is now the proud mother of Samuel Vimes Jnr, but you never know.

Before her marriage to Commander VIMES of the City WATCH and Duke of Ankh-Morpork, she lived alone, apart from thirty-seven dragons and a butler, in the family's town house in Scoone Avenue, Ankh, where she occupied three rooms out of the available thirty-four. It was, and is, a rather pleasant old house with well-designed gardens, owing to one of Lady Ramkin's ancestors shooting 'Bloody Stupid' Johnson (*see* JOHNSON, BERGHOLT STUTTLEY) in the leg when the unfortunate man tried to walk up the drive one day.

Prior to her marriage, both house and gardens were in a state of some disrepair, but a full staff is now employed and Lady Sybil is once again surfacing in Ankh-Morpork society like a submarine in a boating lake. The house is easily identified from the road by the stone dragons on the gateposts. [GG]

Vimes, Young Sam. Son of Sam and Sybil. Much-loved, especially by his father, who obsessed for a while about reading to him – taking great pains to ensure that he was able to read to him as promised. Six o'clock, prompt. Every day. Read to Young Sam. No excuses. Young Sam was very fond of 'Where's My Cow?' But he also takes a very keen interest in poo... as a cheerful six-year-old we find him methodically weighing giraffe poo on a pair of ancient snuff scales. Another favourite book of his is 'The World of Poo'. [T!]

Vincent, Old. An 87-year-old member of the Silver Horde prior to the events of *The Last Hero*. Choked to death on a ~~concubine~~ cucumber. [IT]

Vincent the Invulnerable. Committed suicide by walking into the Mended DRUM and announcing that he was called Vincent the Invulnerable. [SM]

Visit-The-Infidel-With-Explanatory-Pamphlets. Also, in Ankh-Morpork, known as Visit-The-*Ungodly*-With-Explanatory-Pamphlets ('infidel' can get you a thick ear). A constable in the Ankh-Morpork City WATCH, usually just known as Visit, or by his nickname of Washpot. He is a good, conscientious and methodical copper who instinctively respects authority. He doesn't have many friends, perhaps because he has a pathological interest in evangelical religion. He is an Omnian, who in his spare time goes round door-to-door pamphleting with his friend Smite-The-Unbeliever-With-Cunning-Arguments. He spends all his wages on pamphlets and now has his own printing press. The almost genetic Omnian disposition towards envangelism has, in these more relaxed times, moved away from burning people at the stake to merely shouting at them through their letter boxes. [J]

Vitoller, Mrs. Wife of Olwyn VITOLLER, the actor. An intelligent-looking woman with bottomless reserves of patience and organizational ability. And nimble fingers, which she needs in order to get the seat money before Olwyn drinks it. [WS]

Vitoller, Olwyn. Manager of a band of strolling players. Large and fat, with an impressive moustache and a nose that might hide successfully in a bowl of strawberries. Aged sixty, he is the owner of a rich, golden brown and powerful voice. He wears a ragged jerkin, holey tights and a moth-eaten hat. [WS]

Volfssonssonssonsson, Volf. Volf the Lucky. A youngish Vasung warrior from the Hublands. Since he is never seen alive, and even when dead is a man of many parts, the name is probably misplaced. [SM]

Vorbis, Deacon. Head of the QUISITION in Kom, OMNIA. An exquisitor (like an inquisitor, only a lot more so). Well over six feet tall,

with a mild, aquiline face and a body seemingly just skin stretched over bone. He looks like a normally proportioned person modelled in clay by a child and then rolled out.

His ancestors came from one of the desert tribes; he had dark eyes – not just dark of pupil, but almost black of eyeball. This made it very hard to tell where he was looking, because he was apparently wearing sunglasses under his skin.

Vorbis was bald, as were many of the Church of OM's senior members, but Vorbis was bald by design. He shaved all over. He gleamed. He wore a plain grey hooded robe, under which he wore a singlet with nails sewn into it, and carried a steel-shod staff.

He didn't menace. He didn't threaten. He just gave everyone the feeling that his personal space radiated several yards from his body, so that superiors fifty years his senior felt it necessary to apologize about interrupting whatever it was he might be thinking about. Had he not stayed in the Quisition, he could easily have been an archpriest or even an Iam. But he didn't worry about that kind of trivia.

His goal was to become the Superior Iam of the Church, an ambition he achieved for the space of ten minutes. Possibly the most terrifying thing about him was that he was quite genuinely not ambitious for himself. He believed that he was what the Church needed. [SG]

Vortin. Troll dentist and owner of a diamond warehouse in Ankh-Morpork. [SM]

Vul nut. A re-annual plant. Ghlen Livid is made from the fermented vul nut drink they freeze-distil in the AGATEAN EMPIRE. Vul nut wine is particularly exceptional in that it can mature as many as eight years prior to its seed actually being sown. Vul nut wine is reputed to give certain drinkers an insight into the future, which is, from the nut's point of view, the past. [COM]

Vurms. Vurms are somewhat like glow worms, but with a stink that illuminates. They can be found in deep, dark places, where they subsist on the effluvia of any creatures that may arrive there. They are very useful to tomb raiders – who in turn are often very useful to the vurms.

Vyrt. Brother-in-law of King Tepicymon XXVII. An assassin; his influence probably resulted in Teppic being sent out of Djelibeybi to be educated. [P]

There were really only four types of people in the world: men and
women and wizards and witches...

– I Shall Wear Midnight

Wa, Cripple. A beggar who frequented the Pearl Dock, Ankh-Morpork. Well renowned for his floating crap game, which occasionally, owing to its closeness to the dock, resulted in the floating, or at least the gentle bobbing, of participants unmannerly enough to win; he was skilled at switching dice and once diced with DEATH. In person. He had twenty-three people murdered, but did not consider that this in itself meant he was a bad person. [COM]

Waddy. Constable on the old city Watch when Sam VIMES first joined up. [NW]

Waggon, Deirdre, Lady. Author of a book on etiquette. Very necessary in Ankh-Morpork. In a society that includes professional assassins and thieves, the seating arrangements at dinner can take some very careful working out. [MAA]

Wahooni. A vegetable that grows only in certain parts of HOWONDALAND, where it typically reaches twenty feet in length. It is covered in spikes the colour of earwax, and smells like an anteater that's eaten a very bad ant. Its flavour is prized by connoisseurs and makes everyone else want to be sick. It is banned in many of the cities of the STO PLAINS. Ankh-Morpork is affectionately known as the Big Wahooni, in the same way that New York is the Big Apple. [MP]

Wallspur. Prophet of the Omnian religion. [SG]

War. One of the Four Horsemen. (His horse is huge and red, and the heads of dead warriors hang from the saddle horn.) War is a large, jolly anthropomorphic personification, a bit like your old sports teacher in red armour. He does have a habit of losing the thread and not really listening to people. He lives in an ancient longhouse which was full of valhallerian carousing and fighting until his marriage to an ex-Valkyrie, who chucked out what she called 'his no-good friends' and installed a modern black kitchen range where the fire pit had been.

As with many married men of a certain age, War has installed his memory in his wife's head

('Do I like pork?' 'No, dear, it gives you wind.' 'Oh. I thought I liked it.' 'No, dear, you don't.')

Warbeck, Lucy. A young witch and friend of Tiffany Aching. [HFOS]

Watch, the Ankh-Morpork City. Motto: *FABRICATI DIEM, PVNC.*

Strength (according to pre-republican records): one commander, five captains, ten sergeants of varying seniority, and a total of forty corporals, lance-corporals, constables and lance-constables, plus a 'city militia' of varying size, depending on need, made up of civilians.

Together these individuals formed the Ankh-Morpork police force. It consisted eventually of four loosely linked organizations: the Night Watch, the Day Ward (which had more or less the same functions, but the jurisdiction was exchanged at dawn and dusk), the Palace Guard and the Cable Street Particulars.

The Particulars are believed to have been quite an elite force and combined the roles of secret service and government (i.e., whoever was in the palace) office of investigation. Under the administration of Lord WINDER, however, they became an instrument of terror and oppression, which resulted in the burning of their Watch House during the Glorious Revolution. Subsequently restored, it is currently a dwarf delicatessen.

The Palace Guard were (and are) little more than tough men in armour whose job was (and is) to safeguard the life of whoever pays their wages. The Watches were gate guards, kickers

War

of drunks, pursuers of common thieves, traffic controllers, market superintendents and in general the doers of all the tedious jobs of day-to-day city housekeeping.

Taken together they made quite an important body, but the elevation of the THIEVES' GUILD by Lord VETINARI was the final blow to an institution that was already ceasing to have any real function in the city owing to the growth of the Guilds.

For Ankh-Morpork is, in its way, a very democratic place. As it changed from medieval city to the semi-industrialized, multi-species society it is today, there were natural growing pains, resulting in a breakdown of law and order and increasing friction between many more-or-less honest citizens and the Watch. This came to a head one day when a Commander of the Watch, faced with a large and angry meeting which was complaining that, what with all this theft and murder and robbery, no one was making as much money as they ought to, warned the throng 'notte to take the law into their owne handes'.

Legend says that the crowd worked this out silently for a minute or two and then, as one man or woman, rose up and threw the Commander into the river, with a chant of 'If it's not in our hands, whose hands is it in?' After that, the existing Guilds began to police themselves and the Watch became increasingly irrelevant. Lord Vetinari's decision to put crime itself under Guild control knocked away the last support.

In a city which runs on power politics, one man's view of morality and a legal system that is made up on the fly out of pragmatic decisions pasted together with spit, there was no room for people who go around asking awkward questions and arresting people for no more reason than that they were guilty of something. So the city prospered while the Watches dwindled away, like a useless appendix, into a handful of unemployables who no one in their right mind could ever take seriously.

The last thing anyone wanted them to do was to get it into their heads to fight crime, and there is some evidence that Lord Vetinari took

pains to ensure that the Watch consisted of sad drunks, incompetents and petty criminals too unreliable even to find employment in a Guild.

In the case of the Day Watch (as the old Day Ward has become known) this policy seemed to work extremely well, to the extent that they were pretty much like any other city gang. The Night Watch, such as it was, was too incompetent even to manage criminality. Much of this changed when it was joined by CARROT, who triggered a certain phenomenon: when you throw men down hard enough, they bounce.

By a kind of holy stupidity – they believed that, since they were being paid a handful of dollars per month by the city, they therefore had some kind of duty towards it – the Night Watch saved the city from a serious dragon attack.

The effect on their own morale was astonishing, and Vetinari was subsequently unable to prevent the Watch from taking on fresh recruits. His insistence that the recruits consist of representatives of ethnic minorities was probably – considering the kind of ethnic minorities Ankh-Morpork boasts, such as dwarfs and trolls and undead – another attempt to keep it under control. However, fused into something approaching an efficient police force by the suspiciously king-like charisma of Carrot and the cynicism of the then Captain VIMES, they played a prominent role in an attempt upon the life of the PATRICIAN (in thwarting it, that is).

Following the dragon incident, which resulted en passant in the destruction of the old Watch House in Treacle Mine Road, the Night Watch was given, by Lady Ramkin, new premises in Pseudopolis Yard and this is now the official Watch headquarters. Treacle Mine Road is, however, now being reclaimed as another Section House to meet the growing needs of the city.

The Watch is now a modern, go-ahead police force consisting of some one hundred officers (there is a fast turnover, though, because officers with Watch training are frequently 'poached' by other cities). There are Section Houses in Dolly Sisters, Long Wall and Chittling Street. Smaller stations, not permanently manned, are at most of the main city gates.

A River Patrol is sometimes referred to, and is known to have a small office and slipway beside the Mended DRUM, but as far as is known its activities consist wholly of trying to dredge up its boat.

Watch policy (that is to say, Sam Vimes's prejudice) is against undue specialization. There is a small forensics and medical unit (Constable IGOR (*see* IGOR, THE WATCH) and Corporal LITTLEBOTTOM) at the Yard, and a recently formed Intelligence Department for the collation of all those snippets of information garnered on the street by the patrols. Occasional experts are temporarily drafted into a plain-clothes section, still known as the Cable Street Particulars, but Watch policy (*see* above) is also against too much reliance on plain-clothes activity. This may be forced to change as the new Watch becomes more involved in international matters, however, because it appears that Vimes is being groomed for a diplomatic role.

Finally, there is the very recent Traffic Division, also based at the Yard, and masterminded, if that is the word, by Sergeant COLON; it would appear to be a ruse to keep Colon and Nobbs out of the way.

The new Training School, now being established in the old lemonade factory off Knuckle Passage, is temporarily headed by Commander Vimes but the teaching staff is made up of serving officers. New recruits are encouraged to gain experience at all the stations, although in the case of Chitterling Street, which has the notorious Shades and the docks in its section, this may be far more experience than they bargained for. Chitterling Street is considered a very good posting for a young officer seeking promotion, possibly to a better life in the next world.

And now a note about vice. Ankh-Morpork has no Vice Squad, the Guild of Seamstresses having made it clear that they have enough already and don't need any from the Watch. Watch policy is that the Guild is a co-operative enterprise, better run on behalf of its membership than most Guilds, and officers will not therefore become involved except by invitation

or evidence of serious crime.

The day-to-day policing of the salons, houses of negotiable affection, hot bath lobs, parlours, spikies, molly houses and premises of extremely good repute that form the Shades' most energetic trade is left to the Guild, and their enforcers Dotsie and Sadie, locally known as the AGONY AUNTS. They may be considered as highly-specialized constables, whose job is to protect Guild employees from the more enthusiastic customer, and are best left alone, especially Dotsie if you see her left eye start to spin.

THE WATCH OATH

'I, (recruit's name), do solemnly swear by (recruit's deity of choice) to uphold the Laws and Ordinances of the city of Ankh-Morpork, serve the public trust, and defend the subjects of His/Her (delete whichever is inappropriate) Majesty (name of reigning monarch) without fear, favour, or thought of personal safety; to pursue evildoers and protect the innocent, laying down my life if necessary in the cause of said duty, so help me (aforesaid deity). Gods Save the King/Queen (delete whichever is inappropriate).'

Since Ankh-Morpork has not had a reigning monarch for centuries, recruits are advised to read the oath exactly as printed.

The new recruit will also be asked to take the King's Shilling. The origins of this tradition are also lost in the smogs of time, but there is a shilling (five pence in new money) kept at the Watch headquarters for the purposes and recruits are requested to take it after uttering the oath and then to return it immediately so that it can be taken by the next officer. A chain is attached to it to ensure that it isn't taken too far.

WATCH EQUIPMENT

One Shirt, Mail, Chain
One Helmet, Iron & Copper
One Breastplate, Iron
Breeches, Knee, Leather, Watchmen for the
    Use of

Cape, Rain, Leather, Watch Officers for the Use of

Sandals, Leather, Watch Officers for the Use of (Summer)

Boots, Leather, Watch Officers for the Use of (Winter)

One Sword, Short, or

(One Axe, Battle, Dwarf Officers for the Use of, only)

(One Club, Troll Officers for the Use of, only)

(One Adapted Paper-knife, Gnome Officers for the Use of, only)

One Truncheon, Oak

One Emergency Pike or Halberd

One Crossbow, or

(One Crossbow, Siege, formerly Carriage-Mounted, Triple Stringed 2000 lb, with Windlass, Double-Action, Troll Officers for the Use of, only)

One Hourglass

One Bell, Hand, Brass & Wood

One Sewing Kit (zombie officers only)

One Pot Ceramic Cement (golem officers only)

One Badge, Office of, Night Watchman's, Copper

Specialist equipment, issued as standard to officers on patrol from Chitterling Street and the River Gate sub-station and as required by other officers with business in the Shades area:

One blanket, wool, blue, 18" x18" (bogey-men, for the existential confusion of)

One religious symbol of Watchman's choice (vampires, for the discouragement of).

One discourse of pure reason (vampires, for the discouragement of)

THE BADGE OF THE CITY WATCH – A HISTORY

The Ankh-Morpork City Watch was founded, in 1561, by King Veltrick I. It was originally established to look impressive during a state visit by the then Empress of Sto and Officers were kitted out with full infantry armour including a burnished copper helmet and a copper shield embossed with the legend 'Royal Ankhe-Morepork Citie Watch', the Royal coat of arms and the motto of the Veltrick family – 'Make the Day, the Moments Pass Quickly' (Fabricati Diem, Puncti Agunt Celeriter).

Veltrick I was murdered by his son, with the assistance of the Empress of Sto, four days after founding the Watch. Veltrick II did not share his father's interest in having a smart police force, and the Watch was largely forgotten. Over the years that followed, much of this original equipment was lost. Sometimes damaged during a dangerous arrest, sometimes used to weigh down an officer whose body was being consigned to the Ankh to keep him quiet, sometimes sold off to pay for more pressing needs, such as food or warm clothing.

When Veltrick III took the throne in 1572, he was approached by the city's merchants and agreed to make a modest allowance for the continued running of the City Watch. It was he who commissioned the striking of the first Watch badge, a plain disc or shield of copper (representing the shield which they had originally carried). This disc was stamped with AMCW (for 'Ankh-Morpork City Watch') and the officer's number. These badges were commonly in use by the City Night Watch until recently, although only a handful have survived the intervening years. Vimes certainly clings to his.

After the Watch was instrumental in saving the city from domination by a sixty-foot fire-breathing dragon, the Patrician commissioned a new badge to reflect the increased importance of the Watch to the city, and to allow its numbers to be expanded. Duke Vimes continues to hold his original Watch badge, which is now the only known example outside the Patrician's personal museum in the Palace.

Last year, in recognition of the much-enlarged Watch, the badge was further redesigned as the first stage of the creation of a new corporate identity for the Ankh-Morpork City Watch. This is likely now to include the introduction of new uniforms, warrants and equipment, and has been achieved after discussions between Lord Vetinari and Captain Carrot Ironfoundersson. The new badge also incorporates the new Watch motto: 'The Streets Are Always Safe for Honest Folk' – *VIAE SUNT SEMPER TUTUS PRO HOMINIBUS PROBIS.*

Watchtower, Brother. A member of the Elucidated Brethren of the Ebon Night. A bulky man. [GG]

Weasel, The. A small, cunning and brown-clad swordsman. He and Bravd the Hublander encountered Rincewind and Twoflower, robbing Twoflower of his watch. [COM]

Weatherwax family. Magical aptitude appears to be genetic, and the Weatherwax family (found around the RAMTOPS, particularly in LANCRE) has provided at least two witches of extreme power and one Archchancellor of Unseen University. Unlike the Oggs (a family which traditionally throws up witches but has no recorded wizards) the Weatherwaxes are not gregarious, even amongst themselves.

Weatherwax, Alison. A Weatherwax of whom little is known, but who should be included out of completeness and because of the mystery attached to the name.

The registering of births and deaths is not legally compulsory in LANCRE but is invariably done out of social pressure. Even the deaths of former residents a long way off are generally recorded whenever the news turns up, for completeness. It is certain that the birth of an Alison Weatherwax was recorded some 125 years before the present, and equally certain that no death has ever been recorded. This makes it just possible that Granny Weatherwax's own grandmother is still alive, somewhere.

Weatherwax, Esmerelda. Granny Weatherwax. Known to all, and not least herself, as the most competent witch on the Discworld.

Granny Weatherwax is the daughter of Violet Weatherwax, and was initially trained in witchcraft by Nanny Gripes, and subsequently other witches who taught her all they knew, after which she taught herself and was a remarkably apt pupil. Witches rarely acknowledge anything as definite or binding as a law, but it is generally accepted that, although witch skills tend to run in families, a witch should be trained by someone who is not a relative and witchcraft certainly should not be passed from mother to daughter.

She is nominally the village witch of BAD ASS in the kingdom of LANCRE, although for practical purposes she regards the whole kingdom – and, indeed, anywhere else she happens to be – as her rightful domain. She lives in the woods outside the village in a traditional, much-repaired witch's cottage, with beehives and a patch of what might be medicinal plants called the herbs (the patch is very thick, tends to move when there is no wind, and passers-by swear that the small flowers it occasionally produces turn to watch them). (*See also* GRANNY'S COTTAGE.)

She owns a broomstick, originally borrowed from an urban witch called Hilta GOAT-FOUNDER but technically not the same one because it has been entirely replaced over the years by spare parts. Despite the best efforts of dwarf engineers everywhere, it cannot be started without a considerable amount of running up

Esmerelda 'Granny' Weatherwax

and down with it in gear.

Granny Weatherwax's personal history is obscure, a fact which clearly suits her. It is known that she remained at home when her elder sister, Lily, left Lancre in dubious circumstances, and there is some suggestion of cruelty in the family. She nursed her mother until she died.

Beyond that, the picture is of a formidable character with every necessary attribute for the classical 'bad witch' – a quick temper, a competitive, selfish and ambitious nature, a sharp tongue, an unshakeable conviction of her own moral probity, and some considerable mental and occult powers, including a piercing blue cut-you-off-at-the-knees gaze. But, in fact, Granny Weatherwax's practical history puts her on the 'good' side of the ledger, in the same way that a cold shower and brisk run are good – they might sting a bit at the time but you'll feel all the better for it later.

She owned a kitten, given to her by Tiffany Aching, and called, by her, 'YOU'. [ER]

Weatherwax, Galder. Supreme Grand Conjurer of the Order of the Silver Star, Lord Imperial of the Sacred Staff, Eighth-Level Ipsissimus and 304th ARCHCHANCELLOR of Unseen University. An elderly, powerful and impressive-looking man, even dressed as we first saw him in a red night-shirt with hand-embroidered mystic runes (from which bony legs protrude), long cap with a bobble, Wee Willie Winkie candlestick and fluffy pom-pom slippers. He smoked a pipe the size of a small incinerator and was a distant relative of Esme Weatherwax – a cousin, it is believed. [LF]

Weatherwax, Lily. Elder sister of Esmerelda 'Granny' Weatherwax.

A fairy godmother. She was banished from the family home by her mother when she was just thirteen, after which she has had a speckled and profitable career as a witch and lady of fortune. Discworld society, while not formally offering much in the way of opportunity and careers to women, is all the more accessible to a woman of keen intelligence and flexible morality. Three husbands were acquired in the course of her progress; she has buried all three, and at least two of them were already dead.

Give or take the odd laughter-line and wrinkle, she is Granny Weatherwax to the life, although she looks younger than her younger sister. Moralists would say that this is because sin is easier than virtue, but moralists always say this sort of thing and some sin is quite difficult and requires specialized equipment.

She ran the city kingdom of GENUA with a sugary kind of cruelty, and she was an expert at mirror magic, so that she could observe the world through anything that can hold a reflection. This, in a contest with her sister, turned out to be her undoing – Lily had become so good at thinking of the world in terms of reflections that she had lost sight of the real one. She is still referred to in the present tense because, if she has in fact died, there has certainly been no body found.

While there is no Discworld concept of 'black' magic (*see* MAGIC), the use of magic to steer the lives of other people for your own benefit is regarded in the same way (certainly it is by Granny Weatherwax, except of course on those occasions when it is she who is doing it). Lily is probably a good example of a Discworld 'wicked witch' – the criterion here being less what it is that you do and far more what you had in mind when you did it. [WA]

Weavall, Mr. A bald, short-sighted, ninety-one-year-old man, who Tiffany Aching used to visit with Miss LEVEL. His wife Nancy and children, Toby and Mary, are all dead. He comes into a large sum of money and marries the Widow Tussy. [HFOS]

Weaver. A thatcher in Lancre. Married to Eva. He is a member of the Lancre Morris Men. [LL]

Weems. One of the mercenaries hired by HERRENA to capture RINCEWIND. He had a room-temperature IQ. [LF]

Weezen. A hunter from Slice, who once shot a hare in the leg when Granny Weatherwax was 'borrowing' it. [LL]

Welegare. Revd Welegare was the priest at the temple previously frequented by Arthur and Doreen Winkings (*see* NOTFAROUTOE, COUNT AND COUNTESS). [RM]

Wen. Wen the Eternally Surprised. He founded the order of History MONKS, wrote the Books of History to tell how the story should go and sawed the first Procrastinator from the trunk of a wamwam tree. He was bald as a coot and looked like a young man who had been young for a very long time. He never raised a hand to any man in his life, although he is traditionally held to be the inventor of Deja Fu, a hands-free fighting technique. He has an apprentice – Clodpool.

Wen fell in love with and married TIME (in her incarnation as a beautiful if somewhat sad woman) and was/is the father of Lobsang LUDD and Jeremy CLOCKSON. [TOT]

Wert, Jiglad. A member of the Brotherhood of the Hoodwink – the HOODWINKERS. [LF]

Wesley, Jed. Blacksmith in the Effing Forest and, with his brother, Crucible, a pioneer of the history of the railway. He was Blacksmith of the Year three years running in Scrote. Crucible was the brains of the outfit, but they met their end in the early frenzy of interest in the highly dangerous steam power. Hence their staus as 'pioneers'. Survived by their mum. [RS]

Wheedown, Blert. Author of a guitar primer and a highly skilled maker of guitars. When Music With Rocks In hit Ankh-Morpork he found that, for a certain type of guitarist, how the instrument looks is far, far more important than how it sounds. It made him want to cry, especially since it made him rich. [SM]

Wheelbrace, Eric. Champion walker and supreme champion of the right to roam at will, despite all obstacles – wires, fences, trolls, battles, ravines, etc. He disappeared when attempting to walk across the DANCERS in Lancre. [TGL]

Wheels, Gabby. An elderly farm worker who helps with the harvest on Miss Flitworth's farm. He hardly ever speaks, and so he is called 'Gabby' because of that famous sense of humour for which country people are so well known. [RM]

Whelk, Brother. Teaches Comparative Religion in the Citadel of KOM. [SG]

Whemper, Goodie. The witch who trained Magrat GARLICK. A great collector of books about MAGIC (she had about twelve, a considerable number for a witch). She was a research witch (*see* RESEARCH WITCHCRAFT) and she died in an accident while testing whether a broomstick could survive having its bristles pulled out one by one in mid-air. The answer, apparently, was 'no'.

Mention of her name is always followed by 'may she rest in peace'. Witches do not follow any religion, but that is no reason, they say, to deny anyone some peaceful rest. [WS]

Whiteface, Dr. Head of the FOOLS' GUILD. He is a white-faced clown – deadpan white make-up, thin mouth painted into a wide grin and delicate black eyebrows. He wears a pointy hat and shiny white clothes. In short, he's the clown all the other clowns are afraid of. Clowns are very possessive about their make-up but remarkably careless of their names (there are vast armies of Joeys and Boffos, for example) and it is very likely that 'Dr Whiteface' is the generic name for the head clown. [MAA]

Whitlow, Granny. A witch. She used to live in the gingerbread cottage encountered by RINCE-WIND and TWOFLOWER. The art of residential confectionary now seems to have died out on Discworld. Healthier modern variants, such as the houses of cheese and crispbread, never really proved popular. [LF]

Whitlow, Mrs. Housekeeper at Unseen University and commander of its below-stairs servant army. She is a very fat woman (restrained by whalebone) with a face full of chins and a ginger wig. Her glossy skin looks like a warmed candle, and she has an unwise attraction to the colour pink for clothing and furnishings. She can certainly loom – though mostly only horizontally. There was presumably a Mr Whitlow once upon a time, but he is never discussed. She is the subject of some mild undirected fantasies among senior members of the faculty, especially after her behaviour during the craze for Music With Rocks In. [ER]

Wiggall, Mr. Tutor employed by Lord SWIVEL to educate his sons. He was a keen archaeologist. The two older boys gave him the uninspiring nickname of 'Wiggler'. [TSC]

Wiggs, Jocasta. A trainee Assassin and a member of a famous Guild family. She once had a fairly messy encounter with Sam VIMES during a Guild practical exercise. [NW]

Wiglet, Billy. Very short Watch constable. At the time of the events in *Night Watch*, he had been in the Watch for two years. He used to be a fruit porter down the market but he got 'a bad back and a bad chest what with all the cold mornings'. Wiglet was so short that he'd once been accused on navelling a sergeant, being far too short to eyeball anyone. [NW]

Wilkins, Jimmy. Ankh-Morpork Foot-the-ball player. At one point imprisoned in the TANTY for eating someone's nose. [UA]

Wilkins, Mr. He once called Granny WEATHERWAX a domineering old busybody. She made him think he was a frog; the spell lasted a couple of days. [WA]

William the Gonnagle. The ninety-six-year-old battle poet and record keeper of the Nac Mac Feegle clan near Tiffany's village. He is neater in appearance and speaks more precisely than other Feegles. [WFM]

Willie, Boy. Member of the Silver Horde; aka Mad Bill and Wilhelm the Chopper. A rather dried-up old man, but known as Boy Willie because he was (at under eighty) the youngest member of the Silver Horde. He wore very thick boots because he had both legs shorter than the other, a very rare medical condition. [IT]

Willikins (1). Lady Ramkin's butler, a most polished retainer who started with the Ramkin family as the scullery boy. He is fat as butter.

During the events of *Jingo*, he signed up with Lord Venturi's Heavy Infantry, and found that his expertise with the carving knife was a good training for the battlefield. He also used to belong to the Shamlegger Street Rude Boys, where his weapon of choice was a cap-brim sewn with sharpened pennies. [J]

Willikins (2). One of VITOLLER's strolling players, who specializes in female roles. [WS]

Willy. Willy the Pup is a member of the Ankh-Morpork DOG GUILD. [MAA]

Wilph. One of VITOLLER's band of strolling players. [WS]

Wimbler, Sergeant. A past member of the Ankh-Morpork City Watch. [MAA]

Wimsloe. A member of VITOLLER's band of strolling players. [WS]

Winder, Lord. Patrician of Ankh-Morpork during the early events of *Night Watch*. He was unpleasantly plump, with the pink jowliness of a man of normal build who had eaten too much rich food, and extremely paranoid. This was because people were trying to kill him. [NW]

Windling, Mr. A lodger at Mrs Arcanum's, who holds down an unspecified clerical job.

The best way to describe Mr Windling would be like this: you are at a meeting. You'd like to be away early. So would everyone else. There really isn't very much to discuss, anyway. And just as everyone can see Any Other Business coming over the horizon and is already putting their papers neatly together, a voice says If I can raise a minor matter, Mr Chairman . . .' and with a horrible wooden feeling in your stomach you know, now, that the evening will go on for twice as long with much referring back to the minutes of earlier meetings. The man who has just said that, and is now sitting there with a smug smile of dedication to the committee process, is as near Mr Windling as makes no difference.

And something that distinguishes the Mr Windlings of the universe is the term 'in my humble opinion', which they think adds weight to their statements rather than indicating, in reality, 'these are the mean little views of someone with the social grace of duckweed'.[TT]

Winkings, Arthur and Doreen. *See* NOTFAR-OUTOE, COUNT AND COUNTESS.

Wintersmith. A sort of deity, or legendary figure. The bringer of winter. He has a challenging encounter with Tiffany Aching and, at one point, makes her snowflakes that look like her. A good trick, but an impractical present. [W]

Wintler, Mr. Josia Wintler (aged forty-five) of 12b Martlebury Street, Ankh-Morpork, is a small man, with a beaming red face – one of those people blessed with the permanent expression of someone who has just heard a rather saucy joke. He specializes in growing amusingly-shaped vegetables. [TT]

Winton, Mad Al. One of the SMOKING GNU, with Alex CARLTON.

Wisdom. Wisdom comes from experience. Experience is often a result of lack of wisdom. Wisdom is also a lot wiser the further away it is; any old thing written down by some bald man with lots of Zs and Xs in his name is bound, under this rule, to sound a whole lot wiser than the same thing written down by the man next door.

This applies especially if the putative wise man lives up above the snowline somewhere. No one says 'If he's so wise, why isn't he on the beach?'

Wistley, Shaker. Boot-fetishist in Creel Springs, near Lancre. [WA]

Witch, The. A shape made of water-deposited limestone at one of the lesser-known entrances to the LANCRE caves, which is in a narrow valley in the most mountainous region of the country; it looks like a seated old woman. Although there is no formal prohibition on men using this entrance, very few venture very far inside. There is always some pressing reason to go back.

Among the caves accessible from this entrance is one which, because of some curiosity of the rock, is totally impervious to thought.

Witches and Witchcraft. *See* witches by individual name, and extensive entries under MAGIC.

Witch's cottage. Although the basic unit of witchcraft is the witch, the basic *continuous* unit is the cottage. The cottage may have different incumbents over the years, but people seeking cow cures and other items will go to it as much as to the witch.

A witch's cottage is a very specific architectural item, to the extent that 'Middle Period Witch' is a recognizable style. The chimney twists like a corkscrew. The roof is thatch so old that small trees flourish in it, the floors are switchbacks, which creak at night like a tea clipper in a gale. If at least two walls aren't shored up with baulks of timber then it's not a true witch's cottage, but merely the home of some daft old bat who reads tea leaves and talks to her cat.

Despite some popular misinformation, there have been few cottages made out of gingerbread, a singularly impractical building mate-

rial outside those areas where the high ambient magic can compensate for the tendency of the walls to go stale and soggy.

Chicken legs (or duck, in swampy areas) are a popular addition.

Witches' cottages get very sensitive to the moods of their occupant. The home of Granny Weatherwax is so typical of the type that the more detailed information found under GRANNY'S COTTAGE can be taken to apply to the homes of most witches.

Witch Trials. A major Lancre festival. A general get-together when witches from all over the Ramtops come and meet in a typical witchy atmosphere of sisterhood and goodwill – i.e. all nice smiles over the top of a seething mass of envy, scurrilous gossip and general touchiness. The witches show off tricks and spells developed during the year in a spirit of friendly co-operation to see who is going to come second to Granny Weatherwax, although this is all in fun and not a serious contest. And if you believe that, there is no hope for you. The Trials are followed by a bonfire and more gossip. [SALF]

Withel, Stren. In his time, the second-greatest thief in Ankh-Morpork. A cruel swordsman and a disgruntled contender for the title of nastiest man in the world. He has one eye, and a scar-crossed face, and he dresses in black (he was thrown out of the ASSASSINS' GUILD for enjoying himself too much). [COM]

Withel, Theda. A milkmaid who became a famous actress in moving pictures. She was called Ginger by her friends, but adopted – or at least had adopted on her behalf – the screen name of Delores de Syn. She was around 5"2 tall and, although she was not beautiful, the magic of moving pictures could give you real trouble in believing this. The word 'vivacious' springs to mind. Current whereabouts and occupation unknown, but they probably do not involve any kind of livestock. [MP]

Wizards. *See* wizards by individual name, and extensive entries under MAGIC.

Wizards' Pleasaunce. A small, newt-haunted meadow in a horseshoe bend in the ANKH near Unseen University. On summer evenings, if the wind is blowing towards the river, it is a nice area for a stroll. Traditionally, wizards are allowed to bathe naked in the river from there. None in recent history has taken advantage of this privilege. Jumping up and down on the Ankh does not have the same appeal, in any case. [S]

Wonse, Lupine. Former Secretary to Lord VETINARI. Wonse was one of life's subordinates, who rose from his childhood in the SHADES. He was neat, and always gave the impression of just being completed. Even his hair was so smoothed-down and oiled that it looked as though it had been painted on. As the Supreme Grand Master of the ELUCIDATED BRETHREN OF THE EBON NIGHT, he was responsible for the summoning of a great dragon to try and usurp the PATRICIAN. He achieved an accidental death while in WATCH custody owing to the literal-mindedness of the then Lance-constable CARROT, who threw the book at him. [GG]

Worblehat, Horace, Dr. B.Thau, D.M. There is a rumour that the LIBRARIAN was once Dr Horace Worblehat, but no one utters this out loud. Dr Worblehat is dimly remembered as being quiet, polite and generally the kind of person you cannot remember in the school photo. He was born in Moon Pond Lane, Ankh-Morpork, next to the saddle-makers.

Worde, William de. *See* DE WORDE, WILLIAM.

Worm Herding. Somewhat of a lost art. A worm piper working a trained team can do wonders for soil aeration. Sadly, no longer do herds of up to five million worms shake the earth and uproot trees with their passage. [TDA]

Worrier, Lappet-faced. Also known as the Lancre Wowhawk, i.e., similar to a goshawk but less forcible. A hawk. Small and short-sighted. It prefers to walk everywhere, and it faints at the sight of blood. It is a carnivore permanently on the look-out for the vegetarian option. It spends much of its time asleep and, when forced to find food, tends to sit on a branch out of the wind somewhere and wait for something to die. When it is on a perch, it will often end up sleeping upside down. It would take several Worriers to kill even a small sick pigeon, and they would

Wow-Wow Sauce

probably do it by boring it to death. The only way you can reliably bring prey down with a Wowhawk is by using it as a slingshot. Peculiar to LANCRE, where it is the hawk that queens are allowed to fly. [LL]

Wow-Wow Sauce. A mixture of mature SCUMBLE, pickled cucumbers, capers, mustard, mangoes, figs, grated WAHOONIE, anchovy essence, asafoetida, sulphur and saltpetre. Much admired by Mustrum RIDCULLY, current ARCHCHANCELLOR of Unseen University.

Wow-Wow Sauce is one of those entities which, like chess, has an existence that spans worlds and dimensions. On Earth it was pioneered by Dr William Kitchiner (1775–1827), although without the grated wahoonie and several of the more explosive ingredients.

The only condiment more dangerous than Wow-Wow Sauce is the rare Three Mile Island salad dressing.

WOW-WOW SAUCE:
THE OFF-DISCWORLD VERSION

Unlike Mustrum Ridcully's more explosive creation, this is not very hot and can safely be eaten near a naked flame.

> *Butter or, for non-wizards, the substitute of*
>   *choice, a lump about the size of an egg*
> *Plain flour, 1 tablespoon*
> *Beef stock, (1/2) pint*
> *English mustard, 1 teaspoon*
> *White wine vinegar, 1 dessertspoon*
> *Port, 1 tablespoon*
> *Mushroom concentrate, 1 tablespoon*
> *Freeze-dried parsley, 1 heaped tablespoon*
> *Pickled walnuts, chopped, 4*
> *Salt, freshly ground black pepper, to taste*

Melt the butter or butter substitute in a saucepan. Stir in the flour and work in the beef stock. Stir continuously on a moderate heat until you have a smooth, thick sauce.

Stir in the made-up mustard, the wine vinegar, the port and the mushroom concentrate. Add a sprinkling of salt and freshly ground black pepper, and continue to cook the mixture for about 10 minutes.

Add the parsley and the walnuts; warm them through, and serve.

This sauce, when added to roast beef, will earn a vote of thanks from the ghost of the steer. We are unable to comment on its keeping qualities – the question has never arisen.

There are a number of recipes for Wow-Wow Sauce. Its apparent inventor, Dr Kitchiner, used pickled cucumbers and capers in preference to the walnuts – we felt they obscured some of the delicate flavours. But feel free to experiment. Worcestershire Sauce has been suggested as a substitute for the mushroom concentrate and port, but some of the delicacy of the flavour might again be lost. Big changes in the taste of the sauce can be made by quite small variations in the proportions of the vinegar and the mustard – generally, the higher the proportion of wine vinegar the sharper and more piquant the sauce (a tarter version can be made by increasing the wine vinegar to a tablespoonful and reducing the mustard to half a teaspoon).

Dr Kitchiner, incidentally, would have been welcome at Unseen University. He was in the habit of travelling with his own invention, the 'portable magazine of taste'; this consisted of twenty-eight bottles of favoured condiments, such as essence of celery, pickled cucumbers and, of course, the sauce.

For those brave souls who, in the age of the microwave dinner, wish to get the whole thing right, we offer this recipe for mushroom concentrate (there are many others):

Put about six large button mushrooms into a bowl and sprinkle on some salt. Leave them for about three hours and then mash them. Cover the bowl and leave overnight. Drain off the liquid into a saucepan (energetically straining off the mushroom pulp through a sieve will extract more of the liquid). Boil, stirring all the while, until the volume is reduced by about a half. This should produce about a tablespoon of the essence for your sauce.

Wrangle, Tom, Captain. An officer in Lord Selachi's Light Infantry during the events of *Night Watch*. He attended school with Major

MOUNTJOY-STANDFAST and Wrangle, the major knew, was a lot brighter than him. [NW]

Wuffles. Lord VETINARI's pet dog. A small, almost toothless and exceedingly elderly wire-haired terrier with a bristly stub of a tail, who smells bad and wheezes at people. He also had halitosis. He was sixteen years old. Wuffles slept like a dead dog, with all four legs up in the air. Wuffles died some time before *Making Money*. There is now a little grave in the palace grounds. Lord Vetinari goes there once a week and puts a dog biscuit on it – Tracklement's Yums (bone-shaped – but never the yellow one because Wuffles didn't like them). [S]

Wxrthltl-jwlpklz. Demon summoned by Granny WEATHERWAX, Nanny OGG and Magrat GARLICK. [WS]

Wyrmberg, The. A mountain that rises almost one half of a mile over the green valley where it stands. It is huge, grey and upside-down. At its base it is a mere score of yards across. Then it ascends through a clinging cloud, curving grace-fully outward like an upturned trumpet until it is truncated by a plateau fully a quarter of a mile across.

There is a tiny forest up there, its greenery cascading over the lip. There are buildings and a lake. There is even a small river, tumbling over the edge in a waterfall so wind-whipped that it reaches the ground as rain. There are also a number of cave mouths, a few yards below the plateau. They have a crudely carved, regular look about them. The Wyrmberg hangs over the clouds like a giant's dovecote.

The rock contains many corridors and rooms. In its hollow heart is a great cavern where the DRAGONS – the Wyrms – roost. Sunbeams from the myriad entrances around the walls criss-cross the dusty gloom like amber rods in which a million golden insects have been preserved. In the upturned acres of the cavern roof are thousands of walking rings, which have taken a score of masons a score of years to hammer home the pitons for. These rings are used with hook boots to walk across the ceiling. There are also eighty-eight major rings clustered near the apex of the dome – huge as rainbows, rusty as blood. Below are the distant rocks of the cavern floor, discoloured by centuries of dragon droppings.

The dragons themselves are clearly *Draco nobilis*, who have a permanent existence here because of the extremely high level of residual magic in the vicinity (surviving in much the same way as certain deep-sea creatures survived in the presence of a warm-water vent in the sea bed). [COM]

On the fabled hidden continent of XXXX, somewhere near the rim,
there is a lost colony of wizards who wear corks around their pointy hats
and live on nothing but prawns.

– *Reaper Man*

XENO

Xeno. An Ephebian philosopher and author of 'Reflections'. Small, fat and florid, and with a short beard. [P]

However, the events of *The Last Continent* have made it more than clear that nothing people had heard about XXXX was an exaggeration.

XXXX. Continent, somewhere near the Rim. It reputedly contains a lost colony of wizards who wear corks around their pointy hats and live on nothing but prawns. Some of this is true (*see* BUGARUP, BUGARUP UNIVERSITY). There, it was said, the light was still wild and fresh as it rolled in from space, and the wizards surfed on the boiling interface between night and day.

It was believed that XXXX has been the subject of at least two expeditions from Ankh-Morpork; the first, several thousand years ago, was led by a sourcerer and the second, some five hundred years before the present, was never heard of again.

Although the continent received many ship-wrecked mariners, because of the permanent ring of storms around its coast, the same storms made it practically impossible to get home again (until the events of *The Last Continent*). The few stories that filtered back, telling of giant leaping rats, ducks with fur, no wings and four feet, and huge flightless chickens, suggested to the hearers that the place may be entirely mythical.

Just then, Tiffany looked down and in a slight greenish-yellow haze saw a cat, pure white and as aloof as a duchess, staring at her. It was Granny Weatherwax's cat, You.

– *The Shepherd's Crown*

Yen Buddhists. The richest religious sect in the universe. They hold that the accumulation of money is a great evil and a burden to the soul. They therefore, regardless of personal hazard, see it as their unpleasant duty to acquire as much as possible in order to reduce the risk to innocent people. Many major religions, after all, stress that poverty is a stand-by ticket to salvation. [WA]

Yennork. A yennork is a werewolf who is not the classic biomorph (human-shaped but with the ability to change into a wolf at any time) nor a *wereman* (like, say, LUPINE). A yennork is unable to change. They are either stuck as a human all the time (like ANGUA's sister Elsa), or have to spend all their time as a wolf (like Angua's brother Andrei). Technically, the yennork does change at full moon, but because its biological make-up lacks a cogwheel somewhere, it changes from the shape it is in to *the same shape again*, and doesn't notice. Because some yennorks may not even realize that they are technically werewolves, and will live and breed quite happily as a human or a wolf while innocently passing on the complex werewolf gene, they are believed to be the reason for the many gradations and varieties – and also why a werewolf may occasionally crop up in a family with no known werewolf history.

The efforts of the 'pure bred' biomorphs to keep their line free of the taint of yennockism has been responsible for some very strange political thinking.

Yeti. A form of troll that lives above the snow line. They are broadly like a city troll, but rolled out thinner, although a thick coat of fur appears to give them bulk. Yeti are very tall – more than twice as high as a normal person – and most of that extra height is in their skinny legs and arms. Their feet are huge (of course). Their stride is a like a continuous series of leaps from one foot to the other and they can run at about 30 m.p.h.

The yeti of the Ramtops is one of the few creatures to utilize control of personal time for genetic advantage. The result is a kind of physical premonition – you find out what is going to happen next by allowing it to happen. Faced with danger, or any kind of task that involves risk of death, a yeti will *save* its life up to that point and then proceed with all due caution, yet in the comfortable knowledge that, should everything go pancake-shaped, it will wake up at the point where it saved itself, with, and this is the important bit, knowledge of the events which have just happened but which will not now, as a result of foreknowledge, happen. This makes perfect sense, because of QUANTUM. [TOT]

Ymitury, Archmage of. A powerful wizard, parted from his staff, his belt of moon jewels and his life, by the WEASEL and BRAVD the Hublander. Ymitury does not feature in the records of Unseen University, and in any case any wizard who could be tricked out of his staff by a couple of wandering mercenaries probably did not deserve to have it in the first place; it is likely he was some sort of charlatan or possibly even a foreigner. [COM]

Ymor. In his time, the greatest thief in Ankh-Morpork, and one of the last independent gang leaders to merge with the THIEVES' GUILD. His headquarters were in the leaning tower at the junction of Rime Street and Frost Alley. [COM]

Ynci the Short-Tempered. Apparently a past queen of LANCRE A beefy young woman sporting a winged, spiked helmet and a mass of black hair plaited into dreadlocks with blood as a setting lotion. She was heavily made-up in the woad-and-blood-and-spirals school of barbarian cosmetics. She wore a 42D-cup breastplate and shoulder plates with spikes. She had knee pads with spikes on, spikes on her sandals and a rather short skirt in the fashionable tartan and blood motif. She carried a double-headed battle-axe. Her war pony was called Spike.

In the strictest sense, she never existed. She was invented by King LULLY I of Lancre because he thought the kingdom needed a bit of romantic history. But she has an official portrait in LANCRE CASTLE's Long Gallery, some armour in its armoury (in fact made by one of the

Ogg family at the King's instruction), and she features prominently (because of that breast-plate) in Birdwhistle's '*Legendes and Antiquities of the Ramtops*'; there is therefore rather more evidence of her existence than most people leave behind them; in these circumstances actual reality is more or less irrelevant. [LL]

Yob Soddoth. An outer-dimensional monster, recognizable from his distinctive cry: 'Yerwhatyerwhatyerwhat'. [MP]

You. White cat given by Tiffany ACHING to Granny WEATHERWAX. Its mother was Pinky, the Widow Cable's cat. Named You by Granny Weatherwax – as in 'You! Stop that!' and 'You! Get off there!'. When it came to names, Granny didn't do fancy. [W]

You Bastard. A camel. The greatest mathematician in the world. The origin of his name lies in the fact that camels believe that they really

are called whatever it is people say to them most often. [P]

You Vicious Brute. A camel and, like all camels, an accomplished mathematician. Created the Theory of Transient Integrals, and spent most of his life carrying a man who could count to twenty only because he wore sandals. [P]

Yoyo, de. The de Yoyos are a noble family with a seat near Pseudopolis. Their fortunes have risen and fallen regularly. Perhaps this is why they have produced many explorers and adventurers, who have discovered obscure areas of the Disc hitherto known only to natives, peasants and other people whose opinions are too insignificant to count. The head of the family is titled the Compte (Kompt) de Yoyo; the current head, Guy de Yoyo, is a lecturer at the ASSASSINS' GUILD (Modern Languages and Music). He is certainly a great traveller; he was a guest at the famous Samedi Nuit Mort Ball in GENUA. [WA]

Ysabell. DEATH's adopted daughter. When first introduced, she was a sixteen-year-old young woman with silver hair, silver eyes and a slight suggestion of too many chocolates. Not, of course, a blood relation to the Grim Reaper – no real explanation has been given as to why he saved her as a baby when her parents were killed in the Great NEF.

It says a lot for Ysabell's basic mental stability that she remained even halfway sane in Death's house, where no time passes and black is considered the appropriate colour for almost everything. She certainly developed an obsessive interest in tragic heroines and also a fixation for the colour pink.

She married MORT and became Duchess of Sto Helit. Killed in a coach crash. [LF]

"Sing? Never mind sing. Have you ever seen a zombie try to play a guitar? It's helping him find his fingers afterwards that's so embarrassing."

– Reaper Man

Zacharos. A blacksmith used by URN and Sergeant SIMONY to help build the Disc's first, and possibly last, 'tank'. [SG]

Zakriah. A druid who helps BELAFON to repair a stone circle. [LF]

Zeb. 'False' prophet of the Omnian religion. [SG]

Zemphis. Walled town on the ANKH. It lies at the junction of three trade routes (apart from the river itself), and is built around one enormous square, which is a cross between a permanent exotic traffic jam and a tent village.

The only place that was of any significance in Zemphis was Downsized Abbey. It is a ruin now, the monks long gone; these days it is more of a souk, a medina, a heaving bazaar, reminiscent of the Shades of Ankh-Morpork on their holidays. Nothing is still. Silence is a rare blessing. And everyone is a trader. It seems that sooner or later everything and everyone could be bought and sold. And, if necessary, made to disappear. [ER]

Zen. A sub-sect of the Klatchian philosophical system of SUMTIN, noted for its simple austerity and the offer of personal tranquillity and wholeness achieved through meditation and breathing techniques; an interesting aspect is the asking of apparently nonsensical questions in order to widen the doors of perception. Learning how to beat six heavily armed opponents with your bare hands while occasionally doing unnecessary backward somersaults does not, strangely enough, appear to be in the introductory teachings. [WS]

Zephilite, Brother. Brother Zephilite of KLATCH left his vast estates and his family and spent his life ministering to the sick and poor on behalf of the invisible god F'rum. He did many good works, was kind to animals, was renowned for his piety, simple wisdom and generosity, and all in all certainly magnified the name of a god generally considered unable, should he have a backside, to find it with both hands, should he

have hands. It is a sad fact that gods often don't deserve their believers. [S]

Zetesphut. Past King of TSORT. [M]

Zlobenia. Militaristic country, ruled by Prince HEINRICH, and separated from its warlike neighbour, BOROGRAVIA, by the river Kneck. Its chief export is the hand-painted clog. [MR]

Zodiac. There are sixty-four signs in the Disc zodiac. These have included:

Celestial Parsnip, The
Cow of Heaven, The
Flying Moose, The
Gahoolie the Vase of Tulips
Knotted String, The
Mubbo the Hyena
Okjock the Salesman
Perhaps Gate, The
Small Boring Group of Faint Stars, The
Two Fat Cousins, The
Wezen the Double-Headed Kangaroo

It would be more correct to say that there are *always* sixty-four signs in the Discworld zodiac *but* also that these are subject to change without notice. Stars immediately ahead of the Turtle's line of flight change their position only very gradually, as do the ones aft. The ones at right angles, however, may easily alter their relative positions in the lifetime of the average person, so there is a constant need for an updating of the Zodiac. This is done for the STO PLAINS by Unseen University, but communications with distant continents (who in any case have their own interpretations of the apparent shapes in the sky) are so slow that by the time any constellation is known Disc-wide it has already gone past. This does at least mean that astrology on the Disc is a dynamic thing and not a repository for some rather unimaginative mythology, but it does rather reduce the science to something on the lines of 'Look! There! No, *there*! Where I'm pointing! *There*! Doesn't that look like a crab to you? Oh, too late, you've missed it.'

Zombies. Human beings who continue to walk and talk after deaths. Typically, zombies are people with strong, enduring personalities. The method for creating zombies seems to vary, and can include magic, disruptions to the life force on Discworld or sheer stubbornness.*

Zoon, Amschat B'hal. A liar (*see* ZOONS). Bearded and tanned and dressed like a gypsy; he has a lot of gold teeth and hands heavy with rings. He runs and owns a barge which trades up and down the ANKH. He lives on the barge with his three wives and three children. [ER]

Zoons. 'You can always trust a Zoon', they say. They are an absolutely honest race; the average Zoon can no more tell a lie than breathe underwater. There is no physical reason for this fact. It simply seems that most Zoons cannot grasp the idea that something may be described as other than what it is. This is a drawback in a trading race, so once the Zoons discovered the essential role played by mendacity, the tribal elders began to encourage likely young Zoons to bend the truth ever further on a competitive basis.

They introduced the office of tribal Liar, which is subject to much competition. (The Zoons' most famous liar was Rolande Pork, with 'My Grandfather Is Seventeen Feet Tall'.) The Liar represents the tribe in all its doings with the outside world. [ER]

Zorgo. A retrophrenologist in Knuckle Passage, Ankh-Morpork. [MAA]

Zweiblumen, Jack. Name applied to TWOFLOWER when, because of a brief dimensional crossover, he found himself on an aircraft instead of a dragon. He wore britches which ended just above his knees and a vest of brightly striped material, plus a little straw hat with a feather in it. For an explanation of the phenomenon, *see* RJINSWAND, DR. By virtue of this nom d'avion, Twoflower manages to be the last entry in the A to Z. [COM]

---

* Mr. Slant, Ankh-Morpork's most respected zombie, for example, refuses to die until his descendants make reimbursement to his law firm for conducting the defense at his own execution trial.